Thomas Adolphus Trollope

Lindisfarn Chase

A Novel

Thomas Adolphus Trollope

Lindisfarn Chase
A Novel

ISBN/EAN: 9783337033156

Printed in Europe, USA, Canada, Australia, Japan

Cover: Foto ©Andreas Hilbeck / pixelio.de

More available books at **www.hansebooks.com**

LINDISFARN CHASE.

A Novel.

BY

T. ADOLPHUS TROLLOPE.

NEW YORK:

HARPER & BROTHERS, PUBLISHERS,

FRANKLIN SQUARE.

1864.

LINDISFARN CHASE.

BY T. A. TROLLOPE.

CHAPTER I.

SILVERTON AND ITS ENVIRONS.

I DOUBT much whether I could invent a fiction that should be more interesting to my readers than the authentic bit of family history I am about to offer them. The facts happened, and the actors in them were, with very little difference, such as they will be represented in the following pages. But although nearly half a century has passed since the circumstances occurred, it has been necessary, in order to justify the publication of them, to make such changes in names and localities as should obviate the possibility of causing annoyance or offence to individuals still living. The episcopal city in, and in the neighborhood of, which the events really took place, shall therefore be called Silverton; and it shall be placed in one of our south-westernmost counties, where no search among the county families will, it may be safely asserted, enable any too curious reader to identify the real personages of the history.

The ancient and episcopal city of Silverton is one of the most beautifully situated towns in England. Seated in the midst of a wide valley on the banks of a river, which about a mile below the town becomes tidal, and three miles further reaches the sea, its environs comprise almost every variety of English scenery. The flat bottom of the valley is occupied with water-meads, rendered passable to those acquainted with the locality and impassable to strangers, by a labyrinthine system of streams and paths diversified by an infinity of sluices, miniature locks, and bridges removable at pleasure after the fashion of drawbridges. The town itself, with the exception of the physically and morally low parts of it lying immediately in the vicinity of the bridge over the river Sill, is built on a slight elevation sufficient to raise it above the damp level of the water-meadows. The highest point of this eminence was once entirely occupied by the extensive buildings of Silverton Castle. Now the picturesque ivy-grown keep only remains; and the rest of the space backed by the high city wall, which on that side of the city has been preserved, forms the admirably kept and much admired garden of Robert Falconer, Esq., the senior partner of the firm of Falconer and Fishbourne, the wealthy, long established, and much respected bankers of Silverton.

On ground immediately below the site of the old castle, and sufficiently lower for the two buildings to group most admirably together, stands the grand old Cathedral, with its two massive towers, one at either angle of the west front, which looks toward the declivity and the valley. The space between the Cathedral and the site of the castle is occupied by that inmost sanctuary and privileged spot of a cathedral city, the Close. The old city is not in any part of it a noisy one. For though it was formerly the seat of a prosperous cloth trade and manufacture, commerce and industry have long since deserted it, preferring, for their modern requirements, coal measures to water-meadows. But a still deeper quietude broods over the Close. The beautifully kept gravel walk—it is more like a garden walk than a road—which wanders among exquisitely shaven lawns, from one rose-covered porch to another of the irregularly placed prebendal houses, is rarely cut up by wheels. The Deanery gardens, and those of two or three other of the prebendal residences run up to a remaining fragment of the old city wall to the right hand of the castle-keep, as those of Mr. Falconer, the banker, do on the left-hand side of the ancient tower, supposing the person looking at them to stand facing the west front of the Cathedral.

It is a pleasant spot to stand on, and a pleasant view to face;—it was so forty years ago, and I suppose it still is so, despite the cutting down of canonries, and other ravages of the Ecclesiastical Commissioners. If one stood not quite opposite the centre of the west front of the church, but sufficiently to the left of that point to catch a view of the southern side of the long nave, and the southern transept with its round-headed Saxon windows and arches,—for that part of the building belonged to an earlier period than the nave ;— of the mouldering and ivy-grown, but still sturdy-looking and lofty keep of the old castle on the higher ground behind ;—of the fragments of city wall to the right and left, covered with the roses and other creeping plants of the banker's garden on the one side, and of those of the cathedral dignitaries on the other ; —of the noble woods of Lindisfarn Chase on the gentle swell of the hill, which shut in the horizon in that direction at a distance of some seven or eight miles from the city ;—and of the sleepy, quiet Close in the immediate foreground, with its low-roofed, but substantial, roomy, and exceedingly comfortable gray stone houses showing with so admirably picturesque an effect on the brilliant green of the shaven lawns, which run close up to the walls of them ;—if one stood, I say, so as to command this prospect, one would be apt to linger there awhile.

Suppose the hour to be ten A.M. on a September morning. The last bell is ringing for morning service. Dr. Lindisfarn, in surplice, hood, and trencher-cap, is placidly sauntering across the Close from his house, next to the Deanery, with a step that seems regulated by the chime of the bell, to take his place as canon in residence at the morning service. Dr. Theophilus Lindisfarn, Senior Canon, is, literally if not ecclesiastically speaking, always in residence. For he loves Silverton Close better than any other spot of earth's surface ; and keeps a curate on his living of Chewton in the Moor, some fifteen miles from the city. Dr. Lindisfarn, stepping across to morning service, pauses an instant, as he observes with a slight frown an insolently tall dandelion growing in the Close lawn ; and makes a mem. in his mind to tell the gardener that the Chapter cannot tolerate such slovenly gardening. A little troop of choristers in surplices and untasselled trencher-caps, headed by old Peter Glenny, the organist, are coming round the northern corner of the west front from the schoolroom. The Rev. Mr. Thorburn, the Minor Canon, who has to chant the service, is not yet in sight ; for he was officiating as president of a glee club till not the smallest of the small hours last night, and being rather late this morning is now coming up the hill from the lower part of the town, at a speed which will just suffice to bring him to his place in the choir in time to dash off with

" Enter not into judgment with thy servant, O Lord," at the exact instant that the bell sounds its last note, and Dr. Lindisfarn at the same moment raises his benignant face from the trencher-cap in which he has for a moment hidden it, on entering his stall, moving as he did so with a sort of *suant*, mechanical, yet not ungraceful action, which seemed to combine a bow to the assembled congregation with a meditative prayer condensed into the briefest possible time. The rooks are cawing *their* morning service the while in the high trees behind Mr. Falconer's house, a large mansion more modern and less picturesque than the canons' houses, a little behind and to the left of the spot where I have supposed the contemplator of this peaceful scene to take his stand. The morning sun is gilding and lighting up the distant Lindisfarn woods ; a white mist is lying on the water-meads ; and a gentle, drowsy hum ascending from the lower districts of the city. The sights and sounds that caress the eye and ear are all suggestive of peacefulness and beauty ; and are poetized by a flavor of association which imparts an infinite charm to the scene.

And there were no heretic bishops or freethinking professors in those days throughout all the land. There was no Broad Church ; and " earnestness " had not been invented. It was a mighty pleasant time ; at least, it was so inside Cathedral Closes. Dissenters were comparatively few anywhere, and especially in such places as Silverton. They were understood to be low and noxious persons, with greasy faces and lank hair who, in a general way, preferred evil to good. It was said that there were some few of these Pariahs in the low part of the town ; and even that they met for their unhallowed worship in some back lane, under the ministry of a much persecuted and almost outlawed shoemaker. But, of course, none of these persons ever ventured to sully the purity of the Close with their presence. The heresiarch cobbler felt himself to be guilty, and slunk by like a whipped hound, if he met any one of the cathedral dignitaries in the street. The latter, of course, ignored the existence of any such obscure and hateful sectarians ; although it was said that more than one denizen of the Close had been known to listen, though under protest, to a story that Peter Glenny had of a scapegrace nephew of his having once entered the conventicle in the lower town, and having then found the impious wretches singing hymns to a hornpipe tune! The base creatures, who were guilty of such enormities, were too few and too obscure to cause any trouble or scandal in the dignified church-loving Silverton society. If a bishop did endow a favorite son or son-in-law with an accumulation of somewhat incompatible preferments, if a reverend canon *did* absent himself for a year or two together from Silverton, or hold preferment with his canonry not strictly tenable with it, leave some of the little churches in the city unserved some Sunday evening, because he was engaged to a dinner-party in the country, or indulge in a habit of playing whist deep into Sunday morning; or if a Minor Canon *were* found hearing the chimes at midnight elsewhere than in his study or his bed, or did chance to get into trouble about sporting without a license, or did stroll into his country church to take some odds or ends of surplice duty in his shooting gaiters, while he left his dog and gun in the vestry,—why, there was no " chiel amang them " to take invidious note of these things, much less to dream of printing them! In short, the time of which I have been speaking, and am about to speak, was that good old time, which *nous autres* who are *sur la retour* remember so well; and which was so pleasant that it is quite sad to think that it should have been found out to be so naughty!

It would seem nevertheless that there had been still better times at a yet more remote period. For there were, even forty years ago, individuals in the Silverton world, who looked with regret at the march of progress, which had even then commenced. And old Dennis Wyvill, the verger, who was upwards of eighty years old, used to complain much of a new-fangled order of the Chapter that the litany should be chanted, declaring that in good *Dane* Burder's days morning service was over, and all said, and the door locked afore eleven o'clock. But thus it is! " Ætas parentum," says the poet in the same mind with old Dennis Wyvill, the verger, " *Ætas parentum pejor avis tulit nos nequiores, mox daturos progeniem vitiosiorem.*"

The progress of time has not quite spared either the material beauty of Silverton or its environs. One or two rows of " semi-detached villa residences," have made their appearance in different parts of the outskirts

of the city, which, however charming they may be as residences to the dwellers in them, do not add to the beauty of the place. One of these more especially has caused the destruction of a clump of elm-trees, which formerly stood near the spot where the fragment of city wall that bounds Mr. Falconer's garden—or, rather, that which was his at the date of this history—comes to an end, and which filled most charmingly to the eye the break in the landscape between that object and the grass-green water-meads below; and has thus done irreparable injury to dear old Silverton. For the rest, the city and its surrounding country are much as they used to be. The woods of Lindisfarn Chase beyond and, as one may say, behind the town, supposing it to face toward the valley of the Sill, are as rich in verdure and as beautiful as ever. The less thickly, but still well-wooded parklike scenery of Wanstrow Manor, the residence, forty years ago, of the Dowager Lady Farnleigh, is unchanged on the more gradually rising opposite bank of the river. The quaintly picturesque view of the water-meadows up the stream, closed at the turn of it westward about two miles above Silverton bridge by the village and village church of Weston Friary, is unaltered. In the opposite direction below the bridge, the population has somewhat increased; and the houses, most of them of a poor description, are more numerous than of yore. And the new cottages, although somewhat more fitted for decent human habitation than the old ones, are less picturesque. Modern squalor and poverty are especially unsightly. It is as if the ill qualities of the old and the new had been selected and combined to the exclusion of the redeeming qualities of either.

Further from the city the aspect of the country is naturally still more unchanged. The rich and brilliantly green meadows and pasture lands in the lower grounds; the coppice-circled fields of tillage of the upland farms, the red soil of which contrasts so beautifully with the greenery of the woodlands; the gradually increasing wildness and unevenness of the country, as it recedes from the valley of the Sill, and approaches the higher ground of Lindisfarn Chase on the Silverton side of the stream; and the curiously sudden and definitely marked line, which separates the Wanstrow Manor farms from the wide extent of moorland which stretches away, many a mile to the northward and along the coast, on the opposite or left-hand side of the little river; all this, of course, is as it was. And it was, and is, very beautiful.

CHAPTER II.

AT WESTON FRIARY.

THERE were two roads open to the choice of any one wishing to go from Wanstrow Manor to Lindisfarn Chase. The most direct crossed the Sill by Silverton bridge and passed through that city. The distance by this road was little more than eight miles. But the pleasanter way, either for riding or walking, was to cross the river at Weston Friary, and thus avoiding the city altogether, and reaching the wilder and more open district of the Chase, almost immediately after quitting the valley at Weston, so as to make the greatest part of the distance by the green lanes and unenclosed commons which at that point occupied most of the space between the lowlands of the valley and Lindisfarn woods. The distance by this route was a good ten miles, however. The highest part of the ground of the Chase, which shut in the horizon to the westward behind Silverton, has been mentioned as being about seven or eight miles from the city. But the fine old house, which took its name from the Chase, was not so far. Nor was it visible from the town. A little brawling stream called Lindisfarn Brook ran hiding itself at the bottom of a narrow ravine between Silverton and the Lindisfarn woods, and fell into the Sill a mile or two above Weston Friary. This little valley and its brook were about three miles from the city, and four or five from the wood-covered summit above mentioned. The ground fell from this latter in a gentle slope all the way down to the brook, with the exception of the last two or three hundred feet, the sudden and almost precipitous dip of which gave the valley the character of a ravine. The house was situated about half-way down this gentle declivity,—about two and a half miles from the top, that is,—and as much from the brook, which was crossed by a charming little ivy-grown bridge high above the stream, carrying the carriage road from Silverton to Lindisfarn. The same little brook had to be crossed by those who took the longer way from Wanstrow, and by those who came from Weston Friary to the Chase; and for foot-

passengers, there was a plank and rail across the stream. Those travelling this route on horseback, however, had to ford the Lindisfarn Brook; and in sloppy weather the banks were apt to be very soft and rotten, insomuch that many a pound of mud from the Lindisfarn Brook ford had been brushed from bedraggled riding-habits in the servants' halls of the Chase and the Manor; for the intercourse between these two mansions was very frequent, and the ride by Weston Friary, as has been said, was, especially to practised riders, the pleasanter.

Indeed, for those who like open country, and have no objection to a little mud and a moderate jump or two, there could not be a better country for a ride than all this part of the Lindisfarn Chase property. In the driest weather the turf of the lanes and commons was rarely too hard, but in wet weather it was certainly somewhat too soft. This was most the case on the Weston Friary side of the Lindisfarn Brook. On the other side the ground rose toward the Chase more rapidly, and, as the higher land was reached, became naturally drier. But though there was a slight rise from the ford on the other side, sufficient to cause the brook to seek its way into the river Sill a mile or two further up the stream instead of falling into it at the village of Weston, this elevation of the ground between the valley of Lindisfarn Brook and the water-mead around the village, was not sufficient at that point to prevent all the intervening land from being of a very wet and soft description. If I have succeeded in making the topography of the environs of Silverton at all clear to the reader, it will be understood that this same swell of the ground, which between Weston and the ford over the brook of Lindisfarn was a mere tongue of marshy soil, rose gradually but rather rapidly in the direction down the Sill, till it formed the comparatively high ground, on which Silverton was built, and from which the Lindisfarn woods could be seen on the opposite side of the valley of the brook, which had there become a deep ravine, as has been described. A good country road, coming from the interior of the country along the valley of the Sill, passed through the village of Weston Friary on its course to Silverton, finding its way along the edge of the water-meadows, and making in that direction also a singularly pretty ride. This road, having crossed the mouth of the brook by a bridge called Paulton's Bridge, nearly two miles above Weston, held its way along the tongue of low land which has been described, keeping close to the bank of the river. Just above Weston, this space between the two streams was not above half a mile in width, and it was all open common, divided off from the road however at that point, by a low, timber fence, consisting of two rails only, which, traced at a period when such land was of small value, left a wide margin of turf along the roadside.

About the same hour of that same beautiful September morning, at which the reader has had a glimpse of Dr. Lindisfarn on his way to morning service at the cathedral,—a little later perhaps; but even if it had still been *Dane* Burder's time, the service could not be yet over,—an old laborer paused in his loitering walk along the road toward Silverton, to look at two ladies on horseback coming at full gallop across the common, followed at some little distance by a groom.

" Now for a jump! " said the old man, as he stood to look ; " there ben't another in all the country has such a seat on a horse as my lady have! And Miss Kate, she's just such another ! "

And as he spoke, the two ladies came lightly over the low rail on to the turf by the roadside, the younger of the two giving a playful imitation of a view hallo, as she cleared her fence, in a voice whose silver notes were musical as the tones from a flute, Lady Farnleigh of Wanstrow Manor, gentle reader, and Miss Kate Lindisfarn, daughter of Oliver Lindisfarn, Esq., of the Chase.

The fence was not much of a jump ; and the whole appearance of the ladies betokened that they were accustomed to much severer feats of horsemanship than that. It was a soft morning, and though the Lindisfarn woods above were glistening in the sunshine, and the old castle keep and the towers of the cathedral at Silverton were clearly defined in the bright air, the mist, as has been said, was still lying in the valley, and glistening drops of the moisture had gathered on the brims and on the somewhat bedraggled feathers of the ladies' low-crowned beaver hats, and on the curls of hair, which hung in slightly dishevelled disarray around their necks. They bore about them, too, still more decided marks of hard riding. Their habits were splashed with mud up to their shoulders, and the lower parts of them were evidently the worse for the passage of Lindisfarn Brook ford. Their whole appearance was such, in short, that had a malicious fairy dropped them just as they were into the midst of the ride in Hyde Park, they would have wished the earth to open and swallow them up. Yet many a fair frequenter of that matchless show of horsewomen, would, more judiciously, have given anything to look exactly, age for age, like either lady. They were both beautiful women, though the elder was the mother of a peer, who had just taken his seat in the House. In fact, the Dowager Lady Farnleigh was only in her forty-fourth year. Her companion was twenty-six years younger. But both were in face and figure eminently beautiful, and did not look less so for the glow which their exercise had called into their cheeks, and the sparkle in their eyes from the excitement of their gallop. Both sat their horses to perfection, as the old man had said ; and both were admirably well mounted,—Lady Farnleigh on a magnificent bay, and Kate on a somewhat smaller and slighter black,—as indeed they needed to be for the work they had been engaged in. Their horses were splashed from fetlock to shoulder, and from nose to crupper ; and the gallop up the rise from the ford, and over the deep turf of the soft common made their flanks heave as their riders pulled up in the road ; and the breath from their mobile nostrils was condensed into little clouds just a shade darker than the white mist that lay on the watermeads. But the eyes in their pretty thoroughbred heads were as bright as those of their mistresses ; and as they turned their heads and erect ears up the road and down the road, as if inquiring for further orders, they seemed rather anxious to be off again than distressed by what they had already done.

" Why, Kate! " cried Lady Farnleigh, in a clear, ringing, cheery voice, that would have been good to any amount as a draft for sympathy on any one within earshot,—" why, Kate, as I am a sinner, if there is not Freddy Falconer coming along the road on his cob, looking for all the world, of course, as if he had been just taken out of the bandbox in which the London tailor had sent him down for the enlightenment of us natives ! Shall we run, Kate, like naughty girls as we are ? —shall we show our Silverton *arbiter elegantia-*

rum a clean pair of heels, or boldly stay and abide the ordeal?"

"Oh, I vote for standing our ground," answered Kate; "I see no reason for running away," she added, laughing, but with a somewhat heightened color in her cheek.

"To be sure! What is Freddy Falconer to you, or you to Freddy Falconer? Them's your sentiments, as old Gaffer Miles says, eh, Kate? Who's afraid? I am sure I am not!" replied Lady Farnleigh, looking half jestingly, half observantly, into her goddaughter's face; —for she stood in that relationship to Miss Lindisfarn.

Kate laughed, and shook her pretty head, putting up a little slender hand in its neatly fitting gauntlet, as she did so, to make a little unavowed attempt at restoring her hair to some small appearance of order.

In another minute the rider, whom Lady Farnleigh had observed in the road, coming up at a walk, reached the spot where the ladies were.

He was a young man of some twenty-seven years of age. It was impossible to deny— even Lady Farnleigh could not have denied— that Nature had done her part to qualify him for becoming the *arbiter elegantiarum* she had sneeringly called him. He was indeed remarkably handsome; fair in complexion, with perhaps a too delicate and unbronzed pink cheek for a man; plenty of light-brown, crisp, curling hair; no mustache or beard, and closely trimmed whiskers ('twas forty years ago); large light-blue eyes, a well-formed mouth, the lips of which, however, were rather thin, and lacked a little of that color in which his cheek was so rich; and a tall, well-proportioned figure;—a strikingly handsome man unquestionably.

Nor had Fortune been behindhand in contributing her share to the perfect production in question. For Mr. Frederick Falconer was the only son and heir of the wealthy and prosperous banker, the senior partner of the old established and much respected firm of Falconer and Fishbourne, of Silverton. And as for Art, her contributions to the joint product had been unstinted, and in her best possible style. Every portion of the costume, appointments, and equipments of Mr. Frederick Falconer and his horse, from the top of the well-brushed beaver to the tip of the well-polished and faultless boot of the biped, and from the artistically groomed tail to the shin-ing curb-chain of the quadruped, were absolutely perfect; and fully justified the anticipatory commendation that Lady Farnleigh had bestowed upon them. And in addition to all this, it may be said that Falconer was an almost universal favorite in the Silverton society—in the "very best" Silverton society, of course. The young men did not admire him quite so much as the young ladies. But this was natural enough. Both sexes, however, of the old, professed an equally favorable opinion of him. He was held to be a good son, as attentive to his father's business as could well be expected under the circumstances, a well-conducted and steady young man, and by pretty well all the Silverton matronocracy a decidedly desirable "*parti.*"

(How naturally we Anglo-Saxon folks speak French whenever we have anything to say of which we are at all ashamed; or any lie to tell!)

"Good-morning, Lady Farnleigh! Good-morning, Miss Lindisfarn!" he said, saluting the ladies with easy grace, as he came up to them. "You are not only riding early this morning, but you have been riding some time earlier; for I see you have crossed Lindisfarn Brook!"

Both ladies gave a nod in return for his salutation, Lady Farnleigh not a distant or supercilious, but rather a dry one (if a nod can be said to be dry, as I think it may), and Kate a good-natured one, accompanied by a good-humored smile.

"You have been riding early too, which is paying this misty morning a much higher compliment!" returned Lady Farnleigh, "for you are already returning to Silverton."

"Yes. I have been to Churton Basset already this morning. My father wanted a letter taken to Quorn and Prideaux there before they opened for the day. Some business of the bank."

"Well, our ride is not so near its end as yours. We are going up to the Chase again, as soon as I have visited an old friend of mine in the village here. Will you ride over the common with us? Come up to the Chase; and Miss Imogene shall give you some luncheon. And you may ride over with me back again to Wanstrow in the afternoon, if you like."

And Kate bowed her backing of the invitation, with a smile that made Mr. Frederick feel a strong inclination to accept it; although, in fact, Kate had intended only to be courteous, and by no means wished to be, on this occasion, taken at her word, or rather at her bow and smile; for she had not spoken.

It was true that Fred had Messrs. Quorn and Prideaux's answer to his father's letter in his pocket; but he had no reason to think that it mattered much whether it reached its destination a few hours sooner or later. And in truth it was the consideration of the nature of the ride proposed to him, rather than any anxiety about the letter, that made him plead the necessity of returning to Silverton as an excuse for not accepting the proposal.

"Well, good-day, then. You are a pearl of a messenger! Give my compliments to your father; and oh, Mr. Falconer! there is a lot of mud in the road by the lock yonder; take care you do not splash yourself. Goodby!"

He understood the sneer well enough; and would have been riled at it, if Kate had not administered an antidote to the acerbity of her godmother's tongue, by giving him a parting nod and a "Good-by, Mr. Falconer," in which there was no acerbity at all.

Nevertheless, as the young man rode off toward the city, and the ladies turned their horses' heads to enter the village of Weston Friary, Kate said, addressing her companion,—

"How could you think of inviting him up to the Chase to-day? As if we had not enough to think of, without having strangers on our hands!"

"Don't be a goose, Kate!" answered the elder lady. "Do you think I imagined that there was the slightest chance of Master Freddy consenting to ride over Lindisfarn Common with you and me? Catch him at it! But at what time do you think your sister may arrive?"

"We have calculated that she may be at the Chase by two. I wanted to meet her in Silverton; but papa thought it best that we should all receive her together at home. We must take care to be back at the Chase by that time. I would not be out when she comes for the world!"

"Oh, no fear! I've only to say half a dozen words to old Granny Wilkins, poor thing, in Weston here, and then we'll go up to the Chase best pace. We sha'n't be long,

since we have not Master Freddy at our heels."

"Why, what a spite you have, godmamma, against poor Mr. Falconer! What has he done to offend you?"

"Nothing in the world, my dear! And I have not the slightest idea of being offended with him. It is true I don't like him quite so much as all the Silverton young ladies do."

"I don't think you like him at all! Why don't you?" asked Kate, with a blunt, straightforward frankness that was peculiar to her.

"Well, I don't like him at all, that's the truth! But you know the old rhyme, Kate,— 'I do not like you, Dr. Fell,' etc., etc. Upon second thoughts, however, I think I *can* tell why I don't like Freddy Falconer. He is a regular "—

"Oh, not a snob, as you said of that superfine Captain Marnisty, the other day. I don't think Mr. Falconer is a snob!"

"No, I was not going to say a snob. Why should you fancy I was?"

"Only because, when you called Captain Marnisty so, you said 'a regular snob,' just in the same sort of way."

"Well, this time I am going to say a regular something else. No, it would not be fair, or true, to say that Fred Falconer is a snob. But I can put what he is into four letters too!"

"Not a fool!" expostulated Kate.

"No, that's not quite it either, though I have known wiser men than Fred. Try again!"

"Dandy has five letters," said Kate, meditatively.

"Yes, and so has scamp; and I do not mean to call Mr. Falconer that either. No, if I must tell you, it is p—r—i—g. Freddy Falconer is a regular prig! And I am not fond of prigs. But Heaven help us all! there are worse things than prigs in the world; and I have nothing to say against the man. Only," she added, after a pause, "to make a clean breast of it, Kate, I have fancied lately that I have seen symptoms of his Sultanship having taken it into his head to throw the handkerchief in the direction of Lindisfarn Chase "—

"I am sure he never thought of such a thing!" said Kate, with a little toss and a great blush.

"So much the better! In that case, Freddy and I shall remain very good friends. He may make love to every other girl in the county for aught I care; but if he meddles with my Kate, *gare la marraine!* that's all! Will you come in with me to see old Granny Wilkins, dear, or sit on your horse till I have done? I sha'n't be a minute."

"No, no; let me come in with you. Granny Wilkins is an old acquaintance of mine." So the groom helped both the ladies to dismount at the door of the cottage; and it was evident from the unsurprised manner in which the paralytic old inhabitant of it received her visitors that they were neither of them strangers to her.

The business with Dame Wilkins was soon despatched, as Lady Farnleigh had said that it would be. It consisted only of the administration of one or two little articles of creature comfort, a trifle of money, and a few of those kind words, more valuable than any of these, when spoken by the gentle and wealthy to the poor and simple with that tact and heartiness which are both naturally inspired by genuine sympathy, but which are as naturally, and with fatal result, wanting to those charitable ministrations, performed as a matter of duty, according to cut-and-dry rules, even though those rules shall have been adjusted in accordance with the most approved maxims of modern social science.

The fact is that there is just the difference between the two things that there is between the workmanship of some old *cinque-cento* artist, and the product of a Birmingham steam factory. There is much in favor of the latter. Millions of the required article are turned out of hand instead of units. There is infinitely less loss of material. The article produced is, according to every mechanical test, even better than the handiwork of the old artist. It is more accurate, its rounds are absolutely round, its angles true angles; each individual article of the gross turned out per hour is exactly the same as every other, and all are adapted with scientific forethought to the exact requirements they are intended to serve. But the old handicraftsman impressed his individuality on the work of his hands,—put his whole soul into it, as we say, more literally than we often think, as we use the phrase. What is the difference between this old sixteenth century—anything,—inkstand, lady's needlecase, or what not, and the article im-

itated from it by our mechanical science? I am not artist enough to say what the difference is; but I see it and feel it readily enough; and so does everybody else. And the market value of the ancient artist's piece shall be as a thousand to one to that of the modern imitation of it. And I know that this subtle difference, and this superior value is due to that presence of the workman's soul, which the best possible steam-engine (having, up to the date of the latest improvement, *no* soul) cannot impart to its products.

The best possible mechanism, whether applied by dynamic science to the shaping and chasing of metal, or by social science to the cheering of poverty and the relief of suffering, must not be expected to do the work of individually applied sympathy, heart and soul. But modern civilization needs beautiful inkstands in millions; and the masses of modern population need ministrations only to be supplied by organized social machinery. Very true! Only do not let us suppose that we get the same thing, or a thing nearly as precious. Maybe we get the best we can. But the human brain-directed hand must come in contact with the material, to produce the higher order of artistic beauty. And individual human sympathy, unclogged by rules, must bring one human heart into absolute contact with another, before the best kind of "relief" can be attained.

Dame Wilkins, however, was the fortunate possessor of the real artistic article, in the kind visits of Lady Farnleigh. But the few kind words, which were treasured and repeated and prized, did not take long in saying; and the two ladies in a very few minutes were mounting their horses again. Miss Lindisfarn was already in the saddle; and Lady Farnleigh was about to mount, when the groom said, in an under voice, "Please, my lady, the tobacco!"

"To be sure! What a brute I am to have forgotten it! Give me the packet, Giles." She took the little parcel Giles produced from his pocket, and returning into the cottage said, "Here, granny. If it had not been for Giles, I should have forgotten the best of my treat. Here's half a pound of baccy to comfort you as the cold nights come on."

"Oh, my lady! That *is* the best! You knows how to comfort a poor old body as has lost the use of her precious limbs. Thank you, my lady, and God bless you!'' said the old woman, as a gleam of pleasure came into her watery old eyes at the thought of the gratification contained in that small packet.

"I say, godmamma dear," said Kate, after a pause, as they were riding at a sober pace through the village, "do you think it is right to give the poor people tobacco? I have often heard Uncle Theophilus say that the habit of smoking is, next to drinking, the worst thing for the laboring classes; that it promotes bad company, encourages idleness, and very often leads to drunkenness."

"Uncle Theophilus may go to Jericho! I am of another parish; and don't like his doctrine! Tell him from me, Kate, the next time he preaches on that text, that the laboring classes are of opinion that there is nothing worse for their superiors than the habit of drinking port wine; that it makes the temper crusty, promotes red noses, and very often leads to the gout!"

"Ha, ha, ha, ha!" laughed Kate in silvery notes, that made the little village street musical; "depend upon it, I will give him your message word for word."

And then after a short gallop over the common, they crossed the ford again, not without carrying away with them some additional specimen of the soil of its banks and bottom, and thence made the best of their way, first over the broken open ground which intervened between the brook and the Lindisfarn woods, and then through the leafy lanes which crossed them, gradually reaching the higher ground, till they came out on the carriage road from Silverton to the Chase, a little below the Lodge gates.

Here Lady Farnleigh turned her horse's head to return to Wanstrow by the road through Silverton, leaving Kate to ride up to the house alone.

"Good-by, darling!" she said; "I wont come in. I know how anxious you must all be. But remember that I shall be anxious also to hear all about the new sister, and ride over the day after to-morrow at the furthest; there's a dear. Love to them all!"

And Kate cantered up the avenue to join the other members of the family, who were, not without some little nervous expectation, awaiting the arrival of a daughter of the house, whom none of them had seen for the last fifteen years.

CHAPTER III.

THE FAMILY IN THE CLOSE.

LINDISFARN house is a noble old mansion, almost entirely of the Elizabethan period, with stately, stiff, and trim gardens behind it, embosomed in woods behind and around them, with larger and more modern gardens on one side of it, and a wide open gravel drive, and a piece of tree-dotted parklike pasture-land in front of the house; beyond which it looks down over the wooded slope descending to the Lindisfarn Brook, and across it to the cultivated side of the hill on the other side of the top of which stands Silverton. The city is not seen from the house. But the old castle keep is just visible as an object on the edge of the not distant horizon.

It is so charming an old house, so full of character, so homogeneously expressive in all its parts and all its surroundings, and every detail of it and the scenery around it is so vividly impressed on my remembrance, that it is a great temptation to try my power of word-painting by attempting a minute description of the place. But conscious of having often "skipped" similar descriptions written by others, I do as I would be done by and refrain. After all, the associations to be found in each reader's memory and reminiscences have to be called on to supplement the most successful of such descriptions. How can I cause to echo in the memory-chambers of another's brain as they are echoing in mine the morning concert of the rooks in the humid autumn morning air, or in the dreamy quietude of the sunset hour,—the barking of the dogs, and the cheery, ringing tones of old Oliver Lindisfarn's voice, which seemed never to condescend to a lower note than that adapted to a "Yoicks! forward! hark forward!" and which, as it used to echo through the great hall, or make the windows of the wainscoted parlors ring again, seemed to harmonize so perfectly and pleasantly with the other sounds! Why, I swear that even the cry of the peacock seems melodious as it comes wafted across forty years of memory! And as for Kate's silver-toned laugh on the terrace in front of the house, as she played with old Bayard, the great rough mastiff, or enticed her bonny black mare Birdie, to follow her up and down for lumps of sugar purloined out of Miss Imogene's breakfast basin; ah me! the old Lindisfarn rooks will never hear *that* again!

Nor shall I—that, or any other like it! And dear old Miss Immy, as she loved to be called, with her little crisp white cap set on the top of her light crisp silver-white curls, three each side of her head, and her round, withered, red-apple like checks and her bolt-upright little figure, and her pit-a-pat high-heeled shoes, and her stiff, rustling, lavender-colored silk gown, which seemed to go across the floor, when she moved, like some Dutch toy moved by clockwork, and her basket of keys, and her volume of Clarissa Harlowe. Accidents many of these things may seem to be; but they were properties of dear old Miss Immy. For they never changed, neither the snow-white cap nor the lavender-colored gown, nor the volume of Clarissa Harlowe. She really did read it! But she faithfully began it again as soon as she had finished the volume. For sixty years I believe Miss Immy had never been seen without her little basket of keys and her volume of Clarissa Harlowe.

I will not, I say, attempt to describe the old place. But I must needs give some account of the inhabitants of it, as they were at the period to which this history refers.

The Lindisfarn property had belonged to the Lindisfarns of Lindisfarn so long that not only the memory of man but the memory of county historians "ran not to the contrary," as the legal phrase goes. The rental at the period of our history was a well paid four thousand a year, and the tenantry were as well-to-do and respectable a body as any estate in the county could boast. Oliver Lindisfarn, the son and grandson of other Olivers, and the lord of this eminently "desirable property," was in his sixtieth year at the time here spoken of. He had married early in life a sister of his neighbor, Lord Farnleigh;—for the old lord had lived at Wanstrow, which was now the residence of the dowager, his widow, the young lord having taken his young wife to reside on a larger property in a distant county. The present dowager, Lady Farnleigh, was therefore the sister-in-law of the lady Mr. Lindisfarn had first married; but not of the mother of the two young ladies, of whom one has already been presented to the reader. They were the offspring of a second marriage. Lady Catherine Lindisfarn had died after a few years of marriage, leaving her husband a childless widower. He had remained such about eight years, and had then at the age of forty-three married a

Miss Venafry, who after two years of marriage left him a widower for the second time, and the father of two little twin-born girls, Catherine and Margaret. Catherine had been the name of Mr. Lindisfarn's first wife, and Margaret that of his second.

Of course the absence of a male heir was a very heavy and bitter disappointment to the twice-widowed father of two unportioned girls. Mr. Lindisfarn's daughters were entirely so; for on Lady Catherine's death her fortune returned to her family; and Miss Venafry had been dowered by her beauty alone. In another point of view, however, the case of Mr. Lindisfarn was not so hard as that of many another sonless holder of entailed property. For the Lindisfarn estates were entailed only on the male heir of Oliver, and failing an heir of the elder brother, on the male heir of his younger brother, the Rev. Theophilus Lindisfarn. If there were failure of a male heir there also, the daughters of Oliver would become co-heiresses. But Dr. Theophilus Lindisfarn, Canon of Silverton, his brother's junior by only one year, had married Lady Sempronia Balstock, much about the same time that his elder brother had married Lady Catherine Farnleigh; and of this marriage had been born a son, Julian, who was about thirteen years old at the time of the birth of Oliver Lindisfarn's daughters. They were born, therefore, to nothing save such provision as their father might lay by for them out of his income; and Julian, when his uncle's second wife died a year after giving birth to these portionless girls, became the heir to the estates, barring the unlikely chance of his uncle contracting a third marriage.

Long, however, before the dowerless little twins were capable of caring for any provision save that needed for the passing hour, their prospects in life became somewhat brightened. When the second Mrs. Lindisfarn died, a sister of hers, a few years her senior, who had been married for several years to a Baron de Renneville, a Frenchman, and who had been Margaret Lindisfarn's godmother, being childless, proposed to adopt her goddaughter. A pressing and most kind proposal to this effect, warmly backed by the baron himself, held out to his child a prospect which the widowed father did not feel justified in refusing. The De Rennevilles were wealthy, and of good standing in the best Parisian society. Madame de Ronneville had not abandoned her religion. She remained a Protestant, and there was no objection, therefore, on that score. So the little Margaret, almost before she was out of her nurse's arms, was sent to Paris, to be brought up as the recognized heir to the wealth of the prosperous French financier.

The prize which Fortune had in her lottery for the other twin sister, Catherine, was less brilliant, but, nevertheless, was sufficient to make a very important difference in her position. Lady Farnleigh, the sister-in-law of Mr. Lindisfarn's first wife, had become the attached friend of his second, and the godmother of little Catherine. And much about the same time that Margaret was sent to Paris, it was understood that a sum of six thousand pounds was destined by Lady Farnleigh as a legacy to her otherwise wholly unprovided-for goddaughter.

This was the position of the Lindisfarn family at the period of Mrs. Lindisfarn's death. But events had occurred between that time and the date at which this history opens which very materially altered the whole state of the case. And in order to explain these, it is necessary to turn our attention away for a few minutes from the family at the Chase, and give it to that of Dr. Lindisfarn, in the Close at Silverton.

The Chapter of Silverton, at the remote period of which I write, was not noted for the strictly clerical character of its members. Public opinion did not demand much in this respect in those days. The Right Reverend Father, who had presided for many years over the diocese, was a well-born and courtly prelate far better known in certain distinguished metropolitan circles than at Silverton. He was known to hold very strong opinions on the necessity of filling the ranks of the established church with *gentlemen*. And though I cannot assert that he required candidates for ordination to forward, together with their other papers, an heraldic certificate of the " quarterings " they were entitled to, after the fashion of a noble German Chapter, yet it was perfectly well understood that no awkward highlow-shod son of the soil, however competent to " mouth out Homer's Greek like thunder," would do well to apply to the Bishop of Silverton for ordination.

The Silverton canonries were very good things; and good things of this sort were, it may perhaps be thought, naturally reserved for those whose worship was rather given to the special patron of good things, Mammon, than to any more avowed object of their adoration. But nobody could say that the Silverton canons were not gentlemen. Nor can it be said that, with the exception of one, or perhaps two, of the body, whose love for good things went to the extent of hoarding them when they had got them, they were otherwise than well liked by the Silvertonians of all classes ; putting out of the question, as of course they *were* out of the question, those few pestilent fellows who sang hymns to hornpipe tunes down in the back slums. They were gentlemen ; and the Silverton world said that they spent their revenues as such, which was what the Silverton world considered to be the main point. Only the worst of it was that Messrs. Falconer and Fishbourne might have had reason to think that some among them pushed this good quality to excess.

Dr. Lindisfarn, it is fair to state at once, to prevent the reader of these improved days from conceiving an unfounded prejudice against him, was perhaps the most clerical of the body in question. Not that it is to be understood by this that any High Churchman or Low Churchman or Broad Churchman of the present day would have deemed poor Dr. Lindisfarn anything like up to the mark of their different requirements and theories. He would have been sorely perplexed to comprehend what anybody was driving at, who should have talked to him of the duty of " earnestness." He found the world a very fairly satisfactory world, as it was, and had never conceived the remotest idea, good, easy man, that he was in any wise called on to do anything toward leaving it at all better than he found it. Nevertheless, he was fairly entitled to be considered as the most respectably clerical of his Chapter, because his tastes and pursuits were of a nature that was not in any degree in overt disaccordance with the clerical character, even according to our modern conception of it. Whereas the same could hardly be said of the majority of his fellow-canons. One was a very notorious joker of jokes,—of very good jokes, too, occasionally, for he was a man of real wit. (N.B. Though a very clever fellow in his way, he was *not* capable of writing some of the best articles in the *Edinburgh Review*.) But nothing in the shape of a joke came amiss to him, be the subject or tendency of it what it might. He preferred good society; but the *profanum vulgus* was not the portion of the vulgar, which he most hated and kept at a distance. Another was known to be an accomplished musical critic, but was thought to prefer Mozart and Cimarosa to Boyce and Purcell, and to have a not uninfluential voice in the counsels of the lessee of His Majesty's Theatre in the Haymarket. Another had been seen on more than one occasion to wave above his head a hat that looked very like a full-blown shovel in the excitement of a hardly contested race at Newmarket. A fourth was universally allowed to be one of the best whist-players in England, and was thought to be in no danger of losing his skill for want of practice, while a fifth was believed to be a far deeper student of the mysteries of the stock-exchange than of any other sort of lore.

Dr. Theophilus Lindisfarn meddled with none of these anti-clerical pursuits. His heart, as well as his corporeal presence, was in Silverton Close, and Silverton Cathedral Church. But his love for the Church fixed itself rather on the material structures which are as the outward and visible signs of its inward and spiritual existence, than on the abstract ideas of a Church invisible. He was a man of considerable learning and of yet greater zeal for antiquarian and especially ecclesiological pursuits. It is in the nature and destiny of hobbies to be hard ridden. This was Dr. Lindisfarn's hobby; and he did ride it very hard. He was far from a valueless man, as a member of the Silverton Chapter. The dean was not untinctured with similar tastes; and with his assistance and support Dr. Lindisfarn had accomplished much for the restoration and repair of Silverton cathedral, at a time when such things were less thought of than they are in these days. He had fought many a hard fight in the Chapter with his brother dignitaries, who fain would have expended no shilling of the Church revenues for such a purpose; and not content with the niggard grants which it had been possible to induce that body to allocate for the purpose, had spent much of his own money on his beloved church. In fact, it was very well known, that the whole of a considerable sum which he had received from an unexpected legacy by a relative of Lady Sempronia, had

gone towards the new panelled ceiling in painted coffer-work of the transept of the cathedral. And indeed it was whispered at Silverton tea-tables that old Mr. Falconer had been heard to say, with a mysterious nod of his head, that the legacy in question had by no means covered all that the canon had made himself liable for.

Mr. Falconer, no doubt, knew what he was talking about, for, besides being Dr. Lindisfarn's banker, he was a brother archæologist. The votaries of that seducing pursuit were far less numerous in those days than in our own; and the erudite canon of Silverton was fortunate in finding a fellow-laborer and supporter where, it might have been supposed, little likely to meet with it,—in the leading banker of the little city. The dean was the only member of the Chapter, besides Dr. Lindisfarn, who cared for such pursuits. But a few recruits were found among the clergy and gentry of the country; and the banker and the canon together had succeeded in getting up a little county archæological society and publishing club.

Dr. Lindisfarn's tastes and pursuits therefore may fairly be said to have been clerical, or at least not anti-clerical, as well as gentleman-like. Nevertheless, the Lady Sempronia, his wife, did not look on them with an altogether favorable eye. And perhaps she can hardly be blamed for her feeling on the subject. The canon's hobby was a very expensive one. The cost of it, indeed, would have done far more than amply maintain the handsome pair of carriage-horses, which Lady Sempronia hopelessly sighed for, and which would have spared her the bitter mortification of going to visit the county members' wives, or Lady Farnleigh at Wanstrow, in a hybrid sort of conveyance drawn by one stout clumsy horse in the shafts, whereas Mrs. Dean drove a handsome pair of grays. Many other of the small troubles and mortifications, which helped to make Lady Sempronia a querulous and disappointed woman, were traceable, and were very accurately as well as very frequently traced by her, to the same source. Upon the whole, therefore, it was hardly to be wondered at that the poor lady should abhor all archæology in general, and the Silverton society and printing club in particular; and that she should have regarded the discovery of a whitewash-covered moulding, or half-defaced inscription as a bitter misfortune, boding evil to the comforts of her hearth and home.

Lady Sempronia's soul was moreover daily vexed by another peculiarity of her husband's idiosyncrasy, which she put down — with scarcely sufficient warrant, perhaps, from the principles of psychological science—all to the account of the detested archæology. Dr. Lindisfarn was afflicted by habitual absence of mind to a degree which occasionally exposed him and those connected with him to considerable inconvenience. His wife held that the evil was occasioned wholly by his continual meditations on his favorite pursuit when his wits should have been occupied with other matters. But the evil had doubtless a deeper root. It is an infirmity generally regarded with a compassionate smile by those who are witnesses of its manifestations. But to a narrow little mind, soured and irritated by other annoyances, and at best placing its highest conception of human perfection in the due and accurate performance of the thousand little duties and proprieties of every-day life in proper manner, place, and time, the eccentricities of a thoroughly absent man were sources of anger and exacerbation, that contributed far more to make the life of the lady who felt them unhappy than they did to affect in any way the placid object of them. Upon one occasion, for instance, her indignation knew no bounds, when, having with some difficulty driven the canon from his study up-stairs to dress for a dinner-party, to which they were engaged, the doctor, on finding himself in his bedroom, had forgotten all about the business in hand, and had quietly undressed himself and gone to bed, where he was found fast asleep, shortly afterward, by the servant sent to look after him. Of course all Silverton soon knew the story, and the ill-used lady poured her lamentations into the ears of her special friends. But Lady Sempronia was not popular at Silverton, even among her special friends; and it may be feared that the Silverton public accorded her on this, as well as on other occasions, less of their sympathy than her sorrows deserved.

For in truth the poor lady had been sorely tried, and her life embittered by far more serious sorrow and severer trouble,—a sorrow that had left its mark indelibly on her heart, and which produced in her mind another source of half-latent irritation against her husband because he did not seem to be equally affected by it; yet it was the greatest common misfortune a man and wife can have to share, —the loss of an only child. And Lady Sempronia wronged her husband in supposing that he did not feel, or rather had not felt, the blow acutely. But some natures are so constituted, that sorrow sinks into them, as water into a spongy cloth; while from others it as naturally runs off, as from a waterproof surface. And it would be a mistake to pronounce on this ground alone that either of these natures is necessarily superior to the other. And then again in this matter the doctor no doubt owed much to his hobby. Serious hard work, it has been said, is the most efficacious alleviation for sorrow, and the next best probably is hard riding on a favorite hobby.

But poor Lady Sempronia had no help in bearing her grief from either one of these; and it was a very heavy burden to bear.

There were circumstances that made it a very specially and exceptionally sore sorrow to the bereaved parents; and these circumstances must be as briefly as may be related. The two brothers, Oliver and Theophilus Lindisfarn, had married, as has been said, nearly about the same time. The marriage of the elder brother remained childless. But to the younger, a son, Julian, was born about (I think, in) the year 1793. Of course the childless wife of the squire was a little envious, and the happy wife of the Churchman a little exultant,—pardonably in either case. As the years slipped away, the probability that the little Julian would be the heir to the Lindisfarn property grew greater. When, he being at the time about five years old, his aunt, the squire's wife, died, his chance was somewhat diminished, for there was the probability that his uncle would marry again. He was about thirteen years old when that event did happen. But when, some two years later, his uncle's second wife died, leaving him, as the reader knows, only two twin daughters, the probability that Julian must be the heir had become all but a certainty.

Under these circumstances, with a silly, adoring, fine lady mother, and an indulgent, placid, absent, archæological father, it is perhaps not surprising that Julian, kept at home in compliance with his mother's urgent desire, to "read" with a tutor at Silverton, went—as the common saying expressively phrases it—to the bad. Of course that downward journey—" to the bad "—took some lit tle time in making. And Julian was just over twenty-one when he reached *the bad* altogether. There were cavalry barracks at Silverton, and there was always a cavalry regiment stationed there. The younger of the officers were naturally enough among the most habitual associates of the young heir of Lindisfarn. And though it may very well be that no one of those young men went altogether to the bad himself, yet there can be little doubt that they helped to forward Julian on his road thither.

His most intimate friend and associate, however, at that time—when he was about from twenty to one-and-twenty, that is to say—was Frederick Falconer. And all those —his parents among the rest—who had seen with some alarm that Julian was becoming very " wild," considered that his intimacy with so steady and well-conducted a young man as the banker's son was, at all events, a good sign. The careful old banker, on the other hand, was by no means equally well pleased with the intimacy between the two young men. It was difficult, however, to interfere to put a stop to it, without taking unpleasantly strong measures, which would have caused much scandal and heartburning and enmity in the small social circle of a little country town. Old Mr. Falconer had, moreover, much confidence in the steadiness and good principles of his son. Some of the young cavalry officers, whose society the two Silverton youths frequented, were men of large means ; and stories were rife in Silverton of orgies and escapades which, in varied ways, involved expenditure on no inconsiderable scale. There were excursions to distant race-courses ; and more uncertain and cautiously whispered rumors of nights spent in rooms of the barracks, when suppers and champagne, in whatever abundance, were the least dangerous and objectionable portion of the night's amusement. Frederick Falconer, however, never exceeded his liberal, but not unreasonably large, allowance, and never appeared in want of money ; and the old banker considered that to be out of debt was to be out of danger, and that a young man who lived strictly within his means, and always made his quarter's allowance supply his quarterly expenditure, could not be going far wrong. There were not wanting in Silverton, however, one or two shrewd old fellows, who observed to one another, that there was such

a thing as being too *steady;* that young as Freddy Falconer was,—three or four years Julian's junior,—it was on the cards that young Lindisfarn might get more harm from young Falconer than the reverse. But of course the prudent old gentlemen, whose observation suggested to them such remarks, were too prudent to make them out loud.

Certain it was, that young Lindisfarn did not imitate his steady friend's prudence in the matter of his expenses. Julian, on the contrary, always exceeded his more than liberal allowance, and was always importuning his father for money. And the easy, absent old canon, careless in money matters and culpably extravagant on his own account, did, without much resistance, and without any such inquiries as he ought in common prudence to have made, supply his son with sums, which at the end of the year very seriously increased the balance against him in Messrs. Falconer and Fishbourne's books. And then " my brother Noll " had to be applied to for assistance. And the jolly old squire—after roaring his indignation in the bank parlor, in tones which made every pane in the windows vibrate, and caused Mr. Fishbourne to shake in unison with them in his shoes, and Mr. Falconer to jump from his chair with the momentary idea of clapping his hand on Mr. Lindisfarn's mouth, before it had made known the business in hand to half Silverton—lent the money out of funds laid aside for the provision of his daughters, and forgot the transaction before the end of the week.

And then it was the same thing all over again, or rather a similar thing on a much extended scale. " *Major rerum nascitur ordo,*" as is ever the case in such careers as Julian Lindisfarn was running ; for the march to the devil always has to be played with a rapidly *crescendo* movement.

And then—and then,—to make a very sad story as short a one as may be,—one fine morning, in the year 1814, Julian Lindisfarn was missing from his father's house, and the bed in which he was supposed to have slept was found not to have been occupied. And it did come to the ears of some of those prudent old observers of their neighbors' affairs, of whom I spoke before, that Mr Thorburn, the Minor Canon, had told Peter Glenny, the organist, that, returning home through the Close late that night, he had seen young

Falconer in close confabulation with Julian in the shade of the wall of his father's house just under the young man's bedroom window. Mr. Frederick, however, was known by his family to have gone to bed in his own room at a much earlier hour; and everybody in Silverton knew that poor Ned Thorburn, though always perfectly good for a catch or a glee till any hour you please in the morning, was apt to be good for little else after twelve o'clock at night; and certainly *not* good as a witness to the identity of a person seen in dark shadow by him, when coming home from a remarkably pleasant meeting of good fellows. And when the facts, which the next day brought to light, were known in Silverton, neither Thorburn, nor Glenny, nor any of those few persons whose ears the report of the Minor Canon's vision had reached, cared to recur to the circumstances.

The terrible facts were shortly these :—

The London mail, which reached Silverton on the very morning on which Julian disappeared thence, brought letters to Messrs. Falconer and Fishbourne, which made it evident that the signature of their firm had been forged to drafts for very heavy amounts on their London correspondents. The execution of the forgery was so admirable that it was no wonder that the fraud had been successful. It is not necessary to detail the circumstances which, even if Julian's flight had not immediately pointed him out as the criminal, abundantly sufficed to bring the guilt home to him. It is sufficient to state that there was no possibility of doubt upon the subject. But it was at the time thought very extraordinary, even supposing that Julian Lindisfarn was gifted with that faculty of imitation, which might have enabled him to counterfeit so successfully the signature of the Silverton firm, that he should have possessed not only such a general acquaintance with the nature of banking business, as should have taught him how to perpetrate the fraud he contemplated, but such a knowledge of the relations between Messrs. Falconer and Fishbourne and the London house as must have guided him in his operations, and above all, the information, which it seemed impossible to doubt that he must have possessed, of the exact time when the course of business communication between the Silverton bankers and their London correspondents must bring the fraud to detection. It was certainly within the limits

of possibility that Julian's flight was accidentally well timed; but it appeared hardly credible that such was the case.

It was a black day in Silverton—that which brought this sad catastrophe to light; for old Dr. Lindisfarn, despite his faults and eccentricities, was a popular man in Silverton, and the old squire at the Chase was more than popular,—he was exceedingly beloved, not only in Silverton, but throughout the county. The poor, sorely-stricken mother, too, though Lady Sempronia was not much liked, could not but be deeply pitied on this sad occasion.

It was indeed a heavy blow on all on whom any part of the reflected disgrace fell. And the partner of the London house came down to Silverton; and there were long, mysterious sittings with lawyers in the back parlor, at Falconer and Fishbourne's; and the downstricken father, with bowed white head, had to be there; and the hearty old squire, of whom men remarked that he looked suddenly ten years older, had to be there. And it was said that the London firm behaved forbearingly and well; and that the Silverton banker had behaved equally well; and though nobody knew what arrangements had been come to respecting the loss of the money, it was known that there would be no prosecution, and that the lamentable facts would be hushed up, as far as possible.

Before long it became known, too, that the miserable young man, who had caused all this wide-spreading sorrow and suffering, had succeeded in making good his escape to the opposite coast of France, in a fishing-vessel belonging to the small fishing-town at the mouth of the estuary of the Sill, about five or six miles from Silverton. Under the miserable circumstances of the case, it was a relief to his family to know that he was out of the country. For those were days in which death was the penalty of forgery, and it was one of the crimes to which it was deemed necessary to show no mercy.

A little later, news reached Silverton, that the lost one had left France for America : and it was known that the heir to the respected old name and fine estate of Lindisfarn was an exiled wanderer, none knew where, in the New World. For if Julian had never scrupled before his fall to importune his father for money, shame, or some other feeling, prevented him from ever making any application to him afterward. Had it been possible to

2

obtain such information as might have made it practicable to communicate with him, he would not have been left without the means of support. But from the day of his escape no word came from him; nor, beyond the fact of his landing in America, could any trace of him be discovered.

And so the little girl at Lindisfarn Chase, Julian's Cousin Kate, then between eight and nine years old, had to be taught that she must forget all about Cousin Julian, and name his name no more. To the child this was of course not difficult. The Silverton public, also, when they had had their talk; when some had declared that they never could have believed such a thing possible, while others less loudly but more pertinaciously asserted that they had all along foreseen that Julian Lindisfarn's career must needs lead to some such catastrophe; and when Mr. Frederick Falconer had expressed to a sufficient number of persons the shock and astonishment which this unhappy business had been to him; had admitted that he knew poor Julian to be more dissipated than he could have wished, but had always deemed him the soul of honor and integrity, and had sufficiently often " prayed God that it might be a warning to him for life of the necessity of care in the choice of associates,"—then Julian Lindisfarn was forgotten in Silverton, and his place knew him no more.

Of course, it was not so up at the Chase; and still less so in the now still and quiet old house in the Close. But, save when the incorrigible canon would now and then throw poor Lady Sempronia into a fit of hysterics, which sent her to bed for eight-and-forty hours, by speaking of his son in total oblivion of all the misery which had fallen on him, his name was never heard.

There was one other house, not in but near Silverton, where the fugitive was not forgotten, nor the sound of his name unheard. There was another chapter in the little edifying story of Julian Lindisfarn's Silverton life, of which very little was known at that time to his friends or to any one in Silverton; and which may here be touched on as lightly, and got over as quickly, as possible; though subsequent events make it absolutely necessary to the understanding of the sequel of the history to give a succinct statement of the facts.

Stretching along the coast and far into the interior of the country, there was a very extensive district of wild moorland, which ran up to within about ten miles from Silverton. Sill Moor, as this tract of land is called, was—and is still in a smaller degree—a peculiar district in many respects; and the few small villages, which are scattered at great distances from each other over its wide surface, are inhabited or were so forty years ago, by a peculiar and singularly wild population. In one of those moor villages, about fifteen miles from Silverton, which it will be necessary hereafter to speak of more at length, there was a somewhat better house than most of the others around it. In that house there lived an old widowed man, whose name was Jared Mallory, and who was, and for many years had been, the clerk of the neighboring ancient church, which was the parish church of an immense district of moorland. The village was called Chewton-in-the-Moor; and the living was held by Dr. Lindisfarn with his Canonry. And in Jared Mallory's lone house lived with him Barbara Mallory, his daughter. And there was no girl in Silverton, or in all the country-side, so beautiful as Barbara Mallory, the wild moor-flower. And on that fatal morning of Julian's flight, he did not make straight for the fishing village on the coast at which he embarked, but went round by Chewton-in-the-Moor. And there in the gray moor mist, a little before the dawn, under the shelter of one of the huge gray boulder-stones that stud the moor, there was one of those partings that leave a scar upon the heart which no after-time can heal. And beautiful Barbara Mallory, as she clung half frantically with one arm to the man, whom the fear at his heels was compelling to tear himself away from her, pressed a child six months old to her breast with the other. But though she was a mother, the villagers still called her Bab Mallory. And the desolation in that lone moorland house was even worse than the desolation in the childless house in the Close.

No more was heard in Silverton of Julian Lindisfarn for three years after the date of his flight. Then came a report of his death, vague and unaccompanied by any particulars; but referring to persons and places, which enabled an agent sent out to America by his family, to ascertain the following facts. After having been about a twelvemonth in the United States, he passed into Canada, and there, it appeared, became associated with a small band of independent adventurers, some twenty in number, bound on a journey into the fur regions of the far north-west. The party made, it seemed, one tolerably fortunate journey, and returned for a second venture in the following year. But having been surprised one night in their camp, on the further side of the Rocky Mountains, by a small band of marauding Indians, not much exceeding their own in number, they had had to engage in a desperate struggle in which several of both parties were slain. Among these was Julian Lindisfarn. Of course as large material interests depended on the fact of his death, it was desirable that the evidence of it should be satisfactory. And that which the agent, who had been sent to America for the purpose, was enabled to obtain, was perfectly so. He had spoken with, and brought back with him the authenticated testimony of three survivors of the fray with the Indians, who had seen him slain by them.

These facts became known to his family in 1817. The unfortunate young man must have been about four-and-twenty at the time of his death. This was the event that so materially changed, as has been remarked, the state of things at Lindisfarn Chase. Mr. Oliver Lindisfarn's twin daughters became the coheiresses of Lindisfarn.

It cannot be supposed that under the circumstances, Julian Lindisfarn's death should have been felt to be otherwise than a fortunate event by most of the members of his family. The Silverton public naturally felt, and said, that it was the best thing that could have happened in every point of view. Some additional tears wetted poor Lady Sempronia's pillow. But it was in the lone house in the moor that Julian Lindisfarn's death caused the sharpest pang.

CHAPTER IV.
THE FAMILY AT THE CHASE.

In consequence of the circumstances of the family history narrated in the preceding chapter, Margaret Lindisfarn was about to return to the home of her ancestors in the recognized position of co-heiress to the family estates,—a sufficiently brilliant destiny, considering that the property was a good and well-paid four thousand a year, unencumbered by mortgage, debt, or other claims of any sort. Had those circumstances not occurred,—had Julian Lindisfarn been still living,—Margaret's position, instead of being a brighter one than that of her sister, as it had appeared to be at the time when she had been adopted by the De Rennevilles, and Kate had only her godmother's six thousand pounds to look to, would have now been a far less splendid one. For shortly before the time at which she was returning from Paris to Silverton, all the magnificent De Renneville prospects had suddenly made themselves wings and flown away.

The large fortune of the Baron de Renneville had been, like that of many another Frenchman bearing a name indicative of former territorial greatness, entirely a financial and not a territorial one. And that incapacity for leaving well alone, which is generated by the habitual excitement of a life spent in speculation, and which has wrecked so many a colossal fabric of commercial greatness, was fatal to that of M. de Renneville. A series of unfortunate operations on the Paris *Bourse* had ended by leaving him an utterly ruined man. And there was an end of all expectations from Margaret's Parisian relatives.

Of course the shock of this calamity was very differently felt from what it would have been, had it occurred during the lifetime of Julian Lindisfarn. It was very materially modified to the young lady herself, and doubtless also to the kind relatives who had stood in the position of parents to her from her infancy, by the knowledge that there was a very substantial English inheritance to fall back on, now that the more splendid but less secure French visions had faded away. Nevertheless, the calamity had been felt very distinctly to *be* a calamity by Margaret. In the first place, she was, of course, laudably grieved to be obliged to part with those who had been as parents to her. In the next place, she very naturally looked forward with anything but

pleasure to a migration from Paris to Silverton, and from the home of an adoptive father and mother, whom she knew, to that of a real father of whom she knew nothing. And in the third place, she estimated with very practical accuracy the difference between an heiress-ship to some six or seven thousand a year, and an heiress-ship to two thousand only. For somehow or other it happens, that this is a point on which the most beautifully *candide* French girls are generally found to possess a singularly sound and business-like knowledge. We are all aware how cautiously and scrupulously the French system of educating *demoiselles comme il faut* labors to fence in the snow-like mental purity of its pupils from all such contact or acquaintance with the world as might involve the slightest risk of producing a thought or a sentiment which might by possibility lead to something calculated to blemish the perfection of that *ingénuité*, which is so eloquently expressed by every well-schooled feature of these carefully trained and jealously guarded maidens. Nevertheless, a due appreciation of the intimate connection between cash and social position is not among the tabooed subjects of any French female schoolroom, whether it be under the paternal roof or that of some *Sacré Cœur*, or other such first-rate conventual establishment.

For various reasons, therefore, it was a black day for poor Margaret when she had to leave her Parisian home for an exile *au fond du province*, as she expressed it, in foggy England. "At the bottom of the province," Silverton certainly was, if the top of it is to be supposed to be the part nearest London. But the Silvertonians had no notion that the "sun yoked his horses so far from" their western city as to justify the sort of idea which Margaret had formed to herself of its remoteness. And least of all had the warm hearts who on that bright September afternoon were expecting the arrival of the recovered daughter of the house at Lindisfarn Chase the remotest idea that the home to which they were eager to welcome her was other than on the whole about the happiest and most highly favored spot of earth's surface.

Kate was, as Lady Farnleigh had promised her she should be, in very good time to join the assembled members of the family before the hour at which Margaret was expected.

They were all in the long low drawing-room, lined with white panelling somewhat yellow with years, and gilt mouldings, the four windows of which looked out on the terrace in front of the house. It was very evident, at a glance, that something out of the ordinary routine of the family life was about to take place. None of those there assembled would have been in the room at that hour in the ordinary course of things. And there was an unmistakable air of expectancy, and even of a certain degree of nervousness, about them all. The old squire had caused an immense fire to be made in the ample grate; and was very evidently suffering from the effects of it. It was a beautifully warm afternoon; but the squire had an idea that his daughter was coming from a southern clime where it was always very hot,—and besides, the making of a big fire seemed to his imagination to be in some sort symbolical of welcome. He was walking up and down the long room, looking out of the windows, as he passed them, wiping his massive broad forehead and florid face with his silk handkerchief, and consulting his watch every two minutes. He was dressed in a blue coat with metal buttons, yellow kerseymere waistcoat, drab breeches, top-boots, and a white neckcloth. His head was bald in front, and the long locks of silver hair hung over his coat-collar behind. It is worth while to specify these particulars of his toilet, for he never appeared otherwise before dinner.

"I am glad you are come, Kate; I began to think you would have been late! And I should not have been pleased at that. I suppose her ladyship would not come in to-day?"

"No. She thought she had better not to-day; I took good care about the time. It's not near two yet."

"It wants thirteen minutes," said the squire, again looking at his watch: "she can hardly be here before two. Go and listen if you can hear wheels, Mat; you have an ear like a hare."

The "Mat" thus addressed was to every other human being in Sillshire, from the Earl of Silverton at Sillhead Park to the hostlers at the Lindisfarn Arms, Mr. Mat. It would have altogether discomposed him to address him as Mr. Matthew Lindisfarn; but he would not have liked anybody save the squire to call him plain "Mat." He was Mr. Mat; and only recognized himself under that name and title. Mr. Mat was a second cousin of the squire; and had been received into the house by the squire's father, when he had been left an orphan at twelve years old, wholly unprovided for. Since that time he had lived, boy and man, at Lindisfarn Chase; and was considered by himself and by everybody else, as much and as inseparably a part of the place as the old elms and the rooks in them. He was about ten years the squire's junior, that is to say he was about fifty at the time of which I am speaking. Mr. Mat, looked at from one point of view, was a very good-for-nothing sort of fellow; but looked at from another, he was good for a great many things, and by no means valueless in his place in the world. He was essentially good-for-nothing at the prime and generally absolutely paramount business of earning his own living. If kind fate had not popped him into the special niche which suited him so well, he must have starved or lived in the poorhouse. He was perfectly well fitted, as far as knowledge went, to be a game-keeper, and a first-rate one. But he never would have kept to his duties. The very fact that they were his duties, and the means of earning his bread, would have made them distasteful to him. Not that Mr. Mat was a lazy, or in some sort even an idle, man. He was capable of great exertion upon occasions. But then the occasions must be irregular ones. His good qualities again were many. He was the best farrier and veterinary surgeon in the country side though totally without any science on the subject. He had a fine bass voice, a good ear, and sung a good song, or took a part in a glee in a first-rate style. He was a main support, accordingly, of the Silverton Glee-club, of which the Rev. Minor Canon Thorburn was president. But unlike that reverend votary of Apollo, Mr. Mat, though he liked his glass, was as sober as a judge. Mr. Mat, though perfectly able to speak quite correct and unprovincial English, when he saw fit to do so, was apt to affect the Sillshire dialect, to a certain degree; and if there chanced to be any person present whom Mr. Mat suspected of finery or London-bred airs, he was sure to infuse a double dose of his beloved provincial Doric into his speech. He had a special grudge against any Sillshire man whom he suspected of being ashamed of his own country dialect. And

Freddy Falconer was the object of his strong dislike mainly on this ground; and the butt of many a shaft from Mr. Mat purposely aimed at this weakness. Often and often when Mr. Fred was doing the superfine, especially before ladies or Londoners, Mr. Mat would come across him with a " We Zillshire volk, muster Vreddy!" to that elegant young gentleman's intense disgust. There was accordingly but little love lost between him and Mr. Mat. And upon one occasion Freddy had attempted to come over Mr. Mat by doing the distant and dignified, and calling him Mr. Matthew Lindisfarn; but he brought down upon himself such a roasting on every occasion when he and Mr. Mat met for the next month afterwards that he was fain not to repeat the offence. Kate, who was a prime favorite with Mr. Mat, and who could hardly do wrong in his eyes, had once ventured to remonstrate with him on these provincial proclivities, upon which he had at once avowed and justified his partiality.

"To think," he said, "of a Lindisfarn lass" —(he always spoke of the young ladies of the family, whether of the present or of former generations, as Lindisfarn lasses;) — "to think of a Lindisfarn lass having no ear vor Zillshire! Vor my part, I zem to taste all the pleasant time I've known, Zillshire man and boy for virty years in the zound of it, and I du love it. I zem it's so homely and friendly-like. And, Miss Kate, yew du love it yourself, yew don't talk like their vulgar London minced-up gibberish."

Mr. Mat in appearance was a great contrast to the squire. He was a shorter and smaller man, though by no means undersized. The squire was six feet one, and broad in proportion. Mr. Mat's head was as black as the squire's was white, and whereas the latter allowed his silver locks to fall almost on his shoulders, Mr. Mat cropped his coal-black hair so short that it stood up bristling like a scrubbing-brush. He had a specially bright black eye under a large and bushy black eyebrow; a remarkably brilliant set of regular teeth; and would probably have been a decidedly good-looking man, if he had not been deeply marked with the small-pox. As it was, it must be admitted that Mr. Mat was far from good-looking. Yet there was a mingled shrewdness and kindly good-humor in his face that made it decidedly an agreeable one to those who knew him; and few ever found Mr. Mat's ugliness repulsive after a week's acquaintance. His dress, like that of the squire, never varied. Before dinner he always wore a green coat with metal buttons, bearing on them a fox's head, or some such adornment, a scarlet cloth waistcoat, a colored neckerchief, drab breeches and long buff leather gaiters. At dinner, Mr. Mat always appeared in black coat and trousers, white waistcoat and neck-cloth; and, curiously enough,—unless Fred Falconer led him specially into temptation,—with perfectly correct and unprovincial English.

There was one other member of the family party present, who, though the reader has already heard of her, merits being presented to him a little more formally. This was Miss Imogene Lindisfarn. She was, to a yet greater degree than Mr. Mat, an inseparable part and parcel of the Lindisfarn establishment. She was, at the time in question, in her seventy-eighth year, and was the squire's aunt. As long as he could recollect,—and much longer, therefore, than anybody else about the place, except old Brian Wyvill, the keeper, a brother of the verger at the cathedral, could recollect —Miss Imogene had kept the keys, made the tea for breakfast, and superintended the female part of the establishment. She was rather short, and still hale, active, and as upright as a ramrod. She always wore a rich lavender-colored silk dress, which as she walked rustled an accompaniment to the pit-a-pat of her high-heeled shoes. A spotless white crape cap, and equally spotless cambric handkerchief, pinned cornerwise over her shoulders, completed her attire. A very slight touch of palsy gave a little vibratory motion to her head, which seemed, when she was laying down the law, as on domestic matters she was rather apt to do, to impart a sort of defiant expression to her bearing. She never appeared without a little basket full of keys in her hand, and the perpetual never-changed volume of Clarissa Harlow, already mentioned, She was the only member of the family who addressed the squire as " Mr. Lindisfarn." Mr. Mat always called him " squire;" and Kate, somewhat irreverently, but to her father's great delight, was wont to call him " Noll." As for Miss Imogene, she had never been called anything but " Miss Immy" by any human being for the last sixty years.

Miss Immy had cake and wine, and a most delicately cut plate of sandwiches, on a tray near at hand, prepared ready to be administered to the traveller on the instant of her arrival. She had also a reserve of tea and exquisite Sillshire cream, in case that kind of refreshment should be preferred; and she had thrice, in the last quarter of an hour, ascertained by personal inspection that the kettle was boiling. Miss Immy had meditated much on the question what kind of refection would probably be most in accordance with the habits of the Parisian-bred stranger; and she had brought all that she could remember to have ever heard on the subject of French modes of life to bear on the subject. But *soupe maigre* and frogs were the only things that had presented themselves to her mind as adapted by any special propriety for the occasion, and as both these were for different reasons out of her reach, she had been forced to fall back on English ideas. But she was not without uncomfortable misgivings that very possibly the foreign-bred young lady might have requirements of some wholly unexpected and unimagined kind.

It was evident, indeed, that they were all a little nervous in their different ways; and very naturally so. Mr. Mat was least troubled by any feeling of the kind; being saved from it by the entirety of his conviction that no human being could do otherwise than better their condition and increase their happiness, by coming from any other part of the world to Sillshire.

At length, Mr. Mat cried, "Hark! There is the carriage! Yes, there it is. They've just passed the lodge." And all of them hurried out to the porch in the centre of the terrace in front of the house, where they were joined by three or four fine dogs, all proving their participation in the excitement of the moment by barking vociferously. Old Brian Wyvill, the octogenarian keeper, came hobbling up after them. Mr. Banting, the old butler, followed by a couple of rustics still struggling with the scarcely completed operation of getting their arms into their old-fashioned liveries, came running out at the door. Coachman and groom had gone with the carriage to meet Miss Margaret at Silverton, and were now coming up the drive from the lodge. The female portion of the establishment had assembled just inside the hall-door, grouping themselves in attitudes which suggested a strong contest in their minds between curiosity and fear, and readiness to take to flight at the shortest notice, on the first appearance of danger.

Crunch went the gravel! Pit-a-pat went most of the hearts there at a somewhat accelerated pace! The dogs barked more furiously than ever. The rooks began flying in circles around their ancient city up in the elm-clump on the left side of the house, and holding a very tumultuous meeting to inquire into the nature of the unusual circumstances taking place beneath them. The squire hallooed to the dogs to be quiet, in a great mellow, musical voice, producing a larger volume of sound than all the rest of the noises put together. The peacocks on the wall of the garden behind the elm-clump, stimulated by emulation, screamed their utmost. And in the midst of all this uproar, Thomas Tibbs, the coachman, pulled up his horses exactly at the door, with a profound consciousness that Paris could do no better in *that* department at all events.

CHAPTER V.

MARGARET'S FIRST DAY AT HOME.

In the next instant, half a dozen eager hands had pulled open the carriage-door; and an exceedingly elegant and admirably dressed figure sprang from it, and with one bound, as it seemed, executed with such marvellous skill that the process involved no awkward movement, and no derangement of the elegant costume, threw itself on its knees at the feet of the astonished squire.

"*Mon père!*" cried Miss Margaret, in an accent so admirably fitted for the occasion that it seemed to include an exhaustive exposition of all the sentiments that a *jeune personne bien élevée* might, could, should, would, and ought to feel on returning after long absence to the parental roof.

Her attitude was admirable. The heavy folds of her rich silk dress fell down behind, sloping out on the stone step as artistically as if they had been arranged by skilful hands after her position had been assumed. Her clasped hands were raised toward the squire's face with an expression that would have arrested the fall of the axe in the hands of an executioner. And her upturned head showed to all present a very beautiful face, in which the most striking feature, as it was then seen, was a magnificent pair of large, dark, liquid eyes.

"My dear child!" cried the squire in a stentorian voice, that made the fair girl at his feet start just a little—(but she recovered herself instantly)—"My dear child! Glad to see thee! Welcome to Lindisfarn. Welcome home, lass!" he continued, evidently desirous of getting her up, if possible, but much puzzled about the proper way of handling her, if indeed there were any proper way.

"*Mon père!*" reiterated his daughter, with a yet more heart-rending filial intonation on the word.

Old Brian Wyvill was affected by it (like the audience recorded as having been melted to tears by a great tragedian's pronunciation of the word "Mesopotamia"), and drew the back of his rough hand across his eyes. The lady's-maid whispered to the housekeeper that it was "beautiful!" But Miss Immy, greatly startled, trotted up to the still kneeling young lady, with that peculiar little short-stepping amble of hers, holding a bottle of salts in her tremulous hand, which she poked under Margaret's nose, saying, as she did so, "Poor thing, the journey! It has been too much for her!"

Margaret winked and caught her breath, and the tears came into her fine eyes. Human nature could not have done less, with Miss Immy's salts under her nose; but she did not belie her training, and showed herself equal to the occasion.

"*De grâce, madame!*" she said, putting aside Miss Immy's bottle with one exquisitely gloved hand. "It is my father I see!" she added, with a very slight foreign accent.

"To be zure, Miss Margy!" struck in Mr. Mat. "To be zure it's yonr vather! And he wouldn't hurt ye on ony account. Don't you be afraid of the squire. He has no more vice in him than a lamb!"

"Don't be a fool, Mat! My girl afraid of me!" shouted the squire.

"My opinion is, the lass is frighted!" returned Mr. Mat, in an undertone to the squire, looking at Margaret shrewdly as he spoke, with the sort of observant look with which he would have examined a sick animal. "Mayhap," he continued in the same aside tone, "it's the dogs. I'll take 'em off."

"I'm right glad to hear you speak English, and speak it very well too, my dear. I was beginning to be afraid you could speak nothing but French," said the squire.

"Oh, yes, sir," said his daughter. She

had now risen to her feet, rather disappointed that her father had not raised her from the ground, and pressed her to his bosom, as he probably would have done if he had not been too much afraid of injuring her toilet,—"Oh, yes, sir, thanks to my kind instructors, I have cultivated my native language."

"That's a comfort," said the squire; "for I am ashamed to say that I have cultivated no other! But Kate there, and Lady Farnleigh, will talk to you in French as long as you like."

Upon this, Kate, who had hitherto hung back, looking on the scene which has been described with a sort of dismayed surprise, that had the effect of making her feel all of a sudden shy toward her sister, came forward, and putting her arm round Margaret's waist, gave her a kiss, saying as she did so, "Shall we go in, dear? You must be tired. And Miss Immy will not be contented till you have had something to eat and drink."

"*Ma sœur!*" exclaimed the new-comer; again compressing into that word a whole homily for the benefit of the bystanders on all the beauty and sanctity of that sweet relationship, and returning Kate's kiss first on one cheek and then on the other.

And then they all went into the drawing-room, the two sisters walking with their arms round each other's waists.

They were singularly alike, and yet singularly contrasted, those twin Lindisfarn lasses,—to use Mr. Mat's mode of speech. Kate was a little the taller of the two; a very little; but till one saw the sisters side by side, as they were then walking across the hall to the drawing-room, the difference of height in Kate's favor might have been supposed to be greater than it really was. Both had a magnificent abundance of that dark, chestnut hair, the rich brown gloss of which really does imitate the color of a ripe horsechestnut fresh from its husk. But Kate wore hers in large heavy curls on either side of her face and neck, while Margaret's was arranged in exquisitely neat bands bound closely round the small and classically shaped head. Both had fine eyes; but with respect to that difficultly described feature, it was much less easy to say in what the two sisters differed, and in what they were alike, than in the more simple matter of the hair. At first sight one was inclined to say that the eyes were totally different in the two. Then a closer examination convinced the observer that in both girls they were large, well-opened, and marked by that specially limpid appearance which suggests the same idea of great depth which is given by an unruffled and perfectly pellucid pool of still water. In both girls they were of that beautiful brown color, which is so frequently found in conjunction with the above-noted appearance. And yet, notwithstanding all these points of similarity, the eyes of the two sisters,—or perhaps it would be more accurate to say the expression of them,—were remarkably different. Those who saw them both, when no particular emotion was affecting the expression of their features, would have said that Margaret's eyes were the more tender and loving. But those who knew Kate well would have said, " Wait till the eyes have some special message of tenderness from the heart, and *then* look at them." Kate's eyes were the more mobile and changeful in expression ; Margaret's, the more languishing. There was perhaps more of intellect in the former, more of sentiment in the latter. In complexion the difference was most complete and decided. Kate's complexion was a brilliant one. Though the skin was as perfectly transparent as the purest crystal, and even the most transient emotion betrayed itself in the heightened or diminished color of the cheek, its own proper hue was of a somewhat richer tint than that of the hedge-rose. The whole of Margaret's face, on the contrary, was perfectly pale. The skin was of that beautiful satiny texture, and alabaster-like purity of white, which is felt by many men to be more beautiful than any the most exquisite coloring. Perhaps this absolute absence of color helped to impart to the eyes of Margaret Lindisfarn that peculiar depth and languishing appearance of tenderness which so remarkably characterized them. Both girls had specially beautiful and slender figures ; but that of Kate had more of elasticity and vigor ; that of her sister more of lithe yieldingness and flexibility. Both had long, slender, gracefully-formed hands ; but those of Margaret were the whiter and more satiny of the two. Both had in equal perfection the beauty of ankle, instep, and foot, which insures a clean, race-horse like action and graceful gait. Yet the carriage of the two sisters was as remarkably different as anything about them. Kate's every step expressed decision, energy, vigor, elasticity,—frankness, if one may predicate such a quality of a step. Margaret's gait, on the contrary, seemed perfectly adapted to express timidity, languor, and graceful softness in its every movement. On the whole, the differences between the two sisters would be what would first strike a stranger on seeing them for the first time. The points of similarity between them would be noted afterward, or might never be discovered at all unless by the intelligent eye of some particularly interested or habitually accurate observer.

And then the somewhat up-hill process of making acquaintance with the stranger had to be gone through. And Margaret did not appear to be one of those who are gifted with the special tact and facilities which make such processes rapid and easy. The cake and wine were administered, Miss Immy standing over the patient the while, with one hand on her hip, filled to overflowing with the kindliest thoughts and intentions, but having very much the air of a severe hospital nurse enforcing some very disagreeable discipline. But Miss Margaret nibbled a morsel of cake, and having put into a tumbler of water just enough wine to slightly color it, she sipped a little of the uninviting mixture.

" Bless me, my dear !" cried the old lady, whose speech was, like that of most of her contemporaries in a similar rank of life at that period, tinctured with a very unmistakable flavor of provincialism, " *Du* let me *pit* a little drop more wine into your glass ; zems to me, it aint fit drink for either man or beast in that fashion."

" *Merci, madame!* Thank you ! I always water my wine so much. I am used to it." said Margaret.

" Well, if you are used to it, my dear ; but to my mind it seems like spoiling *tew* good things. Better drink clean water than water bewitched that fashion ! The Lindisfarn water is celebrated."

" It is very good, thank you, madame."

" Are they well off for water in Paris ?" asked the squire, catching at the subject in his difficulty of finding anything to say to his new daughter.

" Oh, we had always exquisite water, sir ; " replied Margaret with more of warmth in her tone than she had yet put into it. " Madame de R-rwenneville " (this strange orthography is intended, however inadequately, to represent the most perfectly executed Parisian *grasseyement*)—"Madame de R-rwenneville was always very particular about the filtering of the water."

"Filtering!" cried Mr. Mat in a tone of the profoundest contempt. "You can't make bad water into good by filtering, filter as much as you will. We'll do better than that for you here, Miss Margy!"

"I'm very particular about my filtering too, my dear;" said Mr. Lindisfarn; "the Sillshire gravel does it for me. There's my filtering machine up above the house there, all covered over with forest trees for ornament." And the squire laughed at his conceit, a huge but not unmusical laugh, which set every panel in the wainscoting on the wall vibrating.

Margaret opened her fine eyes to their utmost extent, and gazed on her father with astonishment, very near akin to dismay.

"We had very fine forest trees at Paris," she said, after a little pause, "in the garden of the Tuileries and the Champs Elysées."

"Ah! I am longing for you to tell me all about Paris," said Kate; "I should so like to see it. And all about aunt, and poor M. de Renneville. It is very sad. We shall never get to the end of all we have to say to each other!"

"Well! I shall go and beat the turnips in the copse-side twelve acres," said the squire, rising. "Come along, Mat. Call the dogs. Good-by till dinner-time, my dear; Miss Immy and Kate are longing to show you all the old place. You will soon feel yourself at home among us. But I dare say it will seem dull at first after Paris."

And so saying, the squire and Mr. Mat left the room.

"Now, Miss Immy," said Kate, "I shall take possession of Margaret till dinner-time. I'm sure you must have a thousand things to do; and I mean to have her all to myself."

"Good-by, dears; I'm all behind-hand to-day. Phœbe brought in the morning's eggs hours ago; and I have not had time to mark 'em yet. Kate will show you your room, Margy dear. I hope you will find all to your liking. But it's to be thought that our Sillshire ways may be different to your French fashion; but if there is anything we can get, you've only to speak. I did go into Silverton myself yesterday, to see if I could find any French-fashioned things. But I could only find a bit of Paris soap at Piper's, the perfumer's. I got that. You will find it in your room, dear."

And so Miss Immy bustled off on her avocations, leaving the two sisters together.

"Don't let us stay here," said Kate; "come up-stairs and see your room and mine. They are close together, with a door between them. Is not that charming? That is the door of the library," she continued, as they crossed the hall; "we must not go in now."

"Is it kept locked?" said Margaret.

"Good gracious, no! Locked! What should it be locked for?" rejoined Kate with much surprise.

"I thought it might be, as you said we must not go in. Besides, if it is left open, we might get at the books, you know; all sorts of books. Not that I should ever dream of doing anything so wrong, of course."

"Get at the books! Why, Margy dear, what are books made for, but to be got at? I get at them, I can tell you!"

"Oh, Kate! I have never been used to do anything without the knowledge of my dear aunt. What would papa think of you, if he found you out?"

"Good heavens, Margaret, what are you dreaming of?" cried Kate, in extreme astonishment, and coloring up at some of the unpleasant ideas her sister had called up in her mind. "Found me out! found me out in using the books in the library! I don't understand you. I used to be afraid sometimes, some ten years ago, of being found out in *not* using them!"

"But you said we must not go in," rejoined Margaret.

"Because if we once went in, it would take up all the time till dinner; because I want to take you up-stairs first. There are so many things to show you. The library must wait till to-morrow morning."

"We will ask papa, at dinner-time, if I may go there."

"Ask papa! Why, Noll will think you crazy."

"And pray who is Noll?" asked her sister.

"Noll! why, papa to be sure! Don't you know the name of your own father, Oliver Lindisfarn, Esquire, of Lindisfarn Chase? But that is too long for every-day use; so I call him Noll for short."

"Oh, my sister! Respect for our parents I have always been taught to consider one of our most sacred duties. What would papa say, if he knew that you called him Noll?"

Kate stared at her sister in absolutely speechless astonishment and dismay;—dismay at the wide gulf which she seemed to be discovering between her sister and herself, and the long path which would have to be travelled over by one or other of them before she and her sister could meet in that sisterly union of mind and heart which she had been looking forward to with such pleasurable anticipation;—and speechlessness from the difficulty she felt in choosing at which point, of all those suggested by Margaret's last speech, she should begin her explanations.

"If papa were to hear me!" she said at length; "why he never hears anything else. It's as natural to him to hear me say Noll, as to hear the rooks in the rookery say 'caw!' I never do anything,—we none of us here do anything, that the others don't know of." (Here Margaret shot a glance half shrewdly observant and half knowingly confidential at her sister; but withdrew her eyes in the next instant.) "But perhaps things may be different in France," continued Kate, endeavoring to make the unknown quantity of this difference accountable for all that she found perplexing and strange to her in the manifestations of her sister's modes of thinking; "but you will soon get used to our ways, dearest; and to begin with, you must take to calling papa Noll at once. He is such a dear, darling old Noll!"

"I! I could never, never dare to do such a thing. Beside, do you know, Kate," continued Margaret, with no little solemnity in her manner, "I think, indeed I am almost *sure*, that Madame de R-rwenneville would say that it was *vulgar* to do so."

"Oh! then of course we must give it up," said Kate. She could not resist at the moment the temptation of so far resenting the impertinence involved in her sister's remark; but she repented of the implied sneer in the next moment. But she need hardly have taken herself to task, for Margaret replied with all gravity,—

"I think indeed that it would be better to do so, my sister!"

"Nonsense! you're joking. Margy dear. I would not call darling old Noll by any other name, and he would not have me call him by any other name, for all the world. What Madame de Renneville says may be very right

for Paris, but we are in Sillshire here, and have other ways. You'll soon get used to us. See, dear, this is your room!"

It was a charming room, with one large bow-window looking out on the trim and pretty, though rather old-fashioned, garden, on the east side of the house.

"Oh, what an immense room!" cried Margaret. "This my chamber! Why one might give a ball in it. It must be very cold."

"If you find it so, you shall have a fire; but I hardly think you will, our Sillshire climate is so mild,—much milder than London. See, this is my room; just such another as yours, with the same look out on the garden. I hardly ever have a fire. Used you to have one in your bedroom in Paris?"

"No; but then my chamber was a small one, not a third the size of this; and very well closed,—very pretty,—a love of a little chamber."

"I like a large room," said Kate, a little disappointed at the small measure of approbation the accommodation—which she had flattered herself was perfect, and which was in fact all that any lady could possibly desire—elicited from her Parisian-bred sister. "See, here are all my books, and my writing-table. I keep my drawing-table and all my drawing things on this side because of the light; and that leaves plenty of room for the toilet-table in front here. I should never have room for all these things in a small room."

"It seems very nice, certainly. Are you allowed to have a light at night?"

"Why—how do you mean, dear? We don't go to bed in the dark!"

"But I mean, are you allowed to keep your candle as long as you like?"

"Of course I keep it till I go to bed! Don't you do so too?"

"But if you are as long as you like about going to bed, you may do anything you please,—read any books you like, after they are all in bed and asleep. But I suppose," added she thoughtfully, "that the old woman downstairs sees how much candle you have burned."

"What strange notions you have, Margaret," said Kate, almost sadly, as she began to perceive that the distance that separated her from her sister was greater than she had at first seen it to be. "I *am* as long as ever I like about going to bed—which generally

is as short as I can make it ;—and I *do* read
any books I like after they are all in bed and
asleep ;—or rather I wish I did, and should
do so, were it not that I am always a great
deal too sleepy myself. Are you good at
keeping awake? I wish I was! And as to
the old woman down-stairs, as you call her,
that is Miss Immy ; and I don't think she
looks much after the candle-ends ;—though it
must be, by the way, about the only thing
that she don't look after, for she looks after
everything. Dear Miss Immy! I don't know
what Noll and I should do without Miss Immy.
And you must learn to love her as much as
we do."

"Who is she? Your *gouvernante*, I suppose. What a queer name, Miss Immy!"

"Miss Immy, Margy dear, is Miss Imogene
Lindisfarn, the sister of our grandfather,
Oliver Lindisfarn, and therefore our father's
aunt. She has lived at the Chase all her life,
and nothing would go on without her."

"What a strange old woman she seems!
I don't think she likes me by the way she
spoke to me. And who is that extraordinary
looking man, who looked at me as if I had
been some strange thing out of the *Jardin des
Plantes?*"

"The extraordinary looking man," said
Kate, laughing heartily, "is Matthew Lindisfarn, Esquire, commonly called Mr. Mat ;
a cousin of Noll's, also inseparable from and
very necessary to the Chase. We could not
get on without Mr. Mat. You will see him
looking rather less extraordinary at dinner
presently. And you will very soon get to
like him too, as well as Miss Immy."

"Is he a gentleman?" asked the stranger.

"Margaret!" cried Kate, and her eyes
flashed and her color mounted to her cheeks
as she spoke, "did I not tell you that his
name is Lindisfarn? Ask Lady Farnleigh,
or the dean, or old Brian Wyvill, or Dick
Cox, the ploughboy, whether he is a gentleman. But as I said before," she continued,
putting her arm round her sister's waist and
kissing her cheek, "you must get to know
us all and our ways, and then you will understand it all better, and come to be one of
us. Of course it must all be very different
from life at Paris, and all very strange to
you."

"Oh, so different!" said Margaret.

"And then there will be so many other
people for you to know and to like ;—Uncle

Theophilus and Lady Sempronia ;—and first
and foremost my own darling Lady Farnleigh.
And then I must introduce you to all our
beaux! We have some very presentable ones,
I assure you. And we shall have such lots
to do. And now we must be thinking of
dressing for dinner. You have to unpack your
things."

"Are there people coming to dine here to-
day?" asked Margaret.

"No, nobody. There will not be a soul
but ourselves," replied Kate.

"But must we dress then?" asked her
sister ; "why should we do so?"

"Oh, we always dress for dinner ;—that is,
put on an evening dress, you know. Noll
likes it. I think I had better ring for Simmons. She is our maid between us two, you
know. If you don't like setting to work to
unpack, now,—and we should hardly have
time before dinner,—I can lend you anything."

And so a partial unpacking was done ; and
amid perpetual running to and fro between
the two bedrooms by the door of communication ; — repeated declarations that they
should not be dressed in time for dinner, and
warnings from Simmons to the same effect,
followed by fresh interruptions for admiration, criticism, and comparison, the dressing
was at last done, and the two girls hurried
down the great staircase, just as the last bell
was ringing, leaving both their rooms strewed
with a chaos of feminine properties, which
Simmons declared it would be a week's work
to reduce to order.

Of course during the entirety of the couple
of hours thus delightfully spent by the two
sisters, the tongues of both of them were running a well-contested race ; but it is hardly
to be expected that a masculine pen should
undertake to report even any *disjecta membra*
of such a conversation. Simmons, however,
though her tongue was not altogether idle,
employed her eyes and ears the while with
more activity. And a brief statement of her
report, as made that evening to the assembled
areopagus in the servants' hall, may perhaps
afford the judicious reader as much insight
into the character of the newly arrived Miss
Lindisfarn as could be drawn from a more
detailed account of the enormous mass of
chatter that had passed between the two
girls.

Miss Simmons then announced it as her

opinion that Miss Margaret was "a deep one." "'Twere plain enough to see," she added, "that her maxim was, 'What's yours is mine; and what's mine's my own.'"

"Anyways she's a dewtiful daater!" said old Brian Wyvill; "I never zeed in all my life — and that's not zaying a little—anything so bewtiful as when she were a zupplicating the squoire like on the stone steps. 'Twere as good as any play; and I've zeed a many of 'em in my time."

"For my part," said rosy Betty housemaid, "I don't like the color of her!"

"I tell you all," rejoined Simmons, speaking with the authority of a somewhat superior position, "she is no more tu be compared tu our Miss Kate than Lindisfarn church is tu the cathedral of Silverton."

"'Twould be very unreasonable, and very unfair on her to expect she should be," said Mr. Banting; "Miss Kate's Lindisfarn bred!"

"Ay," said the cook, "and Lindisfarn fed! What can you expect from poor creatures that live on bread-and-water supe, and vrogs, with a bit of cabbage on Zundays?"

The self-evident truth of this proposition was recognized by a chorus of "Ay, indeed!"

"She's a sweet pretty lass, anyway," said Thomas Tibbs, the coachman; "and she were Lindisfarn born, if she weren't Lindisfarn bred. And there's a deal in blood."

"Ay! there be," said Dick Wyvill, the groom, a son of old Brian. "But pretty much depends on the way they are broke."

Meanwhile the dinner in the parlor had passed a little heavily. Notwithstanding the near relationship of the new-comer, all the party were conscious of a certain slight degree of restraint. Miss Immy was nervously afraid that her domestic arrangements might fail in some way or other to satisfy the requirements and tastes of her Parisian niece. She had held a long consultation with the cook respecting the production of some sample of presumed French cookery; and no pains had been spared in the preparation of a squat-looking lump of imperfectly baked dough, which appeared on the table under the appellation of a *vol-au-vent*. And Miss Immy was rather disappointed, though at the same time re-assured and comforted as to the future, when Miss Margaret, utterly declining to try the *vol-au-vent*, made an excel-lent dinner on a slice of roast-beef, only requesting her papa to cut it from the most underdone part, and rather shocking all present by observing that she "loved it bleeding."

Hannah, the cook, gave the untouched *vol-au-vent* entire to Dick, the ploughboy, and drew the most favorable auguries as to Margaret's rapid physical, moral, and intellectual improvement, when she heard of the manner in which that young lady had preferred to dine.

Nevertheless, the dinner, as has been said, passed rather heavily. The squire himself was not without anxiety as to the possibility of making his Parisian-bred daughter comfortable, happy, and contented with all at Lindisfarn. And Mr. Mat was tormented by suspicions that the new member of the family might turn out to be "fine," and that Paris airs might be even worse than London ones. And Margaret herself was laboring under the influence of that undefinable sense of uneasiness which the Italians well call "subjection." She had that unpleasant feeling toward Mr. Mat which arises from the consciousness of having greatly erred in one's estimate of the social position of anybody, and perhaps, for aught one can tell, manifested one's mistake. It would have given me a very favorable opinion of the young lady's gentle breeding, if she *had* at once discovered that Mr. Mat, as seen in his green coat and buff gaiters, was to all intents and purposes a gentleman. But it would be hard to blame her too severely for having mistaken him for a gawekeeper. As to her father, she seemed to feel more strongly than ever the utter impossibility of calling him "Noll." It appeared to her that she had never seen so striking an impersonation of aristocratic and respect-compelling dignity; and she was not far wrong.

The evening, too, passed slowly; and at a very early hour it was voted *nem. con.* that the traveller must be tired, and must be wanting to go to bed. But there was one matter which had already given Margaret much pain two or three times during this her first afternoon in her father's house; and when, as they were all taking their candlesticks to go to bed, an opportunity occurred of adverting to the subject, she was determined to attempt a remedy for the evil while it might yet be not incurable.

"Good-night, Margy, my darling, and God bless thee!" said her father, putting one hand fondly on her head, and kissing her on the forehead.

"Good-night, Miss Margy. If you oversleep yourself, I'll give you a rouse in the morning with the dogs under your window," said Mr. Mat.

"Good-night, Margy dear. I trust your bed and all will be as you like it, and that you will sleep well," said Miss Immy.

And, "Come along, Margy dear! We sha'n't get to bed before we have had some more talk, I'll be bound," said Kate.

The utterers of all these kindly "goodnights" had little notion that they were inflicting so many stabs in the heart of the object of them. But so it was; and the reiterated blows were more than she could bear. Was her migration *au fond du province* to involve a transformation of herself into a dairymaid, that she should be called "Margy"? It was too odious. It would be "Meg" next! She could not bear it. And then before strangers too: they would no doubt do the same! Before *des jeunes gens!* She should sink into the earth. So, while the tears gathered in her fine eyes,—"tears from the depth of some divine despair,"—she looked round on the blank faces of the little circle gathered about her, and clasping her hands in an attitude of unexceptionable elegance, exclaimed in tones of the most touching entreaty,—

"Oh! call me Marrguérrwite; not that horrid name. My father! my sister! dear friends! call me Marrguérrwite!" she said, uttering the word in a manner wholly unattainable by insular organs.

The little party looked at each other in blank dismay, while the suppliant continued to hold her hands clasped in a sort of circular appeal.

"My love," said the squire, "you shall be called any way you like best. Let it be Margaret; but I'll be shot if I can say it as you do, not if 'twas to save my life."

"To my thinking, 'Margy' is quite a pretty name," said Mr. Mat, more confirmed than ever in his suspicions of latent "finery."

"But, sissy darling," said Kate, laughing and putting her arm caressingly round her sister's waist, "I am as bad as Noll. I could not say the name as you say it, not if I were to put a hot chestnut in my mouth every time!

But I'll never say 'Margy' again. Let me say Margaret!"

"I think that people ought to be called as they like best," said Miss Immy. "I've been called Miss Immy nearly fourscore years; and I should not like to be called anything else. So I shall always call her 'Margy sweet,' since that is what she likes best!"

And Miss Immy toddled off, holding her flat candlestick at arm's length in front of her, and shaking her head in a manner that seemed to be intended to express the most irrevocable determination.

CHAPTER VI.

WALTER ELLINGHAM.

LADY FARNLEIGH had asked Kate, as the reader may possibly remember, to be sure to ride over to Wanstrow not later than the next day but one after the arrival of her sister. But on the morrow of the evening spoken of in the last chapter, Kate heard her godmother's cheery voice ringing in the hall, asking for her before she had left her bedroom.

She was just about doing so, and hurrying down-stairs to be in time to tell the servants not to ring the breakfast-bell; for her sister was still sleeping and she would not have her wakened, when she found Lady Farnleigh in the hall in her riding-habit.

"What, Kate turned sluggard! you too? We shall have the larks lying abed till the sun has aired the world for them next. I doubted whether I should be in time for breakfast; has the bell rung?"

"No. And I want to prevent them from ringing it this morning. Margaret is still fast asleep, and I wont let her be waked. She had a very fatiguing journey of it, you know."

"But it's past nine o'clock, child. Our new sister must have a finely cultivated talent for sleeping. You were not late, I suppose?"

"To tell you the truth, we were rather late,—that is, she and I were. We had so much to talk of to each other, you know. How good of you to ride over this morning, you good fairy of a godmamma!"

"And like the fairies I get the bloom of the day for my pains. Such a ride! It is the loveliest morning."

"I must send to tell Noll and the others that there is to be no bell this morning, or else they'll be waiting for it. And then we'll go to breakfast. You must be ready for yours."

"Sha'n't be sorry to get it. I had no thought of riding over to-day, you know; but last night I made up my mind to do so, for a whole chapter of reasons."

"Of which any one would have been sufficient, I should hope."

"Nevertheless, you shall have them all. In the first place, I could not restrain my impatient curiosity to see what our new sister is like. In the next place, I thought that perhaps she might ride over with you to-morrow. And in that case, it would be more *selon les convenances*—and we must be upon our P's and Q's with our visitor from Paris, you know— that I should call first upon her. It is not the usual hour for a morning call, it is true; but no doubt she will consider that the *mode du pays*."

"She will consider that you are the kindest and best of fairy godmothers!"

"But I am no godmother of hers, you know, fairy or mortal. But you have not heard all my reasons for coming yet; I am come to ask permission to introduce to you an old and valued friend."

"You are joking! As if there was any need of your asking permission to bring anybody here!"

"Nevertheless, I choose upon this occasion to ask permission;— your father's, at all events, Miss Kate, even if I am to take yours as a matter of course."

"As if Noll would not be just as much surprised at your asking as I can be!"

"Nevertheless, I say again, I choose in this case to let you all know who and what the person is that I propose to bring to you, before I do so."

"Is he something so very terrible then?"

"I had not said that it was a 'he' at all, Miss Kate. However, you are right. It is a 'he'. And as for the terribleness of him, that you must judge for yourself. I have told you that it is one in whom I am greatly interested."

"And surely that makes all other information on the subject unnecessary."

"Thanks, Kate, for thinking so. But I don't think so. Did you ever hear of Lord Ellingham?"

"I have seen the name in the debates in the House of Lords; but that is all."

"Lord Ellingham has been a widower many years; and it is a long time since I have seen him. But his wife was the dearest friend I ever had—not dearer, perhaps, than your mother, Kate; but at all events an older friend. She was the friend of my girlhood, and I lost her before I came to live in this part of the country. She left her husband with four young sons. The gentleman I purpose asking your father's permission to bring here is the third of these. Lord Ellingham, I should tell you, is very far from being a wealthy man,—and his third son is a very poor one, pretty nearly as dependent on his own exertions for his daily bread as any one of your father's laborers. You see, therefore, that my friend, Walter Ellingham, is by no means what match-making mammas call an 'eligible' young man. He has not been found eligible for much either, poor fellow, by his masters, my Lords of the Admiralty. His father is a leading member of the Opposition,—though of course that can have nothing to do with it. The fact is, however, that, at thirty years of age, Walter Ellingham— 'honorable' though he be—is but a lieutenant in His Majesty's navy; and thinks himself fortunate in having obtained the command of a revenue cutter, stationed on our coast here. I found a letter when I got home yesterday evening, telling me all about it. He hopes to be able to come up to Wanstrow the day after to-morrow; and as I dare say we shall frequently see him during the time he is stationed here, I purpose bringing him over to you. And that is the third reason for my morning ride."

"But you haven't said a word, you mysterious fairy godmother, to explain why you thought it necessary to ask a special permission to make us this present. Of course you will send him up to Lindisfarn in a pumpkin drawn by eight white mice, with a grasshopper for coachman. And I do hope he'll have a very tall feather in his cap!"

"Suffice it that in the plenitude of my fairy wisdom I did choose to ask permission before starting the pumpkin. As for the feather in his cap, I have little doubt that it will come in due time. It is some years since I have seen Walter, but from my remembrance of him, I should be inclined to prefer some other trade to that of a smuggler on the Sillshire coast just at present. But what about this breakfast, Kate?"

"I must go and look after Miss Immy.

The event of yesterday has put us all out of our usual clockwork order, I think. I dare say Miss Immy is deep in speculation as to the modes and times at which French people get up and get their breakfasts."

"I shall go and speak to the squire by myself; I suppose I shall find him in the study?"

"Yes, do. And tell him he may come to breakfast without waiting for the bell this morning."

So Lady Farnleigh made her way to the sanctum which country gentlemen will persist in calling their "study," for the purpose of having five minutes' conversation with the squire, on the subject which was uppermost in her mind, in a rather graver tone than that which she had used in speaking to Kate; and the latter went to discover the cause of such an unprecedented event as the non-appearance of Miss Immy in the breakfast-room exactly as the clock over the stables struck nine.

It was very nearly a quarter past that hour, when the family party, with the exception of the new-comer, met in the breakfast-room.

"Why, Miss Immy! it's near quarter past nine, as I am a living man!" cried the squire. "We shall begin to think that you are getting old, if you break rules in this way!"

"Not so old by a quarter of an hour as you make me out, Mr. Lindisfarn!" said Miss Immy, rattling the teacups about. "The clock is ever so much too fast."

"I dare say the sun got up a little before his time when he saw it was such a lovely morning."

"You know I am always in the room by nine o'clock, Mr. Lindisfarn," reiterated Miss Immy, who would have gone to the stake rather than admit that she was late.

"Always! It shall be always nine o'clock when you come into the breakfast-room; as it's always one o'clock in Parson Mayford's parish out on the moor when the parson is hungry. The clerk sets the church clock every day by his Reverence's appetite; and they say there's no parish in the moor keeps such good time."

"I think I must get Mr. Mayford to come and stay with me while at Wanstrow," said Lady Farnleigh, "for our Wanstrow clocks are always at sixes and sevens."

"Ah! but the Wanstrow air is not so keen as it is on the moor. Parson's appetite would be slower in getting its edge; and your lady-ship would be half an hour behind time at least," said Mr. Mat.

"I should get you to calculate the difference, and work out the mean time accordingly, Mr. Mat; will you be my astronomer?"

"You mean gastronomer, godmamma! That would be more what would be needed for the business in hand," said Kate.

"I wonder when Margy will be down. No, I mustn't say that," cried the squire, correcting himself. "Poor lass, I wouldn't vex her for the world."

"Vex her! What should vex her?" inquired Lady Farnleigh.

"She don't like being called Margy," explained Kate; "we quite annoyed her, all of us, by calling her Margy. She has been used to be called Marguérite. And I am afraid I hurt her last night by laughing at her French pronunciation of it—which was very silly of me. But we put it all right afterward."

"And you were half the night in doing it, I'll bet a wager," said the squire; "and that's why she can't get up this morning."

"Yes, we were rather late. Just think how much we have to talk about!" said Kate.

"And no time except last night to do it in," laughed the squire.

"And she must be tired after her journey, poor lass," said Mr. Mat.

"I dare say she is stirring by this time," said Kate; "I will go and look for her."

"I am going into Silverton; has anybody any commands?" said Mr. Mat.

"Of course you will call in the Close, and tell them she is come. Say that we shall come in to-morrow," answered Kate.

"I'll take the dogs and go with you as far as the brook," said the squire.

So the gentlemen took themselves off; Miss Immy toddled off to her usual domestic avocations, and Lady Farnleigh was left alone in the breakfast-room, while Kate ran up-stairs to look for her sister.

In a very few minutes she returned, bringing down Miss Margaret with her into the breakfast-room, where she was presented in due form to Lady Farnleigh. Margaret executed a courtesy, with proper eyelid *manège* to match, to which Mr. Turveydrop, or any other equally competent master of "deportment," would have awarded a crown of laurel on the spot.

"You have had plenty of warm-hearted welcoming to Lindisfarn; but you must let me say welcome to Sillshire, Marguérite; for 'we Zillshire volk,' as Mr. Mat loves to say, look upon Sillshire as a common possession, of which we are all uncommonly proud."

"It is a nice country; I am sure of it, madame,—my lady," said Margaret, correcting herself and blushing painfully.

"Oh, you must not 'my lady' me; Kate here, calls me all sorts of names,—very bad ones, sometimes!" said Lady Farnleigh, with mock gravity.

Margaret threw her fine eyes, eloquent with surprised and sorrowful reproachfulness, on her sister.

"But then," continued Lady Farnleigh, as she shot, on her side, a glance of shrewd observation on Margaret, "Kate has a sad habit of calling names."

"Madame de Renneville strictly forbade me ever to do such a thing," rejoined Margaret: "she always said that there was nothing more vulgar."

"We must send Kate to the school where 'them as learns manners pays twopence extra,'—and pay the twopence for her," said Lady Farnleigh, with a queer look at Kate, while Margaret opened her magnificent large eyes to their utmost extent, in utterly mystified astonishment.

"But however we call one another," continued Lady Farnleigh, changing her tone, "we must learn, my dear Miss Lindisfarn, to be very great friends; for your poor dear mother loved me, and I loved her very dearly. Love between you and me is a matter of inheritance."

"You are very good, madame. I never had the happiness to know my sainted mother," said Margaret, with a sigh, the profundity of which was measured with the most skilful accuracy to the exact requirement of the nicest propriety on the occasion.

"Here comes some hot coffee for you, Margaret dear," said Kate. "We all take tea; but Miss Immy thought that you probably took coffee; and here is some of our famous Sillshire cream. Now what will you have to eat? A fresh egg, warranted under Miss Immy's own sign-manual to have been laid this morning? See, there is the dear old soul's mark! If the egg were to be taken from the nest to be put into the saucepan the next instant, Miss Immy would insist on marking it with the day of the month, before it was boiled."

"Only a bit of bread, if you please," replied the Parisian-bred girl. "And I should like to have a little hot milk with my coffee, if I might."

"Instead of our Sillshire cream? You shall have what you like, darling; but we must keep it a close secret. What will Sillshire say?"

"I am afraid the cream is too rich. I always take coffee and milk and a bit of bread; —nothing else."

"Ah! Sillshire air will soon avenge your neglect of our good things," said Lady Farnleigh. "Do you ride, Marguérite?"

"I have never been on a horse. Madame de Renneville did not consider mounting on horseback in all respects desirable."

Lady Farnleigh and Kate exchanged glances involuntarily, and the former said, "I dare say Madame de Renneville may have been right, as regards Paris; but you can understand, my dear, that it is of course a very different thing here. Kate and I ride a great deal; and I hope you will ride with us. You must learn at once. Mr. Mat will be an excellent riding-master for you."

"It would give me great pleasure to ride with you, Lady Farnleigh," replied Margaret, with just the slightest perceptible accent on the "you;" "but I am afraid I should be very stupid at it."

"Oh, you would soon learn, with Mr. Mat for your master," rejoined Kate.

"Kate was to have ridden over to see me to-morrow," pursued Lady Farnleigh, "and I hoped that you would have come with her; but now it seems you are to go into Silverton to-morrow; and the day after—has Kate told you?—I am going to bring an old friend of mine to make acquaintance with you all here."

"No, I have not told her yet," said Kate. "An accession to our rather limited assortment of beaux, Margaret!—Mr.—or Captain should I say?"

"Captain, by courtesy," said Lady Farnleigh, "though that is not his real rank in the navy. But he is called Captain—the Honorable Captain Ellingham."

"The Honorable Captain Ellingham. Is he the son of a lord, then?" asked Margaret who seemed remarkably well versed in such niceties of English social distinctions, for a young lady whose entire life had been spent in France. But it is to be presumed that Madame de Renneville had given her personal care to that branch of her niece's education.

"Yes, Walter Ellingham is the son of Lord Ellingham; but for all that he is a very poor man, Margaret," replied Lady Farnleigh.

"Are lords ever poor?" asked Margaret, with a surprised and somewhat disappointed expression of face.

"Yes, my dear; a poor lord is unfortunately a by no means unprecedented phenomenon," replied Lady Farnleigh. "And what is still more lamentable, and still more to the purpose, when a lord is poor, his third son is apt to be still poorer."

"And the Honorable Captain Ellingham is Lord Ellingham's third son?" asked Margaret.

"Even so," said Lady Farnleigh.

"Is the Mr. Falconer you were telling me of last night, Kate, a poor man too?" asked Margaret, after a pause.

"I should think not," said Kate; "I don't know at all. I never remember to have heard the subject alluded to. But he is old Mr. Falconer's only child, and I should suppose that he must be rich."

"Oh, yes! there is no mistake about that at all," said Lady Farnleigh; "Mr. Falconer, the banker, is well known to be a very ' warm ' man, and if you are not English enough yet, Margaret, my dear, to understand the meaning of that phrase, you will at least have no difficulty in comprehending what I mean when I say that Mr. Freddy Falconer is an extremely desirable ' parti.' You will find that all the young ladies at Silverton, including your sister," continued Lady Farnleigh, with an archly malicious look at Kate, "consider him such, and all the old ladies, too, —except one."

"You are always to pay implicit attention to all Lady Farnleigh says, sister dear, when she talks common sense," said Kate; "but you are never to pay the slightest attention to a word she utters when she has got her nonsense-cap on. And if you are in any doubt upon the subject, you have only to ask me; for I am her goddaughter, and know the ways of her."

"That is calling me a fool, by implication; and you have been told, Kate, once this morning already, on the authority of Madame de Renneville," said Lady Farnleigh *grasseyant* in the most perfect Parisian style, "how vulgar it is to do so. But I am afraid you are incorrigible. What can we do to improve her manners, my dear?"

"I am sure I shall always be very happy," began poor Margaret, dropping her eyelids, and speaking with a sort of purring consciousness of superiority.

But Kate, who, as she had very truly said, knew the ways of her godmother, and perceived with dismay that she was beginning already to conceive a prejudice against Margaret, hurried to rescue her from the damaging and dangerous position which she saw was being prepared for her.

"Now, you malicious fairy godmother, don't be hypocritical. It was you who told Margaret that I was in the habit of calling you bad names. What could she think? And her remark thereon was very natural. Now I wont let you turn yourself all of a sudden into the shape of a great white cat, and hunt her, poor little mouse, all round the room. I can see by the look of you that that is what you're bent on."

"What would Madame de Renneville say to that?" exclaimed Lady Farnleigh, turning to Margaret with a look of appeal.

"Never mind Madame de Renneville"— began Kate.

"Kate!" cried Margaret, in a tone deeply laden with reproach, but skilfully modulated so as to seem uttered more in sorrow than in anger, and casting her eyes on her sister with an appealing look of warning, reproof, and tenderness combined.

And "Kate!" re-echoed Lady Farnleigh, in a similar tone, and with a similar look.

It became very evident to Kate's experienced perception that her godmamma was getting dangerous, and was bent on mischief. But she was fully determined to prevent, or at all events not to contribute to her sister's becoming the victim of it. It was as much as she could do to prevent herself from laughing at Lady Farnleigh's last bit of parody. But biting her lips to preserve her gravity, she continued,—

"What I wanted to say was, to ask on what authority you include me among the young ladies who are so enthusiastic on the subject of Mr. Falconer's eligibility."

"Kate!" said her incorrigible ladyship again, in the same accent and manner as be-

fore. But having been admonished by a look
of entreaty from her goddaughter, administered
aside, which she perfectly well understood,
she said,—

" Why, do you not think so? Does anybody not think so? Is he not very undeniably an eligible ' *parti* '? Margaret very judiciously asked, before making up her mind
on the subject, whether he, too, was as poor as
Walter Ellingham. But we, who are well
informed on that point can have no doubts on
the subject. Why, old Mr. Falconer must
be made of gold; whereas my poor friend
Walter has but one bit of gold belonging to
him, to the best of my belief. There can be
no doubt, I think, which is the eligible and
which is the ineligible man. It is clear
enough; is it not, Margaret?"

But Kate, who was very anxious that her
sister should not put her foot into the spring-
trap thus laid for her, but who nevertheless
feared, in a manner which she unquestionably
would not have feared a few hours ago, that
Margaret might, if left to herself, run a danger of doing so, once again hurried to the
rescue, by saying,—

" One bit of gold! What can you mean,
you enigmatical fairy? What is the one bit
of gold that Captain Ellingham possesses,
and how did he come by it?"

" Really I do not know how he came by
it; but I never knew him without it. He
always carries it inside his waistcoat."

" What, a gold watch?" asked Margaret,
innocently.

" To be sure, a gold watch," replied Lady
Farnleigh; " what in the world else of gold
could a man have thereabouts? How dull
you are, Kate, this morning!"

" I always am dull at riddles; but we all
know that a man carries a heart inside his
waistcoat; and I suppose that is the article
that your friend has of gold, as you say. I
see, at all events, that he is a favorite of yours,
godmamma."

" He is," said Lady Farnleigh, briefly;
" and you will all of you have an opportunity
of judging," she continued, " whether he deserves to be so; for your father has very kindly
bidden me to bring him to dine here the day
after to-morrow. And now, girls, I shall
leave you; for of course you want to be alone
together. May I ask if Giles is there?"

" Yes. But come down with us to the

stables, and mount there; I want to show
Birdie to Margaret."

Birdie was a beautiful black mare, nearly
thorough-bred, which had been a present
from Lady Farnleigh to her goddaughter;
and of all her treasures it was the one which
Kate valued the most, and was the most proud
of. A competent judge would have found a
long list of good points to admire in Birdie;
but even the most unskilled eye could not fail
to be struck by the exceeding beauty of the
coat, glossier than satin; by the fineness of
the skin, as evidenced by the great veins in
the neck showing through it; by the dainty
elegance of the legs and pasterns; and above
all, by the beauty of the small head, with its
eyes, as keen, Kate used to say, as a hawk's,
and as gentle as a dove's.

Margaret was accordingly much struck by
Birdie's beauty, as the groom walked her
about the stable-yard for the ladies to look
at.

" Oh, what a lovely creature!" she exclaimed; " I do not wonder that you are
fond of riding on such a horse as that. But
it would be a very different thing to ride on any
one of these great clumsy-looking beasts. I
can never expect to have such a horse as that
to ride!" lamented Margaret, as she very accurately figured to herself the charming picture she would make, mounted in a becoming
amazon costume upon so showily beautiful a
steed.

" You shall ride Birdie, sister dear, and
welcome, as soon as you have made some little progress under Mr. Mat's tuition; but I
think you must begin with something a little
steadier; for my darling Birdie, though she is
as gentle as a lamb, is apt to be a little lively,
the pretty creature."

" But I don't like the look of the something
steadier," pouted Margaret.

" Nevertheless, it is my advice, my dear,"
said Lady Farnleigh, " that you do not attempt to mount Birdie till Mr. Mat is ready
to give you a certificate of competency. Birdie
is not for every one's riding."

" But Kate can ride her," returned Margaret, somewhat discontentedly.

" Ay! but Kate, let me tell you," said
Lady Farnleigh, " is about the best lady
rider in the country. Good-by, girls. You
must give me an early day at Wanstrow, my
dear. When shall it be? why not Wednes-

day? I am to dine here on Friday, the day after to-morrow. Will you say Wednesday, Kate? Make your father come, if you can. If not, get Mr. Mat to come over with you. And come early."

"I do not think papa will come," said Kate; "but we shall be delighted. Mr. Mat shall drive Margaret in the gig, and I will ride."

"That's agreed then. Good-by."

"Now shall I show you the garden?" said Kate, after the two girls had watched Lady Farnleigh as she rode down toward the lodge till she was out of sight.

"No, not now, I think. Let us go and finish unpacking and putting away my things. I have ever so many more things to show you. And besides, I want you to tell me all about this Mr. Falconer."

"The all is soon told," said Kate; "but first you tell me what you think of my god-mother; is she not a darling?"

"I hardly know whether I like her or not," said Margaret. "I feel somehow not safe with her; and I can't quite make her out. One thing was quite clear, that she was not well pleased with your calling her a fairy, and making fun of her in that way. Tell me," added she, musingly, after a pause, during which Kate had been pondering whether it would be better to attempt making her sister understand Lady Farnleigh a little better at once, or to leave it to time to do so,—"tell me whether the six thousand pounds that you are to have from her—that is a hundred and fifty thousand francs, is it not?—are settled on you, or only given you by her will?"

"I declare I don't know," returned Kate, surprised; "I had never thought about it. No doubt papa knows all about it. Why do you ask?"

"Oh! only that the one is certain, and the other uncertain; that is all," answered Margaret.

CHAPTER VII.
MY "THINGS."

So the two girls—the Lindisfarn lasses, as Mr. Mat called them, the Lindisfarn co-heiresses, as they have been called in a preceding chapter—returned to the house. It may be as well, however, to explain before going any further that they were not very accurately so called. They were in no legal sense co-heiresses to the Lindisfarn property ; for the entail went no further than the male heir of Oliver, and, failing such, the male heir of his brother. Failing male heirs of both of these, the property was at the disposal of the squire. But nobody had any doubt that his two daughters would inherit the property, as was natural, in equal proportions. Nevertheless, it was in the squire's power to modify the disposition of it in any manner he might think fit. The two girls, on Margaret's proposition, as has been said, returned to their rooms to complete the delightful work of unpacking the Parisian sister's wardrobe, which the dinner hour had compelled them to leave in the midst on the previous evening.

A rapid progress was made in the unpacking ; but the "putting away," did not proceed with equal celerity. There was all the difference that there is between destroying a theory or system, and reconstructing it. Pulling down, alas! is always quicker and easier work than building up. And in the present instance the more laborious and less amusing task was left to Simmons. Of course Margaret had the most to show ; and then her "things" were Parisian "things." Toilettes and demi-toilettes, *toilettes de bal*, and *toilettes du bois, toilettes de matin,* and *toilettes de soir!* A brilliant dioramic exhibition, illustrated, and varied by interspersed disquisitions and explanations of the glories and pleasures of the French metropolis.

Kate's wardrobe contained but one costume which was not outshone by anything in its own department belonging to that of her sister, and which attracted Margaret's special interest and admiration,—her riding-habit and its appendages. Nothing would satisfy her but that Kate should put herself in complete riding-dress ; and when she had done so, Margaret insisted on trying on the habit herself. And then it appeared, and was specially noted and pointed out by the Parisian-bred girl, that her waist was a trifle slenderer than that of her sister ; which produced from Miss Simmons the observation that there was not more difference than there should be for Miss Kate's somewhat superior height ; and the judicially pronounced declaration that " It *have* been considered, Miss Margaret, that Miss Kate's figure, specially a horseback, is the perfectest thing as ever was seen ! "

"Don't talk nonsense, Simmons ! " said Kate ; " but just take two or three pins, and see if you can pin up the habit so as to make it fit Margaret's waist. There ! " she continued, as the handy servant accomplished the task, " did anybody ever see a nicer figure for the saddle ? Now the hat, Margaret. Just the least in the world on one side. That's it. Oh, you must ride. You do not know how the dress becomes you ! "

"Yes, I think I look well in it ! " said Margaret, admiring herself in a Psyche glass, as she spoke. " And it would be better, you know, in a habit made for me."

" And look, Margaret ; I must teach you how to hold up your habit when you walk in it. Look here ! You should gather it in your right hand thus, so as to let it fall in a graceful fold ; do you understand ? "

" Oh, yes ; that is very easy," said Margaret, walking across the room, and catching the mode of doing so gracefully with admirable tact and readiness. " If the riding were only as easy as that ! But Lady Farnleigh showed a *leetle* more of her boot in walking. I think one might venture just to let the instep be seen," she continued, putting out, as she spoke, from under the heavy folds of the habit a lovely little slender foot in its exquisite Parisian *brodequin.*

" Oh, you are beyond me, already, Margaret ! " cried Kate, laughing ; " I never dreamed of considering the matter so artistically. But certainly, it would be a pity to hide that foot of yours more than need be. Only, darling, that charming little French boot would hardly be the thing for our Sillshire riding, let alone walking."

" I can't bear a thick boot," said Margaret. " And, Kate, don't you think that without being *trop hasardé*, one might put the hat just a *soupçon* more on the left side,—so ? There, that is charming ! How well the black hat goes with the *mat* white of my complexion ! Does it not, now ? "

And in truth, the figure at which both the girls, with Simmons behind them, were gazing in the large Psyche was as attractive a one as could well be imagined.

Just as they were thus engaged, having let the day run away till it was near dinner-time, there came a tremendous thump at the door, which made Margaret jump as if she had been struck, while it produced from Kate, to her sister's no little dismay, a laughing, "Come in, Noll! Come in, and see what we are about!"

And in the next instant, the squire, who had just returned from his shooting, was standing in the midst of all the varied display of finery which occupied every chair and other piece of furniture in the room.

"Why, girls, you are holding a regular rag-fair! What, Margy—ret! is that you? I am glad to see that riding toggery makes part of your wardrobe. That is better luck than I looked for. And upon my word, you look very well in it—very well!"

"It is my riding-habit, Noll; Margaret was only trying it on. Does it not become her? She must get one without loss of time."

"Unluckily, I have never learned to ride, papa," said Margaret.

"Oh, we shall soon teach you here, my love. We'll make a horsewoman of you, never fear! I came up to tell you what I have been doing, girls. I asked Lady Farn-leigh, you know, to bring her friend, Captain Ellingham, to dinner on Friday. Well, I thought it would be neighborly to introduce him to some of the people at the same time. So I have asked the Falconers, father and son. I fell in with the old gentleman down at the Ivy Bridge, looking to see if he could find any traces of the graves of some soldiers of the garrison of Silverton Castle, that he says were buried there at the time of the civil wars. And I told Mat to ask my brother and sister-in-law. She wont come, of course. Mat is not returned yet; but we shall know at dinner whether the doctor can come. And as I was coming home by Upper Weston Coppice I met Mr. Merriton, the new man at the Friary, and asked him and his sister."

"Why, we shall have quite a large party, Noll," said Kate. "Miss Immy will say that she has not notice enough to make due preparations."

"Stuff and nonsense! What preparations are needed, beyond having plenty of dinner? I thought it a good opportunity to bring the people together and make acquaintance with these new folks. They are friends of the Falconers; and he seems a very gentleman-like sort of fellow."

The new people thus spoken of were the owners, having quite recently become such—or rather, Mr. Merriton was the owner—of the small but exceedingly pretty and service-able estate and mansion called the Friary, at Weston Friary. Arthur Merriton and his sister Emily had been the wards of the head of the firm who were Messrs. Falconer and Fishbourne's London correspondents; and were the children of an English merchant, settled for many years in Sicily, by an Italian wife. They had been left orphans at an early age; and had been, together with the very considerable fortune left by their father, un-der the care of the London banker since that time. It was only a year since Mr. Merriton had come of age. His sister was two years older, and they had recently come to live at the Friary, the purchase of which had been arranged and concluded on Mr. Merriton's behalf, by Mr. Falconer of Silverton.

"How many does that make altogether?" asked Kate, intent on getting the subject into fit shape for presentation to the mind of Miss Immy.

"I have not counted noses," answered her father; "but it can't be such a large party after all."

"Let us see. We are five at home, two gentlemen and three ladies; and Uncle The-ophilus will make us up half a dozen, three and three. Lady Farnleigh and Captain Ellingham will make eight; and Mr. Merriton and his sister ten; and the gentlemen and ladies are still equal. But then come the two Mr. Falconers, and make us seven gen-tlemen to five ladies."

"And that will do very well. We shall be four old fellows to three youngsters: I and my brother, and Mat and old Falconer; and young Falconer, Merriton, who seems little more than a lad, and Captain Elling-ham."

"Lady Farnleigh did not seem to speak of him as nearly so young a man," replied Kate; "he will be half-way between you seniors and the young men. She spoke of him more as a friend of her own standing."

"Well, her own standing is nothing so very venerable. But she mentioned the age of this Captain Ellingham. He is thirty; and Freddy Falconer is, I know, seven-and-twenty. So there is no such great difference."

"No," said Kate; "that is very little difference. Only one has always been used to look on Freddy Falconer in the light of a young man, and a captain in His Majesty's Navy seems such a grave and staid sort of personage."

"Well, we shall see. But I protest against the mere count of years being considered to decide the question whether a man is old or not; for if that be the case, you will be making me out to be old myself, next! Well, I suppose it is pretty nearly time to go and dress for dinner."

Margaret, who had been apparently occupied during all this conversation between her father and Kate, with trying the effect of divers positions and modes of standing, as she continued to admire the becomingness of the riding-habit in the Psyche, had, nevertheless, lost no word of what had passed. And when the squire left the room, she was engaged in meditating how far the words her sister had used in speaking of Mr. Frederick Falconer might be considered as corroboratory of the half-jesting accusation Lady Farnleigh had brought against Kate, of being included in the number of those who were inclined to consider that young gentleman as a very desirable "*parti*."

"Here, then," she said, when her father was gone, "is another accession to your collection of Silverton beaux, according to what papa says. Have you ever seen this Mr. Merriton, Kate?"

"No, never; neither him, nor his sister. But I had heard of them before. I fancy they are nice people. They are quite new-comers to Sillshire, and know nobody here but the Falconers."

"Do they live in Silverton?" asked Margaret.

"No, they have bought an estate at Weston Friary,—such a charming village down in the valley at the end of the water-meads, not more than a couple of miles above the town. One of our first excursions must be to Weston."

"What, to call on these people?"

"No, I meant to see the village, it is such a pretty place. But now it will be necessary, of course, to call on the new-comers; and we can do that too. The Friary is a sweetly pretty house and grounds."

"Is that the name of their place?"

"Yes. I believe it was a monastery once upon a time. If you want to win the heart of Uncle Theophilus or of old Mr. Falconer, on the spot, you have only to ask them to tell you all about it. Only they are quite sure to tell you different stories; and you will mortally offend either of them if you give credence to the story of the other."

"One must speak to them separately then," said Margaret, apparently with all seriousness. "But you said," she continued, "that it was an estate that Mr. Merriton had bought?"

"Yes, the estate is called the Friary Estate from the name of the house. It is a small estate; but full of such pretty bits of country. It is quite celebrated for its beauty in the county."

"Then I suppose Mr. Merriton must be rich; or at least a man of independent property?"

"I suppose so," answered Kate; "but I have not heard any one say anything on the subject."

And then Margaret divested herself of the riding-habit, after a last long and wistful look in the glass, and inwardly-registered vow that she would allow no disagreeables to interfere with her learning to ride as quickly as possible, and the girls proceeded to dress for dinner. And that ceremony passed somewhat more pleasantly than it had done yesterday. Margaret delighted Mr. Mat by asking him if he thought he could, and kindly would, undertake the office of riding-master on her behalf; and much talk passed between them on the subject. Then there was talk about the dinner-party on the day after the morrow. The doctor, Mr. Mat brought word, would come. But Lady Sempronia excused herself, as usual, on the plea of indifferent health. And then the excursion into Silverton for the morrow was talked about and arranged. The squire, who rarely was seen in Silverton High Street, except at times of Quarter-Sessions, or other suchlike occasions, excused himself: and Mr. Mat declared, also, that if his services were not wanted, he had much to do at home; and none of his hearers were so unkind as to ask him what it was. Miss Immy, on the other hand, declared that it was absolutely necessary that she should go to Silverton, even if she were to go alone, with a view to matters connected with the next day's dinner. It would be absolutely necessary, she said, to send a message down to Sillmouth, if they wanted a decent bit of fish; and even so the people made a favor of it. For of late years all the best fish was sent off to London, in a way that used not to be the case when Miss Immy was young, and which she seemed to think involved much tyranny and overbearing injustice on the part of the Londoners against the "Zillshire folk."

"Come, Miss Immy," said the squire, apologetically; "the Londoners never refuse to let me have the pick of their market for my cellar."

"But fish is not wine; and wine is not fish," said Miss Immy, distinguishing and separately emphasizing the two propositions by a distinct system, as it were, of little palsied shakes of the head applied to each of them. "And I should think, Mr. Lindisfarn, that you were the only person who had ever supposed them to be so," added the old lady, with much triumph.

So it was arranged that the carriage should be ordered, and that the two young ladies should accompany Miss Immy, and should be deposited at the doctor's house in the Close, so that the new-comer might make acquaintance with her relatives, and also with Silverton, to any such extent as opportunity might be found for doing, while Miss Immy was driving about the town intent on her household cares.

CHAPTER VIII.

MARGARET'S DEBUT IN THE CLOSE.

THOMAS TIBBS, the coachman at the Chase, held as a fundamental axiom, that any man as wanted to drive from the Chase to Silverton turnpike in less than an hour and twenty-five minutes, had not no business to sit behind a gentleman's horses. If called on to pursue the subject, he was wont to do so after the same fashion of dialectic that Miss Immy had used with regard to the fish and the wine. "A gen'elman's carriage," he would justly observe, "is not His Majesty's Mail; and His Majesty's Mail is not a gen'elman's carriage—leastways, not a gen'elman's private carriage," he would add, to avoid the possibility of leading to any unfavorable conclusion as to the gentility of the first gentleman in Europe. "Whereby it's not the value of five minutes you has to look to, but the condition of your cattle," said Thomas Tibbs. The hill up from the Ivy Bridge over the Lindisfarn Brook to the turnpike that stood just where the city wall had once crossed the present road, was a very steep pitch; and upon the whole, the hour and twenty-five minutes claimed for the work by Thomas Tibbs was not an unreasonable demand. His further unalterable allowance of five minutes from the turnpike to the door of Dr. Lindisfarn's house in the Close may seem to have been more open to exception. But Thomas Tibbs, who would have looked down with intense contempt from the altitude of a superior civilization on the Celtic endeavor to hide inefficient poverty under false brag by "keeping a trot for the avenue," maintained that "any man who knew what horses was, knew the vally of bringing 'em in cool;" and nothing could tempt him to exceed the very gentlest amble between the Silverton turnpike and the canon's door.

From which circumstance it follows that, although the Lindisfarn ladies had bustled over their breakfast in a manner that suggested the idea of a departure for the Antipodes, and Miss Immy had descended to the breakfast-room with her round brown beaver hat and green veil on, and an immense parasol, and three or four packages in her hands, and had entered the room giving a string of directions to Benson, the housekeeper, as she walked,—notwithstanding all these efforts, the cathedral service was over at Silverton, and Dr. Lindisfarn had returned to his study —it not being a Litany day—before the carriage from the Chase reached the Close.

Miss Immy refused to alight at the canon's door, alleging that the number of commissions she had to execute would leave her not a minute to spare between that time and three o'clock; at which hour it was arranged that they were to leave Silverton, in order to be in time for the squire's dinner hour at the Chase,—five o'clock extended by special grace on occasion of family progresses to Silverton to half-past five, in consequence of its being every inch collar work, as Thomas Tibbs declared, from the Ivy Bridge to the door of the Chase. The hour which Tibbs claimed as absolutely necessary for his horses to bait, Miss Immy purposed spending, as was her usual practice on similar occasions, with Miss Lasseron, the sister of a late canon of Silverton.

It was perfectly true that Miss Lasseron was the very old friend, and almost the contemporary, of Miss Immy;—true also that Miss Immy very much preferred the nice little dish of minced veal and tall ale-glass full of Miss Lasseron's home-brewed amber ale, with which her friend never failed to regale her when she needed a luncheon in Silverton, to the bit of stale cake and glass of sherry that the Lady Sempronia was wont to produce on similar occasions. Nevertheless, I suspect that Miss Immy's avoidance of the house in the Close, whenever she could decently do so, was in great part due to the small sympathy that existed between her and the Lady Sempronia. The latter dared not say in Sillshire that Miss Imogene Lindisfarn was an uneducated and vulgar old woman. But few who knew her could have had any doubt that such was pretty accurately a correct statement of her real opinion. Miss Imogene, on her side, certainly thought, and did dare to say to anybody who cared to know her mind on the subject, that Lady Sempronia was a feckless and washed-out fine lady, and very stingy to boot. And the Silverton and Sillshire world were much inclined to accept and endorse Miss Immy's opinion. Yet, as regarded the latter part of the accusation, it was hardly a fair one. The Sillshire world did not know as well as the Lady Sempronia that all her stinginess did not avail to bring Canon Lindisfarn's account with Messrs. Falconer and Fishbourne to a satisfactory balance at the end of the year. And those who had a general knowledge of that fact did not call it to mind on occasions when, in justice to the lady, they ought to have done so. It certainly was not Lady Sempronia's stinginess which induced her to drive out, on the rare occasions on which she went out at all, in a shabby old one-horse vehicle, which really made a fly from the Lindisfarn Arms look smart by comparison. And when Miss Piper, the milliner, who had her show-room over the shop of her brother, the perfumer, in the High Street, told ill-natured stories among her customers of the impossible feats she was required by Lady Sempronia to perform, in the way of producing accurate imitations of the new French fashions from materials that had already undergone more than one metamorphosis, it can hardly be doubted that the poor lady would have preferred ordering a new silk, had the choice of

doing so been open to her. It was all very well, as Lady Sempronia had been heard to say, for those to talk whose husbands cared for their families more than for stones and old bones, and all sorts of rubbish ; and who were content with reading what other people had printed instead of printing their own ! And no doubt there was an amount of truth in these lamentations which ought to have obtained for them a greater degree of sympathy than was generally shown to Lady Sempronia. But she was not a popular person at Silverton. And all these things were "trials" to her ladyship. Life indeed seemed to shape itself to her feeling and mode of thought as one great and perpetual "trial ; " and upon the whole she seemed generally to be getting the worst of it.

Kate and Margaret were shown into a long, low drawing-room, looking from its three windows into the extremely pretty garden behind the house. There was an old-fashioned drab-colored Brussels carpet on the floor, an old-fashioned drab-colored paper on the walls, and old-fashioned drab moreen curtains bound with black velvet hung on each side of three windows. Nevertheless, it was, in right of the outlook into the garden and up the exquisitely-kept turf of the steep bank that ran up to a considerable height against the fragment of gray old city wall, and was topped by a terrace-walk running under the rose-clothed southern face of it,—in right, I say, of these advantages, Lady Sempronia's drawing-room was a pretty and pleasant room ; though Kate used to say that it always used to make her feel afraid of speaking above her breath, when she came into it. The world, she said, seemed always asleep there.

There was nobody in the room when the two girls entered it, and the servant went to call his mistress.

" Oh, que c'est triste ! " exclaimed Margaret, as she looked around. " I should die if I were made to inhabit such a room. C'est d'une tristesse écrasante ! "

" And I am afraid poor Aunt Sempronia does not live a very gay life in it. Yet I do not dislike the room. Look at the garden ! Can anything be conceived more peacefully lovely ! " said Kate.

" C'est à mourir d'ennui ! " said Margaret. The two girls were standing looking out of the window with their backs to the door, as

Margaret spoke, and had not heard the noiseless step of Lady Sempronia as she crossed the room toward them. It was evident that she must have heard Margaret's criticism on her dwelling; and the utterer of it felt no little embarrassment at the consciousness that such must have been the case. But, as it seemed, she could not have presented herself to her aunt in a manner more congenial to that lady's feelings.

Margaret blushed deeply, as she performed to Lady Sempronia one of her usual elaborate courtesies, while Kate spoke a few words of introduction. But her aunt, taking her kindly by the hand, said,—

"Come and sit by me on this sofa, my love. It is a pleasure to find at least one member of the family, who can sympathize with some, at all events, of the trials I am called on to struggle against. It is as you say, Margaret; *c'est à mourir d'ennui!* But, unfortunately, *ennui* kills slowly. It has done its work on me in the course of years, my dear. And yet Kate bids me be cheerful,—cheerful in such an atmosphere as this!"

Lady Sempronia certainly did look like one on whom *ennui*, or some such form of mental atrophy, had, as she said, done its work. Miss Immy called it looking "washed out;" and perhaps that phrase may give as good an idea of Lady Sempronia's appearance as her own more refined one. Hers was a tall and remarkably slender figure, with a long face, the thinness of which was made yet thinner in appearance by two long, corkscrew curls of very dull, unshining-looking light-brown hair hanging on either side of it. She had a high-bridged Roman nose, and a tall, narrow forehead, adorned by a "front," which life-weariness had caused to be so unartistically put on, that it hardly made any pretence of being other than it was.

"There can be no doubt that excess of quietude is often very trying to the spirits," replied Margaret, sympathizingly.

"Trying!" exclaimed Lady Sempronia; "indeed, you may say so! Few persons in my station of life have had so many trials as I have, my dear niece. But you, too, have had your trials. It must have been a very severe one to be called on to relinquish Paris to come and live in this remote solitude,—a very great trial. Do you feel the change very painfully?"

"The change is a very great one, certainly," said Margaret, who, remembering that her sister was present, though Lady Sempronia seemed to have forgotten it, could not respond as completely to her aunt's invitation to bemoan herself as she would have been happy to do under other circumstances.

"You will find, my dear, as life goes on, that it is made up of a series of trials. Those who expect to find it otherwise," continued the melancholy lady, with a mild glance of reproach at Kate's face, which was most unsympathetically beaming with health and brightness and happiness,—"those who expect to find it otherwise are but laying up for themselves a harvest of delusions and disappointments. There is to me no more melancholy sight than that of inexperienced youth, rushing forward, as it were, to meet the inevitable trials that await it, in utter unconsciousness of its fate."

"Why, that is just what the poet says, aunt!" cried Kate, with a smile entirely undimmed by any terror at the tremendous prospect before her.

"'Alas! unconscious of their doom
　　The little victims play.
No sense have they of ills to come;
　　No care beyond to-day.'"

"I am glad to see that you are acquainted with the lines, my dear. They are very, very sad ones. You remember how the poet goes on :—

"'Yet see, how all around them wait
　　The ministers of human fate,
　　And black Misfortune's baleful train!'

The following stanzas are very instructive. And the whole poem—it is very short, too short, indeed—would be exceedingly advantageous reading for a young person, every night before going to bed."

"The last lines," continued Kate, "are particularly impressive.

"'Since sorrow never comes too late,
　　And happiness too quickly flies,
. . . where ignorance is bliss,
　　'Tis folly to be wise!'"

"Words uttered in the bitter irony of a broken heart," said Lady Sempronia, with a profound sigh; "and which it would be folly indeed to take *au sérieux!* Tell me, my dear," she added, turning to Margaret, "do you not feel the change from the scenes in which you passed your childhood, to the comparative solitude of your present home, very trying to your spirits!"

"I was certainly very happy in Paris ; and Madame de Renneville and the baron were very kind to me," said Margaret, while a tear trembled in her fine eyes, gathered there not by the words which had been spoken, nor by any ideas called to her mind by them, so much as by the deep tragic tones and profoundly dispirited manner of her aunt. It was a tribute to Lady Sempronia's sorrows and to her eloquence, to which that lady was keenly sensible ; and she already began to feel that her newly-discovered niece was a highly cultivated and charming girl, on whom she might count for sympathy with her in her many sorrows.

Lady Sempronia was very fond of talking of these : indeed, she rarely spoke much on any other subject. But it was remarkable that she never spoke of the one great sorrow, which really was such as to justify her in considering her entire life to have been overshadowed by it. She never alluded to her lost son. That grief was too real, too sacred for idle talk. But of her poverty, her bodily ailments, the misbehavior of the canon in various ways, his absence of mind, his extravagance, his antiquarian tastes, of the troubles arising from the turpitude of all sorts of servants, she would discourse at any length.

"And now, my dear," she said, after some further indulgence in her usual slipshod talk on the miseries of the world in general, and of her own lot in it in particular, "now I suppose you are anxious to make acquaintance with your uncle, the canon. The meeting with a hitherto unknown relative may, in some exceptional cases, be the finding of a congenial and sympathetic heart. But it is far more likely to prove a severe trial." Margaret could not help being struck, as her aunt spoke, with the justness of her observation : but she was not prepared for the candor of what was about to follow.

"It would not be right," continued the Lady Sempronia, "if I were to omit to warn you that the meeting with your uncle is likely to prove a severe trial."

"Dear aunt," expostulated Kate, "I am sure Margaret will love Uncle Theophilus as much as we all do, when she gets to know him."

"My dear!" said Lady Sempronia, turning on her with some little sharpness, "it is

my practice always, both for myself and for those who are dear to me, to prepare against disappointments. It is long since I have been disappointed in anything, and a certain amount of peace of mind may be thus attained. With regard to your uncle, my dear Margaret, we who do know him, as your sister says, are perfectly well aware of the many great and good qualities which he possesses ; but it is nevertheless true, that your first introduction to him may prove a trial. Dr. Lindisfarn is a very learned man,—a man of immense erudition ! Nevertheless, when he comes in to dinner with his surplice on, under the impression that he is entering the choir for morning service, it is a trial ; I confess that to me it is a trial. Your uncle has acquired the high esteem of the whole county, and has received the public thanks of the Chapter for his contributions in time, in knowledge, and in money, to the repair of the ceiling of the cathedral transept. But when I reflect that a small portion of the money so spent would have supplied—among many other matters—the new carpet, which you see, my dear, is so sadly needed for the drawing-room, it is, I do not deny it, a severe trial. When I speak to the doctor upon any subject of domestic interest, and he answers me as if I were talking of things or people of five hundred years or more ago, I do own that it is a very painful trial. In short, my dear, it were weak to conceal from you that in all connected with Dr. Lindisfarn [a very deep and prolonged sigh inserted here] there are many and very grievous trials. And this being the case, it was, I think, my duty to warn you that you would find it *to be* the case. The duty of doing so has been a trial to me ; but I would not shrink from it."

"It has been very kind of you, aunt ; and I assure you that I am not insensible to it," murmured Margaret.

"I suppose Uncle Theophilus has his trials too, for that matter," said Kate.

"I have no reason to think Dr. Lindisfarn exempted from the common lot of humanity," returned Lady Sempronia, with a certain degree of acidity in her manner, yet in a tone of extreme meekness, such as might be supposed the result of long-suffering. "Shall we go to the study ?" she added : "Dr. Lindisfarn does not like to be called into the drawing-room."

So the three ladies proceeded together to

the canon's study. To do this they were obliged to return from the drawing-room into the hall; for, though the study adjoined the latter, there was no door of communication between them. It was a very long room, occupying the entire depth of the house, and lighted by one large bow-window looking into the garden, and by a small window at the opposite end of it looking into the Close. The door opening into the hall was on the left hand of one looking toward the garden, and was near the Close end of the room, so that it was but a step from the hall-door to that of the study. The fireplace was on the opposite side of the room, not in the middle of the wall, but much nearer the garden end; and a double bookshelf, or rather two book-shelves back to back, stood out about two-thirds of the space across the room, so as to partially divide it into two rooms, of which that toward the garden was nearly twice as large as the other. These dividing shelves abutted against the wall opposite the door, so that a person entering could see the entire length of the room; but one sitting near the fire could not see the door, nor be seen from it. The fireplace was merely an open hearth, prepared for burning wood, and furnished with a pair of antique-shaped andirons; for the canon chose to burn exclusively wood in his study, despite the discontent and remonstrances of Lady Sempronia, who declared that the room could be well warmed with coal at very much less cost than it was half warmed with wood. The question of the comparative expense had formed the subject of many a long dispute between them, till the doctor, who, in defence of his own position, had drawn up an exceedingly learned and exhaustive memoir on the progressive difference between the cost of wood and coals from the earliest use of the latter fuel, had spoken on one occasion of the expediency of giving his monograph to the public, as one of the publications of the Sillshire Society. From that time forth the Lady Sempronia, who knew too well that the cost of printing the monograph would more than supply the study fire with wood to the end of the doctor's days, had been silent on the subject.

The exceeding length of the room made the lowness of the ceiling, which the study shared with all the other rooms on the ground floor, seem still lower; and the quantity of heterogeneous articles with which the space was en-cumbered increased the lumber-room like appearance which on first entering impressed itself on a visitor's mind.

Immediately in front of the door, by the side of the window looking into the Close, there was a lay figure, on the shoulders of which were the doctor's surplice, hood, and scarf, and on its head his trencher cap. This somewhat startling ecclesiastical presentation was a device of the doctor's own invention, the object of which was to prevent him, if possible, from forgetting to take off the above-mentioned canonicals when he returned from morning and evening service in the choir. Again and again it had occurred to him to proceed directly to whatever occupation in his study was uppermost in his mind—and had been so, it may be feared, during the hour spent in the choir—without divesting himself of any of these garments. And as the occupations were often of a nature involving contact with dusty tomes and dustier relics of antiquity,—and, as even when this was not the case, the doctor, finding the folds of his surplice under his hand very convenient for the purpose, was apt to wipe either his pen or the dust with them, as the case might require,—considerable inconvenience arose from the neglect. At length it occurred to him that if he had, standing immediately before his eyes, as he entered his room, such a representative of himself, as it were, which he would be always accustomed to see at all other times of the day dressed in full canonicals, and which, when thus presenting itself to him naked, would seem to ask for its usual clothing, he could not fail to be reminded of what he had first to do, before returning to his studies. And the scheme had answered well, except as regarded the bands; and that small article of church costume mattered less. The only evil arising from forgetfulness in this particular, was, that it sometimes happened that the doctor came to his dinner-table with two or even three pairs of bands around his neck, one falling over his coat collar behind, another under one of his ears, and a third in its proper position; for they would wriggle round his neck, and as it never occurred to him to imagine that any such phenomenon could have taken place, when on going to church he found no bands in front, he would put on a pair without any inquiry respecting the disappearance of their predecessors.

The doctor always wore gold spectacles; and as his habits made it absolutely necessary for him to possess three or four pairs of these, a similarly monstrous hyper-development would occur in respect to them, as in the matter of the bands; for, when one pair had by accident, or by the action of his hand when raised to his brow in thought, been pushed up out of their proper place on to his forehead, he never thought of looking, or rather feeling for them there, but forthwith put on a second pair. Lady Sempronia declared that she had seen her husband with one pair on the top of his bald head, another across his forehead, and a third in their proper position, and protested that the melancholy and monstrous sight had been a particularly severe trial to her.

The study was, like that of other gentlemen of similar tastes, crammed full of all sorts of queer odds and ends, which were regarded with much aversion by the Lady Sempronia. But there was one peculiar feature in the contents of the room which stirred up her bile, and grieved her heart to a much greater degree. This was the long rows of the paper-bound volumes of the different memoirs which her lord and master had contributed to the Silverton Archæological Club. It must be admitted, unhappily, that the rows were very long. By the help of the cross-shelves, which have been mentioned as standing out across the room, the study afforded accommodation for a very considerable number of books. But alas! the inner side of these shelves, or that looking toward the garden window, was almost entirely occupied by those costly and learned publications. It is true that the mass of them diminished gradually; but the process was a very slow one. And the long rows of identically similar volumes were a sore offence to poor Lady Sempronia's eyes. The doctor did his best to get rid of them; for no visitor, who could by any possibility be supposed to take any interest in such matters, left the house without a presentation copy of one or more of them. But at length it came to pass that the satisfactory disappearance of the volumes led to an alarmingly unsatisfactory result. The stock in hand of the canon's "Memoir on Panelled Ceilings in Coffer-work as Exemplified in Buildings of the Norman and Ante-Norman Period," began to run so low, that visions of a second edition began to

float before the author's mind, to the unspeakable horror of Lady Sempronia. It had been the most expensive of all the doctor's publications, for colored lithograph illustrations had been found absolutely necessary. And the first hint that the learned world would probably expect a second edition of that highly appreciated work had been one of Lady Sempronia's severest trials. The rest of the hated volumes, of which in her unforeseeing ignorance she had watched the gradual disappearance with satisfaction, suddenly became valuable in her eyes; and she adopted every means of preserving and husbanding the precious remainder of them. She had never before condescended to know even the titles of any of the canon's publications. But now, whenever there was any probability that the doctor would offer any of his works to a visitor, Lady Sempronia would interpose with, "Not the Coffer-work Ceilings, Dr. Lindisfarn. You have only one copy left!" And in fact but one copy remained on the study shelves; for on the first appearance of the danger, the lady had gradually carried off to her secret bower two or three copies at a time, all the remainder of the edition, to be produced, if need were, one at a time, and always under protest, so as to stave off the evil day when the doctor should be able to declare that the work was absolutely out of print.

The canon, though shorter and smaller than his brother, had been a well-looking man in his day. He had a high, delicately formed nose, a particularly well-cut and finely-shaped mouth, and a classical outline of features generally. Though very bald, and limping a little in his gait, in consequence of a fall from a ladder in the cathedral, when he had been engaged in directing and superintending some restorations of his beloved church, he was still a very distinguished-looking man. He always wore a large quantity of snow-white but perfectly limp and unstarched muslin, wound round and round his throat, and a large prominent shirt-frill protruding between the sides of his black waistcoat. A black body-coat, very wide in the skirt, black breeches, black silk stockings, somewhat negligently drawn over very handsome legs, gold knee and shoe buckles, which Lady Sempronia in vain strove to induce him to discard in favor of the more modern fashion of shoe-ties, completed his costume.

Margaret was a little startled on entering the study to see a figure in full canonicals and trencher cap motionless in front of her, and gave a perceptible little jump.

"No, dear," said Kate, "that is not Uncle Theophilus. That is only Canon Lindisfarn. May we come in, uncle?" she continued; "I know you are in your old corner behind the books there. Aunt and I have brought Margaret to see you."

"Come in, Kate, come in!" said a voice from behind the screen of books. "You are always welcome, my dear. But who is Margaret you speak of?"

"Why your niece, to be sure," cried Kate, leading the way round the screen, while Lady Sempronia whispered to Margaret, as they followed,—

"I told you it would be a trial, my dear."

"Don't you remember that you have a niece just returned from Paris?" continued Kate.

"To be sure I do! to be sure I do—now you mention it. Welcome to England, and welcome to Silverton, and welcome to Silverton Close, my dear! What a happiness it must be to you to find yourself at home once again!"

"It is a great pleasure, sir, to become personally acquainted with relatives, whom I have already learnt to venerate," said Margaret.

"I can't think," said the canon, after looking at Margaret in an earnest and yet wool-gathering sort of manner,—"I can't think for the life of me, who it is she reminds me of. There is some face in my memory that hers seems to recall to me."

"They say we Lindisfarns are all more or less alike," interposed Kate, fearing whither her uncle's remembrances might be leading him; "and all the people up at the Chase declare that Margaret and I are as much alike as two peas."

"Then I am sure they do you great injustice, sister," said Margaret, eagerly. "How can they compare your fresh-colored face to my poor white cheeks? I do not know how I came by them. It is just as if they had coquettishly fashioned themselves to please the people they grew among. For the Parisians admire white faces and not red ones. But I am sure I envy Kate's roses."

"There are white roses and red roses," said the canon, "and I'm sure I don't know that

anybody ever yet decided that one was more beautiful than the other."

"Talking of roses, by the by," said Kate, who did not like the turn the conversation was taking, "what about the cuttings you were to prepare for me, aunt? Suppose you and I go and look after them in the garden, and leave my uncle and Margaret to complete their acquaintance."

Kate was desperately afraid that the canon's half-recalled memories, which she had little doubt had been roused by a likeness between her sister and Julian, would stumble on, till they blundered on something which might throw Lady Sempronia into a fit of hysterics, and send her to bed for a week; and was anxious, therefore, to get her out of the danger. And her aunt, who never felt particularly comfortable or happy in the study, yielded at once to Kate's lead, merely saying to the doctor, as she left the room,—

"Not a copy of the Coffer-work Ceilings, Dr. Lindisfarn; remember you have but one copy left!"

"Lady Sempronia is reminding me," said the canon, in reply to a look of inquiry from Margaret, when they were left alone together, "that I must not offer you a copy of one of my little works, which has been so successful with the public that it is nearly exhausted. But the caution can hardly be needed; for it can scarcely be expected that a young lady should interest herself in matters of antiquarian research."

"Oh! there you are wrong, uncle," cried Margaret, who always was a far glibber talker in a *tête-a-tête*, be it with whom it might, than under any other circumstances. "And specially you do me wrong; for I take particular interest in all such matters. *J'aime la rococo à la folie!*" she added, clasping her admirably gloved hands together, bending her graceful figure a little forward, and throwing an expression of intense enthusiasm into her beautiful eyes.

The doctor, though a competent reader of French, was by no means a sufficiently instructed student of French things and phrases to be aware of the amount of distance lying between a Parisian lady's love for "*rococo*," and a taste for antiquarian research. But he knew very well, that he had never seen anything more lovely than his niece looked as she made her profession of admiration for his favorite studies.

"I really think," he said, in the zeal of his delight at the prospect of such a disciple, "that the last copy of my dissertation on Coffer-work Ceilings could find no more worthy destination than the shelf which holds your own special books, my dear. The book is now a rare one; and will, I doubt not, be there in good company."

"Not for the world, uncle, not for the world! I shall come here and ask you some day to lend me your own copy for a quiet hour in the garden. But I would not for any consideration carry off a copy which you will surely need to give to some great man of learning. Besides, what would Lady Sempronia say? But there was a subject about which I was very anxious to ask you; for I can get no information up at the Chase. Is it not true that the mansion called the Friary at Weston was once a monastery? I *should* so like to know all the history of it!"

"And I should so like to tell you," cried the canon, in the greatest glee. "You are quite right, my dear girl. It is one of the most interesting places in the county! Indeed, I have thought for some time past of making it the subject of a monograph."

Margaret had not the remotest conception of the meaning of a "monograph;" nor was she aware how safely she might have simply avowed her unacquaintance with the word, without pleading guilty to any very disgraceful ignorance; but she thought she might say,—

"Oh, that would be delightful, uncle! But what I should like best of all, if it were possible, would be to visit the spot with you,—you and I together, you know, so that you might explain everything to one."

"And why not? Nothing more easy! I have not yet made acquaintance, by the by, with the new owners of the place."

"Oh, that you will do to-morrow, uncle. Mr. and Miss Merriton are to dine with us. You will meet them, you know. And then I shall very soon afterward come to claim your promise of a day at the Friary."

"And I shall be delighted to keep it. Perhaps if I decide on writing on the subject, you might assist me with your pencil. Do you draw, my dear?"

"Yes, I have learned. I can draw a little. I should be so glad to be permitted to be of use. To study, and be directed by you, uncle, would be so delightful."

"And what could give me greater pleasure than to direct your studies? We will attack the Friary together. It really ought to be illustrated, the more so that I am not unaware that there are sciolists in this very city of Silverton, who hold some most absurd notions respecting certain portions of the ancient buildings. Yes, yes, my dear, with my pen and your pencil, we will attack the Friary together. To think of your having already cast your eye on the most interesting bit of antiquity in the county, you puss!"

And then Lady Sempronia and Kate came and tapped at the window from the garden; and the former told Margaret to come and have some luncheon in the parlor. And the doctor dismissed his newly found niece with the profound conviction that she was not only the flower of the family, but the most charming, the most highly gifted, and by far the most intelligent girl it had ever been his lot to meet with.

"Well, how did you and uncle get on together?" asked Kate. "Did you make friends?"

"I hope so," said Margaret; "as far as a learned man could with a very ignorant young girl. He was very kind to me."

"Did he offer to give you any of his books?" asked Lady Sempronia, well aware of the channel by which the doctor's kindness was wont to manifest itself.

"Yes, aunt. He was generous enough to offer me the last copy of his memoir on Ceiling-work Coffers. But of course, after what you had said, I would not let him do anything of the kind. What a pity it is that such an excellent man as my dear uncle should fail to recognize the good sense of abstaining from wasting his money on such things!"

And then the carriage came to the door with Miss Immy, precisely at three o'clock; and that very punctual lady sent in a message to Lady Sempronia, regretting that the immense amount of business she had had to transact in Silverton had made it impossible for her to leave herself time enough to alight —setting forth the absolute necessity of being at the Chase and dressed for dinner in time, not to keep the squire waiting beyond the half-hour of grace allowed them, and begging the young ladies to come out without delay.

So then there was a kissing bout, and Lady

Sempronia turned to kiss Margaret a second time, as she was leaving the room, while Kate was already hurrying across the hall to the carriage, and as she pressed her hand, trusted that they should see much of each other.

"Perhaps the house in the Close, and such little distractions as Silverton could offer,—dull enough though they generally were, God knew,—might sometimes be a change from the profound seclusion and monotony of the Chase."

And, "*Ah, ma tante! Comme vous êtes bonne pour moi, vous!*"

And so upon the whole (putting out of the question, of course, the tender affection of her father and sister), Margaret's *début* at the house in the Close had been a more successful one than at the Chase.

CHAPTER IX.
THE PARTY AT THE CHASE.

MISS IMMY considered "a trial" to be a matter inseparably connected with the Assizes, and in some less perfectly understood manner dependent on Quarter Sessions. She never used or understood the word in any other sense (unless as meaning simply an attempt); and in her own private opinion, uncommunicated to any human being, she attributed Lady Sempronia's constant use of the term to the shocking and fearful impression which had been made upon her especially weak mind (as Miss Immy considered it) by the idea of the thing, at the terrible time when it was a question whether her own son might not have to undergo the ordeal of it. Miss Immy had no idea that she herself had any trials, or she certainly might have considered it to be one, when, on the next morning, the morning of the party, it was made evident at breakfast that the squire had entirely forgotten all about it.

"Would you be so kind, Mr. Mat, as to mention to Mr. Lindisfarn, once every half-hour during the day, that he has to entertain friends at dinner to-day, and that he will get no dinner before six o'clock?"

"I'll try and remember it, Miss Immy, this time," said the squire, laughing; "and if I don't, it will be my punishment to expect my dinner at five and have to wait an hour for it,—a penalty that might suffice for a worse crime!"

And then the squire took his gun, and calling to the dogs to join him, was seen no more till he met his guests in the drawing-room.

Miss Immy had very many things on her mind, and was in a state of much bustle and business-like energy all day. She was wont very scornfully to repudiate the new-fangled heresy, which teaches that the genteel mistress of a family should disavow any labors of the kind, and be supposed to delegate all such cares to subordinate ministers—existing in the Olympus of the drawing-room in a very Epicurean and non-providential condition of godship. She had been irritated by such affectations on the part of others—of Lady Sempronia especially—into a habit of making a special boast before her guests of the part she had personally taken in caring for their entertainment; and it was observable that on such occasions, she always spoke in her broadest Sillshire Doric.

Kate, on whom none of these cares fell, had her day at her disposition, and to Margaret's great surprise proposed to Mr. Mat a ride to Sillmouth. There was a fresh breeze blowing, and she should like, she said, a gallop on the sands to see the big waves rolling in. Mr. Mat was always ready for a ride with Kate; so Birdie was saddled, and away they went.

"Surely, it is a bad day to choose for such a ride," said Margaret.

"Just the day made for it!" cried Kate. "I know our Sillshire coast; and I know what a tide there will be tumbling in with this wind."

"Yes, I dare say; but you will come back with your face as red as beet-root, and people coming here this evening! Besides, I wanted to consult you about a hundred things."

"Oh, my face must take its chance, as it always does. And we can talk as much as we like to-morrow. We shall have all the morning before going over to Wanstrow."

"To-morrow! but I wanted to talk about my dress for this evening," pouted Margaret.

"Your dress! but you have got such lots of beautiful things. Any one will do."

"Any one! That's very easily said. But it depends on so many things."

It was very natural that Kate, who was going to meet only old friends, with the exception of Captain Ellingham and the Merritons, and who was going to do nothing but what she was perfectly well used to, should feel more at her ease about the event of the evening than Margaret, who was going to make her first appearance at an English dinner-party among a roomful of strangers. But the "so many things" that Margaret spoke of included sundry considerations and speculations of a kind that had never entered the English-bred girl's philosophy.

"But I shall be home in plenty of time to dress," she said in answer to her sister's last remonstrance; "and then we can settle what dress you shall wear."

So Kate rode off; and Margaret was left to meditate on her evening "trials" in solitude, broken only by the not altogether sympathizing companionship of Simmons.

Had it entered into Kate's head to imagine that the morning would appear tedious to Margaret, she would not have left her. But it was so much the habit of the family to go each one his own way, and she was so used to being left alone to her own morning occupations herself, that it never occurred to her that it was necessary to stay at home because her sister did.

Nor did it seem that her counsel was really needed in the matter of the dress; or at all events, was so urgently needed as to be waited for; for when she returned from her ride she found the great question decided, and every article of Margaret's evening toilet carefully laid out on her bed.

Kate did return from her seaside gallop with her face not only red but rough; for her ride had answered her expectations to the utmost; and not only the boisterous south-west wind, but the salt spray also had lashed her cheeks. And it needs a painful effort of impartial truthfulness in a chronicler, who owns a very strong special liking for Kate Lindisfarn, to admit that this was not the only respect in which the advantage was with Margaret, when the two girls went down to the drawing-room. Margaret's dress was the production of a Parisian artist, and fitted her fine shape as smoothly and somewhat more tightly than her skin. Kate's, alas! was but the chef-d'œuvre of Miss Piper, the Silverton milliner. It was a pretty light-blue silk dress, a shade or two lighter than the wearer's eyes, which, whatever her complexion may have been, were decidedly none the worse for her ride. They danced and laughed, and flashed with health and good humor and high spirits. Blue was Kate's

favorite color, and it always became her well. But Miss Piper's handiwork did not escape Margaret's criticism in more respects than one; and it must be admitted that the young lady was a very competent critic.

"What will become of me, if I am to wear dresses made by the person who made that?" cried she. "Why, it fits about as well as a sack, Kate, here under the arms. It makes your waist look thick, or rather gives you no waist at all! And you must admit that it is cut odiously round the shoulders."

"Poor Miss Piper!" said Kate, laughing. "She thought that she surpassed herself when she turned out this dress; and I thought it a very pretty one myself. But I can see very well that it does not fit like yours. And then, you know, I have not such a slender waist as yours; we proved that by the riding-habit. And as for the shoulders, I suppose it is cut about as low as they are worn hereabouts. We are provincial folks, you know. But you may depend upon it, we are not so ignorant, any of us, as not to see how exquisitely dressed you are. I never saw such a fit. And how it becomes you!"

Margaret was in truth looking exceedingly lovely. She had selected a black silk dress; perhaps from having been led to think of the ivory whiteness of her own skin in connection with her prognostications of the effect of the morning's ride on her sister's. At all events, the choice was a judicious one. Not only the complexion of the face, but the perfect creamy whiteness of the magnificent throat, and as much as could be seen of the shoulders, was shown off to the utmost advantage by the dark folds of the material in juxtaposition with it. As before, Kate wore her beautiful hair in ringlets, while Margaret's somewhat darker locks were, quite unusually for Sillshire, bound tightly around her small classically shaped head, not only displaying to advantage the beauty of it, but adding in appearance to her height. Kate was in fact the taller of the two girls. But what with this difference of headdress, what with her somewhat more slender figure, and what with the additional advantage given to this by the cut and admirable fitting of her dress, anybody who had seen the two otherwise than absolutely side by side, would have said that Margaret had the advantage. Kate wore white silk stockings and kid shoes; Margaret, black silk—of that very fine and

4

gauzy quality which allows a sufficiency of the whiteness of the skin beneath to shine through the thin covering to turn the black almost to gray—and black satin shoes. And here again, alas! she had the advantage over our Sillshire Kate. And men will be so stupid in these matters! I would lay a wager that either Captain Ellingham, Fred Falconer, or Mr. Merriton, the latter especially,—he was the youngest,—would have said the next morning that Margaret had the prettier foot; whereas all that could have been said in justice was that she had the prettier shoe. In this matter Sillshire could not compete with Paris. And it may be possible that the active habits of Sillshire life had added something to the muscular development, and therefore to the thickness of the country-bred foot, which had done more walking, running, jumping, riding, swimming in its life than any score of Parisian young ladies' feet. At all events, the exquisitely beautiful slenderness of the by no means short but well-formed foot and high, arched instep, which showed itself beneath the folds of Margaret's black dress, was shown to the greatest possible advantage by the skill of the Parisian Melnotte of that day.

Upon the whole, the contrasted style of their dresses added so much to the real differences between the two girls, and the contrasted style of their manner added so much more, that no stranger would have guessed them to be sisters, much less twins. As to this latter matter of bearing, gait, and all the innumerable and indescribable little details which make up what is called manner, there was more room for difference of opinion. Every man admires a Parisian dress or shoe more than a Sillshire one; but some men—and not Sillshire men only—may prefer the Lindisfarn-bred to the *Chassée-d'Antin*-bred manner. Margaret herself, however, had no doubt at all upon this department of the question, any more than upon the other. And her last final glance at the Psyche glass in her chamber sent her down-stairs by Kate's side in high good-humor.

When they entered the drawing-room, they found Miss Immy and Mr. Mat, with Lady Farnleigh and Captain Ellingham. The squire had not yet come into the room. There was a fire in the grate; for, though it had been hitherto lovely September weather, the day had been boisterous and windy,—the first

foretaste of autumn. Lady Farnleigh and Miss Immy were sitting near the fire, and discussing a method, said to be infallible, for keeping eggs fresh longer than any other way; and Miss Immy was declaring her conviction that a fresh-laid egg was a fresh-laid, and a stale egg a stale egg, despite all the cleverness and contrivances in the world. Mr. Mat and Captain Ellingham were talking in the embrasure of a window near the door. When the girls came in, however, and went to join the ladies on the rug before the fire, the two gentlemen came forward, and Captain Ellingham was presented by Lady Farnleigh to both the young ladies. There was not the slightest difference in her manner in either case; but she introduced the stranger first to Kate. And a slight shade passed over Margaret's heart, not over her face,—*pas si bête!*—as the reflection occurred to her that Kate had no right to be treated as if she were the elder sister.

Margaret saw enough of the captain with half a glance, however, to make up her mind at once that as far as he was concerned, any little matter of this kind was of small importance to her. Knowing how poor a man Captain Ellingham was, it was quite a satisfaction to her—almost, one might say, a relief—to find that no amount of dangerous attractiveness had been thrown away upon him. And yet all women, and even all young girls, would not have been at all disposed to subscribe to Margaret's opinion on this point. Captain Ellingham was one of those men who seem to impersonate the *beau-idéal* of their calling. He looked exactly what he was,—every inch a sailor. He was of middling height, very broad in the shoulders, with not an ounce of superfluous flesh on him. His coal-black hair and whiskers, of which he wore rather more than was at that time usual among landsmen, were already beginning to be slightly streaked with gray. His cheek was dark by nature, and bronzed by exposure to weather. The large, good-humored mouth, showing every time he smiled a set of magnificently regular teeth, was supported by a massive square chin, the fleshlessness of which, and of the jaw behind it, caused the lower edge of the latter to show an angle as clean and well-defined as the right angle of a square piece of iron; and it looked as hard and firm as that. But the eyes were the principal feature of his face. They were large brown eyes, which, when they looked anybody in the face without any reason for special expression, gave the impression that nothing could ever make them wink. When they were under the influence of any particular attitude of mind, it was strange how varied, and indeed how contradictory, the expression of them could be. Men said—his own men, the crew of his ship especially—that Captain Ellingham had the eye of a hawk. Others said—not men so much—that Captain Ellingham had an eye like a stag. For the rest he had that sort of quick, decided manner, and that extra and superfluous amount of movement in his bearing, gait, and action, which is apt to characterize temperaments of great energy and nervous excitability. Upon the whole, one might say that Captain Ellingham was not, perhaps, a man to fall over head and ears in love with at first sight, but one with whom it would be very specially difficult to struggle out of love again, if once an adventurous heart should have advanced far enough to begin to feel the power of attraction.

Captain Ellingham, on his side, was one of those men particularly apt to fall in love, as it is called, at first sight, but not irretrievably so. There was too much depth of character, too much caution, too much shrewd common sense, and too strong an admiration for, and cleaving to, and need of, nobleness and goodness for that. So that, in point of fact, his tendency to love at first sight amounted to little more than great susceptibility to every form of female charm, joined to that proneness to poetize each manifestation of it into a conformity with his own ideal, which generally characterizes such temperaments.

Lady Farnleigh's spirit, if any amount of " medium " power could cause it to look over the writer's shoulder as the words are formed by his pen—(would that it could do so! ab, would that it could!) — Lady Farnleigh's spirit, I say, would be very angry at the breach of confidence. But the fact was that, as they returned together in her ladyship's carriage to Wanstrow that night, Captain Ellingham admitted that, of the two charming girls he had seen, he had been most struck by that exquisitely lovely sylph in black ;— certainly the most beautiful creature he had ever seen ! Whereupon that somewhat free-spoken lady had told him that he was a great

goose, and knew about as much of women as she did of haulyards and marlingspikes.

Very short time, however, was allowed him for any quiet comparison of the two Lindisfarn lasses, before the rest of the guests began to arrive. The first comers were old Mr. Falconer and his son. The latter is already in some degree known to the reader. The first thing that struck one in the former, was his adherence to the then all but obsolete fashion of wearing a *queue*, or pigtail, and powder. He was a tall, florid, well-preserved old gentleman, somewhere between sixty and seventy, who, having lived among the clergy of a cathedral city all his life, had acquired naturally in a great degree, and affected in a still greater, a clerical tone of manners and sentiments. Nothing pleased old Mr. Falconer more than to be mistaken for a clergyman.

Mr. Freddy, whose drawing-room get-up was in all respects on a par with that of his morning hours, and on a level with his reputation, after he had greeted, with salutations accurately and gracefully adapted to the special fitness of each particular case, all his old acquaintances, was of course presented first to Margaret and afterward to Captain Ellingham ;—the first by Kate, with a very gracious " My sister, Mr. Falconer. Your Parisian reminiscences [Mr. Freddy had spent a winter in Paris] will make you seem almost more like an old acquaintance than any other of her Sillshire friends." The other introduction was performed less graciously by Lady Farnleigh, as thus : " Mr. Falconer, the Honorable Mr. Ellingham, in command of His Majesty's Revenue Cutter, the Petrel, on the Sillmouth station."

Lady Farnleigh always called Lieutenant Ellingham Captain, like all the rest of the world. I do not know why she chose not to do so on this occasion ; and I suppose that Freddy Falconer could not have told why either. But he observed it ; and hated Lady Farnleigh for it more than he did before. It was because he hated her, and not, to do him justice, from any vulgar reverence for her superior rank, that his bow to her had been markedly lower than to any other person in the room.

Next arrived Dr. Theophilus Lindisfarn, bringing with him, not indeed the precious memoir on Coffer-work Ceilings, but another, on " The Course and Traces of the Ancient

City Walls of Silverton," as an offering to Margaret, the ceremonious presentation of which before the assembled company, and the consequent pouncing on her by old Mr. Falconer, not a little disgusted that sylphlike creature, and wreaked on her some measure of punishment for the false pretences which had brought it upon her. She had reason to suspect, too, that there was more of the same sort of annoyance in store for her; for the canon had entered the room bearing in his hands a carefully packed and sealed brown-paper parcel, looking very much like a brick in size and shape, which he had carefully deposited on a side-table, saying with sundry winks and nods and mysterious smiles, that there was something for their amusement in the evening, which he believed some, at least, of those present (with a very flatteringly meaning look at Margaret) would appreciate.

Then came in the squire, with a rush and a circular fire of apologies.

"A thousand pardons, Lady Farnleigh! You have tolerated my ways so long that I hope you will bear with them a little longer, and give up all hope of seeing them mended. How do, Falconer? I am not absolutely unpunctual though. It is not six o'clock yet! Wants two minutes!"

"And a half, Mr. Lindisfarn!" said the old banker, in a comforting, encouraging sort of tone, as he consulted his chronometer.

"Thank you, Falconer. And a half! Who calls that not being in time? How do, brother? How is Lady Sempronia? Not equal to the trial of coming up to the Chase, eh?"

And then the squire was introduced to Captain Ellingham—duly called so this time —by Lady Farnleigh; and welcomed him to the Chase and to Sillshire with a charming mixture of high-bred courtesy and friendly cordiality.

"And now, Mat, ring the bell, and tell them that they may let us have dinner, there's a good fellow. You must be all half-starved."

"But we are not all here, Mr. Lindisfarn," said Miss Immy. "We are expecting Mr. Merriton and his sister from the Friary, Lady Farnleigh. Mr. Lindisfarn asked them himself; and now he has forgotten all about it!"

"Bless me, so I had! Don't tell of me, anybody! But they ought to have been here by this time. I hope they don't mean to bring London ways into Sillshire, and understand one to mean seven when one says six."

"Our clocks are too fast, Mr. Lindisfarn. I told you so the other day," pleaded Miss Immy.

"Not if they make it now only two minutes past six," said Mr. Falconer, again consulting his infallible watch.

"Not a bit of it," said the squire; "and perhaps the best way of showing them that six means six in Sillshire would be to go to dinner."

But the squire was persuaded to allow a little law on the score of the defaulters' being strangers, and this the first time of offending. And happily a carriage was heard crunching the gravel outside the drawing-room windows before another ten minutes had passed,—which, however long they may have seemed to the seniors of the party, passed quickly enough with some of the others.

And then Mr. Merriton and Miss Merriton were announced. They were entire strangers to everybody in the room except the Falconers, and except in so far as a casual meeting had introduced Mr. Merriton to Mr. Lindisfarn. And there was consequently a little excitement of expectation among the party assembled, to see what the new-comers into the county were like. And in the next instant it was recognized by all present that they were, at all events, remarkable-looking people.

Arthur Merriton, though a smaller and slighter man than either Captain Ellingham or Fred Falconer, would have been thought by many a more remarkably handsome man than either. He would probably have been more generally thought so in England than among his mother's countrymen, where the peculiar type of his beauty is much more common. Fred Falconer's brown locks and carnation-colored cheeks would have attracted more admiring eyes among the beauties of the Conca d'oro, and the carefully-blinded windows of Palermo, than the raven's-wing curls, the brilliant dark eyes, and the thin, transparent-looking sallow cheeks, and finely-formed but yellow-white brow of the son of a Sicilian mother. In person and figure he was delicately and slenderly made, with small and well-shaped hands and feet. His manner was unexceptionably gentleman-like; but there was a nervousness about it that seemed half excitability and half shyness, as he went through the ordeal of being presented to the various individuals of his new neighborhood.

And this peculiarity of manner was yet more marked in the case of his sister. She was very small, moreover, and really fairy-like in figure, which increased the effect of her shrinking timidity and nervousness of manner. Her little figure, in its almost miniature proportions, was exquisitely perfect; but the face had peculiarities which prevented it from being beautiful. The large, fair forehead, which seemed first to attract anybody who saw Miss Merriton for the first time, was too large, and too square, and too prominent for the small face. The eyes had also the rare defect of being too large. But perhaps their size alone would not have seemed a fault, if they had not also been too prominent, and what the French call à fleur de tête. The other features of the face were good and delicate. Exceeding delicacy, indeed, was the prominent and paramount characteristic of the entire face and figure.

The hair was most remarkably abundant, and beautiful in quality, and as black as night. The whole face, except the lips, was entirely colorless.

The ladies and the young men had had time to note all this; and the old men had had time to think to themselves, "What a very strange-looking little body!" when the dinner-bell at length rang.

Mr. Lindisfarn gave his arm to Lady Farnleigh; Mr. Falconer took Miss Iumy; Dr. Theophilus seized on Margaret, to her exceeding great disgust, making her feel as though she should burst into tears amid the sweet smiles with which she looked up into his face, and pretended to coax him, as they walked to the dining-room, to tell her what was inside the brown-paper parcel; Captain Ellingham's character of stranger, as well as his rank, secured him Kate's arm; Freddy Falconer had Miss Merriton under his care; and so, with Mr. Merriton and Mr. Mat bringing up the rear, they went to dinner.

CHAPTER X.

AT DINNER, AND AFTERWARD.

IT was somewhat contrary to rule; but the head of the table at the Chase was always occupied by Miss Immy. It was so for that good old conservative reason, that it always had been so from time immemorial. And the arrangement was a good one, under the circumstances, on one account, at all events,—that it obviated any difficulty as to the question to which of the twin Lindisfarn lasses should be assigned that post of honor. So Miss Immy sat at the top of the table, with the canon on her right and the old banker on her left hand, exactly as she had done on many a previous occasion. And next to Dr. Lindisfarn, of course, sat Margaret. On the right hand of the squire was Lady Farnleigh, and opposite to her Miss Merriton, with Fred Falconer by her side. One place therefore remained vacant between him and Margaret. On the opposite side of the table, to the right of the squire, that is to say, next to old Mr. Falconer, sat Kate, with Captain Ellingham on the other side of her. So that on this side of the table, also, there remained one vacant place between Ellingham and Lady Farnleigh; and all the party were seated except the two luckless unmated cavaliers, Merriton and Mr. Mat. It was an anxious moment for Margaret, while it remained in doubt which of the two unseated ones would find his place on her side and which of them on the other. Had she found herself between the doctor and Mr. Mat, the swelling indignation at her gentle heart must have brimmed over at the eyes. She had already suffered from fate almost as much as she could bear; and had endured it with the smiles of the red Indian at the stake.

As it was she was rewarded for her heroism. Of the two places that remained unfilled when Merriton and Mr. Mat entered the room together, closing the procession from the drawing-room, Mr. Mat saw at a glance the advantages and disadvantages attached to each of them, and like an old soldier lost no time in seizing on that which pleased him best. Mr. Merriton, even if he had had any preferences on the subject, was far too shy and nervous to have acted with promptitude for the gratification of them. Mr. Mat had the choice, therefore, of a place between Lady Farnleigh and Captain Ellingham, or one between Margaret and Fred Falconer, and did not hesitate an instant. Mr. Mat had got no

further yet, as regarded Margaret, than the unwilling admission to himself that she did not *zem* like a Lindisfarn lass, and the feeling that he could not quite make her out. But Mr. Freddy Falconer was his abomination. On the other hand, Lady Farnleigh was a great favorite of his, and she always made much of Mr. Mat; while of Captain Ellingham he had liked well enough what little he had seen of him during their short conversation in the drawing-room before the other guests had arrived.

So Mr. Mat slipped round the table to the vacant place on the side opposite the door of the room, before Mr. Merriton had time to see where there was any place for him at all; and Margaret was made happy by finding the evidently "eligible" Mr. Merriton by her side.

If only she could have changed places with him! She would then have been what the moralist tells us nobody is,—*ab omni parte beata*,—with Merriton on one side and Freddy Falconer on the other! That was what she would have liked, if she could have had it all her own way. She would have preferred, too, if she could not have both those good things, to have had Fred Falconer by her side, rather than Mr. Merriton. She had not, it is true, any accurate data of the kind which alone ought to determine the choice of a well-brought-up and thoroughly prudent young lady in a case of the kind. Fred Falconer was the only son of a rich banker. Mr. Merriton was the only son of a merchant who must be presumed to have been rich also, and had just bought an estate. It was impossible to say. It was a case of doubt, in which it was perfectly permissible to suffer one's self to be influenced by mere personal inclination, and Margaret felt far more inclined to like Falconer. To her thinking he was out of all comparison the handsomer man of the two; and then he had *l'usage du monde*, as she said in discussing the matter afterward with her sister.

Nevertheless, she was tolerably well contented with the goods the gods had provided her in young Merriton. Things had looked much worse! What would it have been, if she had been, as seemed at one moment so likely, shut up between her uncle and Mr. Mat? And then an impartial consideration of the entire situation required that much weight should be allowed to the position of the rival forces on the battle-field. And with this she was tolerably contented. If she could not have the incomparable Frederick, it was far better that he should be given up to that absurd and childish-looking Miss Merriton than to Kate; especially bearing in mind those hints that had fallen from Lady Farnleigh on the subject! She admitted to herself that she could not have managed Kate's place better, if the arrangement had been left entirely to her own discretion. She was separated by the entire length and breadth of the table from Fred Falconer, and was between his father, and that disagreeable-looking Captain Ellingham, who was of no use, but might possibly serve the purpose of making Falconer jealous. Margaret was also well pleased to be placed at a good distance from Lady Farnleigh.

"You would not have had such a fish as that, Mr. Lindisfarn, I can tell you," said Miss Immy, as the canon began to cut up the turbot, under the watchful eye of his brother antiquary opposite, who jealously observed the distribution of the dividend of fin,—"you would not have had such a fish as that, Mr. Lindisfarn, if I had not spoken to Cookson myself about it; it is no easy matter to get a bit of fish, nowadays, Lady Farnleigh. It all goes to London."

"It would not be a bad plan for the Silverton people to subscribe and rig out a fishing-boat of their own," said Mr. Mat.

"The Londoners would out-bid you, sir. Fish like everything else *will* go to the best market," said old Falconer.

"And if your fisherman were to catch not on his own account but on yours, I am afraid the Silverton subscription boat would hardly get a fair share of the fish," said Captain Ellingham.

"I am content to leave the matter in the hands of Miss Immy and Cookson," said the doctor; "for I never ate a better fish in my life."

"Lady Farnleigh tells me that you are a great swimmer as well as an accomplished rider, Miss Lindisfarn," said Captain Ellingham to Kate. "Are you fond of the sea in any other way,—boating or yachting?"

"I have had very little opportunity of trying," answered Kate;—"never in anything larger than one of the small Sillmouth pilot boats; but I liked that very much,—almost as much as a gallop on land."

"I wonder whether I could induce you and your sister to take a day's cruise in my cutter. I am sure we could persuade Lady Farnleigh to do *chaperone*."

"I should like it of all things," said Kate; "it would be a great treat."

"We will consult Lady Farnleigh then, and ask your sister after dinner. The only thing is to choose a good day. It would be desperately dull work for you to be becalmed."

"Such a day as to-day would be the thing; would it not?" said Kate.

"Well, you may have too much of a good thing, you know. There must have been a good deal of sea off the coast to-day."

"Indeed there was! I can answer for that. Or perhaps I should say that there seemed to be to my ignorance."

"Were you down on the coast to-day?"

"Yes, I and Mr. Mat got a gallop on the Sillmouth sands. I went because I was sure there would be great waves with this south-west wind, and I am so fond of seeing them tumble in on the shore."

"What! You knew it was a sou'west wind then? I thought landsmen never knew what wind was blowing."

"But I am a landswoman, you know. And I assure you, that we up at the Chase here are apt to know more about the wind than they do in Silverton."

"Yes, I suppose you must get the most of it up in the woods above the house. What magnificent old woods they are!"

"You must tell Noll that. He is very fond and a little proud of the Lindisfarn woods."

"And may I ask who Noll is?"

"Noll is the elderly gentleman at the bottom of the table, whom all the rest of the world beside me call Oliver Lindisfarn, Esquire. Papa, Captain Ellingham was struck by the beauty of the Lindisfarn woods."

"You must see them by daylight, and ride through them," said the squire. "There are some very fine trees among them. But you could see very little as you drove up to the Chase this evening."

"I walked up the hill, and enjoyed the twilight view most thoroughly. And then, you know, we sailors have cats' eyes, and can see in the dark."

"If you care about that sort of thing," said old Mr. Falconer, "you should not ride, but walk, through the woods on Lindisfarn brow, as we Silverton people call the crest of the hill above the house yonder. There are some of the finest sticks of timber in the county there; but the squire wont cut a tree of them."

"No; there is another old stick must be felled first, before the axe goes among the oaks on Lindisfarn brow," said the squire.

"But is it really true that cats can see in the dark?" asked Miss Immy; who had been meditating on that assertion since Captain Ellingham had made it.

"It is generally said so; but at all events a sailor is obliged to do so, more or less," said Captain Ellingham.

"I wish I could," returned Miss Immy, meditatively; "for I am always afraid of setting my cap on fire when I carry a lighted candle in my hand."

"The boundary line of the Lindisfarn Chase property ran very close behind the site of the house, once upon a time," said old Mr. Falconer, "and all the woods on the hill were part of the property belonging to the Friary at Weston. But at the dissolution of the monasteries, the Lindisfarn of that day obtained a grant of all that portion of the land which lies on this side of the Lindisfarn Brook. It has often seemed odd to me, that, having sufficient interest to obtain so large a slice of the spoil, he did not find means to add the whole of the Friary estates to Lindisfarn."

"I don't think the old boundary line ran quite as you conceive it to have done, Falconer," said the doctor. "There is no doubt about the line as far as the corner of the Weston warren; but supposing us to take our stand at that point," etc., etc., etc.

And the two old gentlemen, who rarely met without a battle royal on some point or other of the manifold knotty questions with which the "paths of hoar antiquity" are strewn quite as thickly as they are with flowers, entered forthwith into a hot dispute, carrying on the fight across Miss Immy, who kept turning from one speaker to the other, with her little palsied nodding of the head, as if she took the most lively interest in the matter in hand, and was very much convinced by the arguments of each speaker in succession.

Margaret, meanwhile, between whom and Mr. Merriton a very few absolutely matter-of-course words only had passed, seized the opportunity afforded by Mr. Falconer's expression of surprise that some ancestors of hers had not found means to monopolize the whole of the ancient Friary property, to say to her neighbor, speaking in a very low and gentle voice, which contrasted with the rather loud tone in which all the rest of the conversation had been carried on,—

"I am sure it is better for all parties that my ancestors did not add the Friary to Lindisfarn. Do you not think so, Mr. Merriton? I am sure it is of more advantage to the inhabitants of the Chase to have some other neighbors besides the good people of Silverton, than to have a few more acres."

"At all events," replied Mr. Merriton, blushing painfully up to the roots of his black hair as he spoke, "it would have been in every point of view a misfortune for me, Miss Lindisfarn."

"I have never been at the Friary yet; but I am told that it is the most beautiful thing in the county;" rejoined Margaret, in the same low tone of voice.

"You have never been to the Friary? And living within five miles of it!"

"But I am a more recent inhabitant of Sillshire than you are, Mr. Merriton. This is only the fourth day from my arrival at Lindisfarn."

"I thought you had lived here all your life," said Mr. Merriton, simply.

"No, indeed!" replied the young lady, with an intonation in which might have been detected some manifestation of a consciousness that her neighbor's supposition was not a complimentary one; "my whole life has been passed in Paris; and I assure you," she added in a yet lower and more confidential tone, "that I find myself quite as much in a strange land here as you can do. Does not Miss Merriton find all the things and all the people here very"— she hesitated a little before adding—"very different from what she has been used to?"

As Margaret had not the remotest idea what manner of people, or things, or places Miss Merriton had been used to, the remark was rather *hasardé*, as Margaret would have said herself. And the consciousness that it was so prompted her to add, "I suppose you have lived in London?"

"For rather more than a year past we have done so; and at different times in my life I have been in town, and in other parts of England before. But the greatest portion of my life has been passed in a different clime."

There was in the last words Mr. Merriton had spoken, and in the manner which accompanied them, enough to have afforded a shrewder and more experienced observer than Margaret a key to one phase at least of his character ; but she was not equal to the perception or to the application of it. And he was probably a little disappointed when she replied simply :—

" Have you, too, lived in Paris, then ? "

" No, Miss Lindisfarn, not in Paris. My home was under a more genial sky."

Margaret gave him a quick, sharp, sidelong glance out of the corner of her eye, and from under the shelter of its long silken lash ; but as this showed her nothing in Mr. Merriton's remarkably handsome face but an expression which seemed to her one of intense sadness, and as she did not see her way at all clearly in the direction which their conversation was taking, she changed it by referring to the safer topic of the Friary.

" Is your new home as beautiful a place as I have been told it is, Mr. Merriton ? I think I should be more inclined to accept your opinion on the subject than that of—people who have known little else than Sillshire."

" Yes, it is very pretty ; a very pretty house and grounds. But I hope, Miss Lindisfarn, that there is no need for you to take anybody's opinion save your own, on the subject. I trust I may soon have the pleasure of showing it to you."

" You are very good. I should so like it ! Indeed, my uncle, Dr. Lindisfarn, had promised to ask your permission to take me there with him. I believe," she added, turning her head toward him, so as to look away from her uncle on the other side of her, and speaking in a very low voice, " that it is considered that the Friary is interesting in some antiquarian point of view."

There was no fear that her uncle might overhear any of her conversation with Mr. Merriton ; for he was far too busily and too loudly engaged in his dispute with Mr. Falconer carried on across the table.

" Yes," said Mr. Merriton ; " I dare say it may be so ; for, as the place was once a monastery, there must be a history attached to it. Do you interest yourself in such pursuits, Miss Lindisfarn ? "

This was rather a difficult question for Margaret to answer. There was in the matter itself something, and in the tone of Mr. Merriton's last speech more, to disincline her to reply in the affirmative, and she was afraid with her uncle so close to her to answer as she would have done under other circumstances. And then there was the prospect of the part she would have to play when the odious brown-paper parcel should be opened after dinner in the drawing-room. So after casting a rapid glance at her uncle, and having thus ascertained that he was thoroughly absorbed in his conversation about the ancient boundary line between the Lindisfarn property and that of the old monks, she ventured to say,—

" Oh, I am a great deal too ignorant to understand anything, or, indeed " (almost in a whisper), " to care much about any such matters. But my uncle is very fond of them : and I try to interest myself as much as possible in them to please him, you understand. When any one is kind to me, I am sure to take an interest in what interests them. That is a woman's nature, you know, Mr. Merriton."

" We must talk to your uncle after dinner, and arrange for a visit to the Friary. It ought to be very soon, before this beautiful weather is over."

" And you must make me acquainted, too, with your sister, Mr. Merriton, when we get into the drawing-room. I am dying to make friends with her. I am sure we shall suit each other."

Margaret was in truth anxious to have the means of interrupting or impeding in some way the apparently very promising flirtation which had been progressing during dinner between that young lady and Mr. Frederick Falconer, and which had by no means escaped her observation.

" Yes, I hope you will like my sister," replied Mr. Merriton ; " but you must have the kindness and the patience to make yourself acquainted with her first. Emily is very timid, very shy, very retiring."

Margaret thought to herself that Mr. Falconer had, without any very great amount of perseverance, contrived to overcome those barriers to acquaintanceship with Miss Merriton ; but she only said,—

" Oh, I am sure we shall understand each other."

Lady Farnleigh, the squire, and Mr. Mat had been all this time discussing the alarming increase in the depredations of poachers, since the conclusion of the war, and the necessity of taking some steps, which Lady Farnleigh was reluctant to adopt, for the protection of the game on the Wanstrow Manor Estate. So that, what with the eager antiquarian discussion at the head of the table, the *sotto voce* conversations between Margaret and Mr. Merriton, and between Fred Falconer and Miss Merriton, and the tripartite poaching debate at the bottom of the board, there was every opportunity for Kate and Captain Ellingham to have enjoyed as undisturbed a *tête-à-tête* as any similarly circumstanced individuals could have desired. Yet it somehow or other came to pass that they did not make the most—or even much—of it. After the talk between them about the proposed excursion in the cutter, the conversation had languished. Captain Ellingham had eagerly asked whether Margaret liked the sea as well as her sister, and expressed his hope, rather more earnestly than seemed necessary, that she should be of the proposed party; and then little more than a few "mere words of course" now and then had passed between them. Captain Ellingham's attention, in fact, was engrossed by the couple who sat opposite to him, Margaret and Mr. Merriton, and by the apparently very confidential nature of the conversation that was going on between them. He seemed unable to take his eyes off Margaret, and was, in fact, acquiring that certainty that she was the most beautiful creature he had ever seen, which he expressed afterward to Lady Farnleigh on their way home.

This might suffice to account for the fact that the conversation between him and Kate had languished during the dinner-time. But to tell the whole truth, Kate was on her side, not to the same extent, nor so undisguisedly, but very similarly guilty. Whereas anybody might have seen that Captain Ellingham was observing Margaret with undisguised admiration, and uneasiness at the closeness of her *tête-à-tête* with the man by her side, nobody save a very fine and intelligent observer could have noted the occasional little lightning-quick and furtive glances which Kate sent into the corner of the table opposite to her, on an errand of discovery respecting the nature of the intercourse going on between Frederick Falconer and Miss Merriton.

Was that, then, a matter of such vital interest to Kate Lindisfarn? The question is one which cuts rudely into the very centre of the triply guarded citadel and mystery of a young girl's heart. It is hardly a fair question. Vital importance! No, certainly: it was not a matter of *vital* importance! Well, but that is a mere quibble—a riding off on the exact sense of a word. Was it a matter of such great interest to her to know what Mr. Falconer was saying to Miss Merriton? No; she certainly did not at all wish to overhear any part of his conversation. Was Kate in love with Fred Falconer? There, that is plain!

No! the rude question may be answered as plainly. No; she was not in love with Fred Falconer. If he had proposed to Miss Merriton to-morrow, and married her next day, Kate's next gallop on Birdie would not have been perhaps a whit less joyous, or her rest at night a whit less unbroken. Still, Kate could hardly, at the time in question, be said with truth to walk the world fancy-free. But that pretty and dainty word expresses fully and entirely the whole state of the case. Kate was not altogether fancy-free. And Lady Farnleigh's observations and inuendoes upon the subject had not been altogether groundless. Poor Kate! Mr. Frederick Falconer was about as worthy of her as a black beetle might be supposed worthy to mate with a "purple emperor" butterfly. But he was very handsome, very gentlemanlike, very well thought of by everybody of their little world; could make himself very agreeable (when Lady Farnleigh was not present; when she was, some mysterious influence prevented him from doing so), and Kate had never seen anything better. So there is the truth. If it be insisted on, that the very inmost chamber of her gentle, pure little heart be made the object of a "domiciliary" police visit, "documents" might be found there of a "compromising" character, so far as the fact goes that she did feel a sufficient interest in Fred Falconer to be disconcerted—no, that is too strong—displeased,—even that is too decided ;—to be curious about—yes; we will say to be curious about—that gentleman's very evident and perfectly well characterized (as the naturalists say) flirtation with Miss Merriton.

And then came the time, very soon after the cloth was removed, and always precisely at the same number of minutes after it, when

Miss Immy rose and led the ladies out of the dining-room. And the dispute between the doctor and the banker raged more furiously than ever. And the squire and Mr. Mat set themselves to investigate Mr. Merriton's ideas on the subject of poaching and game-preserving. And Fred Falconer, taking his glass in his hand, went round the table to Captain Ellingham, and made himself very pleasant in all the many ways in which an old resident can do so to a new-comer into any social circle. Captain Ellingham went into the drawing-room thinking that the banker's son, though a little foppish, was a very good and agreeable sort of fellow. And Freddy—who on his side considered himself to have discovered that Captain Ellingham had fallen in love at first sight with Margaret Lindisfarn—had just carelessly dropped a word to the effect that he thought he rather admired Miss Kate most, for his part, but they were both truly charming girls, and had received an invitation from Captain Ellingham to make one of the professed party for a cruise in the cutter.

As soon as ever they got into the drawing-room, Captain Ellingham lost no time in proposing his scheme to Margaret, who declared at once that it would be delightful. But instead of confiding her delight in the project to him, as he would have liked, and making the arrangement a little matter between themselves, she chose to accept it with such loud and open-mouthed expressions of "how charming it would be," and such a proclamation of the "delicious idea Captain Ellingham has," as made all the room parties to the talk between them, and to Ellingham's annoyance rendered it impossible not to ask also the Merritons.

And then all the young people got round Lady Farnleigh, and without much difficulty obtained her consent to act as lady patroness, and *chaperone* general of the party. And then the day was to be fixed ; and Lady Farnleigh insisted on turning the scheme into a picnic-party, and undertaking herself to arrange with Miss Immy all about their several contributions of comestibles.

"I should not permit anybody but you in all the world, dear Lady Farnleigh, to treat my ship in such fashion. But you are privileged !"

"Of course ; that is why I choose to exercise my privilege. Go and ask Kate there, and she will tell you that my part here is to be fairy godmother, and always to do as I please."

And Ellingham did go and tell Kate what Lady Farnleigh proposed, and what she had said. And that gave rise to a little conversation between them, from which it appeared that they both of them cordially agreed in one point at least,—a hearty and admiring love for Kate's godmother.

Lady Farnleigh having sent off Ellingham on the above errand, stepped across the room to the place where Miss Merriton was sitting, and taking a seat by the side of her, proceeded to make acquaintance with, and take the measure of, the new-comer into Sillshire.

Margaret was then left, to her intense satisfaction, between Fred Falconer and Mr. Merriton, and, showing her ability to deal with all the requirements of that pleasurably exciting but somewhat difficult position with consummate tact and ability, was accordingly enjoying herself to the utmost—when all was spoilt by that abominable brick in the brown-paper parcel ; for a brick it turned out to be ! Margaret could have cried ; and the two young men devoutly wished the learned canon and his brick under the sod from which he had poked it out. But they did not know that Margaret had brought the brick down on their heads by her own false pretences and cajolery.

She had her punishment. On proceeding with much ceremony to the opening of the parcel, which in fact contained a brick with certain mouldings around it, on which he founded a learned and large superstructure of hypothesis concerning the date of the old castle keep at Silverton, the doctor, while saying that he thought the very remarkable relic he had there must be interesting to all the party, declared that to one of them at least he was very sure it would be a treat. And then Margaret had to endure a martyrdom of a complicated description. She had in the first place to fence so skilfully with her uncle as to conceal, as far as possible, her absolute and entire ignorance of even the sort of interest which was understood to attach to such relics. But this was the easiest part of her task ; for the doctor loved better to talk than to listen, and was quite ready to give his audience unlimited credit for comprehension of and interest in the subject. But she had to endure also what she acutely felt to be the ridicule, in the eyes of the *jeunes gens* (as she would have said) who were present, of the *rôle* of blue stocking and *femme-savante* which was thus thrust upon her,—a *rôle* which was superlatively repugnant to her, and unassorted to everything that she would have wished to appear in their eyes.

However, by dint of meaning and appealing looks distributed "aside" (if that phrase may be used of looks as well as of words) with consummate skill, and little purring, coaxing speeches to her uncle, and a liberal use of a whole arsenal of the prettiest and most innocent-looking *minauderies* and little kittenish ways imaginable, she came out of the ordeal better than could have been expected, and if not without suffering, yet with little or no damage in the eyes of any one there.

And then came a simultaneous ordering of carriages, and departure.

Dr. Theophilus Lindisfarn packed up his brick while the ladies were cloaking themselves, and carried it off as his sole companion in the little one-horse shandridan that so vexed the soul of Lady Sempronia.

Lady Farnleigh and Captain Ellingham got off next. The only part of the talk between them that interests us has been already given to the reader. Lady Farnleigh was more provoked by her friend's preference for Margaret over her own favorite than the few words she had uttered indicated.

"To think," she said to herself in her meditations on the subject, "that men, and men of sense, too, should be fooled by their eyes to such an extent; and by the look, too, not of a pretty girl, but of a pretty dress! For Kate's the finer girl, two to one! It was all that chit's Parisian get-up. Hang her airs and graces! She did look uncommonly well though, that is undeniable." And then Lady Farnleigh, being thoroughly minded not to be beaten in the game which she clearly saw was about to begin, and which she was bent on playing to her own liking, fell into a meditation on the possibility of obtaining for her favorite those advantages which seemed to have done so much for Margaret. But in those days of four-and-twenty hours' journey by mail between London and the provinces, it was not so easy a matter to accomplish anything in this line as it might have been in our day of universal facilities.

There was a similar discordance of opinion between the two occupants of the Merriton carriage, as it returned to the Friary. Miss Merriton and her brother, indeed, both agreed in praising the kindness and friendliness of Lady Farnleigh; but when the former was enthusiastic about the charmingness and such-a-dear-girl-ness of Margaret, who had entirely captivated the timid little Emily, as she had set herself to do, her brother would only answer by praises of Kate. In this case the captivating had been a more unconscious and unintentional process on the part of the captor. When Mr. Merriton had twice during his conversation with Margaret at dinner alluded to his home "in other climes," and "more genial skies," and had taken nothing by the effort (for such an advance toward intimate talk was an effort for him), save an unsympathizing inquiry whether he had lived in Paris, he, as he would himself have expressed it, "felt himself chilled." But when he had afterward in the drawing-room, on Kate's addressing to him some words about the Friary, put out a similar feeler for sympathy to her, it had been responded to by an enthusiastic declaration on Kate's part that she longed to see Italy; that it was the dream of her life to be able to do so some day, and that she should tease Mr. Merriton to death by asking him all sorts of questions on the subject, and all sorts of assistance in her difficulties with her Italian studies.

And so Mr. Merriton was then and there inextricably lassoed, and captured on the spot.

In the comfortable, well-appointed carriage which conveyed Mr. Falconer and his son to their home in Silverton, a few words passed before the senior composed himself to sleep, which it may be as well for the purposes of this history to record.

"I was not so hard at it with the doctor—who upon some points *is* the wrongest-headed man I ever knew—at my end of the table as not to have observed that you were making up to Miss Merriton very assiduously at the other," said the father.

"She seems a ladylike, agreeable girl enough, though very shy," answered Mr. Frederick.

"Yes, I dare say. But you will do well, Fred, to remember that there is such a thing as falling to the ground between two stools. What do you suppose Miss Lindisfarn thought of your very evident flirtation?"

"There are two Miss Lindisfarns now."

"Yes, more's the pity! If these French

people—what's their name?—had not gone the wrong side of the post, it would have been on the cards that the squire might have been persuaded not to divide the property; seeing that Miss Margaret would have been amply provided for. But now!—it is a thousand pities!"

"Ay! the Lindisfarn property as it stands is a very pretty thing indeed—a prize for any man."

"*Half* of it is a prize for any man, you mean—for any man who can win the hand of either of the young ladies."

"I only meant that the property is one which any man might be proud to be at the head of."

"And if any man were to marry one of the heiresses, who had a command of ready cash equal to the share coming to the other of them,—who knows what arrangments might be made to prevent the splitting or selling of the estate?" observed the old banker.

"What is Miss Merriton's fortune?" asked his son.

"Miss Merriton has twenty-five thousand pounds in her own absolute disposition," replied the senior, uttering the words slowly and deliberately; "but what is that to the half of the Lindisfarn property?"

"It is about one thousand a year instead of about two thousand," said Mr. Frederick.

"Exactly so," said his father; "to which it may be added that Miss Kate Lindisfarn has her godmother's six thousand pounds."

"Which would very likely be conditional on the young lady marrying with her godmother's consent, seeing that it is not settled money," returned the young man.

"Possibly, but I should say not likely," replied his father. "Besides, Fred, I imagined that you had reason to think that you did not stand badly with Miss Kate; and this newly arrived young lady"—

"Well, sir," returned his son, after a pause, "to speak out frankly, and make no secrets between us, this is the state of the case. Kate is a charming girl. Nobody can feel that more strongly than I do. And it may be, as you say, that I may have reason to flatter myself that I am not disagreeable to her. But there is another lady in the case, with whom I do *not* flatter myself that I stand at all well. In a word, I am quite sure that if Lady Farnleigh can keep me and Kate asunder she will do so; and I fear

that she *may* have the power to do it. Kate is very much under her influence. Now there can be no doubt at all that Miss Margaret Lindisfarn is also an exceedingly charming girl,—to my thinking even more fascinating perhaps than her sister,—and you can easily understand, sir, that under these circumstances it may be well to have two strings to one's bow."

"That's all very well," said the old gentleman. "And now I will tell you with equal frankness what seems to *me* the state of the case. In the first place, when I was a young fellow, I do not think I should have allowed very much weight to the prejudices of a godmamma in such a matter. In the next place, bear this in mind: that though either of Mr. Lindisfarn's daughters may be considered a desirable—a *very* desirable match, there are reasons for considering Miss Kate, the more desirable of the two. Not to speak of Lady Farnleigh's six thousand pounds,—though that would be a very comfortable assistance in any scheme for obtaining the entire property,—I think that it would be far more possible to persuade the old squire to leave the acres and the old house to Kate, with a due sum of money equivalent to Margaret, than *vice versâ*, and very naturally so. And to speak with perfect frankness, my dear boy, *that* is the stake to play for. It is not merely the money, though a good match is a good match; and either of these young ladies would be a very good match. But, thank God, I shall leave you in a position which makes a good match what you may naturally look to. But to be Falconer of Lindisfarn Chase—that would be a thing worth trying for! such a position in the county! In fact, I don't mind owning that I could quit the scene with perfect contentment, if I could live to see you established in such a position. Nor do I mind saying that—supposing, as I have no doubt, that you and I go on together as well as we always have done—the ready cash, which would suffice to buy one-half of the property, should not be wanting, if you should ever be lucky enough to need it. As for Miss Merriton, though all very well in the way of a match, she is not to be mentioned in the same day with either of the Lindisfarn girls, and no great catch for you in any way. And now, my dear boy, if you'll allow me, I'll go to sleep till we get to Silverton."

And so Freddy meditated during the remainder of the short journey on the words of paternal wisdom which he had heard.

At the Chase, the squire and Miss Immy went off to their respective chambers as soon as ever the last of their guests was gone. Mr. Mat walked out muttering something about seeing all safe; but if the whole truth is absolutely to be told, he went and smoked a pipe in the stable before going to bed.

The two girls went up to their adjoining rooms, but could hardly be expected to go to bed till they had, at least compendiously, compared notes as to their impressions during the evening.

Margaret made no allusion to her antiquarian trials, nor to the projected visit to the Friary. The invitation of Captain Ellingham was talked of, and a more mature consideration of it deferred till the morrow, on account of the lateness of the hour to which the debate had already lasted. The most interesting part of the conversation, however, of course turned on the different estimates formed by the two girls of their new acquaintances. But without reporting at length all the chatter of agreement, disagreement, and comparison of notes, which went to the expression of their opinions, the net result may be summed up with tolerable accuracy thus:—

Margaret declared that Mr Merriton was an exceedingly agreeable man, evidently highly instructed, very gentlemanlike, certainly very handsome, and unquestionably the nicest of the three young men of the party. Mr. Frederick Falconer was very handsome and very nice too. Captain Ellingham she could see nothing to like in at all, except his invitation to go on board his ship, which would be charming, as the others were all invited.

Kate said, on the contrary, that she had been much pleased with all she had seen of Captain Ellingham; that, of course, as far as liking went, she could not be expected to like him so well as her old friend, Freddy Falconer; and as for Mr. Merriton, he had seemed to her very good-natured, but more like a schoolboy who was a rather girlish one than like a man.

And so ended the dinner-party at the Chase.

CHAPTER XI.

MR. MERRITON PAYS SOME VISITS.

WHAT with the talk about the proposed sailing excursion under Captain Ellingham's auspices, and what with the calamity of the learned canon's brick, nothing had been settled on the evening of the party at the Chase about the visit of Margaret and her uncle to the Friary. Margaret had been as careful to make her communication to Mr. Merriton on that subject private and confidential as she had been, when spoken to by Captain Ellingham respecting the sailing project, to make all present parties to the conversation. She had also avoided saying one word about any such idea to Kate. And her project was to find the means of availing herself of Lady Sempronia's invitation to the house in the Close, and to go with her uncle thence to the Friary, so as to have the visit, and the opportunity all to herself.

All her scheme was foiled, however, by Mr. Merriton, as is apt to be the case when two parties to an arrangement do not desire precisely the same results from it. Mr. Merriton liked the idea of bringing some of his new neighbors together under his roof on the occasion which had been thus prepared for him. It saved him from the necessity of taking the more decided and self-asserting step of inviting them on no other plea than the simple one of coming to pay him an ordinary visit. It made a reason for their being there; and if the gathering were made to grow out of what Margaret had said to him at dinner, the great point would be gained of throwing mainly on Dr. Lindisfarn the onus and responsibility of finding amusement or employment for the people when they were there.

Besides that, Mr. Merriton began to feel very strongly that the only part of such a plan which could afford any gratification to himself, would be lost if Kate were not to be of the party.

So on the following morning the new master of the Friary ordered his phaeton—Mr. Merriton had passed too large a portion of his life abroad to be much of an equestrian—with the intention of driving, or being driven, rather, over to Wanstrow. Lady Farnleigh had very graciously and kindly made acquaintance both with him and with his sister on the previous evening; and it was absolutely necessary to go and call on her.

The house and grounds of the Friary were close to almost in the village of Weston, which was surnamed from the ancient monastic establishment. And Weston was situnted, as has been said, in the valley of the Sill, about two miles above Silverton Bridge, at a bend in the river just about the spot where the widening of the valley has given rise to the creation of a system of water-meads. These water-meadows fill the whole bottom of the valley all the way from Weston to Silverton, lying on the right-hand side of the river, as one pursued its course for the two miles to Silverton, and the five more that remained of it before it fell into the sea at Sillmouth. The road ran along the left-hand side of the valley, at a somewhat higher elevation than that of the water-meads; and the river ran between the road and the meadows, dammed up to a level a little above that of the latter. The bend in the river at Weston was to the right hand of one following the stream of it; turning the upper part of its course, therefore, toward the Wanstrow and away from the Lindisfarn side of the country. And the village, with its pretty spired church, stood on the left bank, on the outside of the elbow of the bend of the river, and was visible from Silverton Bridge: whereas the ancient Friary itself, and accordingly Mr. Merriton's house and grounds, were on the right bank, enclosed within the elbow of the stream, and were not visible from any part of the city.

Indeed the house was not visible, or scarcely at all visible, from the village on the opposite side of the stream, it was so completely embowered in trees; and in one direction partially hidden by a jutting limestone cliff, which had been evidently, even to non-geological eyes, the cause of the sudden change of direction in the river's course at Weston. On the Lindisfarn and Silverton side of the river the color of the soil was red; but on the Wanstrow side the limestone, which seemed to form the substructure, and to constitute the prevailing ingredient in the surface soil of the district, gave that side of the country a paler, grayer, less rich and less picturesque look than that for which the Lindisfarn side was so remarkable. The Wanstrow side was also much more sparsely wooded.

But these remarks, which apply to all that district on the left bank of the river as soon as ever the valley of the Sill is left and the upper ground reached, are not applicable to the valley itself, to Weston, or to the Friary grounds.

The limestone cliff, which has been mentioned, and which just at that turning-point of the stream has been denuded by the action of the river, and rises t t about a hundred and fifty feet in heigh. s there a feature of very considerable beautyt n the landscape. It is entirely and most richly covered with ivy and creeping plants of many kinds, hanging in great festoons, and which, availing themselves of every projection or inequality in the face of the rock to mass themselves around it, make it the savings-bank for a gradually and slowly-increasing treasure of gathered soil, and then root themselves afresh for a new start in the hoard thus collected. Close at the foot of the cliff runs the river, which, as soon as ever it has got round it, slackens its speed, widens its course, and having passed its tussle with that hard limestone opponent, goes more lazily, quietly, and smilingly, to the peaceful work of irrigating the water-meads.

There are no water-meads above the bend in the river and the limestone cliff. The character of the upper part of the valley is a different one. And I have sometimes felt inclined to regret that there is no view of the two-mile vista of water-meadows, with Silverton at the end of them, from the Friary. The cliff, which shuts out this view, is in itself a great beauty; and one cannot have everything. Above Weston the tillage comes down nearer to the river, on the Lindisfarn side, leaving only a narrow strip of meadow, which is not water-mead, but pasture land. On the Wanstrow side,—the side on which the Friary is,—the same limestone formation, though not rising to the same height, nor rising with the same degree of precipitousness, as it does to form the cliff, shuts in the valley for a few miles, making the rise from it exceedingly steep. On this side the space of pasture ground between the river and this rapid rise is wider. This was the home farm of the old monastery, and now forms the park attached to the residence. The high bank, which has been described as shutting this ground in, and which is, in fact, the prolongation of the limestone cliff that a little lower down turns the river, is entirely covered with thick wood;—not with such magnificent forest as clothes the top of Lindisfarn brow; but with trees of very respectable bulk and growth, amply sufficient to shut in the Friary park with a very beautiful boundary, and to exempt it entirely from that somewhat colder and bleaker look which the country assumes as soon as the valley has been left, and the Wanstrow upper grounds approached.

Mr. Merriton's way from the Friary to Wanstrow crossed the Sill twice at starting. There is indeed a road which climbs the bank that has just been described, piercing the coppice which covers it. But it is a mere cart-lane, and exceedingly steep. The cliff which has been so often mentioned opposes an insuperable barrier to all progress down the valley on the Friary side of the stream ; so that it is necessary for any one who would go otherwise than on two legs or on four from the Friary to the upper country behind the bank and the woods and the cliff which hem it in, first to cross the Sill by a bridge which is the private property of the owner of the Friary, and then, after passing through the village, to recross it by the bridge which has been mentioned in a former chapter as forming a part of the pleasanter though longer of the two routes between Wanstrow and Lindisfarn Chase. On the lower side of the cliff, which shuts off the upper from the lower valley of the Sill,—on the side of the water-meads and off Silverton, that is to say, —the land rises from the river to the Wanstrow high grounds much more gradually.

By this road, therefore, Mr. Merriton proceeded in his phaeton, lolling comfortably back in one corner of the luxurious vehicle, but occupied more with thinking about how and what he should say to Lady Farnleigh, than with enjoying the beauty of his drive. This became less as he left the valley of the Sill behind him, and climbed to the more open downlike region of the limestone hills. The Wanstrow farms were well cultivated, and there was much to gladden the eye of an agriculturist in the district through which the road passed. But it not only looked but felt bleaker as the upper ground was reached, and Mr. Merriton with a shiver put on a cloak which had been lying on the seat beside him.

It was almost all, more or less, collar work from the bridge over the Sill, to the lodge gates of Wanstrow Manor, a distance of about five miles. The park in which the house stands is of considerable extent, and not altogether devoid of fine timber in widely scattered groups. But it is very different from the richly wooded country on the other side of the valley around Lindisfarn. Immediately behind the house, which is situated on the highest swell of the open, downlike hill, there is rather more wood, serving to give it a little of the shelter it so much needs, from the north. But it is little more than a large clump of elms. The house is a modern one, of very considerable pretension, and containing far more accommodation than its present single inhabitant needed or could occupy. But the only special beauty or recommendation belonging to it is its southward view of the coast and the sea. The village and little port of Sillmouth are visible from it, as well as a considerable extent of the coast-line on the further or Silverton side of the estuary, comprising those sands over which Kate had had her gallop on the day of the dinner-party at the Chase. The shore on the other or Wanstrow side cannot be seen from the house, because, though in fact nearer to it as the crow flies, it is hidden under the limestone cliffs which rise from the shore to the eastward of Sillmouth. The sea-view from the house beyond, and to the westward of that little port, is a distant one ; but not too much so for it to be possible to see the white line of the breakers as they tumble in on the sands at low water, and on a black, sea-weed-mottled line of low rocks when the tide is at its highest.

Lady Farnleigh was mostly Kate's companion in her rides on the Sillmouth sands ; but she used to say, that on occasions when she was not so, she could equally well see all that her goddaughter was doing from her drawing-room windows, by the aid of a good telescope.

The sea is visible from the road through Wanstrow Park for a mile or so before the house is reached ; and Mr. Merriton, whose Italian-grown nerves were very quickly made sensible that it could be felt as soon as seen, drew his cloak closer about him, as he congratulated himself on the very remarkable difference of climate between the snuggery of the Friary and the magnificence of Wanstrow Manor.

There was a garden on the west side of the house which was in part sheltered by it, and which partook of the protection afforded by the high trees behind it. And Lady Farnleigh used to do her best to make it pretty and fragrant ; but she declared that it was a pursuit of horticulture under difficulties which were almost too discouraging; and often, when comparing the gardens at the Chase with her own infelicitous attempts, would threaten to give up the struggle altogether, and depend wholly for her flowers on supplies from Lindisfarn.

She was in this garden, lamenting the mischief that had been caused by the high wind of the day before, and trying to devise with the gardener new means of shelter for some of her more delicate favorites, when Mr. Merriton arrived. He was shown into the drawing-room; and the servant, finding that her ladyship was not there, preceded him through the open window into the garden.

"How kind of you," she said, after they had greeted each other, "to come up out of your happy valley to visit these inhospitable mountains! Look what the storm of yesterday has done; and at the Friary I dare say you hardly felt it it all. Our friends at Lindisfarn hear the wind up in the woods above them just enough to make them rejoice in the comfort of their sheltered position. You at the Friary neither feel nor hear it. But here we are in a different climate. Look at my poor geraniums!"

"Even to-day I felt the wind sharp enough as I drove through the park. But at all events, Lady Farnleigh, you have the compensation of a magnificent view! Really the position of the house is a very fine one. The park seems to extend nearly—or quite, does it?—to the coast."

"Yes, I am monarch of all I survey up here (except the sea by the by), and my right there is none to dispute, except this terrible southwest wind: and Captain Ellingham says we are going to have more of it."

"Raison de plus that you should kindly accede to a request I bring from my sister, that you will join our friends at the Friary in passing a day at the Friary. My sister would have accompanied me to wait on your ladyship; but she is very delicate, unhappily, and was really afraid of the drive this morning. Perhaps you will kindly accord her an invalid's privilege, and take the will for the deed."

"By no means let Miss Merriton come up here as long as this wind is blowing. I shall be delighted to see her as soon as I can say, Come! without the fear of exposing her to the climate, which is, joking apart, as differ-

ent from that of your valley as the north of England is from the south. I shall have great pleasure in coming down to the Friary, I am sure."

"It seems that Dr. Lindisfarn had purposed bringing Miss Margaret, who takes an interest in such things, to the Friary to explain to her all about the old monastery, you know, and the traces of the ancient building which yet remain."

"Miss Margaret takes an interest in such studies; does she?"

"Yes," replied Mr. Merriton, quite innocently; "she was speaking to me about it at dinner yesterday, and I intended asking the doctor after dinner; but then we were all occupied with other things, and I had no opportunity. And then Emily and I thought it would be much pleasanter if we could induce the others of the party to join in the scheme, and share the benefit of the doctor's explanations."

"Delightful! I shall like it above all things. We will have a regular *matinée archéologique!*"

"I hoped to have found Captain Ellingham here, that I might have persuaded him to join us."

"He is gone down to Sillmouth to look after his ship. He will be here to dinner this evening, and I shall have much pleasure in conveying your invitation to him. But when is it to be?"

"Well, any day that would be most convenient to all of us. Perhaps, as he is the only one who is likely to have avocations that might absolutely make any day impossible to him, it would be as well to consult him first on that head."

"You are very kind; and I am sure he will feel it so."

"Would you kindly undertake then to fix a day with him? It is a pity I did not find him though; for I meant to have returned through Silverton, and fixed the day with the rest of the party; but I shall not know what day to tell them."

"I'll tell you, Mr. Merriton, what I can do for you, which would facilitate matters. I had intended to have asked all our little circle to spend a day with me up here. And I, too, thought I had better make sure of Captain Ellingham for the same reason that you have given. And we fixed this morning on next Wednesday. Now I will give up Wed-

5

nesday to you; so you will be sure of Elling-ham for that day. And it will be better, too, for all concerned to come to me when this terrible wind shall have changed. If that will suit you, you are welcome to Wednesday."

"How very kind of you! Yes, that would suit us perfectly. Will you then kindly charge yourself with my message to Captain Ellingham? We hope to see him on Wednesday, and would have fixed some other day, if you had not kindly given me the means of knowing that that day would suit him."

"With pleasure; and I am sure he will have great pleasure in coming to you."

"We ought not to be later than one o'clock. There are plenty of old holes and corners to look into. There is a queer place at the further end of the park by the river-side, which they call the Sill-grotto, and which they say was once a chapel. That will have to be visited, I suppose?"

"Of course it will. Dr. Lindisfarn will not let you off a single bit of old wall, or a single fragment of old tradition about the place. No; one o'clock will not be too early, if the doctor is to be allowed a fair course and no favor."

"Let it stand for one then. I am so much obliged to you, Lady Farnleigh."

And then Mr. Merriton got into his carriage and drove to Silverton. His purpose had been to call first on the canon, as the first idea of the party had in some sort originated with him. But it was the hour of the afternoon cathedral service when he arrived in the city, and the doctor was in church.

So he went first to the banker's house in the immediate neighborhood of the Close; and there, banking hours being over, he found the old gentleman in his learned-looking library, solacing himself after the labors of the ledger with more liberal studies.

"Can't well be with you by one," said Mr. Falconer, when he had heard his visitor's errand. "Business first, you know, and pleasure afterward. I can get away, perhaps, in time to be with you by three. Fred will not fail you at the earlier hour;—not a doubt of it, bearing in mind the attractions you hold out to him! He has ridden over to Lindisfarn now. I will give him your invitation, and think I may venture to say that he will be only too happy to accept it."

"You are intimate with the family at the Chase, I believe, Mr. Falconer?" asked Mr. Merriton, thoughtfully.

"Oh, of course! Naturally so. We have been life-long neighbors, and that in a country neighborhood makes a tie that it does not always in cities. Fred and Kate Lindisfarn have grown up from childhood together. And naturally enough they are very great friends," said the old banker, looking up into his guest's face with a knowing glance and smile, which were intended to insinuate what he did not venture to assert in words. "That is all as might naturally be expected, you know," he continued; "and I think I may venture to promise you that when I tell Fred who the members of your party are, he will be punctual enough in waiting on you."

Mr. Merriton was much too young and too guileless a man to be able to conceal from the shrewd eye of the old banker the annoyance that the impressions thus conveyed to him inflicted on him. The old man saw the state of the case perfectly well. "Oh! that's it; is it?" he said to himself. "The more necessary to let him understand that Miss Kate is not destined to be his. It will be as well to give Fred a hint too."

"Well," said the young man somewhat sadly, "I must go and do the rest of my errand in Silverton. I have to ask Dr. Lindisfarn. And oh, by the by! you can tell me, Mr. Falconer; ought I to ask Lady Sempronia? Does she ever go out?"

"Ah—h! You are going to ask the doctor; are you? Yes, naturally—naturally; of course you would. You can't well do otherwise."

"Oh, I had no thought of leaving him out; it was Lady Sempronia that I was in doubt about. The whole idea of the thing began with the doctor, I may say. He is to give us an explanation of all the history and antiquities of the old place!"

"Ah! I see. I see it all. Yes; he will give you the history, never fear; all after his own fashion too!"

"I thought you and Dr. Lindisfarn were great friends?" said Mr. Merriton, innocently, and much surprised at the spitefulness of the old banker's manner.

"Friends! Dr. Lindisfarn and I! To be sure we are,—very old friends. I have a very great regard for Canon Lindisfarn; he is a most worthy man. But that does not blind me to the monstrosity of the errors his wrong-headedness and obstinacy often run him into in matters of archæological science. Now as regards the history—the extremely interesting history of your property of the Friary!—it is sad,—really now quite sad, to think of the number of blunders that he will circulate through all the county by the means of your party next Wednesday. For these things spread, my dear sir! They are repeated. False notions are propagated. They run under ground like couch-grass. They become traditional. And he will have it all his own way!—I'll tell you what, my dear sir, I must be there! I must manage to be with you somehow by one o'clock. I'll not be late, my dear Mr. Merriton. You may count on me."

"So much the better. But about Lady Sempronia?" said Mr. Merriton.

"Oh, ask her, by all means. She goes out very little, and will probably not come; but you can ask her, you know. She is a poor inoffensive, invalid woman, but I have known her uncommonly shrewd sometimes in seeing through some of her husband's fallacies, when more learned people have been led astray by them. She is no fool, is Lady Sempronia. Ask her by all means."

So Mr. Merriton stepped across to the canon's house,—the distance was too small to make it worth while for him to get into his carriage,—devoutly wishing that Mr. Frederick Falconer was resting after life's fitful fever in any vault of the old church, beneath the shadow of which he was walking, à son choix, and cursing the provoking impossibility of not asking him to join the party at the Friary.

The canon had just returned from the afternoon service, and had gone into the study. Mr. Merriton was shown into that room, and found the doctor engaged in transferring his canonicals from his own shoulders to those of his wooden representative.

"Ah, Mr. Merriton! how are you? Come in, come in! This is a contrivance of mine to prevent me from forgetting to take off my surplice, which I otherwise was apt to do!"

"Ah, having your head full of more important things, Dr. Lindisfarn! Yes, I can understand that. I came to speak to you about the visit which Miss Margaret Lindisfarn tells me you were good enough to purpose making with her to my house."

"Aha! the little puss is anxious for the treat, is she? You would be surprised, Mr. Merriton, at the interest—the intelligent interest, I may say, though she is my own niece—that that young girl takes in pursuits and studies which some frivolous minds are apt to consider dry. Yes, I had proposed asking your permission to bring Miss Margaret to the Friary, for the purpose of illustrating to her on the spot the very interesting history of the house."

"And when she mentioned the project to me, it struck me and my sister that it would be a great pity not to give others of our friends an opportunity of profiting by the occasion; and we have asked Lady Farnleigh and the rest of the party at the Chase to come to us next Wednesday. May we hope to see you on that day, and will one o'clock be too early?"

"No; you are very good; Wednesday will suit me very well. There is the afternoon service at the cathedral, to be sure; but in such a case—that can be managed. Do you expect all the party at the Chase?"

"I hope so. I have only secured Lady Farnleigh, Captain Ellingham, the Falconers, and yourself. I will go up to them at the Chase to-morrow."

"Falconer will not be able to come to you at one o'clock, you know. He cannot get away from business so early; and perhaps, between ourselves, that is just as well. The best fellow in the world, Falconer! A good, friendly man. But he has a mania for meddling with matters that are quite *ultra crepidam*. A most excellent man of business! But *optat ephippia bos piger!* you understand, Mr. Merriton. And my friend Falconer does not show himself to advantage in the *ephippia!* Ay, ay! You may depend on it, I'll be punctual at one. And—under all the circumstances it would be very desirable that we should all be punctual at that hour. Don't you see, Mr. Merriton?"

Mr. Merriton thought that he *did* see, although he had not the remotest idea what place, or thing, or circumstance that *ephippia* was, in which Mr. Falconer was said not to shine. Was the *ephippia* perhaps another name for the Friary? He thought he saw, too, that it was best to say nothing of Mr. Falconer's determination to meet his enemy on the ground at all costs. So he merely answered,—

"I had hoped to have the honor of being

presented to Lady Sempronia, and to have persuaded her to join our party."

"Her ladyship, I grieve to say, is very much of an invalid. She will be most happy, however, to make acquaintance with you and Miss Merriton. But I fear she would hardly be able to see you now ; and I do not think that there is much chance of her feeling well enough to join your party on Wednesday. I will give her your kind message, however."

"And pray say that were it not that my sister is also much of an invalid, she would have returned Lady Sempronia's card in person instead of deputing me to do so. She hopes, however, to be able to come into Silverton in the beginning of next week, and will then wait on Lady Sempronia."

And then Mr. Merriton drove back by the road along the edge of the water-meadows to the Friary, disconsolately meditating on what he had heard from Mr. Falconer respecting his son's intimacy at the Chase. For Merriton had brought away with him thence a very severe wound ; and *hærit latiri letalis arundo!*

"Well, Arthur," said Miss Merriton, as he entered the drawing-room at the Friary ready for dinner, "what have you done? Has anything gone amiss? You seem out of spirits."

"The people are all very civil. Lady Farnleigh was especially so. To prevent any *pasticcio* about fixing the day, she gave up, or put off rather, a party at her own house for next Wednesday, giving up that day to us. So it is fixed for Wednesday, and to-morrow I will go up to the Chase. All the rest have accepted."

"But what is it that has vexed you, Arthur? for I can see that something has."

"No; it's your fancy. All the people seem inclined to be very kind. There's nothing amiss that I know of."

"I am sure something has annoyed you, Arthur," persisted his sister, looking him in the face ; "tell me what it is !"

"I do not know why I should look annoyed, I am sure. I might look surprised ; for I did hear something that surprised me in Silverton."

"What about?" asked his sister.

"Oh, nothing that concerns us at all. It seems that Falconer and Miss Kate Lindisfarn are to make a match of it : that is all.

And I confess it does seem to me that he is not half good enough for her. I think I never saw a girl who made so strong an impression on me."

If Merriton had not been so much engrossed by his own emotions as to be rendered for the time unobservant of those of others, he might have been struck by the fact that his communication produced a somewhat stronger effect upon his gentle sister than appeared wholly attributable to her sisterly interest in his feelings. A sudden and deep flush passed over her delicate and pale face, leaving it the next instant a shade paler, perhaps, than it had been before. She only said, however, after a few moments' pause, during which she succeeded in recovering her composure, or at least the appearance of it,—

"But how did you hear it, Arthur? Remember, a great deal of groundless nonsense is apt to be talked on such matters ; and it is very unlikely that anything should be really known on the subject unless they are absolutely engaged to each other ; I do not believe that is the case."

"Engaged! No, I don't suppose they are engaged, or the fact would be simply stated."

"What did you hear, then, and from whom?"

"From old Falconer, when I invited him and his son to come here on Wednesday."

"What did he say !"

"Well, upon my word, I hardly know what he said. But he gave me the impression that it was a sort of understood thing that his son and Miss Lindisfarn were to make a match of it."

"Miss Kate Lindisfarn?"

"Yes, Miss Kate Lindisfarn. Oh, he spoke of Miss Kate clearly enough? He talked—that reminds me—of their having been near neighbors all their lives, and of their having been brought up together, and of their being great friends. But somehow or other, he left the impression on my mind that he meant more than all that. I did not notice," he continued after a pause, "anything between them last night ; did you?"

"No, I can't say that I saw anything of the sort," replied his sister.

"He sat next me at dinner," she continued, with a recurrence in a slighter degree of the blush which the first mention of the subject had occasioned her; "and after dinner he seemed to me to be talking much more to the other sister."

"But that might have been mere civility to a stranger newly come among them. The other sister, Miss Margaret, seemed to me to have very little in her."

"Oh, I thought her a very nice girl!"

"She has lived, she told me, all her life till now in Paris; I never like French women. They never have any sympathy with anything, or person, or subject outside of the barriers of Paris."

And then the brother and sister went into the dining-room; and the presence of the servants prevented any further conversation upon the subject of the Lindisfarn lasses.

Frederick Falconer had in the mean time ridden up to the Chase, as has been seen, bent on acting upon the sage hints that had been thrown out by his father over-night as they were returning together from the dinner-party, with some little modification of his own. He perfectly recognized the justice of the old gentleman's reasons for thinking Kate the more desirable match of the two. But he could not bring himself to make quite so light, as his father was disposed to do, of the opposition which he well knew awaited him on the part of Lady Farnleigh. He had far better means of knowing, as he said to himself, how great her influence over her goddaughter was. And besides, though he was by no means deficient in a sufficiently high appreciation of his own advantages, and was not without a certain degree of hope that Miss Lindisfarn was not altogether indisposed to like him, yet he was far from having the same degree of confidence on the subject that he had chosen to manifest in speaking to his father. And then, again, he really was powerfully attracted by Margaret's beauty and manner, and had already begun to draw comparisons between the two girls entirely to the advantage of the new-comer. He had spent the whole of the two hours he had passed at his desk in the bank that morning, before he had stolen away from it to ride up to the Chase, in reviewing the grounds of such a comparison. Both girls were handsome,—there was no doubt about that. But he thought that the more delicate and less rustic beauty of the Parisian had more attractions for him. Then there was no denying that she had more style, more grace, more

of *le grand air*, said Freddy to himself, calling up his own French *savoir* and experiences. He had a notion, too, that her ways of thinking and tastes were probably better adapted to his own. There were things in Kate that he did not altogether like; that violent passion of hers for tearing over the country like a female Nimrod, for instance—her way, too, of blurting out whatever came into her head, often with a certain look in her eye as if she were laughing at one. He had seen no symptom of anything like this in Margaret. In fact, the meaning in her eyes, as far as he had seen—and it must be admitted, that she *had* the most exquisitely expressive eyes that were ever seen in a human head!—had been characterized by anything but an expression of ridicule when they had rested on him.

In short, though perfectly well aware that it behoved him to win the heart and hand of Kate, if he could, he had pretty well made up his mind that it would be a far more agreeable task to him to win those of Margaret. But there was something in Mr. Frederick's constitution and natural disposition which disinclined him from paying much attention to that part of his father's counsel which had alluded to the danger of falling between two stools. Two stools seemed to Mr. Freddy so much better and safer than only one. Surely, it was not prudent to put all one's eggs into one basket! Surely, two strings to one's bow were admitted to be a good thing! He could not bring himself to back himself frankly and heartily to win with the one horse, to the entire giving up of all hopes of the other. The unknown quantities that entered into the problem to be solved were so much larger than the known ones that he felt it to be far the most prudent plan to keep the matter open as long as might be, make what progress he could, without committing himself irrevocably on either side, and be guided by circumstances.

It would be far from wise, too, to disregard such a *pis-aller* as Miss Merriton. *Pis-aller!* Twenty-five thousand pounds absolutely her own, and her brother looking as if a good sharp English spring might make an end of him? A very pretty *pis-aller*, indeed. It was all very well for his father to talk in that way, when he had set his heart on going in for the whole of the Lindisfarn property. But there was many a slip between *that* cup and the lip. Miss Merriton was a very charming little girl. He had a strong persuasion that he might have her for the asking; or at least that, after a due period of service for such a pretty little Rachel, he might make sure of her. And it would be very unwise to throw such a chance to the winds before he was sure of something better.

It was in this frame of mind that Mr. Frederick locked up his desk, after sitting at it for a couple of hours, and slipped out of the bank to order his horse and ride up to the Chase. Mr. Falconer senior was very indulgent to his son and heir as to the amount of attendance he exacted from him at the bank, if only the hours spent away from it were used advantageously in a social point of view; and he was especially well pleased at all times, and more particularly after the conversation of the night before, to know that his son was up at Lindisfarn Chase.

So Mr. Frederick had arrived there, still looking, as Lady Farnleigh had said, for all the world as if he had just been taken out of the bandbox, in which a London tailor had sent him down for the enlightenment and instruction of Sillshire, just as the ladies were about to sit down to luncheon.

CHAPTER XII.

FRED'S LUNCHEON AT THE CHASE.

MR. FREDERICK FALCONER arrived at the Chase just as the ladies were going to sit down to luncheon. The ladies were Miss Immy and the Lindisfarn lasses. And they were about to partake of that meal specially sacred to ladies and ladies' men alone. It was a great opportunity for Freddy. There was neither Lady Farnleigh nor Mr. Mat. In the presence of either of those persons, Mr. Freddy was, as the old story records Punch to have declared himself to have felt when Mrs. Carter, who translated Epictetus, was among his audience,—unable to " talk his own talk." Freddy Falconer could not talk his own talk when either Lady Farnleigh or Mr. Mat was present.

But on the present occasion all evil influences were absent, and all good ones were in the ascendant. There were Miss Immy in high good-humor ; there was the minced veal and mashed potatoes, beautiful golden-colored butter and the home-made loaf, a currant tart, and a bowl of Sillshire cream : There was the decanter of sherry for Miss Immy, the small jug of amber ale for Miss Kate, the *carafe* of sparkling water for Miss Margaret. The malignant fairy godmother was far away up in her wind-swept garden at Wanstrow ; the squire was beating the turnips in a distant field, and the odious Mr. Mat was trudging by his side. Had ever a ladies' man a fairer field ? Nor can it be by any means said that he had *no favor !*

Both the young ladies, as we already know, were more or less favorably disposed toward him, each after her own fashion. And Miss Immy was one of those who are disposed to allow their fullest weight to the claims of old neighborhood and long acquaintanceship. Freddy Falconer, too, had in her eyes the paramount advantage over either of the other two young men who had been there the previous evening, of being thorough Sillshire. Captain Ellingham and Mr. Merriton were both strangers and new acquaintances, which made a very notable difference to Miss Immy.

" And what do you think of our new importations in Sillshire ?" asked Kate, when Fred had been cordially asked to take some luncheon, and was comfortably established by the side of one of the young ladies, and opposite to the other. Kate was sitting opposite to Miss Immy, and Margaret on the side of the table nearest the fire, between them. Mr. Fred, therefore, took the goods the gods provided him—i. e., minced veal, potatoes and sherry, currant tart and Sillshire cream—in a position yet more shone on by the rays of beauty than that of Philip's warlike son at the royal feast for Persia won !—a position more brilliant, but more difficult also than that of Alexander.

" What do you think of our new importations into Sillshire ?" said Kate.

" The Merritons, or Captain Ellingham ? Which are you alluding to ? "

" To both. But you knew the Merritons before ; did you not ? "

" Not I ! I never set eyes on either of them till they came down here. They were old friends, I fancy, of our business connections in London. I think my father had seen Mr. Merriton in London."

" Quite a young man he seems," said Kate.

" Oh, yes ! A boy rather, one might say. He has just come of age. And upon my word, he looks as if an English winter would do for him. Poor fellow ! I should say he would have done more wisely to settle in his mother's country,—in Italy,—where he has spent most part of his life."

" Oh, in Italy ?" said Margaret. " He told me yesterday at dinner that he had lived abroad ' most of his life.' "

" Yes, and when a man has done that, he is rarely fit for English life in any way."

" Oh, don't say so, Mr. Falconer ; or I shall fancy that I am not fitted for English life, or that you don't think me so," said Margaret, with a look of the most tender appealing reproachfulness in her eyes, as pathetically eloquent as if she had been expecting her doom from the arbiter of her destiny.

" Nay ! it is quite a different thing in the case of a lady," said Freddy, coloring a little. " The foreign ways and manners, which are apt to make a man perhaps not altogether—what ladies like in this country—or gentlemen, indeed, either, for that matter—only serve to add new grace to one of the other sex. Besides, there is a vast difference between Italy and Paris. There is, as all the world knows, no charm equal to that of a Parisian woman," said Mr. Freddy, with the enthusiasm of intense conviction.

" Is there no chance, then, for poor home-bred Sillshire volk ?" asked Kate, with a laugh in her voice, and roguish quizzing in her eyes, and just the least little bit of pique in her heart.

"Now, Miss Kate, you know how far that is from my feeling in the matter! Surely, you and I are much too old friends to misun-. derstand each other upon such a point."

The position was a difficult one. The worst of it was, that there was no possibility of making any by-play with the eyes! What the tongue says may almost always be modified sufficiently for all purposes, if one can but find the means of supplying a running commentary with the eyes, addressed to one special reader. But Fred's situation, with one lady opposite to him, and one at right angles to him, shut him out from that resource ;— unless, indeed, from such very limited use of it as could be resorted to by seizing and making the most of the opportunities afforded him by the momentary employment of one of the two pairs of bright eyes, under the cross-fire of which he was sitting, on a plate or a drinking-glass. And even so there was very little good to be done with Kate in this fashion, unless it was in the way of laughing. Kate would laugh with you or at you, with her eyes, as much as you pleased ; would answer a laugh in your eyes, and answer it openly or aside, as the case needed. But she did not seem to understand any tenderer eye-language. Or if she did, she would not talk it with Freddy Falconer, old friends as they were.

And that was the reason why, after that luncheon-table campaign was over, Fred felt that he had made more progress that day with Miss Margaret than with Miss Kate.

As regarded Mr. Merriton, however, he found the latter more inclined to agree with him than the former. Notwithstanding Kate's wish to be good-natured, and to make herself and their new neighbourhood generally agreeable to the strangers, and the reality of the interest she had expressed to Mr. Merriton about Italy and Italian places and things, he had seemed to her rather a feckless sort of body—rather a poor creature. And Kate was about the last girl in the world to like a man who belonged in any degree to the category of " poor creatures," or to admit that the absence of manliness and vigor could be atoned for by elegance of manner and advantages of person. She was not disposed to undervalue his capacity for assisting her in her study of Dante. But she would have been

more inclined to like him, if her attention had been called to his capacity for riding well up to hounds. Doubtless she would have preferred a cavalier equally calculated to shine in the field and in the study ; but if one good quality out of the two could be had only, I take it Kate would have decided for the hounds, and Dante would have gone to the wall. I do not say, be it observed, that Kate Lindisfarn was a very charming girl because of this ; I only say that she was a very charming girl, and that such was the case.

As for Margaret, she would have cared nothing at all about the riding to hounds ; and truth to say, very little indeed about the capacity for understanding Dante. And, as we know, she was " a very charming girl," too. But some of the value of that phrase of course depends upon the object on whom the charm operates, and by whom it is recognized. Now there can be no doubt at all that Margaret was a very particularly charming girl to Mr. Falconer, despite her disagreeing with him about Mr. Merriton.

" For my part," said she, shooting across the table one of those glances with which young ladies, who are properly up in all the departments of eye language, know how to render such a declaration rather agreeable than otherwise to the receiver of it,—" for my part, I think you are too hard upon poor Mr. Merriton. It is unfair to expect that he should possess all the advantages which can only come from a wider and larger knowledge of the world."

" Really, Miss Margaret, I had no intention of being hard on him," said Falconer, returning her look with interest, " and I shall have less inclination than ever to be so, of course " (eye commentary here, intelligible to the merest tyro in that language), " if you take him under your protection."

" I did not mean to say a word," put in Kate; " and really I don't think there is a word to be said against his manner. It is that of a very young man, that is all."

" That is it," said Margaret avec intention, and looking as she spoke, not at her sister, but at Falconer ; " I never can find such mere boys very agreeable."

" I agree with Mr. Frederick," said Miss Immy ; " my notion is, that if the poor-wished lad had been born and bred in Zill-shire, he would not have looked for all the world as though he had lived on sugar and water and sweet biscuits all his life, like Miss Lasseron's Italian greyhound!"

"And what about the other new-comer among us?" said Falconer, not addressing himself to any one of the party more than to another. "What of Captain Ellingham?"

"Now that is being harder than ever upon poor Mr. Merriton, to bring the two men into contrast in that way," cried Kate.

"Well, I confess I cannot agree with you there, Kate," said her sister. "If there is any hardness in the matter, I think it is all the other way, for my part."

"Oh, Margaret, how can you think so!" said Kate, with some emphasis.

"And I do not think Mr. Falconer had any notion of making a comparison that would be disadvantageous to Mr. Merriton, at all events," added Margaret.

"Indeed I had not," replied Falconer. "I found Captain Ellingham markedly civil; and I have not a word to say in his disparagement in any way. I do not doubt that he is a most able and meritorious officer, notwithstanding the position he occupies in the service. Of course, from merely passing an evening in a drawing-room with two men, one can form no opinion except as to their general exterior agreeability; and as far as that goes, I confess that I think Merriton has all the advantage."

"Why, what in the world did you see in Captain Ellingham to make you take an aversion to him?" asked Kate.

"I did not take an aversion to him the least in the world, I assure you, my dear Miss Lindisfarn! On the contrary. But it seems that I only shared the impression he made upon your sister."

"I own that I did not see anything particularly attractive about him, notwithstanding all that Lady Farnleigh said in his praise," said Margaret.

"Is he a great friend of Lady Farnleigh's, then?" asked Falconer.

"Oh, yes, and according to her, he is a *chevalier sans peur et sans reproche*,—a mirror of all the virtues! I dare say he may be; but "—

"Oh, Lady Farnleigh's approbation is quite sufficient to secure to the fortunate possessor of it that of your sister, Miss Margaret," said Falconer, with some little appearance of pique in his manner. "When you have been a

little longer an inmate of the Chase, you will doubtless make that discovery for yourself."

"And if I pinned my faith upon anybody's judgment in all the world, I am very sure that I could not have a safer and better guide," cried Kate with some vehemence; "and I have no doubt Margaret will discover that too, before she has been here long. Perhaps I should be wiser," she added, with a momentary half-glance at Falconer, "if I followed her guidance in all cases more implicitly."

"I am sure no one could doubt the excellence of Lady Farnleigh's judgment on any subject," said Freddy, looking rather discomfited; "but probably she was speaking of Captain Ellingham as of an old friend and contemporary of her own."

"Hardly that, I should think," said Kate. "Why, how old a man should you take Captain Ellingham to be?"

"Well, he is one of those men who may be almost any age; but I should say he must be on the wrong side of forty," said Falconer.

"Impossible!" cried Kate. "I am no judge of people's ages; but to my notion Captain Ellingham seems quite a young man."

"A young man, Kate! Why, he is quite gray. I declare he looks every bit as old as Mr. Mat!"

"He certainly *is* very gray, both on the head and about the beard," said Freddy; "but that is not the worst of it. There are certain lines about the face "—

"I don't think a man's appearance is at all injured by a few gray hairs among the black ones; and as for the lines, a face is far more interesting to me, that looks as if the owner had been doing something else all his life than thinking of taking care of it!" cried Kate, in her usual impetuous way, having been provoked into saying more than she would otherwise have done by the spitefulness of Falconer's remarks, and by his attack on her with reference to Lady Farnleigh.

"Oh! if Kate prefers gray-beards, there can be no more to be said on the subject, you know, Mr. Falconer. *Affaire de goût!* We have only to remember it and to respect it, *n'est-ce pas!*" said Margaret.

"But is there nothing worth talking of except beards, either gray, black, or brown? What of the other new arrival? What of Miss Merriton? On that subject I am sure

Mr. Frederick ought to be able to enlighten us; for he was studying it all dinner-time."

"What else was there for me to do, unless it were to eat my dinner in silence?" remonstrated Falconer. "My opinion was not wanted in the discussion that was going on about poachers, between your father and Lady Farnleigh and Mr. Mat. I could not venture to do Mr. Merriton such wrong as to prevent him from consecrating all his attention to Miss Margaret, as he seemed so particularly well inclined to do. What else remained for me, except to do the civil, as indeed I was in every way bound to do, to Miss Merriton?"

"Of course you could do no otherwise," said Margaret; "and now give us the result of your investigations."

"The result is very soon and very easily stated," replied Freddy. "Miss Merriton is a perfectly ladylike, well-educated, very timid, very shy, and, I should say, very uninteresting young lady. There is no fault to be found with her; but neither is there anything except negative good to be said of her."

It seemed to be more easy for the little party around the luncheon-table to come to an agreement on this subject than it had been on the, it must be supposed, more interesting topic of the lords of the creation; for there was little dissent from the judgment pronounced by Mr. Frederick on the quiet and unobtrusive little creature whose chief title to notice in the world—her twenty-five thousand pounds in her own absolute disposition—he had not deemed it necessary to touch on in summing up her claims to consideration.

And then the ladies rose to quit the table, and Mr. Frederick took his leave, and rode back slowly to Silverton, pondering many things in his mind. His visit had very manifestly done little towards forwarding his views, as far as they coincided with those of his father. He had accomplished as serious an amount of flirtation with Miss Margaret as could have been expected from the circumstances. But he had, if anything, lost rather than gained ground with Miss Kate. The progress in either case was, however, he said to himself, probably infinitesimal. But he thought that the advance he had made toward attaining a necessary and accurate view of his position, and of the state of the game, was greater and more important.

"Lady Farnleigh means Kate for her penniless *protégé*, Captain Ellingham." That was the first *datum* which he thought might be, with tolerable certainty, deduced from his observations. "She has already begun to work towards that end, and has already achieved a commencement of success. How fierce the little lady was when I ventured to sneer at her being led by the nose by her godmother! And I did not see the least sign which could encourage me to think that I can fight against that influence with success. No; to be honest with myself and keep clear of delusions, no sign; as long as I had the field all to myself, it might have been different—*might* have been. But now it would be a race carrying very heavy weight.

"Then," continuing his meditations, " on the other side, there *are* signs. I have done more with Margaret in two days than I have done with Kate in twice as many years, by Jove! The fact is, there is more sympathy between us. Put all considerations of prudence out of the question, I swear I would not hesitate a minute. What a graceful, elegant-mannered, intelligent, exquisitely pretty little creature she is! I am strongly inclined to think, let the old gentleman say what he will, that Margaret should be my game—out and out, without any shilly-shally.

"The one seems possible enough; the other looks to me very much like being impossible. If that detestable old woman up at Wanstrow means to make her marry Ellingham,—and I have very little doubt upon that point,—she will succeed in doing it. I don't think she could turn Margaret round her finger in that way. There is a different sort of character there.

"And suppose I determine to play for Margaret out and out, and throw over at once all hope of the other: is the speculation so much worse an one? That old Wanstrow woman's six thousand pounds are not worth counting. Pshaw! But about the place. Every word my father says about the importance of such a prize is true. The old boy is right enough there. But would it be so much more difficult to win Lindisfarn with Margaret than with Kate? I doubt it. Specially if I am to assume that Kate marries Ellingham. How is he, a man without a penny in the world, to find the means of paying half the price of the Chase estates? A good fifty thousand would be needful, if a penny. Would it be likely that such a man should see his interest in causing the estates to be sold? With delay, uncertainty, expense? Would it not be very much more likely, supposing that he were to marry one girl, and I the other, that he would be exceedingly glad to accept the old gentleman's cash to the amount of half the value of the property? Is there any ground for imagining that the squire would make an objection to such an arrangement, if desired by all the parties concerned? I cannot see it. If he held by the old name, I should make no difficulty about accommodating him. 'Falconer Lindisfarn, Esquire, of Lindisfarn,'—that would do remarkably well. Or 'Sir Falconer Lindisfarn!' better still; and why not? Yes, I think, I *think* that will be the game, the more prudent as well as the pleasanter game to play. Honestly, I do think so. But what about that fellow Merriton? Kate would never marry him. Is there any danger of his cutting me out with Margaret? She was more inclined to like him than that boisterous, violent, upright and downright Kate! But I have a great notion that that was all *à mon adresse!* She has far more manner, far more knowledge of the world than her sister in that respect. And I fancy, too, that she is one who would have the sense to know on which side her bread is buttered. And I hardly think Merriton would be in a position to make her mistress of Lindisfarn. I don't know; I must ask my father how that is; but I think not. Besides, I do flatter myself that I could cut out that boy!"

So, by the time Freddy had reached his father's door, he may be said to have pretty well made up his mind to enter himself, as he phrased it to his own mind, for the Margaret sweepstakes in thorough earnest, make a straightforward race of it, and run his best.

Frederick Falconer was, it will have been seen, a shrewd man, not under the empire of self-delusion, and with a considerable gift of seeing characters and things as they really were. The net result of what had taken place at the luncheon-table at the Chase as regarded the others of the party who had been sitting at it, was not very different from what he had felt it to be. But he had not only made progress with the one sister, but had in a yet greater degree advanced his sup-

posed rival's cause with the other. Kate had felt much more disposed to feel a liking for Captain Ellingham after that luncheon than she had previously. She had defended him; —a very strong tie of attachment for natures like Kate's. She had thought that he was being unfairly and ungenerously run down. And—strongest contribution of all to the net result—she had been made to feel as if he were on the side of her godmother, and the others on the contrary side.

On the following day, the Lindisfarn ladies had another guest at their luncheon-table. Mr. Merriton drove up to the Chase, as he had told Lady Farnleigh he would do, to give his invitations to the Friary for the following Wednesday. They were given and accepted, as far as the younger ladies were concerned (for Miss Imny pleaded important engagements at home; and all the ladies declared that they could not answer for the squire, but thought they might for Mr. Mat), rather to Margaret's disgust. She accused Mr. Merriton in her heart of being very stupid for not preferring to have her and her uncle there alone, as she had projected and prepared for him. And, moreover, she did not look forward with any pleasure to what she feared would probably happen when the whole party should be there together. She did not at all like being trotted out in the character of an archæological blue-stocking. The double necessity and incompatibility of hiding her utter ignorance and indifference on the one hand, and making them evident on the other, was embarrassing and disagreeable.

Nevertheless, it was impossible to refuse; and the Lindisfarn lasses promised to be at the Friary at one o'clock on the Wednesday, either under the escort of Mr. Mat, or, if that should fail them, with Lady Farnleigh.

Margaret, being out of humor, had rather snubbed Mr. Merriton. But he had proposed to Kate to show her and explain to her on Wednesday a volume of "Piranesi's Views in Rome." And on her replying, in her good-humored, lively way, that she should enjoy nothing so much, and should greatly like to see the Eternal City, he had gone away more in love with her than ever, and dreaming of the delight of returning to Italy with such a bride, and initiating her into all its glories, beauties, and enjoyments.

CHAPTER XIII.

THE PARTY AT THE FRIARY.

LADY SEMPRONIA, when at dinner the canon had communicated to her Mr. Merriton's invitation, rather to her husband's surprise, signified her intention of accepting it.

"I hardly hoped," he said, "and did not give Mr. Merriton much hope, that you would be induced to go to the Friary; but you are quite right, my dear, to look upon this occasion as a somewhat extraordinary one. There is not a more interesting locality in the country, and I flatter myself that I shall be able to make the day a profitable, and indeed a memorable one for all present."

And during all the intervening days the doctor was in a state of pleasurable excitement and anticipation, and worked hard to have every part of the subject in a complete state of preparation. He would have given a good deal to have secured the entire absence of Mr. Falconer. But he reckoned, taking the usual habits of that archæological financier as a base for his calculations, that he should have a good two hours and a half before him, ere the banker could arrive.

It was not without considerable disquietude and surprise, therefore, that just as the modest one-horse chaise which was conveying the canon and Lady Sempronia to the Friary was jogging along the main street of the little village of Weston, while it yet wanted five minutes to one o'clock, the doctor saw the banker's handsome carriage, with its smart pair of bays, dash past and turn at the end of the village down the road to the private bridge over the Sill, which leads to the Friary house.

"Good heavens! there is Falconer!" he exclaimed, turning pale. "But it is impossible! It can't be! It must be Frederick, and the carriage is going back for his father. Odd that the young man should not have ridden over, too; but I suppose as the carriage was ordered out, he thought it as well to make one job of it."

"And if it were Mr. Falconer," said Lady Sempronia, "what then? I cannot see, Dr. Lindisfarn, that you can pretend to a monopoly of all the old stones in the county, though no doubt you are the only individual in it who would deprive your family of necessaries to spend your substance on such things. Mr. Falconer can afford to play the fool."

"That is fortunate, my dear," returned the doctor; "for it is what he assuredly very often does."

And then, when the canon's carriage drove up to the door of the Friary, at which Mr. Merriton was standing to receive his guests, the doctor, as he alighted, saw behind him the pig-tail and the florid, complacent face and the well-grown, black-silk-encased legs, of the Silverton banker. Giving a silent shake of the hand to his host, for he could not at the moment spare time or words for a longer greeting, and leaving him to receive and welcome Lady Sempronia as best he could, he made one stride toward his enemy, crying out, "Is it possible, Mr. Falconer? You here at this time in the morning? In truth this is a—a circumstance"—the word pleasure stuck in the veracious doctor's throat—"which I had not expected. I hope that Mr. Merriton is aware that you have broken in upon all your habitudes,—innovated on the practice of—how many lustres shall I say?—in order to wait on him!"

"My friend Merriton is, I trust, aware, doctor, that I would do more than that for him, if need were," said the banker, with a bow and a sly wink aside to the young man.

"I am quite aware, my dear sir," said Merriton, returning the banker's telegraph, "how much Mr. Falconer is deranging his usual habits in order to give us the pleasure of his company. It is *very* kind of him "

"But business, Mr. Falconer! What will the bank do without you?"

"Oh, the bank can take care of itself, for once and away, doctor. The fact is, if Merriton will forgive me for confessing the entire truth," continued the banker, eying his victim with a sweet and complacent smile, "that, had our meeting here to-day been of merely an ordinary festive character, I might have contented myself with enjoying such share of it as I could have come in for after business hours. But when it became known to me that the party were to have the treat of inspecting the antiquities of the Friary under your auspices, doctor, and the advantage of your explanations of them, I could not resist the temptation of being present. I could not indeed!" And then Mr. Falconer took a long pinch of snuff with an air that included in it the expression of a defiance to mortal combat. And the mortified canon knew what was before him, and saw that the treat to which he had been looking forward with so much pleasure had been snatched from his grasp.

Not that he was afraid of his adversary, or at all disinclined to a fair stand-up fight with him for any number of hours by the Friary clock. That also was a pleasure in its kind; but it was of a different sort from the more luxurious and seducing one which he had promised himself, of having it all his own way, and leading a troop of admiring and unquestioning women from one subject of his learning and eloquence to another.

And then they passed on to the drawing-room, where Mr. Frederick was found busily engaged in prosecuting those investigations into the social qualities of Miss Merriton, which had hitherto only led him, as he had assured the ladies at the Chase, to the conclusion that she was a wholly uninteresting little body.

And then came Lady Farnleigh and Captain Ellingham and not very long after them the Lindisfarn damsels with Mr. Mat. It was nearly half-past one before they arrived; and there was a chorus of outcry at their unpunctuality.

"Not like you, Kate, to be the laggard! And it was to be one o'clock, military time. We have already had the first of our course of lectures," said Lady Farnleigh.

"Ah! I was not on Birdie, you see, godmamma. When I am, I can answer for my time. But we had to come all round by Silverton; and Thomas must be answerable for the delay."

"Thomas is as regular as clockwork; and if you had started in time, you would have been here in time," rejoined the doctor, not in the best possible humor, though he had no longer reason for being anxious to begin the day's amusement punctually.

"Well, uncle, we will behave better another time."

"No, no, put the saddle on the right horse," said Mr. Mat; "Thomas Tibbs is no way in fault; nor is Miss Kate. We had to wait half an hour for Miss Margaret."

"Why, I am sure we came down together; didn't we, Kate?" said Margaret, blushing very red, and shooting at Mr. Mat out of those fine black eyes of hers a look of which it might have been said not only in the Yankee tongue, but in good English, that it was "a caution!"

"Yes," said the abominable Mr. Mat, quietly; "you came down the stairs together, because Kate waited for you. But it was you and not Kate, who tried on three dresses before you could please yourself. Ask Simmons else."

"There never was half an hour spent to better purpose, if Simmons spoke the truth," whispered Frederick, at Margaret's side. "What a lovely toilet!"

"Do you like it? Then I am sure I don't mind how long I kept that old bear waiting," returned Margaret, in the same tone; "not that what he says is true, though. But is he not an insufferable old nuisance?"

"Our likings agree," said he; "Mr. Mat is a particular aversion of mine; and he knows it well enough. There is no love lost between us. Strangely enough, your sister is fond of him."

"Oh, Kate is so odd,—so odd in many things. I am afraid she and I shall find many points of difference between us."

"It will be a great advantage to your sister—your return home, Miss Lindisfarn. If she would endeavor to form her manner from yours, it would be everything to her."

"Of course I have had great advantages, which poor Kate has not shared. But I flatter myself that the generality of the good people here are not so capable as some persons" (eye practice!) "of seeing the deficiencies."

"Would you be better pleased for her sake, that all the people here should be blind to the differences between you, Mademoiselle Marguérite?"

"I am afraid that would tax my charity too severely," answered she, in a tone so low that it was almost a whisper. Then she added, in a rather, but very little, louder voice, "You called me Marguérite! You are the only person here that does. I like it so much better than that odious Margaret, as they call it! Do call me always Marguérite." Whether this was to be taken as a permission to call her by her Christian name, or merely as a request to be addressed in French instead of in English, she skilfully left it to the gentleman himself to decide.

Then, it having been resolved by general vote that one portion of the avowed business of the day should be done before going to luncheon, and that it would be very pleasant to break their archæological investigations by that agreeable diversion, the doctor arose, and proceeded to unroll a large plan which he had brought with him, while most of the party crowded around him.

"Where is Margaret?" cried the doctor; "Margaret, my love; here is your place, by my side. You are to be my fellow-laborer, you know, in illustrating the Friary as it deserves."

Margaret groaned softly, and looked up into Frederick Falconer's face with an appealing expression of intense annoyance in her eyes, which made them look lovelier, he thought, than he had ever seen them yet, as she said, "I must go, I suppose! It is very provoking. Mind, I trust to you to save me from this horrid bore, if any chance of extricating me should offer."

"Would that I could," whispered Fred.

And then the doctor, with his victim by his side, unrolled his topographical plan, and began :—

"The plan of the actually existing buildings,—just put your hand on the paper, my dear, to hold it open, so that they may all see it; "—Margaret, admirably prompt to extract from unfavorable circumstances all the little good they might be capable of yielding, laid a beautifully white and slender hand, with long, slender fingers, flat on the paper, taking off her glove for the purpose, as if the service demanded of her could not have been performed otherwise; and the doctor proceeded :—

"The plan of the modern part of the actually existing buildings has been traced here in black, while that of those portions of the ancient monastery which have perished has, as far as it has been possible to discover the position of them, been laid down in red lines. The part of the plan colored green represents those portions of the actually existing house which were part of the original building. It will be at once perceived, therefore, that the entire wing, including the drawing-room in which we are at this moment assembled, is of modern construction,—comparatively modern that is to say, dating probably from the early part of the seventeenth century."

"I am sure you will forgive me, my good doctor, for interrupting you," said Mr. Falconer, "but it is impossible to hear that statement laid down in so unqualified a manner, without pointing out that there are grave doubts"—

"Thank you, Falconer," cried the doctor, turning on him with the aspect of a boar brought to bay, "I am perfectly aware of all that you would say. I said probably— probably from the beginning of the seventeenth century. We shall go more accurately into the examination of that question, when we shall have brought our investigations down to that time. You will become aware of the advantage of chronological treatment in matters of this kind, when you have applied your distinguished erudition to more of them. Allow me to proceed."

Mr. Falconer was a man of bland manners, and particularly prided himself on suavity of demeanor à toute épreuve. But those of the party who knew him well were made aware by a little vibratory motion of his pig-tail, that he was restraining himself from giving way to his indignation with difficulty. He succeeded, however, so far as to permit no outward demonstration of the tempest that was raging within him to appear, beyond a satirical smile, as, having first soothed his nervous system with a pinch of snuff, he said,—

"I bide my time then, doctor!"

"I was about to point out to you," resumed the doctor, "that only the kitchens, the pantry, the small room adjoining the kitchen on the south side, used, I believe, by the late owners as the housekeeper's room, and possibly still appropriated to the same purpose"— The doctor paused, and directed an inquiring glance at Miss Merriton, thereby causing his hearers to do the same, to the exceeding annoyance and discomfiture of that little lady, who had been surreptitiously engaged in the background in condoling in whispered accents with Lady Sempronia on some of that lady's trials. She felt like a schoolboy, who has been suddenly "set on" at the moment when, having been absorbed in the pages of a novel dexterously hidden beneath his Virgil, he has not the remotest idea of "the place." Lady Sempronia would have prompted her, but was no better informed of the matter in hand than herself.

"The room next the kitchen," said Lady Farnleigh ; " is it still the housekeeper's room ? "

" Yes, that is the housekeeper's room. Is she wanted?" asked poor Miss Merriton, sadly fluttered.

" Not yet. Not at present, thanks," resumed the doctor. "The housekeeper's room —I was saying that the kitchens, the pantry, the housekeeper's room, and the northwest and northeast walls of the present dining-room, or part of them at least, are the only portions of the present house which belong to the ancient monastery."

But at that point of his discourse *pœna pede claudo* overtook the doctor. The bland but inly raging old banker had bided his time, as he said, and found it !

"Excuse me, doctor," he cried, pushing forward to the front of the little group to lay his fingers on the plan ; " excuse me if I say that I feel sure the time will come when your persevering studies will convince you of the danger of laxity of statement in topographical details. The only parts of the present house included in the old monastery ! What! Is there not the wash-house? One of the best characterized remnants in the place ! "

" Now, my dear Falconer, I do hope that you will permit me to proceed with my statement of the facts. I am well aware, of course, that the foundation of the wall of the present wash-house "—

" You know, Dr. Lindisfarn, how deep a respect I entertain for the profundity of your erudition and the accuracy of your research ; but I must be permitted to say that any one who fails to see at a glance the contemporaneousness of the present walls with the foundation on which they stand, must be ignorant of the very A B C of archæology ! "

" I know no man for whose opinion I should have a greater deference on a matter of this kind than yours, Mr. Falconer. But really the grossness of the error into which you have fallen upon the present occasion is a melancholy warning of the consequences of rash and too hasty induction."

" Rash induction, my dear doctor ! I find in Pringle's ' Survey of the Suppressed Religious Houses of the Hundreds of Perribash and Warlingcombe,' a plan, which gives "—

" Indications of walls, of which the ancient foundations still remain ! I dare say you do. I flatter myself I am acquainted with Pringle's work. But Battledore, in his ' Peregrinations and Perlustrations of the Valley of the Sill '—a somewhat rare work, which you probably have never seen, Falconer, for a small edition only was privately printed ; but I shall have much pleasure in showing you a copy,—Battledore clearly shows that the building which had existed on those foundations was in ruins in his time."

Margaret, who all this time had been dutifully holding open her uncle's plan with her fair hand outspread upon it in the manner which has been described, thinking when the dispute between the rival antiquaries had reached that point, either that her services were for the moment no longer needed, or that a sufficient time had been allowed for all present to admire the beauty of her hand, withdrew it from the paper, which immediately rolled itself up against the fingers of the doctor, who had been holding it on the other side. Margaret, who was already gently withdrawing herself from the prominent position she had been made to occupy at her uncle's side, feared that the coiling up of the paper would draw his attention to her desertion. But she need not have alarmed herself. He was far too intent on the battle which had begun to rage to think about any such small matters. Feeling the plan roll itself up into a *bâton*, he grasped it, as he turned upon his adversary, who was unprovided with any such weapon.

" Very cleverly done," whispered Frederick in her ear, as drawing back from the place she had held, she found herself again by his side. "And now, while my father is telling him how Shuttlecock points out that Battledore knew nothing at all about it, we may escape."

" Have you any idea what it is all about ? " asked Margaret, confidentially.

" Not the least in the world ! But I hope the fight will last all the remainder of the afternoon. It wont hurt them ; and it will be a great blessing to us. Don't you think we might steal out upon the lawn through this open window ? There is a beautiful greenhouse ; let me show it to you, while the war is still raging over the foundation of the wash-house."

" The phrase ' ruins,' my dear doctor," said the old banker, with a smile of infinite superiority, " is a very vague one. In this case it was, in all probability, used by the writer whom you cite,—and who is perfectly well known to me, though I have not much opinion of the reliability of his work,—to express the condition of the roof." Here the old gentleman took a pinch of snuff, and looked round on the bystanders with an air which seemed to call their attention to the fact of his having utterly demolished his opponent. "But with regard to the walls," he continued, "I think—I *do* think, that the evidence of your own senses, my dear doctor, would be sufficient to convince you that they are of the same date as the foundations on which they rest. If our kind host will permit us to institute an examination on the spot"—

"Oh, by all means," said Mr. Merriton; "the entire house is at your disposition. If you will step this way"—

And the combatants accordingly followed him to the back part of the house, which stood very close to the cliff which has been described, and occupied the site of the refectory and adjoining buildings—buttery, hatches, and so forth—of the old monastery. But it may be feared that when they reached the battle-ground itself, a great portion of the interest of the fight was lost. Were there ever knights who would not have taken their lances from their rests, and ceased poking each other, if all the spectators had retired from the lists? And unhappily not a single soul of those assembled in the drawing-room at the Friary cared sufficiently to know when the wash-house was built to follow the combatants. There was still Mr. Merriton for umpire, and the dispute had, therefore, to be carried on; but it is permissible to suppose that if it had not been for his presence the fight would have languished.

As it was, the remaining members of the party, who were left in the drawing-room,—Lady Farnleigh, Miss Merriton, Lady Sempronia, Kate, Mr. Mat and Captain Ellingham,—were left to their own devices by the—it is to be feared, not unwelcome—diversion.

"We must not regret, Miss Merriton," said Lady Farnleigh, "that the great question of the antiquity of your wash-house, which seems so doubtful, should be finally set at rest, as it no doubt will now be; although we are deprived, in consequence of the difficulty, of the benefit of the doctor's guidance. I propose that we put the time to profit by investigating, as best we may by the light of nature, that charming fragment of the old cloister that forms the northern boundary of your lovely flower-garden."

"That is the only bit of the antiquities of the Friary that I care about," said Mr. Mat; "and I do think that flower-garden is the prettiest spot in all Sillshire."

"Don't you think we may venture, Miss Merriton, to conduct our own researches in the flower-garden without inquiring what Pringle and Battledore have written upon the subject?" said Lady Farnleigh.

"If Lady Sempronia feels equal to strolling so far," said Miss Merriton, turning to that plaintive lady, by whose side she was sitting on a sofa, listening with admirable patience and sympathy to the tale of her various trials.

"I am afraid," said Lady Sempronia, whose mind was full of the impending danger that the doctor might be stimulated into composing a monograph on the date of the Friary wash-house, "I am afraid that I must not venture out in the sun. It is very powerful at this hour. But pray do not let me detain you, Miss Merriton."

"But perhaps Lady Farnleigh, who is doubtless far more competent to act as guide than I am, will excuse me. If she would kindly undertake the office of *cicerone* I should prefer remaining indoors myself," said Miss Merriton.

"Oh! I am thoroughly competent, I assure you," rejoined Lady Farnleigh. "If I have only your permission, I undertake to do the honors of the gardens *on ne peut mieux*."

So Lady Farnleigh, Kate, Mr. Mat and Captain Ellingham, walked out into the garden by the same window through which Margaret and Frederick Falconer had passed. The latter had, however, gone into the conservatory, which occupied the space of some forty feet between the house and the fragment of the ancient cloister to which Lady Farnleigh had alluded.

The flower-garden in question was worth a visit; and none the less so that the place was well known to all the *partie carrée* who now entered it, except Captain Ellingham. It is indeed as lovely a spot as the imagination can well conceive. Completely shut in on the Silverton side by the lofty jutting limestone cliff, close round the base of which the water ran in a deeper and swifter stream than in any other part of its course, it was enclosed on the side opposite to the front of the house by the river, the opposite bank of which was fringed with a luxuriant plantation of rhododendrons all the way from the private bridge leading to the village, to the spot where it disappeared round the cliff, Over the top of this flourishing plantation the spire of Weston church was visible and behind it the higher and more distant parts of the broken open ground, with its patches of broom, which intervened between the valley of the Sill and the woods belonging to the Chase, and behind them again an horizon formed by the lofty summit of Lindisfarn brow.

On the opposite side to the river, the flower-garden was shut in by the house, by the conservatory,—one end of which abutted on it,—and by the old fragment of cloister, consisting of three arches, and a small portion of the back wall of the cloister, which had, however, been restored and completed by masonry of recent construction, and on which the other end of the conservatory rested. The three isolated arches of crumbling gray stone, standing thus on the exquisitely kept sward of the lawn, and serving as a support for a variety of flowering creepers, were the pride and beauty of the garden. They stood at right angles, as will be understood, if I have succeeded in rendering the above account of the locality intelligible, to that face of the cliff which shut in the garden; and which, itself richly clothed with a wilder and more exuberant growth of coarser creeping plants, was so beautiful an object as to make it questionable whether man's handiwork or nature's had contributed most to the ornament of the little paradise encircled by them both. The remaining side of the enclosed space—that looking toward the upper valley of the Sill and the pasture ground on its banks, which was once the home farm of the monastery, and now the park attached to the modern residence—was only partially shut in by plantations, of horse-chestnut and birch chiefly, so as to leave peeps of the distant view in this direction.

"I do think Mr. Mat is right," said Kate, as they all four stood on the lawn in front of the three old arches, which were probably indebted for their preservation, so many years

after the destruction of their fellows, to the support and protection derived from the cliff against which the last of them rested. " I do think this is the prettiest spot altogether that I ever saw."

"It really is a most perfect thing in its way," said Captain Ellingham, who, to tell the truth, though nobody but Lady Farnleigh had observed it, had been in not the best of all possible humors since they had arrived at the Friary; for, instead of attending to the doctor's exordium as he ought to have done, he had been watching Margaret—that "most beautiful creature he had ever seen in his life"—and all her ways and works, and he did not like what he had seen. He was not pleased with the incident arising from the tardiness of their arrival. Not that he in the least blamed Margaret for the delay of the half-hour employed in the trying-on of three dresses; for he agreed with Falconer in thinking, though he had not said it, that the result produced was well worth the time employed to realize it. But he had not been pleased with her allowing the blame to be cast on her sister, and still less with a certain expression of face which he had noted when Mr. Mat had so brutally betrayed her secret. Then again, though he had much admired the exquisite little hand, so skilfully laid out (literally) for admiration on the doctor's topographical plan, he had most ungratefully felt annoyed at her for the manner of the exhibition of it. And it cannot perhaps be said that he was altogether unreasonable in withholding his entire approbation in either case. But he was far more displeased at certain other things that had fallen within the scope of his observation, with which he really had no right to find fault. He had noted all the little by-play and whispering with Falconer, and had judged it from a stand-point of moral criticism which his judgment would hardly have placed itself on, if he had been himself the culprit in Falconer's place. He had marked also her escape out of the window, followed by him; and it sufficed to bring his indignation and his ill-humor to its climax. And although the sins she had been guilty of would only have confirmed him in the opinion that she certainly was one of the sweetest creatures on earth, if he instead of another had been the accomplice of them, as it was, he began to ask himself whether Lady Farnleigh had not been right, when she called

6

him a goose in the carriage as they were returning from the Chase.

The honorable Captain Ellingham, though doubtless, as Fred Falconer had said, a very meritorious officer, was, it is very clear, a quite exceptionably unreasonable man when the question was one, not of haulyards and marling-spikes, but of pretty girls.

CAPTAIN ELLINGHAM'S ill-temper was beginning to give way before the influences of the charming scene around him, and the thoroughly good-tempered, joyous, and open-hearted enjoyment of it by his companions ; and he was gradually coming round more and more to the opinion that Lady Farnleigh had expressed as to the merits of the Lindisfarn lasses, and as to his appreciation of them, when a circumstance occurred, which, though it suddenly changed the immediate current of all his thoughts, yet eventually operated to complete Captain Ellingham's conversion to his old friend's opinion.

The face of Weston Rock, as the cliff which has been so frequently mentioned was called by the educated classes—though the country-people generally nicknamed it the " Nosey Stone," from the manner in which it stood out from the hillside behind it—the face of Weston Rock, which looks toward Silverton, is, though very steep, not altogether precipitous. The most prominent part of it,—the ridge of the nose, as it were, —which is washed at its base by the river, is for more than half of the height from the water a naked and absolutely precipitous rock. The upper portion of this side of the cliff above this naked wall of rock is very little less steep ; but it is covered with a growth of creeping plants, which do not, however, sufficiently lessen its precipitous character to render it possible for any human foot to traverse it. On the other face of the cliff, that which overhangs and forms the boundary of the Friary gardens, the lower portion of the height is nearly as steep as that which overhangs the river ; but it is not, like that, utterly devoid of inequalities on the surface and ledges, which in some degree break the face of it. The upper portion on this side is not so entirely precipitous ; it is covered not only with a profusion of creeping plants, the long trailing branches of which hang down over the lower part, but over a considerable portion of its surface with patches and tufts of rank, coarse grass and herbage. So that it is possible on that side to descend from the top by the aid of the partial foothold, and the vigorous vegetation of the creepers. Nevertheless, considering that any one attempting such a feat has some seventy or eighty feet of utterly unclimbable precipice beneath him, the edge of which he is approaching as he descends, and bearing in mind that the crumbling of a tuft of couch-grass, or the breaking of a twig, may accelerate his approach to its edge in such sort as to hurry him over it, the descent of the Nosey Stone, even on this its least terrible side, is an undertaking in which one would not wish unnecessarily to engage.

The little party standing on the lawn in front of the old cloister arches, and consequently within a few feet of that face of the cliff which has been last mentioned, were speaking, as everybody always does speak in such cases, of the exceeding knowingness exhibited by the monks in the choice of their situations,—how sure they always were to select the choice bits of all the country-side for their homesteads, and how perfectly well they understood all the points that go toward making any spot specially eligible for a habitation,—when suddenly they were startled by a rustle, a rush among the brushwood on the face of the cliff above their heads, and in the next moment the fall of a heavy substance with a dead sounding *thud* on the turf of the lawn at their feet. It was a young lamb ; and it lay on its side, giving only one or two convulsive movements with its hind legs— for the fall had killed it.

" Poor little thing ! " said Kate, running forward, and stooping over it to see if it was indeed dead ; " it must have strayed from the mother in the field above. I think it is dead ; look, Mr. Mat, see if the fall has quite killed it."

" Killed it, sure enough," said Mr. Mat ; " lambs don't fall as cats do ! "

" It is well for it, poor little beast, that it is killed," said Captain Ellingham, " for of course its bones must be broken."

Just then Margaret and Falconer emerged from the conservatory, where they also had heard and been startled by the noise of the fall. They came forward toward the spot where the others were gathered round the body of the unlucky little animal, with an eagerness of inquiry as to what the matter was, and what had happened, which had somewhat the appearance of being in a certain measure prompted by a feeling of the desirability of diverting the attention of the party away from their own simultaneous re-appearance, after their period of retirement.

"Good gracious!" cried Margaret, when the nature of the accident had been explained to her, "what a mercy it is the creature did not tumble on any of our heads! It might have killed us on the spot!"

But as Margaret uttered the words, moralizing the event after her own fashion, Captain Ellingham suddenly cried, "hush!" lifting his fingers as he spoke; "Hush! I thought I heard a voice up there! Yes! there it is again,—a sob, as of a child crying. Is there any possibility that a child should be on the face of the cliff?"

"Hardly," said Mr. Mat; "more likely the voice you heard was from the top. Very likely some little shepherd or shepherdess, who has discovered the misfortune that has betided one of the flock."

"God grant the child, if it be one, may not come too close to the edge of the cliff!" said Lady Farnleigh. "It is a dangerous place. And it strikes me that, unless the voice were quite at the very edge of the precipice, it could not be heard here."

"So I should say, too," replied Ellingham. "And yet I can hear it now,—evidently the voice of a child crying. Hist! Do you not hear it?"

"There! Oh, yes! To be sure I do. It is a child crying."

"Yes! I can hear it, too, now, very plainly. I think it must have come nearer," said Lady Farnleigh.

"What can we do to find out where it is?" cried Kate, turning to Captain Ellingham, who was still bending his ear to catch the sounds that were at one moment more, and at another less, distinctly audible.

"Do the ladies and gentlemen of Sillshire always go into committee instantly on the spot every time a little *gamin* cries, to investigate the cause of the phenomenon?" said Margaret, tittering.

"Yes, they *du!*" cried Mr. Mat, turning on her fiercely, and speaking in his broadest Doric; "yes, they du, Miss Margy, when 'tis at the voot of the Nosey stoan they hear it! Why, the poor child may be zearching for the lamb to the top of the cliff, and come to vall over in the zame manner, he might!"

"I believe," said Captain Ellingham, who had been attentively listening, "that the voice must be on the face of the cliff; I do not think we could hear it as we do, if it was from anybody on the top. The sound would be too much impeded by the intervening mass of the hill, which prevents a person on the top from being visible."

And as he spoke, Captain Ellingham drew back from the face of the cliff toward the bank of the river, in order to be able to scan the whole surface of it with his eye. If the cliff had been naked, it would have been of course easy to do this in an instant; but the overgrowth of creepers, and brambles and brushwood was in some parts quite abundant enough to hide a child or even a man among it. But after carefully and earnestly gazing for a minute or two, Captain Ellingham cried out,—

"Yes! yes! I think I see him, or her, whichever it is!"

"Where, where?" cried Kate, running out from under the cliff to the place where Ellingham was standing, still intently examining the face of the rock.

"There: a couple of fathom or so above the line where the vegetation ends and the naked rock begins. Do you see a large patch of yellow flowers? Lift your eyes in a perpendicular line from the spot where the conservatory joins the old arches of the cloister, till you come to a noticeable clump of yellow flowers"—

"Yes, oh, yes!" cried Kate, doing as she was bid; "I have them!"

"Well, just above and a little to the right of that clump of flowers, I saw the bushes move, and I am almost sure that I caught a glimpse of a dress!"

"But, good Heaven!" cried Kate, turning pale, "if there is a child, or even a man there, how are they to get away? They must be in fearful danger!"

"It is a child's voice—and I think a girl's," said Ellingham.

"Good Heaven! What is to be done?" asked Lady Farnleigh, looking in a scared manner from one to the other of the two gentlemen;—the two; for, though there were three present on the lawn since Falconer had come out of the conservatory with Margaret, her eyes seemed to confine her appeal to Mr. Mat and Captain Ellingham.

"'Tis a bad place to get tu," said Mr. Mat. "She, ev it is a girl, might get tu the top the zame way she got down; though perhaps she might vind it difficult to du so. But the worst is, that mayhap she don't know—pretty zure, indeed, she don't know—that the naked rock is ten or a dozen voet below her. And ev she goes on pushing and moving among the bushes, she may vall any minute. Ev she would remain quite still till we could get to her with ladder and tackle, we might take her off the cliff safe enough."

"But how could she ever have got there, Mr. Mat?" asked Kate, in much distress; "do you think she fell over the edge of the cliff?"

"No! Depend upon it she clambered down after the lamb that we saw vall. It is not so very difficult to get down by help of the bushes, and climb up again, ev you know what you are about, and what sort of place it is. I've been all over the vace of the cliff after bird's-nests and blackberries, when I was a boy, time and again. She is uncommonly near the top of the naked rock though! And if she comes down any lower, God help her!"

"Shall I try to hail her? We could make her hear well enough; but it is a question whether we may not frighten her."

"Had you not better send a servant to the village, and tell the people to go and look after the child?" said Margaret.

"Tell ye what," said Mr. Mat, "better let me try to speak to her. She'll understand our Zillshire speach better. I should be less likely to frighten her than you. If we can only make her keep herself quite quiet till we can come tu her, it will be all right enough."

"There! there! now I see her plain enough," cried Captain Ellingham; "it is a little girl sure enough! I see her red dress."

"If she don't bide still, it is all up with her! She moved a couple of voot nearer the top of the bare rock then!"

"Good Heaven!" cried Lady Farnleigh; "call to her, Mr. Mat! call to her, at all hazards! tell her not to move hand or foot for her life! I see the poor little thing plain enough; Do you not see, Kate?"—

And she turned, as she spoke, to where Kate had been standing on the lawn; but Kate was no longer there. They had all been looking up eagerly to the face of the cliff, and neither Ellingham nor Mr. Mat had seen her go.

"Kate is gone into the house," said Margaret; "she ran off without saying a word. No doubt she has gone to tell the servants."

Mr. Mat, putting his hands to his mouth so as to make them serve, as far as might be, the purpose of a speaking trumpet, hallooed to the child, whom they could all now see perfectly well, to remain quite still; to take the best hold she could on the biggest bushes near her, and hold on without attempting to budge till help could reach her.

But while he was calling to her—whether or not it may have been that she was startled by the voice from underneath her—she made another movement, which brought her two or three feet nearer to the limit of the bushes, and to the commencement of the bare rock—and certain destruction.

Lady Farnleigh covered her eyes with her hand, and uttered a shuddering cry.

"By Heaven? she will be killed before our eyes!" cried Mr. Mat. "You run, Falconer! run for your life to the top of the cliff, by the path on the other side—you know, the path from Weston water-meads up to Shapton farm;—and get down to the child by the bushes. You'll be faster than me; and I'll be trying to get at her from below. Run for dear life, lad!"

But as he spoke, and while Lady Farnleigh was wringing her hands in distress, Miss Margaret was so overcome by her feelings that she suddenly threw herself backwards into Frederick Falconer's arms, and went off incontinently into violent hysterics.

"It is impossible that I can leave Miss Lindisfarn in this state," replied he, to Mr. Mat's appeal; "impossible, or I would go at once."

"Oh! don't leave me! for pity's sake don't leave me!" shrieked the young lady, opening her fine eyes for a moment—just long enough to shoot up into the face which was hanging over her a glance which was not altogether hysterical in its expression,—no-

cording, at least, to the strictly medical view of such matters.

"Put the lass down with her back on the turf!" said Mr. Mat,—in extreme disgust; "put the lass down!—what hurt can she take?—and see if you can help to save this poor child's life!"

"Oh! don't leave me! don't leave me!" sobbed Miss Margaret.

"Not for all the world," replied Freddy, in an intensely expressive whisper, with eye expression to match. "It is impossible for me to leave her," he said aloud, in answer to Mr. Mat; "don't you see that it is?"

Captain Ellingham had in the mean time contrived to clamber to the top of the half-ruinous arches, and was seeing whether it was possible for active limbs and a sure eye to scale the face of the cliff by that help.

"It is out of the question," cried Mr. Mat; "I tell you it is impossible! Wait while I run into the house to see what ladders they have."

"And ropes," returned Captain Ellingham. "Above all, a good coil of rope."

"Where's Kate?" cried Mr. Mat, as he turned to run into the house.

"I did not see her leave the lawn; I suppose she went into the house," returned Lady Farnleigh. "No doubt she went to get assistance. Since that gentleman does not choose to risk his precious limbs to save a poor girl's life," continued she, looking with a curling lip to the spot where Falconer was hanging over the reclining form of Miss Margaret, "you had better get some one of the servants to hasten to the top of the cliff and try to get down to her. Ellingham will be the man to climb it from below, if any human being can."

"Do you continue to encourage her to hold on for life, but to make no attempt to move, Lady Farnleigh; I will run and see what tackle can be got. You can make her hear you."

And, so saying, he and Mr. Mat hurried off together into the house.

In a very few minutes all the others of the party had run out from the house and were assembled on the lawn. As soon as ever Mr. Merriton understood the nature of the case, and the desirability that some one should, if possible, get to the top of the cliff, and attempt to descend thence to where the child

was, he started off to make his way to the place.

"Take the gardener with you, Arthur, to show you the path up the cliff, and the spot at the top from which you must try the descent," said little Miss Merriton, with quiet presence of mind. "And make him run his best. You can run well, Arthur."

And then, quietly stepping into the house, she called all the men-servants and maids, and set them to work to drag out feather-beds and mattresses, and spread them at the foot of the cliff.

"In case the poor little thing should fall, it might be the means of saving her," she said to Lady Farnleigh. "I fear she would not fall sufficiently clear of the rocks to escape fatal injury; but it is a chance the more in her favor."

While this was being done, Captain Ellingham and Mr. Mat were busily engaged in splicing together two long ladders, which had been brought out on to the lawn.

"Can you judge the height with your eye, captain?" said Mr. Mat; "do you think we have length of ladder enough?"

"It is very difficult to say. I don't know. We must try it. If I can only get to the lowest bushes, I'll answer for the rest."

"How can you possibly take the child off the cliff, when it will be as much as ever you can do to hold your own footing on it?" urged Mr. Mat.

"Only let me get at her; and I'll answer for the rest. I'll manage it, either upward or back by the ladders. Now for it, let's try the length!"

They raised the two ladders, tied together, with some difficulty, only to find that they were some ten or twelve feet too short for the purpose. The lowest of the bushes grew at least that distance above the topmost rung of the ladder; and the child was now about half as much, or perhaps rather more than half as much, as high again above the commencement of the growth of plants.

"I'll tell you what it is," said Ellingham; "there is but one thing for it. We must get the ladders up and stand them on the top of the old cloister wall!"

"I doubt it," said Mr. Mat; "I doubt our raising the ladder there; and if you do succeed in getting it on end, it will be no joke attempting to go up it."

"Not a bit of it, only let us get the ladders up! I'll go up them safe enough! I'm good at a balance," returned Ellingham.

"Well, we can but try," said Mr. Mat. So, aided by the servants, the two gentlemen essayed, and by dint of great exertion, succeeded in raising the ladders against the cliff from the top of the crumbling old wall. Mr. Mat placed himself at the foot of the ladder, in order to hold and steady it to the utmost of his power and strength. But the task of ascending the two ladders, hastily lashed together, raised against an uneven surface of bare rock, and standing on the top of a rotten and crumbling old wall, was not an agreeable one; and all the other individuals of the party assembled on the lawn looked on with breathless anxiety while Ellingham was about to attempt it.

All of them were there, with the exception of Frederick Falconer and Miss Margaret. For after Fred had declared, in reply to the appeal made to him for assistance, that he could not leave Margaret, and had pledged himself to that young lady herself not to "desert her," finding it unpleasant under the circumstances to remain under the observation of the people congregated on the lawn, specially of Lady Farnleigh and Mr. Mat, he had half carried half led the drooping and still hysterical girl into the drawing-room, and was there administering such bodily and mental consolation and comfort as her case required.

Ellingham was on the wall at the foot of the ladder, adjusting a coil of rope around his shoulders and neck in such a manner as to interfere as little as possible with his freedom of action, and was on the point of starting on his perilous enterprise, when the attention of those on the lawn was drawn to a movement among the bushes and brambles at the top of the cliff, just above the spot where the child was still clinging for dear life to the shrubs and crumbling soil, only a few feet above the commencement of the wholly naked part of the cliff. In the next minute it was evident to all of them that it was Kate Lindisfarn, who was about to attempt descending the cliff to the child by the same path by which the latter had reached her present position of danger; who *was* attempting it rather; for, without any hesitation or pause, she began descending among the bushes.

Yes, it was Kate sure enough! Her light-blue silk dress was distinguishable enough and was unmistakable.

"No, no! Back, go back!" screamed Lady Farnleigh with the utmost power of her voice, and striving to enforce her words by waving signals with her hands. But Kate paid no attention to the warning, if she heard or observed it.

"O God! she will be killed! she will be killed!" screamed Lady Farnleigh, in an agony of distress.

"Let her try it, God bless her!" cried Mr. Mat from the cloister wall, with much emotion; "Kate has a sure foot and a steady eye. She is Sillshire, Kate is!"

"Wait till I can join you, Miss Lindisfarn! Wait a moment!" shouted Captain Ellingham, as loud as he could. "Tell her," he added to those below, "for God's sake, to wait a minute till I can get to her!" and he hastened up the ladder.

Kate, however, either did not hear or did not pay any attention to any of the entreaties or warnings or advice screamed out to her, but continued her way down the cliff in a direct line to the spot where the little girl was clinging.

It thus became a sort of race which would reach the child first; and as Ellingham at the top of the ladder, and Kate descending the cliff, neared one another, they came within easy speaking distance of each other and of the object of their exertions.

The last step from the ladder to the face of the cliff was an exceedingly difficult one to make—was indeed more of the nature of a jump from the ladder into a bush, with the necessity of instantly on reaching it taking means with both hands and feet for retaining a position on the face of the cliff. None but a man of tried nerve, and sure of himself and of the perfection of the service he might expect at need from all his limbs, would have dreamed of attempting it. By none whatsoever could it be done without extreme danger. Kate had reached the spot where the child was, and had already clutched her arm with one hand while she held on to a bush above her with the other, before Ellingham had made this desperate jump; and she called to him not to attempt it.

"Don't risk it, Captain Ellingham, there is no need! I can get back with her to the top very well. It is all easy, after this first bit is passed. Go down the ladder, for Heaven's sake! and send somebody round to meet me at the top of the cliff."

"No, no! I can jump it! I can't let you risk clambering to the top without help. It is one thing to make your own way, and quite another to drag another person with you. Here goes!"—

"Oh, don't do it!" shrieked Kate, hiding her eyes with her hand. But in the next instant the spring had been made, and he was standing clinging to the bushes in comparative safety by her side. A shout from those on the lawn below, and a special hurrah from Mr. Mat, showed the interest with which Ellingham's progress had been watched. His success, moreover, besides securing his own safety, was a tolerably sufficient guarantee for that of Kate, and the child whose danger had caused so much trouble and distress; for it was pretty clear that the man who had accomplished the feat of activity that they had just witnessed, would not fail in the far easier task of assisting his two charges to the summit in safety.

And then, with very few words between them, save such as were needed for directing them to place a foot here, and grasp a twig there, and one or two little attempts on Kate's part at protesting against Ellingham's determination to place himself, as they struggled upward, between them and the precipice, so that he might have a chance of repairing the mishap of a slip of the foot, or the failure of a hand grasp, the three of them reached the top in safety.

Then, indeed, there were words to be said. There was the frightened child to be interrogated in the first place. It appeared that the case was exactly as Mr. Mat had guessed it. The pet lamb had straggled over the brow, gradually finding its way down the steep among the herbage; and the child had wandered after it, almost equally unconscious of the danger she was approaching, till the increasing steepness of the slope, and the crumbling of the soil under her feet, and the impossibility of retracing her steps, revealed it to her.

A few minutes after they had reached the top, Mr. Merriton, breathless, and the gardener came up. The former threw himself down on the ground as soon as he saw them; it was very evident that he had done his utmost to reach the spot in time.

"Oh, Miss Lindisfarn! What a relief it is to see you in safety! Captain Ellingham, I congratulate you; but I cannot help envying you your good fortune!" he panted out.

And then they returned at their leisure to the Friary, taking the little girl with them as their prize and proof of their prowess.

And Kate admitted, in going down the steep path on the Silverton side of the cliff to the water-meadows, that an arm would be acceptable to her; and the path was difficult enough to make her sensible that she had a very firm one supporting her, as they returned to the friends who were so anxiously awaiting them.

It is not necessary to set forth in detail how, during the rest of the afternoon, the adventure of the Cliff pushed the projected antiquarian investigations aside, somewhat to the disgust of the two seniors of the party,—how Kate and Captain Ellingham were (to speak in Twelfth-night phraseology) king and queen of the evening,—or how Margaret and Fred Falconer discreetly kept themselves as much as possible in the background, sufficiently consoled for that position by the fact of occupying it together.

It will be enough to state that, though Mr. Frederick was exceedingly well pleased to have made such progress, and so coupled himself with the Lindisfarn co-heiress as to make him feel tolerably sure in his enterprise, and though he was genuinely and honestly much attracted by the beauty which, during the little comedy of the afternoon, Margaret had submitted to his attention under a variety of interesting circumstances and combinations,—nevertheless, he was very sensible of the cost at which he had bought this success as regarded the heiress; and he was not pleased with her for having been the cause of his making but a sorry figure before the rest of the assembled party.

Might not he also, just as easily as Merriton, have run to the top of the cliff and played a creditable part, without troubling himself with the danger of descending it?

As for Captain Ellingham, it may be said that, before leaving the Friary, he had become entirely convinced that he was, or rather, had been, the goose which Lady Farnleigh had called him, and was very earnestly purposed to be so no more.

Kate for her part was somewhat silent and thoughtful as she returned in the carriage to the Chase; and part of her thoughts were that her godmamma had been well within the mark when she had characterized the Silverton *arbiter elegantiarum* in a word of four letters. She began to fear indeed that it would need six; and one of them a double-u to do it rightly.

THAT gathering at the Friary for archæological purposes, which were so little served by it, was a memorable one to several of the persons who had been present at it.

It was very memorable to little Dinah Wilkins, the child who had so nearly come to grief on the Nosey Stone, and whose indiscretion in straying thither had produced—as indiscretions will—so much trouble, and so many consequences, to people with whom it would have seemed that she and her indiscretions could have had so little to do. She turned out to be a granddaughter of old Granny Wilkins, at Weston, Lady Farnleigh's old pensioner, very well known to that lady and to Kate, and a still greater object of interest therefore to the latter, as soon as, in the progress of that heroic descent of the face of the cliff, she had got near enough to her to recognize her. It was a memorable day to little Dinah Wilkins, not only from the fright, the danger, the minutes of mortal anguish—hours they had seemed to her—during which she had been expecting to slip from her precarious position, and be dashed to instant death, every moment; not only from the incidents of that wonderful rescue by the exertions of the gentlefolks, the history of which, and the interest attending it, made the cottage of old Granny Wilkins a centre of attraction to half Weston for days afterward; but memorable also from the permanent influence the circumstances exercised in shaping the future course and destinies of the child's after-life, in a manner which may, perhaps, be told in a future chapter—or which possibly may not find any place for telling in the course of this narrative, seeing that, though they were curiously mixed up with the subsequent history of several of our *dramatis personæ*, they are not essentially necessary to the understanding of the main thread of the narrative.

The archæological meeting *manqué* was also a memorable day to Arthur Merriton. The incidents of it acquired for him a place in the Sillshire social world and in Sillshire opinion, which the peculiarities of his character and position might otherwise perhaps have been slow to win for him. Captain Ellingham perceived and said that he was "a fellow of the right sort!" Mr. Mat declared that he had the true stuff and the

making of a Sillshire man in him. Lady Farnleigh said it was a great mistake to suppose that real manliness of character, and all the best qualities generally included in the term, were only to be found allied with one class of idiosyncrasies and one set of habits and pursuits, or were incompatible with nervous shyness and dreaminess of manner and mind. And she unreservedly admitted to Kate that this second admirer of hers was not a prig, nor anything describable by any such obnoxious four letters. And the good opinion of Lady Farnleigh and Mr. Mat, operating both separately in different spheres, and also with mutually corroborating force in the same sphere, could go a long way toward making a good position for a man in Silverton and its neighborhood. But what was the use of being recognized to be a fellow of the right sort, and to have the true stuff in him, to a man who, for his own part, recognized only this,—that he was desperately in love, and that there was very little or no hope for him. And that was the frame of mind in which Arthur Merriton had walked down from the top of the Weston Cliff to his own beautiful house at the foot of it, with the gardener and little Dinah Wilkins following behind him, and Kate Lindisfarn and Captain Ellingham, arm in arm, in front.

It was characteristic of the man, that he perceived at once, or imagined that he perceived, that his case was hopeless. Many a man would not have admitted for himself, or judged for another that it was, or ought to have been so. All that large and potent class of considerations, which have so great and often so paramount a share in managing Hymen's affairs, and which make Dan Cupid laugh at his business-like brother Godship for always going about with a parchment deed under his arm, and a pen stuck behind his ear—all considerations of that sort were entirely in Merriton's favor. Of course his eyes were opened as to Falconer's business at the Chase, and his chances of winning the hand of Kate Lindisfarn. But this view of misery had only dissolved itself to make way for the appearance of a succeeding view, as terrible, and more substantial. Ellingham was evidently the rival he had to fear. Old Mr. Falconer might talk and nod and smile meaningly to the end of time if he pleased; but after that arrival at the top of the cliff together, with Dinah Wilkins in their joint charge, and that walking down into the valley arm in arm, as they returned from their joint exploit, Arthur Merriton judged it to be a hopeless case. He knew that Ellingham was a very poor man; that Miss Lindisfarn was an heiress of no small mark and position; that his own status in the matter of fortune was such as in the opinion of a prudent father might justify him in pretending to her hand. He knew—I suppose—that he was a very good-looking fellow. Many girls —young ones chiefly of the sentimental sort, who admire " sallow, sublime sort of Werther-faced " men—would have considered him a much handsomer man than Captain Ellingham. He was well educated, cultivated, gentlemanlike, and could read Dante with Kate, which Captain Ellingham could not. And Kate liked reading Dante, and that sort of thing, too. But Merriton judged all this to be of no avail; and deemed his love hopeless. " Faint heart never won fair lady ! " says the proverb—half-true, keeping its promise to the ear and breaking it to the sense like a Sibylline oracle, as is the wont of such utterances of the wisdom of ages. I think I have seen the faint heart win, when the confident one was nowhere! But it all depends on what it is that is to be won. You may catch gudgeons with bait that wont do for trout. Fred Falconer in Merriton's place would not have deemed the matter hopeless, nor have given up the game. But if Ellingham had been at the bottom of the sea—having reached that destination, it is to be understood, before, not after, that memorable archæological party—I think the fainter heart would have had the better chance of winning the fair lady.

Arthur Merriton, however, being Arthur Merriton and not Frederick Falconer, did feel, as he walked down behind Kate and Ellingham, that it was a hopeless case; and, it may be feared, did not feel in a particularly affectionate frame of mind toward little Dinah Wilkins whom he had toiled so hard to preserve.

To Captain Ellingham the day was an especially memorable day. It is more than forty years ago, and the gallant captain was on the wrong side of thirty at the time; but he has not forgotten that day, not any smallest detail of the incidents of it, yet! To him also it was a day of a great unsealing of the eyes. If his destiny had been so malignant as to have accorded him at once his heart's desire, and thrown the lovely Margaret, the " most beautiful creature he had ever seen in his life," into his arms as soon as his eye had fallen in love with her ! If there had been no fairy godmother to tell him that he was a goose, and knew nothing about the matter, and he had been allowed to follow his own blind fancies—to think of the wreck ! But what about the matter as it stood now? As to the two girls—" Lombard street to a China orange ! " as people used to say in those days. There could be no doubt about it, as he saw the matter now, that Kate was not only, as Lady Farnleigh declared she was, the finer girl of the two, by daylight, but the noblest-hearted, the bravest—(it is a mistake, *royez vous, Mesdames*, to suppose that any man, except one whose weakness inclines him to mate with something weaker still, admires a woman for being cowardly ; so you may as well dispense with all those little tricks and prettinesses, the scope of which is to make it evident that your nerves are not equal to meeting a mouse in single combat)—the truest—he would have said the jolliest, but that the vigor and aptitude of that expression as applied to a young lady, had not been discovered by that backward and slow generation— the best, the dearest girl in all creation. That was a fact never more to be disputed or doubted, clear as the sun at noonday.

But what then? How did that very evident fact—evident to others as well as to him, unfortunately—interest him? Was it to be supposed that the co-heiress to the Lindisfarn estates would be permitted to marry a man, who, despite the noble blood in his veins, and the aristocratic prefix to his name, was absolutely dependent for his bread on a profession, which had hitherto afforded him so little of that necessary article? That animal Falconer, who had been intimate with them all his life, was, as far as fortune went, in a position to calculate on the approbation of the lady's family. There might be a hope, perhaps indeed a lurking conviction, at the bottom of his heart, that Kate was not the girl to give her heart to such a man as Mr. Frederick Falconer. But then there was Merriton ; a gentleman, a real good fellow, a man of fortune, a much better looking fellow, as Captain Ellingham reflected again and again, than he was, far more calculated by his education and pursuits to adapt himself to one side of Kate's character and tastes; and it was plain to see that he was desperately smitten with her. Captain Ellingham went over all these considerations carefully and dispassionately, as he thought, while he sat the following night? long after he ought to have turned into his cot, by the light of a smoky lamp, in the not very magnificent cabin of His Majesty's revenue cutter, the *Petrel*. And he, too, though few braver or bolder men stepped a deck in the English navy, was faint-hearted in this matter of winning an heiress.

In fact, if an elderly gentleman *qui mores hominum multorum vidit et urbes* — which means, "who has observed the loves and the love-making of many men and women" — might have the pleasant privilege of whispering a word of counsel in a transparent pink little ear, he would say, "Give that faint-heart-and-fair-lady proverb the lie; and of two aspirants, incline rather, *cæteris paribus* (which, being translated, means, supposing both of them to possess a similar number of thousands a year, and an equally heroic outline of face), to give the preference to the faint-hearted over the confident-hearted swain."

Captain Ellingham *was*, as has been said, faint-hearted in this matter, and dared not allow himself to believe that Kate Lindisfarn, so beautiful, so much admired, so gay, so light-hearted, so fancy-free, with every right to look forward to a brilliant position in life, could be brought to think for an instant of *him*, a rough sailor, hardly a young man in the eyes of a girl in her teens, with a rough brown face, tanned and bronzed and hardened by exposure to wind and weather; at odds with fortune, too, and not the better fitted for shining in drawing-rooms, or winning the ear of youth and beauty, by the discipline of his long tussle with that fickle jade. Pooh, pooh! what had he to do with falling in love with heiresses in their teens? *That* was his proper place (namely, the sufficiently dull and dreary-looking cabin of his cutter), and his profession the only mistress he should think of wooing.

And Kate? Was the day of the archæological visit to the Friary a memorable one to her also? Fancy-free, Captain Ellingham had called her, in his mental survey of all the conditions of the case that made up his hopelessness. *Was* she so wholly fancy-free? The amount and extent of fancy captivity which could be predicated of her in the case of Fred Falconer has been explained, with, it is hoped, sufficient care to avoid representing it to have been more than it really was. But how about it *now*? That day of archæological investigation, if it had eventually failed to finally settle the great question of the date of the Friary washhouse, had, nevertheless, done much toward the investigation of some other things. It had been a great day for the unsealing of blinded eyes. Several persons saw several things clearly which they had never seen before. And I think we may say that thenceforward Kate was fancy-free as regarded Freddy Falconer. He had both done and left undone much which had contributed to this result. And Kate was safely enough off with the old—no, I must not say that. The cautious old proverb does not hit the case. Besides, it would insinuate what I have no right to insinuate at this stage of Kate's history.

Still all this beating about the bush does not answer the question whether Kate Lindisfarn was fancy-free from and after that day at the Friary?

Well! It is so difficult to be categorical in such matters. Merriton, who walked behind her and Ellingham, as they returned from the top of the cliff, had a strong opinion upon the subject. I am sure he would have boxed his own ears rather than have suffered them to catch a word of conversation that was not intended for them. Yet he *did* form a very strong opinion. But then, on the other hand, he was very far from being an impartial observer. It is certain that Kate was remarkably and, for her, singularly silent and abstracted as they returned in the carriage to the Chase; for Mr. Mat told Lady Farnleigh afterward that, finding that Kate would not talk, and not feeling any inclination to talk with Margaret, with whom he had been not a little disgusted in the course of the day, he had pretended to go to sleep, but had remained quite awake to the fact that hardly a word passed between the sisters on their way home.

And then again, judging from the sequel, if it did not date from that day, we know that it was there soon after.

What was where?

Pshaw! You know what I mean. There

is no doubt that she was fond of him during that ensuing winter, I suppose.

Ah! but in these heart histories chronology is everything. Let us be chronological, whatever we are. Was Kate Lindisfarn fancy-free when, having assisted Ellingham in getting little Dinah Wilkins to the top of the cliff, and being assisted by him in getting herself up, and having exchanged congratulations, etc., and panted in unison when the top was reached, and having walked down by the steep path arm in arm back again to the Friary, and having, with all due mutual self-denegations, and "No! it was you, who," and "Don't you remember?" and so forth, shared between them the applause and hero-worship of the rest of the party during the remainder of the evening, they separated with not unmeaning touch of palm to palm at parting—was Kate fancy-free *then*, I say? That is the question.

Well, we know what girls are. It has been said, "Tell me who your friends are, and I will tell you what you are." And it might with quite as much truth be said, Tell me whom a girl falls in love with, and I will tell you what she is; or, *vice versâ*, Tell me what she is, and I will tell you with whom she is likely to fall in love. A pleasing exterior, a handsome face, and well-formed person, are naturally, and in accordance with superior arrangements, the wisdom of which we cannot and may not question, potent conciliators and attracters of woman's love. But there is no more significant symptom of the high level of moral character and nobility of heart prevailing among Englishwomen than the all but universality of the sentiment which makes an absence of these advantages, if compensated by a touch of heroism, more acceptable to them than any perfection of personal attraction in combination with a manifest deficiency of all heroism.

The quick sudden heart-beat; the violent ebb of the blood, which left the cheek deadly pale, to be succeeded in the next instant by a rush of the rich color to face and brow and neck; the mixture of exulting pleasure with the short, sharp agony of terror, which had caused Kate to shade her eyes with her hand, at the moment that Ellingham had made his desperate leap from the ladder to the bush on the cliff face beside her,—all this told of a sympathy between their two natures deeper and far more powerful than any such mere

liking and inclination as might have been produced by the ball-room wooing of the most faultless of Hyperions. And if exactitude of chronology in the matter of the birth of young love in this case be insisted on, my impression is that the register may, with the greatest chance of absolute accuracy, date from the moment when Captain Ellingham alighted in the bushes from that perilous jump.

Just as if any fellow would not jump into any bush for such a prize!

Yes, my ingenuous young British friends! There are plenty of you who would, and some who get the chance, and do such things. And a discriminating and appreciating public in crinoline and pork-pie hats does accordingly adore those of you who do them, and generously give credit for good intentions to those of you who don't get the chance of doing them. But somehow or other that—one would say upon the whole, perhaps, not specially profound—pork-pie-hatted public does, mark you, contrive most astonishingly to nose the hollow pretences of those few among you who, having the chance, would do nothing of the kind.

And then the party at Wanstrow came off. And Margaret had to be asked by the hostess in a clear and ringing voice, before all the assembled party, whether she had entirely recovered from her indisposition at the Friary. And Freddy had to be complimented as audibly upon the admirable skill and tact he had shown in managing and tending symptoms, which the habits and ways of the Silverton young ladies—doubtless by reason of the fine Sillshire air and climate—had probably never given him any opportunity of studying.

Lady Farnleigh took very good care upon this occasion that Ellingham should have Kate for his neighbor at dinner; and his inquiries about little Dinah Wilkins, and Kate's replies and her report of all the gratitude and the wonder and the blessings which she was charged to convey to him from old Dame Wilkins, and from the child's mother, made them feel like old friends, who had a variety of subjects in common between them. And then the sailing party had to be talked over. And Captain Ellingham explained that it was not so much the quantity as the quality of the wind that might make the excursion disagreeable to ladies. And he inquired how far

Kate would choose to brave the chance of a ducking, as the cutter was apt, under certain conditions, to be wet.

"As for being afraid of anything a capful of wind is likely to bring you, that I know I need not suspect you of, Miss Lindisfarn," said he; "but you may not like to get wet through with salt water. And what about the others?"

"Oh, Margaret will be ready whenever you give the word. I don't think she would mind a capful of wind, as you call it. Why do sailors always talk of caps full of wind?"

"I cannot tell what the origin of the term may have been; a corruption from some very different word, perhaps. But it is curious how nearly definite a quantity it signifies in nautical language."

"And what amount of trouble would a capful of wind give the *Petrel?*" asked Kate.

"Oh! no trouble at all, except to cause the helmsman a little extra vigilance and activity. The *Petrel* is a capital sea boat; but she is what we call lively, apt to jump about a good deal, and wet her decks when there is any sea; and that, you know, would not be pleasant for ladies."

"But then it comes pretty nearly to waiting for a calm; and there would be no fun in that. I should so much better like to make acquaintance with your pet *Petrel* when she is in one of her lively moods. What signifies a little wetting? One does not catch cold with salt water, they say; and we should come home and get dry."

"But you forget, Miss Lindisfarn, that I cannot answer for the movements of my *Petrel* with the certainty you can count on Birdie. We may go out with a wind and not be able to return quite so soon as we expect. I strongly recommend, especially if we are to take a windy day, that everybody should take a change of clothes with them."

"Yes, that would be the plan! And if we got kept out all night, what capital fun it would be! Do, pray, Captain Ellingham, let us choose a day when there is a capful of wind. I should so like to see the *Petrel* lively."

"Well, if Lady Farnleigh will consent, I have no objection. Only remember that wind is one of those good things that you may have too much of."

"Oh, what a very cautious and prudent man you are!"

"That is a high compliment to a sailor. Pray make that opinion known to my Lords of the Admiralty."

And Lady Farnleigh's consent was obtained for the selection of a day, when, if possible, without having too much of a good thing, the *Petrel* should be seen in one of her livelier moods. And the proposed excursion came off accordingly. And the *Petrel* retained sufficient discretion amid her liveliness to bring them all back to port before nightfall, although rather in a bedraggled condition, as Captain Ellingham had predicted. And Kate had rendered him more desperately in love with her than ever by the intoxication of high spirits with which she had enjoyed her sail. She declared that it was glorious, and she was almost inclined to think even better than being on Birdie, when she was at her liveliest.

And thus—sometimes in one way, and sometimes in another, sometimes at Lindisfarn, sometimes at Wanstrow, sometimes at the Friary, and once or twice in Silverton—all the members of the little circle with whom the reader has been made acquainted saw a good deal of each other during the remainder of the autumn months, and through the winter. But as the only net result of all this was to render more definite, clear, and palpable to themselves and to the friends around them those relations of the parties to each other which were foreshadowed by the previous intercourse between them, and which the judicious reader has already distinguished spinning themselves out of the filaments of fate in the *chiaro-oscuro* of the future, it will not be necessary to follow with historical accuracy all the pleasant processes of this destiny-spinning.

It will be sufficient for our purpose to present a brief and succinct, but accurate, report of the state of the warp and woof which had been produced, by the time when the birds begin to sing, by all the sailing and riding and walking and talking and dancing and laughing and pleasant intercourse of all kinds which go to the spinning of fate's filaments in this department of human affairs.

Frederick Falconer, like a sensible and businesslike man, who, when he has made a resolution, acts up to it, had consistently carried out the programme he had drawn up for himself. Forsaking all others, he had steadily set himself to the work of winning Margaret

Lindisfarn. And that work had to all appearance progressed satisfactorily, not only to the principals themselves, but to the lookers-on at the game. We have obtained a sufficient peep into the sanctuary of Kate's heart to assure us that her whilom admirer's far more declared and evident homage to her sister awakened no shadow of jealousy or pain there. Lady Farnleigh's declaration that Freddy Falconer might make love to any girl in the county, for aught she cared, provided he did not do so to her goddaughter, seemed to include her goddaughter's sister in its license. The young gentleman stood well, as has been said, in the Silverton public estimation ; the old banker was well known to be a very warm man ; and there appeared to be no reasons of any sort why Miss Lindisfarn's family should not consider that his only son was a very proper match in all respects for one of the co-heiresses. Mr. Frederick's own sentiments on the matter we are already in possession of. As to those of Margaret a greater degree of reticence and more reserve are proper in handling the delicate topic of a young lady's feelings upon such a subject. Nevertheless, perhaps the judicious reader may have acquired a sufficient insight into Miss Margaret's idiosyncrasy to enable him to estimate pretty accurately the state of her feelings and the nature of her views. There can be no harm in saying that she really did like Frederick very much. She thought him very agreeable and very handsome. But it will of course be understood—at least by those who are conversant with the system on which Margaret had been educated, and with the results of it on the development of docile and well-disposed pupils—that it would have appeared to her the height of unworthiness, and even of indelicacy, to permit such feelings and considerations to stand in the way of her transferring her affections to a worthier object,—say a wealthy peer of the realm, or a commoner with a hundred thousand a year,—should such a one present himself before the final adjudication of the prize.

As to Kate—what can be said ? The subject is a less pleasing one, both for the veracious historian to set forth, and for the well-regulated mind of the reader to contemplate. A right-minded heroine, who has any claim to the title, and behaves herself as such, never allows herself, as we all know, to feel the slightest preference for any individual of the other sex until she has received a declaration of love and demand for her hand in due form. Then and thereupon, she may, if she think fit, forthwith feel and acknowledge the tender passion in any degree of intensity. The " popping of the question " is supposed to act, in short, like the opening of an Artesian well, through which, when it has once reached the secret reservoir of the still waters, hidden from every eye, deep, deep away below the surface, they rush forth with impetuosity and in the most copious abundance. Till that last bit of the lover's work has been accomplished, no sign of the living water rewards his toil. This is the true and correct theory of love, as practised and understood by the most authorized heroines.

But poor Kate's education had not, unhappily, been such as efficiently to prepare her for the vocation. She was impetuous, we know. She was apt to permit the consciousness of a pure and guileless heart to hurry her into a practice of following its dictates, without waiting to compare them, as she should have done, with the text of the laws made and provided for the regulation of a heroine's sentiments.

In short,—for the truth must come out, sooner or later,—by the time the spring came, Kate was thoroughly in love with Captain Ellingham, though he had said no word of love to her. Not but that she had kept her own secret so well that he had no suspicion of it ; whereas he had by no means been equally successful in keeping his. Women are more lynx-eyed in these matters than men. Though she would not allow it even to her own self in the secrecy of her maiden meditations, at the bottom of her heart there was a consciousness and a persevering little voice that would not be silenced, which told her she was loved.

And she was happy with a very perfect happiness in the consciousness of it, although he had spoken no word, and although she was perfectly aware of the bearings of that businesslike aspect of the matter, which to him seemed a well-nigh insuperable barrier between them. She knew perfectly well her own position and the value of it. She knew his position ; and felt upon the subject as a loving woman in such circumstances does feel. Nor did she conceive that there was any great difficulty to be overcome in the matter. She had no doubt that it would all come right.

Was there not the fairy godmother, who saw it all, of course, though she said nothing, and understood it all?

And as for Ellingham himself? His part in this stage of the drama was a less happy one. He had suffered himself to become irremediably engrossed by a passion which he greatly feared must be a hopeless one. And the sort of manner and tone and conduct which his fear caused him to impose on himself toward Kate would have either puzzled, or offended, or pained a girl more on the lookout for flirtations, more on the *qui vive* to watch for the manifestations of admiration and the results of it, either for the encouragement or discouragement of them—more self-conscious, in a word, than Kate was in this matter.

And yet, notwithstanding Ellingham's fears and discouragements, it was impossible for him not to perceive a difference in Kate's manner toward him and toward Arthur Merriton. But with self-tormenting perverseness, he told himself that this was only caused by poor Merriton's assiduous and unconcealed admiration. It was plain enough there was no hope for him; and that Kate found it necessary to show him as much. Probably, if Merriton were as cautious and self-restrained in his manner toward her as he himself was, her tone toward him would be as frankly friendly as it was toward himself.

And thus is completed, I think, the *carte de tendre* as laid down from a survey of the hearts of the principal members of our *dramatis personæ* in the early spring of the year following Margaret Lindisfarn's return to her paternal home.

CHAPTER XVI.
WINIFRED PENDLETON.

On one evening of the March of that spring, Lady Farnleigh and Captain Ellingham had been dining, and were about to sleep, at the Chase. Notwithstanding that matters between Kate and Walter Ellingham must be considered, as appears from the general survey and report made in the last chapter, to have been in a less advanced and less satisfactory position than those of Margaret and Fred Falconer, nevertheless, it had come to pass that Ellingham was on terms of greater intimacy with the other members of the family at the Chase, and was a more frequent visitor there, than Falconer. This had no doubt

in some degree arisen from the circumstances which caused him often to be a sleeping as well as dining visitor at the house. There was no reason why Fred Falconer should sleep at the Chase. There was his home in Silverton between five and six miles off, his horse ready for him, and a good road all the way. And though it had been the habit, in old times,—that is to say, in the times before Margaret came home from Paris,—for him to be a frequent guest at the Chase, it had never been the practice for him to sleep there.

The case of Ellingham was different. He had no home save his ship, lying off in Sillmouth Roads. It was between eight and nine miles to the landing-place in Sillmouth harbor, and then there was a dark and most likely very rough row off to his ship at the end of that. Then, again, it had always been the practice, during many years, for Lady Farnleigh to sleep at the Chase after dining there in winter. And such visits were very apt to be prolonged to a second and a third day or more. Lady Farnleigh was the solitary inhabitant of the fine large house up at Wanstrow, and it was very lonely and very dreary and very storm-blown up there in winter. It was much pleasanter to spend a long winter's evening in the cheery pleasant drawing-room at the Chase, amid the sociable family circle there. And though occasionally Kate went to stay for a few days with her godmother, and sometimes, but more rarely, the whole family party at the Chase were induced to pass an evening at Wanstrow, by far the more common practice was for Lady Farnleigh to be staying in the house at Lindisfarn. And as Ellingham mostly came thither with her, and from the very close intimacy and friendship subsisting between them was naturally considered as belonging in some sort to her suite, it had followed that the same invitations and arrangements which made her so frequently an inmate of the house, had extended themselves naturally to him.

Then, again, he got on better with the other members of the family. Fred Falconer could hardly have been said to be much of a favorite there, except in one gentle breast. He was always a welcome guest, it is true. Of course he was, because he always had been so, from the time when he used to ride over on his little pony, with a servant walking by his side and holding the rein. His father was a much respected neighbor and old friend. Nobody had anything to say against Freddy himself. Of course he was a welcome guest. Miss Immy perfectly well remembered the days when she used to give him cake and cowslip wine, and other suchlike dainties in the housekeeper's room. And the squire had been accustomed to "only Freddy Falconer," for the last twenty years, and never felt that his presence entailed the least necessity for abstaining from his after-dinner nap. Nevertheless, it has been seen that Mr. Mat and he did not get on well together, and that Lady Farnleigh had a sort of prejudice against him. Curiously enough, too, another class,—on whose idiosyncrasies and likes and dislikes we are apt to speculate with much the same sort of curiosity with which we regard the ways and instincts of creatures of a different species, so cut off from all community of sentiment, and all intelligible interchange of idea and feeling are they,—the servants, did not like Freddy Falconer.

All these different people liked Ellingham. He and Mr. Mat had come to be hand and glove. Miss Immy had begun to think him real Sillshire. And thus it had come to pass that he had become more domesticated in the house, and more intimate with them all than Falconer, although the acquaintanceship of the latter had dated from so much earlier a period.

The same concatenation of circumstances, by the by, served in a great degree to account for the imprudence with which he had gone on during all the winter falling deeper and deeper and more inextricably in love with Kate. He had not, like Falconer, and like the young shopman who takes his sweetheart out for a walk on Sunday, gone on a love-making expedition with malice prepense, and self-conscious determination. He had been drifting into love, insensibly making lee-way, all the winter.

It was March; and both Ellingham and Lady Farnleigh had been staying for the last few days at the Chase. Falconer had dined there on the day before, and on the morrow Lady Farnleigh was to return to Wanstrow, and Captain Ellingham to his ship.

It was an exceedingly rough and boisterous night; and such weather was seasonable, for it was about the time of the equinox. The wind sighs a differently modulated song in woods of different kinds. Theocritus talks

of the sweet murmuring of the fir-tree; and Alexander Smith tells how

"Wind, the mighty harper, smote his thunder-harp of pines."

But there were no pines on Lindisfarn brow, though there were a few behind, and on the left side of the house. The long moaning, however, rising from time to time into a fierce provoked roar, which continued to encircle the house like a live thing piteously seeking an entrance,—this remonstrating moaning and angry roaring came from the oaks on Lindisfarn brow. The squire would be sure to be out the very first thing on the morrow morning, and up among his beloved woods on the brow to see what mischief had been caused by the storm. He would wince sometimes, as he sat in his chair of an evening, when the winds were keeping it up and making a night of it in the Lindisfarn woods, from a fellow-feeling for his trees, and sympathy with the torment they were undergoing from the tempest.

It was a night of that kind; and the squire and Captain Ellingham and Mr. Mat were sitting over their wine before a huge fire of logs in the low-roofed, oak-panelled, old-fashioned dining-room at the Chase, and the squire was lamenting the mischief that was being worked among his trees; and the captain was hoping that old Joe Saltash, his second in command on board the *Petrel*, had made all snug and was all right in Sillmouth harbor. The ladies had gone to the drawing-room. Miss Immy, scorning to lie down on the sofa, and sitting bolt upright on it, was nevertheless fast asleep, with her volume of "Clarissa Harlowe" by her side. Margaret was reading at one side of the table, and Lady Farnleigh and Kate were sitting on the opposite side of the fireplace to Miss Immy, and were talking together in low voices, when the servant came into the room, and said,—

"Please, Miss Kate, Mrs. Pendleton is here; and is very wishful to speak to you if you would be so kind. She's in the housekeeper's room."

"You don't mean to say, George, that Mrs. Pendleton has come up to the Chase, now, in this weather?"

"Yes, Miss; she has just come in. She says she was blowed away almost; but she aint none so wet. It's more wind than rain."

"Tell her I'll come to her directly, George. I suppose there is a good fire in the housekeeper's room?"

"Yes, miss."

"What can have brought her up to the Chase at this hour, and on such a night as this?" said Kate to Lady Farnleigh, as the man left the room.

"Some trouble or other, I suppose. I am not sure that I quite approve of your seeing so much of Mrs. Pendleton, and making such a pet of her as you do, Kate."

"Oh, I can't give up poor dear Winifred! It is out of the question," answered Kate.

"Well, no. I don't want you to give her up; you can hardly do that for auld lang syne sake. But I don't half like that husband of hers. Besides," added Lady Farnleigh, with an arch look at Kate, and a laugh in her eye, "however tolerant and willing to wink one may have been when one had no concern with the collection of His Majesty's customs, we are enlisted on the other side now, Kate!"

Kate laughed and colored, as she replied, "I don't know that I have changed sides at all. At all events, I must go now and see what Winifred wants."

Margaret had raised her eyes from her book while the above conversation had been passing, just sufficiently to have shown to anybody who had been watching her, that she had paid attention to it; but she made no remark on anything that had been said.

Winifred, it must be explained, had been Kate's nurse for many years. She was the daughter of an old forester in the squire's employment, to whose care his dearly loved woods were intrusted, who had passed a long life in the service of the squire and his father, and was a specially valued and favorite servant. Winifred Parker, the Lindisfarn forester's daughter, had been a very beautiful girl, when at eighteen she was engaged by the late Mrs. Lindisfarn as under nurse to her twins. Very shortly after that, three events happened. Mrs. Lindisfarn died, as we know. One of the twins, Margaret, was shortly afterward, as we also know, sent away to Paris. And very speedily after that, old John Parker, the forester, met with his death from the fall of a tree, which he was engaged in felling. He was not killed on the spot, but had been removed to his cottage, where the squire and Miss Immy and Mr. Mat, greatly grieving, had all of them

jointly and singly promised the dying man that his children (he was a widower, and had, beside Winifred, another daughter and a son) should be cared for, and not suffered to come to want. None of the three who had thus promised, were people at all likely to forget a promise given under such circumstances, or satisfy themselves with any grudging or merely perfunctory performance of it. The other children were well cared for, and Winifred, who had already made herself a favorite in the household, was retained, a greater favorite than ever, as special attendant on the little Kate.

In that position she had remained, endearing herself to all the family, and especially to her little charge, improving herself considerably in many respects, and giving perfect satisfaction to everybody who knew her, for between eleven and twelve years; that is to say, till she herself was thirty years old, till Kate was twelve, and till a period about six years previous to the date of the events that have been narrated in these pages.

To the entire satisfaction of everybody who knew her, I have written; and on the whole, such may fairly be said to have been the case. Yet during most of those years there had been one subject on which Winifred and her kind friends and protectors had differed. Even in this matter, however, she had been so reasonable, so good, so docile, that the difference, far from having caused any quarrel, had turned itself rather into a title the more to their affection and interest in her. Winifred had been a remarkably beautiful girl; and it is hardly necessary to say that this one subject of trouble arose from the source from which most of the troubles that assail pretty girls are apt to spring.

There was a certain Hiram Pendleton, respecting whom the pretty Winifred held the conscientious and wholly invincible opinion that he was in all respects the finest and noblest being that had ever stepped this sublunary globe. The family at the Chase thought that he was not so in all respects. That he was one of the finest in some, was very evident to all who looked at him. A handsomer presentation of a young sailor—Pendleton was a Sillmouth man, and that was his condition of life—it would have been difficult to conceive. Nor had the friends and protectors of Winifred anything very strong to urge against him in other respects. Still there was enough, they thought, to cause and justify their unwillingness to give into his keeping so great a prize and so precious a charge as their pretty and much petted Winifred.

In the first place, Hiram Pendleton had somewhat sunk in the social scale. Winifred was indignant that what was due to misfortune should be made a matter of reproach against her hero. To a certain degree, perhaps, she was right. Perhaps not altogether so. Hiram's father had been a boat-owner; but somehow or other the son had fallen from that position, and had been constrained, or had chosen (he and Winifred said the latter), to make one or two voyages before the mast. He was, at all events, such an A. B. that he could at any time command his pick of employment in such a capacity. But he was said to be "wild;" and I am afraid the truth is that pretty girls—even those who are as good as Winifred Parker was—are apt to prefer wild men to tame ones; just as I do ducks, and for the same reason,—that there is more flavor about them.

And then again there were rumors as to the not altogether avowable nature of the voyages in which Pendleton had been engaged. One thing, however, was certain; and it outweighed a whole legion of facts, even if they had been authentically ascertained ones, on the other side of the question, in Winifred's opinion. And this undeniable truth was that every time he had returned to Sillmouth, he had again and again urged his suit with indefatigable perseverance and constancy. Winifred was only two-and-twenty when Hiram Pendleton first fell in love with her; and she was nearly thirty before she accepted him. And all that time she had been in love with him; and all that time she had waited, and made him wait, in obedience to the wishes and advice of her friends at the Chase; and all that time Pendleton had been constant.

He did more to win his love besides showing himself a pattern of constancy. He manifested signs of becoming a steady and reformed character. He came home from his last voyage with a good bit of money, and announcing his intention to go no more a-roaming, he invested his savings in the purchase of a neat fishing smack and tackle, and settled himself as a scot and lot paying inhabitant of Sillmouth.

Could any Jacob serve more faithfully for his Rachel?

In fact, Winifred Parker's friends did not feel themselves justified in any longer resisting the match. If Hiram Pendleton's start in life had been somewhat amiss, he had amended it and reformed. If all the parts of the career by which he had reached his present position could not bear close scrutiny, that position was at all events now a respectable and responsible one. And, as Winifred Parker often said, and yet more often thought to herself, such constancy as Hiram had shown in his courtship of her was rarely to be matched. So the marriage took place at last, with the still somewhat reluctantly given consent of the Lindisfarn family, when Winifred was at least old enough to know her own mind; for she was upon the verge of thirty. She had, however, lost none of her remarkable beauty; for it was real beauty, and not mere prettiness; no *beauté du diable*, to disappear with the evanescent bloom of girlhood, but the more durable handsomeness arising from fine and regular features, perfect health, and admirably well-developed figure. Winifred Parker had been one of those pretty girls, who, having in them the promise of perfect womanhood, can hardly be said to have reached their culminating point of loveliness till that has been attained.

She was between five and six and thirty, and had become the mother of two fine boys and a girl, at the time when she presented herself on the stormy night in question at the old house in which she had passed, so happily, the best years of her life. But it would have been difficult to meet with a handsomer woman of her sort than Winifred Pendleton was and looked, after her walk up from Silverton to the Chase that stormy night.

She was, as the servant had said, not very wet; for the storm was as yet more of wind than of rain. But of the former there was enough to increase very considerably the fatigue of a stout walker, and to produce a glow and redness of coloring in her cheeks, which somewhat exaggerated the always healthy and fresh-colored appearance of them. Her bright black eye, beaming with shrewdness, intelligence, and energy, was not so large as beautiful eyes are often seen in individuals of the Celtic and Latin races, and not unfrequently in favorable specimens of the high-bred classes of our own much-mixed blood. The dark eyes of the large liquid type, such eyes as Margaret Lindisfarn's, are rarely seen among those classes of our population which represent with least admixture the Saxon element of our ancestry.

A great abundance of glossy, but not very fine black hair, blown into considerable disorder by her walk through the storm, added to her appearance that grace of picturesqueness, which belongs, by prescription, to gypsies, and suchlike members of the anti-scot-and-lot-paying classes, but which is hardly compatible with the demureness of thorough respectability. The large mouth was one of great beauty and sweetness. Any child or dog would have unhesitatingly accorded implicit trust and affection to the owner of it. The tall figure, with its well and fully-developed bust, round and lithe but not too slender waist, and its general expression of springy, elastic strength and agility, was the very perfection of womanhood,—a sculptor's model for an Eve.

But why did Lady Farnleigh suppose at once that trouble of some sort was the cause of Mrs. Pendleton's visit to the Chase? And why did she disapprove of Kate's closeness of intimacy with so old, so meritorious, and so well-loved an humble friend of her family? And what was the meaning of her joking, but not the less seriously meant, allusion to the collection of His Majesty's revenue, and to the share which Captain Ellingham had in the due accomplishment of that collection?

The truth was, in one word, that the Honorable Captain Ellingham, commanding His Majesty's revenue cutter *Petrel*, and Hiram Pendleton, were enlisted on opposite sides in the great and permanent quarrel arising out of that matter of collecting His Majesty's revenue. Pendleton, the bold and able seaman,—not unacquainted, if all tales were true, with lawbreaking in the course of his professional career, the capitalist in possession of a fishing smack and nets, and a small sum into the bargain, safely stowed away (not in Messrs. Falconer and Fishbourne's books), had been led into embarking his courage, his seamanship, and his capital in the then promising and tempting profession of a smuggler. And it is not to be understood

that the pretty Winifred either put her apron to her eyes, or gave any other indication of considering herself an unfortunate and miserable woman, or went with whining who-would-have-thought-it complaints to her friends at the Chase, or with a long face to the parson, the magistrate, or any other authority whatsoever, or went to the dogs. Hiram Pendleton had been as constant a husband as he had been a lover. He was as much in love with his wife, and she with him, after some six years of marriage, as they had been for the six years before it. And under these circumstances, if Hiram had thought fit to levy war against the sacred person of Majesty itself, instead of only against Majesty's revenue, Winifred would have stuck to him and backed him.

Nor must it be supposed that, in those days of oppressive and excessive custom duties, the trade and position of the bold smuggler was regarded by any class of the public quite in the same light as it is in our better-instructed, more legality-loving, and more politico-economical times. Although, of course, persons in the position of Lady Farnleigh and Squire Lindisfarn could not but disapprove of the smuggler's trade, shake their heads at his doings, and seriously lament that their former misgivings with regard to Pendleton should have been thus justified, there was, even in their sphere, no very strong repugnance to the man or his illegal enterprises; and Winifred's old friends, when Mr. Mat would from time to time come home from Silverton or Sillmouth with some story of a successfully run cargo, were apt, though with due and proper protest and disavowal, to feel more sympathy with the bold and fortunate smuggler than with His Majesty's defrauded revenue.

Kate had been always specially daring and outspoken in her illegal sympathies, protesting loudly that smuggling was as fair on one side as the press-gang on the other; that one was no more wrong than the other; that those who pulled the longest faces were ready enough to buy a French silk dress or keg of French brandy; and that, for her part, she was not going to give up dear old Winifred for all the custom-house officers in the kingdom. And so a very considerable amount of friendship and intercourse had been kept up between Kate and her old nurse, notwithstanding that the latter had become a daring smuggler's wife; and though the young lady's visits—generally accompanied by Mr. Mat, whose sympathies and moralities upon the subject were quite as faulty as Kate's—though the visits, I say, to Mrs. Pendleton's pretty and picturesque cottage under the rocks at the far end of Sillmouth sands were generally made, and understood to be made, when the master of it was away, it had nevertheless occurred that a bow, returned by no unfriendly nod on the part of the fair lady, had more than once passed between her and the owner of Deepereek Cottage.

In a word, the family at the Chase, and Kate more especially, had determined not to give up their old and much-valued protégé, notwithstanding the regretable, but in those times and those latitudes not unpardonable and not very severely reprobated, courses into which her husband had fallen. And an amount of toleration and even sympathy for Mrs. Pendleton's family interests and prosperities and adversities, had been felt and even professed by Kate (who was apt to profess all she felt on most subjects), greater than perhaps might have been the case if the young lady had been better aware of all that the life and pursuits of a smuggler involve and may lead to; and at the same time an amount of winking at illegalities, which they were bound to discountenance, had been practised by the elder and more responsible members of the family, which worshipful and law-abiding people in this improved age of the world's history will perhaps consider as scarcely justifiable or prudent.

And now came new circumstances, which had a tendency to complicate these relationships. It was quite clear that between Captain Ellingham and Hiram Pendleton there could be neither truce nor toleration. And, as Lady Farnleigh said, " they "—that is, she and her goddaughter, and the rest of the family at the Chase—were now enlisted on the other side. As her ladyship had also remarked, when first speaking to Kate of Walter Ellingham, it was bad to be a smuggler on the Sillshire coast, when the *Petrel* and her commander were on duty on that station. And it was likely to be difficult to cultivate friendly relations with both parties.

And now what, under these circumstances, could Mrs. Pendleton want this stormy night up at the Chase?

CHAPTER XVII.
A HARD, HARD TASK!

KATE found Mrs. Pendleton waiting for her in the housekeeper's room, a little snuggery looking out on the back of the house, toward the woods therefore, which came down to within a short distance of the mansion on that side, and toward the high forest-covered ground of Lindisfarn brow. So that on this side of the house the moaning and roaring of the storm-wind was yet more loudly heard than in the front. But though the casements rattled and shook as if every now and then they were assailed by a sudden push from the outside, the little room was cheerful with a bright fire; and Mrs. Pendleton had been already supplied with a steaming pot of tea, and a plate of bread and butter.

" Why, Winifred ? " cried Kate, bursting into the room through the door, much as the wind was striving to do at the opposite window; " what in the world brings you up to the Chase on such a night as this ? What a walk you must have had ! "

" 'Tis a terrible night, Miss Kate, sure enough ; not for them as is safe and snug on shore. I think nothing of the walk, though the wind does blow off the brow up here enough to take one off one's legs. But it must be an awful night at sea ! "

" Where is Pendleton ? " asked Kate.

" Over the other side, and safe in harbor at this time, I hope, Miss Kate. But he'll be coming across to-morrow night; and they wont ask no better than a spell of this same weather ; for the night's as dark as pitch, and they are not afeard of wind, you know, miss."

" It would be on the quarter in coming over, as the wind is now ; would it not ? " asked the young lady.

" Yes, and that's one of the lugger's best points. Only there is a little too much of it. But if the wind lasts, or if there is any wind at all that will any ways serve to make the coast with, they will be coming over to-morrow night, sure enough."

" Don't you wish the job was done, and the lugger lying asleep under the Benniton Head rock, and Hiram safe and dry in the cottage ? "

" Where's the use of wishing, Miss Kate ? I might spend my life at it. When I was first married to a sailor,—let alone one as the wind isn't his worst trouble !— I thought I'd never sleep through a dark night again, and felt every puff of wind as if the belaying pins was fixed in my heart. But one gets used to it. But I *do* wish, Miss Kate," she added, looking with earnest eyes into Miss Lindisfarn's face, " that the job was over this time! I do wish it! "

" Is it anything more than usual? " asked Kate, with a glance toward the door, and in a lower tone than before.

" Well, Miss Kate, to come out with it, at once,—for I know we can trust you, and it's over late now to begin having secrets between you and me,—that is what brings me up to Lindisfarn this night."

" What do you mean, Winifred? Is there any trouble? " asked Kate, in a sympathizing manner.

" I'll tell you what it is, Miss Kate," said the smuggler's wife, who had thrown off her cloak, and rising to her feet as she spoke, came one step nearer to the spot at which Kate was standing at the opposite side of the housekeeper's little tea-table, for she had not taken a seat on coming into the room,—" I'll tell you what it is, Miss Kate. If I do not succeed in preventing it by my walk up here to-night, there *will* be trouble, as sure as the trees are troubling in the storm on Lindisfarn brow this night? "

" What can you mean, Winifred? and what can your walk up here to-night have to do with it? " asked Kate, who was beginning to feel a little alarm at the woman's manner.

" It's a big job that's to come off to-morrow night. There's some strange hands in it. The venture is as much as some on them is worth in the world. And, Miss Kate," added Winifred, speaking in a solemn manner, and with special emphasis, while she looked with a fixed and determined, but yet wistful, glance into Kate's eyes, " they don't mean to be beat."

" I don't understand you, Winifred," returned Kate, while a feeling of vague alarm rising gradually in her heart, and betraying itself in her manner, showed that she did partially understand the possible trouble to which Mrs. Pendleton was alluding.

" Miss Kate," said she, still looking down from her somewhat superior height into Kate's eyes with the same fixed and meaning look, " the men mean to bring the lugger in, and run the goods."

" In a dark night like this," said Kate,

" they will have a good chance of doing so, as they have had many a time before."

" Ay, Miss Kate, please God they be not meddled with, the lugger will come in with the tide, while it is as dark as pitch, and all well. But—it 'ill be bad meddling with them."

" And who should meddle with them? " said Kate, with a sudden feeling that Lady Farnleigh's lightly uttered words might have more meaning in them than she had thought of attributing to them.

" The revenue officers, to be sure, miss, and those as has the business to protect the revenue," returned Mrs. Pendleton, shrewdly observing Kate's face.

" Well, and if the *Saucy Sally* "—that was the name of Pendleton's lugger—" gets scent of anything hailing from the custom-house, she will show them a clean pair of heels, as she has so often done before," said Kate.

" Ah, but the *Saucy Sally* don't mean to do nothing of the kind this time. I tell you, Miss Kate, they mean to bring in their cargo whether or no! "

" How, whether or no? If the revenue officers are on the look-out, they must stand off and try another chance."

" But I tell you, Miss Kate, that is not what they mean. They mean to come in. If they can come in quiet, well. There'll be a bit of bread for the wives and children, and nobody the worse or the wiser. But if they are meddled with, there'll be trouble. That's where it is," said Mrs. Pendleton.

" Why, you don't mean to say, Winifred. that they would dream of open resistance to the king's officers? They could not be so mad! "

" I don't know about mad, Miss Kate ; but I zem I know which would be the maddest, them as is wishful to earn a bit of bread for their families, or them as poke their noses where they've no need, to hinder them. But you may rest sure, miss, if the *Saucy Sally* is meddled with to-morrow night, there'll be trouble."

" But you must persuade your husband not to be so foolhardy, Mrs. Pendleton. I can hardly believe he can think of it," said Kate.

" Persuade him! How am I to persuade him,—even putting he was a man to mind a woman's tattle in such matters,—and he over in France? Besides, it does not depend on him altogether; I said there were others in it. And zems to me, Miss Kate, that you know enough of Hiram to judge that if others are for venturing a bold stroke, he is not the man to preach to them to hold their hands!"

"I should hope, Winifred, that he was not a man to join in any violence, which might lead to dreadful consequences," said Kate, with a painfully rising sense of the disagreeable possibilities that were beginning to loom above the horizon of her imagination.

"Might lead!" cried Winifred Pendleton, with a look and an accent that were almost a sneer. "You don't know what men are, Miss Kate; let alone men such as they are, who have known what 'tis to have the law against 'em and not for 'em. Law is a very good thing, Miss Kate, for them as has got all they can wish for in this world. But Pendleton is not the man to stand by quiet, and see his own seized beneath his nose, not if I know anything of him. No more aint those that are with him."

"But, my dear Winifred, what is your object in telling me all this, except to frighten me and make me unhappy? It could not be to tell me this that you have walked up from Sillmouth such a night as this," said Kate, becoming more and more uneasy, though she hardly knew, with any degree of precision, now what she heard could affect her.

"I did walk up from Sillmouth, a good eight miles to-night just on purpose to tell you this, Miss Kate," said Mrs. Pendleton, with the deliberate kind of manner of a person administering a dose and waiting to see the effect of it.

"And what possible object could you have in doing so?" asked Kate, looking at her in great surprise.

"I thought, Miss Kate, that maybe our hearts might pull the same way in this matter," replied Mrs. Pendleton, dropping the lashes over the fine but perhaps somewhat bold eyes with which she had been till now observing her quondam mistress.

"Hearts pull the same way! Of course they do! You know how dearly I have at heart all that interests you. But I don't understand you. You are not like yourself to-night. You speak as if there were something behind that you were afraid to tell me. Has anything happened?"

"No, miss, no! nothing *have* happened.

But, my dear Miss Kate, don't you know what is likely to happen when men come to fighting! If you don't know, can't you guess, what a woman must feel when the father of her children is at that pass, when if it does come to a fight, it wont end without lives lost?"

"But, gracious heavens! Winifred, why will your husband be so rash—so mad? If you have no power to stop him, what is to be done? and what on earth did you propose to yourself in coming here? If papa could help, I am sure he would. If Hiram could be arrested and kept safe till this mad scheme is blown over—but you say he is over in France?"

"Yes, miss, Pendleton is over the other side; and I don't think that any good could be done by arresting him, even if he was here; thank you kindly, all the same," said Winifred, casting down her eyes with a mock-demure look that had a strong flavor of irony in it. "Hiram is a bird of that sort, you see, Miss Kate," she added, "as it don't come easy putting salt on their tails. No, Miss Kate, if any good is to be done, it's you that must do it. And it did come into my head—or into my heart more like—that you and I, miss, might have pulled together in this bad business."

"I help you? and pull together? What can you mean, Winifred? You have got something in your head. Why don't you speak it out plain? You know you can trust me."

"If I did not know that, I should not have said what I have said," replied Mrs. Pendleton, looking full into Kate's eyes with a steady and searching gaze. "And I know well enough that if you could do a good turn to either me or mine, it isn't a little either of trouble or cost that would stand in the way. I know that, Miss Kate. Don't you think I ever forget it, or ever shall. But it isn't trouble or cost that will serve the turn to-night."

She spoke these words simply and naturally, and then hesitated, and once again cast her eyes down to the floor. After a minute she went on, without raising them,—

"It's not to be thought, Miss Kate, that when men come to a desperate fight—and if there *is* a fight it will be a desperate one—the danger's all on one side."

She paused and looked up furtively into

Kate's face, from under her eyelashes. But she could detect neither intelligence of her meaning, nor any other emotion beyond that of the sympathizing distress with which Kate had heard the whole of her story, in her features, as she answered,—

"Of course that must be so. But the king's officers are almost sure to be strong enough to make the odds terribly in their favor."

"Would it seem so terrible to you, Miss Kate, that the odds should be on that side?" asked her companion, with a repetition of the same furtive examination of her face.

"I suppose it ought not to seem so," said Kate, simply; "I suppose one ought to wish that the supporters of the law should be stronger than the breakers of it. And God forbid that there should be blood shed on either side! But you know, Winny, well enough, that as long as it was merely a question of playing hide-and-seek with the custom-house people, which side of the game I wished well to."

"But if it's not a game of hide-and-seek, but a very different sort of game," said the woman, speaking with hurried vehemence, but still without looking up; "and if," she went on, in a lower tone, "that other game has to be played out with His Majesty's revenue cutter, the *Petrel*"—

And again she stole a look at Kate's face, and this time saw, by the bright red flush that suffused the whole of it, that a portion, at least, of the ideas that she wished to suggest had found its way into Kate's mind.

"Ah, I had not thought of that! In that case," she added, while the blush, which a different sentiment had called to her cheek in the first instance, was detained there by a feeling of displeasure with her companion of which no shadow had till then crossed her mind,—"in that case," she said, coldly, "I should think far worse, than if I had not known it, of the chances of the men rash enough to attempt such a struggle."

This reply called up Winifred's eyes from off the ground, and roused a new feeling of a different kind in her heart; and the rich color came into her cheeks also, as she said,—

"You take it with a very high hand, miss! There are not many men, either in His Majesty's service or out of it, who would find it a joking matter or child's play to fight out a fair fight with Hiram Pendleton, let alone

them as are with him! I did not come here to ask for mercy, but to prevent mischief on one side as well as t'other. There's other women besides wives, who might chance to get broken hearts out of to-morrow night's work—if such work is to be."

"I don't know what you mean, Mrs. Pendleton!" said Kate, scarlet, and now thoroughly angry; "I don't know what it is that you are daring to insinuate!"

"Forgive me, my dear young mistress! My dearest Miss Kate, forgive me!" cried Winifred, catching Kate's hand, and looking up with tears in her eyes; "God knows, I had no thought to offend you. I would rather cut my tongue out. But why should it be an offence to you, between you and me, your own poor old Winny? Wouldn't it be a good thing to prevent this bloody work, if we could? And believe me, believe me, my dear young lady, it will be as bad for one side as for t'other!"

"But what right have you to speak as you did, Winifred?" said Kate, relenting, though still much annoyed and offended. "Of course it would be good to prevent bloodshed, if there were any way of doing it. But what reason or what right have you to suppose that I should be especially interested in the matter, beyond what every person would naturally be? And, above all, what possible reason can you have to imagine that I should have any means of influencing the matter one way or the other?"

"I'm sure I don't know why you should be so angry with me, miss, for saying to you what all the folks are saying about to one another. You can't think that it is any secret in Silverton that Captain Ellingham worships the ground you tread on. You can't expect folk to shut their eyes; and I don't see, for my part, why you should wish them to!"

"The people talk nonsense, as they generally do! But you ought to know better than to repeat it to me, Winifred. Besides, you spoke of—of my breaking my heart for Captain Ellingham—as if I were likely to break my heart for any man!"

"Well, I had no right to say that, miss, and I humbly ask your pardon. Not but 'twould seem natural and right enough to me for a girl, let her be the first lady in the land, to care about such a one as Captain Ellingham, and be mad for the love of her!"

"But even supposing that one must naturally, as you say, Winny, follow from the other, what business has any one to impute any such sentiments to Captain Ellingham?" asked Kate, who did not succeed in disguising from her old nurse and humble friend that she *did* feel an interest in investigating that part of the question.

"What business? Well, I do believe that gentlefolk think that poor folk haven't no eyes! servants specially; and they made of nothing else, as one may say! Why, Miss Kate, do you think that the sailors took no note of their captain that time when the whole lot of you went for a cruise aboard the cutter? There was no lack of other ladies aboard, and pretty ones too; but there wasn't a man or boy of the cutter's crew, from that crossgrained old Joe Saltash, the mate, down to the cabin-boy, that could not see where the captain took his sailing orders from, or who was admiral on board. Bless you, Miss Kate, sailors have eyes! ay, and tongues too! How long do you suppose the *Petrel* might be lying in Sillmouth harbor, before it was all over Sillmouth that the revenue captain worshipped Miss Kate Lindisfarn's shoe-tie? Show his sense! the Sillshire folk say. And I suppose, Miss Kate—if I might venture to say it, without your eating me up alive for it,—that you didn't look at him as if you hated him!"

Kate was blushing brightly as Mrs. Pendleton spoke; but she did not appear to be angry this time.

"But even supposing," she said, "that all this was true, instead of being the silliest nonsense that ever was talked, what would it avail toward preventing what you fear to-morrow night, Mrs. Pendleton?"

"Don't call me Mrs. Pendleton, dear Miss Kate, please don't, or I shall think you are still angry with me. How avail? Why, if what I have said was true, it wouldn't be pleasant hearing for you to be told the first thing you open your eyes in the morning that Captain Ellingham's body had been found washed ashore during the night, with a couple of pistol bullets in it, and a gash over the forehead!"

"Good heavens, Winifred! How can you talk in such a way?" replied Kate; and her cheek grew pale as she spoke. "Of course, it would be dreadful to hear it, whether all that trash were true, or as false as it is."

"Well! that's what you are like enough to hear, Miss Kate, if nothing is done to prevent it. And I don't suppose you'd think it was made much better, if you was told that Hiram Pendleton's corpse was lying stark on the sands as well!"

"But what can possibly be done to prevent such horrors!" cried Kate, wringing her hands in distress.

"Why, where is the captain now, at this present speaking?" said Mrs. Pendleton.

"Here at the Chase, in the house," answered Kate.

"Ah, to be sure! here at the Chase, a-taking his wine comfortably along with the squire," continued Mrs. Pendleton. "And if he was a-doing the same thing at the same hour to-morrow night, the *Saucy Sally* would have run her cargo before midnight, and no harm done to nobody in all the blessed world!"

"But I know Captain Ellingham means to be off to Sillmouth the first thing to-morrow morning," returned Kate, shaking her head sadly.

"And how much trouble, I wonder, would it take them eyes of yours, Miss Kate, to make him change his mind, and stay at Lindisfarn?" said Mrs. Pendleton, looking wistfully into the eyes she spoke of.

"Ah!" cried Kate, blushing and drawing a long breath, as if she suddenly perceived for the first time the whole of Mrs. Pendleton's drift and object in coming up to the Chase.

"No, Mrs. Pendleton, that plan wont do! Even if I were to make the attempt, as you would have me, I could no more prevent Captain Ellingham from doing his duty than I could move Silverton Cathedral!"

"All nonsense! I beg your pardon, Miss Kate; but you know nothing about it. Many's the better man than Captain Ellingham that has forgotten all about duty, as you call it, on a less temptation! And where's the special duty of his going out one particular night?"

"I am afraid," returned Kate, thoughtfully, "that he would not be here so quietly to-night, and intending to go out, as I know he does, to-morrow night if he had not some information."

"God help him, then, and my husband, too! They wont both come ashore alive! More likely neither of them; and God help me and my children! Miss Kate, you could do this good job if you tried," added Winifred, clasping her hands, and looking with wistful earnestness into Kate's now painfully distressed face. She shook her head sorrowfully, but with a severe expression on her features, as she said,—

"Nothing that I *could* do would produce the result you wish, Mrs. Pendleton."

"Result I wish! Why, great Heaven, Miss Kate, 'tis the lives of both of them! Consider how you'll think upon my words, when it is too late! When the captain's body is picked off the sand and carried feet foremost, and the white face, with the dripping black hair falling back from it, upward to the sunlight; and my man is laid in his bloody coffin, and I am a broken-down and broken-hearted woman, without a bit of bread to put into my children's mouths," said Mrs. Pendleton, putting her handkerchief to her eyes: "you'll say to yourself, Miss Kate, *I* did all that good work. *I* sent the captain to his fate, when I knew it was waiting for him. *I* brought Hiram Pendleton to his death! 'Twas *I* that made Winifred, old John Parker's daughter, a broken widow, and her children orphans! I did it all, for I might have saved it all, and wouldn't! —Oh, Miss Kate, think, think of it! What's a bit of a girl's pride, or just a taste of a blush, maybe, making you look more lovelier to him than you ever looked before—what's this, I say, to men's lives? Think of it, for Heaven's love, my dear Miss Kate! And don't you go for to think that the king's men are going to have it all their own way. I tell you that the chance is against them. Our fellows are a strong lot—some new hands, strangers, among them—and they wont make child's play of it. As sure as Captain Ellingham tries to stop the *Saucy Sally* to-morrow night, he's a dead man!"

Kate, whose distress had been rising to a pitch of agony while Mrs. Pendleton had been speaking these words, remained silent for a while at the conclusion of them, while her working features showed how great was the effect of them upon her.

"You do not know, my poor Winifred," she said at length, "you cannot guess, how painful it will be to me, how much it costs me to make the application you urge me to do. But," she added, while something that was almost a sob half choked her utterance, "I will not, I dare not have it on my conscience that I have refused, in order to spare my own feelings, to make an attempt at averting these dreadful misfortunes. I will do as you would have me, my poor Winifred, though it is a hard, hard task. I must leave you now. Good-night. Rest yourself well before you start on your return; and if you like, one of the men shall walk over with you —or, better still, I am sure Mr. Mat would let you have the gig."

"God bless and reward you for your good deed, Miss Kate, and grant that you succeed!" said Winifred, with the tears in her eyes,— "and thank you kindly, miss; but I do not want any help to get home. There's not a foot of the ground that I don't know, better than e'er a man about the place: and I'm noways afraid of the walk."

"Good-night, then. It shall be done before he goes to-morrow," said poor Kate, in a tone which might have led a bystander to imagine that the deed to be done was something of a very tragic nature indeed.

And then she had to return to the drawing-room with as cheerful a face as she could manage, fully purposed to do the spiriting which she had undertaken, but intending to set about it, as perhaps the reader need hardly be told, in a somewhat different fashion from that contemplated by her *ci-devant* nurse.

CHAPTER XVIII.

KATE'S ATTEMPT AT BRIBERY AND CORRUPTION.

It was impossible for Kate to find any opportunity of making the contemplated attack on Captain Ellingham that evening. When she returned to the drawing-room, the gentlemen had come in from the dining-room and were listening to a song by Miss Margaret. It was the celebrated air from *Robert le Diable* that she was singing; and she sang it well and very effectively, but with that thin and *criarde* voice, which French teaching and sentiment and practice seem always to produce, and with abundance—ill-natured or severe critics of the English school might perhaps have said, with too great abundance—of that dramatic effect, of which the song is so especially susceptible. It was Margaret's favorite song and her main *cheval de bataille*, not only because it suited her voice, but also, as she would observe, with a very business-like appreciation of the subject in all its parts and bearings, because it suited her face and eyes. When she gave the "*Grâce! grâce, pour moi, pour toi!*" with all that eyes as well as voice could do to emphasize the poet's words and give irresistible force to the prayer, Kate could not help wishing that her sister had to make that appeal for, "*grâce pour moi, pour toi*," which it would be her task to make to-morrow morning to the man who was then listening to it. Captain Ellingham did listen to Margaret's song with pleasure and interest; keenly and critically, one would have said, to look at him observing her the while, with a curious and slightly smiling expression of countenance. He applauded her at the conclusion of her song; but he did not approach the piano, nor make any offer to turn over the leaves of her music-book. Fred Falconer was not there to hang over her chair, and turn the eye part of the stage business into a duet with her. But Margaret was too well-drilled and well-educated a girl not to do her work conscientiously and to the best of her power under all circumstances. The same spirit prompted her that moved the old mediæval artists to carve and finish cornice and moulding, even in parts which from their position could never meet the eye, as carefully as in those portions of the work which were destined to universal admiration.

And then, after Kate's song, Mr. Mat sung his favorite "Cease, rude Boreas," which was assuredly appropriate enough to the occasion; only Boreas did not cease by any means, but quite the contrary.

And after that, Kate sung that pathetic old Sillshire ditty of the sad mutiny time,—" Parker was my lawful husband!"—which, as Mr. Mat said, had the property of always compelling him to "make a fool of himself." It was natural enough that the matter of which Kate's mind and heart were full, should have suggested to her memory that eloquent though homely lament of a wife sorrowing for a condemned and guilty husband. And if Kate had been an even permissibly artful girl, instead of the utterly unscheming and thoughtlessly open creature she was, it might be supposed that she had selected her song with a view to preparing Captain Ellingham's heart for the assault to be made upon it. If she had had any such idea in her head, she might have fancied that her song had answered its end. For she sang it with infinite pathos; and the eyes of the commander of the *Petrel* did not remain any drier than Mr. Mat's.

And then came the time for the flat candlesticks and the good-nights. It was quite clear that nothing could be done in the matter that night. Kate had hardly supposed that there was any possibility of getting an opportunity before the morrow. Then she knew it would be easy enough. Only the deferring her hard, hard task till then involved the suffering of a night of wakeful anxiety and thought.

In the morning, it would be an easy matter to find an opportunity for a *tête-à-tête* with Captain Ellingham. He was to drive over to Silverton in the gig, starting from the Chase at eight in the morning, before the family breakfast hour. The same thing had occurred more than once before; and Ellingham had declared that he did not want breakfast,—always breakfasted later,—liked a drive or a walk before breakfast, etc., etc. But it was in too violent contradiction with the habits and traditions of all Miss Immy's life and experience for this to be permitted; and an early meal was on the table at half-past seven for the departing guest. Upon one of these occasions Kate had come down to make Captain Ellingham's breakfast for him; and she felt that there would be nothing remarkable in her doing so now. Nevertheless, she seemed to herself a guilty thing, compassing some forbidden machination as she went down to the breakfast-room; and she felt quite sure that her face was betraying the agitation of her mind.

Of course, the reader does not imagine, as the pretty forester's daughter imagined, that Kate had any intention of playing the Circe to Captain Ellingham, and seeking to detain him at Lindisfarn by the exercise of her fascinations upon him. Her plan, poor child! involved a much greater degree of *naïve* ignorance of the world and of things. The first scheme, as Winifred imagined it, would have been simply impossible of performance. Her own was infinitely distasteful to her.

Captain Ellingham observed at once, as she entered the breakfast-room, that her look and bearing were not marked by her usual bright animation and cheerfulness.

"I am afraid, Miss Lindisfarn, you are not quite well this morning. If that is so, I should be so grieved to think that you had got up earlier than usual on my account," said he.

"I have had a restless night," said Kate, in her direct and simple way, driving straightway at her object; "but it would have made the matter no better to have stayed in bed this morning; for I have been kept awake by thinking of something that I wanted to say to you before you went away to Silverton."

"I should think myself most unfortunate," replied Ellingham in much surprise, "if any fault of mine can have made it necessary to say what is disagreeable to you."

"Oh, no, indeed, Captain Ellingham. And yet it is very disagreeable to me to say what I must say. And nothing but a belief that it is my bounden duty not to shrink from doing so would induce me to speak to you of it."

"Be assured, Miss Lindisfarn," rejoined he, speaking gravely, and in greater astonishment than ever, "that anything you wish to say to me will"— He was rather at a loss how to proceed, but after a moment's hesitation, continued,—"be listened to by me in whatever manner and frame of mind you may wish me to hear it."

"Thank you, Captain Ellingham. I was sure you would be kind about it, whether you may think it right to—to act in one way or another," said Kate, feeling some little comfort from the consciousness that she had surmounted the difficulty of beginning, but still very nervous.

"I feel sure that I shall think it right to do what you think it right to wish me to do," Miss Lindisfarn," said he, still speaking seriously, and it seemed to her ear at the moment, she fancied, somewhat coldly. It was impossible that the overture could have been received more courteously. Still it seemed to her as if his grave seriousness opened her eyes yet more than they had been before to the gravity of the matter she had to communicate to him.

"I hope so. For indeed, indeed, Captain Ellingham, nothing would have induced me to speak to you on such a matter except a feeling that I should have been acting wrongly in not doing so."

And as she spoke, poor Kate felt that her agitation was increasing,—that the tears were rising in her throat, and that she could with difficulty prevent them from brimming over at her eyes.

"What is the nature of the business?" said he in a softer and kinder voice; for he perceived her distress.

"Is it not part of your duty here, Captain Ellingham, to prevent the smugglers from—from doing their smuggling?"

"That is not only a part, but I may say pretty well the whole, of my duty on the Sillshire coast. It is for that purpose that the *Petrel* is here," replied he, smiling, and somewhat relieved at this discovery of the nature of the subject in hand, though still as much surprised as ever.

"And the government tries, I know, always to take away from them the things they want to smuggle?" said Kate.

"Tries to? I am afraid, Miss Lindisfarn, you Sillshire volk, as Mr. Mat says, don't always wish us revenue officers all the success we deserve, and are apt to laugh at us when we don't succeed. Yes, the government *tries* to take away all smuggled goods, as you say; and tries its best, though it does not always succeed," said the commander of the *Petrel*, becoming still more at his case respecting Kate's business.

"Yes, I know. They try to hide the things and you try to find them. If they succeed, they sell them at a good profit; and if you succeed, they lose them, and I don't suppose the king is much the richer."

"Ah! Miss Lindisfarn, I am afraid it's too clear on which side your sympathies are!" cried Ellingham, laughing.

"But it cannot be the intention of the king or the government," continued Kate, without manifesting the least inclination to share her companion's cheerfulness; "it cannot be their wish, for the sake of a few yards of silk, or a little tobacco, to take away or even to risk human life."

"Ah, my dear Miss Lindisfarn," returned he, reverting at once to all his previous seriousness of manner, and beginning to have some inkling of a suspicion of what sort the business in hand might be, "I am afraid you hardly see the matter in its right light. The government assuredly has no wish to take away men's lives, as you say; but law must be enforced, and its supremacy vindicated at all hazards and at all cost,—at all costs, you understand me?"

"I understand, of course," said Kate, whose misgivings as to the success of her enterprise were already beginning to be increased by the tone and scope of Captain Ellingham's words,—"I understand that if you catch the men in the act of smuggling, you must prevent them; you cannot let them carry their plans into effect. That would be too much to expect,"—a smile passed over the revenue officer's face, as she said these words :—"but if it were known beforehand, that a lamentable sacrifice of life would be the certain result of interfering with the smugglers in any particular case, surely, it would be right—and humane—and best in all ways to—to—to avoid such a misfortune!" and Kate, as she came near the end of her little speech, had clasped her hands, partly in sheer nervousness, and partly from an unreasoned impulse of supplication, while she gazed with wistful and now palpably tearful eyes into his face.

Captain Ellingham dropped his before her gaze, and remained silent for some seconds. Then looking up at her with a full and frank glance, and speaking very kindly and gently, but still gravely, though with a quiet smile, he said,—

"I am very much afraid, my dear Miss Kate,"—it was the first time during the interview that he had called her so, and Kate felt grateful for the friendliness implied in that manner of address,—"I am very much afraid that you have engaged in an attempt to induce an officer in His Majesty's service to act in gross violation of his duty,—a high crime and misdemeanor, Miss Kate!" he added, while he allowed the kindly smile to temper the severity of the words. "I am quite sure," he continued, with more entire seriousness, "that you would not, as you said, have spoken to me on this matter if you had not thought it right. I feel sure, too, that I may safely adhere to what I said just now,—that I shall think it right to do, what you think it right to wish me to do,—after a little reflection. Consider, Miss Lindisfarn, what the result would be, if smugglers were allowed to effect their purpose whenever they chose to say that they would use violence in carrying it out if necessary. Why, your good sense will show you in an instant that not a yard or a pound of goods that came into the kingdom would pay duty. The custom-house might shut up shop, and the government might whistle for the revenue. I am sure you must see this. If these men resort to violence, and if life be lost in enforcing the law, their blood will be on their own heads. Unless they use violence, no greater misfortune can ensue than the capture of their goods, and themselves."

"But they will use violence, deadly violence! They are desperate men!" cried Kate, wringing her hands. "Can nothing be done to prevent bloodshed?"

"My dear Miss Kate," said Ellingham, while the genial smile came back again to his features, "I am very much afraid that you know more about these desperate men than you ought to know! As for what can be done to prevent bloodshed,—it is very simple. The desperate men have nothing to do but to take to an honest calling, or at all events, to steer clear of the Petrel,—which I tell you frankly I think they will find it difficult to do?"

"But I must not betray them," cried Kate, while a new terror rushed into her mind; "at all events, it cannot be right for me to betray them!"

"Certainly not; you have betrayed nobody, and you shall betray nobody. To show you how little there is you could betray, let me ask you—without wishing for any answer though—"whether your conversation with me this morning is not the result of one you had last night with a certain Mrs. Pendleton in the housekeeper's room? Oh! I am no eavesdropper," he continued, as the blood rushed into Kate's face; "but Lady Farnleigh mentioned in the drawing-room the purpose for which you had left the room. She told me, too, all the good reason you have for being warmly interested in, and attached to, your old nurse. But it is Mrs. Pendleton's misfortune to be the wife of perhaps the most dangerous and determined smuggler on all the coast. We have long had our eyes upon his movements. Come! I don't mind playing with my cards on the table; and so far giving the fellow a chance of avoiding bloodshed if he chooses to profit by it. We have information that the *Saucy Sally* is to run over from the other side to-night; we know all about it. And, as sure as fate, if she attempts it, she will fall into our hands; and if the men are rash enough to make a fight of it, they must take the consequences."

"It is very, very dreadful," said Kate, wringing her hands in great distress. "I know they mean to fight desperately."

"And would Miss Lindisfarn, after telling me that fact, propose to me to keep purposely out of the way of this very desperate gentleman?" said Captain Ellingham, looking with a fixed and almost reproachful gaze into Kate's eyes, while a slight flush came over his brown cheek.

"I was told a great deal," said Kate, and the sympathetic blood rushed, as she spoke, all over her own face and forehead, "about the danger that the king's officer might run as well as the smugglers. But of course I knew that was no part of the subject on which it was no use to speak to you,—however painful a consideration it may be to others," she added, hurriedly and in a lower voice, dropping her eyes as she did so.

"Thank you, Miss Lindisfarn!" said Ellingham shortly, giving her a little sharp nod as he spoke. "But supposing I *had* kept out of the way when a dangerous duty was to be done?"

"Nobody in the world would have supposed," replied Kate, speaking rapidly, with a sort of angry defiance in her manner, and looking up while the blush returned again to her cheeks, "that Captain Ellingham was moved by any consideration save that of sparing others."

Ellingham bowed slightly; and his own color went and came in rapid alternation.

"I could not count, I am afraid," he said, "on all the world taking so favorable a view of such conduct as you might be kind enough to adopt. At all events," he continued, speaking in a more simple and businesslike tone, "putting all such personal considerations out of the question, this is simply a matter of duty, which must be done as such. I am sure that you must now see, my dear Miss Kate, that any alternative is wholly out of the question. Perhaps," he added, again changing his manner, "I need hardly say, that if this were a matter in which any earthly consideration could induce me to act differently from the course I proposed to follow, I should deem it the greatest happiness to be guided by your wishes. But duty must be done. And I have, at all events, the consolation of being sure that in doing mine, I shall have Miss Lindisfarn's well-considered approbation."

"Alas! yes! I cannot say that it is not so. And I fear I have only done mischief and not good by my interference," said poor Kate, with a dejected sigh.

"Nay, not so at all," replied Ellingham. "All this fellow Pendleton's movements were known to me, as I told you. We should have been on the lookout for him to-night, at all events. On the contrary, I have stretched a point in favor of your *protégés*, Miss Lindisfarn;" (the bright arch smile again here;)—"I give them the advantage of knowing that they are expected. You may communicate the intelligence to them, and let them profit by it to keep out of my way, if they like; I assure you I am showing them a favor rarely practised by an officer of the revenue service!"

"But the men are on the other side of the water, in France!" said Kate.

"I know that, of course. But these people have always codes of signals, and means of warning their friends. Without that, they would never beat us, as they do sometimes. Let your friend, Mrs. Pendleton, be told that the *Petrel* is wide awake. She will know very well how to make use of the information. And now, my dear Miss Lindisfarn, it is time for me to be off. A thousand thanks for your kindness and hospitality! I wish I could have pleased you better in this affair. Good-by."

"Good-by, Captain Ellingham! I *do* know that you are doing right;—and that it was very wrong and—very silly in—in anybody to try to make you do otherwise," stammered Kate as she gave him her hand.

And so the gig rattled off with Captain Ellingham, who, somehow or other, was in particularly high spirits during his little journey to Sillmouth, and felt as if he would not have the fact of his morning's *tête-à-tête* breakfast cancelled, or the remembrance of it obliterated from his mind for all the *Saucy Sallies* that ever skulked into a port.

And somehow or other, more strangely still, Kate, though her enterprise had so signally failed, and though she was very painfully apprehensive of what the coming night might bring forth, caught herself, to her own considerable surprise, looking back with a feeling of pleasure on certain passages of that abortive attempt at bribery and corruption, to which she had looked forward with such unfeigned terror.

CHAPTER XIX.
KATE'S RIDE TO SILLMOUTH.

THE pleasure, vivid as it was, with which Kate recalled certain words and tones and looks of that breakfast-table *tête-à-tête* conversation, had to be put away in a cupboard of her mind marked "Private"—the public are not admitted here"—for future use. The more pressing business of the moment was to put to whatever use it might haply serve the information which Captain Ellingham had given her leave to convey to the smugglers. It would have been necessary, indeed, in any case, to give Winifred tidings of the result of her conversation with the commander of the *Petrel*. So as soon as the family breakfast was over, Kate followed Mr. Mat out to the stable-yard, where his miscellaneous duties of the day generally began, and asked him if he could manage to ride over to Sillmouth with her.

"I must see Winny Pendleton this morning, Mr. Mat," said Kate. "I am afraid there is likely to be bad work to-night between Pendleton's boat and the revenue cutter."

"Was that what Winny was up here about last night?" asked Mr. Mat.

"Just that, poor soul! It seems that her husband has got other men associated with him worse than himself, and that they are determined to fight with the revenue men, if they are meddled with. Winny wanted me

to persuade Captain Ellingham to keep out of the way of the *Saucy Sally*. 'Of course, it was impossible for him to think of doing anything of the kind; and I have sad misgivings something bad will happen to-night."

"Is Pendleton going to run over to-night?" asked Mr. Mat.

"Yes. That was what Winny told me. And I know the *Petrel* will be on the lookout for him. Oh, Mr. Mat, it's a bad business! I wish to Heaven, poor Winny had never married that man!"

"Ah! It's too late wishing about that now. She has made her bed, and must lie on it. And there are worse fellows of his sort than Pendleton is," said Mr. Mat.

"Can you ride over with me this morning to Sillmouth, Mr. Mat? I must see her, though I have nothing to tell her to comfort her, poor soul!"

"Of course, Miss Kate, I'll go with you. I'll have the mare and Birdie saddled directly."

So Kate and Mr. Mat made their way to Sillmouth and then galloped over the two miles of fine sands which lie between that port and the rocks, but rise from the water's edge immediately beyond Deep Creek, from the bank of which little gully a pretty zigzag path leads to a sheltered nook of flat ground, about half-way up the cliff, on which the smuggler's cottage was built. It was niched in so close to the face of rock rising above it, and so far back, therefore, from the edge of the precipice below it, that it was barely visible from below; and it would hardly have entered into the imagination of a stranger to the spot, when on the shore below, that there was a human habitation half-way between him and the top of the cliff above him, had not the little zigzag path unobtrusively suggested that it must lead to something.

The path was hardly practicable for horses; and though Kate had frequently protested that she was sure Birdie would carry her up safely, Mr. Mat had always utterly set his face against any such attempt. The usual practice, therefore, was—if neither of Winny Pendleton's children could be seen, as was often the case, playing on the sea-shore—for Kate to hold Mr. Mat's horse while he went up to the cottage and sent down one of the boys to relieve her of it and of Birdie.

On the present occasion, this was not necessary; for Winny had been anxiously on the lookout for a visit from the Chase; and on the first appearance of Kate and Mr. Mat on the sands below had sent down one of her sons to hold their horses for them.

They found her in a great state of anxiety and agitation; and, as we know, they had no comfort to offer her.

"God help them, Miss Kate!" said the poor wife, sitting down in the darkest corner of her little parlor, and putting up her apron to her eyes,—"God help them! and I say it for one side as well as for the other. It will be a bad and a black night for some of us."

"But why not take advantage, Winny, of the information I am permitted to give you?" urged Kate. "Captain Ellingham says that you have the means of letting the men know their danger by signals, or in some way, and that you can warn them off the coast. Why not do so?"

"It's not information I wanted from the king's officer, any more than he wanted it from me," said the smuggler's wife almost, with a sneer. "If he knows what we're doing, we know what he's doing. The men are quite aware that the cutter will be on the watch for them. That's why they're determined to fight!"

"But if they could be warned, and not attempt to get in to-night, they might find a time when the cutter is off its guard," urged Kate.

"'Tisn't so easy to catch Captain Ellingham off his guard. That's why we are driven to fight for it. Our men are peaceable enough. They don't want to make any mischief. If they can anyways get in to-night without striking a blow, they will. And they'll have all the information of the cutter's movements that can be given them. But, oh, Miss Kate, he is a difficult one to deal with, and I'm sore, sore afraid that bad will come of it!"

"I did all I could for you, Winny," said Kate, sadly. "I will still hope that in the dark night they may slip in without being seen. We must go now. Of course, I would tell you the upshot of the promise I gave. And, Winny," added Kate, as she turned to leave the cottage, while the consciousness that the words she was about to speak did not tell the whole or even the main part of the truth, caused her to blush all over her face,—"of course, I shall be very anxious to hear your news of the night. If, as please

God it will yet be, all is well, come up yourself to the Chase. If anything," she added, putting an emphasis on the any, "should happen, don't fail to send up a messenger the first thing. He shall be well paid for his trouble."

So Kate and her companion mounted their horses at the bottom of the path, and turned their heads homeward. That two-mile reach of sands between Sillmouth and Deep Creek was such a well-established and sure bit of galloping ground for the two riders, that Birdie and Mr. Mat's mare laid their ears back and started off as usual as soon as ever their riders were on their backs, without waiting for whip or spur. But it is probable that if they had not done so, they would have been allowed to traverse the ground at a listless walk; for neither Kate nor Mr. Mat were in a very blithe frame of mind. Kate was miserable, probably for the first time in her life; and she was surprised to find how completely her unhappiness seemed to make even her limbs listless and unfit for their usual work. For the first time in her life, a gallop on the Sillmouth sands seemed to have lost for her its invigorating tonic and inspiriting efficacy.

They neither of them spoke as long as the gallop lasted; but when they drew up at the entrance of the little fishing-town, through which they had to ride before reaching the road leading along the bank of the estuary of the Sill to Silverton Bridge, Kate pointed with her whip to a tall sail far out in the offing, as she said, sadly, "There's the cutter. Would she were back in harbor again! Is it not dreadful, Mr. Mat? Think of that poor woman, with her children in the cottage there, waiting for the chances of the night, watching the movements of that ship, and knowing that it is bent on the destruction of her husband; knowing that he is braving mortal peril in the pursuit of a livelihood for her and her children! What is to become of them if the chance goes against him?"

And the words as she uttered them suggested to her mind the possible alternative; and Winifred's words of the preceding evening recurred to her,—those words which had made her so angry,—"There's others besides wives may chance to get broken hearts from to-morrow night's work!" She clearly admitted to herself that Winifred spoke the truth;—henceforward—since that conversation of the morning, Kate said to herself; but that was, it may be believed, an error; there could be, at all events, however, no mistake and no self-deception any longer on that point. Yes! that night's work might bring a broken heart to another as well as to Winifred Pendleton. But Kate did not render to her own mind a full and consistent account of all the feelings that moved her to add,—as she looked out wistfully to the sea where the large white sails of the cutter were showing themselves clearly marked against the heavy dun clouds of the horizon,—

"I suppose that there is but little hope for smugglers in a struggle with the king's officers, Mr. Mat? The chances must be all against them?"

"Why, yes; 'tis to be thought they must be; but there's this, you know: the king's officers are noways desirous of taking life if they can help it. They would rather bring their men in prisoners, if they can anyway manage it. But with the smugglers, mind you, it is different. They are fighting with desperation and hate and rage in their hearts. There's no taking prisoners with them; it's down with you, or down with me. And there's the thought, that if they are taken prisoners 'twill go worse with them than if they are killed in the fight and get all their troubles over at once. All this, you see, Miss Kate, makes a fight with the smugglers a desperate and chancy piece of business."

Kate turned pale as she listened to this exposition of a revenue officer's dangers, which Mr. Mat would have spared her, if he had had any notion that his words were falling on her heart with the numbing effect of ice-drops. Observing, however, as they stopped to pay the turnpike, which is just outside Sillmouth on the Silverton road, how pale she was, Mr. Mat endeavored to draw some encouragement from the signs of the weather.

"It is as likely as not," said he, "that there may be no mischief after all! It'll be just such another night as last night,—as dark as pitch. The wind is getting up already, and look at that bank of black clouds out seaward. A dark night and a capful of wind, those are the smugglers' friends! And I should not be surprised if the *Saucy Sally* were to slip in, and get her cargo well up the country before they can catch her."

"God grant it!" cried Kate, fervently; and a more piously earnest prayer for the success of a lawless enterprise against all law and order was never breathed.

"At what time do you think we might get news of the upshot, whatever it may be, up at the Chase, Mr. Mat?" asked Kate after they had ridden awhile in silence.

"As soon as ever there is any of us stirring, if Winifred sends off a messenger at once. There is a little bit of a late moon; and it will all be over, one way or the other, before that rises. I should think Winny might send off somebody by four o'clock, and then we should get the news up to Lindisfarn by seven. They'll be up and stirring in the cottage yonder all night, never fear!"

"You will be on the lookout, Mr. Mat, I dare say," said Kate again, after another long spell of silence between the riders; "for you are as fond of poor Winifred as any of us. Would you come and tell me in my room, as soon as you have heard anything. You will find me up and dressed."

"Sure I will, Kate! sure I will! And I'll be on the lookout, never fear!" replied Mr. Mat, who, if he had been a less thoroughly simple and unsuspicious creature, might have been led by the somewhat overdone hypocrisy with which Kate affected to limit her anxiety to the fate of Winny Pendleton, and by her desire to receive the tidings in the privacy of her own room, to the spot in Kate's heart where her secret was hidden away from all eyes. It is just so that a silly bird, which has made its nest in the grass, indicates the whereabouts of it to her enemies, by her anxious flutterings to and fro about the spot.

The remainder of the ride up to the Chase was passed in silence. And then Kate spent the rest of the hours before dinner-time in strolling out alone to the top of Lindisfarn brow. She was too restless to be able to remain quietly at home; she wanted to be alone, and she turned her steps through the fine old woods to the crest of the hill, that she might the better scan the signs of the weather.

In that department the promise of the coming night was all that she could wish. The breeze was rapidly rising; and though Kate was not enough of a sailor to know whether the wind which was careering so wildly over Lindisfarn brow, and making the old woods groan and sough and sway to and fro, like a mourner in the excess of his grief, was a good wind for the run from the opposite coast to that of Sillshire, she was quite sure that there would be enough of it out at sea ; and she gathered some comfort from the reflection that if the wind did not serve to blow the *Saucy Sally* at the top of her speed into safety, it might be sufficiently strong in the opposite direction to prevent her from running into danger. And the night promised to be not only wild, but "dirty," as sailors graphically call it, and as dark as the most desperate doers of deeds that shun the light could desire. Great massive banks of heavy clouds were heaving themselves up with sullen majesty from the seaward horizon, rearing themselves into the semblance of great black cliffs and rocks, varying the outline of their fantastic forms continually as the storm-wind drove them, but steadily coming onwards and upwards toward the zenith. Once or twice, as Kate looked out from the vantage ground of a rocky ridge, which topped Lindisfarn brow, and raised its naked and lichen-grown head among the surrounding woods, the sky to seaward and the cloudbanks were lit up momentarily by sharp flashes of forked lightning, — not the playful, hovering, dallying, illuminating summer lightning of southern climates, with its manifold tints of every hue, from that of red-hot iron to violet, but sharply drawn, vicious looking dartings of fire, dividing the black clouds like the lines of cleavage in a crystal. And before she had returned to the house, the big raindrops had begun to patter like the dropping shots of distant musketry among the leaves far overhead.

It was as Mr. Mat had said, just such another night as the last had been ; only that the equinoctial storm seemed to have gathered additional strength and fury from its lull during the daylight hours. And Kate, as she lay awake during the interminable seeming hours of that long night, listening to the noises of the tempest, devoutly hoped, that the war which those who were occupying their business in the great waters must needs wage with the elements, would avail to prevent a more disastrous and dangerous warfare between man and man.

Toward morning, the wind fell, and a pale watery-looking beam from the feeble crescent of a waning moon came timidly and sadly wandering over earth and sea, as a meek and sorrowing wife may creep forth at daybreak to look on the home-wreck that has been caused by the orgy of the preceding night.

But Kate said to herself, that the night's work, whatever might have been its result, was done by that time ! As she thought what that might be, which that sad, colorless moonbeam had to look down on at that hour, a cold chill seemed to dart through her heart. Sleep had not come near her while the storm had lasted ; but now while she was counting the weary hours that must elapse before she could receive the tidings that the morning would bring her, she fell asleep.

CHAPTER XX.
DEEP CREEK COTTAGE.

WHEN Kate opened her eyes on the following morning, a ray of bright sunshine was finding its way into her room between the imperfectly closed shutters ; and it was a minute or two before her waking senses could establish the connection between the dreary sounds and thoughts which had occupied her last conscious moments and the cheerful brightness that wooed her waking. She was soon recalled, however, to all the cares and troubles from which she had escaped for a few hours ; for Simmons was standing by her bedside with a folded note in her hand.

"What time is it, Simmons?—late surely?" she asked, hurriedly, as she remembered the anxieties of the hour.

"No, miss : not late ! but please, miss, Mr. Mat told me to wake you if you was not awake yet, and to give you this note, miss, as a boy from Sillmouth has brought up this morning."

"Just open the shutters, Simmons," said Kate, striving to speak in her ordinary manner, while a cold spasm clutched her heart. "Give me the note, and then run down, there's a good girl, and tell Mr. Mat that I am going to get up directly," she added, anxious to obtain a moment's unobserved privacy for reading the dreaded tidings.

The note, written by Winifred, who, among other accomplishments acquired during her residence at the Chase, possessed that of very tolerable penmanship, ran as follows !—

"MY DEAREST YOUNG LADY,—Thanks be to God, things is not so bad as they med have been, though there's trouble enuff and like enuff to be more of it in store. The revnew cutter chased the *Saucy Sally*, but it blowed great guns all night, and Hiram says there aint no revnew craft on the water as can overhaul the *Saucy Sally* in such whether as last night. The cutter is back in harbor again this morning, I hear, and job enough they had to get her there. The *Saucy Sally* come into the creek like a bird, and though I says it as maybe shouldn't, there isn't many sailors afloat or ashore neither as would have brought her in the way Hiram did. But there's neither fair play nor honor among them custom-house folk. When the cutter saw how the game was, and found out that it wasn't none so easy to put salt on the tail of the *Saucy Sally*, they burnt blew lights and fired signal guns to the coast-guard lubbers on shore, and jest as the men was a-getting out the cargo comfortable and up the cliffs, down comes a party of the king's men, and there was a fight—more's the pity! It wasn't our men's fault. And the coast-guarders was beat off, and the cargo safe up the country. But too of the men was carried off, badly hurt. And too was hurt on our side simily. Hiram was one, as he is sure to take the biggest share, when there's blows a-going. But his hart aint nothing to signify much, God be praised! And then comes the worst at the last, as it generally do. The other man hurt was a stranger as took on with Pendleton in France. Him and Pendleton was both brought into the cottage; and the frenchman I am sadly afeared, has got his death. And to make it worse he can't speak a word of English, and what in the world am I to do? My dearest Miss Kate, if you would, you and Mr. Mat, have the great kindness and charity to ride over and look in. Somebody ought to speak to this poor frenchman, and he a-dying, as I am sorely afeared. The men are all away with the things up the country, and the place is as quiet as if there was not such a thing as a pound of contraband baccy in all creation. Pendleton is not here, no one but this poor frenchman. For Hiram and the rest of the men must take to the moor for a spell. And so, my dear young lady if you would look in, you would do a Christian charity to this poor frenchman, a-dying without opening his mouth to a human sole, and a loving kindness to your faithful and dewtiful old servant to command,

"WINIFRED PENDLETON.

"P. S. Pray du! there is a dear, good young lady, my dear Miss Kate. With speed."

Kate read this letter with feelings of the most heartfelt relief. And when she reached the conclusion of Winifred's story, she may be held excusable if the ill-news contained in it was not sufficient to throw any very extinguishing wet-blanket upon the great gladness which the former part of the letter had caused her. She was very sorry for the unfortunate Frenchman; but if he would needs thrust himself where he had so little business to be, what could he expect? and it was, at all events, a comfort that if the protection of the king's revenue required him to be killed, the captain and crew of the *Petrel* had had nothing to do with the killing of him.

Kate was, however, in a mood to do anything in her power for any human being, especially for her old favorite Winny;—which amounts, indeed, to little more than saying that she was herself again. She determined, if she could induce Mr. Mat to consent, of which she had never very much doubt, let the matter in hand be what it might, to ride over again the same ground she had traversed the day before, immediately after breakfast; and she pleased herself with thinking what a different ride it would be from that of yesterday.

She showed Winifred's note to Mr. Mat, who had already learned from the bearer of it the general upshot of the night's work,—that the *Saucy Sally* had landed her cargo; that the smugglers had escaped from the pursuit of the cutter, but had been attacked by a party of coast-guardmen on land; that two of the latter and two of the former party had been hurt; that one of these was Hiram Pendleton, but that his wound was of no great consequence, and that he had been able to escape to the moor with the rest of the men implicated in the affair. Mr. Mat had heard nothing of the other wounded man; and when he learned the nature of the case from Kate, he expressed his thankfulness for the providential dispensation which had ordained that the principal sufferer should be a Frenchman, but at the same time assented to Kate's proposition that it would be but an act of common charity to see what could be done for the wounded man, though decidedly resenting and repudiating Kate's mention of him as a "*fellow-creature.*"

So Birdie and Mr. Mat's mare were saddled after breakfast, and again found themselves, after a quicker and a brisker ride than that of yesterday, at the foot of the little zigzag path which led to the smuggler's cottage.

There was no need for Mr. Mat to go up first; for both Winifred's boys had been on the lookout for their arrival, as Mrs. Pendleton had had very little doubt that her letter would avail to bring Kate thither very shortly. The good dame herself was waiting for them at the top of the path, and poured forth her thanks for their prompt acquiescence in her prayer.

"No, he is alive," said she, in reply to Kate's first hurried question,—" he is alive; but I am afeared he wont last long; he is a deal weaker than he was when he was brought in. And doctor says he can't live. I am so thankful you have come, Miss Kate!"

"Could not the doctor speak to him in his own lingo?" asked Mr. Mat.

"What, old Bagstock, the doctor to Sillmouth? Not he! not a word, no more than I can. But I'll tell'ee, Miss Kate, I've a notion the man understands what is said in English, though he wont let on to talk it."

"Ah! like enough, like enough! They are a queer set," said Mr. Mat.

"Would you please to come in and see him, miss?" asked Winifred; for the preceding conversation had taken place in the little bit of flower-planted space at the top of the zigzag path, between the edge of the cliff and the cottage.

"Yes; I will go in with you," said Kate; "but I was thinking, Winny, that anyway the poor man ought to have some better advice than old Mr. Bagstock. I would not trust a sick dog in his hands."

"It needs a deal of skill to cure a sick dog," said Mr. Mat, "because they can't speak to you, to tell you what is the matter with them. And a Frenchman is all the same for the same reason. Go in to him, Kate; you can speak to him. For my part, I'll stay here; I should be no use."

And so saying, Mr. Mat sat himself down in a sort of summer-house in Mrs. Pendleton's garden, constructed of half an old boat, set on end on its sawed-off part, and richly overgrown with honeysuckle,—a fragrant seat, commanding a lookout over coast and sea that many a garden-seat in lordly demesnes might envy,—and having comfortably established himself there, drew from his pocket a supply of tobacco and the small instrument needed for the enjoyment thereof—(for Mr. Mat was like " poor Edwin," of whom Dr. Beattie sings in his famous poem of " The Minstrel," that he was

> " No vulgar boy ;
> Dainties he heeded not, nor gaud, nor toy,
> Save one short pipe ! ")

and proceeded to spend a half-hour, if need were, which he was sure not to find a long one.

Kate went with Mrs. Pendleton into the cottage.

It consisted of two rooms down-stairs, and two rooms up-stairs, together with some conveniences for back-kitchen, etc., in the form of a " lean-to," built at the rear between the cliff and the front rooms. Of the two rooms down-stairs, one was floored with flagstones, and served as the living room of the family. The other was boarded and sanded, had a colored print of Nelson over the mantlepiece; two bottles with colored sands arranged in layers within them, and two dried star-fish on it; a green baize-covered round table and two Windsor chairs in the centre of the room; a brilliantly painted japanned tea-tray leaning against the wall behind a large Bible—both articles alike deemed too good and splendid ever to be used—on a side table. This room was always kept locked, and served for nothing at all, save keeping up in the minds of the members of the family a consciousness of social dignity, and assuring their social *status* among their neighbors by the possession of a parlor. The profession of the head of the family, it must be remembered, made some such sacrifice to public opinion more necessary than it might have been in another case; for though, as has been said, the trade of a bold smuggler was looked on with much indulgence in those days and in those parts of the country, still such an amount of prejudice against the respectability of a career of lawbreaking existed as would place a smuggler with a parlor only on the same level of respectability as a law-abiding mechanic without that aristocratic appendage.

It would be an error, therefore, to say that the sanded parlor of the smuggler's cottage served no purpose, even if those august occasions were forgotten, when Mr. Pendleton, in great state, smoked a long pipe and drank brandy and water in company with some not too narrow-minded dealer in any of the articles respecting which Mr. Pendleton and the custom-house authorities were at variance. That bold smuggler and very specially ablebodied seaman was always on these occasions dressed in a full suit of black cloth, and got up generally in imitation of a Dissenting minister. He assumed this costume and the title of Mister together, and never at such times smoked anything shorter than a full-lengthed half-yard of clay, with a red stain at the end of it, which he hated. And altogether he was very unhappy during these periods of relaxation and enjoyment; but indulged in them occasionally because he deemed it right to do so.

The two upper rooms were the sleeping-chambers of the family; and when the wounded stranger had been thrown upon her hospitality, it would have been easy for Mrs. Pendleton to have arranged a bed in the sanded parlor, and so avoid the necessity of turning any of her family out of their sleeping-quarters. But that would have involved sacrilege in the desecration of the parlor to ordinary and secular uses, and was not to be thought of.

So Mrs. Pendleton had turned her boys out of their room, and had put the stranger in their place. It was a room that many an inhabitant of princely palaces in the streets of cities might envy! Not very large and not very lofty; but with such a window!—a good-sized casement window looking out on the little plot of garden ground, and beyond it over such an expanse of varied coast, and almost equally varied, and, what is more, changefully varied, sea and sky, as few windows could match. And every sweet, invigorating, health-laden breeze from the ocean came fresh from its dalliance with the wave-tops into that chamber; and though the storm-winds also howled around it, and passionately shook it, and beat against it, the inmates of it were well used to the roughly musical lullaby, and slept none the less soundly for it.

But the storm of the two preceding nights had entirely expended itself. The ocean, like an angry child, had forgotten all its so recent fury, as quickly as it had yielded to it, and was shining in the mid-day sunshine. And a soft wind from the south was blowing gently into the open window immediately opposite to the sick man's bed. The casement was low; and the old-fashioned bed was high; so that the occupant of it, propped up by pillows which rested against the white-washed wall behind the bed, could see, not indeed the garden-plot immediately beneath the window, or indeed any part of the coast-view stretching away on either side of it, but the distant sea, with its shimmering paths of light and shade, and the white sails of the ships and fishing-smacks as they turned up their canvas to the sunbeams, like sea-birds turning in their flight, or, in obedience to an "over" of the helm, dwindled to a barely visible speck on the horizon.

The stranger, who had fought among the foremost and fiercest in the fray with the coast-guard men, had received two bad hurts: one on the temple and side of the head, and one in the chest. His head was bound up, not very neatly or skilfully it would have seemed to scientific surgical eyes, with a superabundance of linen cloths, which still showed in parts of them the stains of the blood which had soaked them through when they were first used to stanch it. The other wound had been doubtless treated in a similar manner; but it was covered by the bed-clothes, and therefore contributed no part to the ghastly appearance of the patient, as he lay gazing wistfully over the expanse of the waters which had borne him to this sad ending of his career.

For he had no doubt that he was dying; and old Bagstock's shrugging declaration, that he did not see that there was anything to be done for him, did but needlessly confirm his own conviction.

Old Mr. Bagstock was a "general practitioner" of the sort that general practitioners mostly were in remote districts and among poor populations forty years ago. Old Bagstock was not the only general practitioner at Sillmouth. The other was young Rawlings; and there was all the difference between them, to the advantage of the latter, that the two epithets denoted,—a difference which, at just about that period in the history of medical science and practice, was far from a small one. But old Bagstock almost exclusively commanded the confidence and the adherence of the maritime population of Sillmouth. Sailors are especially tenacious of old ways and habits. Old Bagstock had brought the greater number of the Sillmouth sailors, fishermen, and smugglers into the world; and they seemed to feel that that fact gave him a vested right to a monopoly in seeing them out of it. A number of things old Bagstock had done, and a number of people he had known before that Rawlings had been ever heard of, were constantly cited as incontrovertible arguments to the disfavor of the latter. And sailors have a very strong conviction that people die "when their time is come," and are much more inclined to attribute to that fact the death of any patient whatever, than to any lack of skill in the doctor.

As for old Bagstock himself, he held a not widely different theory, especially as to the roughs of the not very select circle of his practice. He considered that if a smuggler got a mortal wound, it was useless to try to cure him of it; and if he got a wound which was not mortal, he was so hard and hardy and tought hat he was sure to recover from it. And it is probable that his practice was more accurately squared to the logical consequences of this theory, in cases where there was small prospect of much or any remuneration for his care, and most of all in that of a stranger and a Frenchman, of whom no one knew anything, and for whose doctor's bills it was not likely that anybody he could get at would choose to be responsible.

So, when the wounded man had told Pendleton, before he had started for the moor, that it was all over with him, and Pendleton, whose traffic on the other side of the water had enabled him to comprehend a few words of French, had told the same to his wife, who repeated the same thing to the doctor, old Bagstock had perfectly acquiesced in the opinion; and having somewhat perfunctorily stanched the flow of blood, and bound up the wounds, had taken himself off to some more medically or pecuniarily promising case. And it having been settled thus *nem. con.* that the wounded man was to die, Mrs. Pendleton, in her husband's absence, and her anxieties about the consequences and responsibilities that might fall upon her, as a result of the death taking place in her house, was exceedingly comforted and tranquillized by the appearance of her kind friends from the Chase.

CHAPTER XXI.
A GOOD SAMARITAN.

KATE knew perfectly well, when she started from the Chase on her present errand of kindness towards her old favorite, and of Christian charity toward the wounded stranger, that the business was not a pleasant one. And it was not without considerable shrinking and nervousness that she followed Mrs. Pendleton up the steep and narrow staircase of the cottage, and entered the chamber in which the sick man had been laid. But she had not been prepared for the shock which the sight of the patient occasioned her. The spectacle was one entirely new to her; and the first impression that it produced on her mind was that too surely the man was dying.

The blood-dabbled cloth around his brows, the long locks of coal-black hair escaping from under it, on the side of the head which was not wounded, and the black unshaven beard, added by the force of contrast to the ghastly paleness of his face. He had large dark eyes, which must have been handsome, when seen under normal circumstances, but which now, sunken and haggard as they were, and with a wild and anxious-looking gleam, the result of fever, in them, only served to add to the weird and fearful appearance of his face.

"Tell Mr. Mat," said Kate, turning back with a little shudder to Mrs. Pendleton, as she was following the young lady into the room, "not to leave the garden; he may be needed."

She would have been puzzled to account rationally for the impulse which induced her to say this. It was, in fact, merely the instinctive connection between a feeling of alarm, and the desire not to be alone in the presence of that which causes it. Mrs. Pendleton looked round in her turn, to one of her boys, who, childlike, had crept, with feelings of awe, up the staircase after them, and said,—

"Go down, Jem, into the garden, and tell Mr. Mat that Miss Lindisfarn begs he will keep within call, in case she might want him."

The wounded man turned his head quickly toward the door, at which the two women were standing, as the above words were uttered, and gazed earnestly at them for a few moments, and then, with the restless action peculiar to pain and fever, turned his face toward the wall on the farther side of the bed.

"You are badly wounded, I fear," said Kate, in French, and in a trembling voice, as she stepped up to the bedside.

"Yes, to death!" answered the sufferer in the same language, casting his eyes up at her face for a moment, and then uneasily resuming his former position. He had only uttered three words; but the intonation of them seemed to Kate's ear to carry with it strong evidence that the stranger belonged to a more cultivated social grade than that to which the Sillmouth smugglers usually belonged. It might be, however, Kate thought, that they managed matters connected with the education of smugglers better in France.

"I came to see what could be done to cure you, or, at least, to comfort you," she said, in a voice indicating even more misgiving than before; for the stern shortness of the man's manner was discouraging.

"Nothing can be done for the first, and little enough for the last," he said, turning restlessly and impatiently on the bed.

"Did the doctor say when he would come back?" asked Kate, turning towards Mrs. Pendleton, who was standing at the bed-foot.

"No, Miss Kate, he didn't. I zem he thought there was no use in coming back again," returned Winifred, shaking her head sadly.

"But it is impossible," returned Kate, "to leave a man to die in this manner. What are we to do? I declare, that old Mr. Bagstock has no more humanity than a brute, to leave a poor man in this state."

"Well, miss, for the matter of that, Dr. Bagstock knows if a man must die, he must! And what's the good of running up expenses and wasting time for nothing? Dr. Bagstock have a deal to do, and heaps o' people to see tu. And poor folk cant have doctors a-fiddling about 'em, just to amuse their friends, the way rich folks du. If Bagstock could ha' saved his life, he'd ha' done it."

"You were not able to speak to the doctor?" said Kate interrogatively, turning to the patient, and speaking, as before, in French.

"What was the need of speaking?" returned the sufferer, testily. "I want no doctor to tell me that I am dying. I feel the life ebbing out of me."

"You must have lost much blood!" said Kate, to whose mind the stranger's phrase had suggested the idea.

For all reply, he faintly raised one hand, which was lying outside the bedclothes, on the coverlet, to his head, and let it drop again heavily by his side.

"But the wounds have been effectually stanched, I suppose?" returned Kate, who was striving to apply her very slender stock of surgical ideas to the question, whether indeed it was necessary to abandon all hope of saving life.

"I wish you would send the woman to get me a glass of fresh water. That in the bottle here is hot," said the patient.

"He wants to drink, Winny; and he says this water is hot. It is the fever, you know. Go, there is a good soul, and bring him some fresh from the spring."

Mrs. Pendleton took the bottle in her hand, and left the room, without speaking. As soon as her step had been heard descending the stair, which passed immediately on the other side of the wall at the bed-head, the stranger turned his face to the side of the bed at which Kate was standing, and looking up wistfully at her, with the gleam of fever in his restless eyes, said in English,—

"I wish I could speak with you privately. Find some means of sending that woman out of the room."

"You can speak English, then?" said Kate, much surprised.

"I can; but have no wish to do so before these people. You spoke of comfort! You may give some to a dying man, if you will do as I have asked you. You can do so in no other way."

"Certainly, I will do as you desire," replied Kate, not without a little trepidation and beating of the heart; "but," she added, as the idea suddenly flashed across her mind, "I have a friend here with me—a relative; he is a gentleman whom you could trust implicitly—with anything," she added, hesitating a little, "that ought to be told to an honorable gentleman,—and who has more experience, and would be of more use than I could be "—

"No," said the dying man, decisively; "if you will do the charity I have asked, it must be done as I have asked it, and no otherwise."

Mrs. Pendleton's step, returning with the water, was heard on the stair as he finished speaking; and Kate, turning with a light step to the door, met her on the landing-place just outside of it; and taking the water-bottle from her hands, whispered to her,

"Go down-stairs, Winny, and leave me with him for a little while. He says he wants to speak to me alone. I suppose he has something on his mind. Perhaps he wants to ask about a priest. I suppose he is a Catholic. But, Winny, whatever you do, don't leave the house ; so that, if I call, you may hear me and come directly. Mind, now ! "

Mrs. Pendleton gave her a reassuring look and nod ; and Kate, with a feeling of no little nervousness, returned to the stranger's bedside.

" Is the door shut ? " asked the stranger.

" Yes, the door is shut ; and Mrs. Pendleton has gone down-stairs. You cannot be overheard," said Kate.

" You have already perceived," said the man, after a pause of some little duration, while he had apparently been hesitating how to enter on what he wished to say,—"you have no doubt already understood that I am not what my comrades of last night supposed me to be, and that I have reasons for wishing them not to be better informed ? "

" Of course, I suppose so, from your leading them to imagine that you cannot speak English," replied Kate.

" I joined a smuggling venture from the opposite coast as a means, the only one open to me, of coming here unknown to those who might recognize me,—for I have been known in the country formerly,—and of securing an unquestioned return by the same means together with—a person whom I wished to take back with me. All has been frustrated by last night's unlucky work."

He paused, exhausted apparently by the few words he had spoken, or, perhaps mentally occupied in arranging what he had to say, so as best to place the matter before his hearer, and then proceeded with considerable hesitation,—

" The woman here called you Miss Lindisfarn ? "

" That is my name,—Kate Lindisfarn," replied she.

" And she sent a child to give a message from you to Mr. Mat in the garden ? "

" She did so ! "

" That, then, must be Mr. Matthew Lindisfarn, of the Chase. And you have come all the way from Lindisfarn Chase, eight or nine miles from this place, to see me. I know the country, you see, and something of the people."

" Certainly, you must be a Sillshire man. But in that case have you no friends here, who, even if you wished to avoid them before, ought to be made acquainted with your present condition ? "

" I have relatives here,--who would by no means thank me for making myself known to them, or to anybody else. Nevertheless, it is needful that they should be hereafter made aware that I was living this day, and that as soon as I am dead they should know that I am alive no longer. You will see, therefore, Miss Lindisfarn, that my object is to tell you who I am, and to obtain your promise to keep the information secret until I have breathed my last. Will you promise me to do so ? "

" I will keep your secret," said Kate, " if it is not wrong to do so, and if it is not evidently my duty to disclose it."

" You will be well aware, when you have heard it, that the keeping of it is essential to the welfare of all parties concerned, and that the disclosing of it could only serve to cause misery and distress."

" In that case," returned Kate, " you may certainly depend upon my not disclosing it."

The stranger paused again for some minutes, and turned away his face toward the wall on the opposite side of the bed to that on which Kate was standing. Then turning his face and wistful, feverish eyes again toward her, by rolling his head on the pillow, he said,—

" You have an uncle, Miss Lindisfarn, Dr. Theophilus Lindisfarn, living in the Close, at Silverton ? "

Kate, wondering greatly, made no reply, till he added, " That is so, is it not ? "

" Yes," she then said ; " Dr. Lindisfarn in the Close is my uncle."

" And Lady Sempronia, his wife, lives there also ? "

" Of course she lives there also," said Kate, in growing astonishment.

" I did not know whether she was yet living," said the stranger ; and then from want of strength or some other reason, he paused again. After a while, he continued,—

" Has Dr. Lindisfarn, in the Close, at Silverton, any children ? "

" He has none now. He had a son once, who died, many years ago."

" Can you tell me when and where he died ? " asked the stranger, looking up at her.

" I do not know exactly when ; it was several years ago ; and I believe that he died in America."

" Do you know at all the manner of his death ? "

"Yes; he was killed by the Red Indians, in a hunting excursion."

"Do you know how that information reached his family?"

"Not exactly. I know only that pains were taken, and people were sent to America to find out the facts, and that it was considered certain that he had died as I have said."

"Nevertheless, he did not die in that manner," said the stranger, with a heavy sigh.

The truth then flashed upon Kate, that the man who was speaking to her from his dying bed, was indeed that lost cousin, whose existence, whose death, and whose history and memory had always been to her imagination shrouded in a veil of mystery. She knew only that such an one had lived, had died, and for some vaguely understood reason was never mentioned by any one of the family; though it is possible that, if her mind had been set to work upon the subject, Kate's slender knowledge of the line of descent and of real property might have sufficed to make her aware that the existence of her cousin would affect her own position as one of the heiresses of the lands of Lindisfarn; still, never having been taught to look at the fact of his disappearance in its connection with that subject, and not having any precise knowledge of the real state of the case, the sudden conviction that her cousin was living, and was there before her, did not present itself to her mind as bearing in any way upon that matter. There was no mixture, therefore, of any baser alloy in the feeling with which she replied to his last words, "Can it be possible that you are he,—Julian, my lost cousin?"

"It is possible! it is so!" he replied, without manifesting the least share in the effusion of feeling with which Kate had spoken. "The information brought from America was incorrect. I was nearly but not quite killed by the Indians. They strike less heavily than the king's custom-house officers. Worse luck! I survived that time; and I am, still living for a little while, Julian Lindisfarn."

"But, gracious heavens! you must have some better assistance—I must send"— cried Kate, turning hastily toward the door.

"Stay!" said the dying man; "no better assistance could be of any service to me; and remember your promise!"

"I will keep it faithfully. Be assured of that. There is one person indeed to whom I should wish to tell the secret,—my sister, and "—

"Ah! your sister Margaret? She is no longer then in France?"

"No; she is living now at the Chase; and I should like to tell her,—I have no secrets from her,—I should not like to keep this from her;—and of course the secret would be as safe with her as with me."

"Well, do as you will. But remember that you will produce nothing but distress if my being alive here becomes known to the rest of the family."

Kate would, as may be supposed, have bargained for including her godmother in her confidence; but to her great regret Lady Farnleigh was no longer in Silkshire. On the morrow of that stormy March evening, which she was spending at the Chase, she had started for her son's residence in a distant county, in order to be present at the christening of his first child. Possibly, if Lady Farnleigh had been within reach, Kate might not have insisted on telling the secret to Margaret; but, as it was, she felt that she must have some sharer in it, and that it would be very painful to her to keep it from her sister.

"I will be careful," she said, in reply to her cousin's last words; "but I must send at once for better medical help."

And so saying, Kate hurried down to Mr. Mat, who was placidly smoking his pipe in the old boat turned into a summer-house, and begged him to ride as fast as he could to Silverton, and bring back with him if possible Dr. Blakistry.

Now Dr. Blakistry was a very well-known name in that day. He was one of the first surgeons in England; but his delicate health had two or three years previously compelled him, to the great regret of a large circle of London friends and patients, to settle himself in the west of England.

"You know, I suppose," said Julian Lindisfarn, when Kate, having despatched Mr. Mat on his errand, hurried back to the patient's bedside, "why I went away from Silverton?"

"No; I have never heard any of those circumstances spoken of. I know only that for some reason no mention was ever made in the family, of the son of Dr. Lindisfarn, who was supposed to have died in America," said Kate, sadly.

The wounded man, still moving his head with fevered restlessness on the pillow, turned his eyes away from her, and remained silent for a while. Then again looking up at her, he said,—

"I know right well that this doctor you have sent for can only say the same as the other said. I feel that I am dying! Therefore, it will all soon come to the same thing. But since you know nothing about me, or my story, cousin, all I need say is, that if you were to save my life by bringing this other doctor to me, every one that bears the name of Lindisfarn would consider that you had done the worst day's work you ever did in your life, and had caused a misfortune to the family that you could never remedy!"

"But—surely—it all seems so shocking and so incredible!" said Kate, whose head was whirling with the strangeness of the revelation that had been made to her.

"Do not alarm yourself!" said Julian, in a tone that seemed, weak as it was, to have more of irony than of sympathy, or any other feeling in it; "it will all be well very shortly. Only remember that you will not only break your promise to me, but bring all kinds of trouble and distress and heartbreak upon all connected with us,—with you and with me, if you reveal to any human being the fact of my being alive and here."

"I have promised," said Kate; "but it is clear that the first and most pressing need is to procure you better medical help than you have yet had! Who can say what the result may be?"

"You can understand, of course, cousin," resumed Julian, looking up at her, "that if I had lived, as, four-and-twenty hours ago, I had as good a chance of doing as another,— it would have been right that you and all the family should know that I was living. It was my intention to have found the means of making the fact known to them all. But now it becomes necessary to let it be known that my death will not make that change to you which you might naturally expect it to do."

He ceased speaking, and again remained silent for some minutes; while Kate, altogether mystified by what he had been saying, was doubting whether he were not becoming light-headed, and thinking whether she were not perhaps doing mischief by allowing him to go on talking. Presently he continued,—

"I have been thinking that it is not necessary for me now to tell you circumstances, which—have nothing pleasant about them in the telling; but if you would kindly take a small sealed packet from the breast-pocket of that jacket there, which they took off me this morning, and keep it safely till I am dead, and then give it to my father, Dr. Lin-disfarn, all that is needful would then be known and done. And you might do as you please about letting them all know that you were aware that the wounded smuggler who was dying at Sillmouth was Julian Lindisfarn. Will you do this for me, cousin? All I ask is that you tell no human being that I am lying here, till all is over; and that you will give that packet then, and not till then, to Dr. Lindisfarn."

"But if, as I still trust in God, you should not die, cousin?"

"Well, everything is possible! In that case, then, you will be almost equally soon free from your promise; for if I should not die, I shall very soon be away from this. I should in that very improbable case reclaim my packet; and you would be at liberty to do just as you thought fit about telling or not telling anything of our strange meeting here."

Kate took the packet as her cousin desired, and again assuring him that she would faithfully keep the promises she had given him, told him that she would then leave him, as it was not good that he should talk any more.

"Who is this doctor you have sent for, cousin?" he asked, as she was leaving the room.

"A Dr. Blakistry,—a very famous surgeon, who came to settle at Silverton two or three years ago."

"Good; there is no chance then of his recognizing me,—though as Mrs. Pendleton failed to do so, it is little likely that anybody would. Can he speak French?"

"I should think so. In all probability, more or less;—enough to communicate with you. Good-by, cousin. God bless and preserve you! I cannot remain here till after the doctor has seen you. But I shall take care to have his report sent to me; and I shall be sure to come and see you to-morrow."

"I expect no to-morrow; but I think all has been said that needs to be said. Good-by, cousin!"

And so saying, he turned his face to the wall.

Kate had not long to wait, after leaving the sick-chamber, before Mr. Mat returned from his two-mile ride to Silverton, saying that Dr. Blakistry would not fail to be there within an hour or an hour and a half at the outside.

So Kate and Mr. Mat rode back to the Chase; the former much oppressed by the novel and unpleasant feeling of having a secret to keep, and Mr. Mat attributing Kate's silence and absence of good spirits to the painful nature of the Good Samaritan's duty on which she had been engaged.

CHAPTER XXII.

MAIDEN MEDITATIONS NOT FANCY-FREE.

The first thing Kate did on reaching her own room, when she returned from her expedition to Sillmouth, was to place the packet, which had been intrusted to her, in her desk, which she always kept locked. The envelope was not very much larger, though somewhat thicker and more bulky, than an ordinary letter. The next thing was to draw the bolt of her own door, and sit down to meditate on the strange adventure of the morning, and on the facts which it had brought to her knowledge.

She had truly said that she was ignorant of the circumstances which had led to her cousin's quitting Silverton. But she had a vague knowledge that they were of a calamitous and disgraceful kind. And the shocking things that he had said respecting the feelings with which tidings of his return would be received by his family seemed to confirm but too clearly the worst surmises she could form on the subject.

Then came the sudden thought, was it possible that the stranger was not in reality her Cousin Julian after all,—that the latter had really died, as had seemed so certain, in America, and that the man she had spoken with had, for some motive of fraud, wished to personate him?

But a few moments' reflection led her to reject any such hypothesis. The manner and mode of speech, which proved that he certainly did not belong to the class of life in which she had found him ; the correct knowledge he had possessed of persons and things connected with the family, and his evident fear of being recognized as the man he professed to be, all contributed to confirm Kate in the conviction that it was assuredly her Cousin Julian with whom she had spoken. The letter, too, with which he had intrusted her, would doubtless contain evidence of his identity.

But while the considerations which led her to this conclusion were passing through her mind, the thought of the motives that might induce any one to attempt such an impersonation was also naturally presented to her ; and this led her all of a sudden, as she sat meditating somewhat desultorily on all the strange facts and occurrences of the morning, to the recognition of the bearing that Julian's life must have upon the position in the world

of herself and her sister. It was curious that this had not struck her while she had stood by the bedside of her cousin It was not that his death would put matters back again in *statu quo* ; for she had refused to admit to herself that his death was certain. But not even when the wounded man had spoken words calculated to place the matter before her mind, had she sufficiently put away from its front place in her thoughts the immediate misery of the sufferer before her, for her to be able to seize that aspect of the circumstances.

Now the truth flashed upon her, as a precipice suddenly reveals itself to a man wandering about among thick brushwood on its summit. It seems wonderful that his eye should not have caught sight of it before. All of a sudden, one step among the bushes brings him face to face with it.

Suddenly, as she sat thinking over all that had happened that morning, the truth flashed upon her that she was no longer heiress to any portion of her father's estates ! It was a tremendous shock. Kate Lindisfarn was as far as possible from being a worldly-minded or mammon-worshipping girl. She had indeed had so little experience in her life of the difference between poverty and wealth, that it was hardly a matter of merit in her to be free from an overweening regard for the latter. Nevertheless, the fact that suddenly reared itself up naked and clearly defined in the path of her mind was a terrible one, and gave her a violent shock.

Then in the next instant rushed into her mind also a whole troop of thoughts, which changed the sudden pallor caused in her cheeks by the first dismay to a hot, painful flush.

Ellingham !—It would have been a vain hypocrisy for Kate to pretend to her own heart to doubt that Captain Ellingham loved her. He had never told her so. Quite true ! And till he should do so, it was for her to seem unconscious of the fact. But it was useless to play this proper little comedy before her own heart. She knew that Ellingham loved her. And some girls, perhaps, would have rejoiced that now " the dross that made a barrier between them was removed," etc., etc., etc. But Kate was not sufficiently romantic to view the matter in that light. She had not the slightest suspicion that Captain Ellingham had loved her, and would in due course of time ask her to be his wife, for the sake of her fortune. But she was perfectly well aware that he was a very poor man, in a position in which poverty is especially undesirable ; she understood perfectly well that it might be right and prudent for him to marry under favorable circumstances as regarded fortune, when it might be impossible, or at least highly imprudent, to do so otherwise. Above all, she felt that in any case, whatever her sentiments and opinions might be on such a point, if she were called on to consider it, it was not for her to reflect on it under the present circumstances. It was for the consideration of another person ; and what mainly imported to Kate was that it should be placed before him for consideration. It was dreadful to her to think that as matters stood at the present moment she should appear to him in a position and under circumstances that were not her own. She was winning his heart—she knew, at the bottom of her own, that she had already won it —under false colors and false pretences. She felt as if she were an impostor ; and the thought, as it passed through her mind, made her check tingle. It was shocking to her to think that she had during all this time been appearing to the world as the heiress to a handsome fortune, whereas she was in fact nothing of the kind. And it was far more terrible to think that she must continue to do so knowingly until she should be liberated from her promise, and set free to tell the truth by her cousin's departure from Sillshire —or by— It was revolting to her to contemplate release from her position in that other direction. Release from the odious necessity of secrecy would be afforded by her cousin's death. But as regarded her own position and expectations,—what was that which Julian had said about his death causing no difference to her and which now recurred to her mind in a different train of ideas from any with which she had connected it when she had first heard it ? What was the meaning of those words ? But this was not what was pressing on her for immediate consideration. Her mind revolted from contemplating Julian's death as certain, and from calculating on the consequences that might result from it. She was very far from imagining or attempting to persuade herself, that a fall from the position of one of the Lindisfarn heiresses to that of an almost undowered girl was a trifling matter, or other than a very

serious misfortune and calamity. But it was most true that as she sat in the chair before her little drawing-table, absorbed in these meditations, the idea of continuing to represent herself, or suffering herself to be represented, to her lover as what she was not—for she did not attempt to disguise from herself that she knew him to be such—was infinitely more terrible. This was the matter that pressed for instant solution. What was she to do ? What line of conduct to pursue ? Oh that she had not bound herself to secrecy ! And yet the truth of Julian's declaration that trouble and distress would be caused to everybody whose well-being she was bound most to care for, by a discovery of his presence, was evident. What was she to do ? Oh that Lady Farnleigh had not been so unfortunately called away ! Had she been in Sillshire, Kate would doubtless have stipulated that she should have been made a sharer in the secret. She might have been safely trusted. She would have known how to release her goddaughter from her false position as regarded the only person whose continuance in error respecting her real prospects for a day or two more or less much signified to her.

Then her mind reverted to the conversation at the breakfast-table on the yesterday morning, and passed in review all those passages of it which have been described as having been put by in the hiding-places of her memory for future use ;—but not for use under such circumstances as the present !—and the tears gathered slowly in her eyes as she thought of the pleasure they had given her, —of the upright, loyal heart of that brave man, who, as Kate's own heart with instinctive sympathy told her, could not have "loved her so much, loved he not honor more,"—of the hard, dangerous, and thankless nature of that "duty" to which he was so loyally true, and of the fond, sweet thought that she, even she, was to be the reward which fate had in store for him, and the means of placing him above the necessity of so ungrateful a task !

The hot tears rose and gathered and brimmed over on the peachlike cheek, the rounded swell of which no sorrow had ever yet mined. The sensation of them on her face recalled her mind from its truant wandering to the needs of the present. She dashed away the tears with an angry action of her hand.

"What a fool I am," she said aloud, "to let myself think of things that might have been, when there is so much need of thinking of things as they are!"

Something must absolutely be done!—something;—but what? It was absolute torture to her to think of herself as receiving the homage and the wooing—there was no use or honesty in mincing the phrase; it *was* wooing that Captain Ellingham had been offering to her; and she dared not deny to her own heart that she knew it was so—of Captain Ellingham, when he was led to suppose that she was an heiress of large fortune, and she was in possession of the truth that nothing of the sort was the case. It was torture—intolerable torture to her. But what could she do?

Could she write to Lady Farnleigh?—not to betray her cousin's secret in defiance of her solemn promise; that was impossible,—but some sort of letter, couched in mysterious terms, which should induce her to intimate to Captain Ellingham that he had better not think of proposing t) her (Kate); for that she was not what she seemed to be! And she really took pen in hand to essay the composition of such a letter; and after two or three trials, gave up the attempt in despair. How was it possible for her to request that Captain Ellingham should be warned that he had better not offer to her, before he had ever uttered a word of the kind? How was she to inform her godmother of the fact that she was not her father's heir in any manner that should appear sane, and should not at once bring upon her such an inquiry and examination as would make the keeping of her secret impossible?

Had her godmother been there present, it might have been possible—it seemed to Kate—so to speak to her as to obtain her assistance, without divulging the secret she was bound to keep. But it was impossible to do this by letter.

And then she had—and had had ever since the *tête-à-tête* of the breakfast-table—a lurking consciousness that this offer from Captain Ellingham, which she would now give worlds to stave off, was not very far away. It was a lurking, vague, unavowed consciousness, which would never have shaped itself into definite form before her mind, but would only have flung a rose-colored light of unquestioned happiness over her life, like the golden glory

thrown far and wide over the landscape by the lambent summer lightning, had it not been condensed into fear by the new circumstances of her life. But now, should the offer come,—it was agony to think of it!—what should she do? What she must do was clear, so far. She must refuse—but without assigning any reason—any motive! It was very cruel—very dreadful—and after all that had come and gone! And thereupon a crowd of little minute consciousnesses came flocking into her mind,—memories of looks and glances, emphasized words charged with an amount of meaning accurately gauged and weighed by the self-registering and miraculously delicate crossometer of a young girl's fresh heart, pressings of the hand so slight and shy that they did their work rather by electric than by dynamic force, yet did it surely, and left marks on the memory never more to be cancelled,—all these stored treasures, each labelled with its date as accurately as Miss Immy marked her eggs, came thronging into her mind from their separate memory cells. They had so often been summoned forth in Kate's hours of reverie and self-communion, that it was natural for them to come as usual now. But now they were not wanted. They might go back—poor faded treasures!—to their hiding-places; treasures ever, and not to be destroyed, save with consciousness itself; but no more, never more to be reviewed on memory's gay and gala days,—relics only, sacred though sad, to be brought forth in seasons of the heart's fast-days and humiliations.

And again, as she forcibly thrust back these remembrances into the deepest recesses of her mind, the tears overflowed upon her cheeks; and again she angrily shook them from her, and accused them of interfering with the active measures it behooved her to take. Yet, what active measures? Again, what—what was she to do?

And Margaret too? Yes! How was that to be done? There was Margaret to be talked to. How glad Kate was that she had stipulated that her sister should be told; she had done so at the moment merely from the feeling that she liked to have no secrets from her sister, and from the desire to have some one to help her in sustaining the weight of it. The necessity that Margaret also should be made aware of what her true position was, with a view to properly regulating her conduct toward others had not then occurred to her. But now it was but too clear to her, when she turned her mind to that part of the sea of perplexities which surrounded her, that Margaret was in the same difficulty with regard to Falconer that she was in regard to Ellingham. Kate had seen, with no reason or inclination to regret or object to it, that Falconer had been very evidently paying assiduous court to her sister, and that Margaret had been very abundantly willing to accept as much of his homage as he chose to bring to her shrine. Kate could not doubt that Frederick Falconer purposed making Margaret his wife. In his case, it is true, there could not be the same difficulty in marrying an undowered wife as in the case of Ellingham. Frederick Falconer would be abundantly rich enough to marry a girl without a fortune, if he chose to do so. But, somehow or other, though she had never put into tangible form any ideas in her mind upon the subject, she felt as if she had had a revelation on the point, that Freddy Falconer would not so choose. She felt far more certain of it in his case than she did in that other, which she would not permit herself to scrutinize more narrowly. And she did not feel any necessity for laying heavy blame on Frederick on that account. Doubtless his father would wish him to increase his wealth by marriage. But the conviction that it would not suit Mr. Frederick Falconer to marry a girl without a penny, that he would never have sought her sister's love, had he supposed her to have been such, and that he would consider himself to have been cruelly deluded,—or at all events, a most unfortunate victim of error,—if he were to propose to her under such circumstances,—all these considerations made her feel very acutely the absolute necessity of in some way preventing him as well as Ellingham from proceeding in the path in which both of them were so evidently advancing under erroneous impressions.

Frederick had been up at the Chase that day, as Kate knew. She and Mr. Mat had met him riding down the hill near the ivy bridge over the Lindisfarn Brook, as they were returning from Sillmouth. God grant that nothing decisive had passed between him and Margaret that day! Kate thought that nothing could have happened, or Margaret would doubtless have rushed into her room in-

stantly on her return to tell her of it. But then Kate had only known her sister for a few months. And it may be that her security based on this presumption was not founded on a rock.

Kate looked at her watch, and saw that her sad and painful musings had lasted more than two hours. It was time to dress for dinner; and Margaret would doubtless be coming up-stairs in a minute, if she were not already in her room. But there was no time now for the conversation that must take place between them, and which would necessarily be a lengthy one. It was best to defer it till they should again be alone together before going to bed. It was painful to Kate to have to sit with her sister through the evening with the consciousness of the blow it would be her duty to inflict on Margaret, all unconscious the while of the evil coming upon her. She had a sort of unreasoned and unavowed, but none the less irresistible, conviction, moreover, that the news of the change in her position would be a more dreadful and stunning blow to Margaret than it had been to herself; and the necessity of inflicting this blow was not the least part of the more instant and immediate cares and sorrows that were pressing upon her.

She set about the work of dressing with that languid distaste for the exertion which petty cares of the kind are apt to produce in those who are suffering from the pressure of serious troubles. Margaret came into her room before she was quite ready to go down, charmingly dressed as usual,—for she had become quite reconciled to the pleasing toil of making habitually an evening toilet,—and evidently in high spirits. Kate was sure that her interview with Fred Falconer had been a pleasant one, at all events; for when by chance there were any thorns among Margaret's roses, however few or small they might be, she was apt to give unmistakable evidence of having suffered from them for some time afterward.

"What! not ready, Kate? And you are always lecturing me for being behindhand! Why, it is two hours or more since you came home. What have you been about? And you seem to be all in the dumps too."

"My morning's work at Sillmouth was not a pleasant one, you know," said Kate, blushing with a sensation quite new to her, as the consciousness of playing the hypocrite with her sister, though only for a few hours, passed over her mind.

"And I am sure I don't see why you should meddle with such disagreeable people. I own, for my part, I do not think it a proper sort of thing at all. And it only shows what poor dear Madame de Renneville always used to say,—that one never can step, were it only a hair's breadth, out of one's own proper sphere, without being punished for the indiscretion in some way or other."

"But perhaps it is not always quite easy to know what is one's proper sphere, and what are the limits of it," said Kate, with a sigh, as she once again put a wet towel to her eyes, before going down-stairs. "Come, dear, I am ready now," she added. "Let us go down. I must tell you all about my morning's adventure before we go to bed to-night."

And then, for the first time in her life, Kate had to pass the evening in the family circle with the heavy sense of a secret to be kept from all those dear and familiar friends, who had no secrets from her, with whose hearts she had ever had all in common. And the weight was very grievous to her.

CHAPTER XXIII.
SILLSHIRE *versus* PARIS.

At last the long evening wore itself to its close; and the two Lindisfarn lasses went up to their adjoining rooms together.

"Now, then, Margaret," said Kate, as they reached the top of the stairs together: "I must tell you all about my ride to Sillmouth this morning; I should have told you before, dear sissy, if there had been any opportunity."

"Why! is there anything to tell that signifies?" returned Margaret, opening her great handsome eyes in astonishment.

"Yes, there is a good deal to tell," said Kate, with a sigh; "come into my room with me, darling, or let me come into yours; for we must have a long talk together."

"Not very long, I hope, for I am very sleepy," said Margaret, yawning; "but how strange you look, Kate! What is it? Is anything the matter?"

"You need not come up till we ring, Simmons," said Kate, as Margaret followed her into her room.

"You can go into my room, Simmons, and put my things into my drawers the while; for they are all over the room. I could not find the dress I wanted for dinner."

Simmons went as directed to repair the disorder in her wardrobe made by Miss Margaret, who was, as that experienced lady's-maid declared, a regular untidy one; and Kate, before sitting down in the same chair in front of her little drawing-table, which she had sat in during her two hours of meditation before dinner, shut the door of communication between the two rooms; while Margaret, much wondering what was coming, and fearing a preachment on sundry small matters of which she was conscious, and which she surmised might not be altogether to her sister's liking, installed herself in the large chair that stood before Kate's toilet-table.

"Miss Immy has been telling tales, I suppose!" thought she to herself. "Who could have guessed that the old thing was spying all the time that she seemed fast asleep?"

"You know that Winny begged me to go over to her at Sillmouth to see a poor man who had been wounded in a fray with the coast-guard men, and who was lying in danger of death in her cottage?" began Kate.

"Yes, I know. And I must say that in your place, Kate, I should not have dreamed of doing anything of the sort," said Margaret, thinking it wise, in case Kate meditated a preachment, to be beforehand in occupying the attacking ground.

"I think, dearest, that you would have done so in my place. You cannot feel, you know, towards Winny Pendleton as I do; and therefore you cannot tell how strongly I felt called upon to do as she wished. I assure you, it was a very unpleasant task; though I little thought, when I started on the errand, what a surprise was awaiting me!"

"What was it?" asked Margaret, while her now thoroughly awakened curiosity expressed itself in her widely opened eyes.

"Do you ever remember to have heard, Margaret, that our uncle, Dr. Lindisfarn, once had a son?" asked Kate.

"No, never. I thought he never had had any children," replied Margaret, with increasing astonishment.

"You might very well never have heard of it; but our uncle had a son, called Julian. I can remember seeing him when a little girl.

He was then a grown-up young man. All of a sudden he left Silverton, and we saw no more of him. He got into trouble of some sort. I believe he did something wrong. I do not know what the story was: but I know there was great grief and sorrow about it. I believe it half broke poor Aunt Sempronia's heart. But there was a great mystery on the subject; and after he went away, nobody ever spoke of him; and it was as if he were dead. After a time, there came news that he *was* dead, really. He was killed, it was said, by the Red Indians in America. People declared that they saw him killed, and from that time, till now, I have never heard his name mentioned. But, Margaret, darling," continued Kate, taking her sister's hand in hers, and looking earnestly into her face, "the wounded man, whom I was called to see at Sillmouth this morning, was our Cousin Julian!"

"You don't say so!" said Margaret; "how very odd!"

"It was a strange chance, indeed!—the stranger that it *was* a chance," replied Kate; "for nobody knew, and nobody knows now who he is; and he had nothing to do with sending for me. But he happened to hear Winny call me by my name, and then he discovered himself to me."

"And it was all untrue, then, about his being killed in America?" said Margaret.

"It was a mistake. He was nearly killed, but not quite; and he recovered. He did not tell me the particulars of the story."

"And now he is come back to his father! But how did he chance to be wounded with the smugglers?" asked Margaret, whose curiosity, excited by the strangeness of the story, did not seem to be mixed with any other emotion.

"He had joined the smugglers in their venture as a means of coming over here from France secretly; but he was not coming to his father; he does not wish anybody to know that he is here; and from the manner in which he spoke, I fear that much trouble and distress would come of its being discovered that he is in the neighborhood."

"Why did he tell you who he was, then?" asked Margaret.

"Partly, as it seemed to me, as far as I could understand him, because, though he was very anxious that it should not be known that he was in Sillshire, as long as he lived, he wished that it should be known who he was after his death; and partly, because he felt how needful it is that we should be made aware that he was not killed by the Indians, as was supposed. I made a condition with him, that I should tell you; but I promised, faithfully to tell nobody else, and promised for you, that you would keep the secret also."

"Why is it so needful for us to know that he was not killed? If he does not mean to come back to his father, why could he want any of us to know that he is alive? I do not see any good in our knowing it," said Margaret, raising her eyebrows with a little shrug.

Kate's heart failed her as she answered, "Don't you see, dear Margaret, the difference it makes to you and me? Don't you perceive that if our Cousin Julian is alive, neither you nor I are heirs to our father's property?"

Margaret's habitual paleness became lividness as she said, "Nonsense, Kate! It can't be true! Do you believe that people's fortunes can go backwards and forwards in that way? If that were the case, how could any man know what a girl's fortune was? Besides, the property belongs to our father. Do you suppose that anything can touch our *dot?*"

"Dearest Margaret, I fear it is but too clear that if uncle has a son, the daughters of my father do not inherit the property. The lands of Lindisfarn go to the male heirs of my grandfather."

"And what, then, do we inherit? What is our *dot* to come from?" asked Margaret, while a dreadful spasm was clutching her heart with an icy grip.

"Alas! sister dear, if there is a male heir to the property, we have no inheritance. There is no source from which any dower for us, as it is called in English, can come."

"It is too horrible to be true," said Margaret, looking and feeling as if she must fall from her chair. "I cannot believe it. It is too wicked!"

"But, dearest Margaret, *who* is wicked? Nobody has done anything they ought not to have done. According to the law, Uncle Theophilus having a son comes to the same thing as if papa had a son. That is all. Everybody knows that if we had a brother, we should not be heiresses to the estate."

"It is horribly wicked!" said Margaret, as the tears gathered in her eyes; "the law is abominably wicked,—the law of this vile, barbarous country!"

"Oh, Margaret, Margaret! don't say such shocking words! Think that it is England, Sillshire, our own native land!" remonstrated Kate, who was almost as much scandalized as if her sister had spoken of their own father in similar terms.

"I hate England! It is a vile, horrid country to make such wicked laws; I don't believe it can be true!" said Margaret, now fairly sobbing, and with the inconsistency of passion.

"It is very dreadful to me to hear you speak so, Margaret! But I don't wonder at your feeling it hard. It *is* hard; very hard, because of the disappointment and the false expectation. But that is not the fault of the law, nor of England."

"It is the fault of this bad and wicked man, who was obliged to go away, and who pretended he was dead, and now comes back to rob us of our father's property."

"It is not his fault that we are not heiresses; nor is it his fault, though it arises out of his fault, that we have been led into error," said clear-headed, direct-minded Kate. "Poor Julian did not, as you say, Margaret, pretend to be dead. If fault there were in the matter, it was in those who believed his death on insufficient grounds."

"You have no feeling, Kate,—no feeling at all," sobbed Margaret, "to talk in such a way! I say it is wicked, horribly wicked that poor girls should be robbed of their own father's fortune in such a way! And I say it *is* a vile, hateful country, where such things can be done. And I love France a thousand times better, and always did, and always shall,—a thousand, thousand times! a thousand, thousand times, I do! I hate England, and all the people in it!" cried Margaret, in the impotence of her rage. She was suffering pain; and the first impulse of some natures, when they suffer, is to inflict, if it be within their power, pain on others. Margaret did feel just then that she hated England; but the passionate assertion of it was prompted by the bad instinct that would fain avenge on Kate the pain she was suffering.

"Dear sister," said Kate, taking her hand, and looking into her face with the tenderest sympathy, "I *do* feel for you! It is very, very hard to bear! You will not speak as you do now, when you have time for reflection."

"Yes, I shall! I shall always speak so! It is right to speak so! It is wicked. And I hate everything that is wicked! And so would you, too, if you were good yourself. Didn't I tell you that no good could come of your going to see smugglers and vulgar people? And now see what has come of it!" said Margaret, in a bitterly reproachful tone.

"Nay, sister dear! what has come of my visit to Sillmouth is not that we are no longer heiresses of the Lindisfarn property, but only that we know the fact that such is the case. And that is evidently an advantage,—and perhaps a very great blessing! Don't you see, Margaret, that it is so?" continued Kate, after a pause, looking earnestly into her sister's face.

"A blessing to know this horrible misfortune? Are you mad, Kate, or are you only mocking me?" said Margaret, casting a passionately reproachful glance at her sister from amid her tears.

"Not mad, dear Margaret. But just think a little what the consequences of not knowing our position with regard to our expectations of fortune might be! It is bad enough, —very, very grievous and distressing, that others should not be equally well aware of it. And I trust that erelong there may be no necessity for further concealment on the subject. But it might be very much worse, if we were ourselves ignorant of the fact. Don't you see this?"

"I don't know what you mean! I only know that I have been robbed and wronged and shamefully, most shamefully treated! Poor Madame de Renneville! How little did she think what fate she was sending me to in England!"

It was difficult for Kate, amid her own distress, and in her anxiety, to lead her sister to contemplate the subject of their disinheritance with reference to the circumstances that had pushed themselves into the foreground in her own mind,—it was difficult for her to listen with equanimity to speculations as to what Madame de Renneville might have thought about the matter. She strove, however, to do so; having, at all costs, to bring Margaret to the consideration of the matter from that point of view which appeared to her the most urgently to require immediate attention. She felt considerable difficulty in doing this. A tingling blush on her cheek had been simultaneous with the first birth in her own pure, loyal, and uncompromisingly honest mind, of the thought that it behooved her to guard a man, who had never spoken to her of love, from the danger of doing so under a false impression of her position. Maidenly feeling had produced the blush, and had caused the pain which had accompanied it. But it had not blinded her to the straight-forward, honest duty of preventing a step which in her heart she knew to be imminent, and which she knew was about to be taken by one under a delusion. She had suffered no sentimental mock-modesty to stand in the way of her being honest and true for her-self; and now she had to be equally frank in the case of her sister. But she did not the less feel the difficulty. And Margaret's apparent obtuseness to any idea of the sort made this difficulty greater to her. It seemed as if she must have been over-bold to be struck at once by the possibility of a danger, which did not apparently suggest itself to the more delicately unconscious mind of her sister. Yet it was certain to her that Margaret had fully as much reason to apprehend such a misfortune as she had. She was perfectly well aware that it was quite as likely that Margaret might any day receive an offer from Falconer as she herself from Ellingham. Could it be that Margaret was wholly un-conscious of this? Was it necessary for her to open her sister's eyes to the fact as well as suggest to her that the fact constituted, under the circumstances, a danger, which it was her duty to guard against?

" But the worst of the matter, sissy dear," she began, again taking the hand which Margaret in her petulant outburst of temper had snatched from her,—" the worst of the matter, by far, is that this unfortunate change in our positions may—you know, darling—may have an influence on others as well as ourselves."

Margaret turned her eyes sharply on her sister's face with a look of shrewd and keen observation for an instant before she replied.

" You mean that girls without a *dot* have no chance of marrying creditably ! Of course I know that ! There was no need of casting that in my teeth. I know what you are thinking of, Kate. You have Lady Farn-leigh's six thousand pounds to fall back on. It is at least something. I have nothing ! There is no need to remind me of it."

" Oh, Margaret, Margaret ! " cried Kate, inexpressibly shocked, and in the voice of one who is assailed by a sudden spasm of bodily pain, and the silently rising tears filled her eyes as she looked into her sister's face with a piteous expression of remonstrance against the cruelty of this speech.

" Well, you know, that must make a great difference. It would be affectation to pretend to forget it," rejoined Margaret, feeling some little compunction for the bru-tality of the words which had given Kate such a sharp pang. " But, at all events," she continued, " we have the advantage of a good appearance for the present. The main point is when girls have no fortune, to keep the fact from being generally known, as far as possible. And in this respect, at least, our position is a favorable one. For it does not seem to enter into the plans of this horri-ble cousin to make his existence known for the present, at any rate. So that we shall at all events have a respite, and — who knows "—

Kate gazed at her sister as she thus spoke, and after she had finished, with absolutely speechless astonishment, which sank grad-ually to a persuasion that there was some mis-understanding between them somehow.

" Don't you understand me ? " said Mar-garet, with petulant impatience, in answer to her sister's look.

" I think, Margaret, we don't understand each other," replied Kate, whose brain felt confused by a whole host of conflicting thoughts and feelings. " I cannot suppose that you could wish that any man should "— here the tingling blush came again into Kate's cheek—" should ask you to be his wife," Kate went on more boldly, her steel-true hon-esty of purpose coming to her aid, " under the impression that your position as regards fortune and expectations was different from what it really is. You would wish, undoubt-edly, to prevent such an error by every pos-sible means in your power. You would wish to save him from the unfair and very embar-rassing necessity of declaring himself unable to carry out an intention formed under dif-ferent circumstances, and yet more to save yourself from the possibility of the horrible suspicion that you sought to incite a proposal by letting it be supposed that you had advantages to offer which you knew that you had not. Think of the horror of such a position, Margaret!" said Kate, as the burning blood flushed afresh all over her neck and face and forehead.

"Indeed, Kate," returned her sister, "I think we do misunderstand each other. We look at all these questions from such different points of view. I confess that to my mind, and with the principles in which I have been brought up, there is a degree of indelicacy in a girl thus setting herself to weigh and estimate the motives that may lead a gentleman to pay his addresses to her. You know, my sister, that the English are considered to be a nation of shopkeepers, and to look at everything with a trading eye. And in what you say I see the truth of the reproach. In France a *demoiselle bien elevée* never meddles with any of these considerations. All such matters are arranged by her parents; and it is surely more proper and more delicate to leave it to them. And I must own that the insular shopkeeping spirit, which shows itself in calculations beforehand as to how much of the love of a *futur* may have been excited by your fortune, and how much by your own *beaux yeux*, is to my feeling revolting."

"I don't think, Margaret," said Kate, after a minute's thoughtful pause, and feeling a little puzzled and much pained, "that I quite follow your ideas. For my own part, I don't so much care whether the spirit in which we have to act in this matter is a shopkeeping spirit or not, so that it be a straightforward, honest one. I had much rather—God knows how much rather!—avoid, as far as one can, speculating on the supposed intentions of this or that man in a question of this sort, and very much more abstain from taking any active step in consequence of such suppositions. The course which a girl should pursue in these matters seems to me a simple one enough. I think she should take care to appear to everybody to be what she really is in all respects, and, until her love is sought for, take no other care. And generally, as regards the external matters of fortune, this is the simplest and easiest thing in the world. But we are placed in an exceptional and very painful position. If we were at liberty to disclose Julian's secret openly, our course would be at least easy and clear. If we had

neither of us "—here the rich blush returned—"any reason to imagine that—that our position as regards fortune was of any interest to anybody in particular, we might be content to allow the error of everybody with respect to us to continue for the short time that Julian's safety—for I suppose his safety is in question—will require the secret to be kept. But if that is not the case, Margaret," Kate continued, looking fixedly and with earnest seriousness into her sister's face; "if we either or both of us have in our inmost hearts reason to suppose that there is any one to whom the question of our heiress-ship to these estates may be a matter of great importance, you will surely agree with me that, whether it be dictated by a shopkeeping spirit or not, what we ought to have most earnestly at heart should be to find some means of preventing that somebody from saying or doing anything which—they might, perhaps, not do, if they were aware of the truth."

"I, for my part, even if I could agree to all you have been saying," replied Margaret, "have not the remotest idea, thank Heaven, that I am a subject of interest to any man who would be mercenary enough to be influenced in his feelings by the amount of fortune I may possess."

"I hope so, with all my heart, dearest; but you see at once, that if that is the case, the knowledge of your want of fortune, when it shall become known, will make no difference; and you will be spared the horror of having received and accepted such a proposal when made under an impression which you knew to be delusive."

"But if the fact of this odious man's existence must not be revealed?" urged Margaret.

"That makes the difficulty and the cruel embarrassment!" returned Kate; "the only thing I can think of, is to try to act in such a manner that nothing may be said—to give no opportunity—to discourage anything that might lead to—to anything of the sort," said the poor girl, twisting her hands together in the extremity of her distress and embarrassment. "One thing is quite clear," she continued, after a pause, and speaking more energetically: "that if unfortunately any proposal were made to either of us before we are at liberty to reveal the truth, it must be met by a rejection."

"On what ground, pray?" asked Margaret, shortly.

"Ah! that makes the misery of it! We can assign no ground. It is horrible in any case not to be able to tell the truth; and worst of all in such a case as that. It would be absolutely necessary to refuse, and absolutely impossible to give the real reason for refusing. And this is what makes it so very, very much to be prayed for that no such question may be raised before we are at liberty to tell the truth to all the world. One thing only is quite beyond doubt; namely, that a rejection could be the only answer. Think what it would be to accept such a proposal, made in the persuasion that it was offered to the heiress of Lindisfarn, and accepted by you with the knowledge that you were no such thing! I think it would kill me on the spot!"

"You have very high-flown sentimental notions, Kate. Do you mean to tell me now, in earnest, that if Captain Ellingham were to offer to you to-morrow morning, you should refuse him?"

"Most unquestionably I should," said Kate, while a cold thrill shot through her heart at the thought of it.

"And without telling him any reason, or at least without telling him your real reason for doing so?" pursued Margaret.

"I should. How could I do otherwise? I should at least know that the time would come, when he would know the real reason—no, I don't mean that;—perhaps he would not ever know that! But at least I should have saved him from forming an engagement under a mistaken notion, and I should have saved myself from the intolerable suspicion that it was possible that I wished him to do so. Of course, Margaret, you would be obliged to do the same?"

"I can't say what I should do! I can't calculate and arrange beforehand, as coldly as you do, Kate, what I should say on such an occasion. The most delicate and proper course, I believe, would be to refer to papa for an answer."

"But not when you know that there are material circumstances of which papa is ignorant," urged Kate.

"Really, Kate, I don't know what I should do! But I own I do not see the necessity of debating what course I ought to pursue if an offer should be made to me, which never has been made, and which it is not likely ever will be made!"

"Oh, Margaret!"

"Besides, what is the use of all this, if, as you say, this Julian is dying? If he dies, all this trouble and misfortune has passed over."

"But, in the first place, Margaret, I don't like to build hopes upon my poor cousin's death; in the second place, even if he were to die, the mischief that I dread either for you or for myself may arise first; and in the third place, although he said he was dying,—and when I first saw him I thought that certainly he must be, he looked so ghastly,—still before I came away, I began to have hopes that he might recover. He had seen nobody but old Bagstock—he is an old doctor at Sillmouth, who is good for nothing;—but I sent Dr. Blakistry to him, who is a first-rate surgeon, and I do not think it at all unlikely that his life may be saved."

"It would be much better for everybody if he were to die!" said Margaret.

"Oh, Margaret, you must not talk so! It seems like murder to wish that another person may die! Besides, I am not sure,—I don't understand the matter—but he said something about his death not making any difference to us. Perhaps he may have sold or in some way made away with his right to the property."

"Good heavens, Kate! Could he do that?"

"I don't know; I am very ignorant of all such matters; certainly he did say that his death would make no difference; and I understood him to allude to the inheritance of the estates."

"It is very, very dreadful, and I declare"—

"What were you going to say?" asked Kate; for Margaret broke off her sentence in the middle.

"Never mind! I don't know what I was going to say. It's time to go to bed; and I want to think over the shocking news you have given me."

And Margaret, as she spoke, got up from her chair, and taking up her candlestick from Kate's toilet-table, turned to go to her own room.

"When do you think you are likely to hear

the result of the visit of this doctor you have sent to our cousin?" she asked, as she was leaving the room.

"I hoped I might have heard to-night. To-morrow morning no doubt I shall get a message," replied Kate.

"Of course you will tell me directly."

"Of course. But oh, Margaret dear, do not let your heart wish for the death of this unfortunate man!"

"It seems to me that we are the unfortunates, rather! Good-night. We shall probably know something in the morning."

"Good-night, dear! And oh, Margaret, do think over the absolute necessity of avoiding any proposal, while all remains in doubt and we are bound to secrecy, and of refusing it, if unfortunately it should come!"

"Yes! I will think of it. Good-night!"

And so the sisters parted for the night; and no doubt Margaret *did* meditate long and deeply, while probably some not unpardonable tears wetted her pillow, on the important tidings that had been communicated to her. But it may be surmised that her night thoughts did not tend exactly in the direction Kate would have wished. Indeed, certain glimpses into the interior of Margaret's heart and mind, which had been afforded to Kate by some passages of the above conversation, had been the second painful shock her mind had undergone that day. She felt that there were many points, and indeed whole ranges of subjects, on which there was neither sympathy nor possibility of agreement between them. But she was still unaware of the wide divergence of feeling and opinion, and of the amount of difference in the course of action which this might lead to, in the important circumstances now before them.

CHAPTER XXIV.
THE LINDISFARN STONE.

As Kate was going across the hall into the breakfast-room, with more of heavy care on her brow and trouble in her heart than she had ever known a short day or two ago, the following note from Sillmouth, which had been brought up by a messenger early that morning, was put into her hand.

It was from Dr. Blakistry, and ran thus:

"MY DEAR MISS LINDISFARN,—

"Mrs. Pendleton—your old nurse, as she tells me, and a very decent sort of woman, though a smuggler's wife—has requested that before leaving her house I would write to you my report of the patient I have just been visiting. I am happy to tell you—though I trust, my dear young lady (and you will forgive an old man for saying so much) I trust and suppose, that you have no interest in him beyond that of simple humanity—that he is likely to do well, and recover. He fancied that he was dying,—the result of great loss of blood and consequent weakness and depression, and of the shock to the nervous system. With due care, and a common amount of prudence, he will, I doubt not, be back again in *La belle France* in a month's time, and will, I hope, stay there ; for though I saw enough to make it evident to me, that he does not belong to the same class of life as the men with whom he has been associating, I did not see anything to lead me to think the gentleman an acquisition to Sillshire.

"Believe me, my dear Miss Lindisfarn,
"Very faithfully yours,
"JAMES BLAKISTRY."

Kate hurried up-stairs again to show the note to Margaret, who had not yet left her room.

"So *that* chance is gone!" said Margaret, in much depression of spirits, and looking as if she had passed a sleepless night.

"Oh, Margaret, we ought to be thankful that the temptation to wish for this poor cousin's death has been removed from us."

"You see what the doctor says. He does not seem to have been prepossessed in his favor, by any means."

"But, Margaret, another part of the note is most important to us. Do you observe Dr. Blakistry says that he may get well enough to return to France in a month? It will be a whole month, therefore, before we are at liberty to tell the fact which will make our own position known to everybody. This is very, very hard. It is dreadful!"

"Yes! it will be a month," said Margaret, with a thoughtful rather than with a distressed expression of face ; "before we are at liberty to make it known that we are portionless! A month is a long time."

"Dreadful! It makes me almost desperate to think of it! How will it be possible to avoid"—

"To avoid what?" said Margaret, pettishly.

"What I was talking to you of last night, you know, dear!" said Kate ; while a misgiving as to her sister's feelings and ideas upon the subject, almost as painful to her as any of the many painful phases of the situation, came across her mind.

"Do you know, Katey dear," returned Margaret, "it seems to me that we must each of us manage our matters in the miserably unfortunate circumstances which have fallen upon us, according to her own light; on one thing you may rely,—and it seems to me that it is all you ought to ask of me,—I will faithfully keep my promise to you. You may be sure that the secret is safe with me. I shall not mention the fact of our Cousin Julian's existence to a single soul till you tell me I am free to do so!"

"Of course I know that you will keep your promise. But, Margaret dear, that is not the point I am anxious about. You know that is not it!"

"Well, as to the rest, I must say it seems to me that the best plan would be for us not to interfere with each other. The two cases, you must remember, are widely different. Captain Ellingham—I presume it is for him that you are so desperately alarmed—is a poor man. Lady Farnleigh, you know, very properly told us so when she first brought him here. Whether she would not have done better and acted a more friendly part under the circumstances than she abstained from bringing him here at all, is another matter. I, at all events, have no reason to complain of her imprudence in doing so! But Mr. Falconer—for I wont pretend not to understand that you are thinking of him, in your sermons to me—Mr. Falconer is not a poor man,—very far from it! And that makes such a difference as to change entirely all the considerations that ought to govern one's conduct in the matter."

"But oh, Margaret, you would not have him propose to you, thinking you an heiress, to find out his mistake afterward? It would be impossible for you to accept him under such circumstances. It would be dishonoring to you, and to all of us!"

"You go upon the supposition, Kate, that Mr. Falconer is as mercenary as"—

Kate gave a start that was almost a bound; and there was a something in the glance of her eye that Margaret had never seen there before, and that probably had never been there before,—a something that warned her to stop short in what she was saying; and to continue,—

—"That is I don't mean to express any opinion of anybody else; I only mean that you argue—you must admit you do—upon the supposition that Falconer is actuated by mercenary motives in his attentions to me. Now I don't think that is fair, or charitable, or delicate. I entirely refuse to believe anything of the kind. It would have been impossible for me to have listened to him for an instant otherwise; for my own heart revolts so instinctively from any mixing of worldly considerations with matters that should be regulated by the purest impulses of the affections only, the whole of my nature rebels so strongly against the shopkeeping spirit in which, as I have always heard, such things are regarded in England, that I cannot submit to be guided by any maxims drawn from such notions."

"That seems all very right," said Kate, sadly, and somewhat mystified by the grandiloquent sentimentalities of Margaret's oration, delivered with a tone and manner which would have compelled Madame de Renneville to have clasped her instantly to her bosom, if she could have heard it; "but yet," she added, timidly,—

"There is the bell!" interrupted Margaret, glad to avoid what she knew Kate was going to say, just as well, or perhaps more clearly than Kate knew it herself; "we must make haste down, or we shall be late, and papa will be angry."

"Yes, we must go!" said Kate, ruefully; "and mind, dear, we must keep the best countenance we can. It is very difficult to have trouble at heart, and not show it in one's face!"

"I dare say it is at first, to those who have not had the advantage of the best education," said Margaret, "but Madame de Rrwenneville always insisted on the necessity of being able to do so, to a *jeune personne bien elevée*."

Kate did *not* say "Hang Madame de Renneville," or any feminine equivalent for that masculine mode of relieving the feelings, and I do not know that I have any stronger evidence of the angelic sweetness of her disposition to lay before the reader.

So the two girls went down to breakfast; and Kate had to stand a fire of questions from her father about the wounded stranger; and declarations that he should be obliged at last to forbid her visiting Deep Creek Cottage; for that that fellow Pendleton would end by making the county too hot to hold him; and that if he did it would be a good riddance for Winifred; that things were coming to a pass which would make it absolutely necessary for the gentlemen of the county to set their faces more decidedly against smuggling, etc., etc., most of which the jolly old gentleman had said from time to time for the last twenty years, and notwithstanding which, his fine old florid, benevolence-beaming face, with its adornment of silver locks, remained set much as it ever had been and was likely to continue set, as long as he was lord of Lindisfarn.

"Any commands, ladies?" said Mr. Mat, as they were leaving the breakfast-table. "What is it to be this morning, Miss Kate, a gallop over the common to Weston? I think you seem to want one; you look as if this Sillmouth business had fretted you."

"No, thank you, Mr. Mat. Birdie has done her twenty miles yesterday and the day before. I think I shall have one of my rambles in the woods this morning."

"And I was going to try if I could coax Mr. Mat to drive me over to Silverton. I promised Aunt Sempronia that I would pay her a visit."

"Of course I'm ready, Miss Margaret," said Mr. Mat, with not the best grace in the world; "but if another day would do as well, there is a matter I wanted to see to at Farmer Nixon's at Four-tree Hollow "—

"Come now, Mr. Mat," returned Margaret, utterly throwing away upon the savage a glance which she deemed, and which ought to have been, irresistible, "you forgot all about Farmer Nixon and Four-tree Hollow, when it was a question of riding with Kate."

"Ah, but Miss Kate, you see," returned Mr. Mat, pausing when he had got thus far, and scratching his black scrubbing-brush of a head with the end of one fore-finger, while he looked at Margaret with a *naïveté* utterly unconscious of any offence in what he was saying, pointing at the same time with his thumb toward the door by which Kate had left the room,—"Miss Kate, you see—is Miss Kate; and there is not another such between this and London!"

Never had Madame de Renneville's golden rule respecting the advantages of the *Volto sciolto, pensieri stretti*, to a *jeune personne bien élevée* been more necessary to her pupil than while she replied, with a smile of undiminished sweetness,—

"Oh! I know I must not pretend to rival Kate in your affections, Mr. Mat "—

"Nay, Miss Margaret," replied the untamable savage, shaking his head, "there's not the lass, nor the lad either, above ground who can do that; for I do love her better than all the world! But if you have promised her ladyship in the Close "—

"Yes, indeed, Mr. Mat; I know my aunt is expecting me," replied Margaret, who during the past winter had followed up the good impression she had made in the Close at her first visit, and had made many visits to Silverton in consequence. Indeed, she had in that manner found the means of doing a considerable portion of the flirtation with Fred Falconer, which had been requisite for the advancing of matters between them to the point at which we found them, when making the survey for our *carte de tendre* in the present spring. It was true, therefore, in a certain sense, for Margaret to say that her aunt was expecting her, inasmuch as she certainly expected to see her in the Close again erelong. But it was not true that any special arrangement had been made for Margaret to come to Silverton on that day.

"Well, then," said Mr. Mat, in reply to Margaret's declaration to that effect, "of course I'll drive you over. I suppose I had better order the gig round at once?"

"I heard you asking Mr. Mat to drive you over to Silverton," said Kate, who was putting on her walking things when Margaret came up-stairs to prepare for her visit to Silverton; "I should hardly have wished, I think, in your place, to go there to-day, if I could have avoided it. Of course you will take care to say no word that might lead to the discovery of our secret. It will be best to say nothing about the smuggling, or the wounded man, or the fight, or anything about it. Neither my uncle nor Aunt Sempronia will in all probability have heard a word of it."

"I will take care," said Margaret.

"And Margaret, dearest," added Kate, looking earnestly and beseechingly at her sister; "of course it will be wise under the circumstances to avoid any chance of seeing Fred Falconer!"

"I never seek to see him," replied Margaret, with a toss of her head; "how can you suppose that I should do such a thing?"

"I don't suppose you do, sissy dear; but

I think that, as things are, it would be prudent to seek, all you possibly can, *not* to see him. Think how you would be distressed if—if he were to say anything, you know!"

"I know what I am about, Kate!" said the *jeune personne bien elevée*, who did such credit to her Parisian training.

Pretty much depends, as Dick Wyvill, the groom, had justly remarked, on "the manner in which they are broke."

So Kate went out for her solitary ramble among the woods above the house, and Margaret got into the gig with Mr. Mat for her drive to Silverton. The former directed her steps in the same direction as she had done on the afternoon previous to the great storm, during which the *Saucy Sally* had escaped from the *Petrel.* Now, as then, she gradually climbed the hill by the zigzagging wood paths, till she reached the naked rock jutting out from the soil composed of slaty *débris* and vegetable mould, the remains of many a generation of oaks, that formed the topmost height of Lindisfarn brow. Upon the former occasion she had gone thither with the intentional purpose of looking out at the signs of the weather. Now it was an in-look into her own heart that mainly interested her, and for the sake of which she had come out for a solitary ramble in the woods; and she wandered up to the summit of the brow, careless of the direction she was taking.

The huge limestone mass, which formed the Lindisfarn Stone, as it was called *par excellence*, rose out of the earth by a gradual and moss-grown slope on the side looking away from Lindisfarn house, from the gently-swelling wooded hill that sloped down to Lindisfarn Brook, from Silverton, and from the coast. The other side, which looked toward all these places, formed, on the contrary, a precipitous little cliff in miniature, some fifteen or twenty feet in height. And the ground in front of it fell away at its foot in a steep declivity for a further height of another twenty feet or so, at the bottom of which grew the nearest trees. So that a person on the top of the Lindisfarn Stone was on a vantage ground which enabled him to look over the thick forest, and to command a charming view of all the falling ground, and of the opposite side of the Lindisfarn Brook valley up to the old tower of Silverton castle, which could just be seen over the crest of the opposite hill.

Kate climbed to the top of the stone, as she had done on many a former occasion, but never with so heavy and care-laden a heart before; and sat herself down near the edge of it, facing the precipitous side and the well-known view over the woods and fields, which were to be hers no more.

The lord of Lindisfarn was monarch of nearly all that he surveyed from the top of the Lindisfarn Stone: and the spot was one eminently calculated to suggest ideas connected with territorial proprietorship. But Kate had come thither with no leaning toward any such thoughts in her head. Her heart was full of troubles, which, though taking their rise from the same source, pressed upon her immediately under a different aspect.

Oh that she could hide herself, bury herself, lock herself up for the next month to come! There, on the solitary Lindisfarn Stone, she was safe for the passing hour. Would that it were possible to remain there; where at least for the nonce she was secure from the dreaded danger of that pursuit which had so often been—and she blushed as the confession passed through her mind—a source of happiness to her!

She had been sitting thus for some time, letting the minutes heap themselves up into hours, while she mused at one moment on a whole brainful of minute little projects for avoiding all chances of any such interview with Captain Ellingham as might give him an opportunity for saying the words she now so dreaded to hear; and then again on the manner in which it would behoove her to comport herself, and on the words she would have to say, if that terrible misfortune, despite all her efforts to avoid it, should befall her. She tried to figure forth to herself the scene as it would take place, to imagine the words which he might be supposed to say, and those in which she would be compelled by cruel fate —ah, how cruel!—to answer him. And as she placed it all on the stage of her imagination, she rehearsed accurately enough at least one portion of the *rôle*, as she would in all probability play it:—for she wept bitterly.

Presently she was startled by the sound of voices among the trees beneath her, just within the edge of the forest, where it encircled the clear space occupied by the Lindisfarn Stone; and listening with head erect and bated breath, like a hare startled on her form, was able in the next minute to distingulsh those of Captain Ellingham and old Brian Wyvill, the pensioned ex-gamekeeper. " There be the Lindisfarn Stoan, zur ! " she heard the latter say ; " that be the highest ground in all the Lindisfarn land ; and vrom the tep o' that stoan you may zee a'most all the estate. 'Tis a bewtiful zeat to zet on; and Miss Kate comes cp here time and again. I zems we shall vind her here now."

And the next minute the speaker, emerging with his companion from the edge of the wood, espied her on the top of the rock above them.

" There she be, zure enough, capten ! Please, Miss Kate, capten kem up to the Chase a-wanting vor tu speak tu ee, and as yew wos not tu house, I tould un, I thot a cou'd vind ee ; zo we kem up the vorest together."

" It's a true, full, and particular account, Miss Lindisfarn. I did come up to the Chase on purpose to speak to you, and was very unwilling to return and leave my errand unsaid, and so ventured by the help of old Brian to start on an exploring cruise in search of you. May I scale your fortress ? "

" If you can find the way to do so," replied Kate, striving to speak in her usual light-hearted tone, and hoping that he might lose some little time in finding the side by which the stone is accessible, and so give her a few moments to collect herself and dry her eyes. She strove hard to speak gayly, but there was a tremor in her voice ; for her heart was beating as though it would force its way out from her bosom. For a moment she clung to an absurd hope that old Brian Wyvill would remain, and make any *tête-à-tête* conversation impossible ; but in the next, she heard him tell Captain Ellingham that he " med walk cp tu the tep of the stoan on t'other zide ev it," and saw him turn to go down the hill.

Ellingham little thought, when he talked playfully of scaling her fortress, how nearly the words represented the true state of the case, and how much she would have given to have made it absolutely inaccessible to him.

She had little doubt that the misfortune she had much dreaded had fallen upon her already. If she had not been in such a nervous agony of fear, lest Ellingham should propose to her under the present circumstances, she probably would not have felt so certain that it was coming. As it was, she had little doubt of it ; and the fear of the bitter,

bitter draught that was nearly at her lips was so great as to suggest a mad and momentary thought of the possibility of escape from it by throwing herself off the rock from the front of it before her lover could reach the top of it from behind.

Her lover ! Yes. Kate did not pretend to herself to have any doubt about it. There stands the account of her conversation with Ellingham on the occasion of her attempt at bribery and corruption, fairly reported in a previous chapter. One does not find anything like love-making in it ! Lydia Languish could not have scent the faintest odor of "*la belle passion*" in any part of the conversation. The combined ingenuity of Dodson and Fogg could not have extracted from it the faintest indication of a compromising intention. Yet it was after that conversation that Ellingham had felt as if he were walking on air, and had gone off in the gig triumphant and rejoicing. It was when she went up to her room to prepare for her ride to Sillmouth, to carry the tidings of his utter refusal to comply with her wishes, that Kate had first felt the delicious certainty that he was hers, and hers only, forever.

Strange ! How poor imperfectly-articulate, half-dumb lovers do get to understand each other in some way, certainly deserves an enlightened naturalist's attention. The ants, too, how curious is the way in which they evidently communicate intelligence, often of a complicated character, to one another, apparently also in their case by the appropinquation of noses ! I suppose, however, that the ants have expressive eyes Otherwise I have no conception how they manage their confabulations.

Putting out of the question, however, the whole of that intensely interesting subject on which poor Kate so dreaded to hear Ellingham enter, there were topics enough on which it was very natural he might wish to speak to her. They had not met since that memorable conversation at the early breakfast-table. It was very intelligible that they should both wish to talk over the result of the events to which they were then looking forward. Nevertheless, Kate felt sure that Ellingham's present errand was not merely to talk of smugglers and smuggler hunting. She knew—why or how she knew she could not tell—but she had not the slightest doubt that the misfortune, to the possibility of which she had been looking forward as the most terrible that could happen to her, had in reality fallen upon her. Nor did she doubt or waver for an instant in her decision as to the only answer that it was possible for her to make to the communication that awaited her. If only she could have told him the truth!—not *all* the truth,—not the too undeniable truth that she loved him with a passion that paled all else in life, even as a sunbeam pales the dull glow of fire among the ashes on a hearth half burned out,—not this, but simply the truth respecting the vanishing of her worldly wealth! Far, far better, infinitely better would it have been if that truth could have been made known to him before he had set forth on the errand that had now brought him to the Lindisfarn Stone! Failing this, it would have been an infinite relief to her to have been able to tell the truth now, and to attribute her rejection to its true motives. But to be obliged to answer him by an unmotived rejection,—she, in her character of a wealthy heiress, to refuse her hand to the brave man, rich in honor, loyal truth, noble thoughts, and all the treasures of a loving, honest, manly heart—to be compelled the while to hide with jealous care every word,

every action, every glance, that might betray the secret of that yearning love, which seemed to be intensified by the pity she felt for the pang she was about to inflict; to crush deep down into the recesses of the beating little heart, that was bounding in its prison-house with longing to pour itself and all its thoughts and sorrows and troubles into his arms, every indication that she was not in truth the cold mammon-worshipping worldling that she must necessarily appear to him,—this was indeed a cruel, cruel fate!

In a minute or two more she heard Captain Ellingham coming up the sloping side of the rock behind her. She was seated, as has been said, on the verge of the other side, looking towards Silverton, with her back turned to the side from which he was approaching. Every foot-fall, as he stepped hurriedly across the nearly flat top of the huge stone, seemed to strike a blow on her heart. She would have risen to meet him; but it was utterly impossible for her to do so. She sat gazing over the prospect of woods and distant fields as if she were fascinated and rooted to the spot, till she heard his voice by her side.

CHAPTER XXV.

"TEARS FROM THE DEPTH OF SOME DIVINE DESPAIR!"

"HAVE you been able to forgive me yet, Miss Lindisfarn," said the voice close behind and above her in very gentle accents, "for the brutality with which I refused all your requests at the breakfast-table the other morning?"

"Pray don't suppose, Captain Ellingham, that I am not fully aware that it is I who need forgiveness for having ventured to make a suggestion to you which involved a breach of duty. If I had not been worked up to a state of desperation by the terrors of my old nurse, I should not have been guilty of the indiscretion," said Kate.

The reply was a natural one enough, and altogether a sensible and proper one. Yet there was an undefinable something in the tone or manner of it, which rang unpleasantly on Ellingham's ear. It seemed to imply regret that the incident should have occurred at all; whereas he looked back to it with delight, and treasured up every word, and dwelt on every accent with ecstasy. There was a cold, dry, formal tone, too, in the accent with which she spoke, that smote his ear, and distressed him. It was the result of the arduous struggle, that was going on within her, poor girl! to save herself from bursting into tears, and to find strength and sense to answer him calmly and coherently.

"But you see how needless Mrs. Pendleton's terrors were! If it were not that I am perfectly well convinced that Miss Lindisfarn's approbation would be accorded to performance and not to breach of duty, I might be tempted to take credit for having let the smuggler slip through my fingers intentionally in obedience to your wishes. The honest truth is that I tried all I could to catch him, and he out-manœuvred me!"

"I suppose it does not involve a very serious breach of the revenue laws to be glad that the matter ended as it did," said Kate, feeling a little more tranquil, as a faint hope came to her that perhaps, after all, Ellingham's present purpose was only to speak of the affair with the *Saucy Sally.*

"For you, at all events, Miss Lindisfarn, it is, I conceive perfectly lawful to rejoice in the discomfiture of the *Petrel;* but in my case it is not only the revenue laws, but a sailor's professional pride, that stands in the way of my being heartily glad of the *Saucy Sally's* escape. It was a superb feat of seamanship that that fellow Pendleton performed that night; and an admirable boat the *Saucy Sally* must be."

"I have heard she is a very first-rate sailor," replied Kate.

"First-rate indeed! But what a pity it is that such a seaman as that man must be, should be on the wrong side, and break the law, instead of serving his country. There's one thing, at all events, may be said for high custom duties, and the smuggling that arises from them,—no honest trade ever did or ever will breed such seamen as smuggling does. I wish your *protégé*, Miss Lindisfarn, could be persuaded to give it up. I shall surely catch him one of these days, or nights rather;—or if not I, some other fellow on our side."

"Yes; I wish he would give it up, for poor Winifred's sake," said Kate.

All this time Ellingham had been standing by her, as she sat in the position she had first taken on the rock. He was by her side, but somewhat behind her; and she, though she had turned her head a little toward him in speaking, had hardly raised her eyes to his face. He had begun the conversation in the most natural manner, by speaking on the subject which was, of course, one of interest to both of them; but he was now at a loss how to get from it to the real object of his visit. But he had come up to Lindisfarn that day, and had pursued the chase up to Lindisfarn brow, quite determined to do the deed he had, not without very considerable difficulty, made up his mind to do before he returned. Captain Ellingham was not the sort of a man to leave undone that which he had determined to do. He had made up his mind to do it, I say, not without some difficulty, and after a good deal of consideration and hesitation. Perhaps he would not have done so at all without the aid, comfort, and counsel of Lady Farnleigh. There is no means of knowing exactly what may have passed between them on the subject; but in all probability Lady Farnleigh, from the first, intended that her two favorites should make a match of it; and there can be little doubt that it was due to her representations and advice that the poor revenue officer eventually determined to venture on offering to an heiress of two thousand a year. Having made up his mind to do so, and having fixed on the present day and hour for accomplishing the purpose, difficult or not difficult, he meant now to do it.

"Yes; I wish he would give it up for poor Winifred's sake," Kate had said in reply to his last remark, uttering the words in a more simple and natural tone than she had used before.

"Mrs. Pendleton was a great favorite with you all at the Chase, I believe," said Ellingham, advancing a step as he spoke and sitting down on the rock by her side.

The movement revived all Kate's worst suspicions and terrors. She would have risen from her seat, and at once commenced her walk back to the house, so as to have limited the time at his disposition to a few minutes only; but she felt her limbs trembling so, that she did not dare to make the attempt, and remained as if chained to the rock, with her eyes fixed unconsciously and unmeaningly on the little black square on the horizon representing the ruined keep of Silverton Castle.

"A favorite with you all, was she not?" repeated Ellingham.

"Yes, we had all a great regard for her," said Kate, still apparently absorbed in the contemplation of the distant view of Silverton Castle keep.

"And it was for her sake, doubtless, that you were led to feel an interest in the fate of that bold smuggler and very excellent seaman, her husband."

"Of course, naturally. Poor woman! she was in a state of great anxiety and distress."

"Of course. Her whole life must be one of anxiety."

"It was a source of much trouble and regret to us when she married, though her husband was not a smuggler then."

"Did you object then, as her friends and protectors, to her marrying a sailor?"

"Oh, no! But there were then reasons for thinking that he was not a very steady man. I was too young at the time to understand much about it; but I know that my father and Mr. Mat were not altogether satisfied with Pendleton's previous history."

"You would not have objected, then, to the marriage merely on the ground of the man's being a sailor?"

"Oh, dear, no!" said Kate, quite unsus-

piciously; if we could only have felt well assured that he would have continued steadily to follow his business as a boat-owner and fisherman, as he was when poor Winny married him, we should have been perfectly well contented."

"Did it ever occur to you, Miss Lindisfarn, when thinking of the lot of your favorite nurse, to judge of her chances of happiness by putting the case to yourself? Did you ever ask yourself whether you could have been content to take for your partner in life one whose vocation called him to pass much of his life on the ocean?"

"Is it likely," replied Kate, whose heart began here again to beat with painful violence and rapidity,—"is it likely, do you think, that any such idea would present itself to a little girl of twelve years old?"

And no sooner were the words out of her mouth than she could have bitten off her tongue for speaking them; for it flashed into her mind, that they might seem to imply that at her present more mature period of life, such a consideration might have occurred to her. It was, however, impossible to recall them; and Captain Ellingham proceeded hurriedly.

"But since that time the sight of poor Mrs. Pendleton's troubles may have suggested such a thought to you."

"Her troubles have arisen," returned Kate, fencing, and, as she used the simple truth for the purpose, fencing very unskilfully, "not from being the wife of a sailor, but from being the wife of a smuggler."

And again, as soon as the words were past recall, she was horrified by the sudden thought, that they might seem to encourage the idea which she was anxious to discourage by every possible means.

"The thought was never suggested to you, then, Miss Lindisfarn, whether or no you could yourself be ever induced to accept the love of a sailor?" said Ellingham, with a momentary glance into her eyes that would have said all he had to say to the most obtuse of Eve's daughters, even if she had been previously wholly unsuspicious of his intent, and not without a little tremor in his voice.

Here it was then! The dreaded moment was come! What—what was she to reply? Stave off the evil yet a moment longer by refusing to understand him? She hated herself for the cowardly evasion, but adopted it in the extremity of her distress and embarrassment.

"Girls, I fancy, rarely trouble their heads with speculations having reference to such matters, and on cases that do not seem to have any probability to commend them to their notice," she said, turning her face more away from him as she spoke, in a manner that unmistakably indicated the annoyance she was suffering.

"Oh, Miss Lindisfarn, has no probability of such a question being asked of you ever commended itself to your notice? Have you not seen—but it is contemptible of me to embarrass you thus by cowardly shrinking from the subject on which I came here purposely to speak. Miss Lindisfarn," he went on with a sort of hurried desperation, "I came to the Chase this day, and I took the liberty of following you hither, for the purpose of asking you to be my wife. I say nothing about the entirety of my happiness being dependent on your reply; it is of course that it should be so. A man must be a wretch indeed, that could address you, as I am daring to do, were it otherwise. I think you must know that I love you well. Not that any such knowledge can give me the slightest right to presuppose your answer. But it makes it needless for me to try to tell you how much, how entirely, you have become all in all to me. I am not a young man. Most men have loved more than once before they have reached my years; but it is the first-fruit of my heart that I am offering you. My life has not been a prosperous or a very happy one. My path through the world has always been on the shady side of the wall! And the fact that it has been so makes my presumption in asking for the sunshine of your love seem the greater to me. I ask you to smile on a man who has had few smiles from any one. I ask you to take a pale and colorless life, with nothing in it save the one stern presence of Duty, with nothing of present brightness and little of future hope, and transfigure it with the sunshine and warmth and glory of your love! That is all I ask; and I proffer nothing in return save—nothing at all; I have nothing to proffer. What is my love to one who has love and admiration from everybody,—everybody from her cradle upward!"

All this had been poured out with passionate rapidity and vehemence, while Kate kept her face steadily turned away from him toward the distant horizon. He might have supposed that no word of all he had said had reached her ear, so motionless and utterly voiceless she remained! But though she had commanded herself sufficiently to allow no sound to escape her lips, her power of self-control had been limited to the effort needed for that. The silent tears were streaming from her eyes; and she feared even to raise her hand to her face to dry them, lest the motion should betray her agitation.

He had paused a moment or two; but no sound of answer came.

"Is there no hope for me?" he asked, in a tremulous voice; "must the future be a yet more cheerless and hopeless blank to me than the past? Miss Lindisfarn, *is* there no hope for me?"

Still there came no word, and her face was turned away so that he could not see it. But she shook her head with a slow, sad motion, which very plainly expressed a reply in the negative to the question that had been asked her.

"Gracious Heaven! Is that my answer? Do I understand you aright? Miss Lindisfarn!" he continued, in a voice tremulous with the agony of his mind, the tones of which were well calculated to make their way to a tougher heart than that of her on whose ear they fell, "Miss Lindisfarn! is that your sole answer? Have you no word for me?"

But still no other answer came than a repetition of the same slow and sad shaking of the head.

"Then God help me! My life is done!" he exclaimed, in a tone of utter despair; "I ought not to have set my all on so desperate a cast! Miss Lindisfarn, I ought, perhaps, to say that I have not been unaware of the very wide distance placed between us in respect to the goods of fortune. But I have not cared to touch on that head, because I am quite sure that your decision on my fate, be it what it might, would not turn on that consideration"—

Here Kate's agitation became such that her shoulders, which were turned toward him, and her whole person, were visibly shaken by it; and with a great gasping sob there burst from her, as if it had forced itself from her heart against her will, the exclamation, "God bless you, Captain Ellingham, for that word!" and then the pent-up agony could be held in no longer, and she burst into a storm of sobs and tears, so violent as to be wholly beyond her power to control it.

Ellingham was so utterly unprepared for any such manifestation of feeling, so completely amazed and thunderstruck, that he did not at the moment accurately apply her words to the phrase of his that called them forth.

"Gracious Heaven! Miss Lindisfarn, what have I done? What have I said? Why are you so distressed? It is for me to bear, as God shall give me strength, the blow that has fallen on me. I have no right, and, Heaven knows, no wish, to distress you thus."

Still the convulsive sobbing continued despite her utmost efforts to recover control over herself. Ellingham was utterly at a loss what interpretation to put upon her extreme agitation. After another short pause, he said again,—

"At all events, there must be no misunderstanding between us. The matter at stake is to me too tremendously vital. Is it your deliberate purpose, Miss Lindisfarn, to communicate to me in answer to my question, that there is no hope for me?"

She shook her head amid continued weeping, and sobbed out the words, "No hope! No hope!"

"No hope, either now or in the future? If there is any, oh, Miss Lindisfarn, give me the benefit of it, in pity!"

And again the only reply was the same sad shaking of the head, and the words, "None, none!"

"And it is your own decision that you give me, not that of any other person?" urged Ellingham, still at a loss to conceive any explanation of her extraordinary emotion.

She bowed her head once, looking up at him with streaming eyes; for he had risen from his seat on the rock, and was now standing in front of her.

"Your own unbiassed decision?" he reiterated.

"It is my own decision. Nobody has prompted it. Nobody knows anything about it."

"And is there no hope for me that time may produce any change in my favor,—no hope that I may be able to win your affection in return for—not a lightly felt, or lightly given love, Miss Lindisfarn?"

"Oh, pray leave me, Captain Ellingham! I cannot say anything other than I have said. I cannot! Please leave me!"

"But how can I leave you here in the state of agitation in which you appear to be, Miss Lindisfarn?"

"Never mind! It is very foolish of me. But please leave me to myself. I shall recover my—myself in a few minutes! It was the surprise—and—my great sorrow at being obliged to pain you, Captain Ellingham. But—but—I cannot do otherwise; you will, perhaps—no! I was only going to say that —that—it must be as I have said!"

"And I must leave you thus?"

"Yes, please, Captain Ellingham! I shall be better presently, and will then walk down to the house by myself."

"Good-by then, Miss Lindisfarn. I have been the victim of a great mistake, of a monstrous and blind self-delusion! Forgive me for the annoyance I have caused you, and for, the besotted presumption which led me to do it! Farewell, Miss Lindisfarn, and may God bless you, now and forever!"

"Farewell, Captain Ellingham! God bless you too! I pray it very earnestly. And think as little hardly of me as you can. Farewell!"

"Think hardly, Miss Lindisfarn! I can put no interpretation on the manner in which you have received and rejected my suit. That some reason influences you, which you do not judge well to assign to me is, I think, evident. But be assured,—be very well assured that I do not imagine, and never shall or can imagine, that that reason, be it what it may, is of a kind to shake the opinion, that you are—all that my great love has believed you to be."

And with those words he turned and left the top of the rock by the same way by which he had climbed it.

Kate's tears gushed out afresh as he left her, sitting in the place from which she had not moved during the whole of the above conversation; and she looked out eagerly through them to catch sight of him, as he came round the base of the rock, on his way down the hill toward the house, and toward Silverton.

But she was disappointed; for he did not come round the rock, nor descend by that side of the hill; and Kate, therefore, saw him no more.

It was not strictly true, as has been said, that Lady Sempronia expected a visit from her niece Margaret on that particular morning on which she induced the somewhat reluctant Mr. Mat to drive her over to Silverton. Yet it was quite true that the visit was expected, though not by Lady Sempronia. The gentle Margaret, however, had found the means during the past winter of making herself so acceptable to her aunt, that she was always glad to see her. And when upon this occasion she arrived from Lindisfarn, as was usually the case, before the canon had returned from the morning service at the cathedral,—for Mr. Mat in the gig was not so long getting over the eight miles as Thomas Tibbs with the family carriage behind him,—she found as cordial a welcome from her drab-colored aunt, sitting alone in her drab-colored drawing-room, as was compatible with the nature of the person and the locality.

Mr. Mat, it is to be understood, did not come in; but dropping Miss Margaret at her uncle's door, went away to his own affairs; for Mr. Mat entered Lady Sempronia's doors and her presence, to tell the truth, as rarely as *bienséance* would permit. Probably, after putting up the gig at the Lindisfarn Arms, he strolled to the cathedral and lounged in the nave till the Rev. Mr. Thorburn, the minor canon, came out from service, and then adjourned with that musical dignitary to the house of little Peter Glenny, the organist.

Margaret found her aunt a shade or two worse in spirits than usual. In truth, existence and the world in general had but a flavorless, drab-colored, washed-out sort of appearance, as seen from the Lady Sempronia's point of view, it must be admitted. The low-ceilinged, drab-colored drawing-room, with its worn-out carpet and pale-brown curtains and faded furniture, had not on that March morning the cheerfulness due to the sunshine, and the beauty of the garden outside its windows, that it had when the reader first made acquaintance with it. The garden had as yet but little beauty; the morning was raw and chilly, and it is impossible to conceive anything more suggestive of ascetic uncomfortableness than the miserable little bit of half-extinguished fire, which, contained in some wretched contrivance for rendering the proper proportions of the grate abortive, occupied the middle of Lady Sempronia's fireplace. She was sitting, when Margaret entered, in the centre of a large, deep, old-fashioned sofa,—one of that kind which show no portion of uncovered wood in any part of them; and was engaged in manufacturing out of balls of white bobbin a small square of network, destined to be pinned against the back of one of the drab-colored arm-chairs, rather for the concealment of its dilapidations than the protection of its magnificence.

A litter of books upon the table, even if the inmate does not read them, suggests the possibility of doing so, and the idea of the companionship of other minds. A clock ticking audibly on the mantelpiece is not an incitement to uproarious gayety, but it at least conveys an impression of homeliness and life. A cat on the hearthstone, again, is far better than the clock, and contributes much toward mitigating the horrors of such a position as that of Lady Sempronia. But she had none of these alleviations, and as she sat there upright in the middle of the great sofa, placed at right angles to the almost empty grate, and opposite to the window looking into the sunless and flowerless garden, in the midst of the tomblike stillness of the colorless drawing-room, it is hardly surprising if the world in general presented itself to her view as a vale of tears, and on the whole as a melancholy mistake and failure. It is intelligible that under such circumstances the arrival of Miss Margaret should have been felt by her aunt to be a not unwelcome relief.

Lady Sempronia had, moreover, a special trial to lament over on the morning in question. This, indeed, was generally the case; but on the present occasion it was a matter that had particularly tried her temper.

"My position, you see, my dear," she remarked to her sympathizing niece, after the usual condolences which constituted the Lady Sempronia's mode of greeting and welcoming, "is one of peculiar hardship and difficulty. Your uncle, without being *quite* far enough gone to be put under restraint, is nevertheless fully as incapable of managing his own affairs, or of conducting himself with ordinary propriety as most of those who are so."

"It *is* a very vexatious position, dear aunt!"

"Ah, my dear! If you only knew half of what I have to go through! There was yesterday evening! I do assure you it was one of the most painful trials that could be inflicted upon a right-minded person!"

"What was it, aunt?"

"Oh, my dear! Such a scene! so painful! We had a few friends to dine with us; the doctor's doing, as usual. I know too well that our means do not justify us in entering into such expenses. We might do so, of course, with perfect comfort and propriety even, if the money were not all flung away on the most futile absurdities. But, as I say to Dr. Lindisfarn, you cannot burn the candle at two ends at once. You cannot give dinners and print monographs, both."

"That is very true, dear aunt!" said Margaret, shaking her head sympathetically.

"But the doctor thinks differently," pursued the faded lady, with a deep sigh; "and he would have me invite people to dine here yesterday; the dean and Mrs. Barton, Dr. Blakistry, the Polstons from Sillmouth, and one or two others; quite enough to carry the story of what they saw all over the country."

"What was it?" asked Margaret, with an awakening of real curiosity.

"Oh, my dear! We had all gone in to the dining-room; the dean took me, of course, and the rest came in as they chose; for the doctor was not there. He never will do anything like other people! and generally when there are any people here he joins us in the dining-room. Well, my dear, dear Margaret! We were all in our places round the table. Sanders said the doctor was coming, and was holding the door open for him. We all paused a minute, still standing to wait for him, when—oh, my dear child! I shall never, never forget that moment! In walked your uncle. I could see by the look of his eye in a minute that he had no more idea of where he was, or what he was doing than a stark staring Bedlamite—up he walked to his place at the bottom of the table with the same sort of step he has, you know, when he is walking up the nave with his surplice on, and—and—down he went on his knees,

and put his face into his soup-plate, as if it were his trencher-cap! Oh, Margaret! I thought I should have dropped where I stood! The dean behaved very well; but I saw Mrs. Barton give him a look across the table. Then we all sat down; and I was in hopes that that would have recalled him to himself, and to some decent sense of the proprieties of the time and place. But not a bit of it! Presently he stood up, and looked round the table in a calm and dignified sort of way, as much as to ask why the service didn't begin. And that vulgar, coarse wretch, Minor Canon Thorburn, who was sitting near the bottom of the table, called out in his great chanting voice, 'Not a bit of it, doctor! I have chanted the service twice this day, and I'm not going to begin it again!' and that brought him to: 'Ah! bless my soul!' said he, 'dinner-time! so it is! Thorburn and I make it straight between us. He thinks he is elsewhere, sometimes, when he is in church; I think I am in church when I ought to be eating my dinner!' And then there was a tittering all round. But what provokes me past bearing is that your uncle takes all such things as coolly and calmly as if he were doing everything he ought to do! He was not embarrassed, not he! He has no sense of shame!"

"It is very sad," sighed Margaret; "and, aunt dear, talking of that, I think I had better go into the study, before uncle comes home from the cathedral, to put away a few of the remaining copies of the 'Memoir on the City Walls.' He has given away several copies lately, and there are only a few left; and if they run out altogether, he will be sure to reprint it. You know he never objects to my being among his books; and I meant to hide a few copies of the "Town Walls" behind 'Grose's Antiquities.' All the space behind 'Slawkingham's History of Sillshire' is filled with are serve store of the 'Monograph on the Horseshoe Arches at Parbury-in-the-Moor,' which is particularly bad for him to give away because of the colored plate at the beginning!"

It will be perceived, that Margaret had not only acquired a perfect understanding of the home politics of Lady Sempronia's household, but had made herself very intelligently useful in forwarding that much-tried lady's views. When alone with her uncle, she had no scruple in pouring oil on the fire of his antiquarian zeal to the utmost extent that her ignorance of everything connected with the subject would allow. And when she found herself in the somewhat more difficult circumstance of being present at any difference of opinion between her uncle and aunt, she was wont to extricate herself from the difficulty by a masterly silence, dropping her silken lashes over her downcast eyes, with an expression that deplored the existence of a difference, and permitted either party to feel how deeply she lamented the perversity and obstinacy of the other.

"Do, my dear! Go into the study. You have not above a quarter of an hour before the service will be over. I am sure it is a comfort to have any one in the house who so thoroughly understands all the trials I have to go through."

So Margaret left her aunt to her knitting, or knotting, or netting, or whatever the proper term is to describe the fabrication of the reticulated fabric on which she was engaged, and betook herself to her uncle's study. But having entered that sanctum and carefully closed the door, and having taken at random some half-dozen volumes from the shelves and placed them on the floor, she appeared to be suddenly called away from her librarian-like avocation to other cares. First of all she tripped with a step that would hardly have bent the grass-blades beneath it, had her tripping been in a meadow, to the window,—not that looking into the garden, but the opposite one at the other end of the room looking into the Close,—and carefully drawing aside as much as of the muslin curtain which hung before it as would enable her to peep out from the side of it, in a direction which commanded the road leading towards the door of the cathedral, she gazed for half a minute, and, apparently satisfied, dropped the curtain. Then holding back the folds of her pretty lilac silk dress with both exquisitely gloved hands, she put out first one and then the other slender foot, cased in bronze colored morocco *bottines*, the admirable fitting of which showed off the arching of the instep to the greatest advantage. Both were subjected to a close scrutiny, and neither was found to be quite free from dust, while on the heel of one appeared a slight splash. So the pretty examiner darted across the room to a drawer under the shelves in one corner of the library, and sharply pulling it open,

took from it a duster, which the doctor kept there for the behoof of his books, and hastily set to work to repair the mischief her scrutiny had discovered. This happily accomplished, she again returned to the window, and again satisfied herself that there was nobody yet coming across from the cathedral. Just opposite to the door, and behind the lay figure, which has been mentioned in a former chapter as a device of Dr. Lindisfarn's for reminding him to take off his surplice on returning from the choir, there was a small square toilet glass hung against the panelled wall, intended for the doctor's service in robing, though ministering but little to the correctness of his appearance by its hints. It was now, however, consulted by a more docile pupil. Having put all into perfect order at one extremity of her person, Margaret now gave her attention to the other. The edges of the dark bands of glossy hair on her brow had to be just a little retouched; the ribbons of the pretty bonnet to be readjusted beneath the chin; and the set of that *chef-d'œuvre* itself somewhat modified. All this was done with a rapid and sure hand; the result was approved by one intent and searching but all too transient glance;—a second was devoted to an equally rapid dress-rehearsal of a small but exceedingly effective pantomime representation by the eyes themselves; and then the charming performer flitted back to her post of observation at the corner of the window looking on the Close.

Was ever such preparation made before by a dutiful niece for receiving an elderly uncle, and that uncle a canon returning from morning service at his cathedral!

In a very few minutes she dropped the muslin curtain from her fingers, as if it had suddenly burned her; a bright look of satisfaction came over her face, the blood mounted to her fair cheeks just sufficiently to tinge the cream-colored satin of them with the delicate hue of a pale hedge-rose, and her eyes were lighted up with the brilliancy of animation, as she tripped back to the place in the bookshelves from which she had removed the volumes to the floor, and took one of the books in her hand. In the next minute the doctor, having let himself in with his latchkey, opened the door of the study, and was heard saying,—

"Come in, come in, Mr. Falconer! I

shall have much pleasure in showing you the volume. What, Margaret, you here? Delighted to see you, my dear!"

"I was at my old work among your books, you see, uncle; but I did not intend to get caught playing the librarian by any one but you. Mr. Mat was coming in this morning, so I begged a place in the gig."

"And I little thought of the pleasure that was in store for me, when I walked with you across the Close, doctor!" said Falconer.

His eyes and Margaret's had already met and exchanged intelligent greeting and congratulations on the success of the lie that each was telling.

The unsuspicious canon proceeded meanwhile to disrobe himself and robe his lay representative, or as the Rev. Minor Canon Thorburn (more generally called, out of church, Jack Thorburn) used to say with ever new felicitousness on every occasion, turn him from a *lay* into a clerical figure; while the two young people shook hands, with laughing, conscious eyes.

"How good this is of you! You certainly are the best as well as the loveliest girl that ever breathed! Had you any difficulty about the gig?" whispered Falconer.

"Yes, indeed I had! That old brute, Mr. Mat, after offering to ride with Kate, pretended to have business to do, when I asked him to drive me in; and then told me in so many words, that I was mere dirt compared to her—the atrocious old savage! I wouldn't have stooped to ask him, or be driven by him, if it had not been for"— and her magnificent eyes said the rest far more eloquently than the most silver tongue could have done.

"The old savage! And to think of your having exposed yourself to such annoyances"— and Mr. Freddy also concluded his phrase by the same medium of communication,—creditably, yet not in the same style that Margaret did it. She certainly had the finest and most expressive eyes that ever were seen in a human head. They were so beautiful, so tender, so eloquent! They could look anything—save honest.

"And now, sir, that the object has been served, I do not mean to play librarian any longer. So you may put these horrid old books back in their places. I am afraid I have soiled my gloves with them as it is!" said Margaret, holding out the tips of her taper fingers for his inspection in a provoca-

tive manner that made it absolutely necessary for Freddy to assist in the process by subjecting each separate digit to manipulation and minute investigation.

"What exquisite gloves! Paris of course. Well, I do think there is nothing more beautiful in nature than a beautiful hand—when one sees it to perfection," added Fred, as, after satisfying himself that the books had done little or no mischief, he contemplated Margaret's hand, while the extreme tips of its fingers were supported by the extreme tips of his.

"Come, attend to your work! Put the books back again into their places," said Margaret.

"Can't we get away into the garden?" whispered Falconer, as he did so.

"He will drive us away in a minute," returned Margaret, in the same voice; "you'll see!"

"I think I have finished my task for to-day, uncle," she continued, as the doctor, having got rid of his canonicals, came up the room from the further end near the door to his accustomed corner by the fire, and behind the screen of books, that has been described as nearly dividing the room into two; "I thought I should just have time before you came back from church to finish putting the 'Bampton Lectures,' on this shelf in the proper order according to their dates."

"Thank you, my dear! And now you must run away to your aunt; for I am going to be very busy. Mr. Falconer, Lady Sempronia will be delighted to see you in the drawing-room. See, here is the volume we were speaking of. You can send it back to me when you have done with it.

So the doctor was left in possession of his study.

"Can't we get away into the garden?" said Falconer again, as they crossed the hall together toward the drawing-room.

"We must speak to my aunt first," returned Margaret, opening the drawing-room door as she spoke.

"Uncle has been insisting," said she, as soon as Fred had saluted Lady Sempronia, "on my showing Mr. Falconer that point in the corner of your garden from which the old keep tower is visible. I don't suppose he cares much to see it; but *que voulez vous?* I must do as I am bid!" And the wonderful eyes in two consecutive seconds claimed admiration and gratitude from Falconer for the ready lie, and exchanged condolences with her aunt on the boredom of her uncle's antiquarianism.

"Come, Mr. Falconer," she continued, "come and see the tower as it appears from the Close gardens."

So they escaped into the garden, and were soon arm in arm, in a sheltered walk under the old city wall, which there formed also the boundary of the canon's garden, and which was very near the spot from which in fact the keep-tower was visible.

One would have said that Margaret had schemed with right good-will to secure this *tête-à-tête* with Falconer; and yet, now the object was attained, all the abundant cheerfulness and good-humor which had been so apparent but a minute ago, seemed at once to have deserted her, and a pensive melancholy had suddenly supervened in their place; even as the face of the landscape is changed when the sun is hidden behind a cloud. The fine eyes were fixed upon the ground, or raised only from time to time to glance for a moment with an expression of gentle sadness on his face. She answered him in monosyllables, and his most insinuating compliments were only answered with a sigh.

In short, it became absolutely necessary for him to inquire very tenderly what it was that had damped her spirits; had he had the inexpressible misfortune of offending her?

In all probability Mr. Fred Falconer understood perfectly well what the matter was; and interpreted the signs hung out to him with an accuracy and readiness which made all further conversation on the subject superfluous; for kindred spirits understand one another rapidly in these cases. Nevertheless, it was necessary that the little comedy, in which these two talented performers were engaged, should be duly performed.

"No," returned Margaret, looking steadily at the gravel walk, and picking leaf from leaf of a rose, which she had gathered from the creeping plant that almost covered the old gray wall, while she let the pink petals fall one after another, according to the usual stage directions provided for such circumstances—"No; you have neither done nor said anything to offend me" (just the slightest emphasis upon the two verbs); "I should be very ungrateful for much kind-

ness, if I were to say or think so, Mr. Falconer; but"—(eyes, which had been raised for a second with one expressive glance at the words *much kindness*, here glued to the gravel more determinedly than ever).

"But what, my dear Miss Lindisfarn? What was to have followed that little hesitating *but*, so all important to me?"

"Is it so important to you?" (Half a glance from corner of eye in state of liquefaction; extreme tenderness and the purest candid *naïveté* in equal proportions thrown into the voice.) "Can I flatter myself that it is so?"

"Surely, my dear Miss Lindisfarn, surely you must know, that all that concerns your happiness is so to me!" (Intense pathos. Pause on the gravel walk. Gentleman moves slightly in front of lady, and very timidly lays fingers of right hand on back of glove engaged in picking the rose to pieces. Appealing glance, only to be attempted in case of handsome eyes.)

"Is what to you? I do not quite understand you," said Margaret, taking prompt advantage of her companion's imperfect grammatical construction, and at the same time very slightly, and as if unconsciously, withdrawing her hand.

"Nay, you know what I would say! There is something which weighs on your spirits! You may hide it from others,—but do you think, Miss Lindisfarn, that it can be concealed from me? Whatever your trouble may be, can you not confide it to me? Mar— Oh, forgive me, Miss Lindisfarn! I—I— I forgot myself! That sweet, dear name! Marguérite! May I dare—may I call you Marguérite?"

(This is an important point in the play; and according to the rules of this Royal Game of Goose, you stop three turns for the eyes to exchange a glance, to which Burleigh's nod was as a sixpenny pamphlet to a Blue Book of the biggest dimensions. If the lady player be sure of herself, and knows what she is about, she may make the look steady and fixed for five seconds, and make it up of fluttered tenderness three parts, gently reproachful pathos two parts, and ingenuous surprise—be careful about the quality of this last article—one part, dissolved in two drops of *lachryma pura*. N. B. A larger quantity of the liquid vehicle would injure the opera-

10

tion. A gentle heaving of the bosom may be judiciously thrown in. Exhibited in this form, the effect is wonderful.)

Margaret made up the dose with admirable and unerring skill, and administered it with prompt decision.

"Yes! I think it is a pretty name," she said, dropping her eyes as soon as they had performed the operation, "and it is sweet to hear it from the lips of those who— But I don't know if I dare tell you. I don't know if I am doing right. I cannot tell how you may judge me" (emphasis delicate, and not too strong on the pronoun), "if I venture to make the confidence you ask."

"Can you doubt that—Marguérite?" said Falconer with an ardent glance, and uttering the name as if he had received a sharp blow on the second button of his waistcoat, at the moment it issued from his lips. He was doing his best; but the fact is, that he was a very inferior performer to the lady.

"I do think I may trust you to put a kind construction on my venturing to tell you," said she, with a little gush, most delicately and artistically hit off. In fact, the two or three last plunges, which the fine fish on her hook had been making, showed her that the moment had come for winding up line rapidly; "I do think I may venture. You are so good, so kind, so indulgent! The fact is— I have been blamed—cruelly blamed and misjudged—oh! how can I tell it you?—Those I live among are not all as kind to me as you are, Mr. Falconer! Cruel, wicked things have been said about me in connection with you! I am accused of—of—oh! how can I say it?—of allowing you to occupy too much of my attention!—of giving occasion to the coupling our names together by the world. And I am told that I must be more cir—cir —circum—spect! Oh, it is very hard!— very cruel!"

And here the lovely creature's cup of sorrow was too full! It brimmed over! She was sobbing—not aloud, for it was possible that her uncle's study window might be open; possible also that the gardener might be within earshot; but still very unmistakably sobbing.

Falconer had not been paying all the attention to the touchingly-broken utterances of this address which the admirable method of its delivery deserved. The only excuse for him was that he perfectly well knew what she was going to say before she began; and that the moments occupied by the speaking of it were exceedingly necessary to him for the taking of such a rapid and masterly survey of the general situation as should enable him to decide promptly yet prudently on his immediate course of action.

The fact was that he had not intended to make a direct and formal offer of his hand to Miss Lindisfarn on that day. It was not that he at all wavered in his determination of doing so, or had any thought of swerving from the line of conduct he had on mature deliberation traced out for himself in the preceding autumn, and had been conscientiously laboring to carry out all the winter. Far from it! But he was both by nature and by training a cautious man. It was a golden rule of life with him "Not to put his arm out farther than he could draw it back again." And might he not be about to do so? "Never set your name to a contract, Fred, a minute before it is necessary to do so," his father had often said to him. And now the still voice of paternal wisdom whispered in his heart. Yet, on the other hand, "Strike while the iron is hot," was a good maxim too. And it did seem to his best judgment, that the iron was quite hot now. It was good thrift, surely, to make hay while the sun shone! And when could it shine more brightly than at the present moment? And might it not be possible to combine the advantages of both the opposing systems? Might not this feat of ability be attainable by a judicious and bold dexterity? Fred thought that it might. And all these thoughts had passed in his master mind, and his decision had been taken by the time Margaret had got to the end of her delicately confidential communication. He had decided on stretching out his arm; but not so that, if some possible, though highly improbable, contingency should make it desirable, he should be unable to draw it back. Was he after all irrevocably putting his name to a contract, by words uttered only to one pair of ears? So he said, "Base and unmanly!" grinding the words between his clinched teeth; "it is the penalty which hearts that can feel pay to the jealousy of the colder natures which cannot sympathize with them!" (Freddy was fond of that sentence, and set it down in fair round-hand text in his private journal—it is to be hoped not for future use.) "You must know, dear—dearest Marguérite,"—here he took her hand, which she did not this time withdraw,—she knew that she was *en règle*, and that the game was now in her own hands—" that your happiness and peace of mind are dearer to me than my own! If you do not know it, will you believe it? Will you suffer me to persuade you that it is so,—will you give me this little hand, and with it the right to defend you against all, or any, who may dare to breathe a word against you? Marguérite, best, loveliest,—may I say dearest, Marguérite? may I say *my* Marguérite?" (voice suddenly dropped to exquisitely tender whisper.)

Dead silence; a little vibrating tremor commencing in the charmingly gloved hand he now held in both of his, gradually communicated itself to her whole person. Then two little sobs, barely more than sighs; and all executed with faultless perfection. (N. B.—This passage had better not be attempted by beginners. If not handled with consummate tact, it would be a failure. It is true that Margaret was making her *début*. But inborn genius sets aside all rules!)

"Oh, rapture! Am I then, indeed, the happiest man who breathes this day?"

This appeal produced a quivering but very decided pressure of the little lilac-gloved hand.

(This may be very safely executed by any one; and those who feel that they ought not to venture on the more difficult business described in the former paragraph had better proceed at once to this part of the exercise.)

"Look up, my sweet one! Give me one look of those divine eyes! Speak to me, my Marguérite!"

She *did* give him a look. And upon my word, it almost threw his double-entry heart off its balance, and tumbled him into earnestness. Juliet and Ophelia blended in one, were in the look of those large, soft eyes! She knew in her heart at the moment that that look was unnecessary; that she had won her game without it. But she was carried away by the spirit of her part. It was the love of the consummate artist for her art—the irresistible impulse of true genius to revel in the perfection of its own ideal!

The "look," which Frederick had asked for, had been accorded him in such measure that he did not think it necessary to press his demand for a categorical verbal answer any further; but would have been contented to assume that his proposal was accepted, and to carry on the remainder of the interview in the tone suggested to his imagination by the eloquence of Margaret's look. But this did not suit the lady's views. The business part of the meeting was not completed yet in her estimation; and till it should be so, she was, in accordance with the good old saw, in no wise minded to come to the play. So dropping once more the victorious eyes beneath their heavy lids and long lashes, she whispered,—

"You bid me speak to you, Frederick! What can I say, save that I am your own,—yours only, yours ever, through good and ill!"

And as she spoke, she let her hand rest in his, looking into his face with an expression of expectation and waiting for something, that imperatively demanded of him a similarly categorical and solemn declaration.

"My own sweet Marguérite! How can I find words to say how entirely, how devotedly, I am yours?"

"Mine, Frederick, forever, come weal come woe!" she said, clasping her hands together, and looking up into his face with an intensity of tenderness and solemnity combined, that made Freddy feel as if every possibility of retreat was being cut off behind him;—precisely, in short, as she intended that he should feel.

Nevertheless, though the man could not but be affected by the tender earnestness of the lovely creature by his side, the spirit of the man of business so far rallied as to whisper to him that, after all, these fine words were words only, unheard, unwitnessed! It was all right, no doubt. But *if* any hitch—why—

It was singular, however, and surely an evidence of their fitness for each other, that similar thoughts were at that very instant passing through his Marguérite's mind.

Nevertheless, having with a firm hand and steady attention to the main object in view brought the affair to the above favorable point, she felt that the recognized rules of the game did not justify her in refusing to her adorer an admixture of that *post seria ludum,* which happily tempers the business in which they had been engaged as well as most other sublunary matters. She permitted him to encircle her slender and elastic waist with one arm, while fondling with his other hand the dainty little palm passed across from the opposite side, only thinking with a pretty little start that she heard the gardener, when she had reason to fear that he might be rumpling the beautifully arranged folds of her silk skirt. She allowed him to "seal the contract on her divine lips," all according to the well-known rules, merely holding up her hands the while in such a manner as to protect as far as might be from injury the artistic arrangement of her hair, and the perfect set of her bonnet and its ribbons, and recovering and repairing herself after the operation with a manner and action very similar to that of a duck after withdrawing its pretty head from beneath the surface of the water.

Having accorded these favors, however, while meditating on the next step which it was expedient to take under the circumstances, she shook off the sweet forgetfulness and once more returned to business, thus:—

"I have said that I am yours, Frederick, because you bade me say so, and because Heaven knows how entirely it is the truth; but we must not forget that I am promising more than it is in my own power to perform. My heart is your Marguérite's own to give, and she has given it freely, wholly, irrevocably! It is your own, now and forever! But my hand, alas! is not so entirely at my own disposition. My father! You must ask me of him, my Frederick! I have no reason to think that he will refuse you; how should I have any? But it is absolutely necessary to make your demand of him in due form. Trust to me to have prepared him to receive it."

"I had been thinking, my own Marguérite, that it would be well to avoid as long as might be the envious gossip and tittle-tattle of a little country town, by keeping our engagement our own sweet secret for a while."

"Oh, you are so right, so right! It will be the greatest relief. It will need but a word to papa, a hint, that it is as well to let the matter remain between our two families for the present. He will meet your father, you know; and that is all that is necessary. I think you so right."

"You do not think that it would be better to defer the application to your father for a time?"

"Ah no! My Frederick, I dare not! Besides, remember what I was forced, amid

burning blushes, to confess to you at the beginning of our conversation. I should be compelled to fly your society—to keep you at a distance! And how could I submit? How could I live through such a time of trial? No! I fully agree with you as to the outside world; but it is absolutely essential that our two fathers should know the truth."

"I am not sure," said Frederick, hesitatingly.

"Look here, Frederick. I will tell you how it shall be. The morning is the best time to be sure of papa. I will tell him to-night after dinner. I can make an opportunity of speaking to him alone before going to bed. You ride up early to-morrow morning to breakfast, and see my father in his study before he comes out. He is always up some time before the breakfast-bell rings. You shall find the way well prepared for you. And now we must go in. Indeed, we have been an unconscionable time in looking at the keep of the castle! Why do they call it the keep, I wonder? Because it keeps people so long examining it?" laughed Margaret, once again in high spirits and good-humor. And before emerging from behind the mass of trees that had all this time been hiding them from the windows of the house, she permitted Frederick one repetition of the "sealing" process; but positively only once! It was too dangerous to the ribbons to be risked needlessly often.

"I think," said Margaret, as they entered the house, "that I had better tell Aunt Sempronia. She is so good to me; and we can perfectly trust her, dear creature!"

Freddy Falconer was not, upon the whole, discontented with his morning's work; though he had done what he had not come out that morning with the intention of doing. But Margaret was such a darling! He was, as he declared to himself, not without some little surprise, and at the same time a sort of self-congratulation, really and truly over head and ears in love. And then it could not be otherwise than all right. There were the Lindisfarn lands. They were not like M. de Renneville's coupons and actions. They would not be found to have all vanished some fine morning. No, no! It must be all right.

Nevertheless, Mr. Frederick felt that he had put out his arm so far that it would be difficult to draw it back again; and had learned that those who made a point of regulating their conduct by that prudent saw had better not fence with such as are their masters at the play.

FREDERICK passed through the house from the garden without thinking it necessary to be present at the communication about to be made to Lady Sempronia. Margaret told her aunt what had occurred in a few simple words, which marked that gifted young lady's capacity for rightly estimating the characters of those with whom she was brought into contact. Lady Sempronia expressed her congratulations,—of course in the form of condolences,—and signified her entire approbation of the alliance, under the veil of a resigned thankfulness that matters were not worse than they were. Mr. Frederick Falconer was rather a model young man in her eyes, as indeed he was in those of most of the mammas and daughters of Silverton. He always did the proper thing at the proper time and place. He would never, it might be safely predicted, waste his own or his wife's substance in printing monographs upon any subject whatever. He would not go to bed when he ought to dress for dinner. He would not fancy himself in church, or even in his bank, when he was entertaining friends at the bottom of his own table. Her niece's lot in life would be a happier one than her own had been.

There was no difficulty in making Lady Sempronia understand that it would be desirable not to made the news public just at present. She detested the Silvertonian small-talk, in which she had so much larger a passive than an active share ; too much herself not to approve cordially of that measure. And still less was there any disagreement respecting the necessity of not admitting dear Uncle Theophilus to the secret. Of course that would be equivalent to announcing the fact to all Silverton. Margaret told her aunt that it had been arranged between them that Frederick should ride up to the Chase the next morning to ask her father's consent in due form, and mentioned her purpose of telling her father all that had occurred that same night.

So then the two ladies nibbled a morsel of stale cake, and drank a glass apiece of vapid sherry in company : Lady Sempronia invoked a blessing on her niece in tones that would have suited a last parting in Newgate preparatory to an execution of one of the parties in front of it ; Mr. Mat came to the door in the gig, and excused himself from entering on the plea that his horse would not stand (though, to tell the truth, the ostler from the Lindisfarn Arms had found no difficulty in smoking a quiet and meditative pipe while he and the horse had waited at Peter Glenny's door sufficiently long for Mr. Mat, Minor Canon Thorburn, and Miss Glenny, the organist's sister, just to try over again the "Chough and Crow ; " but the horses from the Chase, all of them except Birdie, had a particular dislike to " standing " at the senior canon's door in the Close); and Margaret was driven off homeward.

" Afraid I'm a few minutes late, Miss Margaret ! But we sha'n't be long in getting over the eight miles. You shall have a good half-hour to dress for dinner," said Mr. Mat, touching the horse on the flank as he spoke.

" Oh, please, Mr. Mat, don't drive fast ! I'm always so frightened in a gig. Indeed, I don't want half an hour to dress."

" All right ! " said Mr. Mat, who, with a view to future contingencies, was not bent on making his coachmanship too agreeable to his passenger ; " I never was spilt but three times in my life ; and all three times it was going down from Silverton turnpike to the Ivy Bridge, when I was going home late for dinner. It's an ugly pitch that ! "

" Oh, please, Mr. Mat ! For goodness' sake be careful ! I am sure we can spare a few minutes ! " cried Margaret, grasping the rail by her side, and with difficulty refraining from screaming.

" Not half a minute to spare, if you have got to try on three dresses before you come to the right one to-day, Miss Margaret ! " retorted the horrid brute, speaking in his broadest Zillshire.

Margaret gave him, too, a look,—her second *chef-d'œuvre* in that line to-day ; and nobody who had seen the two could have denied that her own powers in that department were versatile. But Mr. Mat *was* taking care of his driving ; and was none the worse for the fulmination, as he did not see it.

Nothing more was said till they had passed

the Ivy Bridge in safety, and begun on the other side of it the long ascent, mostly through the woods, to the Chase.

"Lady Sempronia in good spirits?" said Mr. Mat then.

"Her ladyship is, I believe, as well as usual," replied Margaret, sulkily.

"Poor soul! that's a bad account," said Mr. Mat.

Margaret vouchsafed no reply to this; and they proceeded up the long hill in silence, and at such a more sober pace as left her mind at leisure to meditate on one momentous question, which had already presented itself to her before she left Silverton.

Was she to tell Kate? and if so, *how* was she to tell her what had taken place? That was the question.

It did not take her long to decide the first part of the doubt. If she did not tell Kate, her father unquestionably would. It might be very easy to lead him to agree in keeping the matter a secret for a time from the public of Silverton. It might be possible to persuade him that the discretion of Mr. Mat and Miss Immy was not to be implicitly trusted. But Margaret knew well that it would seem to him monstrous and out of the question to keep her secret from the knowledge of Kate. It might be dangerous even to propose such a thing. Margaret had taken good care to inform herself of a fact, of which the reader is already aware, which was also perfectly well known to the Falconers, father and son, and which had been the cause of that little prudential hesitation, which had prompted Falconer in his somewhat unsuccessful attempts to avoid committing himself. Kate and Margaret were twin sisters, and all the Silverton world considered them to be co-heiresses of the Lindisfarn estates. It was natural that they should be so; and the squire himself in all probability regarded them as such. But they were not so in the eye of the law. They were not so indefeasibly. Failing a male heir, Mr. Lindisfarn's property was at his own disposition. And it was in his power (and therefore it was an event on the cards) to leave the whole or any proportion of the estate to either one of his daughters, if he should see fit to do so. This circumstance was never very far distant from Margaret's well-regulated mind, and added very remarkably to the binding force of the Fifth Commandment in her estimation and

practice. She well knew how high Kate stood in her father's affection and esteem. There never had been anything in his manner to herself, which was always indulgent and loving, to cause her the slightest uneasiness on the subject; but it did strike her that it might be unwise, as well as certainly futile, to make any attempt at keeping such a piece of family news as that which she was now carrying home, a secret from Kate while telling it to her father.

As to the latter step, it was of course necessary for very obvious reasons. She had understood all that had been passing in her beloved Frederick's mind, just as perfectly as if he had worn glass in front of his breast. His part naturally—and very properly—was to play fast and loose in case of possible accidents. Hers, more especially with the terrible bit of information in the background which she had, and which he had not, was of course to make him fast as words and vows could make him.

It was absolutely necessary, then, to tell Kate the fact of her engagement. And then came the consideration *how* that was to be done. After all that had taken place between the two sisters, she felt that the task was a difficult one. It was true that she had by no means given her sister to understand that she had any intention of ruling her own conduct in conformity with her scruples. On the contrary, she had very explicitly reserved to herself entire freedom of action. She was quite aware, however, how very strongly Kate would be grieved, and indeed outraged, by her acceptance of Frederick's offer under the circumstances of the case. Her indignation she might brave. But would Kate *do* anything? Would she take any steps?

Would it perhaps be possible to make Kate believe that she had told Frederick all the truth, and that he had persisted in his offer undismayed by the intelligence? Yes! Kate was fool enough to believe anything. But then there would be the breach of her solemn promise not to mention the secret of Julian's existence, and far worse, the certainty that Kate would then speak openly to Falconer on the subject. No; that plan was out of the question.

What *could* Kate do to frustrate her schemes, if she were anxious, as there was every reason to suppose she would be, to do so? She could not tell the real facts of the case to anybody, probably for the next month to come. Could she allow Falconer to become aware of the horrible truth, that she and her sister were two portionless girls, in any way without telling him the facts? It might perhaps be possible for her to say, or cause to be said, to him or to his father, enough to alarm him and awaken his distrust and caution. Would Kate take that step, considering the position it would put her, Margaret, in?

Margaret thought on mature consideration that she would not.

To secure this result, however, she must tell her story to Kate pathetically, not defiantly. It must be an appeal *ad misericordiam*. (I am giving Margaret's thoughts, not her words.) She must represent herself, as far as possible, to have been the victim of unlucky chance in the matter of her encounter with Falconer. Then difficulty, embarrassment, fear of having her sacred secret wormed out of her, tender passion, etc., must bear the blame, if any still remained to be borne. Kate was very soft—believed anything she was told—was very pitiful, and easily moved to compassion! And then again, she could hardly in any conceivable way make any such communication to the Falconers, however enigmatical, as should rouse their doubts on the vital subject of the heiress-ship, without exposing to them, either at once or subsequently, the fact that she, Kate, and therefore in all human probability, she, Margaret, also, had been cognizant of the horrible truth at the time when she had accepted, and, as she knew right well at the bottom of her heart, invited, his offer. And would Kate contribute to place her sister in such a position as that?

Margaret, again considering this matter dispassionately and carefully, came to the conclusion that Kate would not do this.

The history of the morning, therefore, according to such carefully arranged version of it as she thought she could manage to concoct, was to be told to Kate; and she must throw herself on her mercy.

And then came the question,—when was this rather formidable and important conversation to take place? It was evidently necessary that it should be done before she spoke to her father. And she had purposed to do that the last thing at night, when the domestic party in the drawing-room were separating. She had promised that Falconer should find the ground prepared for him when he came the first thing in the morning. She rather wished, now, that she had not been in such a hurry, and had fixed a later day, or at least a later hour, for her lover's interview with her father. Could she manage to see the latter in his study as soon as ever he was up, before Fred's arrival? If so, there would be all the night for her talk with her sister. If not, there would be no opportunity for speaking with Kate save the hurried half-hour of dressing for dinner, on the instant of her arrival at the Chase. That would never do. There was not time. Besides, it was so immediate. She felt that she needed a little time to make up her mind to the task, and to arrange her story. There was nothing for it save the other plan. And if Freddy arrived in the morning before she had finished her interview with her father, why, she must trust to Kate, who would then be in her confidence, to receive him, and make him understand that she was even then performing her promise to him, and that the coast would be clear for his attack on the squire in a minute or two. The time left for him to do his work in before the ringing of the breakfast-bell, which was like the trump of fate to the squire, would be short; but perhaps that was all for the best.

So Margaret, much pondering, had finally arranged her programme in that manner, by the time she and Mr. Mat arrived at the Lodge.

"Done the eight miles and a bit in an hour and ten minutes! That's not so bad, Miss Margaret, considering the ground, and that I had your precious safety to think of," said Mr. Mat; "and it wants five-and-thirty minutes to the dinner-bell!"

"Thank you, Mr. Mat. I shall have plenty of time," said Margaret, with a somewhat unwonted degree of cordiality, born of the sense of difficulty and danger which was pressing on her, and seemed to counsel the wisdom of standing as well with all around her as might be.

So she hurried up to her room; and to Kate's somewhat languid questions as to her day at Silverton, replied only that she had a great many things to tell her,—far more than there was then time for; and that they must have a good chat when they came up to bed at night.

Each sister perceived at once that there was something unusual in the manner of the other. And each conceived at once a shrewd suspicion of what she had to hear from the other. Kate's manner was languid, depressed, and that of one exhausted by suffering;—Margaret's, febrile, nervous, and constrained. Both looked forward with no little apprehension and misgiving to the conversation appointed for that night. Margaret had little doubt that Kate had received the offer from Captain Ellingham which she had so much dreaded, and had refused it. And though totally incapable of comprehending many of the feelings which had contributed to make Kate's task a terribly painful one, she understood that it must have been very vexatious. She speculated much on the question what influence Kate's own trouble was likely to have on the mode in which she would receive her confidence; and was inclined to consider that the result would be unfavorable. Surely, the high price which she had paid for the gratification of her own scruples would disincline her to indulgence for another's masterly disregard for them.

Kate surmised and greatly dreaded, yet struggled against believing the extent of the misfortune she had to learn from Margaret's confession. She knew that her sister at least risked seeing Falconer by going to Silverton; she had felt that she would have cut her hand off rather than have run that risk unnecessarily under the present circumstances, and she greatly feared, both from what she had already learned to know of Margaret's character, and from her obstinacy in going to Silverton that morning, that if by ill-hap Falconer had made her an offer, Margaret had not had firmness and high principle enough to refuse it.

Both girls would have given much to have avoided going through the ceremony of the dinner-table, and the subsequent evening in the drawing-room; both equally longed for and dreaded the hour that was to come afterwards. And they walked down to the drawing-room side by side, each with her brain and heart teeming with thoughts and fear and doubts, all relating to the same set of circumstances, and yet all as wholly different the one from the other as if they had been conceived by creatures of two different species.

CHAPTER XXVIII.

THE TETE-A-TETE.

At last the long evening wore itself to an end; and the two sisters went up-stairs together, and turned into Kate's room, for the conversation which both of them almost equally dreaded, though with feelings and from motives as contrasted as it was well possible for them to be.

"You need not wait, Simmons," said Kate, as they entered the room; "Miss Margaret and I want to have a good long talk before we go to bed; and we wont keep you up. We will help each other to undress."

And then, as soon as the servant had closed the door behind her, the two girls sat down,—Margaret in a large easy-chair, that stood at the foot of the bed, and Kate close by her side, but at right angles to the front of the large chair, on a small one, which she drew from the side of her drawing-table.

Kate, who had generally plenty of color in her cheeks, was paler than usual; for she had been and was still suffering much; and was moreover struggling against a sickening dread of what was coming. Margaret, who was usually as white as a lily, had a bright spot of delicate color in the middle of her creamy cheeks, the evidence of a febrile state of nervous agitation. Perhaps both girls were improved in beauty by the deviation from their ordinary appearance.

Kate was the first to speak.

"I know already, Margaret," she said, "that what I dreaded from your going to Silverton this morning has in fact happened."

"Why? What do you know?" replied her sister, quickly and almost fiercely.

"I know that you saw Mr. Falconer."

Kate would have said "Fred Falconer" on any other occasion; as, in speaking to her godmother or to any of her own family, she was ordinarily in the habit of doing. The feeling which made her now speak differently is very readily understood. But Margaret marked and resented the little change.

"How do you know that?" rejoined she, with flashing eyes.

"Because Mr. Mat told me that he saw him cross the Close with my uncle, and go into the house with him, when he returned from the service in the cathedral."

"That odious animal again!" thought Margaret, jotting down the new offence in the long bill against Mr. Mat posted in her memory, and meeting it all the same with prompt payment in ready hatred. But all she *said* was,—

"How does that show that I saw him, pray? When I am at the close, I stay in the drawing-room with my aunt. And Mr. Falconer of course went with Uncle Theophilus into the study."

"Did you not see him, then?" asked Kate, simply and directly.

"That is another matter," replied Margaret, who of course had no intention of denying what she had come there specially to confess; and who had only fenced with Kate's opening in the manner she had done from an instinctive desire to put off for an instant or two more the disagreeable moment which was coming.

"You did see him, then? Of course you did. Oh, Margaret! I wish you had not gone to Silverton this morning. It was very imprudent under the circumstances. I do wish you had not gone," repeated Kate, with so deep a sigh that it was almost a groan.

"Well! I did expect a rather more sisterly reception for what I had to tell you, I do confess, Kate. I come to open my heart to you, and make no secrets between us, and—and tell you everything, and you meet me with reproaches and groans!"

"I meant no reproach, dear; but for Heaven's sake tell me at once what happened!" replied Kate, now thoroughly alarmed by her sister's words and manner.

"Well! What I have to tell is of a kind usually received with a very different sort of welcome, Kate, from that which you seem inclined to accord to my tidings."

"You don't mean that"—said Kate, looking with large and affrighted eyes on the deepening color in her sister's face, and hesitating to shape her dread into words.

"I mean, Kate, that I was quite right in my estimation of the character of Mr. Falconer, as you have suddenly taken to call him. You remember our last conversation here? You remember what I then said of Fred's disinterestedness, and superiority to all mercenary considerations? Well, I was right, Kate, in my judgment of him. That is all."

"Do you mean that you told him of our loss of fortune—or rather of our never having had any fortune at all?" exclaimed Kate, whose fears began to point to a catastrophe in a new direction.

"Kate!" exclaimed her sister, in a tone of strong remonstrance and virtuous indignation; "is it possible that you can suspect me of such baseness? Do you really think that I could have under any circumstances betrayed the secret you confided to me in so solemn a manner? No, my sister, you do not know me!"

"I don't suspect you, Margaret; but I can't understand you! What has passed between you and Falconer? And what proof can you have had of his disinterestedness?"

Thus pressed, Margaret paused a moment before making the decisive plunge, intently occupied with the thought how she could accomplish it most effectively and gracefully. Then, rising from her chair, and flinging herself on her sister's shoulder, so as to hide her face among the abundant curls that hung around Kate's neck, she whispered in her ear,—

"It is all settled between us. We are pledged to each other solemnly and irrevocably! And he is the most generous and most disinterested of men; — and he is coming up to the Chase to speak to papa before breakfast to-morrow morning!"

"Oh, Margaret, Margaret! What does it all mean? Are you sure that— What did you tell him? Without betraying Julian's secret, I don't understand—"

"Why, won't you kiss me and congratulate me, Kate?" said her sister, still hanging round her neck.

"You know, Margaret, that your happiness is as dear to me as my own," replied Kate, kissing her on the forehead in obedience to this appeal; "but I don't understand how Falconer has proved his disinterestedness, or what opportunity there was for anything of the sort, since you did not say a word to him about the change in our prospects."

"Ah, Kate! you will persist in suspecting and misjudging him!" said Margaret, in a tone of deeply sorrowing reproach. "Are you sure, my sister," she continued, drawing back her head, and looking steadily into the innocent, pellucid depths of Kate's honest eyes, as if it were necessary to look very far down, in order to read the truth at the bottom of their wells,—are you sure that there is no feeling at the bottom of your heart, which interferes with your congratulating me on my happiness as frankly and heartily as I had hoped?"

"Oh, Margaret! what are you dreaming of? Only let us see clearly that there has been no mistake, no misunderstanding;—that Falconer knows, that in proposing to you, he is proposing to a girl without a penny of fortune, and I will congratulate you, and rejoice in your happiness, my dear, dear sister, believe me, as I would in my own. But I don't understand it! Tell me, darling, how it came about, and all that passed?"

"Oh, how can I tell you all that he said! I suppose that such matters pass generally very much in the same way. But I can very accurately tell you what he did not say. He did not make any single allusion, much less any inquiry as to fortune or money matters from beginning to end. I assure you he was thinking of quite other things."

Kate's face fell; and a cold spasm clutched her heart as her sister spoke. She had begun to hope from what Margaret had been saying that, somehow or other, though she could not quite comprehend how, it had come to pass that Falconer had become aware of the real state of the case, and had really taken the step Margaret announced him to have taken, with duly opened eyes. But her sister's words cruelly destroyed any such illusion.

"Is that all? Margaret dear, that is not enough. You are deluding yourself. Consider for a moment! Of course Mr. Falconer spoke to you under the full impression that you were the heiress to half papa's property. If nothing were ever told him to the contrary, of course he thought so. He was justified in thinking so. Does not every other human being in Sillshire suppose so? We only — you and I only in all the world know that we have no claim to any such position."

"But why will you persist in attributing your own mercenary feelings to other people?" said Margaret, who found it impossible to keep her temper as much under control as she had purposed doing. "I tell you that Falconer had no such ideas in his mind. You must excuse me if I persist in believing, extraordinary as it may seem to you, that I myself, and not the Lindisfarn acres, was the object of his pursuit."

"You know, Margaret, that I have no wish to say or think otherwise," replied Kate ; " but surely you would wish that any one so addressing you should not do so in ignorance of the truth on such a subject. Think whether you would like the telling him afterwards how the matter really stands. Think how intolerable it would be, and then judge of the necessity for preventing it !"

" But how could I help it? You are so unreasonable, Kate,—so unfair ! You tell me facts with the positive injunction to keep them secret, and then make it a matter of blame to me that I do not blab them on the first opportunity. Would you have had me repeat to Falconer all that I had solemnly promised you to keep secret ? "

" Of course you could not betray poor Julian's secret."

" Then I should like to know what you would have had me do ? "

" You know, Margaret dear, that I foresaw the danger and the difficulty. That was my reason for telling you the facts that had come to my knowledge. I saw that any offer of marriage to either of us, before we should be at liberty to let the truth be publicly known, would impose on us the necessity of refusing it, without being able to explain the circumstances under which we did so. It was very possible that such a difficulty might have fallen upon you, even if you had done all in your power to prevent it. But I would have had you endeavor in every way to avoid it. I would have had you abstain from going to Silverton, as you know, this morning."

" Nothing is easier than preaching, Kate ! I should like to know what you would have done, if the case had been your own? Besides, was it just, or fair, or to be tolerated, that I should shut myself up, and not dare to show my nose out of the lodge gates, because a cousin whom I have never seen has put himself into such a position that his existence cannot be avowed ? Not I indeed ! I hate all such underhand doings and discreditable secrets. It is a sort of thing that I have never been used to."

" I have no liking for secrets of any sort, Margaret ; and God knows that I long for the time when this one may be freely disclosed. But this secret is not of my seeking or making, nor of yours. We could not help

ourselves. And it was very evident that the possession of it might place us in very painful circumstances. That is why I wished you, as far as possible, to avoid the danger you have fallen into. You would go to Silverton ; and it has happened as I feared it might. And now the question is, What do you mean to do ? "

" What is the good of talking in that way, Kate? of course it is out of the question to betray Julian's secret. What do I mean to do ? I have done all that I mean to do. He told me he loved me, and asked me if I could love him. My answer was a frank and honest one. What could I do more ? "

" But surely you must feel, Margaret, that it is impossible for you to let him enter into an engagement to you, supposing you to be heiress to half the Lindisfarn property, and you knowing all the time how sadly different your position is."

" I told you my feelings and principles on such subjects, Kate, when we spoke on this point before. I have been brought up to think that girls have no business to meddle with such matters. It appears to one who has had the advantage of such an education exceedingly indelicate for them to do so. I shrink instinctively from all contact with considerations and business of the kind. I cannot enter into such things."

" It may be," said Kate, with a sort of dreamy musing, "that you are right. But then what was so disagreeable for you to say must be said for you by some one else. Papa must tell Mr. Falconer that "—

" You don't mean to betray poor Julian's secret? Think of the consequences ! " cried Margaret, quickly, and with an alarmed glance at her sister's face ; " surely that is impossible ! "

" Yes, that is impossible. That is what makes the difficulty. But something must be done. Something must be said to Falconer before it is too late."

" What is it possible to say ? " rejoined Margaret, in much alarm. Then, after a pause, during which her whole power of thinking was brought to bear intently on the subject, she added, " If he were the sordid wretch you persist in imagining him to be, it would be quite enough to explain all these matters to him at any time before the marriage took place. But if, as I know right well, no such considerations would have weight with him, it would be as needless as useless to enter into the subject now."

"But, dearest Margaret, you do not seem to see the matter in its true light. Of course it would be out of the question to make a marriage with one who supposed you to be a large heiress, while you were aware that you were nothing of the kind. And of course the marriage might be broken off when that fact could be openly told. But would not such a breaking off be very painful to us all? Would it not be wrong to place any man knowingly in such a position as should compel him to make such a breaking off? But even that is not the worst. I am not so much thinking of protecting Mr. Falconer from the danger of making a bad match. What I am anxious about is that you should not accept an offer, knowing well that it was made in ignorance of circumstances of which you were well aware."

"But I am not supposed to know anything of the kind!" burst in Margaret, surprised into a naïvely sincere avowal of her insincerity; "I should have known nothing of the kind if it had not been for your officious eagerness to tell me bad news. I should have known nothing of the kind; and there would have been no difficulty in the matter," urged Margaret, forgetting honestly, in her indignation, that, had she not received the fatal information from Kate, she would assuredly have been in no such hurry to receive the offer, which she had that day extracted from Fred in so masterly a manner, in the canon's garden.

"Oh, Margaret!" said Kate, sorrowfully; "I told you what I knew, only that you might avoid the embarrassment which you have fallen into."

"I see no embarrassment at all," rejoined Margaret, — "unless, indeed, you should think it right to complete the work you did when you told me this improbable story— which I do not half believe — by publishing abroad that you told it to me."

"Margaret!" almost shrieked Kate, as if she had received a sudden stab; "how can you speak such words? And, oh, Margaret, how can you persuade yourself to enter on such a path of duplicity? *You* will know that you know it if nobody else were ever to know it."

"It is all very fine preaching, Kate, especially in a case that is not one's own. What could I do? You admit that I could not tell him the secret. What was I to do? What answer was I to make to him?"

"I should have declined his offer, Margaret," said her sister, quietly.

"But it was not my wish to decline his offer! And on what grounds too? Was I to tell him I hated him? That would have been a lie. Spoken to as he spoke to me, I could but confess the truth,—that I was not indifferent to him. What would you have had me say?"

"I know that it was difficult," said Kate, speaking still more quickly, and with her eyes cast down to the ground.

"Surely, then, I took the only path that was open to me; all taken by surprise, too, as I was," pleaded Margaret. "I hardly knew what I was saying. I only knew that it was impossible to me to hide the truth from him. Could you expect me to be thinking of fortunes and marriage settlements at such a moment? Don't be too hard upon me, Kate!"

"Heaven knows, Margaret, that I have no wish to be hard on you; but every wish to help you in any possible way. But remember, that it must needs be known that I, at least, was aware of Julian's existence at the time when Mr. Falconer made his offer to you."

"Why should it be known that the man who was wounded by the revenue officers, and whom you visited in his illness at Mr. Pendleton's cottage, was our cousin, Julian Lindisfarn? If he recovers, as there seems to be little reason to doubt that he will, and goes away back again to France, as soon as he is able to move, why should we say anything about the matter at all? Why cause so much unnecessary pain and sorrow to all our relatives? Of course he will come forward in due time to claim his inheritance. There is no chance of his failing to do that. Why need we move in the matter till then? And why need it ever be known to anybody that you were aware of his existence before the time when it may become known to all the family!"

"It is bad enough to have to keep the secret till he goes away," said Kate, with a sigh that was almost a groan; "but, Margaret," she added quickly, and looking keenly into her face,—for the progress of the conversation was rapidly generating very painful misgivings in Kate's mind,—" you cannot dream of absolutely marrying any man. who is under the delusion that you are an heiress!"

" Oh, of course not that!" said Margaret. while a hot flush suffused her face. " When it comes to the business part of the matter, and the lawyers, and all that, of course all such things will be properly explained and put right. But since we cannot tell the real truth at once, and that by no fault of ours, I cannot see that we are bound to make difficulties for ourselves and sorrow and trouble for others by interfering in the matter. Surely, under the circumstances of the case, it would be more sisterly, Kate, to abstain from betraying the fact that I knew of the matter when Frederick proposed to me this morning. I could not tell him, you know. And yet he might think that I ought to have done so. It is very, very hard! I do think, Kate, that you might spare me this."

And as she spoke, she threw those eloquent eyes of hers, with a wistful and almost tearful glance of entreaty in them, on her sister's face, in a manner that Kate's heart could not resist. Kate had but little notion of the falsehood practised by tongues. But that human eyes also should tell lies, was an idea that had never been dreamed of in her philosophy.

She did feel it " very hard," as Margaret had said, that the fatality of circumstances should make it impossible for her to pursue her usual straightforward path of frank and thoroughly open truthfulness. And it did occur to her mind, for a passing moment, that it was " very, very hard " that Ellingham should never come to know that she had made the discovery of her own want of fortune all but immediately before her refusal of his suit. He would come to know it, of course. But what would she not have given for the assurance that he should be made aware that she was in possession of the fatal secret at the time of her rejection of him! And it was very bitter to her to think that this fact might never be known to him. Nevertheless, if consideration for her sister were to prevail so far as to induce her to consent to a suppression of the facts known to her for a longer time than her promise to her cousin rendered necessary, assuredly the gratification of her own feelings with regard

to Ellingham should not induce her to expose her sister's want of openness. And in all probability the sense of self-sacrifice operated in some degree to reconcile her conscience to the connivance with the suppression of the truth, which was asked of her. Had her own interests pointed in the same direction with Margaret's in the matter, it may be safely assumed that she would not have yielded to the latter's pleading.

As it was, she began to feel, as Margaret looked up in her face, that she should not have the courage to condemn her to the exposure that would be involved in the making known her acquaintance with the fact of Julian's existence. The idea of the agony which she would herself have felt if she had accepted an offer of marriage under such circumstances, and had afterwards been discovered to have known all the time that she was a penniless bride, was too vividly present to her mind for it to be possible for her to sentence her sister to it.

" Would to God," she said, looking pitifully at her sister, " that this had not happened! Would to God, that it could have been avoided! "

" But now that it has happened so, you will not denounce me, Kate? " said Margaret, perceiving that her sister's tenderness for her was getting the upper hand in her mind.

" Denounce you, Margaret! "

" You will not declare that I knew this hateful secret, which I had no desire to know, and which I was bound by my promise to you not to disclose? "

" No, I will not, Margaret. I will say nothing on the subject. God forgive me, if it is wrong! I do not see clearly what is right in the matter. I will not say any words that shall bring disgrace or blame upon you."

" And you will not, immediately after Julian's departure, take any steps to noise abroad the fact of his being still alive? You would only be blamed for having concealed it while he was here."

" But, Margaret, that must, at all events, be told. You cannot let things go on, you know, till "—

" Of course, of course, Kate; I know that. But leave the things alone. Let the facts disclose themselves at the proper time. Why should we meddle in the matter? "

"Only, if things were to come to a crisis between you and Falconer, you know, Margaret, before the circumstance of Julian's life had become known, it would, in that case, be absolutely necessary for us to disclose the truth."

"Oh, yes! Of course, of course! But things will not come to a crisis, as you call it, so soon as all that. I am in no great hurry. Depend upon it that Falconer will and shall know the whole state of the case before anything is definitely settled. But promise me that you will not denounce me as having known the truth all the time!"

"But you seemed just now, Margaret, to think that it did not matter whether you knew it or not; and that, in any case, it was no business of yours to pay any attention to it, or to speak to Mr. Falconer on any such subject."

"And so I do think," returned Margaret, sharply; "those are the ideas and feelings in which I have been brought up. But if I have been led astray by the difference of ways and manners in this part of the world, I can't help it! I am quite convinced in my own mind, that the knowledge of Julian's existence and the effect it may have on my fortune will not make any difference in Fred's feelings toward me. To my ideas, it seems absurd to suppose that it could do so. If I am anxious not to be known to have been aware of certain circumstances this morning, it is in deference to your ideas, Kate, rather than to my own."

Kate had nothing ready to reply to this. There was a slippery agility about her sister's fence, that was altogether too much for the steady, straightforward, perfectly open march of ideas that was habitual to her own mind.

"I wish I had not told you anything about it, Margaret!" she said, after musing a little while, and sighing deeply as she spoke. "It did not seem to me at the time at all sisterly not to tell you. But now I think that it would have been for the best to keep it from you. Perhaps I was wrong!"

"I confess I think you were, Kate. I am quite sure that I should have much preferred knowing nothing about it. I hate all business matters."

"I did as I would have wished you to do by me in such a case, Margaret. Nevertheless, I say, perhaps I was wrong. And I will not take upon myself to interfere with your conduct in the matter by any acts or words of mine"—

"That is all I ask of you, Kate. That is my own dear sister!" exclaimed Margaret, with much effusion of manner.

—"Unless, indeed," continued Kate, speaking with evident reluctance, "any acts or words of mine should be necessary to prevent a marriage being absolutely made, without the real state of the case being known."

At the beginning of the conversation between the two girls, Kate would never have thought of making any such proviso as the above. And she would hardly now have admitted to herself that there was any necessity for it. But, despite herself, an unreasoned and unavowed consciousness had come into her mind since the discussion begun, that instinctively prompted her to utter it.

A dark shade passed over Margaret's face, like a cloud before the moon, save that it passed more rapidly than any storm-cloud. It was gone in scarcely more than a second, and the lightning flash from the eyes, that had accompanied it, passed from them as rapidly. But there was a dangerous and scathing look about it, during the moment it lasted, that would have seemed to any more observant and skilled interpreter than Kate, eloquent of anything save sisterly love.

But the cloud flitted past, and the flash died out as suddenly as it had shot forth— and Margaret only said, with a sort of impatient manner—,

"Of course, of course! *Cela va sans mot dire!* So now, dear Kate, we understand each other. I am so glad! And *now* will you not congratulate me on my happiness? for indeed I am very happy."

What could Kate say? She had the most perfect conviction that no marriage would take place between Frederick Falconer and any undowered lady, be she who she might. It was difficult to furnish the congratulations required of her on such a prospect. She could only say that she did most sincerely rejoice in anything which was for her sister's happiness. And that safe generalization passed muster very satisfactorily. Margaret had been victorious in the great battle she had come into that room that night to fight; and she was content.

"And now, Katie dear, it is high time for us to go to bed. Good gracious! it is near one o'clock! And we must both be up in good time before breakfast to-morrow morning. He is to be here to speak to papa in his study before the bell rings. And I have promised that he shall find the way prepared for him; so that I must see papa first; and I had intended to have done so over night. But I would not speak till I had consulted you, dearest, of course. And I could not get an opportunity of doing that till now; so that we shall be pressed for time in the morning. And what I want is, that if I am with papa when he comes, you should receive him, and "—

"You do not want me to say anything to him "—

Again the thunder-cloud passed over the fair face, and the evil-looking lightning flashed from the superb eyes. But it was only for a fragment of a moment.

"Pooh! make yourself easy, Kate! I only want you to compromise yourself so far as to bid him good-morning, and tell him that I am speaking with papa, and that the coast will be clear for him in a minute."

But the statement of the duty thus assigned to her did not by any means tend to make Kate "easy," as Margaret had so flippantly said. It led her, on the contrary, to the consideration that even thus, at the very outset, she would be taking an active part in promoting an engagement between her sister and Falconer, she being in possession of information which she was very sure would have prevented him from contemplating anything of the kind, if he had shared it. Something must, of course, be said on the subject between her and Falconer. And what could she say? How could she so guide herself as not to be guilty, in her sister's behalf, of that which, on her own behalf, she had kept herself clear from at the cost of so much agony and self-denial? *How* was this to be done? And as these thoughts rushed through her brain, her heart sank within her.

But Margaret had meanwhile risen from her seat, and was leaving the room with a nodded "Good-night," as considering that her last words had quite sufficiently settled the programme for the following morning, and that there was nothing more to be said on the subject. Kate felt that it was impossible for her to accept the part assigned to her. A whole vista of similar and still worse

difficulties and troubles opened itself mistily and indistinctly before her. How she should fight through them she did not know, nor could she now pause to consider. But this first step to-morrow morning she felt that she could not take. And it was absolutely necessary to refuse it on the instant.

"Stop, Margaret!" she cried, in her desperation; "stop a moment; that will never do. I would rather not see Mr. Falconer to-morrow morning. I cannot do it; indeed I cannot!"

The words seem plain enough. But words are but symbols, plain only to those agreed upon the ideas they are used to symbolize. One man says, I told such and such things to another; and he takes it for granted that he put into the mind of that other the thoughts that were in his own. But the eye can see only that which it is given to it to see; and the mind can conceive only the ideas which it is capable of conceiving. And Margaret accordingly interpreted Kate's words according to the key supplied by her own head and heart.

"Why, Kate! I had no idea of this," she said, turning round at the door of the room; "upon my word I had not;" and as she spoke, there was a strange contradiction between the expression of her eyes and that of her mouth. The former spoke with their usual eloquence of grave and regretful sympathy, while an irrepressible smile of gratified triumph and conscious superiority mantled about the latter. And it was a curious fact that the former feature told the lie that was needed, in their owner's opinion, for the occasion, while it was left to the latter to tell the unsuppressible truth. In the case of most performers the reverse would in all probability have been the case. It was not so with Margaret. Most of the lies she told were told by her eyes,—those beautiful large eyes,—tender, confiding, beseeching, fierce, vindictive, languishing by turns. They and the expression of them, were more under the perfect and habitual control of the mistress, who made such frequent and such effective use of them than even the muscles of that habitual telltale of the affections, the mouth, which in that lovely young face could speak lies, but had not yet acquired the habit of looking them.

But Kate was too much engrossed by her

own painful thoughts, and too little in the habit of meeting with or suspecting falsehood anywhere, to note that her meaning had been misapprehended. And when Margaret, in accents of ill-concealed triumph and gratification, went on to say that if that were indeed the state of the case, she would not for the world expose Kate to the pain of such an interview; and that, after all, it would be quite sufficient if Banting were to tell Falconer, on his arrival, that Miss Margaret was with her papa, and that the squire would be happy to see him if he would wait a few minutes; Kate was delighted to catch at such a means of escape, and assented thankfully to the arrangement.

So the sisters parted for the night, Kate determining that she would not appear in the morning till after breakfast, when Falconer should have left the house; and Margaret victorious, and congratulating herself on the masterly manner in which she had brought to a successful termination an interview to which she had looked forward with so much apprehension.

But it was long before either of the sisters fell asleep. Kate's mind was busy with painful provisions of the embarrassments and difficulties which seemed to unfold themselves before her in more and more threatening numbers and proportions, the more she meditated on the subject. And Margaret set to work to review her position and Kate's conduct as regarded by the aid of the new light, which, she fancied, had been thrown upon the subject by Kate's last words.

"So, so, so, so!" thought she, "that's the explanation, then, of all the difficulties and scruples and pack of nonsense; is it? Well! It is quite as well to know it. But I think I can distance Miss Kate at one game as easily as I have done at another. Yes! I am glad I know how the land lies!"

CHAPTER XXIX.
SPEAKING TO PAPA.

MARGARET was a frequent offender against that primal law of the Lindisfarn social code, which commanded that all those who lived under it should appear in the breakfast-room, what time the uncorruptibly punctual Mr. Banting, who never delegated that important function to any inferior hand, rang the morning bell. Margaret was a frequent and almost

privileged offender; for how could the great cardinal virtue of coming down to breakfast punctually in time be expected from one who was not only not "Sillshire," but not even English-bred?

But on the morning after the conversation recorded in the last chapter, Miss Margaret was up betimes. The squire was understood to be generally in his "study" half an hour or so before breakfast: and it wanted nearly as much as that to the morning bell-ringing, when Margaret, not altogether without a little quickening of the heart-pulse, but still with an exceedingly creditable degree of self-possession, tripped to the door of the study, and after the pause before it of some half a minute, gave a little tap against the panel with the knuckles of her slender little pink hand.

It was very evident that Margaret's early appearance from her chamber had not been obtained at the cost of any abbreviation of the cares of the toilet. To do her justice, it must be admitted that Margaret had retained enough of English nature and English instinct, amid the influences of her Parisian education, to preserve her from the abominable continental sin of compensating finery for show hours by slovenliness in hours of privacy. She was always *tirée à quatre épingles;—always* dressed with perfect freshness and taste. But on the present occasion, an educated eye would at once have observed that the exquisitely pretty *toilette de matin* in which she appeared at the squire's study door was the result of more than usual care and consideration. There was a candor, gentleness,—nay, even a sort of foreshadowing of young matronhood, in the pale, glossy folds of the pearl-gray silk dress, lighted up, as by a flash of passionate girlhood, by the rich, deep rose-colored necktie, and tiny wrist-knots, which set off so admirably the fair wearer's marble white throat and hands. Then there was a modish little scrap of a rich black silk apron whose girdle helped to call the eye to the outline of the slenderest of waists, while it gave just the slightest flavor of housewifery to the entire composition. The dark satiny hair was dressed as charmingly as usual; but there was a little tribute to sentiment in one smoothly rolled ringlet, rather too regular in outline to be quite innocent of the irons, which strayed from under the mass of plaits and rested on the pearl-gray bodice. In truth, Margaret's costume on the morning in question was a grand success, in which every slight artistic touch had its importance, from the piquant rosette on her slipper to the demure little black velvet *jeannette*, with tiny gold cross and heart, then a recent importation from France, which encircled her alabaster throat.

The squire's hearty, jovial voice from within, in a tone like that of a somewhat modified view-holloa, bade her "Come in, whoever you are," in answer to her modest tap; and on opening the door, she found the old gentleman standing with his legs wide asunder on the rug, with his back to the "study" fire, busy in putting a new lash to a dog-whip, holding the while the end of the bit of whipcord between his teeth.

The squire, with his tall and well-grown person, his clear, healthy, rosy complexion, and his handsome features, with the kindly beam from his honest, laughing blue eye, his pleasant smile, and his reverend silver locks, was as attractive a presentment of age, as was Margaret of youth. But somehow or other, they did not give an impression of being well-assorted. Very great, mysteriously great, is the power of that education which is imparted to human beings by all the united influences of everything that surrounds them during the process of development from childhood to man and womanhood. It is so great as to throw doubt on all our speculations respecting the possible identity or divergence of races. Here were two twin children; Sillshire had made one of them into our darling peerless Kate, and Paris had made the other into our incomparable Marguerite! African and Caucasian! Ham and Japhet! Why, had not the skin of the Paris girl already become of a different color and texture from that of the Sillshire lass? Psychological differences! I should think there *were* psychological differences,—capable of being tolerably satisfactorily described by a shorter word! Physiological characteristics! I only know that Kate used always to seem to carry about with her an atmosphere redolent of hedge-roses and the morning dew on the sweetbrier, while Margaret scented the fanning breeze with *bouquet de millefleurs*. I believe that if her blood had been analyzed, a residuum of the oxyde or chloride of *bou-*

quet de millefleurs, or some such thing, would have been found in it.

Kate Lindisfarn by the side of her father always seemed the due and thoroughly satisfactory completion of an admirably composed picture. The group was thoroughly harmonious. There was no such harmony, no such artistic keeping in the group formed by Margaret and the squire.

None the less kindly, on that account, however, was the squire's greeting as Margaret entered his study on the occasion in question.

"What, Margaret!" he cried, in the mellow but somewhat stentorian tones, to which his Parisian daughter confessed she had not yet been able to accustom or reconcile herself; but he had never once, since that evening of Marguerite's first arrival, relapsed into the sin of calling her "Margy,"— "what, Margaret! you afoot so early this morning? What's in the wind now? And upon my word, what a picture of a dress! I make you my compliments on the success of your toilet, my dear! Come and let me have a closer look at you!"

And as he spoke, the squire, holding the handle of his dog-whip in one hand, and the end of the lash in the other, playfully threw it over her head, so as to encircle her waist, and draw her thus imprisoned towards him. Margaret gave a little uneasy wriggle, very plainly expressive of her not altogether unpardonable fear that the usage she was being subjected to might inflict damage on some portion of the work of art on which so much pains had been bestowed. The squire perceived it, and after impressing one kiss on her forehead, very much with the air and action of a man walking on eggs, released her.

"I wanted to speak to you, papa, if I may; and I thought that this would be the most convenient time for catching you."

"Any time, any time, my dear! But what is it, my dear child?" said the squire, somewhat nervously; for he could not imagine what could be coming, and had a kind of presentiment that something at or about the Chase was going to be complained of.

"I will only trouble you a very few minutes, papa."—

"As many as ever you like, my darling! We have five-and-twenty before Banting rings the breakfast-bell!" said the squire, look-

11

ing at his great silver hunting-watch, and seeming to consider that length of time as an infinity beyond which no imaginable conference could prolong itself.

Margaret did not exhibit any degree of unusual emotion or embarrassment. She did not bite her thumbs, or more elegantly hide her face on her father's shoulder. She cast down her eyes, however, beneath their long and silky lashes, with a very pretty little bending of her arched neck, and twining the tasselled cord of her apron round her two forefingers as she thus stood by her father's side, she said, in a very demure, but yet in a sufficiently businesslike, manner,—

"Yesterday, papa, I received a proposal which, of course, it is my first duty to communicate to you immediately."

"A proposal, my child! What, you don't mean a proposal of marriage?"

"Yes, papa; it was a proposal of marriage. Although, according to the ideas of those among whom I was educated, it is proper that such a proposal should be made in the first case to the parents of the young person, I believe that it is in this country considered permissible to address such a communication to herself."

"Yes," said the squire, scratching his head, and looking at his exquisitely elegant daughter with a mixture of admiration and curiosity, "in this country we generally make love to the girls themselves, rather than to their fathers and mothers. But who is it, my pretty one, who has asked for the present of that pretty little hand? Who is the bold man? And what answer did he get from 'the young person' herself?"

"It is Mr. Frederick Falconer, papa; of course my answer necessarily was that he must apply to you."

"Apply to me? Well! Yes—that is all right and proper, very proper! But I suppose the young gentleman wanted some answer from you first."

"But of course, you know, papa, I could give him none—except altogether conditionally on your approval and pleasure."

"And was he contented with that?" said the squire, with a twinkle in his clear blue eye, and a look which was meant to be the quintessence of archness.

Margaret, however, did not give the slightest countenance to any unbecoming levity, by responding in any way to these demonstrations.

"From all that I have seen of Mr. Falconer, papa, and still more from what I have heard of him, especially from my aunt, Lady Sempronia, since I have been in this country, I should be led to suppose that he would not expect any other reply from me," returned Margaret, with a grave propriety of accent and bearing that the old squire felt to be a slap in the face for his improper levity.

"But if I am to give him his answer, my dear child," he said, more gravely, "I at least must first learn from you what sort of answer you would wish it to be."

"In that, my dear father, I should wish to be entirely guided by your superior knowledge and by your advice."

The squire scratched his head, and stared at her with the blank, puzzled look of a man suddenly called upon to act in the midst of a whole world of circumstances entirely new to him.

"Well! That is all very right and proper," he said at last; "and I am sure, my dear, I shall be most happy—that is, as far as my power goes,—but, you see, the first question is, it seems to me— But what does Kate think about it?" he added, briskly, as the bright idea struck him that her mediation between himself and the embarrassingly superfine propriety of his Parisian daughter might powerfully tend to facilitate matters.

"I believe my sister has a very good opinion of Mr. Falconer," replied Margaret; and a slight passing flush, that passed across her face as she said the words, was the first sign of emotion of any sort which she had betrayed since entering her father's room.

"Yes; I have a very good opinion of Mr. Falconer too," replied the squire. "I have known him from a boy. I never knew any ill of him. And I have heard much good. I believe he has always been a very good son. I don't know that he is exactly the man I should fall in love with, if I were a young lady. But then," continued the squire, quite gravely,—for he had no inclination to incur a second reprimand for levity, and was in truth applying himself to the task imposed upon him to the best of his ability, — "but then God only knows what I should do or should feel, if I were a young lady. I sup-

pose most things would seem very different
to me then, you know. I can't say I like
Fred's seat in the saddle. And Mr. Mat says
he is Jemmy Jessamy. But then perhaps
you don't care about his riding; and you are
not bound to follow Mr. Mat's opinion. If
it were Kate now, the way he sits his horse
might count for something."

"I do not think my sister would consider
Mr. Falconer's mode of riding any objection
to him in the point of view which is now
under consideration, papa," replied Margaret; and while she was speaking, the
slight flush again passed over her face,
accompanied this time by an almost imperceptible toss of the head.

It occurred to the squire's recollection at
that moment, that he had heard his old friend
Lady Farnleigh call Freddy Falconer a prig:
and the thought did flash across his mind for
an instant, accompanied rather than followed
by a self-accusing feeling of penitence for
having conceived it, that perhaps he and his
foreign-bred daughter were all the better
adapted to each other on that account.

But he only said in answer to Margaret's
last words, "I dare say not, my dear,—I
dare say not. And, really, my dear child,
I do not know that I can say anything
more or better to you on the subject than
that, if he has contrived to win that quiet,
undemonstrative little heart of yours, I
do not know of any objection to him.
I do conscientiously believe him to be a very
good young man. And that, I take it, is
about all that I ought to look to in the matter. The rest is your own affair; and can
only be decided by yourself. In this country,
my dear, we think that love should precede
marriage as well as follow it; and I own that
I should be very sorry to see you marry any
man to whom you were not sincerely attached. But if Fred Falconer has really
been able to make himself agreeable to you,
as I said before, I do not know any just cause
or impediment why you two should not
be joined together in holy matrimony;" thus
bringing to a conclusion—neatly and forcibly,
as he flattered himself—the longest oration,
in all probability, which he ever had uttered;
though his sense of rhetorical propriety
would have been more completely satisfied,
if the circumstances of the occasion would
have allowed him to add the words, "he is
now to declare it." Still, the squire was

contented with his effort; and having clearly
expressed his views on the subject, and at the
same time done, as it seemed to his mind, due
homage to the seriousness of the occasion by
winding up his period and the subject with
the time-honored and *quasi* semi-sacred for-
mula he had hit on, he appeared to consider
that he had said and done all that was or
could be then and there expected of him in
the premises.

But it was now Margaret's turn to look
into her father's face with blank and puzzled
surprise. To her comprehension of the matter, he had been babbling upon a variety of
trifling and at all events secondary matters,
to the total forgetfulness of the one thing
needful. Not a word or an allusion to
the point which ought to form the main
and special object of the solicitude of any
right-principled father or guardian! Or
was it that the squire, being as a prudent
father should be, perfectly well-informed as
to the fortunes, prospects, and expectations
of every young man in the neighborhood, and
having the knowledge that things were satisfactory in this respect in the case of Fred
Falconer, thought that she, Margaret, was
too young and too silly to be spoken with on
such a subject? If, indeed, her father were
unprincipled enough to neglect his duty to
his child, and leave her unprotected in this
respect, it was the more necessary that she
should take care of herself. If, on the other
hand, the second hypothesis were the true
one, and the fact were that her father deemed
her still too much of a child to speak to on
matters of serious business, she was not at all
sorry to have an opportunity of showing him
that such was by no means the case.

So she said, first raising her eyes for one
quick, observant glance into his face, and then
dropping them on the floor, as she stood in
front of him, "I suppose, papa, that you
would disapprove of any marriage that was
not a suitable one in point of fortune and
position. I have always been educated to
believe that no happiness can be expected
from any such union, and that nothing is
more unpardonable, in a well-brought-up
young person, than the slightest thought
even of forming such a *mesalliance*. But of
course I know nothing about such matters.
It is my duty to leave all such entirely in
your hands."

The old squire felt as if there would be

nothing left for him but to listen meekly and strive to profit by it, if the astonishingly "well-brought-up young person," standing then on the rug before him, had seen fit to favor him with an exposition of the whole duty of man.

So he replied, with no little feeling of awe for that exquisitely dressed incarnation of perfect propriety, "Of course, my dear Margaret, of course! It is a very necessary consideration. Happily, I believe that in the present case there is no cause for any hesitation on that score. No doubt Master Freddy will be very comfortably well off."

"I suppose, papa, you will think it right to be very explicit in speaking on this topic with Mr. Frederick Falconer?" and the manner in which the name was pronounced succeeded in administering a fitting reproof to the old gentleman for the irreverence he had permitted himself in speaking of his august daughter's intended as Master Freddy."

"Well, my dear: I have always understood, and indeed I may say I know that old Falconer is more than well off,—that he is a wealthy man; and Frederick is his only son. But of course the lawyers must have a finger in the pie, before it comes out of the oven, and it will be for them to look into the matter properly."

"Yes, papa. And is it not the mode in England for the lawyers to write down all about it, before the marriage is arranged?" inquired his daughter, with charming girlish naïveté.

"Quite so, my dear. Settlements, we call them. The settlements must be made properly, of course."

"And all that I have, or ever shall have, must be written down in them, too, must it not, papa?"

"Yes, my dear, I suppose so. I am not much of a lawyer; but I suppose that is the proper way."

"And you call it by such a funny name! Tying up! I have heard dear Madame de Renneville talk of tying up. I remember it because it is such a queer expression. I suppose the lawyers must tie me up, papa?" she said, raising her eyes as she spoke, and shooting point-blank into the squire's face a sunny beam of girlish mirth. And again, the same strange phenomenon occurred, which had been observable in this remarkable "young person" on a former occasion. Her mouth did not join in the smile of her eyes, but remained quite gravely busied about the serious business in hand. It needed, however, a far more observant and skilled physiognomist than the squire to take note of this. He was divided between pleased admiration of the exceeding prettiness of the face and figure before him, and marvelling admiration of the range of knowledge a "*jeune personne bien elevée*," might be expected to possess.

"Yes, my dear! You must be tied up, I suppose, as you say; or at least your fortune must. And, by the by, that brings me to a point which I can hardly say, I think, that I ever considered at all, so much has it always been in my mind as a matter of course. I have but you and Kate, my child, you know, and there is neither oldest nor youngest between ye. Of course, all I have will be yours between you. And the matter never has come into my mind in any other light. But what you say about settlements puts it into my head that the sharing of the property between you is not a matter of course, but depends on my will."

Margaret's eyes were by this time quite concealed beneath their long, drooping lashes; but her mouth was more seriously occupied with the business in hand than ever. For an instant, Margaret feared that she had, perhaps, been injudicious in leading her father, as she had purposely and with admirable skill done, to speak on the subject of his intentions respecting his property.

"Of course," the squire went on to say, "I never had any thought upon the matter but that you would share and share alike. But for that to be so, I must make it so! And if settlements are to be made I must make it so *then*. Afterward I should have no power to alter the arrangement," added the squire, speaking somewhat gravely.

"It would never have entered into my head, of course, papa, to think of, much less to inquire into, your intentions on the subject. Only it seemed possible that Mr. Falconer, or his father for him, might think it right to know my position in this respect."

"Has anything been said to you on the subject?" inquired the squire. He would never have dreamed of making such an inquiry of his Sillshire Kate. But he was beginning to feel as if he should not be a bit surprised if it should turn out to be the correct thing for a "*jeune personne bien elevée*," upon an occasion such as the present, to pull out of a dainty little apron-pocket a rough draft of a settlement ready prepared by her own fair fingers.

"Oh, no, papa! not a syllable! I am sure Mr. Falconer would not have been guilty of such an indelicacy for the whole world! Indeed, I think that in all probability he has not given a thought to the subject. But his father, you know, papa, will probably wish to know."

"Of course, my dear! And it is quite right and necessary that he should know; and quite proper that Mast—that Mr. Frederick should wish to know too. I only said that the matter presented itself to my mind for the first time. Well, I think I may say that I shall be ready to tell Mr. Falconer that I am prepared to settle on you, upon your marriage with his son, one-half of this property. As for what I may be able to do for you during my lifetime, it would require a more leisurely consideration, you know"—

"Oh, of course, papa, of course! I am sure that nothing can be farther from Frederick's intention than to dream of speaking to you upon any such subject when he comes to speak to you this morning."

"This morning! Bless my soul! Is he coming this morning?" cried the squire, rather startled.

"Yes! I have very little doubt that he is at the Chase already, papa! He was so impatient! I could hardly prevent him from coming up here last night. But I thought that it would be more agreeable to you to see him in the morning. May I tell him that he may come in to speak with you, dear papa?" said she, casting a pleading look on the squire as she spoke.

"Of course, my dear, of course I will see him. But stay one moment, Margaret. When did all this happen, eh?"

"All, papa!" she answered, with the prettiest little half-shy, half-laughing glance into his face that it is possible to conceive, followed by the demurest dropping of the conscious eyes to the ground; "I can hardly tell you when it all happened! But it was yesterday at my uncle's in Silverton, that—that—I told him he might speak to you. May I tell him to come in, papa? I am sure he is waiting most anxiously to see you."

"Pray tell him I shall be most happy to see him," said the squire, adding, as he once again looked at his watch; "and, dear me! the sooner the better. We have only five minutes left before the bell rings!"

"Oh, that will be quite enough, papa, to give your consent in!" said the jeune personne with a bright smile, tripping to the door as she spoke.

She found that Frederick had been true to his word,—of which she had not felt absolutely certain,—and had already arrived at the Chase. All had passed exactly as had been settled between the sisters over night. Kate had not made her appearance. She had told Simmons to make her excuses to Miss Immy, and tell her, what was perfectly true, that she had slept all night, and she was now endeavoring to get a little sleep. And Mr. Banting had, as instructed, told Mr. Frederick, on his arrival, that Miss Margaret was in her papa's study, but that, if he would walk into the breakfast-room for a few minutes, the squire would then be happy to see him.

I suspect from a certain look which, though veiled beneath the exterior semblance of perfectly respectful deference, might have been detected hanging about the muscles of Mr. Banting's face, as he communicated this intelligence to Mr. Frederick, that that well-trained domestic knew the nature of the business which had brought the young gentleman to the Chase at so early an hour as well as any of the parties more immediately interested in it. He performed his part, however, with the most undeniable propriety; and Mr. Frederick, looking as little conscious as he could, awaited his summons in the breakfast-room, devoutly hoping that neither Miss Immy, nor Kate, and still less Mr. Mat, might come in and find him there before he should be called to the squire's study.

Margaret, however, flitted into the room while he was still alone there; and Frederick, with a glance that sufficed to prove to her that the care she had bestowed upon her charming toilet had by no means been thrown away upon him, was about to avail himself of some of the little privileges which are usually understood to belong to the prerogative of an accepted lover. But Margaret, with one of those little evolutions which sometimes seem to be as natural and as easy to girls as wriggling is to eels, and sometimes as utterly impossible to them as movement is to the bird fixed by the fascination of the eye of a serpent, escaped him, saying at the same time in great haste,—

"It is all right, my own! I have seen papa! He is expecting you in the study. But he says he has only five minutes to spare before the breakfast-bell rings. And no earthly consideration would induce him to abstain from coming out into the breakfast-room directly it does ring. So make haste. Run along; you know the way. I will wait for you out on the terrace."

So Frederick did as he was bid; and found the five minutes quite enough for the transaction of his business with the blunt and simple-hearted old squire.

"How do, Fred, my boy?" said the old man, extending his hand to him in cordial and kindly greeting; "glad to see you—always; and not sorry to see you on the business which brings you here this morning."

"My dear Mr. Lindisfarn! If I have dared"—

"Ay! Margaret has told me all about it! Well, I see no objection. I have known you, Fred, man and boy, since you wore long clothes; and I do believe that I may as safely trust my girl's happiness to you as to any man. You have been abroad; and sometimes I have thought that you brought home with you some foreign ways and tastes. If it is so, perhaps you and Margaret may be all the better suited to each other. You know pretty well what to look to with her. I have no thought, and never had, of making any difference between my two girls. As to what you can say, on your side, and as to what your father and I can do for the young household before the old birds hop the twig, of course he and I must talk it over together. But as far as I can see, I know of no objection; and I wish you joy with all my heart. So now come to breakfast; for Banting will ring in one half-minute."

Frederick, however, escaped as they were crossing the hall, and ran out to join Margaret on the terrace.

"Nothing can be kinder than your father, my own darling!" he said. "He spoke in the frankest and kindest manner of his intentions towards you in regard to property, and such matters. But of course I cared little to listen to all that, having other things in my head, and was heartily glad when he said that all those subjects must be talked over between him and my father."

"Will you not come in to breakfast, dearest? Kate will not be down. You must submit to be congratulated by them all sometime or other, you know."

"But not this morning, my own darling. I cannot stand Mr. Mat this morning. It is dreadful to have to tear myself away from you. But there would be no pleasure in sitting by you under the eyes of all the party at breakfast; and I am sure you had rather be spared it."

"Well, perhaps you are right! *Au revoir* then!"

And as they had by that time reached the corner of the terrace, where there was a spot not commanded by the breakfast-room windows, or any others likely at that hour to be occupied, she permitted him to encircle her waist with his arm for an instant long enough (*à la rigueur*) for the taking of one kiss, selected out of the whole scale of kisses (which is a long one), with a view to its exact fitness to the proprieties of the occasion, and then dismissed him.

Margaret then returned to undergo the ordeal of the breakfast-room with a calmness inspired by a sense of having been and shown herself perfect mistress of the situation, and having, at least thus far, managed her somewhat difficult affairs with the hand of a master.

Frederick returned to Silverton, not discontented, yet not so thoroughly well pleased with his morning's work as his lady-love. He had a certain sense of having been outgeneralled, which was not agreeable to him rather from the hurt it inflicted on his *amour propre* than from any real reason he had to be dissatisfied with things as they were. He had meant to win Margaret; and he had won her! But had he not unnecessarily "put out his arm further than he could draw it back again"?

It was not till he reached the Ivy Bridge at the bottom of the ascent to Silverton that it occurred to him that what Margaret had said about receiving the congratulations of the party assembled in the breakfast-room implied the abandonment of that plan of keeping their engagement secret which had been agreed on between them.

And Frederick bit his lips as the thought flashed into his mind.

CHAPTER XXX.
THE LINDISFARN JAWBONE.

KATE LINDISFARN was an especial favorite with Dr. Blakistry. There was nothing odd in that ; for she was an especial favorite with all the country-side in general, and with a singularly large number of individuals of all classes in particular. But the doctor, having neither chick nor child, as the phrase goes, and being therefore driven to look abroad for somewhat to care for, to love, and to pet, had enlisted himself in a special manner, and assumed a foremost place in the motley corps of Kate's devoted slaves and adherents.

Not that the strength of this allegiance had been needed to induce Dr. Blakistry to ride out to Deepcreek Cottage and give the desperately wounded man lying dying there, as was thought, the benefit of his skill and care ; for the doctor was a humane man, and indeed somewhat of a medical Quixote, holding and acting on the theory that the diploma which marked him as a student of the laws of nature, and dubbed him as learned in them, constituted, as it were, his letters of ordination as a high-priest in her service, and invested him with the mission, the privilege, and the duty of combating with human (physical) error and suffering wherever it could be met with. He would gladly, therefore, have turned even farther aside out of his way, than it had been necessary to do, to visit the wounded smuggler, in whatever way the knowledge of his case had reached him ; but Kate's summons had the effect of making the case and the patient additionally interesting to him.

And there was yet another cause which, after his first visit to Deepcreek Cottage, had operated to arouse Blakistry's curiosity and give him yet another source of interest in the case. The excellent M. D. was an enthusiast theorist, as M. D.'s mostly will be, who aspire to be anything more than mere rule of thumb practitioners, and as M. D.'s should be, so long as they can love their theories only second best after, and not better than, truth. Dr. Blakistry was an enthusiastic theorist. And some of his theories were wise ; and some were partially so ; and some were but fancy-bred crotchets ; for he was but a mortal M. D. after all.

Well, one of Blakistry's theories was, that certain features of the human face are more liable than others to be changed and modified in the transmission from one generation to another, by all the accidents of education and mode of life ; and that others are much less liable to alteration from such circumstances ; that they are more persistent, therefore, in races of mankind and in families, and more trustworthy as guides to probability in questions of filiation and the like. The jawbone, and especially the lower jawbone was, according to Dr. Blakistry, the most reliable feature in the face for such purposes, being the least liable to alteration by circumstances befalling the individual subsequently to his birth. Now it so happened that the Lindisfarn family afforded the doctor a case strikingly corroborative of his theory. All the Lindisfarns, however unlike they may have been in other respects, had their lower jawbones of the same shape. The peculiarity was sufficiently marked to have become long since notorious in the country ; and of course, to the eye of a scientific observer (and one whose pet theory it especially served to confirm), it was yet more noticeable.

It was not without a start of surprise, therefore, that Dr. Blakistry had, in the first instant of his looking at his patient in Deepcreek Cottage, recognized the true Lindisfarn jaw on his pale and bandaged face.

Dr. Blakistry was displeased. Of course he was ! What business had this smuggler from the coast of France with the Lindisfarn jaw ? Was he to come there with his jaw to spoil, or at least injure, one of the finest illustratory cases of his favorite theory ? And then, as the doctor's active mind went to work upon the subject, he began to think whether it might be possible that the phenomenon under his observation should prove a case in favor of, rather than one militating against, the Blakistry jawbonian theory.

It was a strange coincidence, to begin with, that he should be called by no other than Kate Lindisfarn to visit that jawbone, so unmistakable to him, though others might easily fail to observe it in a face changed by suffering, disfigured by wounds, and partially concealed by bandages. Mrs. Pendleton was Kate's old nurse. True ! But was that fact to be accepted as sufficiently explaining so curious a combination of circumstances ? And then, as the doctor mused on these facts, it occurred to him that he had heard from somebody or other, since he had settled in Silverton, some story about there having once been a male heir to the Lindisfarn property,—a son of the canon's, who had gone wrong, and had died in America,—all long before he, Blakistry, had come into that part of the country.

"Died in America. Humph! Anyway, that fellow lying there with the broken head has the Lindisfarn jaw, if ever a man had! Well, Nature knows nothing about the legitimacy or illegitimacy of marriages and births. Who can tell? Our friend at the Chase there, old Oliver, was young once, and did not marry early, as I have heard. Anyway—Mrs. Pendleton!"

The last words, uttered aloud, were the result of the doctor's soliloquy, or rather of his musings, as represented by the above phrases; and they were uttered as he was on the point of beginning to descend the steep, zigzag path, which led from the smuggler's abode to the bottom of the cliff, where he had left his horse in charge of one of the Pendleton children. He turned back toward the house as he spoke, and Mrs. Pendleton came out and across the little garden to meet him.

"I have no doubt of that young fellow's recovery if due care is taken, as I have told you. The patient's constitution seems to be singularly old for his apparent years; nevertheless"—

And here the doctor, glancing up at the little bedroom window, which was open, at no great distance from the spot where they were speaking, drew Mrs. Pendleton a few steps down the zigzag path, so as to be safely out of the sick man's hearing.

—"Nevertheless," he resumed, "I have little fear but that we shall bring him round. Still as it will in all probability be some time before he is able to be moved, and as it may be that those who love him are in pain and anxiety about him, and as your husband himself will doubtless be anxious to hear how he is going on, it seems very desirable that he should be communicated with on the subject."

"It may be very desirable, sir; so is a many other things in this world; but they can't be had for all that," said Mrs. Pendleton, with rather a hostile and defiant air. "When Pendleton's away," she added, "I never know where to find him; over in France, as likely as not!"

"Look here, Mrs. Pendleton!" said the doctor, gazing steadily, but with a pleasant smile, into her face, and gradually closing one eye till that feature executed a wink that a horsedealer might have been proud of,—"look here! I am not a lawyer, nor a revenue officer, nor a magistrate, nor a constable! I am a doctor. My business all the world over is to cure trouble, not to make it in any way or kind. Doctors are always trusted. You may trust me!"

"And suppose some of them as their business is to hunt an honest man down for striving to earn a bit of bread for his wife and children by honest labor should ask you, in the name of the law, where Hiram Pendleton was a-hiding; what should you say?"

"What should you say, Mrs. Pendleton, if they were to ask you?"

"I should tell them they was come to the wrong shop for information; and if they wanted him, they had better look for him.'

"Well, that is just about what I should say. But they wont come to me; never fear! We doctors are always hearing all sorts of secrets from everybody; but nobody ever expects us to tell them. The world would come to a pretty pass, if the doctors were to tell all they know. No! You may tell me where Mr. Pendleton is, safe enough. If he never gets into trouble till he gets into it through me, he'll do well!"

Thus exhorted, Mrs. Pendleton yielded. Indeed, the view of the medical profession presented to her by no means involved the reception of any new ideas into her mind. Men whose lives are exposed to the risks and chances which attend such a career as that of Hiram Pendleton are in the habit of considering the doctor as a confidant and friend. Old Bagstock would have been trusted by Mrs. Pendleton, and frequently was trusted by the anti-legal world of Sillmouth with a variety of secrets, which His Majesty's revenue officers would have been very glad to get hold of. And Dr. Blakistry had that additional claim to confidence, one which never fails to exert a singularly powerful influence over persons in Mrs. Pendleton's sphere of life,—arising from being a gentleman,—a circumstance of difference between him and Dr. Bagstock, which was not at all the less clearly and palpably recognizable by Mrs. Pendleton because she would have been utterly unable to explain wherein it consisted.

So she said, in reply to the doctor's persuasive words and looks,—

"Well then, the truth is, doctor, that Pendleton is not twenty mile away from here at this moment. He is in hiding out on the moor. I don't justly know where he is at the present speaking; for he is obligated often to change his quarters. But if any one was at Chewton,—that's fifteen miles out on the moor, or thereaway,—they would not be far off from him. And old Jared Mallory, him as is parish clerk at Chewton, is sure to know exactly where he is."

"The parish clerk!"

"Ay, the parish clerk! seems queer, don't it, going to the parish clerk to inquire for a —such a one as Hiram Pendleton? Next a kin like to going to the parson for him! But Jared Mallory is like what you was a-saying, sir, of the doctors. There is no telling the secrets and strange things as old Jared Mallory have a-knowed in his time, of all sorts and kinds, and of a many sorts of persons. And there is no fear of his splitting. But if you whisper in his ear,"—and Mrs. Pendleton whispered the words into that of the doctor,—"'Fair trade and free, says Saucy Sally,' he will bring you to speech with Pendleton."

"Very good! I wont forget. Thank you, Mrs. Pendleton. You shall never have any cause to regret having trusted me."

So the doctor rode back to Silverton in meditative mood, convincing himself more and more irresistibly with every furlong he rode, that either that jawbone he had been looking at was the jawbone of a genuine Lindisfarn, or that there was an end of all scientific certainty in this world.

The next day Dr. Blakistry mounted his horse immediately after breakfast, and turned his head in the direction of the moor. He had first to ride down Silverton High Street, which makes a steep descent just before reaching the bridge over the Sill, and the adjacent low parts of the city, and then to cross the river. On the other side of the Sill the road immediately begins to ascend the high ground towards Wanstrow Manor. But shortly branching off at the lodge-gates, and leaving the park to the right hand, to take a direction nearer the coast, it gradually leaves the cultivated lands behind it, passes

through a border district, in which little low dykes have replaced hedgerows, and feeble attempts at cultivation struggle at disadvantage with the thankless nature of the peaty soil, and then enters on the bleak solitude of the trackless moor,—trackless as far as eye can reach, save for the one good road which crosses the whole extent of it. At long and distant intervals, however, an almost impassable track is met with, leading off from the high-road to some of the few villages buried in the depths of the wilderness. How these lost settlements kept up any communication at all with the rest of the world before the high road, itself a creation of quite modern times, existed, it is hard to say. To the present day the moorlanders are a wild and peculiar people. At the date of the events narrated in this history, they must have been yet more so; and before the construction of the road that now cuts the moor in half, they must have been isolated and wild indeed.

Dr. Blakistry had ridden fast—for there was a cold, raw mist lying on the moor— about eight miles along this modern highroad, before he came to the opening of a very unpromising-looking track turning off from it to the left,—in the direction of the seacoast, that is to say,—at the corner of which was a wan and gibbet-like finger-post, on which the words "Chewton 7 miles" were still with some difficulty decipherable.

The doctor turned accordingly. But the same rapid rate of progress which he had hitherto made was thenceforward impracticable. The track began by making a very steep dip into a boggy hollow, then climbed out of it by a still steeper stair of crags. Here and there, for a short distance, it was possible to trot over a bit of springy, turf-covered peat; but for the most part the track alternated between bog and craggy rocks. For miles there was not a living creature to be seen, nor a sound, save now and then the ripple of a tiny stream, to be heard. Then, on rounding one of the huge boulder-stones, which here and there form landmarks on the surface of the moor, a scanty flock of small sheep, the greater number of them black, were found availing themselves of the shelter from the wind-driven mist afforded by the huge stone, and profiting by the patch of greener herbage which had produced itself by favor of the same protection. And soon after that a church-bell was heard ; and then, among a few trees, a belfry became visible, and the doctor knew that he had at length reached Chewton.

They always rang the church-bell at Chewton at mid-day ; assigning, as the all-sufficient reason for doing so, that such had always been the practice. It cost some trouble to do it, of course. And nobody in the place had the remotest idea of any good being done by it to anybody. But it was not usually done in other parishes ; and it always had been done at Chewton. And Chewton felt a pride and a gratification in these circumstances. In all probability, the isolation of the place had helped to preserve the old ringing of the *Angelus* in Catholic days, athwart all chances and changes, to the present time.

At the entrance of the village, which seemed to be more of a place than Dr. Blakistry had expected, he got off and led his horse. The way led toward the main street of the village, round the low wall of the churchyard. The bell continued to ring as he skirted it ; and a little child sitting on the old-fashioned stone stile over the churchyard wall, and belonging, in all probability, to the ringer at his work within the church, was the first living being the doctor saw in Chewton. It was a magnificent little fellow about ten years old ; and the doctor stopped to learn from him if he could tell the way to Jared Mallory's house. But the words died on his lips, when the child, looking up into his face, upon being spoken to, exhibited to his gaze a perfectly well-defined specimen of the Lindisfarn jawbone !

CHAPTER XXXI.

THE JAWBONE TELLS TALES.

"Why, good heavens!" ejaculated Dr. Blakistry to himself, as he stood with his horse's bridle over his arm, looking down into the wondering, upturned face of the handsome child, as it sat motionless on the stone slab of the churchyard stile,—"why, good heavens, there it is again!"

It meant the Lindisfarn jawbone; for in truth that special form of feature was very markedly traceable, by a practised physiognomist, in the child's face. And a disagreeable thought shot across the doctor's mind, like a cold ice-wind, that it might be possible that the formation in question was merely one feature of a provincial type, and not the special inheritance of a particular family. This, however, was a point to be cleared up, if possible, at once. So the doctor made a dash at the heart of the matter by asking,—

"Can you tell me where your father is, my little fellow?"

"Grandfather is in the church a-ringing the mid-day bell!" replied the child, looking up into the doctor's face with a fearless but much-wondering gaze, and speaking in the broadest and purest Sillshire Doric; "I'm a waiting for him."

"And what is your name, my boy?" returned Dr. Blakistry, smiling kindly.

"My name's July Mallory, and my grandfather is parish clerk of Chewton," said the child, with an assumption of much dignity in making the latter announcement.

"Ay, indeed! And is your father at home, July?" said the doctor.

"Mother is at home," replied the boy; jerking his beautiful gold-ringleted head towards the church-door as he added, "Grandfather is coming home to dinner as soon as he has rung the mid-day bell."

"And where does your mother live, my fine little fellow! I want to see her," said the doctor, stooping to pat the abundant golden tresses that clustered around July Mallory's cheeks and neck, and to get a nearer and more searching look at the shape of the lower part of the child's face as he did so.

Yes; there was no mistake about it! if there were any truth in the doctor's pet theory,—if he were to be delivered from the horrible necessity of violently pulling out one favorite opinion from the fagot of opinions which most men bind up for themselves by the time they have lived half a century in the world,—of violently pulling out this big stick of the fagot, and thus loosening, who could say how irremediably, the whole bundle,—if this evil were to be avoided, it must be shown that little July Mallory was a Lindisfarn.

The reader, if he have not forgotten those particulars of Julian Lindisfarn's early life which were briefly related in the opening pages of this history, will of course have at once perceived that the doctor's theory was in no danger, and that little July Mallory had every right to the feature in question. And there was patent to Dr. Blakistry a concatenation of circumstances, which indistinctly and uncertainly was leading him towards a shrewd guess at the truth. There was that stranger, with the broken head, representing himself as a French smuggler, but marked by the Lindisfarn jaw in the most unmistakable manner. His favorite Kate herself, who was every inch a Lindisfarn, had it not more decidedly. He was summoned by Kate to visit this stranger, and implored by her to send up special news of the result of his visit to the Chase. Then this mysterious stranger was found at Sillmouth in close connection and association with the Pendletons, and Hiram Pendleton, the smuggler, was evidently in close connection with these Mallorys. Then again the little July Mallory had said nothing about his father; had plainly ignored any such relationship, when Blakistry had asked him about his father. That name "July" too. It was a Julian Lindisfarn, as Blakistry distinctly remembered to have heard, who had "gone to the bad," and vanished, having died, as it was said, in America. And now this July, short for Julian, Mallory! Yes; there certainly was a plank of safety for the theory, shadowed out by these circumstances!

"Mother lives in that house there, where the smoke is coming out of the chimbley. That's the rashers as mother is a-frying for dinner. When the smoke comes out of the chimbley like that, when grandfather is a-ringing the mid-day bell in the church, there's always rashers for dinner," replied the young inductive philosopher.

"What, in that large house there, my young Baconian?" said the doctor, smiling to himself, as a man may be permitted to smile who perpetrates so wretched a pun for his own private use alone (for private and unsocial vices cannot be visited by social laws as those are and ought to be which affect society),—" in that house there, with the stone roof?" he said, pointing to one very near at hand, at the bottom of the village street, somewhat larger and more solidly built than the cottages on either side of it, and distinguished from them by being roofed with the gray, rugged flagstones of the moor instead of with thatch.

" Yes," said the child ; " that's where grandfather and mother and I lives ; and I *know* there's going to be rashers for dinner to-day," he added, gazing earnestly at the smoke, and reverting unceremoniously, after the fashion of children, to the point of view which interested him in the matter.

" Grandfather, mother, and I," repeated the doctor to himself. " Not a word about father ? And I *know*," he soliloquized, after a moment's musing, " that you are a Lindis-farn, by the same rule that teaches you that there will be rashers for dinner, my little man !"

" Well, I shall go and see your mother, July," added he, aloud ; " and I dare say I shall see you and your grandfather when you come home to dinner."

And so saying, the doctor giving a pull with his arm to the bridle, which was hanging over it, as an intimation to his horse that it was time to cease tasting the heathery gamy-flavored moorland herbage at the foot of the churchyard wall, on which he had been engaged while his master was holding the above conversation, proceeded to walk in the direction of the house which had been pointed out to him.

Two stone steps, with an iron rail on each side of them, led to the low-browed door in the middle of the front of the house ; and a little wooden paling, very much out of repair, though evidently some two hundred years or so younger than the iron rail and the rest of the house, fenced in from the street a space about two feet wide in front of the dwelling on either side of the entrance. The door stood open ; and the doctor, hitching the bridle of his horse over one of the rails, entered without ceremony. The front-door gave immediate admission to the main living apartment of the house, the " houseplace," as it is emphatically called in the northern

counties. This was the dining-hall and also the kitchen of the inhabitants ; and there, within the shelter of the huge, old-fashioned fireplace, was a woman still young, at least for those who will admit a life of some eight-and-twenty years to be so designated, and, still, far more incontestably, very handsome, engaged, as the youthful inductionist had predicted, in frying rashers of bacon.

" This is the house of Mr. Jared Mallory ; is it not, madam ?" asked the doctor, as courteously saluting the occupant of the chamber, as if she had been reclining on a sofa, and making eyelet-holes in muslin. There was in the remarkable beauty of the woman, and also, as the doctor fancied, in an undefinable something about her manner and bearing, a certain amount of additional evidence in favor of the chance that the Lindis-farn jawbone would be found to be in its right place, and the pet theory be saved after all !

" Yes, sir, this is Jared Mallory's house. Have you business with him, sir ?" replied the woman, making a courtesy in return for the doctor's salutation, civilly, but, withal, in a grave and distant, if not with a repelling manner.

" Yes ; I have ridden over to Chewton from Sillmouth on purpose to speak with him. I am a physician, and a friend of Mrs. Pendleton's, who lives at Deepercek Cottage. My name is Dr. Blakistry."

Bab Mallory, " the moorland wild-flower," —for, as the reader is well aware, it was to her and to no other that the doctor was speaking,—had not thought it necessary to lay aside the occupation in which she had been engaged when her visitor entered. She remained under the deep shadow of the great projecting fireplace, but with the red light of the fire, at which she was cooking, on her face and figure. She retained in her hand the long handle of the frying-pan, constructed of a length which would admit of its being used at a fire made on a hearth raised only a few inches from the floor, without compelling the person using it to stoop inconveniently, but turned herself partially so as to look towards the stranger. The hand unoccupied by the frying-pan was on her hip ; and the quick movement by which this unemployed left hand started to a position a few inches higher up on the side, and was pressed convulsively against it, was, therefore, not necessarily a very noticeable one. And the sudden deadly pallor which, at the same moment overspread the beautiful, but almost olive-colored face, seen as it was in the artificial lurid light of the fire, might easily have escaped the observation of a less keen and practised observer than Dr. Blakistry. Neither of these indications escaped him, however; and connecting them by a rapid and habitual process of inductive reasoning with the words of his which had evidently produced them, the doctor thought he saw in them another gleam of light on the mystery he had ridden across the moor to elucidate, and another probability of salvation for his theory of the hereditary nature of the shape of the jawbone.

The daughter of Jared Mallory, who knew all about the affairs of the *Saucy Sally* and her owners, and who was the mother of that beautiful child yonder with the unmistakable Lindisfarn jaw, was violently agitated at hearing that a physician had come out from Deepcreek Cottage to see her father. Humph!

He paused for some word of reply, which might serve to throw further light on the subject of his speculations, and confirm the suspicions which were now verging towards conviction.

But Bab Mallory had not had the weight of an ever-present secret on her heart for ten long years for nothing; and was not so easily to be thrown off her guard.

"Sweet are the uses of adversity," we are told on high authority, not altogether unbacked by some gleanings from still older wisdom. Yet, upon the whole, it may be doubted, perhaps, whether that opinion be not one of those formed by the world in its younger day, which the advantage of its longer experience and riper wisdom may lead it to modify. Surely, the uses of prosperity are quite as frequently sweet with fruit of the highest and most durable savor. Surely, the "uses" of adversity are quite as frequently, nay more frequently, bitter and evil than sweet. I am inclined to think the greater number of those human plants, which do not thrive to any good purpose in the soil of prosperity and happiness, would grow yet more stunted and deformed in the unkindly soil of adversity and unhappiness. It is old-fashioned physiology, which supposes that cold bleak mountain-tops are the positions most favorable to human health. And I am disposed to think that the psychological doctrines analogous to it are not entitled to much greater weight.

Though Bab Mallory's life up to her eighteenth year had been—not altogether an uncultivated one; for that strange old Jared Mallory, her father, amid his varied avowed and unavowed occupations was not altogether an uncultured man, yet—a sufficiently wild and rough one, she had never known anything fairly to be called adversity till then. Up to that time she had been the wild-flower of the moorland, as healthy morally as well as physically, as lovely, as sweet with as wholesome fragrance as the heather around her. Then adversity had come, and its uses had not been sweet to her. The open, fearless eye of innocence had been changed into the hard, bold eye of defiant resistance. Easy-hearted trustfulness had become ever-present mistrust. The high-spirited self-reliance, which is the substratum of so many a great quality and virtue, had been corrupted into the cankered pride, which seeks refuge from wounds, and at the same time finds an unwholesome nourishment, in isolation.

No; poor Bab Mallory had not been made better by adversity.

Open-heartedness had, of course, gone, together with so much else; and when, after the lapse of a moment, she had recovered from the heart-spasm which Dr. Blakistry's words had caused her, she only replied to them, by saying quietly, as she turned a little more towards the fire and the occupation which made an evident excuse for her doing so,—

"My father will be home very shortly, sir. Will you please to take a seat? Have you been acquainted with Mrs. Pendleton for long, sir?" she added, after a short pause, as the doctor complied with her invitation.

"No, not very long. I had no acquaintance with her, indeed, till I was called to her cottage to visit a wounded man lying ill there, by a young lady who is a friend of mine. But we soon made friends, Mrs. Pendleton and I. It is a doctor's business, you know, to make friends, and be a friend, wherever he goes."

Dr. Blakistry had watched the patient on whom he was operating narrowly, as he spoke; and he had not failed to mark the little involuntary start, though it was a very slight one, which had been elicited from poor Bab by his purposely introduced mention of the "young lady" who had summoned him to the wounded smuggler's bedside.

"Yes, a young lady it was, and a very charming young lady, too, I can assure you, who called me to visit a patient at Deepcreek Cottage!" added the doctor, answering that little start, and choosing to let her know that he had observed it.

"It was very kind of a young lady, and a little out of place, too, was it not, sir, for a young lady to be interesting herself about a poor wounded smuggler?" said Bab, attempting to turn the tables, and do a little bit of pumping in her turn.

"You know, then, that the sick man is a wounded smuggler?" returned the doctor, showing poor Bab at once how little she had taken by her motion.

"It is little likely that he should be anything else!" returned Bab, darting an angry flash of her dark eyes at the doctor as she spoke. But the flash was only momentary, and quickly died out into the quiet, observant look of habitual caution.

The rashers were cooked by this time, and the amount of attention needed for transferring them from the frying-pan to a dish, and placing the latter, carefully covered, by the side of the braise on the ample hearth, supplied an excuse for abstaining from any further reply for a few moments. When the operation was completed she resumed the conversation, having quite got the better of her sudden gust of anger, and again essaying to turn the pumping process on her visitor.

"One need not be very 'cute," she said, "to guess that a man lying wounded in Deepcreek Cottage must be a smuggler;—at least for those who know anything of Hiram Pendleton. But here comes father, sir. I am sorry you should have had to wait so long; but now you can despatch your business at once."

Jared Mallory, who entered with his grandson as she spoke, was a tall and upright old man, considerably older, apparently, than Bab Mallory's father need have been. He looked nearly if not quite seventy. But, though his figure seemed to have shrunk from that of a man muscular and broad in proportion to his more than ordinary height to a singular degree of gaunt attenuation, he bore about him no other obvious mark of decrepi-

tude of age. His attitude was upright, even stiffly so. His head was abundantly covered with long iron-gray locks, which were only just beginning to turn more decidedly to silver. His features were good,—must have been handsome,—and there was an air of superiority to the social position he occupied, and even of dignity, about him, which, though remarkable, did not seem to challenge so much notice, or to be so much out of place, as it might have done thirty years previously. It was in due keeping with one's conception of the village patriarch, if not with that of the parish clerk, or still less with that of the confidant and accomplice of smugglers.

After the first little start of surprise, Mr. Mallory bowed courteously to the stranger in his house, at the same time, however, turning on his daughter a look of very unmistakable inquiry.

"This is Dr. Blakistry from Sillmouth, father, who has ridden over the moor to speak with you about a wounded man, whom he has been attending in Hiram Pendleton's cottage at Deepcreek," said Bab, in reply to the look; and Dr. Blakistry could observe the same sudden manifestation of interest in the old man's face which the same announcement had called forth in the no less carefully guarded features of his daughter.

"Nay, Mr. Mallory," replied Blakistry, "your daughter's interest in my patient at Deepcreek has led her to jump to a conclusion which nothing I have said has warranted."

Bab tossed her head at this, with an air of much annoyance and impatience.

"I said," resumed the doctor, "that I had been attending a wounded man—your daughter here tells me that he is a smuggler; I dare say that may be so—at Deepcreek Cottage, that I was a friend of Mrs. Pendleton's, and that I had ridden over to speak with you."

"I am acquainted with Mrs. Pendleton, sir, and shall be happy to attend to you. Bab, perhaps you had better go into the parlor for a few minutes, and take the child with you.,'

"Oh, no! pray do not do that. You are just going to dinner: I will not detain you more than a minute or two; and I have no further secret than just this, which, as I was told to whisper it, I whisper accordingly."

And the doctor, advancing a couple of

strides to the old man's side, whispered in his ear the passwords, "Fair trade and free, says *Saucy Sally!*"

Bab, who had seemed much more inclined to be guided by the visitor's hint that she might stay than by her father's intimation that she had better go, turned towards the hearth, and stooped to occupy herself with her cookery, but, as the doctor did not fail to perceive, remained eagerly attentive to what was passing.

"All right, sir," said the old man; "and now, since you did not come here to speak of the wounded man at Pendleton's, what is there I can do for you or for Mrs. Pendleton?"

"Why, Mr. Mallory,' said the provoking doctor, "you are as much in a hurry with your conclusions as your daughter! I never said that I had not come here to speak of my patient at Deepcreek Cottage! I only observed that I never told your daughter that such *was* the case."

"Very true, sir! But we uneducated folks are not apt to speak with such attention to accuracy!" said Mr. Jared Mallory, speaking with some impatience, and almost with a sneer, but with the manner and accent of the educated classes to which he was asserting that he did not belong. "May I ask you, then, to state what is the purpose of your visit to Chewton?"

"Well, my principal object in coming here, and that for which Mrs. Pendleton sent me here, was to see and speak with her husband."

"Well, sir!" returned the old clerk; "since Mrs. Pendleton, who I suppose knows what she is about, has sent you here for the purpose, I think I can put you in the way of meeting with Hiram Pendleton; but your ride at the moor is not yet quite at an end, if you wish to see him. He is not at Chewton, nor within six miles of it."

"And I confess to have ridden quite far enough already, considering that I have to ride all the way back again," said Dr. Blakistry.

"I am afraid that you are not likely to see the man you want, without adding another dozen miles or more to your ride, sir," said the old man, with a somewhat malicious appearance of satisfaction.

"And I am thinking," said the doctor, "that perhaps I may be able to do my errand without seeing Mr. Pendleton. But if I am, as I fear, keeping you from your dinner, Mr. Mallory, I will go and have a look at the village, and return when you have done."

"Not at all, sir! By no means! If you will only say at once—or if," he continued, partly in compliance with a look from his daughter, and partly struck by a sense of the discourtesy of his previous proceeding,—"if the moor air has given you an appetite that can content itself with moorland fare,—a bit of bacon and a cut from the loaf,—perhaps you will honor us by sitting down with us, and we can talk of the matter you have in hand, whatever it is, over our dinner."

"Thank you, Mr. Mallory! I confess, that I do feel very particularly well inclined to eat a bit of bacon and a cut from the loaf; and not a very small cut either! I shall be thankful for your hospitality, and we can talk the while, as you say."

An Englishman cannot be surly to a man sitting down at his table to share his meal with him. It is no more possible to him than it is to an Arab to slay the traveller who has sought hospitality in his tent. And the party of four, consisting of old Mallory, his daughter, his grandson, and his visitor, had hardly broken bread around the same table, before the tone of the conversation between them had become less stiff and somewhat more friendly.

"You said rightly enough, Mr. Mallory, that the moor air, and a ride through it, are capital specifics for creating an appetite. And that fine little fellow opposite seems to find the first quite enough for the purpose without adding the second. He was my first acquaintance in Chewton. I found him sitting at the churchyard gate speculating on the fried rashers which he concluded were being prepared for him, from the smoke he saw curling up from your chimney. What a fine little fellow he is!"

"Ay, the child thrives!" replied the old grandfather, somewhat dryly, and with none of the satisfaction in his voice which the remark would seem calculated to call for; while the mother of the boy thus praised fixed her eyes on the plate before her, and remained silent.

No one of these little indications was lost upon the doctor, who saw in them still further confirmation of the truth of his conjectures, and of the consequent salvation of his favorite theory.

"It is strange," he continued, "that the little fellow should bring us back again to the individual we have already so often spoken of, my patient at Deepcreek Cottage. But I can't help being struck by a singular resemblance of feature between the two. I observed it the moment I saw the child. We physicians, you know, are apt to take notice of such things, habituated, as we are, to scrutinize faces and the expression of them closely."

A quick and significant glance passed between old Jared Mallory and his daughter, as Blakistry spoke thus; but it did not pass so quickly as to prevent him from catching it on its passage.

"Other people, I suppose, think less of such chance matters," replied the old man. "You were going to mention the object of your visit to Chewton. If I seem in a hurry to hear it, it is because I shall be obliged to go out again as soon as I have eaten my dinner."

"My business was to find Pendleton, having been directed here by his wife for that purpose. But the truth is that my object in seeing Pendleton was no other than to speak to him about this same patient of mine, the man lying ill at his cottage. And when I said that I began to think that I might obtain the information I wished without seeing him, it was because I fancied that I might learn here all I needed,—perhaps more satisfactorily than from him."

The same quick, sharp glance, this time with a yet more marked expression of agitation in it, at least on the part of the daughter, passed between her and her father.

"If you mean merely because of the chance likeness you fancied you saw between "—

"I have finished my dinner," interrupted Bab, rising from her chair, as she spoke; "and as what you have to say to my father cannot be any business of mine, sir, I will leave you to finish it with him, if you will kindly excuse me. Come, July, I am sure you have eaten enough to last you till supper-time," she added, affecting to look towards the doctor with a smile, which he had no difficulty in seeing was not the genuine expression of the feeling that was in her mind. "I suppose, father," she added, as she turned towards the door of an inner room, "that if Dr. Blakistry brings news that anything has happened or is likely to happen to the wounded man, it will be best to let Pendleton know of it at once."

The doctor perceived at once the anxiety that betrayed itself while striving to conceal itself under the appearance of indifference in these words; and while noting the symptom, and adding it to his stock, hastened to relieve it.

"Oh, no, nothing of the sort. He will do very well, with a little time and good nursing. It was an ugly cut enough though. And if there had been another half-pound of weight on the cutlass that gave it, why, the result might have been different. As it is, I assure you, you have no cause for anxiety," and the doctor looked keenly, but at the same time kindly, at her as he uttered the words.

"Anxiety!" said Bab, with widely-opened eyes, and a toss of her handsome head; yet still, as it were, in despite of herself, lingering to hear what should come next.

"Yes, anxiety. It is very natural. And pray do not think me impertinent, my dear madam, if I beg that you will remain and hear what I have to say. I think it may be interesting to you. And may I hope that you will consider me in the light of a friend in listening to me? I come here only as such, as I went to see the sufferer at Deepcreek Cottage only as such. Doctors necessarily become often acquainted with the secrets of their patients. It is their duty, and, I think I may say, their invariable practice, to respect them. May I then speak to you as a friend?"

The appeal was evidently made to both the father and daughter. They looked at each other with glances of uneasiness, and mutual inquiry; but for a minute or so neither spoke.

"If we are somewhat slow, sir, to reply cordially to such an appeal," said the old man at length, "it is because it is a new and strange one to us. We have not been much accustomed to friends or friendship. We have met with but little of it from those we might perhaps have expected it from. That must be our excuse if we are somewhat slow to expect it from one who is a stranger, and on whom we certainly have no sort of claim."

"One does not always find friendly feeling most in this world, Mr. Mallory, as I should think your experience must have taught you, from those from whom it might most naturally be expected. As for myself, it is little indeed I have to offer, or rather nothing. Circumstances—mainly the one of my having been called to visit the wounded man at Deepcreek Cottage—have brought certain things to my knowledge; and all I wish you to understand is, that my object is to use that knowledge in no wise to the annoyance or harm of you or yours, but, if the possibility should offer, to your advantage. And now I will be perfectly frank with you. I am well convinced that the wounded man whom I have attended is no other than that Julian Lindisfarn, the long-lost son of Dr. Theophilus Lindisfarn of the Close at Silverton. This was my conviction when I set out to come here, to speak to Mr. Pendleton about him"—

"Pendleton knows nothing about him,—that is as to who he is!"—interrupted Bab, hastily.

"In ascertaining that fact, I should not have communicated the information to him," said the doctor. "I have communicated my conviction to you, because I am entirely persuaded that you are also aware of the fact."

"What can the man have said to lead you to imagine such a thing?" said Bab, still keeping up her fence, though evidently feeling herself not far off from the point at which she would be obliged to abandon it.

"Nothing; I told you I would be quite frank with you. My patient has said nothing. But what are the circumstances? I am called to this wounded smuggler by a young lady,—rather a remarkable fact, as you yourself observed. Now that young lady was Miss Kate Lindisfarn."

"And did she tell you that the man she asked you to visit was her cousin?" again interrupted Bab, with a quickness and earnestness that once again betrayed to her shrewd companion her own knowledge of all the circumstances.

"By no means! I am quite certain, and you may be quite certain, that Miss Lindisfarn would not betray any confidence that was placed in her."

"Then what can have led you to"—

"The same process which has convinced

me— Perhaps it would be as well to send my little friend there out to his seat on the churchyard stile again," said the doctor, interrupting himself.

Poor Bab turned pale, and her breath came short; and old Jared looked suspiciously and defiantly at his guest. But he said to his grandson, sternly,—

"Run along out, child! Go and play! You are not wanted here! Now, sir! You were about to say"—he added, as he stepped across the wide stone floor of the kitchen, and closed the door of the house behind the child.

"I was about to say," resumed the doctor, quietly, "that the same process of reasoning which had convinced me that my patient was, in fact, Julian Lindisfarn—or mainly the same—had convinced me that the boy who has just left the room is his son."

"I do not understand very well, sir, what you mean by what you call a process of reasoning, but"—

"He is the son of Julian Lindisfarn," interrupted Bab, drawing herself up to her full height, and looking proudly and defiantly at the doctor; "and I am his mother."

"I was sure of it from his jawbone!" said Blakistry, triumphantly; "that is, sure of the paternity. The other circumstances were deducible from circumstantial evidence."

"His jawbone!" exclaimed old Jared, frowning heavily.

"The most unchangeable feature in all the face, my dear sir! There are scientific reasons, which—in one word, the wounded man is, to any eye capable of tracing a family likeness, evidently a Lindisfarn. And the very handsome child who was here just now is equally so! These things cannot be hidden from the eye of science!"

"But it may be questionable, sir, how far the tongue of science is justified in"—

"Nay, father! If Dr. Blakistry means kindly,—and I am sure he does,—and if he has saved Julian's life"—

"I do not say that I saved his life! Maybe that I did; for the cut was an ugly one, and there was much fever; and I cannot say, —quite between ourselves, you know—quite in confidence, Mr. Mallory,—I cannot say that I have much confidence in the clinical practice of Dr. Bagstock. Still, I do not say that I saved his life."

"At all events, he is saved; and you have

done your best toward it. It is the truth that "—

" Bab ! " interrupted her father, very sharply. " Stop a minute ! I want to speak to you ! "

So saying, he drew her aside to a far corner of the large room ; and the father and daughter spoke a few sentences together in earnest whispers. Then turning again to Dr. Blakistry. she continued,—

" It is the truth, as I was saying, that he now lying at Deepcreek Cottage is Julian Lindisfarn, and that the child is his son. But he is, for reasons which I need not trouble you with, sir, extremely anxious that the fact of his being there should be known to no one, save to his two cousins, the young ladies at the Chase. His secret became known to Miss Kate while she was at his bedside, having been brought there, not by any knowledge or suspicion of the fact, but only by her kindness for Mrs. Pendleton. And Miss Kate bargained for his permission to tell it to her sister. If those young ladies have kept their solemn promise, it is known to no one else. And all that I would ask of your kindness, sir, is to reveal the truth which you have discovered to no one. Much trouble and sorrow would be caused by doing so, and no good to any one."

" You have been aware, then, of all his doings ? " remarked the doctor.

" Oh, yes ! When Pendleton or any one of them are out here in the moor, there is no want of news. I knew all about it except the name of the kind doctor who had come at Miss Kate's invitation to visit him."

" Well, you may depend on my faithful keeping of the secret which the laws of science have betrayed to me. Shall I mention to my patient that I have seen you here ? "

" Perhaps best not ! " said Bab, with a half-smothered sigh.

" Certainly not," added the old man, far more decidedly. " We beg of you to say no word upon the subject of him or of us, to any one, neither to himself, nor to the young ladies at the Chase,—who, of course, know nothing of the facts which have been spoken of here, except that of their cousin's existence,—nor to Mrs. Pendleton, nor to any other person whatever. It is the only kindness you can do us,—the only kindness, at least," he added, in a more kindly tone and

manner, " besides that you have already done in caring for the safety of the father of my daughter's child."

" Be assured, my dear sir, that I will not fail to obey you," said the doctor, pressing the old man's hand, and then taking that which Bab Mallory frankly extended to him.

So the doctor rode back to Silverton in a happier frame of mind than that in which he had journeyed forth. Science had vindicated herself ; and the great theory was justified and confirmed in the most notable manner.

And then the doctor's mind was at leisure to revert to the less exalted and merely social considerations involved in the circumstances of which he had become the depositary. He thought he remembered to have heard that the Lindisfarn property had been entailed on the male heir, who was supposed to have died in America. What a change would be made in a great many things by his reappearance ! And the two persons most concerned knew the facts ! And nobody else knew them, except the queer, isolated people he had just left. A strange position of circumstances enough ! And would the two girls keep the secret ? Of his pet, Kate, he had no doubt. Of Miss Margaret he did not feel so sure. Well, we shall see ! At all events, there was, thank Heaven, nothing for him to do, save simply to do nothing but look on.

So the doctor got home to his quiet, comfortable little bachelor's dinner, in his quiet, comfortable little bachelor's house in Silverton, well contented with his day's work : some of the circumstances connected with which were subjected to his speculations under a new light, and from a fresh point of view, when his housekeeper told him, as she waited on him at dinner, the news of the day in Silverton,—that Mr. Frederick Falconer was engaged to be married to Miss Margaret Lindisfarn.

CHAPTER XXXII.
SETTLEMENTS.

Dr. Blakistry religiously kept the promise he had given, despite the very strong temptation to break it, to which he was exposed by his longing desire to publish to the world the remarkable confirmation afforded to his theory by the circumstances of the story which he had become acquainted with.

He flattered himself at the time, when the gratification arising from the discovery was fresh in his mind, that the consciousness of this triumph of scientific truth under his auspices would abundantly suffice him. But the longing shortly came upon him to enjoy his triumph in the eyes of others. He resisted gallantly, however ; and the possession of Julian's secret continued to be confined to Kate and her sister, the doctor, who was utterly unsuspected of sharing it by the two girls, and the little family out on the moor.

He was not, however, forbidden to think on the strange circumstances of the case ; and considering them in connection with the tidings, now the property of all Silverton, of the engagement between the rich banker's son and Miss Margaret Lindisfarn, his mind dwelt frequently on the great prudence and wisdom his friend and favorite Kate had shown in stipulating with her cousin that she should be allowed to communicate the secret at least to her sister. Had she not done so,—had Miss Margaret been left under the false impression, shared by all the rest of the Silverton world, that she and her sister were co-heiresses of the Lindisfarn property, —she might have been led into forming an engagement, all the parties to which would have been under impressions most painfully different from the reality. As it was, concluded the doctor, it was evident that Falconer had been made to understand in some way that, for some reason or other, his intended bride had no such expectations. And he freely gave that cynosure of Silvertonian eyes credit for a greater degree of unworldliness and disinterestedness than he had ever before been inclined to attribute to him, and felt that he liked him better than he used to do.

The necessary meeting between the squire and old Mr. Falconer had passed off well and easily. The old banker had driven up to the Chase, and been closeted with the squire in his study for a short half-hour ; and the two gentlemen had then come forth into the parlor, where lunch was on the table, with faces which very plainly declared that no difficulties had arisen between them.

"People think," the hearty old squire had said to the cautious man of business who was eagerly marking every word that fell from him,—"people think that my girls are co-heiresses of this property. But as far as I can understand the lawyers' lingo, that is not the case."

"I have always been perfectly well aware of that, Mr. Lindisfarn. People talk carelessly, without, perhaps, knowing the exact meaning of the terms they use," said the banker.

"The state of the case, as I understand it, is this," continued the squire ; "my hands are not tied in any way. It lies with me to bequeath the property as I may think fit."

"Nay, not quite so, Mr. Lindisfarn, if you will pardon me for correcting you on such a point," said the banker, making his pig-tail vibrate with the intensity of his self-complacent, courtly courtesy, as it used to do when he was engaged in the discussion of some point of antiquarian lore with Dr. Theophilus Lindisfarn ; and with a kind of catlike purr in his voice which, somehow or other, seemed to be used as a sort of wadding between his words to prevent them from coming into hard contact with each other,— "not exactly that, Mr. Lindisfarn. Your hands are not tied as regards the division of the property between your children. But I apprehend that you have not the power of willing any portion of it away from them."

"Pshaw ! who the devil ever apprehended anything else ? The property belongs to the girls ; of course it does ; and of course it would, whether I had the power to leave it to the lord mayor or not. But it is in my power to divide it between them as I may think proper. Now, you see, Mr. Falconer, if I settle one-half of the property on Margaret, I put this power out of my hands."

"Undoubtedly, Mr. Lindisfarn,—unquestionably you do. But, if you will forgive me for making the suggestion, one does not quite see how the young ladies can be well and—and—desirably, I will say, settled in the world, without such a sacrifice of power on your part."

"Why, a good settlement on either of the girls, or on both of them, might be made, you know, Mr. Falconer, so as still to leave a considerable portion of the property—say a third of it—unsettled, and still in my own power, as far as bequeathing it to either child goes," said Mr. Lindisfarn, speaking as if he were putting the idea before his own mind for consideration rather than offering it as a suggestion to his companion.

"Such a course might certainly be adopted,

Mr. Lindisfarn ; and it is not for me to make any remarks upon the wisdom or expediency of it," said the old banker, with a certain dry stiffness in his manner, which had not before been apparent in it ; and the purr, in which his words were packed, seemed to have more of the harsh quality of sawdust, and less of the softness of wadding in it ; for this suggestion on the squire's part was exactly what the banker had feared, and had considered as likely to operate to the advantage of Kate, and the disadvantage of Margaret. " Such a course," he continued, " would have the effect of retaining a power of disposition in your own hands. But you must forgive me, my dear sir, if I intimate that an intention on your part to approach the subject from such a point of view, would very essentially modify—necessarily so, as you will of course at once perceive—the views and intentions which I may be disposed to submit to you on my side."

And the old gentleman threw himself back in his chair, and began nursing the black-silk clothed calf of his right leg, looking keenly into the squire's broad and open face, to see the result of his shot.

" And what do I want with any such power, after all ? " continued the squire, musingly, and replying very evidently more to the train of thought that had been going on in his own mind than to the banker's words. " Perhaps it is best to put it out of my hands. They are good girls and good daughters, both of them. I can't say, when I look into my own heart, Falconer," continued the old man, stretching his arm across the corner of the table at which they were sitting, and laying his broad hand on the superfine black cloth coat-sleeve of his companion,—" I can't say honestly that they are both quite the same to me there. It would not be natural or possible that it should be so. Kate—but there, we all know what Kate is. But if my poor Margaret has been turned from an English girl into a French one, it was by no fault of her own. And if it is impossible for me to feel that she is as near to my heart as her sister, it would be unpardonable to make that a cause of still further disadvantage to her. And maybe it is all for the best to put the matter out of my own hands. No man can tell how great a fool he may grow as he gets older, eh, Falconer ? Yes, the most right and righteous course will be to settle the property fairly between them. Yes, let it be settled on 'em both at once, one-half share for each."

Mr. Falconer executed a long series of little bows, as the squire thus delivered himself, which imparted to his pig-tail and his chin an alternating up-and-down, see-saw movement, expressive of the most decided approbation.

" I felt quite sure, my dear Mr. Lindisfarn, that your heart and head would both coincide in leading you to that determination, as soon as the matter was placed fairly before you. I have no such reflections to make. I have but one child. All that I have will be his ; nay, is his in point of fact. No father ever had a better son. He has never given me an hour's anxiety since he was old enough to know right from wrong ! I have no long-descended acres to give him, Mr. Lindisfarn ; you know that. You know who we are and what we are. Traders, Mr. Lindisfarn, mere traders—somewhat warm ! I can leave my son a good name, Mr. Lindisfarn,—and something else besides ; " and the banker performed a very elaborate and significant wink as he spoke the last words,—" something else besides. As regards settlements, you must of course be aware, my dear sir, that it is not quite so simple a matter for a man in business to tie up capital as it is for a land-owner to tie up his acres. It will, of course, be proper that the young lady's fortune should be strictly settled on herself ; and, therefore, there will be the less difficulty in meeting the necessary requirements on our side. But all this will be matter for consideration and arrangement with your solicitors. All I wish is to act as liberally by my boy as it is possible for me to do ; and my full purpose and intention is that he shall possess every farthing I have in the world. Can a father say more, Mr. Lindisfarn ? Can a father, who is a banker, speak fairer than that ? "

The squire, thus appealed to, professed his inability to conceive any fairer speaking in a father and a banker ; and then the two old gentlemen had come out from their conference in the study, into the room where the ladies were at luncheon with Mr. Frederick. The ladies, that is to say Miss Immy and Miss Margaret ; for Kate, who had taken of late to pass much of her time up-stairs, had again to-day excused herself from coming down to luncheon.

"What! Kate not here?" cried the squire, as he entered; and a passing cloud traversed his face. But his genial, kindly good-humor shone out again in the next instant as, going to the back of Margaret's chair, he pinched her cheek—much to the young lady's annoyance, as he would have had no difficulty in perceiving, had he been in front of her instead of behind her—and said,—

"We have been sitting in council upon your case, little lady; and, as far as I can see, we shall manage to find the means of paying the butcher's and baker's bills for the new nest, as far as breakfasts and dinners are concerned; I don't know about luncheons; they are abominable things. Don't you think so, Falconer? I don't think we will allow the young people any luncheon, eh? You don't do anything in this way, I'll be bound!"

"Well, sometimes just one glass of sherry, especially when the Lindisfarn sherry falls in my way, and more especially still when I have the opportunity of drinking a glass with Miss Immy," said the banker, filling a glass, and drawing a chair to the corner of the table by the side of Miss Immy.

"Thank you, Mr. Falconer," said that lady. "Your very good health! And I drink," she continued, raising her glass high in the air with a steady hand, though the brown top-knot of ribbons on her cap shook with the little palsied movement of her head which seemed to impart an expression of invincible determination to the sentiment she uttered, "I drink particularly to the health and prosperity of Mr. Frederick Falconer and his bride."

And the old lady swallowed her glass of sherry with an air of sacramental solemnity.

A glance of mutual intelligence passed between the two objects of her good wishes, which, while contributing to indicate their fitness for each other, did much to manifest their unfitness for communing with the genial, honest hearts around them.

"Hang the old fool!" said the features of the gentleman, as plain as features could speak; while the lady's delicately flushed cheeks and more eloquent eyes managed to express the more complicated sentiment of her shame at being related to such Old-World Vandals, and her conviction that she and her Frederick belonged to a far other and far superior "monde."

It was necessary to say something, however, and the admirable Frederick managed to utter, "Much obliged, Miss Immy—really, —fully sensible—haw!" And then he felt that he had sacrificed himself to the extent required by the occasion.

"Put out my arm further than I can draw it back again," thought the young man to himself; "I should think so indeed! But there!—I can see by the governor's face that it is all right."

So the banker and his son drove home to Silverton together; and their conversation by the way was of a far more sensible nature than that which had passed between the squire and his daughter.

"So that is settled, so far!" said the senior. "You remember what I told you, Fred, once before, when we were driving over this same road together, that I thought Kate the better spec. Well, I can tell you that the old squire was monstrously inclined to fight shy of settling half the property on Margaret. If I had not been very firm with him"—

"But it is all right as it is, I suppose!" interrupted his son. "Half the estates to be settled on Margaret on the day of her marriage! That's the ticket I go for! As for Kate, I took the horse I was most safe to win with, as I told you, sir, before. And besides"—

"Well, it is all very well as it is,—very well; I only hope that I may find old Slowcome as easy to deal with as the squire about settlements," added the banker, with an almost imperceptible sigh.

The old established Sillshire firm of Slowcome and Sligo were Mr. Lindisfarn's solicitors.

"Why," said Frederick, answering rather to the slight sigh, which had not escaped him, than to his father's words, "is there any hitch?"

"No! Hitch! I hope not! I am glad, very glad, on the whole, that you have brought the matter to bear without letting the grass grow under your feet. But—in short, I need not tell you that in our business, what a man can do one day he may be unable to do in another. Circumstances change. Business is very uncertain;—and in ours we are dependent on so many besides ourselves. A man may be struck down at any moment by no fault or imprudence of his own. I have had causes for much serious anxiety of late. Why should I trouble you with them? I trust, I doubt not, all will go well. And I should have said no word of this kind to you to-day, had it been that it is as well to tell you that I shall be very glad to see you safely married to Miss Margaret Lindisfarn, with half the Lindisfarn acres duly settled on her, even if they are tied up as tight as old Slowcome can tie them."

There was much food for meditation for our friend Fred in this speech. He did not like it. He knew his father; and the more he pondered over that knowledge in connection with the words the old banker had been speaking, the more he did not like it. Nevertheless, he thought it best not to push his father for any further explanation of his words; but he inwardly resolved to make that use of the hints thrown out to him which it was evidently intended he should make,—that is, to press his affairs with the heiress to as rapid a conclusion as might be possible.

A cloud had passed over the jolly squire's genial face, it has been said, when on coming out from his study with the old banker, he found that his darling Kate was not in the parlor with the rest of the family party. On several occasions recently, little matters of the same sort had been unpleasant to the squire. He was not one of those men who are quick to observe the actions of those around them, and to speculate on, and draw conclusions from them. But for some days past it had been gradually forcing itself upon his notice that, somehow or other, Kate was not like her usual self. Instead of being constantly seen about the house, and still more frequently heard, she was rarely seen, and hardly ever heard at all. The huge old staircase never echoed now to the carolling of her clear, cheery voice, as she tripped up it to her room, or came dancing down as of old. She frequently made the excuse of headache for remaining in her own room, always (only none but her sister had yet noticed the coincidence) when Falconer was there. Kate with a headache! And yet her looks gave abundant testimony to the genuineness of her excuses.

At last it had entered into the head of the squire that Kate's evident low spirits and unhappiness must be connected with the fact

of her sister's engagement. And the suspicion that she herself was not indifferent to Falconer, came upon him with a bitter pang. Could it be that her young heart had been won by a man, who, to her father's thinking, was so every way not good enough for her? He did not say to himself that, though not fit to tie the Kate's shoestring, he was good enough for Margaret's husband. But unconsciously this was his feeling on the subject. There seemed to be a fitness for each other between him and Margaret, which the squire could feel, though he could not reason on the subject, sufficiently even to formulate the persuasion into words said only to himself. And he had been content therefore to accept the Falconer overtures. But what misery was in store for them all, if it were really true that Kate were pining for her sister's lover.

Mr. Mat to whom alone the squire had dropped a word upon the subject, utterly and most vigorously scouted the possibility of such an idea. More likely Kate was vexed at seeing her sister throwing herself away on such a fellow. Maybe she was down in the mouth, and off her food a bit by reason of Lady Farnleigh's prolonged absence. Kate had been used to be so constantly with her ladyship all her life; it was well-nigh missing her mother like! Or might be, said Mr. Mat, it was nothing at all but just a little trifle wrong in health, as young girls would be, which would all come right again. But let it be what it might, it was not pining after Fred Falconer! What Kate! he, he! Mr. Mat knew better than that.

Meanwhile it was most true that Kate was very miserable. Upon that part of the varied causes for unhappiness that had fallen upon her which more immediately concerned herself, she strove to let her thoughts dwell as little and as rarely as possible. But we all know, alas! how vain such strivings are. And in Kate's case, condemned, as she was, to a degree of solitude to which she was quite unaccustomed, by the other untoward circumstances of her present position, it was less possible than it might otherwise have been to warn the thoughts from off the prohibited ground. The progress of her sister's affairs was a constant subject of uneasiness and alarm to her. And the doubts and difficulties she felt as to her own conduct, and the consciousness that, while action of any kind was impossible to her, even the inaction to which she condemned herself was likely to give rise to ideas and interpretations which it was agony to her to think of, made those weeks a time of great and severe trial to her.

Meanwhile, Dr. Blakistry was assiduously doing his best for the recovery of his patient at Deepcreek Cottage; and his efforts were well seconded by the youth and constitution of the wounded man. He was, in fact, progressing rapidly towards recovery. Dr. Blakistry kept Kate well informed as to the progress of the patient "in whom," as the doctor said, "she had taken so kind an interest." But of course no word was said between them as to the secret which both of them knew, and which one of the two knew to be shared by the other. Nor did Kate see her cousin a second time. No good could have been done by any such visit, and assuredly nothing agreeable could have been hoped for from it.

About three weeks after the date of Mrs. Pendleton's memorable visit to Kate on the night of the great storm,—the night before the affair with the Saucy Sally and the coastguardmen, — Mrs. Pendleton again walked up to the Chase. She brought Kate news of the very satisfactory improvement in the condition of her wounded guest. Dr. Blakistry declared that in a few days he would be able to leave his room. Mrs. Pendleton also handed to Kate a sealed note—of thanks for the kind and charitable attention she had shown to an unfortunate stranger, the good women said,—which her guest had requested her to put into Miss Kate's own hands.

"It is something more important than that," said Kate, when she had read the short note, and tossed it into the fire of the housekeeper's room, in which, as on that other occasion, she received her old nurse's visit. "It is to request me to send back by you a small packet, which he begged me to keep for him when he was persuaded that he was going to die. I will go and get it."

So she went up-stairs to her room, took the little packet from her desk, and putting it into a sealed but unaddressed envelope, delivered it to Mrs. Pendleton.

And within a week from that time,—about a month, that is, after he was wounded,—a second visit from Mrs. Pendleton brought Kate the information that the stranger had at last been pronounced by Dr. Blakistry able to travel, and that he had sailed for the opposite coast in the Saucy Sally the night before.

Mr. Pendleton was a very good husband, as has been said, smuggler though he was; and had no secrets from his wife which it would have much imported to that excellent woman to hear. But he did not think it necessary to overtask female discretion, and torment female curiosity, by troubling her with matters which in no wise concerned her. Thus there had been no reason at all that he should tell her the altogether uninteresting fact that the Saucy Sally conveyed on that same night another, nay, two other, passengers, to the coast of France. When she slipped away from Sillmouth in the first dark hours of a moonless night, she had none on board save the same crew with which she had made her last dangerous voyage. But she did not stand out at once across the channel, as would have been her natural course. On the contrary, Hiram, who stood at the wheel himself, and seemed as able to feel or smell his way in the dark, as he could have seen it, if it had been broad daylight, kept her close in along the coast to the westward, till he was just off a little bit of a creek formed by a small stream which came down from the neighboring moor. Having reached that point, he showed a green light for an instant. It was absolutely a merely momentary flash. But it sufficed for its purpose; for in a very few minutes, the anxious crew of the Saucy Sally could hear the low sound of muffled oars, and in the next, a small boat pulled along-side of them, as they lay to, in which there were four persons ; a woman, a child, a tall old man, and a man who had the appearance of a common sailor.

The French stranger, who had just recovered from his hurts, stood by the bulwark of the Saucy Sally, and tenderly assisted and received the woman as she clambered from the boat up the lugger's side. Then he took the boy from the hands of the tall old man in the boat, and holding the child in his arms, darted down with him into the not very brilliantly lighted little cabin of the smuggler.

The lugger shook out its sails ; and the tall old man in the boat, having regained the lonely beach of that little-frequented moorland shore,

"Walked grieving by the margin of the much-voiced sea"

as long as he could descry the outline of the receding vessel in the darkness; and then returned to a not less lonely home at Chewton, a few miles inland.

CHAPTER XXXIII.

PATERNAL ADVICE.

WHEN the news of her cousin's final recovery from his wounds and departure for France reached Kate, her sister was not with her at the Chase. She had been much at her uncle's house in the Close lately,—an arrangement which had been highly agreeable to all the parties chiefly concerned. It had been a great relief to Kate under the circumstances that the scene of the love-making between her sister and Falconer should be transferred from her own home to the house in the Close in Silverton. Margaret was always better pleased to be in Silverton than at home, where, little as there was to amuse her at her uncle's, the surroundings were still less congenial to her. And now, of course, more than ever, it was agreeable to her to be in the near neighborhood of her beloved Frederick.

To that *preux chevalier* himself it was far more convenient to have his work close at hand. He found it easier to do it, too, amid the gentle dulness of the good canon's house, and under the protecting wing of the feebly sympathetic though profoundly dispirited Lady Sempronia, than amid the rougher, more observant, and less congenial inmates of the Chase. Frederick engaged in making love within possible ear-shot or eye-shot of Mr. Mat, always felt as if he were there with a view to stealing the silver spoons. Kate's palpable avoidance was an annoyance to him. Miss Immy's old-fashioned compliments and courtesies and very effete little waggeries bored and irritated him. And even the jolly old squire's loud and hearty words of greeting or of jest were very distasteful to him. In every respect it was far better that his charmer should be in Silverton. It gave him so many more and easier opportunities of acting in obedience to his father's hint to the effect that he would do well not to let the grass grow under his feet.

The old banker had repeated similar words of advice on one or two occasions, coupling them with hints of a kind which made Fred

very seriously uneasy. He could not avoid seeing, too, that his father himself, though striving hard to keep his usual countenance and manner, was harassed by some cause of anxiety and trouble.

We know how excellent a son Frederick had always shown himself! And in the present circumstances, as always, he did his utmost to comply with his father's wishes. Again and again as they walked together in the friendly shade of the trees under the old city wall in the canon's garden,—the scene of Frederick's offer and of his Marguerite's acceptance of his love,—he implored her to fix the day, and to use her influence to abbreviate the cruelly long delays and procrastination of Messrs. Slowcome and Sligo. And Margaret, if it had been in any wise proper, permissible, or possible, would have replied that he could not be in a greater hurry than she was. In fact, the words of Dr. Blakistry's opinion that her cousin would be well in a month, were always sounding like a warning knell in her ears. As soon as her cousin should have recovered, he would go away; the time for which Kate was bound by her promise of secrecy would have expired, and then—

But Margaret, of course, was far too well bred, and knew her business far too thoroughly to allow herself to be hurried by this urgent motive into any unbecomingly easy accordance of her lover's prayer. Nevertheless, she allowed an admissible amount of sympathy and pity for his impatience to appear. It was with the prettiest play of coyness, and amid blushes and drooping of the eyelashes that she admitted the detestability of Messrs. Slowcome, *père et fils*, and of Mr. Sligo, and the intolerableness of their delays.

At length, one day,—it was towards the close of business hours in the Silverton Bank, —Mr. Falconer sent to ask his son to step into his private *sanctum*. Frederick met Mr. Fishbourne, looking, he observed, very grave, passing out from conference with his chief, as he went in.

"Well, Fred," said his father, as he entered, evidently striving to brighten up a little, and to speak as cheerfully as he could, "I sent for you to ask how affairs are getting on between you and Margaret. You have had her all to yourself for some days past, down in the Close here."

"And I flatter myself I have **not neglected**

my opportunities, sir," replied Frederick, speaking in the same tone. "In fact," he added, a little more seriously, "I have nothing to complain of, and in truth I believe I might have it pretty well all my own way, were it not for that horridly slow coach, old Slowcome. It is to Slowcome and Sligo, sir, that you should address yourself rather than to me, with a view to doing anything toward hastening the match."

"Hasten old Slowcome! Humph! If the end of the world were fixed for twelve o'clock this day week punctually, do you think Slowcome would move one jot the faster, or omit a single repetition of 'executors,' and 'administrators' from his 'draft for counsel'? Not he. Now look here, my dear boy. I am sure you have the good sense to make the best use of any hint I may be able to give you for your guidance, without seeking to ask questions concerning matters which it is better not to trouble you with"—

"Good heavens, father!"—

"Gently, my dear boy, gently! do not agitate yourself. I trust there is no occasion for you to feel any agitation. I hope—I have every hope that all will go well. But there *are* circumstances that make me think it my duty to tell you that if your marriage with Miss Lindisfarn could be hastened, it would be—ahem—prudent to do it!"

"I've told you, sir, that we are only waiting for these troublesome settlements. Once for all, I believe, that as soon as the papers are signed, I may name the day as soon as I like."

"But as far as I see, it may be a month or more before that will be done!" said the old man, fidgeting uneasily in his chair.

"I have no doubt it will!" returned his son; "but what in the world can I do to hurry the old fellow?"

"Nothing; nothing would hurry him! But sometimes," and the old man looked furtively up into his son's face as the latter stood lounging with his arms crossed on the high back of the writing-table at which his father was sitting, "in the days when I was young, an impatient and ardent lover was not always content to wait for the tedious formalities of the lawyers."

"What! marry without any settlements at all!" exclaimed the "ardent lover," staring at his father in open-eyed astonishment, as if he suspected that he was losing his senses.

"Pooh, pooh, without settlements at all! Who spoke of marrying without settlements? In such a case as yours it would of course be all the same thing if the deeds were signed before or after! The substance of them has been all agreed to."

"But would the old people at the Chase consent?" said Frederick, doubtfully.

"Pshaw! consent! Why, Fred, one would think you had the blood of seventy-seven in your veins instead of that belonging to twenty-seven! Of course the old folks would not consent. Of course *I* should not consent! Ha, ha, ha! We did not always ask the consent of papa and mamma in my day."

Frederick, looking down on his father from the other side of the high-backed writing-table, keenly and observantly, as he spoke the above words, did not seem to be at all stirred up by them to any of that hot-headed ardor which the old gentleman appeared to think would become his years. He grew, on the contrary, graver in manner, and felt very uneasy.

"But, suppose, sir," he answered, watching his father narrowly as he spoke,—"suppose my natural impatience prompted me to take such a step as you hint at, is it likely that Margaret would consent to it?"

"Nay, that is your affair,—altogether your affair, my dear boy. I suppose no girl ever consented to such a step unless she were pretty vigorously pressed to do so; but very many have consented."

"Margaret has an uncommonly shrewd head of her own; she has abundance of sound common sense!" said Fred, musingly, and speaking more to himself than to his father.

"I am sure she has! Without it, she would not have been the girl for you, Fred. But what would you have? Girls are romantic—a thing represented to them in a poetical point of view, you know"—

"But again, father, supposing that I could induce Margaret to consent to such a step, would it be, looking at it from our point of view, a safe one?"

"I do not think there would be much danger," replied his father, speaking in a decided and business-like tone, very different from that in which he had been hitherto talking. "I am very much convinced," he continued, "that there would be no danger at all. The old squire, even if he has ever had a thought of anything else than dividing the property equally between the two girls, would never budge from his word given to me. Trust me, the old squire's word is as good as any settlement old Slowcome can make, any day. Certainly, I do not mean to say," continued the old banker, "that the step in question would be one which I should counsel under ordinary circumstances. There would be, no doubt, a certain possibility of risk; and it is always unwise to run any risk, if it can be avoided. But I have already told you, my dear Fred, that there are reasons,—there are reasons. Very possibly, in all probability, there may be nothing in them; but—if you can steal a march on old Slowcome, and do the job, at once, why, I should advise you to do it. We old birds should be very angry, of course," added the old gentleman, with an attempt at a smile, which the evident anxiety in his face rendered a sorry failure; "but we should be very forgiving."

"Well, sir, as you tell me I had better not, I will not attempt to question you; and I will think very seriously of all you have said, and be guided by it, as far as is practicable."

"And look here, Fred," said his father, opening the drawer of his writing-table, and taking from it an unsealed envelope, "I have not calculated at all accurately the cost of posting from here to Gretna. It is a long journey; but I think that there is enough there to do it, if you should happen to need such a thing. Four horses make the guineas as well as the milestones fly. But there would not be much chance of your being pursued. There would only be a bit of a lecture and a blessing, and a laugh against Slowcome, when you came back all tied as fast as Vulcan could tie you."

"Thank you, sir," said Fred, pocketing the bank-notes. "Depend upon it, I will put your advice to the best profit I can."

So the younger man went out, very far from easy in his mind, leaving the senior with his hands deeply plunged in his pockets, and his head fallen forward on his breast, in deep and anxious thought.

In truth, he had but too much reason for anxiety. A most unlucky combination of unfortunate circumstances falling together had, in fact, placed the bank in very critical circumstances. And it was quite a touch-and-go matter with the old established firm to get on from day to day without a catastrophe. Mr. Fishbourne said (to his partner only) that it was quite providential that they had succeeded in weathering the storm as long as they had. But he did not appear to have any comfortable reliance on the stability of the intention of Providence with regard to the old Silverton Bank.

Frederick's favorite time for paying his visits to the house in the Close was the hour of the afternoon service in the cathedral. The spring had not yet ripened into summer; but the season was sufficiently advanced to render the sheltered walk in the canon's garden at that quiet hour extremely pleasant. The doctor was sure to be absent at the cathedral. Lady Sempronia, if she went out at all, did so at that time. If, as was more frequently the case, she did not go out, she was reposing on the sofa in the cheerless drawing-room after the wearing fatigue of doing nothing all day, and recruiting her strength for that great hour of trial and effort,—the dinner-hour.

Frederick was at that time safe, therefore, to find his Margaret at liberty to give herself up entirely to him; and the gathering gloom of evening only served to make the shaded terrace-walk under the old wall all the more delightful.

It was just about the usual hour of his visit, when he parted from his father in the bank parlor; and he walked straight across the Close to the senior canon's house, bent on at once feeling his way toward the execution of the project his father had shadowed forth to him. It was not that he went to the work with a very light heart, or a very good will. But he was profoundly impressed with the conviction that his father would not have spoken in the manner he had, if there had not been very grave reasons for doing so. And with regard to the prudence of the step, as far as concerned Miss Margaret's fortune, he quite agreed with his father in feeling that the old squire's word upon the subject was as safe as any bond.

So he knocked at the door, and asked the servant, who had long since come to understand that the gentleman had the right to make such an inquiry, if Miss Margaret was in the garden.

"Yes, sir; you will find her on the terrace, I have no doubt," said the old man, whose time for translation to a vergership had almost come, smiling knowingly at the visitor.

"Then, if you will let me out, Parsons, I will go into the garden through the study, so as not to disturb Lady Sempronia, if she is at home."

So Falconer passed into the quiet garden, and found Margaret on the terrace-walk as usual. She was at the farther end of it when he came within sight of her, and was reading a note, or paper of some sort, which she thrust away immediately on catching sight of him.

It was natural enough that she should put away anything that she was reading when she came forward to meet him. Nevertheless, there was a something about the manner of the action that caused her fond Fred to take observant note of it. Perhaps it was in the nature of the intercourse between these two young hearts, so specially fitted for each other, as the old squire had observed, that every smallest movement or indication which escaped either of them should be, with the unfailing quickness of instinct, seized on, examined, noted, and interpreted by the other!

The simple fact as to the paper which Margaret, with such conscious but unnecessary haste, concealed at the approach of her lover, is that it was a note from Kate, which had been given to her about a quarter of an hour previously, communicating to her the tidings the former had received from Mrs. Pendleton, of the convalescence and recovery of her inmate.

Of course Margaret had been for some days past prepared for this event, and aware that it would not be deferred much longer. Nevertheless, it gave her a shock to learn that the dreaded moment had absolutely arrived. Would Kate reveal the facts immediately, was the question! Kate urgently desired now that she was free to do so. That her sister, in the note, to return at once to the Chase, that they might talk the matter over together. And Margaret considered that this was a favorable sign. If Kate intended to tell at all hazards, she would rather have done so, thought Margaret, making the error that all such Margarets make in speculating on the conduct of such Kates, without saying anything about it to her.

At all events, Margaret determined to obey her sister's summons and go up to the Chase the next morning. She had sent back an answer by young Dick Wyvill, who had brought in Kate's note on the pony of all work, to the effect that she would be ready immediately after breakfast, if Kate could prevail on Mr. Mat to come in for her in the gig. If not, the carriage must be sent.

She had sent this reply, and was conning over again Kate's note, to see if she could extract from it any evidence of the writer's mood of mind respecting the all-important question, when she saw her lover emerging from the thick clump of Portugal laurels which filled the corner of the garden at the end of the terrace nearest to the house, and hastened forward to meet him.

CHAPTER XXXIV.
DIAMOND CUT DIAMOND.

FREDERICK advanced along the terrace under the city wall, to meet his lady-love, with the slow step and downcast mien of a man thoroughly despondent and broken. Margaret, her hands extended a little in front of her, as in eager welcome, and her face bent forward, came toward him with a quick step, which broke into a little run as she neared him, very prettily eloquent of her impatience to meet him.

The lady was the first to speak.

"Frederick, dear! you seem as if you were not glad to see me! And I,—how I have counted the hours till that came which I might hope would bring you to me! What is it? Is anything the matter?"

"Anything the matter!" re-echoed Fred, in a tone of profound discouragement, taking her two hands in his, and holding her by them at arm's length from him, while he looked into her face with an expression of the intensest pathos and misery,—"anything the matter! Ah, Margaret! But I suppose girls do not feel as men do in these cases, and that it is therefore impossible for you to sympathize with my horrible torture."

"Gracious Heaven, Frederick! Horrible torture! What is it? For God's sake, have no secrets from me! Tell me what is the matter!"

The words and the form of speech, and the manner of speaking them, as far as the by no means inconsiderable talents of the speaker could accomplish it, expressed extreme anxiety and agitation. But I do not think that the lovely white bosom, from which they came, caused the Honiton lace which veiled it to flutter one jot quicker a motion than it had done before.

"The matter, Margaret!" returned Fred, in a tone of worn-out, listless despondency; "the matter is no more than you know—the old story—more delays! no prospect of the end of them that I can see! Oh, Margaret, my heart wearies so for the hour when I can call you mine! I am sick,—sick with the heartsickness that comes of hope long deferred. But you—weeks or months are all the same to you. You can wait patiently; you have no sympathy with my horrible impatience. Ah, Margaret, you do not love me as I love you. It would be impossible for you, if you did, to endure these never-ending, still-beginning delays so tranquilly."

"My Frederick, you are unjust to me! Do you not know that your wishes are my wishes? Do you not know that I would fain do your pleasure in all things? Do not suppose that all this delay is otherwise than odious to me also,—odious to me because I know that it vexes you, my own love!" and the beautiful, dangerous creature looked into his eyes, as she spoke, with a brimming fulness of sympathy and fondness sthat might have melted a heart of adamant.

"Dearest!" said he, passing from the position in which he had hitherto stood at arm's length in front of her, to her side, while he twined her arm under his, and took the hand belonging to it between both of his hands; "my own Marguerite! forgive me, if all I suffer makes me peevish and unjust. But it is too bad. There is no end to it. That old beast, Slowcome has no more feeling than his own great ruler, which I should like to break over his stupid old bald pate!"

"Is there anything new,—any new cause of delay, I mean?"—asked Margaret, with really unaffected interest. For time was most important to her too. Heaven only could know how important it might be! Here was Julian safe away out of England. Kate free to tell the horrid, horrid truth that would ruin everything and drive her Frederick from her side, as if she had the pestilence, at any moment. Who could tell when the thunderbolt might fall, or how much time was yet left her to shelter herself in the haven of matrimony, before the flood should come and devour her, and suck her, with its hideous under-draft, away from that safe harbor forever? Yes, time was fully as important to Margaret as it was to her fond Frederick. If he could have known the sincerity of alarm with which she asked if there were any new cause of delay, he would not have accused her, assuredly, of lack of sympathy with him.

"I do not know. How should I know? I do not understand their abominable nonsense; it seems to me that that brute Slowcome takes a pleasure in making it as longsome as possible. I see no prospect of any end."

"But is there any new cause of delay, Frederick,—anything that they did not know before?" asked Margaret, with real interest.

"No, nothing new, that I am aware of. How should there be? It is all perfectly clear and thoroughly known to all parties concerned. Your father gives you half the Lindisfarn property. My father gives me all he has in the world. The matter is clear enough, I think. As if that could not be written down and signed and sworn to, if they think it necessary, in half an hour, without writing Heaven only knows how many skins of parchment about it! And all to prevent you or me from cheating each other, my Marguerite. Is it not absurd? Is it not too bad that we should have to weary and pine our hearts out for such impossible trash? It is monstrous,— positively monstrous!"

"It is indeed, dearest. But, surely, a great deal might be written in a whole day, even of those horrid parchments, if they would only be industrious about it. When does Mr. Slowcome think it will be done?" asked Margaret, with the prettiest childlike innocence.

"I am sure I don't know! There is no getting anything out of him—the old wretch! He rubs his hands together, and twists his watch-chain, and seems as pleased as possible when he tells me with a grin that, 'Every expedition will be used, Mr. Frederick, that is consistent with the care and scrupulous attention which it is my duty to pay to the interests of my clients, Mr. Frederick. Draft settlement for counsel has been proposed—counsel must have time'— Ugh! I could strangle the brute as he stands before me. Nothing on earth can make him even speak any quicker than his usual little self-satisfied quaver, with a ha-ha-hum between every two words!"

"It is very vexatious," murmured Margaret, with gentle sympathy.

"Oh, vexatious! It is hopeless! I see no end to it. I declare I believe in my heart that old Slowcome knows that it will be another month before the deeds are ready. And all for such nonsense too! If it were really necessary—really something conducive to the happiness or welfare of my darling, I would wait,—I would be patient. But that one's days, which might be days of unspeakable happiness, should be turned into days of weary, wearing suffering, and all for nothing—it is too bad!"

"I suppose that others have had to suffer from the same annoyances. I suppose that these vexations are unavoidable," said Margaret, in a voice that seemed meant to counsel resignation.

"I dare say that there may be other Slowcomes in the world; and I suppose that in some cases it may be necessary to wait for the completion of their work. But the heart-break of the thing is that, in our case, it is all unnecessary, that we are condemned to this horrible delay for the sake of mere compliance with a matter of routine—and that, too, to please a stupid old lawyer, who, of course, sees his interest in considering and representing such ceremonies as absolutely indispensable,—all to satisfy Messrs. Slowcome and Sligo."

"It is very hard," murmured Margaret, administering at the same time a little pressure of her fair fingers against the palm that held them.

"When we know, too, that it is only for the lawyers; that neither your father nor mine would either of them dream of distrusting the other, or fancying it necessary to wait for the signature of papers!"

"Are these bothersome papers always signed before the marriage?" said Margaret, in a very low voice, scarcely above her breath, while she again very slightly pressed his hand with hers.

"I don't know; I should think not! Why, it is just like the huckster, who will not let his goods go out of his hand till the money has been paid over the counter,—it is disgusting!"

"I am sure that there can be no shadow of such feeling either in your father or in mine!" said Margaret.

"Of course not! That is what I say. It is so very hard, so intolerable to be sacrificed to the absurdities and mere blind routine of such an animal as old Slowcome! If I thought for an instant that it was a matter which your dear good father would care about, I should be for submitting with the best grace we could."

"Should be for submitting, Frederick—why, what else can we do, alas? What possible alternative is open to us, save submitting with, as you say, the best grace we may?"

"There is an alternative, Margaret!"

"What do you mean, Frederick?"

"An alternative, which many a loving

couple, who yet have loved less truly, less madly than I love you, have had recourse to."

"For Heaven's sake explain yourself!" and do not, ah, do not speak of your love for me as if it were greater than mine for you. It is not so, Frederick."

"The explanation is a very simple one, Margaret! It is simply to laugh at the lawyers; and leave them to finish their slow work at their own slow pace, and at their leisure."

"How do you mean, dearest?" said Margaret, with a perfection of *ingénuité*, which completely imposed upon her adorer. For now that she was quite sure that Fred was on the road that suited her own views, it was not only needless to lend him any further helping or guiding hand, but was in every way best that she should make a little difficulty in yielding to the proposal which, to her great delight and no small surprise, she saw plainly enough was coming.

"I mean, dearest and best," said Frederick, passing his arm round her waist and drawing her gently to his side, a movement which, under the circumstances of the case, she did not think it necessary to resist entirely, contenting herself with drawing back a little from him, and gazing wistfully and with earnest inquiring eyes into his face the while, as if wholly engrossed by her interest in the reply he was about to make to her,—"I mean, dearest, that after all, it is nothing but our own will that makes us wait the convenience of Slowcome, Sligo, and Co.; that if we two will it so, there is nothing on earth that can prevent our becoming man and wife without asking their permission, and leaving them, as I said, to finish their papers and their signing and sealing at their leisure."

"Oh, Frederick!" cried Margaret, looking at him with admirably counterfeited dismay; "how can that be?" Are not the papers, which those vexatious lawyers are so long about, necessary to the performance of a marriage? Can a marriage be made without them?"

"Why, you dear, innocent little simpleton," said Frederick, with that manifestation of superiority which even if manifested in a more accurate knowledge of the amount of population at Pekin, is so delightful to some men; do you suppose that Slowcome and Sligo, or any of their compeers, are called on to assist in all the marriages that are made? Do you suppose that Dick plough-boy and Jenny dairy-maid trouble the lawyers to draw their settlements before they are made man and wife? And yet, Margaret," continued her mentor, assuming a graver tone of pious-sounding unction, "they are married in the sight of God, and of his church, and of the law of the land, as holily and as irrevocably as any lord or lady in it."

"And is that really so?" returned his pretty pupil, looking up at him with a beautiful commingling of interest and admiration. The Archbishop of Canterbury was not more completely aware of the self-evident nature of the truths her lover was laying down thus authoritatively, than was Miss Margaret Lindisfarn. But the air of nascent conviction was perfect with which she added, "And yet it must be so; of course it must. All the poor people cannot have lawyers bothering for months about them."

"Of course not. I have told you already, these accursed settlements are precautions to prevent me and my father from cheating you and your father, and to prevent you and your father from cheating me and mine! It is humiliating to think of it. That is the meaning of them. It is very proper, you will understand, my love, that these settlements should be made, because men and women are mortal; our parents must die; we shall ourselves die; things must be recorded; and the interests of those that come after us (lady's eyes cast down to the ground here, with an inimitable movement of the head, that was in itself a perfect study) must be arranged, cared for, and protected. It is perfectly right and necessary that these settlements should be made; but there can be no necessity of waiting for them, unless either of us distrusts the other. Can you trust me, my Margaret?"

"Frederick, can you ask such a question?" said, or almost sobbed, Margaret, with a gush of emotion that would almost have carried away old Slowcome himself in its impetuous rush of candor. "Trust you, great heaven! Have I not trusted you? Have I not trusted you with more and better, I would fain hope, than money or acres? I have trusted my heart to your keeping; Frederick, I think I may trust the rest. Trust you! Ah, Frederick, can there be love, where there is not perfect trust?"

And she clasped her two exquisitely gloved little hands together as she spoke, and raised them and her large, dark, liquid eyes towards the sky, while the admirably fitting silk, tight drawn over the well-developed bosom, and the delicate lace that filled the middle space between the two sides of her dress, rose and fell with the panting violence of her emotion. The figure, the expression, the action was perfect, and very beautiful. The play was almost too good for the occasion; it was almost too good for the inferior player who had to play up to her. It was impossible for him not to be moved by the physical beauty of the face and figure before him. But the perfect *vraisemblance* and strength of the moral emotion rather startled and frightened him. He felt somewhat as a mere park rider, who expects his horse to go through the expected *manége* of curvetting and dancing might feel if the graceful creature were all of a sudden to take to rearing in violent and veritable earnest. He began to doubt whether there might not possibly be some difficulty in keeping his seat under all circumstances and contingencies. He pulled himself, however, as well as he could, up to the moral elevation demanded by the nature of the occasion, and replied,—

"Thanks, Margaret, thanks, my own love. It is no more than I expected of you; but your perfect confidence is very touching to me. I shall never forget it. Heaven bless you for it!—What I was about to say to you was, that if, indeed, you place such entire confidence in me, there is, in reality, no reason why we should wear our hearts out by waiting for these dull dogs of lawyers."

"I am quite ready to do anything that you may think best and wisest, my dear Frederick. As I have told you, your wishes are mine. What would you propose to do?"

"Simply to marry,—to be made man and wife, and let the papers be signed afterward when they are ready."

"I suppose our parents would make no objection?" said Margaret.

"In their hearts they would not, we may be very sure. But probably they would be much embarrassed by our making the proposition. In young people,—in those who are in our position, Margaret,—the world easily forgives such departure from the established routine. In our parents the case might not be the same. They might be blamed. No; the way to act—the way in which these things are always done—is to ask no permission at all; to do it—and then come back to be forgiven!"

"Oh, Frederick! Do you think we could venture on such a course as that? It frightens me to think of such a thing!"

"Dearest! There would be nothing to alarm you. It would all be very easy, very simple. You say that you have confidence in me; do you think that I would lead you into trouble or sorrow?"

"Oh, no; oh, no! I *have* perfect confidence in you, Frederick,—in your affection, your sense, your courage. With you I am sure that I should fear nothing."

"If so, my own, we may snap our fingers at Slowcome and Sligo, and name the auspicious day for ourselves."

"Are you really serious, Frederick? But I do not comprehend what it is you would propose to do. Tell me what steps you would think it advisable to take."

"Simply the same steps, Margaret, that are usually taken by so many others in our position; except, indeed, that very many have to contend with the difficulty of the opposition of their families to the match at all; whereas we shall have no difficulties of the sort, or, indeed, of any sort. See now, my love! If, in truth, you have confidence enough in me to be guided entirely by me in this matter, this is what I should propose. We will have no getting out of window, and rope-ladders, and all that sort of thing. All such *grands moyens* are for those who have to fight against the opposition of parents and guardians. We have no need of any such. This shall be our simple, common-sense programme. Some evening—say to-morrow evening—what do we gain by delay?—I will have a post-chaise and the best pair of horses in Silverton at the little door in the garden wall that opens on the lane, near the Castle Head turnpike. Then, after dinner, while the doctor is still in the dining-room or in his study, and Lady Sempronia is taking her after-dinner nap on the sofa, you shall just quietly walk out into the garden, come to the little door in the wall, which I will take care to have open,—I know where the gardener keeps the key,—

and there on the other side you find me waiting for you. You step into the carriage, I jump in after you; and before anybody has observed your absence, we are ten miles or so on our way to Scotland. That is what *I* would do, Margaret; and what we *will* do, if you have that confidence in me you spoke of!"

"I have, I have, Frederick; doubt it not. I have all confidence! But—Scotland! That is a long way off! Why should we go to Scotland?"

"Because, my darling, that is the place where it is easiest for us to be married without any delay. The law is different in Scotland. People can be married there at once. It is not, indeed, absolutely necessary in our case; for we might be married by special license. But there would be more or less of delay. Whereas, in Scotland, we can be made indissolubly man and·wife as soon as ever our feet touch Scottish soil."

"Is it possible! Oh, Frederick, how extraordinary! If anybody but you told me so, I should think they were telling fibs."

(The pretty creature knew all about a Gretna Green marriage as well as any postboy on the last stage over the border.)

"It is not only possible, it is certain; and what is more, very frequently done. Should you be afraid to make such a little trip with me?"

"With you, Frederick, I should be afraid of nothing. I would fly with you to the end of the world,—if I had only had my things ready! How am I to manage about my things?"

"What things, dearest, should you require?"

"Oh, my trunks,—and who is to pack them?—and my toilet things, you know,—and—and—Simmons,—you know?"

"Simmons! what, the maid at the Chase? Are you mad, Margaret? No, that would never do! There can be no maid. We must be all in all to ourselves and to each other. Can you not trust me, my own Margaret?"

Frederick here got possession of her hand again, and pressed it against his heart, looking wistfully into her face, as he spoke, with the most intense expression of supplication he could muster; for he felt that this was the difficult point.

"Go without a maid, Frederick! Oh, impossible! How am I to dress myself? How

am I ever to put on my orange-blossoms and my wedding veil?" she said, disengaging her hand, and clasping it with its fellow, as she held them out toward him in passionate appeal.

"My dearest girl, you do not understand the matter rightly. There will be no dressing for our wedding. You will be married directly you step out of the post-chaise, in the same clothes in which you stepped into it, at the garden-door here. Instead of orange-blossoms and bridal veils you will have panting post-horses, and a village blacksmith for a clergyman. You will have a pretty *toilette de voyage*. Why not the dress you have on? I never saw you look more absolutely perfection!"

"It seems all so strange; and to go away with you, alone, to such a distance!"

"Yes, my Margaret! It needs perfect trust in me. Can you not have that trust?"

"I can, I will, Frederick! I put myself and my destiny wholly, unhesitatingly, into your hands. Am I not your own? I will do all that you would wish me to do."

"Dearest, dearest Margaret! Then listen to me. What time do you come out from dinner!"

"Oh, always before six! When we are alone, Aunt Sempronia always goes into the drawing-room almost the minute the cloth is taken away. Uncle, after a little while, goes into his study, where, to the best of my belief, he falls fast asleep."

"And when you get into the drawing-room?" asked Frederick.

"Oh, aunt fidgets about a little, and scolds if the servants have made too big a fire; and then settles herself on the sofa, and tells me to wake her when the doctor comes in."

"And how long is it generally before he does come in?" asked Frederick.

"Oh, about an hour,—sometimes more; never, I think, less than that."

"Excellent—nothing could be better! Then, when the old gentleman does come in to his tea, and no Margaret is there, it will be some time before they guess that you have left the house; and when at last they come to the conclusion that you are not to be found in it, it will be a long while before they make a guess at the truth."

"Or I could leave a little note on the drawing-room table to say that I had a bad headache, and had gone to bed, but would not disturb her ladyship's nap. Then nothing would be known of my departure till ten o'clock the next morning."

"Admirable! perfect! Why, you little darling, you were born for a conspirator. Nothing could be better imagined! But we must be sure that there is nobody coming to dinner. Is there anybody coming to-morrow?"

"But to-morrow will not do, Frederick!" said Margaret, in a different tone from that in which she had been speaking hitherto, a simple, business-like tone, which at once convinced him that for some reason the morrow would *not* do.

"Why, what is it, dear?" he asked, also speaking in a changed key.

"Because I am to go up to the Chase to-morrow morning."

"Oh, Margaret, that is very unfortunate!" said Frederick, in a genuine tone of vexation and disappointment.

"But it cannot be helped, Frederick. It is all arranged. But I can return here on the following morning."

"And will you do so, my own love? May I depend on your doing so?"

"Frederick!" she said, in a tone of fond reproach.

"And be on your guard, dearest! Take care that Kate does not worm your secret out of you, or make a shrewd guess at it."

"Kate make a shrewd guess,—or worm a secret out of *me!*" said Margaret, in a tone of profound disdain, which had more of genuine feeling in it than any words she had uttered during the whole of the previous conversation with her lover. "Why, Fred, what do you take me for? Am I quite a simpleton?" she added, with a toss of her head that showed she really was indignant at the imputation.

"Anything but that, Margaret, Heaven knows! But it is necessary to be careful," returned he, penitently.

"Never fear; Kate will learn no secret of mine!"

"And you will be here on the following morning, without fail?"

"I have promised you, Frederick; and you may be sure that I will not fail you," said she, giving him her hand, as pledging her faith.

"My own darling! my dearest *wife!* How

can I sufficiently thank you for the sweet trust and confidence you are placing in me? —only by deserving it. And I will deserve it. See now! On the evening of the day after to-morrow, I will be in the lane on the other side of the garden-door, with a carriage and everything in readiness, at six o'clock, and will wait, with what patience I can, till you come. See, the key of the door is always to be found just here," said Frederick, showing her a little cavity in the old wall near the ground; "the old fellow always puts it there, never dreaming that anybody who wanted it, might easily find it there. Now just let us see whether the lock goes easily enough for that little hand to open it—gently—quietly!" said he, as he put the key into her hand; the well-oiled lock was turned with perfect ease. "Capital! that will do. You will remember where to find the key. Perhaps it would be better that I should not attempt to see you on your return from the Chase."

"Perhaps not."

"When do you intend to be back?"

"Oh, to dinner to-morrow! I shall not stay there. I shall say that uncle made me promise to return to dinner without fail. It is only that Kate wants to have a talk about something or other. She is such a bother! Kate is exactly cut out for an old maid, and I believe she will live and die one."

"You don't think there will be anybody to dine here the day after to-morrow?"

"Oh! It is very unlikely. We always discuss such things here ever so long in advance. Oh, no; I think we may be sure that we shall be all alone."

"Then I think that we may consider all as settled? The day after to-morrow, at six in the evening."

"It is very sudden! You will be very good to me, dearest, very indulgent, and very true; *n'est-ce pas, mon bien aimé?*"

"I will, I will, my beloved Margaret, now and ever. How can I ever thank you enough for all your love and trust? Dearest, be very sure that you shall not repent of them."

"I do not think I shall, Frederick. So now, if all is definitively settled, I think we had better go in. It must be nearly time for the dressing-bell to ring."

"Adieu, sweetest! To think that the next time we meet, it will be to part no more till I can call you really, wholly mine!"

13

" *Au revoir! Après demain à six'heures!* " whispered Margaret, as he squeezed her hand in parting at the door of the drawing-room, from which he escaped just as Lady Sempronia was rousing herself and thinking that it was time to dress for dinner.

CHAPTER XXXV.
ONLY TILL TO-MORROW NIGHT!

The next morning, at a rather earlier hour than usual,—it was just as the canon was leaving his house, to step across the Close to morning service at the cathedral,—the gig from Lindisfarn came to the door for Miss Margaret. But there was no Mr. Mat in it. The old groom who had driven in, brought a note from Kate, to say that she had not been able to persuade Mr. Mat to come; but that she had thought it better to send the gig, as Thomas Tibbs, with the carriage, would have been so much slower about it.

Margaret was quite as well pleased to perform the short journey with the groom as with Mr. Mat. Indeed, it was felt by her as an escape, that she was not condemned to the latter penance. Nevertheless, she took it as an affront, and resented the slight accordingly.

She did not take anything with her; for she fully purposed being back again to dinner, as she told Lady Sempronia when she mentioned to her Kate's summons.

Her original plan had been to stay at the Chase for the night, and return to the Close the following morning, as she had said to Frederick. But a little consideration had led her to change it. In the first place, she felt on reflection that it would be very desirable to shorten as much as possible the talk which must pass between her and Kate. There could be nothing agreeable in it; and she had no desire to sustain the part, which she would be obliged to play before her sister, for a greater number of hours than was absolutely inevitable. It would be a great thing to escape the long evening hours, and the *tête-à-tête*, which it would be impossible to avoid, in Kate's room after they had retired for the night.

In the second place, she preferred having a little longer time between her return to the Close and the execution of her momentous project. Fred had told her that "no things" would be needed. But she could not absolutely subscribe to that view of the matter.

There was at least, her *toilette de voyage* to be decided on,—a matter not to be put off to the last minute. As a mere matter of fatigue, too, it would be better to start on her long journey after a day of perfect rest.

Then, again, she was inclined to think, on consideration, that, despite the possible difficulty about stable arrangements, she might find it easier to get back the same day than on the next. There would be the excuse of not having even what was necessary for the night; there would be the keeping her uncle's dinner waiting. She would then probably avoid seeing her father, who would most likely be out, all the time she was at Lindisfarn, and would thus get rid of the danger of objection on his part.

So, taking all these things into consideration, she had determined on curtailing her visit to Lindisfarn to the few hours that she could spend there between the breakfast and the dinner hour at the Close.

"Oh, yes, dear! Be sure you come back!" Lady Sempronia had said. "It would be cruel to leave me all alone, and my poor nerves in the state they are! And your poor uncle is madder than ever about this new whim of his monogram, or whatever it is, he calls it, upon the church at Chewton; such a place, my dear! if you could only see it! and I am frightened to death lest he should insist upon printing it. Oh, you must not leave me!"

"I only hope, dear aunt, that there will be no difficulty about sending me back either in the carriage or with the gig."

"Oh, my dear Margaret, you *must* come back! Stay, perhaps I had better write a line to dear Kate; or would it be best to Miss Immy—only you know"—

"Oh, no! best to Kate, dear aunt; if you would write a line to Kate, it might, perhaps, make matters easier."

So the tearful lady sat down at her little desk, and fishing for a clean scrap of paper, among a tumbled mass of bills of all sorts and sizes, she wrote in the eminently lady-like hand of the last century, in which the body of the letters was scarcely greater in altitude than the thickness of a line, while the tops and tails were of immoderate length, and the lines very far apart, the following note :—

" My DEAR KATE,—Margaret tells me that it is *imperatively* necessary that she should go up to the Chase to-day. It is a sad trial to me to part with her. But, alas, what is life, mine especially, *but* trials! I trust, however, that you will send her back to me this evening. Would that I could send for her! I will not now go into the sad detail of the reasons which make this impossible to me. They are, alas! too well known to you, my dear niece, and to the world in general, the more's the pity. I must trust to your kindness, therefore, and to that of Mr. Mat,—for I know that he is the *Master of the Horse* at Lindisfarn,—not to disappoint me in this. Dear Margaret will explain to you how totally unfit I am to be left alone with your dear uncle, especially at the present moment. Indeed, I do not know what might be the consequences to me! I am grieved to hear that the recent rains are likely to cause very wide-spread *distress*, and perhaps *ruin*, among the agricultural interests. But God's will be done! Tell your dear father so from me, with my kind love. I look to Margaret's return by five o'clock; for you know what your poor dear uncle's temper is if the dinner is kept waiting.

"Your affectionate aunt,
"S. LINDISFARN."

"I don't think Kate will be so cruel as not to send you back to me," sighed Lady Sempronia, as she handed this note to Margaret.

"Oh, no, dear aunt! depend upon it, I shall be back by five o'clock."

So Margaret got into the gig, and was driven in a little less than an hour up to the Chase.

She was in high spirits; or at least in a state of excitement which produced a similar appearance; and had some difficulty in meeting her sister with the depression of manner befitting the part she had to play.

"Oh, Margaret dear! I am so glad to have you at home again. I have so much to talk to you of," said Kate, as she met her at the door.

"And we have not very much time to say it in, Kate; for I must be back again in the Close by five o'clock."

"Back again to-night?"

"Yes. It is impossible to avoid it. See, here is a note for you from my aunt. Poor soul, she is in a very low way! I cannot leave her. You will see what she says. Besides, I have brought home none of my things."

"But, my dear Margaret, how are you to get back again to Silverton this evening?

You know what a bother there always is with Tibbs."

"That is why I spoke about it the first thing, Kate. It must be managed somehow. I suppose I am not in Mr. Mat's good books, by his not condescending to come for me this morning. But you can make him do anything you like."

"I suppose it is impossible to disappoint my aunt," said Kate, with a sigh, as she finished reading her aunt's letter. "But what is it she alludes to as her particular sorrow at this time more than usual?"

"Oh, you know my aunt! She is in a great trouble, just at present, for fear my uncle should take it into his head to print a new paper he has been writing all about an old church at his living in a place they call Chewton,—a most horrid, desolate place, aunt says, out in the moor. The paper is to be read at the meeting of the eccle—eccloy—whatever it is they call themselves, next month; and as uncle is very particularly proud of it, she is in great fear of the probable consequences. And indeed, I may perhaps be of some use; for I have some little influence over Uncle Theophilus."

"Well, I suppose you must go," sighed Kate; "and I will see what can be done about sending you. Perhaps the old pony could be put in the gig, just to take you to Silverton. Come! let us go up to my room. Noll is out with the dogs."

"But had we not better settle first about the gig?" urged Margaret, who was by no means willing to allow any amount of doubt to rest upon the execution of her programme.

"Very well! If you will go up-stairs, and take your hat off, I will go and see about it, and come to you in my room."

Margaret ran quickly up the stairs, and into her sister's room. There her first care was not to take off her hat, but to cast a sharp, searching glance at Kate's table, to see if any note or letter had been left there, according to Kate's careless habits in such matters, which might, even by the outside of it, perhaps, give her some hint of the position of matters with her sister. But there was nothing on the table,—not even the usual litter of Kate's manifold ordinary occupations. The little desk, instead of standing open, was shut up; and there was not so much as a book to be seen lying about. All the drawing things at the other small table were piled into a little heap in the middle of it, and had evidently not been touched for days.

If any more intelligently sympathizing eye than her sister's had looked in Kate's face, the looker would not have failed to be struck by evidence of the cessation of all the ordinary sources of interest and occupation, as legible there as in the condition of her room.

And there were not wanting such sympathizing eyes at Lindisfarn. It was plain enough to more than one loving observer that Kate had been stricken somehow or other, whether in heart or merely in body, and matters were out of joint at the Chase in consequence. Mr. Mat was miserable, and cross to every one but the object of his trouble. He would neglect his dinner, and sit looking wistfully at Kate, as she wearily went through the daily ceremony, and when she and Miss Immy had left the room, would say to the squire,—

" The lass is not right, squire! She is not like herself, no more than I am like the Bishop of Silverton! But as for telling me that she is thinking anything about that fellow Falconer—they may tell that to the marines! I've known the lass from her cradle up. It's as damned a pack of nonsense, squire "—

And Mr. Mat's black eye grew moist under its shaggy black brow as he spoke.

" God grant it may be as you say! " sighed the squire; " anything better than that."

Miss Immy, for her part, threatened Kate with Dr. Blakistry. As yet Kate had, not without difficulty, fought off this strong measure. But Miss Immy was getting really uneasy about her; and it was clear that, unless she could manage to " look like herself again," she would have to submit to a professional visit from the doctor before long.

And the alternative was quite out of Kate's power. She could not look like herself again; for she felt very unlike that former self.

And, worst of all, Lady Farnleigh was still absent. Most unfortunately she had been detained, much beyond the time she had at first intended, by the serious illness of her daughter-in-law. That lady was now, however, much better; and there was a prospect of the " fairy godmother's " return before long.

Kate often sighed as she remembered the happy, careless days, when she had so nicknamed her best and dearest friend, and thought how infinitely greater was her need of such a protectress than she had ever dreamed it could be.

She joined Margaret in a few minutes in her room, going up the stairs much more slowly than she had done.

" I have arranged for you to have the gig for your return," she said, sitting down wearily beside her sister. " Mr. Mat made no difficulty. The gig will be at the door at half-past three."

" Mr. Mat makes less difficulty about sending me away from Lindisfarn than about bringing me back to it. *Cela s'entend!* I dare say there is no love lost between us."

" Oh, Margaret! I am sure that Mr. Mat does not feel otherwise than kindly toward you."

" It matters very little to me how he feels, that is one good thing! But now, Kate, what was your object in making me come up here? "

" Surely, you must know, Margaret. Julian has recovered; he has left England. We are no longer bound by any promise of secrecy; and it is above all things necessary that the error as to his supposed death should be corrected with as little delay as possible. But I was unwilling to take any step in the matter without first speaking with you."

" I suppose it will be necessary that the fact should be known," replied Margaret; " but do not you think that it would be more proper to leave it to him to make the announcement himself? You remember that he told you he purposed doing so."

" Yes; but what I cannot bear is that we should know it and keep the knowledge to ourselves. I cannot bear the burden of the secret any longer, Margaret."

" I do not see that the burden has been a very heavy one to you, Kate. To me it has been different. In the circumstances in which I have been placed, it has been very painful to me to be obliged to keep such a secret to myself. Happily, I know well that the knowledge of it would have occasioned no difference in the conduct of my future husband. Nevertheless, you can understand, I suppose, that it would be unpleasant to me to have to confess that I knew the real state of the case, so early as for my misfortune I did, in consequence of your imprudent visit to that smuggler man's cottage."

"I will not say anything about that, Margaret. I thought it was right under the circumstances to go there, and I went. Now it would be infinitely more agreeable to me—it would be a greater consolation and comfort to me than you can imagine—if I could not only let the fact of Julian's existence be known at once, but also let it be understood that I knew it at the time I did know it. You cannot guess how much I would give to do this. Nevertheless I have made up my mind to abstain from doing it, for your sake; for I can fully feel how dreadful, how intolerable, it would be to you, that it should be known that you had accepted an offer of marriage without saying a word about it, or in any way intimating that your position was a very different one from what it was supposed to be."

"I could not help myself, as I have told you before," said Margaret, sullenly.

"It was very unfortunate," sighed Kate; "but I have told you that I have made up my mind not to say anything about the date at which this important secret reached our knowledge. You must feel, however, dear Margaret, that the time has come when it is absolutely necessary to break off this engagement, and"—

"Break off!—will nothing make you believe, Kate, that all people are not so sordid in their views as you imagine them?" interrupted Margaret, while her cheek flushed up, and her eyes flashed fire. "It is very singular, sister, how particularly anxious you are that the engagement between me and Fred should be broken off; but you may as well give it up as a bad job. Make your mind up to it, once for all, that it wont and can't be broken off."

Kate looked into her sister's gleaming, angry eyes, with a quiet glance of mute appeal, and of sorrow rather than reproach, as she said,—

"Can you not believe, Margaret, that your happiness and welfare are all I wish for or care about in this matter?"

"It don't seem like it"—

"And that when I speak of breaking off the engagement you have made, I mean merely breaking that which was entered into in ignorance of the truth, to be replaced, if the parties to it wish to do so, by a fresh engagement made with full knowledge of the truth? You can't doubt that it is absolutely necessary that no time should be lost in telling Mr. Falconer the truth; and it was about this that I wanted to speak to you to-day."

"I am sure I don't see why you should take so much trouble to meddle with my affairs! I suppose I am the proper person to tell Mr. Falconer, as you call him; and I presume I may be left to do so in my own way, and at my own time."

"But that is just the point, Margaret. Certainly you are the person who ought to tell him. He ought most unquestionably to hear it from no one but yourself. But the time—that is the question. At your own time, you say. When is that time, Margaret? That is what I want to settle with you."

"Now I am not going to be dictated to, as if I were a school-girl and you my mistress, Kate. Remember that you are not even my elder sister, though you seem strangely inclined to take the tone of one. I have just as good a right to preach to you as you to me, remember! I told you from the beginning fairly and honestly, that my views and ideas differed from yours in this matter, and that I intended to be guided in it by my own, and not by yours. That is still my intention, I beg you to understand. I shall choose my time for telling my future husband the whole of this strange improbable story, according to my own judgment and convenience. I presume you will not think fit to take it upon yourself to meddle between us."

"Most certainly, Margaret, I shall not take it upon myself to say anything upon the subject to Mr. Falconer, if you mean that. But I must speak to those who ought necessarily to be made acquainted with the truth in the first instance. I must tell my father and my Uncle Theophilus. And it is this that I was unwilling to do, without having first spoken to you, on purpose that you might have the opportunity of yourself speaking to Mr. Falconer before the facts reach him from any one else. You know my father. Do you think that he would suffer any uncertainty to remain on the subject in the mind of anybody for an hour after he had heard the truth? You know my uncle. Do you think he is likely to keep it secret?

You know what Silverton is. Do you think anybody in all the place is likely to remain in ignorance of the facts four-and-twenty hours after I have told them to papa? And do you see now that I had reason enough to make a point of your coming up here to-day."

Margaret bit her lips till they were white, and remained silent for a minute or two.

"And when *do* you mean to make this communication to papa?" she then asked, keeping her eyes fixed, as she spoke, on the floor.

"I should have done it long ago if it had not been for this unhappy entanglement of yours."

Margaret raised her eyes to her sister's face for an instant, and the forked lightning shot forth dangerously.

"It was only to give you time," continued Kate, with increased and almost tearful earnestness, "that I have abstained thus long. I can abstain no longer! The weight of this secret seems as if it were crushing my heart. I must tell it. But I would fain that you told Mr. Falconer first,—or at least as soon."

"You are very peremptory, Kate! You have got the whip hand of me, and you are determined to use it cruelly,—cruelly!"

"Oh, Margaret, Margaret!" sobbed Kate.

"Yes, cruelly!" continued her sister, speaking with extreme bitterness. "It is your turn now! And I am in your power—to a certain degree—to a certain degree. Well! what time do you condescend to assign to me in your mercy?"

"You are going back to Silverton this evening; it is so far convenient. I thought that it would have been necessary to send for him here. As it is, it will be easier. You will, in all probability, see him this evening."

"You find it very easy to settle it all your way. In all probability I shall do nothing of the kind. I have no reason to think that he will come to my uncle's this evening."

"It would be very easy to send a word across the Close, requesting him to do so."

"Kate! what do you take me for? If you have been brought up to do that sort of thing, I, for my part, have not, and flatter myself that I know what *convenance* requires rather better than to take such a step."

"I can see no objection to it under the circumstances, and for the purpose we are talking about, I confess, Margaret," replied Kate, with a deep sigh. "What would you propose doing yourself?"

"If you will promise me not to say any word till to-morrow evening," replied Margaret, after a few moments of deep consideration, "I will promise you to tell Frederick the first time I do see him. I think it very likely that I may see him in the course of to-morrow,—almost certain. I will be content if you will give me only till to-morrow evening. You may tell papa, and all Silverton, too, if you like, after dinner to-morrow. Will that do?" said Margaret, inwardly congratulating herself on the admirable good fortune which had prompted Frederick to propose the scheme he had, and to fix the execution of it for such an early day. What on earth would have become of her, but for this happy piece of good fortune! As it was, the fatal facts would not be known till they were safe off on their way to Scotland; and when they came back married, Frederick would learn it as a bit of news that had reached Silverton in the interval of their absence.

"Very well," said Kate, slowly and reluctantly; "let it be so, since you are unwilling to release me sooner. Let it remain settled that I tell papa the whole of the facts to-morrow evening after dinner;—papa and Mr. Mat, mind, Margaret!—there must be no more secrets!—and Mr. Mat is likely enough, mind, to have out the gig and drive off to Silverton that same evening, to tell Uncle Theophilus that his son is still living."

"No! you must give me the whole evening," exclaimed Margaret, remembering that Mr. Mat's untimely arrival in the Close might be the means of prematurely discovering her absence from her uncle's house;—"I bargain for the whole evening. Who knows at what time I may see Frederick? He often comes in late. If you wish to be of any service to me, Kate, you must give me the whole evening. You can tell papa the first thing the next morning. That can make no difference, you know, Kate. Let it be the first thing in the morning, the day after to-morrow. And then let Mr. Mat have the satisfaction of telling the world of our ruin as soon as he likes. I will find the means of doing my part before that time.

You pledge yourself, then, Kate, to say nothing till the morning of the day after to-morrow ? "

" So be it, then, Margaret. I promise you that I will keep the secret till that time. Then I shall, without fail, tell papa : and I think it more likely than not, that Mr. Mat will tell my uncle within an hour afterward."

" Let him do his worst ! " said Margaret, bitterly, but yet triumphantly.

" Oh, Margaret, I wish you could think that we all have but one heart and one interest in this sad matter. You may trust me I know what I am talking about, when I tell you that not a soul in this house or in Silverton will feel our misfortune more acutely than poor Mr. Mat."

" Well ! it don't much matter. There is small consolation in his caring about it, whether he does or not; and now, I suppose, our business is settled."

" Yes," said Kate, sadly ; " will you come and see Miss Immy ? "

" I suppose I must before I go back ; it is a great bore. But I want to go into my own room first," answered Margaret, whose mind was busy with the consideration whether there might not be certain small articles at the Chase, which it might be desirable for her to take with her in her flight to Scotland.

Kate accompanied her sister into the adjoining room, and Margaret had some difficulty in making her comprehend that she wished to be there alone. She succeeded at last, and Kate left her, thinking that she wished to commune with herself on the terribly painful task which lay before her.

Margaret hastily bolted the door behind her, and did not come out of her room till it wanted only a quarter of an hour to the time the gig was ordered for her return to Silverton.

CHAPTER XXXVI.
THE TWO SIDES OF THE WALL.

MARGARET returned to her dinner at her uncle's, in the Close, in good time. She was still in high spirits, or, at least, in that state of nervous excitement, which, in some persons, so closely resembles them. She was, at all events, well contented with the result of her visit to the Chase ; and the game she had been, for the last month past,

so desperately playing, seemed definitively to be at last in her own hands.

When she had supposed herself, as all the rest of the Sillshire world supposed her, to be an heiress to landed property to the amount of two thousand a year, she had not been very particularly anxious or eager about Frederick Falconer's proposal. The match seemed a very fair one in a prudential point of view, and the gentleman was by no means disagreeable to her. " She had never seen anybody she liked better," as the classical phrase runs upon such occasions ; but Margaret had been far too well brought up, and had much too strong a feeling of what she owed to herself and to the proprieties of maidenly delicacy, to be in any danger of breaking her pure and gentle heart for any son of Adam. She was quite contented to do her little bit of flirting, and trot out her pretty little airs and graces, and show off her certainly not little attractions, all within the most rigorous bounds of the strictest reading of the code of the *convenances*, and leave the result to work itself out as Providence and the gentleman might decree. But all this was suddenly and tremendously changed by that terrible communication from her sister. Then it became absolutely necessary that this chance should be seized on, and that promptly. It was most desperately a case of now or never with her. Any sin against those *convenances*, which assiduous drilling and the social atmosphere in which she had lived had made a second nature to her, was extremely repugnant to all Margaret's feelings. If the *lex non scripta* prescribed that at any given juncture of her girlhood life, it was permissible for her to allow a creature of the other sex to squeeze her little finger, " all the best and most beautiful feelings of her nature " would have been outraged, if any man should have dared to make the penultimate digit participate in the pressure.

Still, all the little outlook into the world around her, which it had been possible for her to obtain, convinced her that the sacred code of *les convenances* was made and provided for the guidance of *les jeunes personnes* of a certain standing in the social world,—a position from which she was—alas, and alas ! —suddenly and most cruelly hurled. Quite other maxims and rules were needed for the being which she had become,—an adventuress. Yes, not being a young person with expectations, she was an adventuress. It was useless, and mere folly, to blink the fact, or mince the phrase. She was an adventuress; and however painful it might be to one not "to the manner born," it behooved her to act as such. She had accepted the position then *en maitresse femme*, and vigorously set about acting as the exigencies of the part demanded of her.

It had not been a pleasant thing to live through the past month, with the horrible sword of ignominious failure suspended over her head by a thread all the time. Very much otherwise. But now her boldness and her ability seemed about to be rewarded. At last she was in sight of port, and to all appearance safe. And she did feel that she deserved some applause for the manner in which she had steered her bark, in a sea of no ordinary danger and difficulty.

Not that the future was all smooth water. Far from it. Margaret indulged herself in no such weak illusion. Her Frederick would be grievously disappointed, doubtless, when the first news that met him, on bringing his wife back to his native town, would be that he had married a beggar. She had a very strong conviction that her Frederick was about the last man in the world, to commit such a folly and indiscretion. And Margaret was by no means inclined to think the less well of him on that account. No doubt he would be greatly disappointed, — thunderstruck! No doubt there would be unpleasantness. What else could be looked for? Was not all this miserable business calculated to produce unpleasantness of all kinds? Still, she would be a wife ; and she flattered herself that she should know how to use that vantage-ground in such a manner as to make the position not too intolerable a one for her.

It was no use thinking of that, however, now! Sufficient for the day was the evil and the work thereof. What she had now to do was to step boldly forward on the path toward her object. Fate itself seemed helping her. What, what should she have done, had not the delays of the lawyers thus happily tired out Frederick's patience! She had been living in the hope of inducing Kate to keep the fatal secret a little longer! It seemed, however, to judge by her sister's words and manner, in this last interview,

that that would have been a vain hope. What a blessing was the foolish impatience, which would not let that fond fellow Frederick wait for his happiness any longer!

These were the meditations which occupied Margaret's mind during several of the hours of that last night in her uncle's house. The next morning, at breakfast, a new source of anxiety arose. As the doctor and his wife and niece were sitting at their morning meal, the doctor announced his intention of paying a visit, that day, to his living of Chewton in the moor.

"It is absolutely necessary, my dear, though in truth it is a very great trouble. But in the interests of science, you know, I never spare myself."

"Nor others, Dr. Lindisfarn!" said Lady Sempronia.

"My dear, I am sorry to inconvenience • you in any way, though I do not see how it should inconvenience you. It is indispensably necessary that I should verify the accuracy of certain statements and descriptions. I am come to a point at which I cannot get on without another personal inspection of the buildings and localities. Heaven knows I have no liking for the job personally. But when the accuracy and completeness of the work, on which so much depends, are concerned, I cannot hesitate. I was going to mention that I shall not be able to get home to dinner. If I could have gone early this morning, I might have done so. But I wished to be in my place at the morning service. I shall start directly afterward."

"You know best, Dr. Lindisfarn!" said his long-suffering wife, with a resigned sigh.

"We will not have the bore of a regular dinner to-day, my dear," said she to Margaret, as soon as the doctor had left the breakfast-room ; "we will have a cutlet or something at luncheon, and then we shall enjoy our toast and tea."

It was Lady Sempronia's thrifty habit to make the absence of her lord and master at least so far an advantage as to save a dinner by it.

But then it occurred to Margaret that if the ordinary routine of the day were thus altered, her aunt's after-dinner nap would probably share the fate of the dinner, or at least be pushed out of its usual place in the day's programme. And if so, it might very well happen that it would be impossible for her to escape from Lady Sempronia at the right moment. Usually on such occasions as the present, the tea, thus promoted to the position of a meal, was served at seven o'clock. And it seemed likely that at six, the fateful hour fixed for Margaret's escape, her gently fretful ladyship would be awake and in the drawing-room waiting for the repast which such ladies love, and expecting her niece to keep her company.

During the whole forenoon Margaret was in a state of great anxiety, and was eagerly debating within herself the expediency of despatching Parsons with a note to Frederick informing him of the state of the case, and of the probable necessity of modifying their plans to meet the new circumstances.

It was past twelve o'clock, and she had just made up her mind that she would do this immediately after luncheon, when once again fortune stood her friend, and made any such step unnecessary. She was in her own room nervously looking over for the twentieth time every article of the costume she intended to travel in, when she was startled by a little tap at her door. Hurriedly shutting the drawers in which she had laid out most of these in readiness, she told the applicant to come in. It was Lady Sempronia's maid, with,—

"Please, Miss Margaret, my lady bade me say that she is took so bad with her nerves that she will not be able to come down to luncheon. She hopes you will excuse her, and she would be glad to speak to you."

Margaret found her aunt in bed. The prominence with which the dangers to be feared from the growing importance of the doctor's monograph on Chewton Church had been brought before her prescient mind had, as usual, proved too great a trial for her enfeebled nervous system. She had, she declared, a racking headache,—feared she should become hysterical,—felt that her only chance was to keep herself absolutely quiet,—and should not leave her bed any more that day, even if she were able to do so on the morrow.

It was difficult for Margaret to keep the decently sorrowful face of sympathy which this communication required, so great a relief was it to her. Was it possible for anything to be better? Fortune herself seemed to have undertaken the task of taking all diffi-

culties out of the way, and leaving the coast clear for her!

The remainder of the day passed very slowly with Margaret, but not altogether unhappily. She was nervous and excited, but full of hope and confidence. Twice she walked round the garden, and glanced sharply at the cavity in the wall near the little door into the lane, to satisfy herself that the key was there. She longed to take it up, and try it in the lock, but refrained. It was imprudent; and Margaret was a very prudent girl!

At last the feared yet wished-for hour came. At last it wanted only a quarter to six. The note to be given to Lady Sempronia when her ladyship's cup of tea was carried up to her, was all ready.

"DEAR AUNT," it said,
"The shock which has sent you to bed, has reacted—less forcibly, no doubt, than on your delicately sensitive nervous system—on me too. I have a violent headache, and am now going to bed. I have told Elizabeth to give you this when she takes you your tea, and not before, lest you might be getting a little sleep. I hope, dear aunt, that we may both be better to-morrow.
"Your loving niece,
"MARGARET."

This was given to Lady Sempronia's maid with injunctions not to disturb her mistress till tea-time, then to carry her a cup of tea, and give her the note at the same time.

"I have a dreadful headache myself, Elizabeth," added the young lady; "I shall not stay up for tea, but go to my room at once. If I want you to undress me, I will ring, but do not disturb me unless I do; for if I can keep myself quiet and get to sleep, I would not be waked for the world. If it is late when I wake, I will manage to undress by myself."

Then while the servant was going through the hall towards the kitchen, Margaret heavily and wearily dragged herself up half a dozen stairs toward her room. But as soon as ever the swing door which shut off the servants' part of the house had slammed to behind Elizabeth, she turned, and darting light of foot as an antelope, and swift as thought into the drawing-room, passed gently through the window, carefully shutting it after her, into the garden. Then tripping, with short-drawn breath and beating heart, along the dark garden-walk to the little door in the wall leading to the lane, she paused, pressing her hand to her bosom, and intently listening. But no sound broke the silence save the audible beating of her own heart.

She had not waited thus more than a few minutes, however, before the quarter bell in the neighboring cathedral tower, after a strange sort of grating, jarring prelude, as if clearing its voice before speaking, sung out its clear ding-dong!—ding-dong!—ding-dong!—ding-dong!—Four quarters. It was the full time then. Margaret had not been sure whether it might not yet want a quarter to the hour fixed. No! and in the next instant the deeper bass of the hour bell tolled, one—two—three—four—five—six! Of course, she knew very well that the bell was going to strike six. Yet it seemed to her fancy as if that sixth stroke had a fateful clinching power in it, which cast the die of her fate, and made it impossible for her to draw back.

She listened still more intently than before, but heard nothing. Perhaps the carriage had already taken up its position on the other side of the wall; and perhaps Frederick was within a few inches of her on the other side of the door, afraid to give any audible sign of his presence, for fear that it might reach other ears beside hers.

After a few more minutes of intent listening, which seemed to be at least four times as many as they were, she decided that this must be the case, and she determined to open the door. There could be very little risk in doing so; for the lane was a lonely one, but little frequented by day, and still more certain to be undisturbed by night. She turned the key in the lock with the greatest precaution, starting at the little click it made just at the end of the operation, and cautiously opening the door a little, peered out into the darkness of the lane. She could see nothing! And yet she was sure she had counted the striking of the clock aright.

And then a sudden hot flush came over her; and she began to think of the retributive storm of indignation and reproach with which she would visit the delinquent for his unpunctuality as soon as he should arrive.

She all but closed the door, leaving barely a sufficient aperture for her to keep her anxious watch of the lane. And the intolerably tedious minutes slowly accumulated themselves till once again there came the harsh rattle in the quarter bell's throat, preparatory to its clearly chimed ding-dong,—the first quarter after six.

Margaret began to feel both physically and morally very cold. A sickening sensation of fear crept over her. Yet there was no other possible course to follow but still to wait. And Margaret still waited, with a rapidly gathering agony in her heart, a few hours of which might be deemed a fair expiation for many an ill-spent day.

The more Margaret reflected, the more inexplicable it seemed to her. And if she could have perceived what was taking place on the other side of the wall, at the moment she was leaving the house to come out into the garden, she would still have been as much at a loss to understand the meaning of what she would have seen.

The phenomena which presented themselves on that side of the brick and mortar screen fell out in this wise.

At a little more than half-past five o'clock, Frederick, true to his engagements, was giving the last instructions to a well-fed postboy in the yard of the Lindisfarn Arms hostel and posting-house. These instructions were that he should remain in readiness himself, his chaise, and his pair of horses (for Frederick considered that four horses would only serve to attract attention in a manner that was not desirable; and that the notion that four horses can draw a light chaise over a short stage more quickly than two is a mere popular delusion, unless, indeed, the stage should be a specially hilly one), within the safe seclusion of the innyard till six o'clock,—that he should then quietly come out, and proceeding by a certain back way, such as most Old-World English cities are provided with, towards the turnpike at the Castle Head, as it was called, which was very near the embouchure of the lane behind the doctor's garden into the road, should so come on towards the little door from which Margaret was to emerge, telling anybody who might question him—if the questioner were one to whom it was necessary to reply at all—that he, the postboy, was going to carry Dr. Lindisfarn up to the Chase to dinner—a perfectly reasonable and satisfactory reply, inasmuch as the doctor when going to the Chase usually did get into his chaise at the little garden-door, which, opening so near to the Castle Head turnpike, saved him a considerable *détour* through the town.

Nothing could have been better arranged. Jonas Wyvill, the postboy,—he was a cousin, I fancy, of those Wyvills one of whom was a verger in the cathedral, and another a superannuated gamekeeper up at the Chase, and "boy" as he was perennially in professional posting parlance, had long since reached a very discreet age,—Jonas Wyvill had pocketed his retaining fee, perfectly comprehended his instructions, got into the saddle at six punctually, precisely as the cathedral clock—that same bell to which Margaret had listened so nervously—struck the quarters, and quietly proceeded towards the place of rendezvous.

Frederick, fond and faithful, was standing on the other side of the little door at the moment that his beloved was tripping across the garden towards it. In another minute they would have been in each other's arms, and in the next dashing along the road on their way to Scotland.

What could have interrupted so suddenly the course of true love which had run smoothly so very nearly to the point of pouring itself into the ocean of connubial felicity?

Frederick was on the outside of the garden-door, with his ear close to the panel of it. It wanted just one minute to six; when, instead of the light step which he was straining his ear to catch the sound of on the other side of the wall, and which in another minute he would have heard, he became aware of a foot-fall of a very different character close to him in the lane. And the next instant he distinguished in the rapidly increasing darkness old Gregory Greatorex, his father's long-tried, trusty, and confidential clerk.

Old Greg Greatorex was one of those men who look like over-grown and ill-grown boys all the days of their lives. Old Greg was nearly sixty years old, and as gray as a badger. But still his gaunt, shambling figure had the peculiar effect above mentioned. Perhaps it was mainly occasioned by the fact that his body was very short in proportion to his long, flute likelegs. They seemed—those straggling, ill-shapen, knock-kneed, long legs—to be attached to his body rather after the fashion in which those of Punch's *dramatis personæ* are arranged than according to the more usual method of nature's handiwork.

Then he had no beard, or any other visible or traceable hair on his broad white face. Old Greg had lived, man and boy, with Mr. Falconer as long and rather longer than he could remember anything. And it would have been difficult to imagine any command of the banker which Gregory would not have faithfully executed, not exactly from affection for his master,—Greg Greatorex was not of a remarkably affectionate nature,—but simply because it seemed to his intelligence, part of the natural, necessary, and inevitable nature of things that it should be so.

"Come, come away, sir, quick! this instant! Thank the Lord, I'm in time!" panted the old man into Frederick's ear.

"Good God! Gregory, what do you mean? What are you come here for? Why, man, the governor's up to it," he whispered into the old clerk's ear.

"I know! *I* know, sir. The governor has sent me here now. It is a good job I am in time. The old gentleman would have run here himself, only he knew I could come fastest. I never saw him in such a way."

"What's up now, then? What is it, in Heaven's name, Gregory?"

"You must ask your father that, sir. There was no time to tell anything;—it was just touch and go! But all the fat is in the fire some way or another; and if this runaway job had n' come off, you would have been a ruined man, Mr. Frederick. I heard your father say *so* much."

"Good heavens! What am I to do?" whispered Frederick.

"Come away, sir, from here. Come to your father and hear all about it. Anyway, you may be quite sure there is to be no elopement to-night."

"And Margaret?—the lady, Gregory? What in the world am I to do about the lady? She will be here in a minute, if she is not at this moment waiting on the other side of this door."

"Leave her to wait, sir; she will soon find out that something has put the job off."

"She will never forgive me," sighed Frederick.

"It don't much signify whether she does or not, so far as I can understand," chuckled the old clerk. "But you can come and hear what your father has to tell you about it, and thank your stars that this business was put a stop to in time."

"But the chaise will be here in a minute, Gregory. There! it is striking six now! The chaise was to come out from the Lindisfarn Arms as it struck six."

"I'll go and meet it, sir, and turn it back, while you go to your father. It would come up the back lane to the Castle Head, I suppose?"

"Yes, you will meet it in the lane. It is old Jonas Wyvill; you must tell him that it is put off for to-night."

"Or rather that it is *not* 'off'; " said Greatorex, who had recovered breath enough for superfluous words by this time, and for a chuckle at his own wit.

They had withdrawn from the immediate vicinity of the door in the wall as the clock struck, but still spoke in whispers. Had Margaret opened the door a moment sooner than she did, she would have seen the two men, within a few paces of her. But they separated at the mouth of the little lane some fifty yards from the doctor's garden-door, as the last words were spoken,—the old clerk to meet and turn back Jonas Wyvill and the chaise; Frederick to hasten to his father's house in the Close, to learn the explanation of this most unexpected and unpleasant termination of the enterprise which had seemed on the eve of successful execution.

He did for one instant think of seeing his Margaret, and telling her, as best he might, that some *contretemps* had frustrated their plan for to-night, instead of thus brutally leaving her to the agonies of suspense, and slowly-growing conviction that it was a hopeless disappointment. But Frederick was not a very brave man, and he stood in no little fear of his gentle Marguerite. It would not, it may be admitted, have been a pleasant interview; and perhaps braver men than Frederick Falconer might have hesitated about facing the lady in the moment of her legitimate wrath. But it certainly was a cur's trick to sneak off and leave her as he did. But *que voulez-vous?* Figs *wont* grow on thistles.

CHAPTER XXXVII.

OF SLOWCOME AND SLIGO, BUT MORE ESPECIALLY
OF SLOWCOME.

THE business premises of Messieurs Slow-come and Sligo occupied the ground-floor of one of the best houses in the best part of the High Street of Silverton. It was, and was well known by everybody who knew anything in Silverton to be, one of the best, most roomy, and most substantial houses in the old city; but it by no means asserted itself as such by its onward appearance. There was a Grammar School of very ancient foundation at Silverton—so ancient that it looked down on all the crowd of Edward the Fourth and Elizabeth's foundations as mere mushroom growths, —and the venerable and picturesque, but very dingy and somewhat dilapidated-looking, collegiate buildings, stood in the High Street, withdrawing themselves with shy pride, as such old buildings often will, from the frontage line of the rest of the street, and shrinking backwards from the modern light, and the noise, and the traffic, some fifteen or eighteen feet to the rear, so as to leave a vacant space of that extent between the footpath of the modern street and the dark old Gothic frontage, the work of one of those centuries, which, inarticulate as they were in comparison to our own many-voiced times, yet contrived, somehow or other, to make the sermons that their stones preached very unmistakable and eloquent ones.

The old Grammar School had reason to be shy and retiring; for the fact was it had seen much better days. It had been richly endowed and wealthy in its time, with advowsons, and rent charges, and great tithes, and small tithes, and bits of fat land here and there all over the country. But things had gone very hard with the old college at the time of the Reformation. It had not been wholly and solely a school. A chantry with a choral establishment had been comprised in the intentions of the founder,—palpably superstitious uses, and flagrant in proportion to the amount of the wealth devoted to them,— and the old college had been very mercilessly pruned by those to whom all such things were an abomination. There was still one endowed mastership, a piece of preferment in the gift of the Principal and Fellows of Silverton College, Oxford; and there was one fellowship in the same college, to which no one save a scholar of the old school in the

High Street was eligible. Of course the master's son was duly sent up to Oxford to be endowed with this not severely contested fellowship, and, unless when the time came for appointing a new master to Silverton school he was already better provided for, the fellow so elected was usually sent back again to his native city in the character of master of the school.

There was also a "High Bursar" of the college. I do not suppose that many persons in Silverton, with the exception of the local antiquaries and historians, ever heard of this dignitary. What or whether any functions were discharged by the High Bursar, or whether any profit or other advantage accrued to that officer or to the "Grammar School and Chantry of St. Walport de Weston prope Silverton,"—as, despite all changes of manners and creeds, the old foundation still delighted to style itself, whenever its feeble senile voice could find force to make itself heard at all,—I am not aware. Nor do I at all know how, why, or by what authority the High Bursar became such. But I do know what few Silvertonians, I take it, did,—that Silas Slowcome, Esq., was the High Bursar; and I have been told that the memory of man in Silverton ran not to the contrary of the fact of a Slowcome occupying the same position. Nor do I know whether it was by virtue of the office so held that the reigning Slowcome always dwelt in the substantial but dim-looking old house I have been speaking of above, which was next to the school, standing back from the street like it, and which, as the local guide-books tell you, formerly constituted a part of the old foundation. I fancy, that it was, and is, the property of the school still, and probably about the only property remaining to it; and that the rent—not an excessive one probably—paid by the Messrs. Slowcome, with some addition, perhaps, from Silverton College, forms the main portion of the master's money endowment. The whole practice and theory of this High Bursarship is, however, an obscure subject. I know that old Slowcome always went accompanied by a clerk carrying an ancient-looking box, lettered "Grammar School and Chantry of St. Walport de Weston prope Silverton," into the old schoolroom on the morning of St. Walport's day, that he remained there with the master for perhaps three minutes; and that the master always dined with the High

Bursar on the evening of that day. I know, too, that old Slowcome, who had a son a gentleman commoner, at Silverton College, used to go up to Oxford now and then, and always dined at the high table in Hall when he did so. But this, beyond the fact of his inhabiting the old house by the side of the school buildings, is absolutely all I could ever learn about the connection between the High Bursar and the Walport's.

It is not to be supposed that the house as it at present exists is, though evidently older than its neighbors, by any means of the same date as the picturesque Gothic building by its side. No doubt it was entirely changed and modernized, when it was diverted from its original uses to that of a family dwelling-house. And the building as it now is dates probably from the beginning of the eighteenth or the close of the seventeenth century. It is very dingy-looking, especially on the ground-floor; on the upper floors, Mrs. Sligo, who, much to her discontent, is compelled to live there, takes care that all that paint and washing can do to brighten it up shall not be neglected. The windows and door-posts, however, of the ground-floor in the front of the house are yellow with the effect of time. The great black hall-door in the centre, between its heavy stone columns, stands open—like gate of black Dis—at least during business hours, and admits all who choose to enter into a large hall, closed on the opposite side by a modern glazed door, on which is a brass plate, bearing the names of Slowcome and Sligo. One large room to the right of this entrance is, or at least forty years ago was, occupied entirely by a vast quantity of boxes, some of wood and some of metal, with the names of most of the Sillshire aristocracy painted on them. There were heavy bars before the windows of this prison-like room, and other internal precautions both against fire and thieves. Another equally large room on the other side of the entrance was fitted up as a clerk's office, and was tenanted by the younger members of the legal family. The principals of the firm, and the managing clerk, Mr. Benjamin Wyvill,—(it is curious how, in small old-fashioned country towns, not much exposed to changes by emigration or immigration, the same names occur again and again in various strata of the body social) —the principals and Mr. Wyvill, I say, had their rooms at the much pleasanter and brighter-looking back of the house.

The upper part of the building was inhabited, as has been mentioned, by the Sligos; and was in truth a very much better residence than Mrs. Sligo could have hoped to enjoy elsewhere. Nevertheless, that lady, who was not of Sillshire birth, but who held rather a remarkable position in the Silverton world, and who was indeed herself a remarkable woman,—though I fear I may hardly have an opportunity of making the reader acquainted with her in the course of this history.—Mrs. Sligo, I say, was much discontented with the arrangement. The senior partner resided with his wife and family in an extremely pretty little villa residence just outside the town on the top of the high ground behind the cathedral, looking toward the Lindisfarn woods. The firm had been Slowcome and Sligo for more than two generations, the senior partner always maintaining his position in it. The present Mr. Slowcome was an old man, and the present Mr. Sligo a young one, who had inherited his late father's share of the business.

On that same day on which Frederick and Margaret were to have emancipated themselves, in the manner that has been described, from bondage to Mr. Slowcome's parchments and papers, that gentleman was sitting as usual at his work in his warm and comfortable room at the back of the old house in the High Street. There he sat at his library table, thickly strewn with papers, very leisurely writing a letter. Whatever old Slowcome did, he did it leisurely. Whenever any old acquaintance came into his room, he would speak of the tremendous press of business, which made it impossible ever to get away from the office. And, in truth, he never did get away from the office, save on Sundays. There was no vacation-time for him. He lived always in his office from ten o'clock in the morning till five in the evening, and often till a much later hour. For if anything chanced to detain him, his principles as to the duty of punctuality at his own dinner-table proved to be of the loosest description, as Mrs. Slowcome was wont bitterly to complain. And yet when thus enlarging to any chance comer upon the grievous burden of his work, and the insufficiency of the hours of the day for the doing of it, he would spend half an hour in chatting over the subject. He never seemed to be in a hurry, and though always behindhand, always kept plodding on with a slow, steady sort of tortoise-like pertinacity, which, it must be supposed, did contrive to transact the business to be done somehow or other. For Slowcome and Sligo had the business of almost all the gentry of Sillshire in their hands, and the business did not come to grief, and none of their customers ever dreamed of leaving the old firm.

On the contrary, old Slowcome was one of the most highly respected men in Sillshire.

Nor was it at all true that Slowcome was a beast, as Frederick had protested to Margaret, in his indignation,—not at all. Old Slowcome was nearly seventy years old, and he was and had been all his life an attorney-at-law. It is true that he had a bald round head, with a pigtail, rather aggressive in its expression, sticking horizontally out behind it, and a comfortable little round protuberance in front of him, from the apex of which dangled a somewhat exuberant gold watch-chain with three or four extra sized seals appended to it, which swayed and swagged in a manner that perhaps rather too ostentatiously spoke of their owner being able to pay his way, and being beholden to no man ; true also that the extraordinarily ample frills of his shirt-fronts, always exquisitely plaited, perked themselves up rather aggravatingly ; that his white waistcoat, black coat, ditto shorts, with their gold buckles at the knees, black silk stockings, irreproachably drawn over somewhat thick and short legs, and admirably blacked square-toed shoes, all carried with them a certain air of self-assertion ; true, moreover, that nobody ever suspected any past or present member of the firm of Slowcome and Sligo of wearing their hearts upon their sleeves ; and undeniably true that if you asked Mr. Slowcome any question the answer to which you were waiting for with breathless suspense, he would always take a huge pinch of snuff, in the most leisurely manner, before answering you. Still, all these things do not make a man utterly a beast.

It may be admitted, perhaps, that old Slowcome, as observed in his little round, low-backed Windsor chair, in his office, was not apt to strike a student of mankind, visiting him there, as a genial, lovely, or large-hearted specimen of the *genus homo ;* that the specific differentiation was more obtrusively prominent than the generic characteristics, and the man was, in some degree, merged in the

attorney. Yet in that pretty little suburban villa, up near the Castle Head, where the whole place, from the overarched entrance gateway, all round the shrubberies, enclosing the exquisitely shaven lawn, to the porch of the elegant little dwelling, seemed to be one bower of roses, wherein a Mother Slowcome and three blossoming daughters were nested ; there it may be that old Slowcome was recognized as human, and that the man reasserted, for a few all too fleeting hours, his ascendency over the attorney. It is possible to imagine, even, that the time may have been when he himself was impatient for the approaching day of his union with her who has been the presiding genius of Arcady Lodge for now more than forty years,—possible that he, also, may in his green and inexperienced youth, have cursed the law's delay, and the tardiness of the drawers of draft settlements. There must have been memories. Daughters must exercise a humanizing influence even on an attorney-at-law ! He can talk to his sons of capiases, and suchlike ; but he must come out from among these to hold converse with his daughters. Even if rating them for permitting a garrison captain to dangle after them in their progress up the High Street, from the circulating library and fine art emporium of Mr. Glossable to the workshop of little Miss Piper over the perfumer's, he does not, I suppose, ask them *quo warranto* they so offended. No ! there must have been humanizing influences at Arcady Lodge. The mischief was that old Slowcome was there for so small a portion of his existence. And Mrs. Slowcome complained that he got worse and worse, in the matter of coming home too late for dinner. He seemed, literally, to have lost all perception of the lapse of time, and would go on prosing and boring, as if the minutes were not growing into hours the while.

The dinner-hour at Arcady Lodge was half-past five ; and Mr. Slowcome ought to have left his office at four. The great outer door was shut at that time ; and the junior clerk was punctual enough in performing *that* duty. But that did not get old Slow, as the young men in the office called him, out of his room. And people knew very well that he was, in all probability, to be found there long after office-hours ; and would come and knock at the door, to the infinite disgust of the smart young gent who had to open it, and who, after having once replied, "After office hours," as shortly and sharply as the appearance of the applicant made it safe for him to do, dared not answer in the negative to the reiterated demand, "Is Mr. Slowcome now in the house?"

It was just about the hour for shutting, on the day on which Frederick, as the reader knows, did *not* run off with Margaret Lindisfarn, that a person called at the office of Messrs. Slowcome and Sligo in the High Street.

"Mr. *Sligo* is in his room," said the clerk, knowing very well that no visitor, be his errand what it might, would keep *that* gentleman at the office beyond the proper hour for shutting, whereas he might likely enough detain old Slow, and consequently himself, the young gent in question,—which was of much greater consequence,—for the next three hours. Either of the elder clerks of Messrs. Slowcome and Sligo would probably have known the stranger by sight; but the young gent, who had only recently been promoted to his stool, had never seen him before, and could not make him out at all.

He was a remarkably handsome, and yet not a prepossessing, man, even to the not as yet perfectly developed and cultivated æsthetic sentiments of young Bob Scott, the clerk in question. He was unusually tall, and slenderly made. But there was a something sinister in the expression of the handsome features, and repulsive in the swagger of self-assertion, which had been generated by an habitual feeling of the need of it, and which produced its effect on Bob Scott, though he could not have explained as much in words. Then, the style of the stranger's dress was objectionable to men and gods. A somewhat loudly smart style of toilet would not have offended the taste of the youthful Bob Scott. A grave propriety would have commanded his respect. Even consistent shabbiness, though it might have added some sharpness to the tone of Bob's reply, would have failed to arouse the sentiment of suspicion and dislike with which he viewed the applicant for an interview with the head of the firm. A very threadbare pair of Oxford-mixture trousers, ending in still more dilapidated boots, clothed the lower part of his person, and might with propriety enough, have formed the costume of some member of Bob Scott's

own profession, at odds with fortune. But a green cut-away coat, much weather-stained, and a bright blue, exuberant, and very smart neck-handkerchief, seemed quite out of character with any such theory; and a shallow-crowned, broad-brimmed hat, put on very much over one knowing-looking eye, seemed neither to belong to any of the walks of life to which the trousers and boots might be supposed to belong, nor to the "horsy" sporting style of the man's upper habiliments. In short, Bob Scott could make nothing out of him except that he was a very queer customer.

"Mr. *Sligo* is in his room!" said Bob.

"I said nothing about Mr. Sligo," returned the stranger; "I asked if Mr. Slowcome was here. If not, I must go up to him at the Castle Head, that's all."

"Yes, Mr. Slowcome is in. I'll ask him if he chooses to see you," said Bob, sulkily, taking the stranger's measure with a stare that travelled all over him leisurely, without the least attempt to disguise itself.

"What are you going to ask him?" said the stranger.

"Why, if he'll see you, if that's what you want," said Bob.

"See who, you blockhead?"

"Come, I say! I'll trouble you to speak civilly, whoever you are!" remonstrated Bob, in very considerable indignation.

"You don't half know your business, young man. Go and tell old Slow that Mr. Jared Mallory, of Sillmouth, wants to speak to him on business of importance."

"Mr. Jared Mallory, of Sillmouth!" repeated Bob; "oh, how was I to know?"

So he left Mr. Mallory at the door, and in a minute came back to say that Mr. Slowcome would see him.

The reader has already made the acquaintance of one Mr. Jared Mallory; but it will be seen at once that the man standing at the door of Messrs. Slowcome and Sligo's office is not the same individual. It was his son; Mr. Jared Mallory, junior, attorney-at-law, of Sillmouth, was the son of old Jared Mallory, the parish clerk at Chewton, and the brother of Bab Mallory, "the moorland wild-flower," whom we last saw clambering up the side of the *Saucy Sally*, to be received on that vessel's deck by Julian Lindisfarn, on his way back to France.

CHAPTER XXXVIII.
A PAIR OF ATTORNEYS.

MR. JARED MALLORY of Sillmouth, attorney-at-law, had a practice there of a rather peculiar sort, not quite so profitable as it ought to have been in proportion to its extent, and in consideration of the not always agreeable nature of the business involved in it. Still it was a kind of business that suited the man. He was an attorney and so was Slowcome. But the lives and occupations of no two men could be more different; and no amount of reward, in cash, Arcady Villas, and respectability, could have induced Jared Mallory to sit seven or eight hours in a snug, warm office every day of his life. The nature of the population of Sillmouth, and the circumstance of the elder Mallory's connection with one class of its inhabitants, will suffice to explain as far as needs be the general nature of that branch of business to which Mr. Mallory, junior, devoted himself. It was not a class of business which was in the ordinary nature of things calculated to make a man nice or scrupulous; nor was it at all of a nature likely to bring Mr. Mallory into contact with the members of that sleek, prosperous, and eminently respectable firm, the Messieurs Slowcome and Sligo, of Silverton; so that the Sillmouth attorney was very nearly, though not absolutely a stranger to his compeer of Silverton.

"Mr. Mallory, of Sillmouth, I believe," said old Slowcome, half rising from his chair for an instant as his visitor entered, and then very deliberately putting his double gold eyeglass on his nose, and as leisurely looking him over from head to foot.

"Yes, Mr. Slowcome. We have met before— But you gentlemen in our old-fashioned little Sillshire metropolis here hold your heads so mighty high—that "—

"Nevertheless, Mr. Mallory," replied Mr. Slowcome, very deliberately, and almost, we might say, sleepily, and provokingly accepting and avowing as a fact which admitted of no dispute, the Sillmouth attorney's statement of the wide social space which separated them from each other,—"ne—ver—the—less, Mis—ter Mal—lo—ry, I shall be very happy to give you my best at—ten—ti—on."

"Not a doubt about that, Mr. Slowcome !" returned Mallory, nettled, and eying the respectable man with a glance of malicious triumph,—" not a shadow of a doubt or mistake about that, as soon as you shall have heard the nature of my business."

"And pray what may the nature of that business be—a—Mis—ter Mallory?" said old Slow, with the most imperturbable and aggravating composure, speaking the words with a *staccato* sort of movement, as if some self-adjusting utterance measurer were ticking them off and making them up into six-and-eightpenny worths. "You must excuse me if press of business compels me to observe that my time is very precious," he continued, still speaking in the most leisurely manner, and throwing himself back in his chair, as he crossed one fat, silk-covered calf over its brother's knee, and pushed up his gold eyeglasses on his forehead, as if to peer out under them at his visitor.

"Oh, yes. Of course, of course. I'm in a deuce of a hurry myself,—always am ; but duty to a client, you know, Mr. Slowcome, and—very important case—delicate matter ; you understand."

"Ay—ay—ay ! Mister Mallory, I dare say you have many cases of a—hum—de—li—cate description ;" and old Slow nodded his chin and his gold eyeglasses and his bald round head up and down with the slow, regular motion of the piston-rod of a steam-engine.

"Not such as brings me here to-day though, Mis—ter Slow—come," said Mallory, winking at that outraged old gentleman. "I do not wish to be abrupt, nor to distress you more than is inevitable,—in—evitable, I am sorry to say ; but I may mention at once that my business is of a nature calculated to be disagreeable to you."

"Ay,—ay,—ay," said old Slow, without a shadow of variation in his tone or manner. "And what may the disagreeable business be, Mr. Mallory?" he added, nursing his leg with infinite complacency ?

"I believe your firm are solicitors to the Lindisfarns, Mr. Slowcome?"

"Any business matters touching Mr. Lindisfarn, of Lindisfarn Chase, may with propriety be communicated to me, Mr. Mallory, and shall receive my best attention."

"If I am not misinformed, I may consider you as the legal friend of Dr. Lindisfarn, of the Close, also?"

"You may consider me as perfectly ready to hear anything which it may be useful for my good friend, Dr. Lindisfarn, that I should

14

hear," said the old man, with an appearance of perfect nonchalance, though in fact he was observing his visitor's face all the time with the keenest scrutiny.

"The Lindisfarn estates — magnificent property it is, Mr. Slowcome — were entailed, I believe, by the late Oliver Lindisfarn, Esq., the father of the present possessor, on the issue male of his eldest son, Oliver, and failing such issue, on the issue male of his younger son, Theophilus; failing such issue also, the daughters of the elder son become seised in tail. I believe I am correct in stating such to have been the disposition?" said Mr. Mallory, pausing for a reply.

"Very possibly it may have been. I cannot pretend to carry all the dispositions ruling the descent of half the estates in Sillshire in my head, Mr. Mallory. It would be too much to expect, you know,—really altogether too much. And it would be very easy to look into the matter,—if anybody authorized or justified in making the inquiry were to ask for information."

"Quite so, Mr. Slowcome, quite so. I admire caution myself, Mr. Slowcome. There is nothing like it!"

"Well, sir?"

"Well, sir, Mr. Oliver Lindisfarn has no sons. He has two daughters. Dr. Theophilus Lindisfarn had a son, Julian, who, under his grandfather's will, became heir in tail to the estates. I believe that even you, Mr. Slowcome, will have no difficulty in admitting the facts so far?"

"Well, sir?"

"Julian Lindisfarn, the son of Dr. Lindisfarn, of the Close, some ten years or so ago, left Silverton, under circumstances which it is not now necessary to speak of more particularly, and was understood to have afterward died in America."

"Well, sir?"

"The facts as I have stated them are of public notoriety. The heir in tail died; the daughters of the elder brother became heiresses to the estates. Nothing clearer or more simple! But what should you say, Mr. Slowcome, if I were to tell you that Julian Lindisfarn did not die in America?"

"I am surprised, Mr. Mallory, that a gentleman of your experience should put such a question to me!" said old Slow, leaning his head on one side, and smiling pleasantly and

tranquilly at his visitor. "Surely, it must occur to you," he continued, speaking very leisurely, "that I should say nothing at all, not being called upon to do so,—not being called on, you see, Mr. Mallory."

"Well, Mr. Slowcome, say nothing at all. I don't want you to say anything. I give you the information, free, gratis, for nothing. I tell you that Julian Lindisfarn did not die in America. He was supposed to have been killed by the Indians. He was nearly killed, —but not quite."

Mr. Slowcome bowed in return for this free, gratis communication, but said nothing.

"Do you feel called upon, Mr. Slowcome, may I ask, to pay any attention to the statement I have made?"

"Well, really, Mr. Mallory, I cannot say that I do; to speak quite frankly, I do not see that I am called on to pay any attention to it."

It was by this time much too late for Mr. Slowcome, by any possibility, to reach Arcady Lodge, where Mrs. and the three Misses Slowcome were discontentedly coming to the conclusion that they must sit down to table without papa again, in time for his dinner. But he did not on that account show the slightest symptom of impatience, or even accelerate his own part of the interview, either in matter or manner, one jot.

"And yet," pursued Mallory, "the fact would be a somewhat important one to your clients at the Chase, and not less so to those in the Close."

"That is perfectly true, Mr. Mallory; the facts you speak of would undoubtedly have important consequences, if authenticated —if authenticated, you know, Mr. Mallory."

"Oh, there will be no difficulty about that!—authentication enough, and to spare. Julian Lindisfarn was alive at Sillmouth, a few days ago."

"If Julian Lindisfarn be really, as you state, alive, in spite of the very great improbability that he should have, during all this time, allowed his family to suppose him dead, and if he can prove his identity to the satisfaction of a jury, the young ladies at the Chase would consequently not be the heirs to the property."

"And what if I were further to tell you, Mr. Slowcome, that although Julian Lindisfarn was alive, and at Sillmouth,—and I am in a position to prove these facts beyond the possibility of doubt or cavil,—what, I say, if I were further to tell you, that he is now dead?"

" The latter statement would, I should imagine, so far diminish the importance of the former as to make it hardly worth while inquiring whether it could be authenticated or not. The young ladies at Lindisfarn would be heiresses to the property, as they have always been supposed to be; and it would apparently matter very little, at what precise date they became such," said Slowcome, a little thrown off his guard by the prospect, unexpectedly thus hung out to him for a moment, that, after all, there was no coming trouble to be feared.

" Now you must forgive me, Slowcome, if I say that I am astonished that you, of all men in the world, should jump at a conclusion in that way! If it had been the young gent who opened the door of your office to me just now—but, really, for a gentleman of your experience "—

" May I ask what is the conclusion I have jumped at, Mister Mallory?" said old Slow, as placidly as ever, but with a very marked emphasis on the " Mister," intended to rebuke the Sillmouth attorney for venturing to address him as " Slowcome."

Mr. Mallory perceived and perfectly well understood the hint. " Very good," thought he to himself; " it is all very well *Mr.* Slowcome ; but we'll come a little nearer to a level, perhaps, before I have done."

" Why, you have jumped at *this* conclusion, Mr. Slowcome," said he, in reply to the old gentleman's last words,—" that if Julian Lindisfarn died a short time since, it puts matters into the same position as if he had died years ago. Suppose he has left heirs? How about that, Mr. Slowcome?"

" It is true that for the moment I had lost sight of that contingency. But really, Mr. Mallory, this mere gossip, though exceedingly agreeable, I am sure, *as* gossip, is so unimportant in any more serious point of view that one may well be excused for not bringing one's legal wits to bear upon it. No doubt, again, if Julian Lindisfarn has left an heir male, legitimate and capable of being undisputably authenticated as such, that heir would inherit the Lindisfarn property."

" The fact is, Mr. Slowcome, though I could not refrain from being down upon you for making such an oversight, it would have come to the same thing whether Julian Lindisfarn had died in America years ago, or when he did. He has left a son born before he left this country for America."

" A son born in wedlock, Mr. Mallory?"

" Of course. I should not be here to give you and myself trouble by talking of an illegitimate child."

" Am I to understand, then, that you come to me, Mr. Mallory, as the legal representative of the child in question, and that you are prepared to put forward a claim to the Lindisfarn property on his behalf?"

" You could not have stated the case more accurately, Mr. Slowcome, if you had tried for an hour! That is exactly it. I come to make, and in due course to establish, the claim of Julian Lindisfarn, an infant, son of Julian Lindisfarn, formerly of the Close in Silverton, and of Barbara Mallory, his lawful wife, to be declared heir-at-law to the lands and hereditaments of Lindisfarn."

" Son of Julian Lindisfarn and of Barbara Mallory, you say, Mr. Mallory. Any relative, may I ask?" said Slowcome, in the most indifferent manner in the world, but shooting a sharp glance at the provincial lawyer from under his eyebrows as he spoke.

" Yes; Barbara Lindisfarn, formerly Barbara Mallory, the widow of the late, and mother of the present, heir to the property, is my sister. But as that fact is wholly unessential to the matter in hand I did not think it necessary to trouble you with it."

" Nay, it is one of the many facts that may perhaps—*may*, you know—be felt to have a bearing in the case, when it goes before a jury. Miss Mallory, your sister, was a native of Chewton in the Moor, if I mistake not?"

" Yes, she was, though I do not see what that has to do with the matter in hand any more than her being my sister has."

" Not at all, not at all! Only it seems to me as if I could remember having heard something years ago about that unfortunate young man in connection with Chewton in the Moor. Yes, surely, surely, it was at Chewton in the Moor!"

" It was at Chewton in the Moor that Julian Lindisfarn met with Barbara Mallory, if you mean that,—at Chewton in the

Moor that he was married to her, and at Chewton in the Moor that his son was born."

" Ay, ay, ay, ay ! Born subsequently to the marriage, of course ? " said old Slow, with a very shrewd look out of the corner of his eye at the other.

" Subsequently to the marriage ! Of course. Why, what the devil do you mean to insinuate, Mr. Slowcome ? "

" I insinuate ! Oh, dear, me, I never insinuated anything in my life ! When I don't make a statement, I ask a question. I only mean to ask a question for information's sake, you know."

" All right, Mr. Slowcome ; and I am happy to be able to give you the information you wish. Yes, the child, Julian Lindisfarn, was born in due time and season, so as to entitle him as fully to the name as he is entitled to the estates of Lindisfarn."

" And now Julian Lindisfarn, the father, is truly and certainly dead, at last, you say, Mr. Mallory."

" Yes ; he died on the night of the twentieth of this month, at sea ; and his death can be proved by several eye-witnesses of it."

" Have you any objection to say under what circumstances it took place ? "

" None in the world, my dear sir, not the least in the world, if the press of business, and the value of your precious time, which you were speaking of just now, will allow you leisure to listen to such matters."

" Well, I can mostly find time for doing what has to be done, Mr. Mallory. I am naturally interested, you know, in the fate of that poor young man, whom I can remember as handsome a lad as I ever saw. His father is an old and valued friend of mine. And then, you know we are not engaged in business,—mere gossip,—mere idle chat, you know. Of course, when we come to talk of these things in earnest, we must look into documents,—do—cu—ments, Mr. Mallory. which alone are of any avail in such matters. And how did the poor young man come to his death ? On the twentieth—dear me ! Only the other day."

" Only the other day, Mr. Slowcome. Ay ! we are here to-day, and gone to-morrow, as the saying is. And that was specially his case, poor fellow, as one may say, for he was, as I told you, at Sillmouth, and, it seems,

had been ill, or wounded in some fray, or something of the kind, and so had been prevented from returning to France, whence, as I am given to understand, he had come. I have not troubled myself to obtain any accurate information upon all these points, seeing that they do not in any way bear on the important facts of the matter. What is certain is that the unfortunate young man engaged a passage for himself, his wife, and child, by a vessel called the *Saucy Sally*, of which one Hiram Pendleton was master and owner ; that he sailed in her on the evening of the twentieth, in company with Mrs. Lindisfarn and their child ; and that when off the coast of France on that night,—or rather on the following morning—it being very dark and foggy at the time, the *Saucy Sally* was run down by a larger vessel, the *Deux Maries* of Dunkirk, in which accident the passenger Julian Lindisfarn, as well as two others of the crew, perished. The body of one of the two sailors and that of Mr. Lindisfarn were recovered, and identified ; of which due certificates and vouchers can be furnished by the French authorities ; so that there is no doubt of his being dead this time, beyond the possibility of a mistake."

" And the lady who was with him, and the child ? " asked Mr. Slowcome, who had listened to the above statement with more evident attention and interest than he had previously condescended to bestow upon Mr. Mallory's communications.

" The mother and the child were both saved by the exertions of Hiram Pendleton, the owner and skipper of the unlucky craft. He succeeded in placing both of them on the deck of the French vessel, and subsequently in saving himself in the same manner ; though it seems by all accounts to have been touch and go with him."

" Hiram Pendleton ; ay, ay, ay, ay ! So it was Hiram Pendleton who saved the mother and child ? " said old Slow musingly.

" Yes, indeed ; and at great risk of his own life too, so it would seem."

" And lost his vessel ; dear, dear, dear ! " rejoined Slowcome, still musing.

" Yes, saved his passengers, and lost his ship. I suppose the loss will make Hiram Pendleton something like a ruined man."

" I have heard, I think, that he and the king's revenue officers were sometimes apt to differ in their views of things in general."

"Maybe so, Mr. Slowcome. I don't know much of him, and nothing of his affairs."

"No, no, of course not. It is not likely you should. How should you, Mr. Mallory? But now, as to this extraordinary and really very interesting story, which you have been telling me, perhaps it would suit you to mention when the do—cu—ments will be forthcoming. Of course without seeing the do—cu—ments I should not be justified in giving the matter any serious attention at all."

"Well, Mr. Slowcome, as far as satisfying you that you would *not* be justified in omitting to give the matter your most serious and immediate attention, and to lay the circumstances at once before your clients,—as far as that goes, I think I may be able to do *that* before we bring this sitting to a conclusion. Allow me to call your attention, sir, to these two documents, copies, you will observe; I do not carry the originals about in my pocket, as you will easily understand; but they can and will be produced in due time and place;" and the Sillmouth attorney drew from the breast-pocket of his very unprofessional-looking cut-away green coat, a pocket-book, from which he selected from among several other papers, two small strips. "The first," continued he, with glib satisfaction, "is, you will observe, a copy of the marriage certificate of Barbara Mallory with Julian Lindisfarn, Esquire, duly extracted from the register of Chewton Church, by the Rev. Charles Mellish, who performed the ceremony, and attested under his hand."

"Ay, ay, ay, ay! I see, yes. The paper seems to be what you state; and the other?"

"The other is a copy of certain affidavits duly made and attested, sworn by the medical man and nurse, who attended Mrs. Lindisfarn in her confinement, serving to remove any doubt which might arise respecting the date of the child's birth."

"Would it not be simpler and more satisfactory to produce the baptismal register?" said Mr. Slowcome, while closely examining the papers submitted to him.

"Simpler, certainly, it would be," returned Mr. Mallory; "but I do not see that it would be at all more satisfactory. But, the fact is, we have been driven to this mode of proof by the impossibility of finding any register at Chewton."

"Ay, indeed! impossibility of finding any register at Chewton?" rejoined old Slow, with the same appearance of almost careless indifference which he had hitherto maintained; but with the shrewd gleam of awakened interest in his eye, which did not escape the practised observation of his sharp companion. "May I ask if the other document has been confronted with the original record in the register?"

"No such register can be found at Chewton, Mr. Slowcome," returned Mallory. "No doubt the loss of the baptismal register, and that of the marriage register, is the loss of one and the same volume. When old Mellish, the late curate, died, about eight years ago, no register could be found. I don't know whether you are at all aware, Mr. Slowcome, what sort of a person Mr. Mellish was —the strangest creature!—about as much like one of your respectable city clergy here as a tame pigeon in one of your town dovecots is like a woodpigeon. He had lived all alone there out in the Moor, without wife or child, all his life, till he was as wild as the wildest of the Moorfolk. Things went on in a queer way in his parish. If the Saturday night's carouse went too far into the small hours of the Sunday morning, the inhabitants were not so unreasonable as to expect any morning service, and waited very patiently till the Sunday afternoon; and then my father—my father was and still is clerk of Chewton, Mr. Slowcome—my father used to go and see what condition the parson was in, before he rang the bell. Oh, it was a queer place, was Chewton in the Moor, in old Mellish's time! It was thought that he had probably kept the registers at his own residence, and every search was made, but all to no purpose. Births and marriages don't take place in that small population—only a few hundreds, Mr. Slowcome!—so often as to cause the register to be very constantly needed, you know."

"Ay, ay, ay! a very remarkable state of things. And your good father was parish clerk during the curacy of this exemplary gentleman, Mr. Mallory?"

"He was, Mr. Slowcome; and has been so, and is so still, under his successor, a very different sort of a man. If matters did not go on worse than they did in old Mellish's days, it was mainly due to my father, who was far more fitted to be the parson, in every respect, than the drunken old curate, though I say it who should not, Mr. Slowcome.''

"Nay, nay! I do not see any reason why you should not say so, since such was the case. But I suppose that even at Chewton it was the custom for a marriage to be solemnized before witnesses, Mr. Mallory?''

"Well, I should not wonder if that was very much as it happened. With a parson who saw double, one witness would easily do for two, you know ; he, he, he!—but, however, there were two witnesses to my sister's marriage, as you will see by reference to the copy before you. My father took care that it was all right in her case, you may swear.''

"Ay, ay, ay, ay! I see, I see—' James Martinscombe, of the Back Lane, Sillmouth,' and ' Benjamin Brandreth, of Chew Haven.' These witnesses, I suppose, will be forthcoming at need, Mr. Mallory?''

"Martinscombe will not, certainly, poor fellow. He was a friend of mine, Mr. Slowcome, and is since dead. Of Brandreth we have not been able to hear anything. He was a shipowner and master, of Chew Haven ; and, I believe, a friend of my father's. He sailed, it seems, from Chew Haven, some five or six years ago, and has not been heard of since.''

"Dear me! What, neither he, nor his ship, nor any of his crew? Are the shipowners of Chew Haven (I don't know what sort of a place it is) apt to disappear in that way?''

"Chew Haven is a poor little place enough, —just a little bit of a fishing village, at the mouth of the creek that runs down off the Moor past Chewton. And, I take it, the fact was, that Brandreth was in reduced circumstances. I don't know that he was on a vessel of his own when he left Chew Haven and came back no more. No. It would have been satisfactory to find the witnesses, no doubt. But witnesses wont live forever, no more than other men. And failing the living men, I need not tell you, Mr. Slowcome, that their signature to the register is as good evidence as if they were to rise from the grave to speak it.''

"No doubt, no doubt, Mr. Mallory. But we have not got their signature to the register,—only the parson's copy of it —and I have seen only the copy of that, you know.''

"The curate's extract from the register,

duly made, signed, and certified in proper form, will be forthcoming in due time, Mr. Slowcome, and that is undeniable evidence, as you are well aware. Old Mellish's handwriting was a very peculiar one ; and abundant evidence may be got as to that point.''

"Well, Mr. Mallory,'' said Slowcome, suddenly, after a short pause, during which he had all the appearance of being on the point of dropping off to sleep, but was, in fact, deeply meditating the points of the statement that had been made to him,—"well, Mr. Mallory, of course, I can say nothing to all this. You allege a marriage between the late Julian Lindisfarn, recently deceased, under such painful circumstances, and your sister, Miss Barbara Mallory. Of course, every part of the evidence of such a statement must be expected to be subjected to the severest possible scrutiny ; of course, you are as much aware of that as I can be. Of course, we say nothing. You will take such steps as seem good to you ; and, in the mean time, I am much obliged to you for favoring me with this visit. Good-morning, Mr. Mallory.''

"Good-morning, Mr. Slowcome. Of course it would be most agreeable and best for all the parties concerned, if such a family affair could be settled quietly and amicably,—of course it would. But we are ready for war or peace, whichever your clients may decide.''

"Thank you, Mr. Mallory ; of course, in reply to any such observation, I can say nothing,—absolutely nothing, upon the present occasion. Your statement shall receive all consideration, and the family will decide on the course to be pursued. Good-morning, Mr. Mallory.''

And so the Sillmouth attorney bowed himself out, to the infinite relief of Mr. Bob Scott, who had begun to think that, if Slowcome and Sligo intended to keep their office open day and night, he had better look out for another service.

CHAPTER XXXIX.

MR. FALCONER IS ALARMED.

WHEN his visitor was gone, Mr. Slowcome sat still in his Windsor chair, apparently in deep meditation, so long, that the hardly used Bob Scott really began to give it up as a bad job, for that night at least. At last, however, he heard the old gentleman get up from his chair, and proceed to put on his great-coat. So he came out of the dingy, prison-like office, in which he was condemned to pass his days, and which he had already made utterly dark, by putting up the shutters, so that he might lose no time in being off home when at last old Slow should think fit to bring his day's work to an end, and stood by the side of the hall-door, ready to let his master out, and to follow him as soon as he had gone half a dozen steps from the door.

But, just as Mr. Slowcome at last appeared at the door of his room, leisurely buttoning up his great-coat, as he came out into the hall, Mr. Bob Scott was startled by another sharp rap at the door close to him. Springing to open it, with the hope of getting rid of the applicant before old Slow could catch sight of him, he found himself in the worshipful presence of Mr. Falconer, the banker.

Bob Scott's face fell, and the sharp, angry " After office-hours ! " to be accompanied by a slamming-to of the door in the new-comer's face, died away upon his lips.

" Is Mr. Slowcome within ? " said the banker.

" Yes, sir, *he's* within," said Bob, with a deep sigh ; " but I think, sir, he has put his great-coat on to go. It's *long* past office-hours, *you* know, sir. But we don't count hours here, oh, dear, no, nothing of the kind ! "

" Well, ask Mr. Slowcome if he will allow me to speak to him, for just one minute ; I wont keep him a minute."

" Just one minute," Bob muttered to himself, as he turned away to execute the banker's behest,—" just one minute ! As if old Slow could say, ' How do you do ?' under five minutes. It takes him that to open his blessed old easy-going mouth."

" Walk in, please, sir. Mr. Slowcome *has* got his great-coat on, sir ; but he'll be happy to see you," added the despondent youth, returning into the hall.

" Only one word, my dear Slowcome, one word ! No, I wont sit down, thank you ; I only just looked in to ask you how we were getting on ? The young folks are growing desperately impatient."

" Ay, ay, ay ! I suppose so, I suppose so. Well, we were all young once. But, Mr. Falconer," and old Slow deliberately stepped across the room and closed the door, which the banker, meaning only to say one hurried word, had not shut behind him, " I am very glad you happened to look in ; for I have just this instant had a very strange visit, which may very possibly—possibly, I say— cause some little delay in bringing this matter to a satisfactory conclusion."

" Delay ! " replied the banker, evidently ill at ease ; " why, there is nothing wrong, I hope,—nothing "—

" Well ! that we shall see ; I hope not, I sincerely hope not ; but "—

" For Heaven's sake, my dear sir, what is it ? Pray speak out."

" Well, yes, to you, Falconer ; but it is a delicate matter. However, in your position —Lindisfarn settles, you know, half the property on Miss Margaret."

" Yes, a very proper settlement, surely ? "

" Oh, very, very,—if—he have the power to make it ! " said the old lawyer, dropping his words out, one after the other, like the ominous drop, drop of heavy blood-drops on a pavement.

" Power to make it—Lindisfarn ? And you have just had a strange visit ? What is it ? What difficulty or doubt can there be ? "

" I suppose you know the history of the entail of the property ? Male heir of Oliver, eldest son ;—failure of male issue there, male heir of Theophilus, younger son ; failing male issue there, return to female children of eldest brother."

" Yes, yes, of course ! I know all that ; all the country knows it."

" Just so, just so. You no doubt know also the circumstances under which Dr. Theophilus Lindisfarn, having had a son, became childless ; in consequence of which event, the estates reverted to the daughters of the elder brother ? "

" To be sure I do ; nobody better. I remember all the circumstances as well as if they had happened yesterday. I have reason to, by George ! But the poor fellow died ; and there is an end of that—killed in America by the savages. A great mercy, too, for all parties concerned, between you and me, Mr. Slowcome. Quite a providential arrangement ! "

" Oh ! quite so—if it had been carried out. But what if Providence neglected that means of making all snug and comfortable. Suppose the story of the murder by the Indians was all false?"

"What! you don't mean to say"—stammered the banker, turning pale.

"Yes, I do; just so, just that," said old Slow, making a balancing piston-rod of his chin and pigtail; "at least," he added, "that is what I have been told by a man who left this office not two minutes before you entered it."

"Good Heavens! That man alive still! And the result, therefore, is, that the Misses Lindisfarn have no longer any claim to be their father's heirs?"

"Precisely so, Mr. Falconer. That is the very lamentable and unfortunate state of the case."

"But if Julian Lindisfarn were a convicted felon, Mr. Slowcome?"

"But he was not a convicted felon, Mr. Falconer; no proceedings were ever taken against him."

"But it is not too late to do so!" cried the old banker, eagerly, with an excited gleam in his eye.

Old Slow shook his head gently, and a quiet smile came over his face, as he answered,—

"Wont do, Mr. Falconer. There's no hope of disposing of the difficulty in that way."

"Why? If he comes forward to make any claim"—said the other, eagerly.

"You might put salt on his tail; but he has beat us, Mr. Falconer. He is dead now; though he did not die in America."

"But then—if I understand the matter at all, Slowcome, the girls become the heiresses after all."

"You are in such a hurry, Falconer. One is sure to run one's head into some mistake, when one suffers one's self to be hurried. That is why I never do. If Julian Lindisfarn had died without legitimate issue, it would have been as you state; but that, as I am told, is not the case. The object of the man who was here just now was to set up a claim on behalf of a son of Julian Lindisfarn."

"And such a son would inherit to the ousting of Mr. Lindisfarn's daughters?"

"Unquestionably he would; there can be no doubt about that at all," said Slowcome, raising his head and looking point-blank into his companion's face.

"And this statement—or rather all these statements, Mr. Slowcome—did they come to you, may I ask, from a trustworthy source,—from such a source as would lead you to put faith in them?"

"Ah! there we come to the marrow of the question. The gentleman who was kind enough to communicate these facts to me is —not a—person—on whose unsupported statement I should be disposed to place implicit reliance. But neither is he one who would for a moment suppose that his statement could be of any avail. No, he has got his proofs,—his documents."

"You think, then"—said Falconer, cursing in his heart old Slow's dilatory and tantalizing mode of dribbling out the contents of his mind.

"I think, Mr. Falconer,—for to you I have no objection whatsoever to give, not my opinion, mind; for I cannot be expected to have had either the time or the means to form an opinion upon the case as yet; but my impressions, my merely *primâ facie* impressions,—though you will of course understand that I said no word to my informant which could lead him to infer that I either believed or disbelieved any portion of his statement,—my impression is that it is true that Julian Lindisfarn did not die years ago in America, but that he did die, as stated, the other day at sea off the neighboring coast of France. I am further disposed to believe that he really did leave a son behind him, who is now to be put forward as the heir-at-law to the property."

"It is all up, then!" cried the banker, throwing up his hands as he spoke.

"You are in such a hurry, Falconer! You are making a most prodigious jump to a conclusion, and a wholly unwarrantable one. I believe, as I say, that Julian Lindisfarn left a son. Did he leave a legitimate son?" said the lawyer, dropping the words like minute guns, and aiming a poke with his forefinger at the third button of the banker's waistcoat, as he finished them; "that is the question. That is the only direction, to speak the plain fact frankly, as between you and me, in which I see any loophole—any hope."

"But the child is stated to be legitimate."

"*Stated!* of course he is *stated* to be legitimate. What is the use of *statements*. They have more than that. The copy of a document professing to be an extract from the marriage register, duly made and signed by the clergyman, and attesting the marriage of Julian Lindisfarn and Barbara Mallory, was shown to me."

"Barbara Mallory!"

"And I have no doubt but that the original of that document will be forthcoming. Also I have seen the copies of affidavits proving the birth of the child at a due and proper period after the marriage. And I have little doubt but that the date of the child's birth can be substantiated."

"Well, then, where on earth do you see any loophole of hope, I should like to know?"

"Well, Mr. Falconer, it must have occurred to your experience to discover that every document is not always exactly what it professes to be in every respect. I do not know. I cannot say anything. But there are certain circumstances that I think I may call—ahem!—suspicious, in the statement which was made to me. The register, from which the extract certifying the marriage professes to have been taken, is stated to be lost. It may be so; many registers have been lost before now. Of course we shall leave no stone unturned to see whether any hole can be picked in the case put forward. Strict search must be made for this missing register. The father of the woman said to have been married to young Lindisfarn is, and has for many years been, parish clerk of the village where the marriage was celebrated,—a rather ugly and suggestive fact."

"Mallory, Mallory—why, that is the name of the old clerk at Chewton in the Moor, Dr. Lindisfarn's parish!"

"Just so; and the person who was with me just now, and who is getting up this case, is a son of the old man, and brother of the so-called Mrs. Lindisfarn, an attorney—of no very good repute, between ourselves—at Sillmouth. He tells me a great deal—most of which I knew very well before he was born—of the careless and unclerical habits of old Mellish, the late curate at Chewton, which is put forward to account for the loss of the register. If that register could only be found"—

"Please, sir, it only wants a quarter to six!" said Bob Scott, opening the door of his master's room, and making this announcement in the utter desperation of his heart.

"Good Heavens! so late?" exclaimed Falconer, turning as white as a sheet.

"Oh, it is no matter," said old Slow, as placidly as possible; "there is no hurry; there is time enough for all things!"

"I beg pardon, my dear sir. Not another second for the world,—a thousand pardons!"

And to old Slow's no little surprise and perplexity, but to Bob Scott's infinite delight, the banker brushed off in the greatest possible hurry, and almost ran up that short portion of the High Street which intervened between the office of Slowcome and Sligo, and the lane which led from it into that part of the Close in which his own residence was situated.

Only a few minutes to six; Good Heavens! and in another ten minutes his son would be speeding, as fast as post-horses could carry him, toward Gretna, to join himself indissolubly to a girl not worth a penny. Heavens and earth, what a merciful escape! If indeed there be yet time to stop him.

"Gregory, Gregory!" cried Mr. Falconer, bursting into the private parlor at the bank, where he knew that the old clerk was fortunately still engaged with his books, and throwing himself panting on a chair, as he spoke,—"Gregory! Mr. Frederick is going to run off with Miss Lindisfarn from the door in the wall of her uncle's garden in Castle Head Lane, at six this evening. It only wants a few minutes. Run for your life, and stop him; at all hazards, mind you! Cling to him if necessary. Tell him you come from me; and bring him here to me. Mind now, everything depends on your being there in time and preventing his starting. Off with you!"

And that is why and how the elopement did not take place, and Margaret was betrayed in the shameful manner that has been related.

CHAPTER XL.
THE TIDINGS REACH THE CHASE.

"Merciful Heaven!" thought the panting banker to himself, as he sat, exhausted with the unwonted exertion he had made, in the chair into which he had thrown himself while speaking to Greatorex, "what an escape! what a marvellously providential escape! If only Gregory Greatorex is in time! But yes, yes, there is time, there is time. To think that if that young scamp of a clerk had not got tired of waiting, and put his head into the room to say that it was near six o'clock, I should have let the precious moments slip to a certainty. They would have been off, and Fred would have married a beggar. 'Twas a mere chance, too, my looking in at Slowcome's, as I went down the High Street, a mere chance. How thankful we ought to be to a mercifully overruling Providence! A beggar,—yes, those poor Lindisfarn girls are no better,—evidently no better. It is all very well for Slowcome to make the best of it, and talk about a loophole and a hope. Of course, it is his business and his duty to do so. Of course a fight on the subject will suit his book; but it is as plain as a pikestaff that they have not a chance, and that is Slowcome's opinion too. A most wonderful dispensation, truly. There goes six o'clock!" cried Mr. Falconer, jumping from his chair, and going nervously to the window of the room. "Heaven grant that Gregory may have been in time, and that Fred has listened to reason. Oh, yes, he never would! —but I should be very thankful to have him safe here."

And the old gentleman, with his hands plunged into the pockets of his superfine black shorts, kept nervously moving from the window to the fireplace, and from the fireplace to the window, looking at his watch every minute.

"Thank goodness, you are here, my dear boy!" he exclaimed, as Frederick entered the room at last, seizing him by the hand, and shaking it again and again,—"thank God, you are here! Greatorex has done it like a faithful servant! I will not forget him. My boy, what an escape we have had!"

"But will you have the kindness to explain the meaning of all this, sir? You first tell me "—

"Yes, yes, I know, I know. But, my dear boy, such an extraordinary circumstance. You shall hear. There was only just time, barely time to stop you. A minute or two more, and you would have been off, and "—the banker finished his phrase in dumb show, by throwing up his eyes, hands,

chin, and nether-lip, to heaven,—or at least, toward the ceiling of the bank parlor.

"But I'll be shot if I can make out head or tail in the matter!" cried his son.

"Have a moment's patience till I can tell you," remonstrated the senior.

"You yourself put me up to going off with the girl, and then at the last moment— Do you consider, sir, that you have made me behave very ill to Miss Lindisfarn?"

"My dear Fred, let her alone, let her alone. Thank Heaven, you have no need to trouble yourself any further about her!"

"To think of her, poor little darling, waiting and waiting there, at that garden-door."

"My dear boy, she has not a penny."

"Getting into a scrape with her aunt, most likely "—

"I tell you, Fred, she is a beggar!"

"Catching her death of cold in that damp garden "—

"Don't I tell you she has not a sixpence in the world? Do you hear? Do you understand what I say? Not a sixpence! And I have been mercifully permitted to become cognizant of the truth in the most extraordinary manner, just in time,—barely in time to save you from marrying yourself to a beggar. Ten minutes more, and you would have been off; and nothing could have saved you."

"But what on earth is the meaning of all this? Will you have the kindness to explain to me what has happened, or what you have heard?"

"Sit down then, Frederick,—sit down quietly, and you shall hear all. I am so shaken with the surprise, and my anxiety about you, and the run I had, that I am all of a tremor. But once again, thank God, all is safe! Think of my stepping by chance— quite by chance—into Slowcome and Sligo's, as I was walking down the street,—thinking of the job you were after, you dog!—just to ask whether they were getting on with the settlements. I do not know what prompted me to go in. But it is a wonderful instance how a merciful Providence overrules our actions. I think it must have been a feeling that it would be just as well for me to show in that way that I knew nothing about the elopement, you know. So I just stepped in; and Slowcome told me the news."

"What news, in Heaven's name?"

"Do be patient a moment, Frederick? Am I not telling you? 'Settlements!' said Slowcome; 'it will be well if Lindisfarn is ever able to make any settlement at all on his girls,' or something to that effect. And then he told me that he had just had a man with him, who had made a formal claim on the inheritance on behalf of a son of Julian Lindisfarn, who, the man said, had not died in America long ago, as supposed, but quite recently in this immediate neighborhood."

"A son of Julian Lindisfarn!"

"Yes; a son by a certain Miss Mallory out at Chewton in the Moor, his father's living, you know."

"What, a legitimate son?" asked Frederick, eagerly.

"Yes; it would seem so; a son born in wedlock, of Julian Lindisfarn and his wife, Barbara Mallory!"

"His wife? I do remember, sir, that at the time of his unhappy detection and escape, there was something about some girl out on the Moor. Of course, you know, sir, I was not in his confidence, and knew little or nothing about the matter; but I know that he had some tie of the sort out there. But his wife,—is it possible? Well, he was just the sort of man, soft enough and reckless enough to be led into anything of the kind. And to think that his son should now turn up to cut the Misses Lindisfarn out of their inheritance!"

"Ay, indeed! Slowcome talked about some possibility that the child might turn out to be illegitimate after all. But he admitted that the man had shown him copies of documents,—extracts from the register and that sort of thing; and he evidently had little or no hope of being able to resist the claim himself. Yes, the property will to go the child of that scamp, Julian, and Miss Margaret and Miss Kate will be nowhere! Don't you feel, Fred, that you have had a most narrow, a most providential escape?"

"An escape, indeed!" cried Frederick. "It makes my head go round to think of it. But it is very painful, too, to think of that poor girl; she will be furious,—absolutely furious; and will feel that I have used her very ill."

"Pshaw, let her think what she pleases! What signifies it what she thinks? She has not a sixpence in the world, I tell you. She

will have enough to think about as soon as this terrible news reaches her. Of course it will be Slowcome's duty to communicate it to the Lindisfarns immediately. It will be all over the town to-morrow. Good Heavens! I should never have forgiven myself, Fred, if this elopement business had taken place. You will be pleased to hear, too, that there is much less need for any hasty step of the sort. The news from Lombard Street to-day has been very good. I am in considerable hopes that we shall get over the danger with no more damage than a mere scratch. A merciful escape there, too. But it would have made it doubly unfortunate if you had gone and irretrievably linked your fortunes to those of a beggar. As it is, your prospects are as bright as ever. And a word in your ear, my boy! Blakistry told me he did not like the sound of Merriton's cough at all; and look at his narrow chest. In that case, you know, little Emily Merriton would be a prize in the lottery worth catching, eh?"

In fact, the last posts from London had brought the Silverton banker tidings from his correspondents in Lombard Street, which gave him great hope that the serious danger which had threatened him would pass over with very little damage; and for the last day or two his heart had been very much more at ease.

The result of this had been that the old gentleman's mind had returned, with its usual zest, to those learned recreations which were his delight; and he had been able once more to take that interest in the proceedings of the Silverton archæologists, which, during the period of sharp anxiety about the fortunes of the bank, graver cares had put to flight. It was time, too, that he should do so. The great annual meeting of the Sillshire Antiquarian Society was to take place next month. Several important papers from various leading members were to be read, and one especially by Dr. Lindisfarn on the "History and Antiquities of the Church of Chewton in the Moor."

Chewton Church was one of the specimens of ecclesiastical architecture of which Sillshire was most proud. Next to Silverton Cathedral, it was, probably, the finest church in the county. Its remote position had hitherto prevented it from receiving all the attention which it merited. But there were several points of especial architectural and ecclesiological interest attaching to it, and much was expected from Dr. Lindisfarn's promised paper. It was, in a special degree, his own ground, as he was the rector of the parish. He was understood to have bestowed long and careful study on the subject, and a great treat was expected by his learned brethren, and a considerable triumph by himself.

Mr. Falconer did not at all relish the prospect which was so pleasant to his old rival and (archæological) enemy. It was gall and wormwood to him to think that the canon should have it all to himself, and be permitted to walk over the course, as it were. He was sure that Lindisfarn would be guilty of some grievous error, some absurdity or other, which it would be a delicious treat to him to expose at the general meeting of the society,—a very learned man, the doctor; no doubt a very learned man; but so inaccurate, so careless, so hasty in jumping to a conclusion!

The doctor's memoir had, it was well known to his brother archæologists, been some months in preparation; and the banker had already more than once been out to Chewton quietly by himself to ascertain as far as possible the probable scope and line of the doctor's inquiries and researches, and to find, if possible, the means of tripping him up. It was thus that he had become acquainted with the fact that old Jared Mallory was the clerk of Chewton; and had indeed made some little acquaintance with that worthy himself; inasmuch as the banker's inquiries and examinations had necessarily been mainly conducted through him. Now, having his mind more at ease respecting his business anxieties, and returning therefore to his pet object of spoiling, if possible, his rival's expected triumph, he determined to pay another visit to the locality on the following Sunday. That day was the best for the purpose for two reasons; first, because the banker could then absent himself from Silverton for the entire day, without interfering with business; and, secondly, because on that day he could be sure that Dr. Lindisfarn would be safe in Silverton, and that there would be no danger of meeting him on the battle-field. The strange circumstances which he had heard from Slowcome made him curious, moreover, to see that old man again, and possibly also his daughter, the

soi-disant Mrs. Lindisfarn, and the child, who had become all at once of so much importance. The news of the loss of Hiram Pendleton's vessel, and of the stranger, who had taken passage in her back to France, and of the gallant rescue of a woman and child by the bold smuggler himself, had become partially known in Silverton; and it had reached the banker's ears that the rescued mother and child had gone back to the house of the woman's father at Chewton.

Before the Sunday came, however, which the banker had fixed for his excursion, others of those more nearly interested in the extraordinary tale which had been told to Mr. Slowcome were beforehand with him in a visit to the little moorland village.

Of course, Mr. Slowcome lost no time in communicating his tidings to the persons most nearly concerned in them. He had himself, the very next thing the morning after his interview with Mallory, driven up to the Chase, and been closeted with the squire in his study. Thus Kate was forestalled in the disclosure she was, in accordance with the agreement come to with her sister, to have made to her father that same morning. And it became unnecessary for her to say anything on the subject. The news the lawyer brought was necessarily a tremendously heavy blow to the stout and hearty old man. Would to God, he said, that the truth could have been known some years earlier! He might then have been enabled to make some provision for his poor dear undowered girls. It was now, alas! almost too late. He could not expect to hold the property many more years. Still, he might yet do something. Anyway, God's will be done; and God forbid that he should wish or make any attempt to set aside the just right of his brother's grandson.

"Those are the sentiments, Mr. Lindisfarn, which, if I may take the liberty of saying so, I felt sure that I should find in you. At the same time," said Mr. Slowcome, " you will permit me to observe that it is our bounden duty to ascertain beyond all doubt, that the child in question is in truth the legal heir to the estates."

" Is there any doubt upon that point, Slowcome ? "

" I cannot tell you, I am sorry to say, Mr. Lindisfarn, that I have any very strong doubts upon the subject,—or rather, perhaps,

I should say that I have not any very strong hope of being able to prove that any such doubt in my own mind is justified by the facts of the case. But I have some doubt ; I certainly *have some* doubt,—not that the child now brought forward is the son of your nephew Julian Lindisfarn, but doubt whether or no he were really born in wedlock."

" Well, Slowcome ; you know how incompetent I am even to form an opinion upon the subject. Let right be done. That is all I say. And I know I may leave the matter wholly in your hands, with no other expression of my wishes on the subject save that."

" Certainly, certainly, Mr. Lindisfarn. Quite so. Of course I have not had time as yet to make any, even the most preliminary, inquiry in the matter,—hardly even to think of the subject with any due degree of consideration. But you may depend on all being done that ought to be done."

" Thank you, Slowcome. And now comes the cruellest part of the business : I must break the news to my poor girls ! I know my Kate will bear it bravely. And my poor, poor Margaret—hers is a hard case ! But, any way, it is a mercy that this was discovered before she made a marriage under false pretences, as it were. Falconer is now at liberty to do as he likes about it. You will let Mr. Falconer understand that I consider him perfectly released from every shadow of a promise or intention made under other circumstances."

" And now, Mr. Lindisfarn, I must lose no time in waiting on your brother. My first duty was, of course, to you."

So the lawyer bowed himself out ; and the poor old squire went bravely to work at the cruelly painful task before him.

Kate said all she could to comfort him. To her the most painful part of the conversation with her father was the necessity of concealing from him the fact that she already knew all he had to tell her. She doubted long as to her true duty in the matter, and was more than once almost inclined to yield to the temptation of telling him all. But the recollection of her promise to Margaret,— though according to the letter of it, she was now at liberty to speak, and if the facts had not become otherwise known, she would have spoken,—and the thought of the position she would have been placed in by the avowal, kept her silent.

Mr. Mat was absolutely furious,—utterly refused to believe in the legitimacy of Julian's son,—swore it was all a vile plot ; he knew those Mallorys, and knew they were up to anything. He had known poor old Mellish well. He did not believe but that the register could be found. It must and should be found somehow ! In short, Mr. Mat was utterly rebellious against fate and facts.

Margaret of course was still at her uncle's house ; and the task of breaking the news to her would therefore fall on others.

Mr. Slowcome's duty in the Close was of a less disagreeable nature than it had been up at the Chase. Nevertheless, his tidings were not received there with any kind of satisfaction or exultation. It was some little time before Dr. Lindisfarn could be brought to remember all the old circumstances, and piece them together with those new ones which had come to light sufficiently to understand the present position of the matter. When he did so, his distress for his brother and his niece was evidently stronger in his mind than any gratification at the prospect opened before his own grandchild. The thought that his poor lost son—lost so long, and, truth to tell, so nearly forgotten— had been all those years alive (and under what circumstances) and had died so miserably but the other day, and almost within sight of his paternal home ! All this was a stirring up of harrowing memories and painful thoughts that brought with them nothing of compensation in the changed destinies of the family acres.

As for Lady Sempronia, she went into violent hysterics, and shut herself up in her own room, of course. It was a gratification to her that this tremendous trial should be added to her store of such things, much of the same sort as that experienced by a collector who adds some specially fine specimen of anything hideous to his museum.

Dr. Lindisfarn requested Mr. Slowcome to undertake the duty of breaking the news to Margaret ; and the delicate task was accomplished by that worthy gentleman, with all the lengthy periphrasis and courtly pomposity which he deemed fitting to the occasion. It is needless to say that Margaret played her part to perfection. Of course she knew perfectly well from the moment of his solemn entry into Lady Sempronia's drab drawing-room, and still more solemn introduction of himself, every word that he was going to say. But he left her with the conviction that it was impossible for any young lady in her unfortunate position to show a greater or more touching degree of natural sensibility, tempered by beautiful resignation and admirable good sense, than she had done. She had listened with marked attention to the possibilities he had hinted at of error or fraud in the statements made, and had cordially adhered to his declarations of the propriety of taking every possible step with a view to discovering the real truth.

"Ah!" said old Slow to himself, as he left the drawing-room, "such a girl as that, with one half of the Lindisfarn property, would have been a pretty catch for my young friend Fred. It is a sad business,—a very sad business."

But before leaving the doctor's house, Mr. Slowcome caused himself to be again shown into the study; and set before the doctor his very strong desire that Dr. Lindisfarn should himself accompany one of the firm on a visit to Chewton, with a view to seeing on the spot what could be done with a hope of discovering the missing register.

"I would go myself, Dr. Lindisfarn," he said, "if my presence were not imperatively required in Silverton, or if Mr. Sligo were not in every respect as competent as myself to do all that can be done. But it would be a great assistance to us, if you would consent to accompany him, both on account of your knowledge of the people and the localities, and more especially because your authority, as rector of the parish, would be exceedingly useful to us."

To this proposal the doctor, who was by no means loath to pay yet another visit to the scene and subject of his ecclesiological labors, and who began to speculate on the possibility of finding or creating a disciple in Mr. Sligo, made no difficulty. And it was decided that the visit should be made, as unexpectedly as possible, on the morrow.

CHAPTER XLI.

IN MR. SLIGO'S GIG.

THE church at Chewton in the Moor was, as has been said, a remarkable and beautiful building, the lofty nave and side-aisles of which were admirable specimens of the severe and yet graceful style, which ecclesiologists of a later generation than Dr. Lindisfarn have taught us to call "Early English," while the transepts, tower, and chancel evidently belonged to a still earlier period. Had it not been that certain untoward circumstances prevented the publication of Dr. Lindisfarn's elaborate and profound Monograph on the subject, I might have been able to gratify the reader with a more detailed and circumstantial description of this interesting structure than I can now pretend to lay before him. As it is, I must content myself with mentioning one specially curious feature, to the elucidation of which the learned canon had particularly applied himself, and which formed the subject of one chapter of the Memoir, headed, "On the remains of the ancient panelling in the passage leading to the sacristy of Chewton Church, and on certain fragments of inscriptions still legible thereon."

There was in fact at Chewton a singular little building almost detached from the church, at the end of the south transept of which it stood, and which had evidently in old times formed the sacristy, and was now known by the more Protestant sounding title of the vestry,—a thoroughly good Protestant word, though its first cousin "vestment" has a suspiciously Romish twang in the sound of it! Well, this whilom sacristy was reached from the church by a sort of corridor, which opened out of the eastern wall of the transept, and which seemed to be an unnecessarily costly means of communication, inasmuch as a door at the extreme corner of the transept would have equally effected the purpose. But those "noble boys at play," our ancestors, did not always, as we all know, practise an enlightened economy in their playing. The appearance of the detached building and of the corridor was extremely picturesque both on the inside and the outside ; and was universally felt to be so by all visitors. And it does seem just possible that the aforesaid noble old boys spent their money and toil

with the express intention of producing that result.

Anyway, there was the passage, with its remains of cut-stone mouldings and various ornamentation grievously obliterated and destroyed by the layers of Protestant whitewash, which the zeal of many generations of un-æsthetic church-wardens had laid stratum over stratum upon them. And then, near the sacristy door in the right-hand wall of the passage, going toward that apartment, there were still visible through these coatings of a purer faith the ornamented cornices and mouldings of a small but very beautiful arch, which seemed too low to have ever been intended for a doorway. And beneath this arch, there were certain remains of panelling, partially, and indeed almost entirely whitewashed over, on which the greedily prying eyes of the learned canon had detected, in certain spots, where the whitewash had been rubbed off, those fragments of ancient inscriptions, alluded to in the heading to that chapter of the Monograph which has been quoted. The rubbing off of the whitewash had been very partial and irregular but enough of the ancient woodwork beneath it had been uncovered to permit certain remains of painting to be seen, and especially the letters TANTI . . . . VI . . . . . ˙ TANTI . . . . AI . . . . TAN . . . . in an extremely rude and archaic character !

It was known among the Sillshire archæologists, that Dr. Lindisfarn had expended an immense amount of erudition in the elucidation of these mysterious syllables, and had constructed on the somewhat slender scaffolding poles thus furnished him a vast fabric of theory and conjecture, embracing various curious points in the social and ecclesiastical history and manners of the English clergy during the reigns immediately following the Norman invasion ; and a very great treat was expected to result from his labors. It was evident that something was lost between the adjective "tanti" and the substantive "vi"! They could not be joined in lawful syntax together ! And what could the missing word or words have been ? The learned Sillshire world was on the tiptoe of expectation.

More than once already had the doctor strained his eyes to descry if possible the very faintest outline or smallest portion of a letter in the space, which separated those given above; but all in vain! And now he proposed profiting by the trip proposed to him by Mr. Slowcome, to take the opportunity of bringing the younger eyes of the gentleman who was to be his companion to bear upon the subject.

For Mr. Sligo was, it must be understood, quite a young man, and was supposed, indeed, by most of those who knew him, to be able to see as far into a millstone as most men. He was in all respects a very different man from his senior partner, Mr. Slowcome. In contradiction to what had been the practice of the firm for several generations, young Sligo had been educated for his profession, not in the paternal office in Silverton, but in London; and indeed, had only come down to the western metropolis when the sudden death of his father, old Sligo, had opened to him the inheritance of a share in the old-established firm.

Mr. Slowcome did not altogether like young Mr. Sligo. One understands that such should be the case. I believe that old Slow had more real knowledge of law in his pigtail than Sligo had in his whole body. Nevertheless, the younger man came down from London with airs and pretensions of new-fangled enlightenment, and was full of modern instances, and an offensive "*nous-avons-changé-tout-cela*" sort of assumption of superiority, which the greater part—including all the younger portion—of the provincial world were disposed to accept as good currency. Then young Sligo was very rapid; and old Slowcome was very slow; and there were other points of contrast, too marked to escape either the Silvertonians or the partners themselves. Young Mr. Sligo, however, proved himself an efficient and useful member of the firm, keen, active, and intelligent. He was, moreover, "Young Sligo" the son of "Old Sligo;" and that was all in all to Mr. Slowcome. So, though the two men were as different in all respects as any two men could be, they got on pretty well together.

Old Slowcome was admitted to the society of the clergy in the Close, and of the squirearchy in the neighborhood on tolerably equal terms; but this standing had hardly yet been accorded to Mr. Sligo. So that he was all but a stranger to Dr. Lindisfarn when he waited upon the canon immediately after breakfast on the morning subsequent to the conversation between that gentleman and Mr. Slowcome, according to the arrangement which had been made between them.

Mr. Sligo had a very neat gig and a spanking, fast-trotting mare; and his offer of driving Dr. Lindisfarn over to Chewton had been willingly accepted by the doctor. The road by which Chewton could be reached in this manner was, for the latter half of it, a different and a somewhat longer one than that by which Dr. Blakistry had ridden across the moor, the track which he had followed being altogether impossible for wheels.

"I confess, Dr. Lindisfarn," said Sligo to his companion, after they had quitted Silverton, and had exchanged a few remarks on the beauty of the morning, the qualities of Mr. Sligo's fast-trotting mare, etc.,—"I confess that I have hopes of the result of our investigations to-day."

"I am truly delighted to hear you say so!" replied Dr. Lindisfarn.

"I have, indeed; and it is very gratifying to feel that all the parties are of one mind in the matter."

"Oh! there is no doubt of that. All the county are anxious about it."

"No doubt,—no doubt. Our investigation will be a delicate one," added Mr. Sligo, after a short pause.

"Oh, excessively so; you can have no idea to what a degree that is the case!" cried the doctor, with great animation; "the traces are so slight"—

"They are so, that must be admitted; they *are* very slight certainly. Nevertheless, to a sharp and practised eye, Dr. Lindisfarn, if you will not think it presumptuous of me to say so, there are certain appearances which"—

"Indeed! you don't say so?" exclaimed Dr. Lindisfarn, hardly more delighted than surprised; "I was not aware, Mr. Sligo, that you had ever turned your attention to investigations of this character."

"Turned my attention? Why, if you will excuse my saying so, Dr. Lindisfarn, I flatter myself that matters of this sort are my speciality."

"You don't say so! I am truly delighted to hear it. We shall be rejoiced to welcome you among us as a fellow-laborer, Mr. Sligo."

"Any assistance I may be able to give, in

any stage of the business, I shall be proud and happy to afford. I am sure, Dr. Lindisfarn," replied the lawyer, rather surprised at the warmth of his companion's expressions of gratitude.

"You are very kind, I am sure, Mr. Sligo," returned the doctor, drawing up a little; for the young lawyer's proposal of meddling with any other stage of the case had instantly alarmed his antiquarian jealousy, and he began to suspect a plot for robbing him of a portion of the credit of his discovery,—"you are very kind, but I think I shall not need to trespass on your kindness in respect to any part of the matter, with the exception of the researches to be made to-day."

"Oh, indeed, Dr. Lindisfarn! You are the best judge. I may say, however, that when I was with Draper and Duster, all the work of this kind there was to be done passed through my hands. But you know best, sir."

"Draper and Duster,—I do not remember either of the names. Are they members of the Society?" asked Dr. Lindisfarn, much puzzled.

"Yes, sir, they are. Gray's Inn. One of the first houses in London."

"I don't think I quite follow you, Mr. Sligo. I have heard of Gray's Inn, as a place of abode for gentlemen of your profession. But though I believe I know most of the distinguished men who cultivate our delightful science, I do not think that I ever heard of the antiquaries you mention."

"Well, sir,—they do cultivate the delightful science, as you are complimentary enough to call it,—not a little. But I never said that they were antiquaries; and I don't much see what that has to do with the matter."

"Then I am afraid, Mr. Sligo, that we shall differ *toto cœlo* on the most fundamental notions of the spirit in which the pursuit should be taken up and conducted," said the doctor, very sententiously, "unless the light of profound erudition and scholarship be brought to bear upon these investigations, they sink to the rank of mere twaddling and trifling."

Mr. Sligo faced round in the gig at this, and looked at the senior canon with a sharp and shrewd eye, as in doubt whether the oddness he had heard of in Dr. Lindisfarn, did not extend to the length of what he called, in common people, not canons of cathedral churches, stark, staring lunacy. He saw the old gentleman's florid and cleanshaven face was a little flushed,—for the doctor had been speaking with the energy of profound conviction on a point that touched him nearly,—and he therefore answered in a very mild voice.

"It would not become me to differ with you on the subject, Dr. Lindisfarn; far from it. No doubt you are right. I dare say what we have got to do to-day *may* seem twaddling and trifling to a gentleman like you; but I can assure you that it is only by such twaddling and trifling that we have any chance of saving the Lindisfarn property from going to an illegitimate brat."

"Saving the Lindisfarn property! Bless my heart, Mr. Sligo, I was not thinking anything about the Lindisfarn property."

"Then what, in the name of Heaven—I beg your pardon, Dr. Lindisfarn—but what, if you please, have we been talking about all this time?"

"Talking about, Mr. Sligo? Why, about the partially defaced inscription in the sacristy, to be sure. What else should we have been talking about?"

"Oh, dear, dear me. There is a case of mistaken identity now. Why, if you will believe me, Dr. Lindisfarn, I was speaking, and thought you were speaking, all the time about the search for the missing register that we are going to make at Chewton."

"I was mistaken then in supposing that you are interested in antiquarian investigations, Mr. Sligo?" said the old man much disappointed.

"I am afraid so, sir," said Sligo.

"And you never have paid any attention to the deciphering of ancient inscriptions?"

"Not that I am aware of, sir."

Dr. Lindisfarn heaved a deep sigh, but was nevertheless somewhat comforted by the reflection that he was in no danger of being robbed by a rival, if he had no chance of assistance from a brother.

"Nevertheless," he said, "it may be that you might be able to descry with your young eyes what my old ones, though aided by, perhaps I may be allowed to say, no incompetent amount of study, have failed to make out. I will show you the spot, and perhaps you will try if you can discover any further remains of letters."

"With all the pleasure in life, Dr. Lin-

15

disfarn ; and you shall assist me with your authority as rector, and your acquaintance with the late curate's character and ways. I am told he was a very queer one."

"The fact is, I am ashamed to say, Mr. Sligo, that I knew very little about him ; less, perhaps, than I ought to have done. I found him there when I succeeded to the living, which had previously been held by old Dean Burder. He was quite one of the old school, I take it."

"Ah! not very regular in his ways, nor quite up to the mark, I suppose. I believe Mr. Matthew Lindisfarn knew him well ? "

"Yes. I fancy Mr. Mat and poor Mellish used to be rather cronies in those old times. Mellish was very musical, and that was enough for Mr. Mat."

"Oh, musical, was he? But he was a little too fond of this sort of thing, was he not ? " said Mr. Sligo, raising his elbow in a significant manner.

"Ah, too fond of his glass of wine, you mean, Mr. Sligo ? Well, it was said so. I am afraid to a certain degree it was so. We all have our failings, Mr. Sligo."

"Too true, Dr. Lindisfarn. I am not the man to forget it. I only ask these things because they may have a bearing on our present business. Under the circumstances, I suppose that some degree, perhaps a considerable amount, of irregularity in church matters may have prevailed in his parish ? "

"It may have been so. There were never any complaints, however. He certainly was very popular in the parish. The people were very much attached to him."

"Did he inhabit the parsonage-house at Chewton ? " asked the lawyer.

"There is no parsonage-house, unfortunately, nor has there been one for several generations. When the old house fell down in one of the great storms that often sweep this moorland district, it was never rebuilt."

"Are you aware where the late curate did live then, sir ? " asked Mr. Sligo.

"For many years, for all the latter part of his life,—indeed, during all the time that he held the curacy under me,—he lodged at the house of the parish clerk, a man of the name of Mallory, a very decent sort of a person, I fancy."

"O—h ! the late curate lived in the house of Mr. Jared Mallory, did he ? " rejoined Mr. Sligo, with a special expression of voice

and feature, that was quite lost on Dr. Lindisfarn.

"Yes, it was convenient in many ways. Mallory lived in a good house of his own, larger than he needed ; and it was near the church."

"And perhaps all the farther from—you know the saying, Dr. Lindisfarn, and will excuse me for being reminded of it on this occasion," said the lawyer.

"No. I am not aware of any such popular saw or saying ! " replied Dr. Lindisfarn. "But the fact was that it was convenient for him also to be in the same house with the parish clerk, you understand."

"I see, sir,—I see ! many years under this Mallory's roof ; a man of that sort necessarily falls under the influence of those about him,—parish clerk especially ; I see,—I see ! I suppose this is Chewton, down in the hollow here in front of us, sir ? "

"Yes, here we are ; this is Chewton, but you don't get so good a first view of the church coming this way, as by the other road over the moor."

"I suppose our plan will be to drive direct to the clerk's house, sir ? Do you know which it is ? "

"Oh, yes ; follow down the main street of the village straight on ; the church is a little to the left at the further end ; and Mallory's is near the bottom of the street on the left-hand side."

So Mr. Sligo drew his fast-trotting mare and smart gig sharply up to the door of the stone house with the iron rail in front of it ; and rather unceremoniously throwing the reins to Dr. Lindisfarn, and saying shortly, "I will announce you, sir," sprung from the gig, almost before it had stopped, and dashed precipitately into the house, without any ceremony of knocking or asking leave, whatever.

CHAPTER XLII.
LADY FARNLEIGH RETURNS TO SILLSHIRE.

MARGARET waited at the little door leading from the canon's garden into the Castle Head Lane till the cathedral clock chimed the half-hour past six.

It was a raw night, and her bodily condition at the end of that half-hour was not a pleasant one. But her sufferings from that cause were as nothing—absolutely nothing—to the mental torture she endured during at least the latter half of those never by her to be forgotten thirty minutes. Nothing but her own very strong reason for wishing that the proposed elopement should be carried into effect could have induced her to swallow her bitter burning indignation so long, and force herself to take yet a little more patience. We know how important it was to all her hopes that the thing should come off; and very, very cruel was the gradual growth during those minutes of misgiving into despairing conviction that it was not to be. For the first ten minutes, she was very angry with her lover for his ungallant want of punctuality. And as she stood with her ear on the stretch, she kept rehearsing to herself the eloquent upbraiding with which she promised herself to punish his misdemeanor. During the second ten minutes, anxiety was gradually growing into dread ; and during the last ten, she was suffering from the sickening, despairing certainty that all was lost.

Still, the true cause of the miscarriage of her hopes and plans never occurred to her. There was no possibility apparent to her by which the fatal news could have yet reached her lover's ear ; that fatal news which she had all that month past concealed in her heart with a fortitude analogous to that of the Spartan boy, who held the fox beneath his cloak, while he gnawed his vitals. Among all the conjecturings which chased each other tumultuously through her mind during the whole of that night, therefore, the real nature of her misfortune never unveiled itself to her in its full extent.

She stole back to the house as the half-hour struck, shivering without and burning with shame and indignation within ; and succeeded in slinking up to her room without having been seen. It did not very much signify to her ; for if she had chanced to meet Elizabeth on the stairs, she would merely have said that, finding her head very bad, she had gone down to see whether the cool, fresh air of the garden would do it any good.

The next morning, her looks, when she descended to her uncle's breakfast-room, vouched abundantly for the truth of her statement respecting her headache.

Then in the course of the morning came Mr. Slowcome on his return from the Chase, with the great news ; to the communication of which she listened, as has been said, with all propriety. Then the causes of the disappointment of the previous evening became intelligible to her. She had at least very little doubt upon the subject. The truth was known to Mr. Slowcome yesterday. There was very little room to doubt that Falconer had heard it from him, and had thereupon abandoned the projected elopement and the marriage together.

That Falconer should, on learning the real state of the case, give up all idea of the marriage, seemed to her so much a matter of course, and was so wholly conformable to the line of conduct which she would have pursued herself in similar circumstances, that she could not, in her heart, blame him for it. Nor did she pretend to herself that she did so. But it was the manner of the thing. To leave her there, exposed to all the inconveniences, the risks, the mortifications, the uncertainty. It was brutal, it was cowardly, it was ungentlemanlike, it was unmanly. And Falconer's conduct assuredly was all this. And if the gentle and lovely Margaret had had power to give effect to the promptings of her heart, it would have been well that day for Frederick Falconer, if he could have changed lots with the most miserable wretch that crawled the earth.

The next day,—that on which Mr. Sligo drove Dr. Lindisfarn over to Chewton, as has been narrated,—Margaret returned to the Chase. She would have given much to have escaped from the necessity of doing so and of meeting Kate under the circumstances ; but there was no possibility of avoiding it. It was too obviously natural that her father should wish to speak with her ; and in fact the intimation that she had better return home came to her from him. Mr. Mat came for her in the gig, soon after the doctor and Mr. Sligo had started on their excursion.

" 'Tis a bad business,—a cruel bad business," said Mr. Mat, feeling deep sympathy with Margaret on this occasion, though there was generally so little of liking between them, but though very sincerely feeling it, finding himself much at a loss to express it. Mr. Mat could not be considered an eloquent man, certainly, yet he had found no difficulty in speaking out what was in his heart to Kate on this occasion. It was different with Margaret : " A bad business ; and I don't know what I wouldn't ha' done sooner than it should have happened, Miss Margaret. Still, when all is said and done, money is not everything in this world, Miss Margaret, and "—

"I am aware, Mr. Mat," replied the young lady, with tragic resignation, "that virtue alone is of real value, or can confer real happiness in this world."

Mr. Mat gave her a queer, furtive look out of the tail of his shrewd black eye; but he only said, "Ay, to be sure, and with such looks as yours, too "—

"Beauty is but a fleeting flower," said Margaret, in very bad humor, but still minded as usual to play her part correctly, and say the proper things to be said.

"But 'tis the sweetest flower that blows while it does last," said the gallant Mr. Mat.

"I have ever been taught to set but small store by it," sighed Margaret; and then there was a long pause in their conversation, which lasted till Mr. Mat began to walk his horse up the steepest part of the hill, going up from the Ivy Bridge to the Lindisfarn lodge-gates.

"I don't believe it; I wont and can't believe it," he then said, as the result of his meditations.

"Believe what, Mr. Mat?" asked Margaret.

"Believe that the child they want to set up as the heir is your Cousin Julian's lawful son, Miss Margaret."

"You don't say so, Mr. Mat?" cried Margaret, in a very different tone of voice from that in which she had before spoken.

"I *du*," said Mr. Mat, very decisively; "but not believing is one thing, mind you, and finding out is another."

"What do you think is the truth, then, Mr. Mat?" said Margaret, in a more kindly tone than she had ever before used to her companion.

"I don't know; but I zem there's a screw loose somewhere; I don't believe 'tis all right."

"Oh, Mr. Mat! do you think it would be possible to find it out?"

"Ah, that's the thing; they are 'cute chaps; and that fellow Jared Mallory, the attorney, is a regular bad 'un. But maybe the play is not all played out yet. Here we are, Miss Margaret; and welcome home to the old place!"

Kate was on the steps waiting to meet her

sister, and seized her in her arms as she got down from the gig.

"Come up-stairs, dear. Papa is out about the place somewhere. He will see you before dinner."

Margaret kissed her sister somewhat stiffly and ungraciously, and proceeded to follow her up the stairs in silence. When they were together in Kate's room, the latter said,—

"You know, I suppose, Margaret, how the news came out. You are aware that it was communicated to Mr. Slowcome, and he came up here to tell us yesterday?"

"Oh, yes, I know it all!" said Margaret.

"And—and—yourself—your own affairs?" hesitated Kate, whose great anxiety on her sister's behalf would not let her be silent, though she felt a difficulty in asking for explanations which, according to her own feelings, should have come so spontaneously from sister to sister.

"Everything is broken off between me and Mr. Falconer, Kate, if that is what you are alluding to,—broken off now and forever, whatever may be the result of the doubts that have arisen."

"Doubts that have arisen, dear Margaret? I fear the nature of the case has not been fully explained to you. Alas! there are no doubts about the matter."

"I have spoken with the lawyer myself, Kate, and prefer to trust to my own impressions," said Margaret, whose sole idea that there might be any doubt about the matter arose from the words which had dropped from Mr. Mat in the gig.

"I fear that you are deluding yourself with a baseless hope, Margaret," said Kate, shaking her head sadly. "But I know that the change in our position has not been the worst unhappiness you have had to struggle with, dearest Margaret; and my heart has been very heavy for you; for I feared,—I feared, Margaret, as I told you, that he was not worthy of the great faith and trust you placed in him."

"Mr. Falconer has behaved very badly. It would be agreeable to me never, if that were possible, to hear his name again. I hope, at all events, not to have to hear it from you, Kate!" And it was clear that Margaret intended that the whole topic of her engagement should be closed and walled up between her and Kate.

"It was a very great shock to poor papa at first," said Kate; "and it was very painful to me, as you may suppose, to be obliged to conceal from him that I had known it all along; but there was no help for it. But the worst is not over, Margaret; Lady Farnleigh is coming home in a day or two; and I do dread the having a concealment between her and me. It is a great, great comfort that she is coming home,—a comfort that I have been longing for these many weeks. And now the happiness of seeing her is almost all spoilt by the necessity of keeping this miserable secret from her knowledge. And it is not so easy a matter, let me tell you, Margaret, to keep a secret from godmamma as it is from dear old Noll."

"You don't mean to say, Kate, that you are going to break your promise, and betray me! You are not going to put it into the power of that woman to ruin me!"

"Margaret, Margaret—that woman! and ruin you! For Heaven's sake, do not speak in such a way; and worse still, have such thoughts in your heart."

"That's all nonsense, Kate; Lady Farnleigh is not my godmother. It is plain enough to see that she detests me, I saw that clearly the first day I came here; I saw her jealousy for her favorite—as if it were my fault that— I tell you she hates me; and it would be delightful to her to have it in her power to twit and expose me, and—I had rather die than that Lady Farnleigh, of all the people in the world, should know—all about it! I had rather die!" repeated Margaret, with a flash of her eyes that perfectly startled her sister.

On the next day but one to that on which this conversation passed between the two sisters, Lady Farnleigh returned to Wanstrow, and showed her impatience to see her darling Kate under the unhappy circumstances that had fallen upon her by driving over to Lindisfarn that same evening. She arrived at the Chase in time for dinner, but during that meal, of course, nothing was said of the subject that was uppermost in all their hearts.

After dinner, as the ladies were crossing the hall to the drawing-room, Lady Farnleigh made a sign to Kate to let Miss Immy and Margaret go on to the drawing-room, and to escape up-stairs with her to her room.

It was not an unprecedented escapade of her ladyship's.

"And now tell me all about it, my dear, dear girl—my poor dear Kate! Has it hit your father very hard?"

"It was a hard blow at first,—very hard. But you know my dear father,—dear old Noll! You know his cheery, hearty nature. Sorrow cannot stick to him; it runs off like water off a duck's back; his genial strong nature turns it. Nevertheless, I am sure he has felt it deeply; if he could only have known the truth earlier in life, he says. Poor dear, dear Noll! And I cannot say all that I would to comfort him, you see, because the misfortune hits poor Margaret more severely than it does me. Thanks to a certain good fairy that stood by at my christening, you know, I am sufficiently well provided for," said Kate, creeping close up to her godmother's side.

"Sufficiently provided for! You know very little, my poor child, of what pounds, shillings, and pence can do, and what they can't. If you mean that you need never come upon the parish, as far as that goes you may probably be easy. You want but little here below, and all the rest of it, I dare say. But Birdie wants her oats, and plenty of them, and a good groom to wait on her. It is all very fine talking, Kate, and the headings to the copybooks may say what they please; but poverty is a bitter thing to those who have to make acquaintance with it for the first time in the midst of a life of ease and abundance."

"Well, you are a Job's comforter, you bad fairy, I must say," cried Kate, laughing.

"I don't like it, Kate, and I can't pretend to say that I do. It is a great misfortune, and there is no wisdom in pretending to ourselves that it is not so."

"I have still so much to be thankful for,—so much that ought to make happiness," said Kate, with rather suspicious emphasis on the word "ought."

"Yes, that is all very pretty spoken, and proper—and it's true, indeed—which is more than could be said for all pretty and proper speeches. But now, goddaughter, we have got to discuss another chapter. Yes, you know what is coming, Miss Kate; I see your guilt in your face. How dare you take advantage of my back being turned to break my dear friend's heart?"

Kate looked up into Lady Farnleigh's face with an expression that caused her at once to change her tone.

"If I try to laugh, my own darling, it is to save crying," she said, putting her arm around Kate's neck, and pressing the gracious drooping head against her bosom; for they had been standing side by side in front of the low fire in Kate's room. What is it, my Kate? Tell me all that there is in this dear, good, honest heart, which I feel beating, beating, as if it would burst. Tell me all about it, my own child."

It was true enough, as Lady Farnleigh said, that Kate's agitation was becoming more and more painful, as her friend spoke. Her bosom rose and fell with long-drawn sighs, that, despite her utmost efforts to suppress them, gradually became sobs. Slowly the great clear tear-drops which had been gathering in her eyes beneath the downcast lids brimmed over, and rolled down her pale cheeks, till suddenly flinging herself into a chair by her side, she fell into such a storm of hysterical weeping that Lady Farnleigh became at once convinced, not without astonishment, that there was something more than the patent circumstances of the case could account for, to occasion so violent and so painful an emotion. For violence of emotion, hysterics, and the like, and even tears, were quite out of Kate's usual way. It was very evident to Lady Farnleigh, as she looked on the convulsed face and bosom of her dearly loved godchild, with sympathizing sorrow and almost with alarm expressed in her own face, that there was some serious cause for grief here, beyond those of which she was cognizant.

She had heard in a few short lines from Captain Ellingham of his rejection, and of the change of station which he had under happier circumstances looked forward to as such a misfortune, but which he was now disposed to consider as a most lucky escape from scenes and associations which had become intolerable to him. She had heard this, and had heard it with some surprise and a little vexation, but had flattered herself that some of the many misunderstandings, or shynesses, or cross-purposes, which are so apt to interfere with the precise intercommunication of people's sentiments and purposes in such matters, would be found to have caused all the mischief, and a little judicious intermediation would put it all right. But now the fearful state of agitation into which Kate had been thrown by the mere mention of the subject, showed her that it was no mere affair of girlish coyness, or even of the rejection of a suitor whom she could not love. There was something else,—something more than all this; and influenced by the purest and truest desire to find the means of comfort for so great a sorrow, she determined to get to the bottom of the matter in some way.

But it was evident that the heart wound was not at that moment in a state to endure the probe, even in the tenderest hands. So she applied herself to soothing the weeping girl as well as she could, without any attempt to continue the subject.

"You have been too much shaken, my poor Kate, by all these things; we will not speak now on painful subjects. Hereafter, when you are calmer, and your spirits have recovered their usual tone,—hereafter you shall tell me all you can feel a comfort in telling."

"Indeed, indeed, godmamma, I have no *wish* to have secrets from you! I—I "—and hiding her face on Lady Farnleigh's shoulder, she burst anew into a passion of tears.

"There, there, my darling, we will speak no more of it now; another time, another time. There, my Kate, your tears will have done you good, there, you will be calmer now, my child!" and Lady Farnleigh soothed her on her bosom as she spoke, as a nurse soothes a suffering infant.

After a little while, Kate became calmer; and, having dried her tears, but with a still quivering lip, said to her friend,—

"But you know, dearest godmamma, that it was all for the best; what should we have done, think, if Captain Ellingham had been accepted by me, when he supposed that I possessed fortune enough for all our requirements, and then "—

"Do you imagine, Kate, that Ellingham proposed to you because you were an heiress?"

"No, no, that I am sure, quite sure, he did not," replied Kate, with an energy which Lady Farnleigh marked, and made a note of in her mind.

"Well, then?" said she.

"But that is a very different thing from

proposing to a girl supposed to be a large heiress, and then finding that she has nothing."

"Yes, it is different. It would be fair in such a case to give back to a man his entire liberty,—fair too to hold him blameless if he availed himself of it to retire from a position he never intended to occupy."

"But it would be very unfair," exclaimed Kate, "to expose a man to such a painful ordeal."

"Very unfair; but you are talking nonsense, Kate, dear. Such unfairness as you speak of would imply that the lady was aware of the mistake respecting her fortune. Of course, no good girl would be guilty of such conduct as that. But what has that to do with the present case?"

"I only said, dear godmamma, that it was all for the best as it turned out, since Captain Ellingham had no intention of proposing to a girl who had nothing to help toward the expenses of a home."

"That, my dear Kate, is a matter for Captain Ellingham's consideration; and what his sentiments upon that point are, you have no means of knowing."

"I do know, at all events, that he does not imagine that I refused him because I had, or was supposed to have, much more money than he had. I do know that, for he told me so in the most noble and generous manner; and it is a great, great comfort," said Kate, and the now silent tears began to drop anew.

Lady Farnleigh observed the emotion which the mention of this circumstance caused Kate, and added a mem. of it to the note she had already taken.

"If, indeed, you had known of the strange circumstances which have come to light and have so materially altered your prospects, at the time you rejected Ellingham's offer, it would all have been intelligible enough; and it would have been for him to renew his suit under the changed circumstances of the case, or not, as he might think fit; but that was not the case. If he were now to do so, it would be insulting to suppose that you might accept a man in your poverty whom you had rejected in your wealth."

"Oh, Lady Farnleigh, the bare thought is hideous," cried Kate, seeming to shrink bodily, as from a stab, while she spoke,— "hideous; and Captain Ellingham is inca-

pable of conceiving such an idea. He will never repeat his offer. As you say, it would be offensive to me to do so,—in a manner in which it is impossible that he should offend."

Again Lady Farnleigh silently added another note to her mental tablets.

"And what is all this about your sister Margaret?" continued she, willing to lead Kate's mind away, for the nonce, from the subject of her own affairs. "I hear that she was engaged to Mr. Falconer; and what is to become of that engagement now?"

"It is all true, godmamma, too true. She *was* engaged to Mr. Falconer. Papa had given his consent, and the settlements were being made out. But it is all broken off now."

"Oh, it's all off now. And how long had it been on, pray?"

"It is a little more than a month since she accepted him, I think," replied Kate, remembering vividly enough that miserable and memorable day so soon after that interview with her cousin in the cottage at Deep Creek.

"A month ago, was it?" said Lady Farnleigh, musing.

"Yes, about a month ago. But we have seen very little of it all up here at the Chase. Margaret has been almost constantly down in Silverton with Lady Sempronia and my uncle."

"And when did the break-off take place?"

"Oh, just the other day."

"On the news of this unlucky discovery about the property, of course?"

"I presume so, of course. But Margaret is not communicative about it. She does not like speaking on the subject, naturally enough."

"And what did the gentleman say for himself? How well I judged that man, Kate!"

"I have no idea how it was brought about, or what passed. I know that Margaret considers herself to have been very ill-treated. She said briefly that all was off between them, and that she wished she could never hear his name again."

"So, so, so, so. Well, my dear, I dare say she *has* been ill-treated. My notion is, that Master Fred is a man to behave ill in such circumstances. There are more ways than one of doing a thing. But still it is right to bear in mind what we were saying just now, you know, of the unfairness of holding a man to an engagement made under very different circumstances."

"Of course, godmamma. I don't know at all how matters passed between Margaret and Mr. Falconer. The making of the engagement and the breaking of it were both done down in the Close."

—"Unreasonable to expect that a man should consider himself bound by such an engagement under such circumstances," continued Lady Farnleigh, more as if she were talking to herself than to her companion, "and yet a man must be a great cur; I dare say Mr. Frederick Falconer did it very brutally. At all events, he lost no time about it. What day was it that the facts about this new claim were known?"

"Mr. Slowcome came up here to papa, on the Thursday morning. It must have been known to everybody in the course of that day. Mr. Falconer may have heard of it even on the previous evening."

"And *when* did you say the break-off between them took place?"

"I only know that when Margaret came home on the Saturday, she told me that it was all off."

"From the Thursday morning to the Friday night; that was the time he had to do it in. Upon my word, Master Freddy must have shown himself worthy of the occasion! Why, he must have jammed his helm hard up, and laid his vessel on her beam ends at the very first sight of the breakers ahead."

"He certainly could not have lost much time in making up his mind about it," Kate admitted.

"And what had I better say to her on the subject?" said Lady Farnleigh, after a short pause, during which she had been thinking over the circumstances of this broken match, as far as they were patent to her, with a resulting estimate of the actors in the little drama not very favorable to either of them.

"Well, I am sure Margaret would be best pleased by your saying nothing at all."

"Then nothing at all will I say; I am sure there is nothing agreeable or useful to be said; and I have no wish to pain or annoy her. And now I suppose, my pet, that we must go down into the drawing-room. Your father and Mr. Mat will have come in from their wine by this time; and I want to have a little chat with Mr. Mat. I suppose Mar-

garet wont think me a brute for saying no word of condolence to her, respecting the mangled condition of her heart."

"Now, godmamma, I must not let you be savage and spiteful about poor Margaret," said Kate, with a faint attempt at a smile. "I am sure she must have suffered."

"Well! I wont be savage and spiteful; *au contraire*, you unreasonable Kate, was I not debating with myself whether or no it would be more civil to attempt any binding up of her wounds by my condolences? But I suppose not; I do not think it is a case for my surgery; I am sure I wish to be civil, not spiteful. But—there! I don't want to meddle with it. But if you were to hang and quarter me, my dear, I cannot be sympathetic and tearful over the loves of Miss Margaret and Mr. Frederick, whether the course of them runs smooth or crosswise."

So Kate and her fairy godmother went down into the drawing-room; where they found the squire fast asleep in his favorite corner of the fireplace; Miss Immy sitting bolt upright in a small chair at the table, tranquilly reading her "Clarissa Harlowe," with a pair of candles immediately in front of her; Mr. Mat busily engaged in weaving the meshes of a landing-net, at a table by himself in the further part of the room, silently whistling a tune over his work,—if the phrase is a permissible one for the description of a performance which consisted, as far as outward manifestations went, only of the movement of the lips and eyebrows—and Miss Margaret half reclining elegantly on a sofa, unoccupied save in chewing the cud of sweet and bitter fancy. Her attitude was unexceptionable, and her occupation very pardonable. Nevertheless, some hidden consciousness or other made her spring up and reseat herself in a primmer fashion, as the door opened and Lady Farnleigh and her sister came in.

"I was afraid Mr. Banting would have brought the tea in, Miss Immy, and that you would have waited for us," said Lady Farnleigh.

"Oh, dear, no!" said Miss Immy, as if her guest had suggested the most absurd impossibility; "it wants five minutes to teatime yet."

"Indeed! Well, I shall spend these five minutes in a *tête-à-tête* with Mr. Mat, over there at his separate establishment, and try whether I can't make him miss a mesh at least once in every minute."

"Not you, Lady Farnleigh," said Mr. Mat. But, nevertheless, it might have been observed that Mr. Mat's netting made but very little progress from that time till the tea was brought.

CHAPTER XLIII.

LADY FARNLEIGH CATCHES AN IDEA.

LADY FARNLEIGH slept at the Chase that night, as she usually did on the occasion of her visits. She had, also, as her wont was, ridden over from Wanstrow, sending what she needed for her stay at the Chase through Silverton, and retaining her own horse at Lindisfarn, but sending back to Wanstrow the groom who had ridden behind her. At breakfast the next morning she said,—

"I hope you have not forgotten your promise, Mr. Mat. Mr. Mat and I are going to ride into Silverton this morning. It is not very civil, is it, Kate, to run off and leave you in such a fashion the first morning? But I can't help it. I have all sorts of things to do, and people to see, so that there would be no pleasant ride to be got. We will have a good gallop together to-morrow, Katie dear. But to-day I invite only Mr. Mat to ride with me, because there will be nothing but what is disagreeable to be done."

"Always ready for the worst that can happen in your ladyship's company," said Mr. Mat.

Margaret glanced up at Lady Farnleigh's face with a sharp, uneasy look, as the latter had spoken of the various things she had to do and people to see in Silverton; but she quickly dropped her eyes again on her breakfast plate, and did not say anything. As soon, however, as Lady Farnleigh and Mr. Mat had, almost immediately after breakfast, mounted their horses and ridden away towards the lodge on the road to Silverton, and the squire had somewhat listlessly sauntered back into his study, and Miss Immy had bustled off to her domestic cares, Margaret said to her sister,—

"I wonder, Kate, that your favorite god-mamma did not invite you to ride with her; it is so long since you have had a ride together."

"Yes, and I should have liked a good gallop over the common towards Weston well enough," said Kate; "but you heard her

say that she had several people to see in Silverton."

"I wonder who it is she has gone to see?" rejoined Margaret, after a pause.

"How should I know? She has a great many friends in Silverton, and business people to see besides, very likely."

"But all her friends are acquaintances of yours. Why should she not have taken you with her?" persisted Margaret.

"She would easily guess that I am not much in a humor for visiting," returned Kate, "as in good truth I am not."

"I wonder why she took Mr. Mat with her?" still continued Margaret, pondering, and evidently not at all satisfied with Kate's answers. "Will she call in the Close, do you suppose, Kate?"

"Very likely. She did not say anything to me about it," answered Kate, carelessly.

"Did you observe how closely she and Mr. Mat were talking together last night in the drawing-room?" said Margaret, still, as it seemed, uneasy about the visit to Silverton.

"Not particularly. But it is very likely. They are very old friends and allies, my god-mamma and Mr. Mat."

"Yes; but I am sure they were planning something about what they are gone to Silverton for this morning!" said Margaret.

"Nothing more likely. But what in the world have you got into your head, Margaret, about Lady Farnleigh's ride to Silverton?"

"Oh, I know what I know, and I think what I think. I've a notion that she is gone to plot and plan, or meddle, or make in some way about our affairs. And however much you may like that, Kate, I don't like it. I don't like her, as you well know; and I don't at all want her to interfere with any affairs of mine."

"Why, how should she interfere, Margaret? I can't guess what you are thinking of," said Kate, much surprised; "and I am so sorry, more sorry than you can think," she added, "that you have taken such an unreasonable dislike to my dear, dear godmother. You may depend on it, Margaret, that we have not a better friend in the world than Lady Farnleigh."

"That is to say, she is *your* friend," returned Margaret, with a strong emphasis on the possessive pronoun.

"My friend, and your friend, and Noll's friend, and the dearest friend our mother had in the world, Margaret!"

"That's all very well, Kate, for you. But I like choosing my friends for myself," said Margaret.

Meanwhile Lady Farnleigh and Mr. Mat were walking their horses leisurely down the road that led toward the Ivy Bridge.

"This is a very sad affair, Mr. Mat. Do you think the squire feels it very deeply?" said her ladyship.

"It is the worst piece of business that ever happened at Lindisfarn, Lady Farnleigh. The squire—God bless him!—is one of those who think that care killed a cat; and he will none on't. But he feels it,—he feels it for all that, you may depend on it."

"And my darling Kate! she is not like herself,—neither mind nor body. Do you think, Mr. Mat, that she is fretting about it? I should not have thought that it would have affected her so deeply."

"Not a bit of it, Lady Farnleigh. Kate's not a-fretting after the acres. That's another bad matter,—another and not the same."

"How another—what other?" said Lady Farnleigh, who, having been obliged to quit the subject of Ellingham's offer to Kate, in the manner that has been seen, had failed to learn whether the fact had become known to any of the members of the family, and was anxious to ascertain this point.

"Ah! that's the question," said Mr. Mat, with a deep sigh,—"that's just what I should thank anybody to tell me. I don't suppose there's been a day for the last fortnight that the squire and I have not talked it over after dinner. Squire's a deal more down in the mouth about Kate than he is about the property. As you say, Lady Farnleigh, she is noways like the same girl she used to be. Body or mind, be it which it may, or both, she is amiss, and far amiss somehow."

"It is some time, then, that she has been in the state she is?" asked Lady Farnleigh.

"Yes, a spell now,—ever since that silly business of a match between Miss Margaret and Freddy Falconer, ugh!" grunted Mr. Mat, with an expression of infinite disgust.

"Ever since the announcement of her sister's engagement," said Lady Farnleigh, musingly. "It has clearly nothing to do, then, with the discovery of her cousin's marriage, and of the existence of a male heir to the property?"

"Oh, nothing,—nothing at all. That is what I say; it came before all that."

"And there has been nothing to which you can attribute it,—nothing has happened,—nothing of any sort?"

"Nothing that I can think of, and I am sure I never thought so much about anything before, in my life, as I have thought about that. There was that affair at Sillmouth,—at Pendleton's cottage; but there was nothing in that, so far as I can see, to make her out of sorts."

"Oh, by the by! tell me all about that story; it all happened, you know, after I went away."

"Well, there was nothing, as it turned out, to make Kate vex herself. It seems that Pendleton's boat, the *Saucy Sally* he called her, you know, poor fellow!—she was a beautiful boat as ever swam, and she's gone the way of all Sallys, however saucy they be, now,—well, the *Saucy Sally* was going to make a run from t'other side one night, with a big cargo; and the men were determined to make a fight of it, if they were meddled with, the stupid blockheads! And poor Winny Pendleton got wind somehow, that the cutter—Ellingham's vessel, the *Petrel*, you know—would be on the look-out for them. So poor Winny was frightened out of her wits, — natural enough! — and off she starts one terrible blustering night to walk up to the Chase, all a-purpose to beg Kate to try and persuade Ellingham—he was up at the Chase that night, as it chanced—to stay quiet where he was next day, and so let the lugger slip in quietly, and no bones broken; a likely story! and Winny must have been a bigger fool than I took her for, to think of such a thing. However, she did frighten Kate, with her rawhead-and-bloody-bones stories of what would be sure to happen if it came to a fight between the cutter and the smugglers, to such a degree that Kate went to Ellingham and told him all about it, one way or another; I don't know what she said to him. Of course he told her that he must do his duty, come what might. And we, Kate and I, had to ride over to Sillmouth, to tell Winny Pendleton that it was no go; and that if the men would fight, their blood must be on their own heads. And certainly,

Kate was in a desperate taking about it that night. She took it into her head that either Pendleton or Ellingham, or maybe both of them, would certainly be killed. But as good luck would have it, it was a terribly dirty night. The *Saucy Sally* managed to give the cutter a wide berth; and there was no fight at all, except with some of the coastguardmen on shore, in which Pendleton got hurt, and a French chap who was with him got a broken head, which nearly sent him into the next world. Well, the wounded man was carried to the cottage at Deep Creek; and up comes, or sends, Winny again, to say that the stranger is dying,—old Bagstock had given him over, and he could not speak a word of English, and Pendleton was away to the moor, and what on earth was she to do, and all the rest of it,—and would Miss Kate have the charity to come down to the cottage, and speak to the man who was dying without being able to speak a word to a Christian soul? There was no saying no to that. So we had to mount our nags and ride over again. And we found the man bad enough, to all appearance. But Kate, like a sensible girl and a good Christian, as she is, sent me off for Blakistry to mend old Bagstock's tinkering. And Blakistry managed to set the chap on his legs again; and he was on his way back to France, as I hear, in the *Saucy Sally*, when she was lost. That is the whole of the story. And though Kate certainly was very much put about—more than you would have thought—when she feared there was going to be bloodshed, and likely enough lives lost, still, as the matter turned out, there was nothing to vex her at the time even, let alone making her miserable from that time to this. No, no; *that* has nothing to do with it."

"And you can think of nothing else of any sort?" asked Lady Farnleigh, after she had pondered in silence for a few minutes, over all the details of Mr. Mat's history.

"Nothing at all, Lady Farnleigh. Somebody or something did put it into the squire's head, at one time, that she had cast a sheep's eye on that Jemmy Jessamy of a fellow, Fred Falconer, and was breaking her heart over her sister's engagement to him. But, Lord! it was no good to tell that to me! Our Kate pining after Master Freddy Falconer! No, that wont do!"

"No, I don't think that is at all likely. I flatter myself we know Kate, both you and I, Mr. Mat, a little too well to give any heed to *that* story."

"*I* should think so, and I was quite sure you would agree with me, Lady Farnleigh."

"But we are no nearer to guessing what *is* the matter; and something serious there is," said Lady Farnleigh, with grave earnestness.

"Ay, there is, and no mistake about it; sometimes I think 'tis all from being out of health."

"Well, I'll tell you what I will do for one thing,—and the first thing. We will ride first to Dr. Blakistry's, and I will have a talk with him. You shall leave me there for a little time, Mr. Mat."

"Very good, that will suit me very well; for I want to see Glenny about some new glees that our club has been getting down from London."

So that matter being satisfactorily arranged, they rode directly, on reaching Silverton, to Dr. Blakistry's door, and were fortunate enough to catch him before he had started on his round of professional visits. So Mr. Mat went off to his musical friend, and Lady Farnleigh was admitted to a *tête-à-tête* with the doctor.

"Doctor," said she, going directly to her object, after a few complimentary words had been said with reference to her return to Sillshire,—"doctor, I am unhappy and uneasy about my goddaughter and pet, Kate Lindisfarn. She is far from well. Whether the main seat of the malady is in the body or the mind, I do not know; but whichever it may be I equally come to you for help. Is it long since you have seen her?"

"Why, as it so happens, Lady Farnleigh, it is rather longer than usual since I have seen Miss Lindisfarn. It is—let me see— just about a month, or a little more, since I saw her, soon after paying a visit near Sillmouth to a patient to whose bedside she summoned me."

"Yes, I have heard the story of the wounded Frenchman at Pendleton's cottage. Mr. Mat told me all about it as we were riding in from the Chase this morning."

"Of course your ladyship has heard also of the very singular circumstances which have come to light, with the effect of changing in so important a degree the worldly prospects of the Misses Lindisfarn?" asked the doctor.

"Of course. Yes, I have heard the strange story, as everybody in Sillshire has heard it by this time. It *is* a very strange story."

"Has it occurred to your ladyship to consider how far it may be possible that the depressed state of Miss Kate Lindisfarn's spirits may be attributable to this sad change in her social position?"

"The idea has occurred to me, doctor, but only to be scouted the next instant. No, that is not it. We must seek again. In the first place, all my knowledge of Kate's character—and it is a lifelong knowledge, remember, doctor—would lead me to say that such a misfortune would not affect her in such a manner. It is a misfortune,—a great misfortune. Of course Kate would feel it as such. But she would not pine or fret over it. It is not in her nature, I feel perfectly sure of it. But, in the second place, it cannot be that your conjecture is the true one, for another and a perfectly decisive reason. The effect was in action before the existence of the cause to which your suggestion would assign it. Kate's sad loss of spirits and of healthy tone was remarked on at the Chase a month ago or more; and this sudden change of fortune has been discovered only within the last few days."

Dr. Blakistry remained silent for a minute or two before he replied.

"I should be quite disposed to agree with you, Lady Farnleigh," he then said, "that such a cause as we are speaking of would not appear to me to furnish a probable explanation of the phenomena in question. But I think it right—under the circumstances of the case, I think it right—to let you know that you are in error respecting the time at which the knowledge of this sad misfortune may have begun to exercise its influence upon our young friend. The putting you right in this matter involves the disclosing of a secret which was confided to me, and which no consideration would have induced me to betray, were it not that death has made the further keeping of it altogether unnecessary. I do not know exactly by what means the facts which involve the change in the destination of the Lindisfarn property have been made generally known; but—Miss Kate Lindisfarn did not first become acquainted with these facts in the same manner or at the same time. They were known to her and to her sister from the time of that visit of mine to the wounded stranger in Deep Creek Cottage."

"Dr. Blakistry!" exclaimed Lady Farnleigh, in the greatest astonishment.

"It is even so. Miss Lindisfarn is not aware that I am cognizant of the fact that such is the case; but it so happens that I know it to be so. The wounded man to whose bedside I was called was none other than Julian Lindisfarn, the same who is said to have recently perished at sea on his return to France; and Miss Kate was informed by him of the fact, and was made fully aware of the bearing that fact had upon her prospects."

"And Margaret?"

"Was equally made aware of the same facts. She was informed of them at the same time, by her sister, who bargained with her dying cousin, as he then fancied himself, for permission to share the secret with her."

Lady Farnleigh bent her head, and placed her hand before her eyes, as if in deep and painful thought, for some minutes.

"What can have been Kate's motive?" she said at last, raising her head and looking up into the doctor's face, but still seeming to speak more to herself than to him,—"what can have been Kate's motive for keeping this secret from her family and from me?"

"The motive of her secrecy up to the time of her cousin's departure from England is obvious enough. Doubtless she had given the same promise of secrecy to her cousin that was exacted from me. It seems to have been his earnest wish that it should not be known to his family that he was alive and in the immediate neighborhood. But what her motive has been in still keeping silence as to the fact since his departure, and yet more since his death has become known, I cannot imagine."

Again Lady Farnleigh remained plunged in deep thought, resting her head upon her hand for a long time.

At last, suddenly raising her head and speaking with rapid earnestness, as if a sudden thought had flashed across her mind, she said,—

"Can you recollect the exact date of your visit to the cottage at Deep Creek, doctor?"

"Undoubtedly. I can give it you with

the greatest certainty. It was—yes, here it is," said the doctor, referring to a note-book as he spoke, "the date of my first visit to Deep Creek Cottage was the 20th of March last."

"The 20th of March last!" exclaimed Lady Farnleigh, hurriedly searching among a variety of papers she drew from the *reticule* which ladies were wont to carry in those days,—"the 20th of March!" she repeated, looking eagerly at the date of a letter she had selected from among the other papers. "Doctor, I think I have discovered the *mot d'énigme*. I think I see it. I *think* I understand it all. You must excuse me if I make the bad return for your information of keeping my own surmises on the subject to myself. I must do so at least till they are something more than surmises. I *think* I see it all. My dear, dear, darling, high-minded, noble-hearted Kate! And then Miss Margaret! Heavens and earth! You have no idea, doctor, how many things this little secret of yours explains, or how much it is worth. Have a little patience, and you shall know all about it in good time."

"I will bide my time, Lady Farnleigh, with such patience as I may. I only hope that the solution of the mystery is of a nature to bring back the roses to Miss Lindisfarn's cheeks. Sillshire cannot afford to let them wither away."

"That we shall see; I can't promise,—we shall see. But I am not without my hopes. And now, doctor, while I am waiting for Mr. Mat, who is to come here for me,—and I must trespass on your hospitality till he does come; for he is my only squire,—I will ask you to have the kindness to give me the means of writing a letter. I want to post it before I leave Silverton."

And sitting down at the doctor's writing-table, Lady Farnleigh, scribbling as fast as ever she could drive the pen over the paper, wrote the following letter :—

"DEAR WALTER,—If it is possible, come here without loss of time, on receiving this. And if it is not possible, make it so; I want you. *Basta!* come direct to Wanstrow, without going to Silverton at all. I got back here only yesterday. I know you wont fail me; and therefore say no more.

"Yours always and affectionately,
"KATHERINE FARNLEIGH."

She sealed it in such haste and flurry that she burnt her fingers in doing it; addressed

it to "The Hon. Walter Ellingham, Moulsea Haven, North Sillshire," and then jumping up from the table, said, "Where can Mr. Mat be? He told me he was going to Glenny's, the organist's. I suppose they are deep in quavers and semiquavers. And I want to be on my way back to Lindisfarn. If my horse were here, I would ride off by myself."

"Here is Mr. Mat; I am sure he has not suffered himself to be detained from his allegiance long, Lady Farnleigh."

"No, indeed! and I am very rude; but the fact is, Dr. Blakistry, that since I flatter myself that I have discovered what I was in search of when I came here, I am in a very great hurry to go and test my nostrum. Can't you sympathize with that impatience?"

"I can, indeed, and admit it to be a most legitimate one. Mr. Mat," continued the doctor, addressing that gentleman as he entered the room, "her ladyship's service requires that you should sound to boot and saddle forthwith; sorry that it accords so ill with the duties of hospitality to tell you so, but"—

"We must be off, Mr. Mat; I want to get back to Lindisfarn."

"I thought your ladyship had ever so many things to do in Silverton!" said Mr. Mat, staring.

"All that remains to be done now, however, is to put this letter in the post; we will ride by the post-office, and if you are for a good gallop up from the Ivy Bridge to the lodge-gate, I am quite disposed for it."

"With all my heart, Lady Farnleigh. Any pace you like, once we are down the steep Castle Head to the bridge."

"I have heard a queerish thing since I came into the town, Lady Farnleigh. It reached my ears by an odd chance, and I hardly know what to make of it," said Mr. Mat, as they were walking their horses down the steep pitch of hill above mentioned.

"Anything with reference to these sad affairs at Lindisfarn?" said Lady Farnleigh, to whom any other Silverton gossip was just then altogether uninteresting.

"Why, I hardly know; I can't help fancying that it *has* reference to some of us up at the Chase, Lady Farnleigh," replied Mr. Mat, with a shrewd glance at his companion's face. "But you shall judge for yourself. When I went into Glenny's, the organist's, just now, I found old Wyvil, the verger, in his room. 'Here's the man that can tell us,' cried Glenny, meaning me. I saw with half an eye that old Wyvil was vexed, and that Glenny was letting some cat or other out of the bag; but it was too late then to put her in again. 'Tell you what?' said I. 'Why, this,' said Glenny: 'was Dr. Lindisfarn expected to dinner up at the Chase last Friday?' 'Not that I know of,' said I; 'and I certainly should have known if he had been.' 'There now! I thought as much!' said Glenny. 'Why, what about it?' said I. 'Well it is this,' said Glenny, without paying any heed to old Gaffer Wyvil's signs and winks: 'Jonas, at the Lindisfarn Arms,'—that is the postboy, Lady Farnleigh, who is cousin, or nephew, one or the other, to the old verger,—'Jonas,' says he, 'has been telling my old friend here that he was ordered by Mr. Frederick Falconer to take a chaise and pair that evening round to the door in the doctor's garden-wall, that opens into the Castle Head Lane; and if he met anybody who asked questions, he was to say, that he was going to take the doctor up to the Chase to dinner. Well, he was doing as he was ordered,—was coming along the Castle Head Lane just at six o'clock, which was the time he was told to be there,—when he met old Gregory Greatorex, Falconer's confidential clerk, who sent him back all of a hurry, telling him that the chaise was not wanted for that night. Looks queer; don't it?' said Glenny. 'Very queer!' said I. As if all Sillshire did not know that the squire dines at half-past five too! 'I hope you gentlemen wont go for to get a poor boy into a scrape,' said old Wyvil; 'he did not mean any harm by telling me, as we was having a bit of gossip over a mug of beer.' 'Never fear,' said I; 'the boy, as you call him,'—he's sixty if he is a day,—'shall come to no harm.' Now what does your ladyship think of that?" concluded Mr. Mat, looking up with another of his shrewd, twinkling glances.

"Upon my word, Mr. Mat, I hardly know. Was Margaret at her uncle's on that day?"

"Yes, she was, and has been there a deal more than at home lately."

"Was she to sleep there that night?" pursued Lady Farnleigh.

"Yes, and did sleep there!" said Mr. Mat.

"It *is* very odd!" said Lady Farnleigh.

"I see that your ladyship has taken the same notion into your head that came into mine," said Mr. Mat.

"What was that, then?" said Lady Farn-

leigh, smiling, and looking archly at Mr. Mat in her turn.

"Why, what does a postchaise, at a back-door in a by-lane on a dark night, where a young lady is living, mostly mean?" said Mr. Mat.

"It must be owned that it looks very like an elopement, *dans les regles!*" said the lady; "but I confess that that is an indiscretion which I should not have suspected either the gentleman or the lady of, in this case."

"It seems one or both of them thought better of it, anyway!" returned Mr. Mat.

"When was the claim put forward on behalf of Julian Lindisfarn's child first heard of in Silverton?"

"Old Slowcome heard of it from Jared Mallory, the attorney at Sillmouth, that same afternoon," replied Mr. Mat.

"Humph," said Lady Farnleigh, musingly, as she coupled this fact with the information she had just been put in possession of, respecting the date of Margaret's knowledge of the true state of the case concerning her cousin.

"What does your ladyship make out of it?"

"Well, I don't know; we shall see. But I am almost inclined to think, Mr. Mat, that I can make out of it that it was a great pity Mr. Gregory Greatorex did not abstain from meddling with Jonas Wyvil, the postboy," said her ladyship, with a queer look at Mr. Mat.

Mr. Mat's bright black eyes twinkled like two bits of live fire, and a rather grim smile mantled gradually over the hard features of his seamed face, as he answered,—

"What, let 'em do it? 'twould have served Jemmy Jessamy right, if that was what he was up to."

"I am never for separating two young and ardent hearts, if it can anyway be avoided. Don't you agree with me, especially in cases where one may say with the poet, 'Sure such a pair were never seen, so justly formed to meet by nature,' eh, Mr. Mat?"

"Young and ardent hearts be—stuck on the same skewer, the way they do in the valentines!" cried Mr. Mat, with an expression of intense disgust. "I can't say that I can make it out, Lady Farnleigh; they are not the sort, not if I know anything about them," added he.

"Well, perhaps we shall understand it better by and by, Mr. Mat," returned Lady Farnleigh.

And as they reached the Ivy Bridge and the bottom of the hill, while she was speaking, with the long ascent toward Lindisfarn before them, they put their horses into a gallop, and did not draw rein till they were at the lodge-gates.

CHAPTER XLIV.

MR. SLOWCOME GOES TO SILLMOUTH, AND TAKES
NOTHING BY HIS MOTION.

DR. LINDISFARN and Mr. Sligo gained nothing by their excursion to Chewton. Their researches were equally fruitless on the special objects of both gentlemen. The evident priority which the doctor gave to his archæological investigations was a matter of the most intense astonishment, and almost, one may say, of scandal, to Mr. Sligo. That an elderly gentleman in the possession of his senses, so nearly interested as Dr. Lindisfarn was in the result of the examinations which he (Mr. Sligo) was there for the purpose of making, should utterly fail to take any rational interest in the matter, manifestly in consequence of his being wholly absorbed by his anxiety to discover the meaning of certain syllables which in all probability had no meaning at all, and at all events, none that could be supposed to affect the title of any human being to any amount of property real or personal, was a phenomenon so new, so wholly unaccountable to Mr. Sligo, and so distasteful to him, that it made him cross with the doctor. He began to think that the admission that the old canon was in the perfect possession of his senses was an assumption not warranted by the facts in evidence. The doctor, on his part, was revolted by his companion's evident want of interest in the whole question of the mysterious inscription, and the cursory and impatient attention which was all that he could induce him to accord to it. He looked at the wooden panel in question, tapped it with his knuckles, stared, at the doctor's request, at the inscribed letters, and declared that, as far as he could see, there never had been any others; at all events, his eyes could see no traces of any such.

"And now, Mr. Mallory," he said to the old clerk, who, having accompanied the two gentlemen to the church, had been standing by, impassible and grave as a judge, while this examination was in progress,—"and now, Mr. Mallory, if Dr. Lindisfarn is satisfied that there is nothing more to be discovered here, we will, with your leave, return to your house, and resume the subject on which we were speaking."

"As Dr. Lindisfarn pleases," said the old clerk, gravely; "but he, as it is reasonable to suppose, knew the late Mr. Mellish as

well as I did, and in any case I have nothing more to tell about him."

"You admit that the church registers were at one period kept at your house?"

"I have told you that such was the case, since you expressed curiosity upon the subject. There was no question of *admitting* one way or the other in the matter, Mr. Sligo. I have nothing to admit or deny on the subject. The books were at one time kept at my house,—not because it was my house, but because it was the clergyman's lodging. I had nothing to do with the bringing of them there, or with the taking of them back again to the church. The responsibility for the custody of them lay with the parson, and not with the clerk, as you no doubt are well aware, Mr. Sligo."

"Well, well, never mind whether it is admitting or stating; you say that the registers were subsequently taken back to the church?"

"You speak of registers, sir; but I have no recollection of having seen more than one book, and that not a very big one. During the latter years of Mr. Mellish's life, that book used to be kept in the vestry."

"And was always at hand there, I suppose, when needed?"

"I suppose so, sir; but it was often for months at a time together that it was never needed. We don't bury, marry, or christen every day out on the moor here, as you people do in the towns!"

"When was the last time that you have any recollection of having yourself seen the book, Mr. Mallory?" asked Sligo. "How long before the death of Mr. Mellish, now, had you a death, or a burial,—or a christening?"

"I could not at all undertake to say when I saw the book last. Old Farmer Boultby, of the Black Tor Farm, out towards the coast, was, I think, the last parishioner buried by Mr. Mellish, a month or so maybe before his own death. Whether his burial was registered or not, I can't say; nor whether it was done at the time of the ceremony or not. Very often the curate would put the entries into the register afterward." Further cross-questioning of the old man only obtained from him that he "could not say how long afterwards—at any convenient time—he did not mean by that to say when the curate was sober, though it might be that sometimes he was not altogether so at the time of the performance of the function."

In short, all that Mr. Mallory *could* recollect were circumstances tending to show that the whole ecclesiastical administration of the parish was in the greatest possible disorder in every respect in the old times when Mr. Mellish was curate, near ten years ago; and he could *not* recollect any single fact which could help to fix the existence of the missing register at any ascertained date or place. He could remember, however, perfectly well that when Mr. Partloe, who succeeded Mr. Mellish in the curacy, came, there was no book to be found, and Mr. Partloe had procured a new one. Mr. Partloe was a very different sort of gentleman from Mr. Mellish,—very particular, and very regular. The new book was always kept in the vestry, was there now. They were still without any proper chest at Chewton; but the new register was, from the time of Mr. Partloe's coming, always kept in a little cupboard in the vestry, which he had caused to be put up at his own expense. Mr. Partloe had been curate only four years. The register-book had been kept with the most perfect regularity all that time; as it had indeed by the present curate, Mr. Bellings, who had succeeded Mr. Partloe. Mr. Bellings was not at home, having ridden over that morning to Silverton. Dr. Lindisfarn and Mr. Sligo must have met him, had they not come by the other road, which alone was passable for wheels. But it would be easy to obtain an opportunity of examining the new register, which had been kept from the time of the death of Mr. Mellish. Very easy, no doubt; and altogether useless as regarded the business in hand.

What search had been made for the missing register by Mr. Partloe when he came there after Mellish's death, Mr. Mallory could not say, but felt certain that Mr. Partloe must have exhausted every means for finding it, as he was such a very particular gentleman.

Had the old book never been needed in all these ten years? Mr. Sligo asked; had nobody in all that time required to refer to it for the establishment of any of the facts of which it constituted the sole legal record? No, nobody. When folk were dead out in the moor there, nobody wanted to ask any more about them. When folk were married, they got their marriage lines, and that was all that was needed.

"And your daughter's marriage lines, Mr.

Mallory,—of course she had them?" asked Sligo, suddenly.

"No doubt she had them, Mr. Sligo. Of my own personal knowledge I can affirm nothing about it. The whole subject of the marriage was a very painful one to me. I would have prevented it if I could have done so, without the risk of greater evil to my unfortunate child."

"Unfortunate, Mr. Mallory?" cried Sligo. "Well, I don't know what you may call fortunate, but "—

"My daughter was induced to make a marriage, Mr. Sligo, to which her position in life did not entitle her; which she was compelled to keep secret for many long and painful years, while calumny and scandal were at work with her name; which took her husband from her within a few months of their union; which has ended in leaving her a widow,—a widow widowed in such a fearful manner, and compelled by duty to her child to assert its rights with hostility against a family for whom I have the greatest respect, and with a result that is lamented by and is unwelcome to the whole country-side. You must excuse me, Mr. Sligo," said the old man, who had been speaking under the influence of his feelings in a somewhat higher strain than that of his usual talk,—"you must excuse me if I cannot consider the marriage a fortunate one in any respect; and I feel confident that Dr. Lindisfarn will enter into my sentiments on the subject."

"I am sure, Mallory, your feelings are all that they ought to be on the subject. It is an unhappy business. If my poor boy were living, it might have been different. As it is —you see—ha—hum—I wonder, Mallory, whether poor Mellish could have thrown any light on that singular inscription in the vestry corridor?"

"Not he, sir. It is little he thought of such matters," said the old man, glancing at Mr. Sligo as he spoke.

"When was the last whitewashing done, Mallory?" asked the doctor, meditatively.

"When Mr. Partloe first came here, sir. He was a great man for whitewash, Mr. Partloe was, sir, a tidy sort of a gentleman, who liked to have things clean and neat. He had all the passage leading to the vestry and the vestry itself new whitewashed."

"It is very unfortunate," sighed the doctor.

" Very," re-echoed Mr. Sligo, who had been mentally reviewing the total failure of his attempts to learn anything of the history of the missing register.

" Very unfortunate, gentlemen ! " coincided old Jared Mallory, with a placid drawing down of the corners of his mouth, and softly rubbing his palms and fingers together with the action of a man washing his hands with very smooth and easily lathering soap.

And so it came to pass that the senior canon and the junior partner in the legal firm drove back again to Silverton, having accomplished nothing of any sort by their journey.

" I am afraid the document will have to be admitted as good evidence, as it stands," said Sligo, alluding to the extract from the register in the hands of the Sillmouth attorney.

" Yes, indeed ! but as evidence of what ? " returned the doctor. " Any interpretation that can be put upon it must be entirely conjectural. And I confess I am at loss too ffer even a conjecture."

" It is legal evidence of the marriage, that is all," said Sligo, shrugging his shoulders.

" Oh, ah, yes—I see ! " said the doctor.

" No go ! " said Sligo, as he entered Mr. Slowcome's room at the office, on his return to Silverton ; " nothing to be done. That old man, the clerk, mute as a stockfish and sly as a fox. Nothing to be made of him. But I observed one thing, sir."

" What was that, Mr. Sligo ? Come, take a chair and let us go into the matter comfortably."

" No, thank you," said Sligo, who had acquired a horror of getting himself seated at the writing-table in his partner's room, and considered the proposal that he should sit down there much as a sparrow might have regarded an invitation to hold out his tail for salt to be put upon it,—" no, I wont sit down, thank you. I must be off. But I am going to mention that I noticed that there was nothing to be seen at Chewton of the old man's daughter, or the child. So I just said, ' Is your daughter with you, Mr. Mallory ? I should be happy to have an opportunity to pay my respects to Mrs. Lindisfarn ; ' ' Mrs. Lindisfarn, I said, you know, just so. ' Mrs. Lindisfarn is not at Chewton,' said he, as stiff and grim as an old woman in a witness-box, when she don't mean to tell you any-

thing ; ' she is at Sillmouth with her brother.' Well now, that set me thinking, Mr. Slowcome."

" Indeed ; and what did you think, Mr. Sligo ? " replied the senior partner, with much interest.

" Well, nothing for certain,—only a guess ; maybe nothing in it. ' What have this woman and her child been sent to Sillmouth for ? ' said I to myself. Jared Mallory is a bachelor, and a loose one, and a poor one. The woman's home is and has been in her father's house—a very good house it is—at Chewton. What is the nature and character of women, especially of that sort of women that get led away by such chaps as this Julian Lindisfarn seems to have been ? And this led me to guess—a mere random guess, you see, Mr. Slowcome—that it is not unlikely, if there has been any got-up fraud in this matter, that they may think it best to keep the woman out of the way, under the care of that precious scamp Mr. Jared, junior. Twig, eh, sir ? "

Mr. Slowcome took an enormous pinch of snuff very slowly and deliberately ; and having thus stimulated his brain, and carefully brushed away every scattering atom of the dust from his shirt-frill and waistcoat with dainty care. answered Mr. Sligo's rapid and elliptical exposition of his ideas.

" I think I gather your meaning, Sligo ; you consider it probable,—or at least possible, for I am quite aware that you put forward this theory as mere possibility,—you think it possible that the young woman may have been removed and placed in her brother's charge, from fear that she might be disinclined, or only partially inclined, or weakly inclined, to engage in the fraud, and might perhaps, if judiciously handled, be induced to make a clean breast of it, and tell the truth."

" Pre-cisely so, sir. That is what came into my head. Think there is anything in it, sir, eh ? "

" I am not at all prepared to say there may not be. It is a very shrewd idea, Mr. Sligo, and well worth acting on. It would be very desirable that you should endeavor to see this young woman."

" Job for the head of the firm, sir," said Mr. Sligo, shaking his head. " You must see her yourself, sir."

" Why should I do it better than you,

Sligo? I am sure you have always shown yourself"—

"Very good of you to say so, Mr. Slowcome; but in this case—beautiful woman—don't you see? Two sorts of 'em! If she is of the sort to prefer doing business in such a case with the junior partner, you understand, Mr. Slowcome, why then she is not of the sort that we shall get the truth of this business from. If there is to be any hope of that, she must be of the sort that would prefer to speak with you on the matter. Twig, sir, eh? Fatherly dodge—daughters of your own. Your entire turn-out, sir, worth anything for such a business! See it in that light, sir? You'll excuse *me!*" and Mr. Sligo winked a running commentary as he delivered himself of these suggestions, which greatly added to their suasive force.

"I think I catch your idea, Mr. Sligo," said Mr. Slowcome, in a dignified manner; "and upon the whole I am disposed to think that you may be right. I dare say you *are* right. I will try to see the young woman myself. I do not, I confess, much like the idea of being seen knocking at the door of Mr. Jared Mallory, junior. Nevertheless, in our good client's interest, I will undertake the job."

Mr. Slowcome did undertake the job the next day, driving, or rather being driven, over to Sillmouth in his well-known carriage, with the large, sleek, well-conditioned powerful roadster, driven by the Aready Lodge hobbledehoy in livery, for the purpose. Of course, every man, woman, and child in Sillmouth—or at least all those who were in or looking out into the street, which comprised the major part of the population—became aware of the advent of the great Silverton lawyer; and when the handsome carriage and the big horse and the hobbledehoy in livery drew up at Mr. Jared Mallory's door, that gentleman was standing at it to receive them.

"Mr. Slowcome, upon my word! quite an unexpected honor, I am sure. Will you walk in, sir?"

So the head of the respectable Silverton firm had to walk into the disreputable looking little den, which his professional brother of Sillmouth dignified by the name of his office.

"Touching the business of the Lindisfarn succession?" said Mr. Mallory, when they were seated in the dirty little bare room, with the air of a man who had affairs of various kinds pending, to which the visit of the Silverton man of business might perchance have had reference.

"Yes, Mr. Mallory, touching the business of the Lindisfarn succession," said Slowcome, and there stopped short, like a man in the habit of feeling his way with those he spoke to as cautiously as a skilful pugilist makes his play before his adversary. But he was not likely to get anything by any such tactics from the man against whom he was now pitted.

"I shall be most happy, Mr. Slowcome, to give my best attention to any overture you may be desirous of making," said Mallory, sitting on the corner of the plain deal table in his office, and swinging one long leg to and fro in a devil-may-care sort of manner, which especially scandalized the sense of propriety and irritated the nervous system of old Slow, who was seated in the one arm-chair the mean little place contained.

"Overture, Mr. Mallory?" said he, thus driven; "I have no overture to make. It is not a case for anything of the sort. In a matter of this kind, Mr. Mallory, where it will become necessary for an excellent and highly respected family to—to—to open its arms, as I may say, to a new member, to one whom none of them have ever before seen, of whom they have known nothing, you must feel that it is very natural that interviews should be desired. My present mission here is, therefore, to see Mrs. Lindisfarn, and "—

"Oh, I see! respectable family opens its arms by power of attorney. Family solicitor — Mr. Jared Mallory—honor to inform Messrs. Slowcome and Sligo that that cock positively declines to fight!"

"What *do* you mean, Mr. Mallory?" said Mr. Slowcome, staring at him in unfeigned amazement.

"It is no go, Slowcome!" returned the other, closing his left eye, as he nodded at his visitor knowingly; "not a chance of the shadow of the tithe of a go. Why what *do* you take me for, Mr. Slowcome, to imagine that I should allow you to tamper, sir, with my witnesses in that manner?"

"Tamper, Mr. Mallory? Take care, sir, tamper!"

"I will take care, Mr. Slowcome, devilish good care. As for the expression—withdraw it with all my heart, if it riles you—parliamentary sense— But Mrs. Lindisfarn is not visible this morning, Mr. Slowcome. No, not so much as the tip of her nose!"

So Mr. Slowcome's fatherly bearing, his unblemished character and white waistcoat to match, his shirt and gold buckles, and his pigtail were all unavailing, and he had to pack all these properties into the carriage with the stout cob and the hobbledehoy for driver, to be driven back again to Silverton, having taken absolutely nothing by his expedition.

CHAPTER XLV.

THE FAIRY GODMOTHER AT HER SPELLS.

As Lady Farnleigh and Mr. Mat were riding up from the lodge gates, they met Mr. Merriton riding down the hill from the house.

"How do, Merriton; sorry to have been out when you called. Found the ladies, I suppose, more to the purpose, eh?" said Mr. Mat.

"Thank you. Lady Farnleigh, happy to see your ladyship back in Sillshire again—good-morning," said Mr. Merriton, rather shortly, and rode on.

"Better fellow that than I thought him when he first came here!" said Mr. Mat.

"Oh, I rather like Mr. Merriton. I quite think that he and that quaint little sister of his have been acquisitions to us," said Lady Farnleigh.

"Do you remember that day at the Friary, when little Dinah Wilkins all but fell over the face of the Nosey Stone?"

"To be sure I do! I shall not forget it in a hurry."

"Well, Merriton behaved well that day—very differently from some others that were there. Yes, I like Merriton. Seemed to be out of sorts just now, I thought."

"In a hurry to get home, perhaps."

Lady Farnleigh and her squire had ridden from Silverton up to the Chase in less than an hour, and they found Miss Immy and Miss Margaret still sitting in the dining-room at the luncheon-table. Kate, as had been so often latterly the case, was not there.

Lady Farnleigh declared that her ride had made her hungry; and Mr. Mat so far derogated from his ordinary habits as to sit down at the table, and draw a plate toward him in rather an apologetical sort of manner.

"So you have had Mr. Merriton here? Did you give him some luncheon, Miss Immy?" said Lady Farnleigh.

"He did not come into the dining-room, Lady Farnleigh. I asked him; but he refused," said Miss Immy, feeling that she had been rather injured by the rejection of that middle-of-the-day hospitality, which she regarded as more especially and exclusively her own affair.

"I don't know what you have been doing or saying to him," said Mr. Mat; "but as we met him going down to the lodge, he seemed quite out of sorts. Have you been unkind to him, Miss Margaret?"

"Really I know nothing about it, Mr. Mat," said Margaret, tossing her head. "Mr. Merriton's visit was not to me, nor to Miss Immy, indeed, as far as that goes. His business here, whatever it may have been, seemed to be of a very exclusive nature. And if you want to know anything about it, you had better ask Kate. I have no doubt she will tell you, and explain why Mr. Merriton was out of sorts—if he were so."

All this was spoken with a peculiar sort of sourness, and with sundry tosses of the head, the observation of which caused Lady Farnleigh to bring her luncheon to a rather abrupt conclusion, and leave the room, saying, "Where is Kate? In her own room, I suppose, according to her new bad habit. I shall go and look for her. I want to speak to her."

Lady Farnleigh did find Kate in her own room; but, contrary to her usual habit, she was locked in. The door resisted Lady Farnleigh's quick, impatient, push preceded by no knock.

"It is I, Kate. Open the door, darling, I want to tell you all about my expedition to Silverton."

Kate came to the door at once, and Lady Farnleigh saw at a glance, when she opened it, that her pet and favorite had been crying.

"What is it, my darling?" she said, coming in, and at the same time rebolting the door behind her,—"what is it, my Kate? All alone! and tears, tears, tears,—you who used to be all smiles and laughter from one week's end to another. My child, this will not do. Has anything vexed you this morning, dear? What is this about Mr. Merriton? We met him, Mr. Mat and I, as we came up the drive from the lodge; and he seemed to be very unwilling to give us a word more than a passing greeting. And when Mr. Mat remarked down-stairs that he seemed to have been all out of sorts, Margaret tossed her head, and said, in her sharp, disagreeable way, that Mr. Merriton's visit had not been to her, and that you could doubtless explain all about his being out of humor."

"It is true, godmamma! He came here to me," said Kate, hanging her head in a very penitential sort of attitude. "He would not be shown into the drawing-room, but asked to see me; waited in the hall till I came down, —for I was up here at the time,—and then asked if he might go with me into the library."

"So, so, that speaks plainly enough for itself, my dear," said Lady Farnleigh, drawing a chair close to Kate's, and making the latter sit down by her, and taking her hand between both her own caressingly; "I quite understand all about Mr. Merriton's visit to the Chase now, my dear; so I will not ask what it was he said to you in the library; but what was it you said to him?"

"Indeed, godmamma," said Kate, looking up sadly enough into Lady Farnleigh's face, but striving to force a feeble smile athwart the remnant of her tears, "it would not be at all fair to Mr. Merriton to tell the story so shortly. He spoke to me in the kindest and most delicate manner. You know how shy he is! He seemed hardly able to speak at all at first; and I was quite unable to give him the least bit of help. But when he had once begun, he got on better, and I assure you I was quite touched by his kindness."

"Well, dear! And I suppose his kindness consisted in throwing himself and his hand and his heart and everything else that is his at your feet," said Lady Farnleigh, willing to get a smile of the old arch and gay sort from Kate by any means; but the strings of the finely-tempered instrument were unstrung, and could not give back to the touch their old music.

"That was the upshot of it, I believe, godmamma. But he did it with such good feeling and delicacy. He spoke of the change that had occurred to us,—my sister and me, —apologized for venturing to do so on the score of its inevitably becoming the gossip of the place, and confessed that that circumstance had given him courage to do so at once, what he had hitherto not dared to do.

But he said it so well, far better than I can repeat it. He never supposed for an instant he said, that such considerations could make any difference in my decision on such a point; but my family might consider that under the present circumstances he was not making a proposal which could be blamed on the same grounds, at least, as it might have been had he made it previously."

"All spoken very much like a gentleman, as Mr. Merriton unquestionably is. And what did my little goddaughter say in return for so many pretty speeches?" said Lady Farnleigh.

"Oh! I told him, godmamma, you know, that it was out of the question. I spoke as civilly—indeed, as kindly as I could."

"You say 'you know, godmamma!' just as if I knew all the secrets of that little hide-and-seek heart of yours, my Katie. I thought I did once. But there is something there now that godmamma, fairy she be, knows nothing about. How should I know that it was out of the question? Mr. Merriton is a gentleman, and I believe a very worthy man, and certainly he is what is called a very good match, especially so under our present circumstances. And I suppose, too, that he wanted to have it explained to him a little, why it was perfectly out of the question? Did you say nothing on that head?"

"What could I say, godmamma, but that, though I esteemed him much, I did not feel toward him as I must feel toward the person I could accept as a husband? That was in truth all there was to be said about it. Was it not, godmamma?"

"I suppose so, Katie dear. And you probably had the less difficulty in saying it that you had already been called upon to say the same thing once before to another aspirant?"

"Godmamma!" cried Kate, with a great gasp, while the tell-tale blood rushed with tumultuous force over her neck and shoulders and forehead and cheeks, to leave them in the next moment ghastly white, and she began to shake all over like an aspen-leaf.

Lady Farnleigh almost repented of the success of her stratagem, when she saw the excess and genuineness of the distress she had caused her favorite. Nevertheless, having gone so far, she would not abstain from pushing her test-operation to its extent.

"Forgive me, darling!" she continued; "I would not pain you needlessly for the world, Kate ; you know I would not. But it did not seem to distress you to speak of this other rejection. What difference could there have been in the two cases?—unless, indeed, that Merriton could not have imagined that he was rejected on prudential considerations."

"But he did not think that !" sobbed Kate, with difficulty forcing out the words between the hard and quick-drawn breathings that were alternately extending and contracting their coral-pink delicately-cut nostrils.

"That is what I say, my dear," returned Lady Farnleigh, wilfully mistaking her meaning, with cruel kindness, " I say he could not have imagined that."

"I mean," cried Kate, almost driven to bay by the extremity of her distress, " I mean that *he* did not imagine that—*the other.*"

"Oh, Ellingham ! No, it is not in him to harbor such a thought of a girl he loved. But it was not so self-evident as in the latter case. I suppose the answer you gave, dear, was much about the same in either instance ? "

"Godmamma !" exclaimed the poor girl, in the tone of a prisoner crying for mercy from under the cords of the rack. " You said," she added, after a short pause, " that that subject should not be spoken of between us again."

"At all events, Kate, you must admit that it is impossible for me to avoid seeing that there is a remarkable divergence in your mode of feeling and speaking of the two events. The account you give me of them is much about the same of one as of the other in all material points. But yet they appear to affect you very differently. As to Ellingham, I should not have mentioned the matter again, were it not that I had to tell you that I must return to Wanstrow to-morrow morning the first thing after breakfast, because I am expecting him there. He is going to pay me a visit."

Kate kept her face resolutely bent downwards, so that it was impossible for Lady Farnleigh to see the expression of it ; but she could see that her announcement was making her goddaughter tremble in every limb.

"I thought it best to mention it to you, darling, that you might not be exposed to meet him unexpectedly. You must prepare yourself to do so ; for of course it can hardly be but that he will come over to the Chase."

"I do not think that he will come here, godmamma," said Kate, in a voice scarcely above a whisper.

"It may be so, my Katie. Nevertheless, my own impression is that he *will* come here. —it is my very strong impression that he will come. It is best, therefore, that you should be prepared to meet him, little one," said Lady Farnleigh.

"I should be glad to be spared doing so just yet, if it were possible," she said, huskily, for the words seemed to stick in her parched throat ; " could I not remain up in my own room here, godmamma ? "

"My child, you cannot live shut up in this room. You must learn to meet him. And besides—what would you do, Kate, if he were specially to ask to see you ? "

"Oh, godmamma ! It is quite out of the question that he should do that,—quite ! " said Kate, in somewhat stronger tones.

"I do not think so, my dear. On the contrary, I think it extremely probable that he will want to speak to you ! "

"I cannot fancy that he would do such a thing, godmamma. You do not know— What makes you think that he is likely to do so ? "

"Simply my knowledge of his character, my dear. I have known Walter Ellingham all his life. I love him nearly if not quite as well as I do you, my pet ; and if I am not mistaken in him, he *will* come here, and will want to speak to you ; so you had better, as far as may be, make up your mind as to what you will say to him in return."

"But what can he want to say to me, godmamma ? " said Kate, while her cheeks tingled, and she drooped her face yet more upon her bosom ; for the slightest shadow of a shade of disingenuousness was new and painful to her, and the truth was, that Kate knew very well what it was that her godmother supposed Walter Ellingham might have to say to her.

"My notion is, my dear, that he will want to ask you yet once again, before giving up all hope, whether you will be his wife. My notion is, that he is coming to me at Wanstrow for that express purpose and no other ! Therefore, I say again, my Katie, that it would be well that you should be in some degree prepared as to the answer you will give him."

"How would it be possible for me to give him any other answer than I gave him before? How would it be possible, godmamma?"

"My dear, how can I answer such a question, when I do not know what the answer was, nor what your motive for giving it to him was? It very often is possible for a young lady to change her mind, and give an answer to such a question different from her first one."

"But even if it were possible that I should change my mind,—even if it were possible that I should wish to give a different answer, how could I do so? Could I accept an offer as a comparatively unportioned girl which I refused as a rich heiress? Would it not be to give everybody the right to think that the change in my conduct was produced by the change in my fortunes? Oh! dear, dear godmamma!" cried Kate, hiding her face on Lady Farnleigh's shoulder, "I do think that I would rather be burned alive at the stake, than that he should think that!"

"Ah! rather than 'that he should think it! It would not so much matter about the rest of the world. Well, it may be that he may have something to say to you on that head. So I wont press you now to decide what answer you should give him, before you have heard what he may say to you," said Lady Farnleigh, quite sure now, if even she had had any doubt before, that Kate's rejection of Ellingham had been caused solely by her knowledge of the fact of her cousin's being alive, and of the consequences of that fact as regarded her future fortunes, and by her certainty that Ellingham was addressing her in ignorance of those circumstances. "And now, my dear, to change the subject," continued Lady Farnleigh, "what do you think that I heard, or rather that Mr. Mat heard, in Silverton to-day. It concerns—or at least I am entirely persuaded that it concerns—your sister Margaret; and yet I would give you a hundred guesses to guess it in!"

"What was it, godmamma—what did you and Mr. Mat hear?" said Kate, looking up with genuine alarm in her face.

"Why simply this: that a few nights ago, —the very night, it would seem, before Mr. Slowcome came up here to tell your father about your unfortunate cousin's having left

an heir,—Mr. Frederick Falconer ordered a chaise and pair from the Lindisfarn Arms to take up its station at nightfall at the back door of your uncle's garden, which opens into the Castle Head Lane. That is all, —no, by the by, not quite all,—and that the post-boy had orders to say, if anybody asked him any questions, that he was going to take Dr. Lindisfarn up to the Chase to dinner, where, Mr. Mat says, he was in no wise expected that evening. "What do you think of that, Kate?"

"Why, it looks—I am utterly amazed! But, godmamma, Margaret and Frederick Falconer had papa's consent,—and—everything; I cannot understand it. But was it —do you think? And why, if so, did nothing come of it? And Margaret—oh, it cannot be what we had in our heads, godmamma. It is impossible. There is some mistake. It is impossible!" reiterated Kate, as she remembered what had passed between Margaret and herself the day before that fixed for the suspected elopement. "And yet again," she said, as it occurred to her that it was possible that Margaret might have told Frederick the secret according to her compact, that Frederick might have felt therefore that his father would never consent to his marriage with a portionless girl, and that he might have planned an elopement to avoid his father's opposition. And it suddenly darted into her mind, that if such indeed had been the facts, Frederick Falconer must be a far more disinterested and nobler fellow than she had ever given him credit for being; and yet, almost at the same instant, there shone clear across her mind the conviction that it could not be; that Freddy Falconer was in reality Freddy Falconer, and not another; and the whole story seemed utterly unintelligible to her. "But at all events, nothing came of it," continued she, looking into Lady Farnleigh's face; "how is that to be accounted for?"

"I confess that it is all very unaccountable!" returned Lady Farnleigh; "but as for the coming to nothing of the scheme, whatever it may have been, the same gentleman calmed the storm who had raised it,—that is to say, dismissed the post-chaise. Or at least it was dismissed by the confidential clerk of the bank, Mr. Mat says."

"But that might have been old Mr. Falconer's doing, you know, godmamma ; old Mr. Falconer may have found it out, and put a stop to it."

"Humph !" said Lady Farnleigh. "What may have been the gentleman's motive," she added, after a pause, "either in planning such an escapade or in abandoning it, I cannot presume to guess. But what about Margaret? She of course, knew nothing, so soon as that, of the change of fortune that was hanging over her?" added her ladyship, looking shrewdly into Kate's face as she spoke. "What should we have to think of her, if it were possible to suppose that she had obtained knowledge of the facts? Of course, you had heard no word that could lead you to imagine that such a plan was in contemplation !" said Lady Farnleigh, looking into Kate's face, which was burning with the painful blushes that her companion's words respecting the possibility of Margaret's knowledge of the secret had called into it. It was a comfort to her to be able to say frankly, in reply to the last question of her godmother, that no syllable of the kind had reached her ears ; and that the whole thing seemed to her so improbable and incomprehensible that she still thought there must be some mistake about it.

"Suppose," said Lady Farnleigh slowly, and looking at Kate as she was speaking,— "suppose that Margaret had in some way obtained a knowledge of the fatal secret, and was therefore willing to consent to an elopement, in order that the marriage might be made irrevocable. before that knowledge reached other people. And suppose that it did reach the gentleman just as he was on the point of starting?"

"Good heavens, Lady Farnleigh, but that would be to suppose Margaret guilty of conduct too dreadful to be possible !—and it would make out Frederick Falconer to be a great deal worse than I have ever thought or think him."

"Well, my dear, I hope you may be right ; we shall see. But as regards Margaret, Kate, which is what most interests us ; does it not appear to you that the conduct which you stigmatize as too atrocious to be possible would be but the natural sequel to the accepting of an offer at all under such circumstances as those in which Margaret was placed, if indeed she had a previous knowledge of the important facts in question ? Would not this elopement, if elopement there really were in question, have been the only means of attaining the object which a girl accepting an offer under such circumstances must have had in view ? "

"But," pleaded Kate, turning very pale, and feeling deadly sick at heart, "may we not suppose—is it not possible, that is—that she might have been led into the weakness of accepting an offer made to her—that is, supposing always that Margaret could have known of the secret of Julian's being alive so far back as when the offer was made "— and Kate's conscience smote her as she spoke the words,—smote her on both sides from two different directions ; both for her want of candor towards Lady Farnleigh, and for abandoning Margaret so far as even to admit the above case hypothetically ; "is it not possible," she continued, avoiding her godmother's searching eyes in a manner she had never, never done before, "that Margaret might have been led into accepting his offer by the difficulty of knowing what answer to make to him ; it *would* be very difficult you know, godmamma !" and Kate remembered, as she spoke, *how* difficult, how cruelly difficult, it was. "She might have been, as it were, surprised into accepting, from not being able to assign the real cause for her refusal ; and without any intention of suffering the matter to go on, you know, godmamma. Might it not have been so ? "

Lady Farnleigh noted in her mind Kate's hypothetical admission, and her assumption that Margaret could not have told the simple truth to her lover, forgetting that Lady Farnleigh could not have comprehended any such motive for silence, if she had not been informed of all the circumstances of the case. Lady Farnleigh, I say, noted all this and smiled inwardly at Kate's clumsy attempt and manifest incapacity for dissimulation. Lady Farnleigh felt that it might have been easy, by availing herself of these inconsistencies, to force Kate to a confession of the whole truth ; but it did not suit her present purpose to do so. She was contented with obtaining light enough to enable her to perceive with very tolerable accuracy and certainty the whole of the story. It was pretty clear to her that Kate's knowledge of the facts learned in the cottage at Deepcreek had constrained her to refuse an offer which she would otherwise, to the best of Lady Farnleigh's judgment, have accepted; and that Margaret's knowledge of the same facts had led her to act in a precisely contradictory manner; and further that Kate was prevented from now avowing that her knowledge of her cousin's being alive dated from the time it did by her anxiety to defend and spare her sister.

And to tell the truth in all its ugly nakedness, Lady Farnleigh was by no means distressed, as she undoubtedly ought to have been, at the discovery of much that was base and bad in Margaret. Besides the six thousand pounds which she had long ago settled on Kate, Lady Farnleigh had a few other thousands over which she had entire control, and of which her own son had no need. Now what Lady Farnleigh wished to do, what it would have been a pleasure for her to do, in the unhappy mischance which had fallen upon her friends, would have been to add these thousands to the little provision she had already made for her darling goddaughter. But she had conscientiously felt that this would not have been doing the best she could for the children of her dearly loved friend, the late Mrs. Lindisfarn. She felt that it would have been under the circumstances to treat Margaret hardly. And she had determined that she would virtuously abstain from doing her own pleasure in this matter, and would do strictly that which she believed to be right. But now, if indeed Margaret had been guilty of such conduct as that which seemed to be proved against her, that would surely be a most righteous judgment which should assign to her favorite the means which would facilitate the union she (Lady Farnleigh) had set her heart on, and should declare one so unworthy to have forfeited all claim on her. And people like their own way so much, and Lady Farnleigh was so strongly addicted to following hers, that—to tell the honest truth, as I said before—it was by no means disagreeable to the self-willed lady to find that she might be justified in following her devices in this matter.

So, having from her conversation with Kate,—a conversation which she would fain have spared her goddaughter, if she could have done so, but which it was absolutely necessary for her to have, before she could judiciously say what she proposed saying to Ellingham—acquired the information, or rather the confirmation of her suspicions, which she needed, she only replied to those last words of Kate's very lame and ineffectual pleading for her sister, by saying,—

"Well, my dear, it may have been as you say. It is possible, as far as we know at present. But we shall see. We shall know all about it before long."

"And you must think as leniently as you can, dear godmamma, of Margaret, even if it should turn out that she has acted foolishly in this matter. The circumstances in themselves, you see, are very difficult; and then you know"—and there Kate paused awhile, as not knowing very well how to put into words the ideas which were in her mind, or perhaps not having conceived them clearly, —"poor Margaret is so different,—has been brought up with such different ways of thinking, and we can hardly tell how far many matters would present themselves to her under a different aspect from what they would to our minds. I do think that great allowances ought to be made; don't you, godmamma?"

"Very true, my dear; Margaret, as you say, is very different," replied Lady Farnleigh, looking fondly at Kate, and speaking in a half-absent sort of manner, which showed that more was passing in her mind than was set forth in her words. "And, by the by, where is she, I wonder?" she continued, rousing herself from her musing; "I must speak to her about all this"—

"What, now, godmamma?" interrupted Kate, in a voice of considerable alarm.

"Don't alarm yourself, my dear, I only want to say a few words to her about the match she was about to make, and the breaking off of it. It would be unnatural for me to leave the house without doing so. Where do you think she is now?"

"Down in the drawing-room with Miss Immy, in all probability."

"I would go down to her," said Lady Farnleigh; "but I don't want to speak to her before poor dear Miss Immy, who would not hear half what was said, but would think it necessary to take part in the conversation. Could not you go down, Kate, and ask her to come up here, just for a chat, you know?"

Kate looked rather doubtful as to the task assigned to her, but went down-stairs to perform it without making any further observation. And in a few minutes she returned with her sister.

CHAPTER XLVI.
THE FAIRY IN HER WICKED MOOD.

MARGARET, as it may be supposed, had not been passing happy hours since her return home on the morning after the abortive scheme of elopement. She was in truth very exceedingly miserable. Blank despair as to the future; ever-present fear of the exposure each passing hour might bring with it; a feeling of hostility against and separation from those around her, who should have been near and dear to her; a consciousness that she stood alone in the midst of that family who seemed all to feel together, to act together, and to understand each other so perfectly; and lastly, a burning and consuming rage and intensity of hatred against the false traitor, who had foiled her schemes, dashed down her hopes, and brutally and knowingly exposed her to the suffering, the mortification, the affront, the ridicule of such a catastrophe as she had undergone;—all these unruly sentiments and passions were making Margaret supremely miserable, during those days of hopelessness, and yet, in some sort, of suspense.

Lady Farnleigh's presence at the Chase had added a new source of annoyance and disquietude to all those which were tormenting her. She had an instinctive dread and dislike of Lady Farnleigh, and it seemed to her as if it were fated that the dreadful exposure which was hanging over her should be made to fall upon her by no other hand.

It may readily be imagined, therefore, that when Kate came into the drawing-room, where Miss Immy was sitting bolt upright at the table in the middle of the room, tranquilly perusing the pages of "Clarissa Harlowe," and Margaret was sitting on a sofa by the side of the fireplace with a book hanging listlessly from her hand, while her restless thoughts were occupied on a very different subject, and walking up close to the latter, said in a low and rather hesitating voice,—

"Margaret, dear, Lady Farnleigh is going to leave us early to-morrow morning, and she wants before going to have a chat with you;—so much has happened, you know, since she left Sillshire,—and she thought that you would like better to come up to my room, where we can be snug by ourselves, you know—will you come?"

Margaret's first impulse was to refuse the invitation. She looked up sulkily and defiantly into Kate's face, as the latter stood over her, anxious and ill at ease.

"Do come, there's a dear! she is so kind," said Kate, still speaking very low, while Miss Immy remained profoundly absorbed in her well-known romance.

"Oh, very kind,—so kind,—especially to me!" sneered Margaret. And as she spoke, the spirit of defiance rose in her, and a feeling that what she dreaded must needs come, and that less of torture and suffering would arise from meeting her enemy and doing battle on the spot than from suspense and fear and the consciousness of appearing to be afraid,—a feeling very similar to that of an animal hunted till it turns at bay,—took possession of her, and she added, "Yes, I will come! It will be the sooner over."

And getting up from the sofa as she spoke, and flinging the volume in her hand on the place from which she had risen, she drew herself up slowly, and as if lazily, to her full height, and stalked haughtily and sullenly to the door.

Kate followed, not a little dismayed at these indications of her sister's state of mind, and looking forward with anything but pleasure to her share in the coming interview. It was no small relief to her, therefore, when, as she was following her sister up the stairs, the latter suddenly turned, and with lowering brow, said,—

"Lady Farnleigh is in your room, you said, I think?"

"Yes, in my room, Margaret. She is waiting for us there."

"But if I am to be lectured, I prefer that it should not be done before lookers-on. You saw her by yourself, and have made good your own story. I will see her alone, too, if I am to see her at all. I will go into my room, and she may come to me there, or, if you like to be shut out of your room for a few minutes, I will go to her there."

"To be sure, Margaret, if you wish it! You can go into my room. I will not come; I will go down-stairs to Miss Immy," said Kate, absolutely cowed and frightened by Margaret's tone, and the haughty, lowering scowl that sat upon her brow.

It was impossible that the grace and beauty of movement assured by Margaret's perfect figure and bearing should ever be absent from her. And as she entered Kate's room, with bold defiance in her large, dark, open eyes and in the carriage of her head and neck, with sullen but haughty displeasure on her beautiful brow, there was something grandly tragic in her whole appearance, worthy of the study of a Siddons. Lady Farnleigh could not help looking at her with a glance in which a certain measure of admiration mingled with her disapproval and dislike. And Margaret, as she entered, eyed her enemy—as she was determined to, and was perhaps partly justified in, considering her—with the look with which a *toreador* may be supposed to regard his adversary in the ring.

"Thank you for coming up to me, Margaret," said Lady Farnleigh; "I thought that we could have a little talk about all this untoward business more comfortably up here than in the drawing-room. Is not Kate coming?" she added, as Margaret closed the door behind her.

"No, Lady Farnleigh, she is not! I told her that if you had anything to say to me about—matters that concern me only, I chose, if I heard it at all, to hear it alone."

And the tall, slender figure, in its black silk dress, remained standing—in an attitude that might have become Juno in her wrath,—in front of Lady Farnleigh.

The latter raised her eyes to the pale, handsome, lowering face, with an expression of surprise in them, and gazed at her fixedly for a moment or two, before saying,—

"Well, perhaps you were right.—perhaps it will be better so. You spoke as if you had doubted, Margaret, whether you would consent to talk with me at all upon the events that have been happening here. It would be very reasonable that you should have such a feeling as regards any stranger—any one out of your own family—except myself. Perhaps I ought to recall to you the facts that give me a right to consider myself entitled to such exception."

"Yes, Lady Farnleigh; I should like to hear that!" replied Margaret, drily, and all but insolently.

"When your dear and admirable mother died, Margaret," returned Lady Farnleigh, after holding her hand before her eyes for a moment of thoughtfulness, "leaving you and Kate motherless infants, I promised her to act a mother's part toward you as far as should be possible. I have done so as regards your sister to the utmost of my power, with your good father's sanction and approv-

al, ever since. I have, as you well know, had no opportunity of keeping my promise to your mother as regards yourself, hitherto. But now that circumstances have brought you back among us, and more especially now that a second series of unforeseen and unfortunate occurrences have unhappily changed the brilliant prospects that were before you, it would be a great grief to me if anything—either in your conduct, or your will—should prevent me from being to you what I trust I have always been to Kate."

For an instant the latter words suggested to Margaret's mind the possibility that Lady Farnleigh meant to tell her that if she was a good girl, there should be six thousand pounds for her, also, as well as for Kate. But a moment's consideration convinced her that if Lady Farnleigh had more money to leave, it would be all for Kate; and even if she had been inclined to suppose that the chance of such a piece of good fortune was before her, her imperious temper, and the spirit of defiant rebellion which seemed to her to be her only refuge in the storms that were about to break over her, were at that moment too strongly in the ascendant, and too entirely had possession of her soul, for it to have been possible for her to suppress them, even for the sake of securing it. The utmost she could bring herself to do, was to say, with sullen majesty, and without taking a seat,—

"What was it you wished to say to me, Lady Farnleigh?"

Kate's fairy godmother, though one of the kindest and lovingest natures in existence, was not endowed with a very meek or long-enduring temper; and Margaret's sullen and evidently hostile manner and words were rapidly using up the small stock of it remaining on hand. So Lady Farnleigh replied, with more acerbity in her tone than would have been the case if that of Margaret had been less provocative,—

"I fear, Margaret, you have been acting far from—judiciously, let us say, in the matter of this match with Mr. Falconer, which is now, I am told, broken off."

"I must take leave, Lady Farnleigh, to think that I have been sufficiently well instructed in all that propriety requires of a young lady on such occasions, to make it unnecessary for me to consult the opinion of—persons whose authority I certainly should never think of preferring to that of the dear friends who superintended my education."

" And you think those friends would have approved your recent conduct?"

" I do not see what there has been to blame in it. When addressed, in a manner which the ways of this country render permissible, by a gentleman whom I was justified in considering a good and eligible *parti*, I gave him only a conditional assent, leaving him to seek his definite answer from papa."

" Quite *en regle*, Miss Margaret! But do you think that you were justified, under the peculiar circumstances of the case, in giving that conditional assent and sending the anxious gentleman to ' ask papa ' in the manner you speak of,—justified, not by the conventionalities of this or of that country, but by the laws of simple honesty and honor?"

" Simple honesty and honor, Lady Farnleigh!" cried Margaret, while the blood began to mount rapidly in her beautiful pale checks, and to tingle there very unpleasantly.

" Yes, Margaret, honor and honesty. Was it honorable or honest to accept such a proposal, knowing that the maker of it was under grievously erroneous impressions as to the circumstances which made you an ' eligible *parti*,' as you phrase it, in his eyes?"

" You allude—rather unfeelingly, I must say, Lady Farnleigh—to the great misfortune which has fallen upon my sister and me. But you perhaps are not aware, having been absent from Sillshire at the time, the proposal in question was made, and the reply to it, which you are pleased to criticise, given, before the facts you refer to were known," said Margaret, still doubting whether Lady Farnleigh were indeed in possession of the real facts of the case,—not seeing, indeed, any possibility by which they could have reached her,—and determined to fight her battle with a bold front to the last.

" Margaret!" said Lady Farnleigh, in reply, looking her steadily in the eyes as she spoke, " the facts I refer to were not known to Mr. Falconer, or to any one else in Silverton, at the time when he made his proposal to you; but they WERE KNOWN to you!"

Margaret almost reeled under the force of this direct and terrible blow. Her first impulse was to hide her burning face with her hands and rush out of the room; but it was

only the weakness of one moment. In the next she attempted to hurl back the accusation which she could not parry.

" Honor and honesty!" she said, with a cold, withering sneer upon her brow and lips. " With what sort of honor and honesty have I been treated? With what sort of honor and honesty has your favorite Kate and have you yourself, Lady Farnleigh, treated me? My sister runs to you with tales which, as far as there is any truth in them, she was bound in the most sacred manner and by the most solemn engagements to keep secret; and you avail yourself of your position and superior experience to worm out from her the means of injuring a friendless girl, whom you cannot forgive for having what your *protégée* never had nor never will have. Honor and honesty, indeed!"

" If you had a tenth part of your sister's honor and honesty in your heart, Margaret, it would not occur to you to suppose that she had betrayed your secret to me. She is not even aware that I know it. But it so happens that I do know that you were made acquainted with the error as to your Cousin Julian's death, and were perfectly aware of the result which that must exercise on your own position, about a month before your acceptance of Mr. Falconer's offer."

" I knew only what Kate knew also,—knew nothing, indeed, but what she told me."

" Quite true, Margaret. Kate had the same unfortunate knowledge that you had, —and you both of you used it in your own fashion."

" Used it! Why, what could I have done, I should like to know? I don't know whether the spy and informer from whom you have obtained your information, Lady Farnleigh, told you also that I was bound not to divulge the fact of my cousin's being alive,—that it was impossible for me to do so. What could I do then? I waited—how impatiently none will ever know—for the moment when it would be permitted me to tell Mr. Falconer the truth, and was compelled to content myself in the mean time with the conviction, that his motive in addressing me was not money, and that the discovery that I had it not would not change his sentiments toward me."

" And are you still supported by that conviction, may I ask?" said Lady Farnleigh, unable to prevent a certain amount of sneer from betraying itself in her tone.

"Of course I cannot suppose, Lady Farnleigh, that Mr. Falconer can be so base as to dream of retreating from his engagement because it turns out that I may be less richly dowered than he had imagined. It is hardly likely that, if I could have conceived him to be capable of such conduct, I could for an instant have listened to his addresses."

There was an audacity of falsehood in this speech which provoked Lady Farnleigh into pushing Margaret more hardly than it had been her intention to do when she began the conversation. She could not refrain from saying,—

"But surely, your conviction must have been somewhat shaken upon the subject, when the gentleman failed to keep his appointment at six o'clock, at your uncle's garden-gate; particularly when you remembered that that sudden change in his plans, which left you so cruelly in the lurch, took place just about the time when the news of your not being the heiress to your father's acres became known in Silverton."

"It is infamous! It is shameful!" screamed Margaret, throwing herself suddenly on the little sofa by the side of Kate's fireplace, and bursting into a flood of tears—very characteristically feeling the exposure of her having been duped and ill-treated far more keenly than the detection of her own sharp practice toward another. "You wicked, wicked woman!" she cried, "spying and setting traps for people, and then triumphing in their ill-fortune. It is too bad,—too bad. I shall die,—I shall die! I wish I may! Oh, why was I ever sent to this horrid country and this cruel house!"

And then her passionate sobbing became inarticulate, and she seemed in danger of falling into a fit of hysterics.

"I don't think you will die, Margaret," said Lady Farnleigh, it must be admitted somewhat cruelly; "but perhaps it might be better if you had your stay-lace cut. I will go and send Simmons to you."

And so the executioner of this retribution left the victim writhing, and convulsively sobbing in the extremity of her mortification, and the agony of her crushing defeat.

CHAPTER XLII.

AT THE LINDISFARN STONE ONCE MORE.

NOTWITHSTANDING the very decided conviction that Margaret's conduct richly deserved far more severe and more serious punishment than the *mauvais quart d'heure* which Lady Farnleigh had inflicted upon her, the fairy godmother, on rejoining Kate, felt rather repentant and annoyed that hers should have been the hand, or rather the tongue, to inflict even that modicum of retribution. She was evidently "out of sorts," when she went down-stairs and found Kate in the drawing-room.

"Margaret has been behaving excessively ill, my dear," she said, in answer to Kate's questioning look,—"most ungraciously and ill-temperedly to me; but that is nothing; she has been behaving most unpardonably to Mr. Falconer,—behaving in a manner amply justifying any abruptness of breaking off on his part, and you may depend upon it that he will not be remiss in availing himself of the justification. To think of her accepting the man, when she knew all about the change in her position, and knew that he did not know it!"

"Godmamma!" said Kate, aghast.

"Yes, Miss Kate. Do you think I am a fairy godmamma for nothing?"

"I cannot smile about it, godmamma," said Kate, sadly.

"In truth, my dear, it is no smiling matter. I am deeply grieved; and I am sure that your father will feel it sorely."

"But, godmamma," said Kate, timidly and hesitatingly, after a pause; "did Margaret tell you she was aware of Julian's secret at the time of the offe.?"

"No, Kate, she did not," replied Lady Farnleigh, looking into Kate's face with a shrewd glance, half aggressive and half arch, "she did not tell me; but I knew all about it, for all that."

"You did not tell me that, godmamma," returned Kate, a little reproachfully; but feeling at the same time, despite her vexation at Margaret's detection, an irrepressible sensation of relief at the reflection that Lady Farnleigh, though she had not chosen to say so, must be cognizant of the fact that she, also, was in possession of the same information at the time when she had refused Ellingham.

"You know then also, I suppose," continued Kate, after a pause of some seconds, "that Margaret was not at liberty to tell Mr. Falconer the real state of the case when he proposed to her?"

"Yes, Kate, I know that too," answered Lady Farnleigh, with the same look, half affectionate and half quizzing, which her face had worn before; "and I admit that the situation was a cruelly painful and very difficult one;—or at least that it would have been so to some people."

"Margaret did not know what to do, you see, godmamma. What could she have done?"

"Refuse him, my dear!" said Lady Farnleigh, shortly.

And then there was silence between them for a long while.

Lady Farnleigh started, as she said she would, immediately after breakfast the next morning on her return to Wanstrow Manor. And at an early hour on the following—the Monday—morning Captain Ellingham arrived there, as she had expected. The station to which he had been moved from Sillmouth was on the northern coast of Sillshire, whereas the latter little port is situated on the southern side of that large county. The distance, therefore, which he had had to travel in obedience to Lady Farnleigh's behest was not a very long one. It had so happened that the exigencies of the service had permitted him to start for Wanstrow almost immediately on the receipt of her letter; and he had not lost many hours in doing so.

I hardly think that there is any necessity for relating the conversation which passed between him and Lady Farnleigh on his arrival. For the gist of it may be inferred from what subsequently happened. And it was, at all events, a short one; for it was barely twelve o'clock when he reached Lindisfarn.

Margaret had declared herself ill, as ill at ease enough she doubtless was, ever since her stormy conversation with Lady Farnleigh, and had secluded herself in her own room. The squire was busy in his study, as he had been for many more hours in the day than he was in the habit of spending within doors, ever since that ill-boding visit from Mr. Slowcome. Mr. Mat was absent for the day. He had taken a horse early in the morning, before Kate was down, and had told the servants that he should not come home till the

evening, and possibly not till the morrow. Miss Immy alone pursued the even tenor of her way, uninfluenced, though assuredly not unmindful of the misfortune that had fallen on the family. But that even tenor of her daily occupation prevented her from being ever seen in the drawing-room till after luncheon. And Kate therefore, since Lady Farnleigh's departure, had felt unusually lonely and depressed in spirits.

After having, as soon as breakfast was over on that Monday morning, vainly attempted to compel her mind to fix itself on her usual employments in her room, she gave up the fruitless struggle, and yielding to the restlessness which was upon her, strolled down into the stable to try if she could get rid of half an hour in the society of Birdie.

The stables at Lindisfarn were not placed at the back of the house, so as to be out of sight of the approaches to it, partly, probably, because there was no space there, unless it were made by the sacrifice of some of the noble old trees of the Lindisfarn woods, which just behind the house came down almost close upon it and upon the gardens; and partly, perhaps, because the Lindisfarn who had raised the handsome block of buildings which contained them was disposed to consider that department of his mansion quite as much entitled to a prominent position as any other. So it was, however, whatever the cause, that at Lindisfarn the stables stood at right angles to the front of the house, the front stable-yard (for there was a back stable-yard behind, which served for the more unsightly portions of a stable-yard's functions), —the front stable-yard was divided from the drive by which the entrance to the mansion was reached, only by a low parapet wall. There was a broad stone coping on the top of it, which made a very convenient seat for Bayard, the old hound, who was wont to lie there on sunny days, with his great black muzzle between his huge paws, meditatively, by the hour together.

It was one of the first genial mornings of spring in that southwestern country; the old hound, whose muzzle in truth was beginning to have more gray than black in it, had taken his favorite seat on the low wall in the sunshine; and Kate, leaving the stable-door open, had come out to bestow on her other playfellow a share of her attention.

She was sitting on the wall in front of the

fine old dog, and was, in fact, giving him such portion of her attention as she could command. It was but a small share, and evidently much less than old Bayard was disposed to content himself with ; for he had stretched out one magnificent fore-arm and paw till it rested on Kate's lap, and he was shoving his cold nose into her hand as it rested on the edge of the coping stone, evidently bent on recalling to himself his mistress's wandering thoughts. But they were roving far away, and would not come back for all old Bayard's wistful caresses, favorite as he was.

She was sitting thus when the sound of a horse's feet, coming in a sharp canter round a curve in the road from the lodge-gate, fell on her ear and on old Bayard's at the same moment. The ground fell away very steeply from the terrace in front of the house to the lodge ; and that part of the bending road which the rider was passing was hidden from the spot where Kate and Bayard were, by a large mass of very luxuriant laurustinus and Portugal laurel. Kate's first notion was that Mr. Mat was unexpectedly returning, and very hurriedly ; for it was not like him to gallop his horse up to the door, and leave him steaming hot. But Bayard knew better. The hoof-falls that disturbed his reverie were, he was quite sure, the produce of no hoofs that lived in *his* stables ; so he roused himself, jumped down from the wall, and uttered a short, interrogative bark. In the next instant, a horse at full gallop swept round the large mass of evergreens ; and in the next after, the seaman's horsemanship of Captain Ellingham, aided by the effect of the stable-scent on his steed's organs, brought him to a stand sharply at the spot where Kate and her companion were.

The latter alone seemed to be at all inclined to practise the hospitable duties proper to the occasion. After a very short and perfunctory examination of the strange horse, Bayard at once showed his recollection of Captain Ellingham, and welcomed him to Lindisfarn. But if Kate did not turn and run, it was only because her feet seemed rooted to the spot on which she was standing.

" Captain Ellingham ! " she said, and could proceed to no further greeting ; for her tongue clove to the roof of her mouth.

" Miss Lindisfarn," said Ellingham, dismounting, " I was anxiously debating with myself, as I rode up the hill, whether I could hope that, when a message was brought you that I was here and begging to see you, you would grant me an interview or not. Now my good fortune has secured for me the chance of at least preferring my petition in person. May I hope that, when I have found somebody in the stables to take my horse, you will allow me to speak with you for a few minutes? For that is the sole object of my coming hither ; and I know it will be a potent backing of my request, when I assure you that I am here in accordance with the counsel and wishes of Lady Farnleigh."

" It is a potent backing, Captain Ellingham," said Kate, who had had time to recover herself in some degree while Ellingham was speaking ; " but there is no need of any such to make me say that you are welcome at Lindisfarn."

A groom came out from the stables, and took Captain Ellingham's horse from him, as Kate spoke ; and she was leading the way towards the front-door of the house, when he said,—

" Miss Lindisfarn, I shall be delighted to see all my kind friends here, *after* I have had a little conversation with you alone. It is for that purpose that I have come here, with the approval of our dear and excellent friend, Lady Farnleigh."

" If she wishes—that is, if you think ; Captain Ellingham—that Lady Farnleigh would think—I am sure—if there is anything"—stammered Kate, making, for such an usually straightforward speaker, a very lame attempt at any intelligible utterance.

" When the sentence that has been pronounced on a criminal, Miss Lindisfarn, is by any good hap to be reversed," said Ellingham, coming to her assistance by taking upon himself the active share of the conversation, which he seemed somehow to be much more capable of doing satisfactorily than he had been on the last occasion of a *tête-à-tête* between him and Kate,—" when sentence upon a criminal is to be reversed, it is usual and right that the revised decision should be pronounced, as far as may be, before the audience which was present at the first. Would you object to walk with me ? " he continued, meaningly, after a considerable pause, " through the woods up to Lindisfarn brow ? "

Kate shot one short, sharp, inquiring glance

at him from under her downcast eyelashes, as she said, " If you like, I will walk with you up to the brow, Captain Ellingham; but I am afraid there can be no reversal of anything that ever passed there."

" I cannot submit to have my appeal dismissed without, at least, a hearing of the grounds on which it is urged."

And then they walked on a little way side by side in silence, till Kate, feeling that the silence was acquiring a force with a geometrical rate of progression, as it continued, in that mysterious way that such silences do increase the intensity of their significance by duration, and determined therefore to break it at all hazards, said,—

" How different these woods are looking from what they were when we were last up here together! Do you remember all the traces of the recent storm?"

" Yes, indeed! and how the poor old woods had been mauled and torn. I hated these fine old woods then; but I have no spite against them now."

" Hated Lindisfarn woods? And I do so love them! Why did you hate our old woods? And what has brought you into a better frame of mind?" said Kate, more quietly than she had spoken before.

" I felt spiteful against these hills and woods, and against all the beautiful country they look down on, because all these fine Lindisfarn acres were so many ramparts and bulwarks and fortifications, all increasing the impossibility of scaling the fortress, which all my hope of happiness depended on my conquering—on which my hope still depends! But I do not hate the Lindisfarn acres any longer; for they no longer stand between me and my goal."

" Oh, Captain Ellingham!" said Kate, almost too much agitated to speak, yet dashing out in desperation to defend the Lindisfarn acres from any such maleficent influence; " You told me, you know"—

" Yes, Miss Lindisfarn, I told you that I was well persuaded that your rejection of my suit, though it was altogether unassigned to any motive, did not rest on any cause of the kind I have been alluding to. I was and am thoroughly convinced of that fact. And for that reason, Miss Lindisfarn, I should not now venture to renew my suit, if the only difference in our position toward each other were that produced by your having then been

supposed to be one of the heiresses to all this wealth, and your now not being imagined to be such any longer. Your rejection of my suit was not caused by the wide difference in our fortunes, as they were supposed to stand then; therefore I should not be justified in renewing it merely because that wide difference has disappeared."

" I am glad to know that!" said Kate, very tremblingly.

" Yes, I know that," said Ellingham, laying considerable emphasis on the verb. "And therefore I must find another excuse for daring to ask you to reconsider the decision you then gave me. Miss Lindisfarn, this is the excuse : you did not refuse me here last spring because you deemed yourself to be richly endowed, but in part, at least, because you were aware that you were not so. May I not hope that that was the real deciding reason? Is that so?" he added, after a considerable pause, during which Kate could not find courage and calmness enough to venture on a reply, although the thoughts and feelings which were making her heart beat were assuredly not of a painful nature.

" Is not that true, Kate?" he said, again, whispering the last word so low that it was barely audible.

" It is true," she whispered, tremulously, in a scarcely louder tone ; " but where is the change? I was then, and am still, unpossessed of wealth."

" Where is the change! why, in this; that you knew that I then supposed I was asking a great heiress to be my wife ; you could not explain to me that fact,—I know why now. Now we both know all about this terrible secret. Now that at least need be no barrier between us. Now there is no mistake. Now I am asking Kate Lindisfarn, no heiress at all, if she will bestow,—not all these beautiful woods and fields, which weighed so heavily on my heart that I hardly dared ask at all before,—but her hand, rich only with a priceless heart in it, upon a rough sailor, who has little to offer in return save as true and strong a love as ever man bore to woman."

He had got hold of her hand while speaking the last words ; and she did not draw it away from his, but turned her face away from him. And he made no attempt to draw the trembling little hand he held nearer to him, but let his own follow it to where it hung beneath her averted and drooping face. And in that position he felt a wet tear fall on the hand which held hers.

"Have you no answer for me, Kate?" he whispered again.

"I wish I could have answered before I knew anything about the change in the destination of these woods," murmured Kate, very plaintively.

"You wish that!" he cried; "then this little hand is my own." And he snatched it to his lips and covered it with kisses, as he spoke. "Dear, dearest, generous girl! But do not be selfish in your generosity, my Kate. Remember how much sweeter it must be to me to ask you for your love, when there can be no thought,—not in your noble heart, my Kate but in the suspicions of the outside world—that I am asking for aught else."

They had by this time reached the Lindisfarn stone, and were sitting side by side just where Kate had sat on the day she had refused him.

"This used to be a very favorite seat of mine; but I have never been here since," said Kate, without any previous word having been said in allusion to any former occasion of being there. But there was no need of any such explanation of her meaning; and the mysterious magnetism which so frequently and so strangely makes coincidence in the unspoken thoughts of two minds was on this occasion less inexplicable than it often is.

"But now will you henceforth take it into favor again, Kate?"

"I wish it was going to remain *ours*," said Kate, leaving Ellingham at liberty to understand the communistic possessive pronoun as referring to Kate and the members of her family, or as alluding to a closer *bi-partite* partnership, according to his pleasure.

"We will make the gray old stone ours," said Ellingham, accepting the latter interpretation, "after the fashion of poets in old times, and jolly tars in these days." And he took a pocket-knife from his pocket as he spoke. "Now then I will carve 'Kate' on the stone, and you shall cut 'Walter,' and we will put a pierced heart above them, all in due style."

"But I can't carve, especially on this hard rock," said Kate, smiling.

"Oh, I will show you how. See there is my 'Kate' in orthography very unworthy of the dear, dear word. Now you must put 'Walter' underneath it. I will help you."

And he put the knife into her hand, and proceeded without the least hurry about bringing the operation to a conclusion, to guide the taper little fingers to scratch the required letters on the stone.

"There," he said, when the word was completed; "now read it, 'Kate and Walter.' Come, sweetest, you must read it. It is a part of the ceremony."

So Kate, tremulously whispering, read "Kate and Walter," thus pronouncing for that sweet, formidable, never-to-be-forgotten first time the name which was thenceforward forever to be the dearest sound for her that human lips could form.

K. T. A.—*Kappa, tau, lambda!* three Greek letters, my dear young lady readers, the full and complete significance of which, as used to convey a compendious account of the remainder of the above-described scene, may be with perfect safety left to the explanation of your unaided intelligences, when it has been briefly mentioned that they stand for the words "and all the rest of it."

CHAPTER XLVIII.

MR. MAT COMMITS SACRILEGE AND FELONY.

MR. FALCONER, senior, did not go to Chewton on the Sunday, as he had purposed. He was prevented from doing so, and went on the next day,—that same Monday on which Mr. Mat was absent all day from the Chase, and on which "Kate and Walter" held their second session on the Lindisfarn Stone.

Mr. Mat had said nothing to anybody respecting his errand; but the fact was, that he also had determined on going over himself to Chewton; not with much hope of being able to effect any good, where wiser heads had failed, but still anxious, as he said, to see, if he could, what those Mallorys were up to.

Mr. Mat had known Charles Mellish, the late curate, well, in days gone by; and to tell the truth, they had, more often than was quite desirable,—at all events, for the reverend gentleman,—heard the chimes at midnight together, both in Silverton and out at the curate's residence at Chewton. Music was the chief tie between them. Poor Charley Mellish,—for he had been one of those men to whom that epithet is always applied, and who are always called by the familiar form of their Christian names,—poor Charley Mellish had possessed a grand baritone voice, which made very pleasant music when joined with Mr. Mat's tenor.

Mr. Mat had often stayed for two or three days together out at Chewton, in those pleasant but naughty old bygone times, and knew all Mellish's ways and habits, his carelessness and his irregularity, but knew, also, as Mr. Mat was thoroughly persuaded, and loudly declared, that poor Charley was utterly incapable of permitting or conniving at any fraud, either in the matter of the registers intrusted to his keeping, or in any other. Mr. Mat had a very strong idea that the register, which would prove whether the propounded extract from it were truly and honestly made or not, must still be in existence, and might be found, if looked for with sufficient patience and perseverance.

It thus came to pass that Mr. Falconer, senior, and Mr. Matthew Lindisfarn were journeying toward the remote little moorland village on the same day. But they were not travelling by the same road, nor exactly at the same hour.

Mr. Mat's way lay, indeed, through Silverton, and coincided with that of the banker till after he had crossed the Sill by the bridge at the town-foot, and traversed most of the enclosed country intervening between the river and the borders of the moor. After that, Mr. Mat, being on horseback, pursued the same route which Dr. Blakistry had taken on a former occasion; whereas the banker in his carriage followed the lower road, by which Dr. Lindisfarn and Mr. Sligo had travelled.

Mr. Mat and the banker might therefore have fallen in with one another, had it not been that the former started on his journey at the earlier hour, and had already passed through Silverton when the banker was still finishing his breakfast.

Mr. Mat took his ride leisurely, being much longer about it than Dr. Blakistry had been,—not because he was the inferior horseman of the two—quite the contrary; Mr. Mat was in those days one of the best riders in Sillshire, and could have, without difficulty, found his way across and over obstacles that would have puzzled the M. D. But he rode leisurely over the moor because he so much enjoyed his ride. It so happened, that he had never been at Chewton since his old crony Charles Mellish's death. And every mile of the way waked up whole hosts of long sleeping memories in Mr. Mat's recollection.

The ten years that run from forty-five to fifty-five in a man's life are a terrible decade, leaving cruelly deep marks in their passage, often accomplishing the whole job of turning a young man into an old one. And these were about the years that had passed over Mr. Mat's head since he had last ridden that well-known road from Silverton to Chewton.

Not that these years could be said to have turned Mr. Mat into an old man, either. He was of the sort who make a good and successful fight against the old tyrant with the scythe and hour-glass. His coal-black, spikey, scrubbing-brush of a head of hair, was as thickly set and as black as ever. His perfect set of regular white teeth were as complete and as brilliant in their whiteness as ever. His shrewd and twinkling deep-set black eye was as full of fire and as bright as it had been when last he rode that way. And his copper-colored, deeply-seamed, and pock-marked face was not more unsightly than it had ever been. And Mr. Mat always carried a light heart beneath his waistcoat, which is as good a preservative against age as camphor is against moth, as all the world knows.

So he rode through the keen morning air of the moor, reviewing his stock of recollections athwart the mellow sunshine-tinted Claude glass which memory presents to eupeptic easy-going philosophers of this sort, carolling out ever and anon some fragment of a ditty, with all the power of his rich and sonorous tenor.

> "There's many a lad I know is dead,
> And many a lass grown old !
> And as the lesson strikes my head,
> My weary heart grows cold ; "

he sung, as he turned his horse's head out of the main road across the moor into that breakneck track, by which we have seen Dr. Blakistry pick his way. But the stave was carolled forth in a manner that did not seem to indicate a very weary or cold heart in the singer's bosom ; and Mr. Mat, as he sat on his well-appointed steed, with his white hat just a little cocked on one side, his whip under his arm, and his hand stuck into the pocket of his red waistcoat, certainly did not present to the imagination the picture of a sorrow-stricken individual.

A couple of rabbits ran across the path, startled from their dewy morning nibble by his horse's tread ; and Mr. Mat broke off his song to honor them with a view-halloo that made the sides of a neighboring huge rock—a " tor," in the moorland language—re-echo again.

" And when cold in my coffin," he shouted again,—" when cold in my coffin— Ha ! Miss Lucy ! mind what you are about, lass ! turf slippery; is it ?—When cold in my coffin, I'll leave them to say, he's gone ! what a hearty good fellow ! "

" El—low ! " said the echo off the gray tor side.

" What a hearty good fellow ! " repeated Mr. Mat, in a stentorian voice, stimulated by the echo's second.

The good resolution thus enunciated seemed, however, to have been uttered by Mr. Mat, rather in the character of the late curate than in his own proper person ; for he continued soliloquizing a train of reflections, which that view of the sentiment he had been chanting inspired him with.

" Yes, he was a hearty good fellow,—poor Charley ! as good as ever another in Sillshire,—not a morsel of vice in him—not a bit ! They got hold of the wrong bit of stuff, maybe, to make a parson out of. Poor old Charley ! He's gone,—what a hearty good fellow ! How often have I heard him sing that. Well ! well ! Now he *is* gone. And we are all a-going !

> ' And so 'twill be, when I am gone
> Those evening bells will still ring on !
> Some other bard will walk these dells '—

Hup ! Miss Lucy ! what are you about, lass ?

> ' And sing your praise,'sweet evening bells.'

And I wonder whether another as big a rogue as that old Mallory will pull your ropes, sweet evening bells ? There's some devilry of some sort at the bottom of this business. I am sure of it,—sure and certain ; but it's deeper, I am afraid, than anything I can get to the bottom of."

And with these thoughts in his head, Mr. Mat came in sight of the tower of Chewton Church, and in a few minutes afterwards, pulled up at the house of Mr. Mallory, the clerk,—pulled up there more because it had always been his habit to do so in old times, when Charley Mellish lived in that house, than for any other reason ; though, in fact, anything that Mr. Mat was come there to do could only be done by addressing himself to the old clerk. But the fact was, that Mr. Mat did not very well know what he had come there to do. He had yielded, when he made up his mind to ride over, to a sort of vague and restless desire to do something, a conviction that all was not right, and a sort of feeling that it might be possible to find out something if one were on the spot.

It was about eleven o'clock in the forenoon when Mr. Mat reached Chewton, and hung Miss Lucy's rein on the rail in front of Mr. Mallory's door. He knocked at the door with the handle of his whip ; and it was instantly opened to him by the old man himself.

" Mr. Matthew Lindisfarn ! why "—

" What has brought me here ? you were going to say, Mr. Mallory ; after staying away ten years or more ! Well ! a little of remembrance of the old times, and a little of interest about these new times. That's about it, eh ? '

"The old times and the new times are pretty much alike, as far as I can see, Mr. Mat. A little more rheumatism, a little more weariness when one goes to bed, and a little more stiffness when one gets up in the morning; that's the most of the difference that I can see."

"Well! there is no jolly, good-humored, smiling face looking out of that window over the door up there, where poor old Charley's face used to be, when I rode over, three or four hours earlier than 'tis now, mayhap, and he would welcome me with, 'Chanticleer proclaims the morn!' Does that make no difference between the old times and the now?"

"You don't seem much changed, Mr. Mat, anyway," returned the old man, looking at his visitor with a queer sort of interest and curiosity; "you are pretty much as you were, I think, coat and waistcoat and all!"

"Pretty much; and I don't see that ten years have made any great improvement in you, Mr. Mallory. I don't see a mite of difference, to tell the truth."

"I don't know that there is much, Mr. Mat, barring what I told you just now," said the old man.

"And I don't suppose," said Mr. Mat, shutting one bright black eye, and putting his head on one side with an air of curious speculation, as he eyed the tall, grave old man with the other,—"I don't suppose, Mr. Mallory, that these ten years have made either of us a bit the better or the wiser. I can't say that I am aware of their having had any such effect on me, for my part."

"Well, Mr. Matthew, I should be sorry to think that, for my part. But then I'm nearer the great account, you know," said the clerk, with a touch of official sanctimoniousness.

"So that it is about time to think of making up the books, eh, Mr. Mallory? Well, that's true. But, bless your heart, there's no counting in that way. Think of that poor young fellow lost at sea the other day,—my cousin—a far-away cousin, but still my cousin, Mr. Mallory—and your son-in-law, as I understand, Mr. Mallory. Think of him!" said Mr. Mat, thus suddenly bringing round the conversation to the topic which was uppermost in his mind, by a bold stroke of rhetoric, which he flattered himself would not have disgraced the leader of the western circuit, "there was a sudden calling to account, Mr. Mallory."

"Ay, indeed, Mr. Matthew," said the old clerk, leisurely, folding his hands in front of his waistcoat, and twirling his thumbs placidly as he stood in front of his visitor, in the middle of the flagged floor of his large kitchen and entrance hall; for the two had by this time entered the house; but the old man had not invited his self-hidden guest to be seated,—"ay, indeed, Mr. Matthew, and it's what they are specially liable to, 'who go down to the sea in ships, and occupy their business in the great waters.'"

"Such queer business, too, by all accounts," said Mr. Mat.

"Indeed, I am not much in the way of hearing reports here," rejoined Mr. Mallory, indifferently.

"Very true, Mr. Mallory; out in the moor here, you know. But be all that how it may, it is necessary now to see that the rights of the child—your grandson, Mr. Mallory, and my far-away cousin—are properly settled. That is the feeling of all the family; and perhaps it is all for the best that there should be a male heir for the old place and the old name," said Mr. Mat, whom nobody, and least of all himself, would ever have supposed to have so much Jesuitry in him.

"Of course Mr. Oliver Lindisfarn, and the doctor, my honored master, can only wish that right should be done. Queer enough that the child should have the rector and the clerk of Chewton for his two grandfathers, is it not, Mr. Matthew? I suppose the settlement of the question don't make much more difference to either of them than it does to the other! I have had all the sorrow of the business; and I sha'n't have any of the advantage— No, not all the sorrow, either; for Dr. Lindisfarn had his share too, no doubt; and he will get as little good from it as I shall."

"Of course, of course, Mr. Mallory; and all you can wish is what all the parties concerned wish in the matter,—that the right thing should be done."

"I can safely say, Mr. Matthew, that that is my feeling. But to tell you the truth, I feared, from what I have heard my son say,— the lawyer at Sillmouth, Mr. Matthew,—that the family would make some attempt to dispute the boy's title," said the old man, looking keenly at Mr. Mat.

"I am sure the squire at the Chase has no wish to dispute anything that is not fairly disputable," rejoined Mr. Mat; "but as far as I can understand, there arises some doubt and difficulty about a missing register. If that could be found, I fancy it would make the thing all clear and plain."

"No doubt, Mr. Matthew, no doubt. But how to find it? that is the question. You knew poor Mr. Mellish, nobody better; and you knew his ways. Like enough to have made the old register into gun wadding, for want of better," said the clerk.

"No!" said Mr. Mat, shaking his head very decisively,—"no, Charley would never have done that. He would never have done anything that could bring no end of wrong and trouble to others."

"But you know, Mr. Matthew, that half his time he did not know what he was doing," said the clerk, with a sad and reproachful shake of the head.

"No, not so bad as that! Come, come, Mr. Mallory, don't stick it on to him worse than it was, poor fellow. I have seen him with a drop or two too much now and again towards the small hours. But not in the morning; not when there could ever have been any question about gun-wadding. No, no! Charley never made away with the book in any fashion, I'll lay my life! It must have been in existence somewhere or other when he died; and if it could be found, it would make this child's rights as clear as day, and spare all further trouble about it."

It was now old Mallory's turn to scrutinize his companion, which he did to much better purpose than simple Mr. Mat had done, observing his features furtively and keenly out of the corner of his eye, with a shrewdness calculated to detect an *arrière pensée* in a deeper dissembler than Mr. Mat.

"At all events," he said, "it is exceedingly vexatious that the register cannot be found. I have done my utmost long ago, as well as recently, to find it. And I shall be very much surprised if anybody else ever finds it now."

"Have you any objection to let me go up-stairs into the rooms he used to inhabit? I should like to see the old place again for 'auld lang syne' sake. You know, Mallory, how many a jolly night I have passed in those rooms in old times."

"Ay, Mr. Matthew! it were better if I had not any such to remember. They were sad doings; no credit to the house, nor to the parish, for that matter!" said the old clerk, casting up his eyes in pious reprobation.

"I am sure the next parish was never any the wiser for that matter. It must have been a roystering rouse with a vengeance, that the silence of Sillmoor could not swallow up and tell no tales of! And as for the people here, you know whether they loved poor Charley, or were likely to think much ill of him, poor fellow, with all his faults. May I go up and have a look at the old rooms?"

"Yes, Mr. Matthew, I have no objection whatever. You can go up-stairs if you wish it. I will wait on you. But the room has been used since Mr. Mellish lived in it."

"Both the rooms he occupied?" asked Mr. Mat.

"No, not both of them. The sitting-room has been occupied since by my daughter when she was here. But the room beyond, the bedroom, where he died, has never been used since. We have more space in the house than we need."

So they both went up-stairs; and Mr. Mat, under cover of indulging in the reminitcences of his dead-and-gone jollifications, cast his eyes sharply about him to see if he could get any hint of a hiding-place or repository in which it might be possible to suppose that the missing register might have been hidden and lost. In the room which had been the curate's sitting-room, no trace of his occupation remained. It had very evidently long since passed under feminine dominion, and had been, it may be hoped, purified, during the reign of the moorland wild-flower, from all odor of the naughty doings witnessed in that former phase of its existence. It was not so, however, in the inner room, in which the poor curate had slept, and had died. There everything had remained to all appearance exactly as he had left it. On a nail in the white-washed wall by the side of the old bedstead, just in the place where Roman Catholic devotion is wont to suspend a little vase of holy water, still hung the Protestant curate's dog-whip. On the wall opposite to the bed, and at right angles to the window, was scrawled in charcoal on the white surface a colossal music score, with a number of notes rudely but very clearly, legibly, and correctly placed on the lines of it. The main direction in which poor Mellish's efforts at discharging his duty in the matter of instructing his parishioners had developed themselves, was in attempting to get up a choir, and to teach a class of the boys to sing. And this bedroom had been the poor fellow's school-room, and the huge score and notes on the wall his lecture-board.

Poor melodious Charley! He was willing to teach what he best knew; and whether Sternhold and Hopkins supplied all the exemplars commended to the voices of the ingenuous moorland youth, it were invidious too closely to inquire.

On another side of the room was a large worm-eaten chest, on which Mr. Mat's eye fell immediately. He lifted the creaking lid eagerly; but there was nothing but dust and one old rusty spur in a corner inside. And a smile passed over the face of Mr. Mallory as he let the lid and the corners of his own mouth fall at the same time.

There was no other shade of a possibility that the missing volume might be found in the curate's bed-chamber; and Mr. Mat turned with a sigh—quite as much given to the memory of his old friend as to the failure of his present hopes—to follow Mr. Mallory down the stairs, when, just as they reached the stairfoot, the unusual sound of carriage-wheels was heard outside Mr. Mallory's door.

"I suppose it must be that lawyer come back again," said the old clerk. "He was here the other day, wanting to find this same unlucky register, and he seemed for all the world to fancy that I could tell him where it is. As if I would not find it if I could! I know as well as he does—better for that matter—that it would set all right. I am glad that you should happen to be here, Mr. Matthew, when he pays us his visit: he may look where he likes, for me."

So saying the old man went to the door, and there found, instead of the lawyer he expected, Mr. Falconer, senior, all smiles and bland courtesy.

"Mr. Mallory, your servant. I dare say you can guess my errand; and— But whom have we here? Mr. Mat, I declare! Dear me! Why, Mr. Mat, are you going to enter the lists with us? Have you turned ecclesiologist? Have you visited the church, eh?"

"No, sir, no! we have not been near the church. Mr. Matthew Lindisfarn was here upon another matter. What, you want to have one more look at the famous inscription, sir; is that it?"

"That is what I wish, Mr. Mallory; if you will be so obliging as to afford me the opportunity of doing so."

"Good-morning, Mr. Falconer. I know nothing about the inscription, and I am not turned any ologist of any sort, that I know of. But you might guess what brings me here. I wanted to have a look with my own eyes after this plaguey register. You know all about it, no doubt. All Sillshire knows it by this time."

"Ay, ay, I understand; a bad business, Mr. Mat, a bad business! Truly grievous! But my little matter is a question of some interest between Dr. Lindisfarn and myself and some others, walkers in the paths of hoar antiquity, Mr. Mat."

"What, all across the moor here away?" said Mr. Mat, with a puzzled air.

"Yes, indeed. These pleasant paths have led us on this occasion all across the moor out to Chewton. And now if you like to step across to the church, and if Mr. Mallory will be so obliging as to accompany us with the keys, I shall have pleasure in showing you the famous inscription, which is puzzling us all; and who knows but you may hit upon some suggestion that may help us?" added the old gentleman, patronizingly.

"With all my heart, Mr. Falconer. I used to know the church well enough at one time, years ago. Will you open it for us, Mr. Mallory?" said Mr. Mat.

"I must be going to the church myself in a minute or two, gentlemen," said the clerk; "for it is time to ring the noontide bell. The sexton is a laboring man away at his work; so I always ring the bell at midday."

"Ah, yes! I remember it," said Mr. Mat; "there always used to be noontide bell at Chewton. So you keep up that old fashion still, eh, Mr. Mallory?"

"Dr. Lindisfarn would not have it dropped on any account, sir; and indeed you might say the same almost of a many of the older parishioners. They hold to the noontide bell very much about here. There always *has* been a noontide bell at Chewton-in-the-Moor, time out of mind."

Thus talking the clerk and his two visitors strolled leisurely across the village street, and along the churchyard wall to the old-fashioned stile over it, formed of huge slabs of stone from the moor,—that stile on which Dr. Blakistry had found little July Lindisfarn—or July Mallory, as the case might be—sitting and speculating on rashers in the coming time. July was there no longer, having been removed, with his mother, to Mr. Jared Mallory's house at Sillmouth.

The clerk opened the church, and admitting the two gentlemen into the body of the building, betook himself to the belfry, to perform his daily duty.

"This is indeed a fortunate chance, my dear sir," whispered Falconer to Mr. Mat, as soon as they were left alone, "an opportunity I have never enjoyed before. At my former visits here I have never been able to examine the curious relic of which I spoke to you except under the eyes of the man who has just left us—a creature of the doctor's, of course—worthy, excellent, good man, Dr. Lindisfarn, I am sure. I have the utmost regard for him. But crotchety, my dear Mr. Mat,—I do not mind saying it to you,—decidedly crotchety upon some points; erudite, but de-ci-ded-ly crotchety. Now in the matter of this inscription our dear doctor has formed a certain theory,—it is not for me to say whether tenable or not, at least, not here nor now," said the banker, with a meaning look at his companion, which, however, was meaningless for Mr. Mat,—"a certain theory," continued the banker, "which might most judiciously be tested by the removal of a small portion of the coating of plaster which covers the ancient woodwork. But this I have never been able to attempt, as you will understand, in that man Mallory's presence. Even if he had allowed me to do so, which I do not think, any discovery which I could make would have been immediately communicated to the doctor, you see; and in these matters one wishes, you know—naturally—you understand"—

Mr. Mat understood nothing at all. But he very docilely followed the lead of the old banker, who, as he spoke the last words, had brought him into the corridor leading to the vestry, and stopped short in front of the partially discovered panel which appeared to be let into the wall under the low ornamented arch, in the manner which has been previously described. There, unquestionably enough, were to be seen the mysterious syllables, on which all the senior canon's superstructure of learned dissertation and con-

jecture was founded: "TANTI . . . VI . . . TANTI . . . VI . . . TANTI" And both above and below them were the half-obliterated remains of figures or painted symbols of some sort, which really looked more like hieroglyphics than anything else.

"There, sir, is the celebrated Chewton inscription," said Mr. Falconer, "and I am bound to admit that I do not think there can be any doubt or discrepance of opinion on the reading of the letters. They read most undeniably 'TANTI VI TANTI VI TANTI;' but the doctor has never adverted to the probability that the letters ' v, i,' thus singularly repeated, and especially found thus in conjunction with the adjective ' tanti,' which signifies, my dear Mr. Mat, ' so many,'—' so many,' " repeated the banker, holding up his fore-finger in a manner intended to demand imperatively a strong effort of Mr. Mat's mind for the due comprehension of that important point,—"the very great probability, I say, that these letters ' v, i' may be simply Roman numerals."

All the while the learned banker was setting forth his opposition theory in this manner, Mr. Mat was observing the panel in question more narrowly and with a greater appearance of interest than could have been reasonably expected from a man of his tastes and habits. Stooping down with his hands resting upon his knees, so as to bring his face nearly to a level with the letters, he stared at them, while a close observer might have marked a gradually intensified gleam of intelligence first glimmer in his eyes, then mantle on his humorous puckered lips, and lastly illumine in its completion his entire visage.

"Now what I wish," continued Mr. Falconer, "and what I propose doing, with your kind aid, Mr. Mat, now that the clerk's absence has given us the opportunity, is just to rub, or scrape off a little—just a leetle—of the whitewash here, to see if we can discover any further traces. Don't you think we might manage it, Mr. Mat?" said Mr. Falconer, coaxingly.

"All the world says you are a very learned man, Mr. Falconer, and the doctor another; and learning is a very fine thing. But what would you and the doctor and all the rest of the big-wigs say, if I was to tell you, without any rubbing off of whitewash at all, what comes next after the words you see there?"

said Mr. Mat, putting both his hands in his waistcoat-pockets, balancing himself on the heels of his boots, and looking at the banker with merry-twinkling, half-closed eyes, and his head thrown back.

"Say Mr. Mat?" replied Falconer, apparently quite taken aback with astonishment,—"say?—why, sir, I should say that any such statement was worth just nothing at all without verification. For my own part, I frankly admit that I do not perceive, nor indeed can imagine, the possibility of a conjecture"—

"Well, look ye here, Mr. Falconer, my conjecture is this : I am of opinion that the next letters after those where the whitewash has been rubbed off will be found to be *v, i,* over again, and then *t, h, i, s ;* now if that turns out to be right when we rub off the whitewash, I think you ought to make me president of the antiquarian society, or the devil is in it."

"My dear sir," said Falconer, becoming very red in the face, and more distant in his manner, from annoyance and astonishment, and finding himself, as it were, shoved aside from his place of learned superiority,—"my dear sir, I must confess I do not understand you ; I know not what notion you have taken into your head ; I must protest"—

"Well, Mr. Falconer, I have told you what the next letters will be found to be. Now we'll proceed to verify, as you say."

And Mr. Mat as he spoke, drew out from his pocket one of those huge pluralist pocket-knives,—a whole tool-box of instruments in itself,—which such men as Mr. Mat love to carry about with them ; and having pulled out from some corner of its all-accommodating handle a large wide-bladed hack-knife, proceeded with no light or delicate hand to scrape away a further portion of the coating of whitewash which covered the board.

Falconer looked on, aghast with dismay and horror.

"Mr. Mat, Mr. Mat! Good Heavens! what are you about? What will the doctor say? Gently, gently, at all events ; or you will destroy whatever remains of antiquity time may have spared."

"Not a bit of it, sir," said Mr. Mat, scraping away vigorously ; "there! now, sir, look and see if I was a true prophet. There they are! There are the letters I told you wo

should find,—'*v, i ; t, h, i, s ;*'—plain enough ; aint they ?'"

Mr. Falconer put on his gold eyeglasses, and peered closely at the place where Mr. Mat had laid the wood bare. He read the letters, as deciphered by Mr. Mat, without any difficulty.

"My dear sir," he said, tremulously, while his hands before and his pigtail behind began to shake in unison with the excess of his perplexity and astonishment, "I confess I do not understand it,—I am at a loss,—I wash my hands of the matter. You must account for what you have done to the doctor ; I fear he will be greatly displeased, I—I—retire baffled !—I can offer no conjecture—ahem ! '"

"Oh, I'll be accountable to the doctor! Why, I thought that he was worriting his life out to find out what this writing meant. I thought that was what you all of you wanted ? " cried Mr. Mat. "But I'll tell you what it is, Mr. Falconer," he continued, selecting, as he spoke, another instrument from his pocket arsenal, "I mean to verify this a little more. I am going to have that board out, inscription and all. Why, it's an old acquaintance of mine, Mr. Falconer, the old board, and the inscription, as you call it, and the whole concern. Bless your heart, I know all about it! What do you say to this now, by way of a learned explanation ?" And with a very reprehensible forgetfulness of the sacred character of the building in which they were standing, and throwing himself into an attitude meant to be in accordance with his words, Mr. Mat made the groined roof of the fine old church ring again with the well-known old burthen, "Tantivy, tantivy, tantivy ! This day a stag must die ! "

"Ha, ha, ha, ha ! " he laughed uproariously ; "to think of poor Charley's music-score coming to make such a piece of work ; ha, ha, ha, ha ! "

"That is all very well, Mr. Mat," said Falconer, seizing, with a transient gleam of hope, on a point which seemed to afford the means of hitching a difficulty on to Mr. Mat's explanation of the celebrated Chewton inscription ; "but you will do me the favor to observe that the cabalistic word taken from the art of venerie which you have cited, ' tantivy,' must be held to be written as pronounced, with a *y* at the end ; whereas the letters painted on that panel are *v, i.*"

" Tell ye, Mr. Falconer, I saw him paint it —helped him to do it. Fact was, the parish boys used to puzzle themselves with the *y* at the end ; so he wrote it *i*, comes to the same thing, you know. Poor Charley was always wanting to teach a lot of the parish boys to sing,— all he did teach 'em, or could teach 'em, I suppose, for the matter of that. But singing he did understand, nobody better. Poor fellow ! many's the glee he and I have made two at. Well, his plan was to paint a few bars of some easy song or other, with the words,—there, you can see the notes plain enough !—and paint it all so big that the whole of his class could read it at once. That was what this board was for. If you will go up into the room in old Mallory's house, where poor Charley used to live, you may see just such another bit of music done on the wall with charcoal. I was up there just now, before you arrived, and there is the poor fellow's handiwork on the wall pretty nearly as fresh as ever. Yes, there it is, music and all, plain enough," continued Mr. Mat, who had, all the time he was talking, been vigorously working away at the board, and had at last succeeded in wrenching it away from the wall,—" there is poor Charley's class-board, ' Tantivy, tantivy, tantivy, this day a stag must die !' Now, Mr. Falconer, don't I deserve to be made perpetual president of the learned Society of Antiquaries of Silverton, eh ? What do you say to the verification now, Mr. Falconer ? "

" It is truly a very extraordinary explanation of the mystery,—very unexpected and extraordinary indeed. Nevertheless, Mr. Mat, I am sure that you will forgive me, if I declare myself to be speaking strictly under reserve, and refrain from pronouncing at present any definitive opinion. I fear, as I before observed, that the doctor, who is rector of this church, you must remember, Mr. Mat, will be very seriously displeased at the—the somewhat precipitous and violent steps which have been taken for "—

" For the discovery of his favorite mare's nest, eh ? Well, I must take the blame of that. But now, Mr. Falconer," continued Mr. Mat, changing his manner entirely, and speaking very seriously, " I'll tell you what it is ! I've got a mare's nest here as well as the doctor. I did not wrench that board

out of its place only to show you what it was. I know the old board that my own hands had helped to paint well enough, directly I saw it. But something else came into my head at the same time. You have heard all about the missing register, and how much may depend on the finding of it ! Well, now I remember how this place in the wall used to be before Mellish had the board put up there. There was a space under this stone arch here, as you may see now, and at the bottom of it a stone trough like a small conduit. Well, when Charley had done with the old board, and the boys had got pretty perfect in ' This day a stag must die,' he scrawled that other lesson on the wall, as I was telling you just now, and I never knew nor cared what had become of the board ; for though I was often over here in those days, my visits were not for the purpose of going to church, more shame for me. But I recollect as well as if it was yesterday, hearing Mellish complain, time and again, that there was no proper place in the vestry for the keeping of the register book. And when I saw the board put up here so as to shut in a snug place under the old arch, and yet so as to leave an opening a-top,—for, as you may see, this board did not close up the arch ; that must have been done afterward, and I dare say our old friend who has just done ringing the bell could tell us the when, and maybe the wherefore,—when I observed all this, you see, having the matter of the register more in my mind than the inscription, it came across me like a flash of lightning that it was very likely Charley had put the board up here to make a place, and a very snug, safe place, too, for keeping the register in. It was just like him, always full of contraptions, and a deal cleverer with his hands than he was with his head, poor fellow."

Just as Mr. Mat had completed his explanation, the two violators of the fabric of the church were rejoined by the old clerk. And a wrathful man was he, when his first glance showed him what had been done. Perhaps there was something more, besides anger, in the pallor that came over his rigid old face, and the dilation of his still fiery, deep-set eyes.

" What is this, gentlemen ? " he said, in a voice tremulous with passion. " Sacrilege ! You have committed sacrilege, gentlemen, and abused the trust I placed in you, in allowing you to remain in the church."

" Mr. Mallory, I protest "— began the banker, with formal pomposity.

" Gentlemen," interrupted the gaunt old man, still shaking with rage, " you must answer for this outrage as best you may. You must be accountable to the rector of the parish—and to the law. I must insist upon your leaving the church instantly—instantly ! " he reiterated, coming forward a step as he spoke, so as to advance towards placing himself between Mr. Mat and the partially disclosed aperture which the removal of the board had occasioned.

" Certainly, Mr. Mallory, certainly," said Mr. Mat, taking a rapid stride forward as he spoke, so as to be beforehand with the old man, and to place himself close to the spot from which the board had been taken ; " I did this job. Mr. Falconer had no hand in it at all. I will be answerable for it. But before I go I must just see what lies buried among the rubbish there behind the boarding, only for the sake of antiquarianism, you know."

And while the words were yet on his lips he plunged his hand into the trough of the monk's old conduit, still hidden behind a second board, which had been placed below the old music-score, and in the next minute drew it forth with a small vellum-bound volume in it.

Holding his prize aloft with one hand, Mr. Mat put the thumb of the other to his ear, and uttered a view-halloa which might have waked the ancient monks from their tercentenary slumber.

Mr. Falconer, not a little scandalized, but quite awake to the possible importance of the discovery, held up his hands, partly in dismay and partly in interest.

Mallory became perfectly livid, and trembled visibly in every limb. He strove with might and main, however, to speak with stern calmness, as he said,—

" Mr. Matthew Lindisfarn, I require you to give up that volume instantly to me. If indeed it be a register, I, in the absence of the rector and the curate, am the legal and proper guardian of it. Mr. Falconer, I appeal to you ! "

" I wash my hands—indeed, I have once already stated to Mr. Matthew that I wash my hands."

" And I will wash mine when I get back to the Chase ! " cried Mr. Mat, still holding high in the air the dusty and cobweb-mantled volume, and making for the door of the church.

Mallory rushed forward to intercept him, with an agility that could not have been expected from his years, crying out,—

" Mr. Lindisfarn, I warn you ! This is sacrilege and felony ; felony, Mr. Lindisfarn ! Take care what you are about. Mr. Falconer, you are a magistrate, I call upon you."

" Good-by, Mr. Falconer ; I'm off ; no time to lose—see you in Silverton. Beg pardon, Mr. Mallory, but this book must go to Silverton, felony or no felony."

And so saying, he darted out of the church-door, and across the street to the rail where he had left Miss Lucy, and was in the saddle in the twinkling of an eye.

" Now, Miss Lucy, old girl, put the best foot foremost ; " and turning in his saddle as he started at a gallop, he saw his two recent companions standing at the church-door, staring after him open-mouthed.

" Yoicks ! Yoicks ! hark forward ! " he cried, once more flourishing his prize in the air before their eyes, and then carefully securing it within his coat, gave all his attention to guiding Miss Lucy across the moor, at what would assuredly have been a break-neck pace to most riders.

CHAPTER XLIX.

MR. SLOWCOME COMES OUT RATHER STRONG.

The flanks of Miss Lucy were streaming as she stood at the door of Messrs. Slowcome and Sligo's offices in the High Street, about half-past one o'clock on that Monday morning. Mr. Mat had ridden the fifteen miles from Chewton in one hour and a quarter ; but had nevertheless found time to reflect, as he rode, that after all he did not know what the register might prove, or whether it might be found to prove anything in the matter of the succession of the Lindisfarn property. He remembered with some misgiving that in truth he did not know with any certainty whether the dusty volume he had drawn from its hiding-place was any parish register at all or no ; and justly considering that it would be very desirable to ascertain what might be the real facts in these respects before carrying his prize to the Chase, where probably nobody would be able to understand anything of the matter, he determined very judiciously to submit the volume in the first place to the learned scrutiny of old Slow.

Hurriedly throwing Miss Lucy's rein to a boy in the street, who, like every other boy in the streets of Silverton, knew both Mr. Mat and Miss Lucy perfectly well, he rushed into the open door, and made straight for that inner one of glass, which gave immediate admittance to the sacred presence of the heads of the firm, quite regardless of the remonstrances of the outraged Bob Scott, who in vain tried to stop him.

"Sir, sir, Mr. Mat!" cried Bob, in his capacity of Cuberns, "they are engaged. Mr. Slowcome has people with him on business, and Mr. Sligo is with him too; you must wait, if you please," said the junior clerk, rushing out from his den on the left-hand side of the entrance.

"Can't wait; who's with him?" said Mr. Mat.

"Why, Mr. Jared Mallory, of Sillmouth!" whispered Bob, with an air of much mystery.

"All right!" cried Mr. Mat, with his hand on the lock of the glazed door; and in the next instant he was in the innermost shrine of Themis.

Mr. Slowcome was sitting in his accustomed chair, wheeled round a little from the writing-table, so as to face the Sillmouth attorney, who was seated opposite to him, while Mr. Sligo was standing dangling one leg over the back of a chair, on the rug before the fireplace.

One would have said to look at the three that both Mr. Slowcome and Mr. Mallory were exceedingly enjoying themselves, and that Mr. Sligo was much amused by watching them. And in this case Mr. Slowcome and not Mr. Mallory was the hypocrite. That latter gentleman was very thoroughly enjoying himself, and seemed entirely to have got over that appearance of being ill at ease, which a consciousness of his unprofessional and out-at-elbow-like shabbiness inspired him with on his first visit to the offices of the prosperous Silverton firm. He sat thrown back in an easy attitude in his chair, with one knee crossed over the other, with one hand in his trousers, while the other was caressing his chin; and he was eying old Slow with the look of a man who has forced

his antagonist into a corner, and triumphantly watches his struggles to escape from that position. But old Slow afforded him as little as possible of this triumph. He, too, seemed perfectly at his ease, and at all events, was not hurried into speaking or moving one jot beyond his normal speed. Mr. Sligo was biting his nails, and looked like a terrier watching for the moment when a baited badger might give him an opportunity for dashing in upon him.

"How do, Slowcome?" cried Mr. Mat, nodding to Mr. Sligo. "Who is this gentleman?" he continued, staring at the visitor to the firm : "Mr. Jared Mallory, I should say by the look of him."

"You are right, Mr. Matthew Lindisfarn, though I can't say I should have known you by the look of you, if I had not known you before !"

"We were engaged, Mr. Matthew, in discussing, quite in a friendly way, and without prejudice to any ulterior proceedings which it may be necessary to take in the matter—without prejudice, Mr. Mallory"—

"Oh, quite so," snapped Mr. Mallory, with the rapidity of a monkey seizing a nut.

"We were engaged in discussing this matter of the disputed succession—not but what I am premature in calling it so," pursued Mr. Slowcome, as if he were speaking against time, and would beat it out of the field, "but this question, which may become such—may unfor-tu-nate-ly become such—respecting the Lindisfarn property."

"Quite so," put in Mr. Sligo, like a pistol-shot.

"And I am come to help you," said Mr. Mat, briskly, drawing a chair between Mr. Slowcome and Mallory.

"Ay, ay, ay, ay," said Mr. Slowcome; "Sligo, Mr. Matthew has come to help us."

"More the merrier," said Mr. Mallory.

"Perhaps better see member of firm confidentially. My room at your service, Mr. Matthew," suggested Mr. Sligo.

"Look at that, Mr. Slowcome," said Mr. Mat, producing his book, and utterly disregarding the caution of Mr. Sligo.

"A remarkably dirty volume," said old Slow, taking it between his finger and thumb, and laying it gingerly on the desk before him. "Have you a duster there, Mr. Sligo? Be so good as to ring the bell."

"Let me look at it, Mr. Slowcome; I am not so dainty," said Mallory, stretching out his hand towards the volume.

"Nay, Mr. Mal-lo-ry," returned Slowcome, waving him off with an interposing hand; "let us keep our hands clean if we can,—clean if we can, you know, Mis-ter Mal-lo-ry. What does the volume purport to be, Mr. Matthew?"

"It has not purported anything yet. That is what I brought it here for, that you might see. But if I am not mistaken, Slowcome, that is the missing register of Chewton church."

A sudden change, transitory as a flash of lightning, passed over Mr. Mallory's face, and he again stretched out his hand toward the little volume, which had by this time been duly divested of its dust and cobwebs, saying, as he did so,—

"Indeed, Mr. Matthew; that would be most satisfactory to us all."

Mr. Sligo sprung forward to interpose, and snatch the volume himself. But old Slow was beforehand with them both, quietly letting his fat white hand fall upon the volume as the words passed Mr. Mat's lips.

"Dear me, dear me," he said, without the change of a demi-semi-tone in his voice, "and where did you obtain the volume, Mr. Matthew Lindisfarn? That is if you have no objection to answer the question, you know."

"Oh, no objection in life," said Mr. Mat, readily; "I committed felony to get it. At least, so that gentleman's worthy father told me."

"Ay, ay, ay, ay. Dear me, dear me; you removed the volume from the parish church of Chewton, and Mr. Mallory, senior, who is, I understand, the clerk of that parish, expressed an opinion—a *primâ facie* opinion of course—that the removal of it amounted within the meaning of the statute to felony. Ay, ay, ay, ay! Your good father amuses his leisure hours with the pleasing study of the criminal law, Mr. Mallory?" said Slowcome, bowing to the Sillmouth attorney with a perfection of bland courtesy.

"Little study needed to tell that stealing a parish-register is felony, I should think," snarled Mallory.

"Very true, Mis-ter Mal-lo-ry, very true indeed. We will, however, examine the volume, at all events. We can hardly make felony of that, Mr. Mallory; can we?"

And thus saying, old Slow carefully and leisurely adjusted his gold eyeglasses, and proceeded to look at the book, from which he had not once removed his hand, during the above conversation.

"Most assuredly this is the register of births, deaths, and marriages of the parish of Chewton, ranging over all the time with which our present business can be concerned, Mr. Matthew," said he, after a leisurely inspection.

Mr. Mat's eyes twinkled, as he said,—

"I knew poor Charley Mellish could never have done anything wrong about it in any way "—

"No suggestion of the kind, Mr. Mat. Register lost, all about it, no case," interrupted Mr. Sligo precipitately, and thereby averting a storm of virtuous indignation, that was on the point of bursting from Mr. Mallory.

"And where was the mislaid volume found, Mr. Matthew?—always supposing that you have no objection to reply to the question," said Slowcome.

Mr. Mat related the scene in Chewton church as compendiously as he could, not omitting the old clerk's violent opposition to his taking away the book, and concluded by asking the legal oracle what he thought about it.

Mr. Slowcome had, while Mr. Mat was telling his story, handed the important book to Mr. Sligo, with a look, and the one word "Sligo," as he put it into his hands. And Mr. Sligo had in about a minute afterwards, while Mr. Mat was still speaking, returned the volume open to Mr. Slowcome, with his forefinger pointing carelessly to one of the late entries on the page. Old Slow glanced at the passage pointed out to him, while he said, in answer to Mr. Mat's final question,—

"Well, Mr. Mat, I am bound in justice to your friend Mr. Mallory, senior, of Chewton, to say that I am of opinion that the abstraction of the register does bear a *primâ facie* similarity to a case of felony."

"*Primâ facie* and *lasta facie*, too, I should say!" cried Mr. Mallory; "now look'ee here, Mr. Slowcome," he continued, "this may come to be an ugly business, you see. Of course we cannot put up with such a document as that being left in the power and at the discretion of our opponents. Out of the question, no saying what may have been done already, no offence." (Luckily for Mr. Jarad's bones, Mr. Mat had no conception of his meaning.) " But look'ee here, Mr. Slowcome, matters may be arranged ; no wish to press hardly on a gentleman much respected in the county. Let the register be immediately sealed and returned to the clerk of Chewton, and we consent there shall be no further notice taken."

" That is a very handsome offer, very handsome and friendly, Mr. Mallory, indeed ; but would it not," and here Mr. Slowcome paused to savor a huge pinch of snuff, and carefully fillipped away a grain or two from his immaculate shirt-frill before proceeding,— " would it not, I was about to observe, have an awkward appearance of compounding a felony, Mr. Mallory, since we are driven to use such hard words ? "

"I'll tell you what it is, gentlemen, all three of you," cried Mr. Mat, striking his hand on Mr. Slowcome's table as he spoke, " if I have committed a felony, I'll be shot if it shall be for nothing ! And that register shall be examined before either it or I leave this office ! "

" We don't *shoot* felons in this country, Mr. Mat," said old Slow, while an earthquaky sort of movement, originating in the inside of him caused his ponderous watch-chain and seals to oscillate, and indicated that old Slow conceived himself to have perpetrated a joke.

" And very few documents of any description that ever find their way into *this* office, go out again unexamined ! " said the younger partner, with a hard look at Mr. Mallory.

" Very right, Sligo ! very judiciously observed indeed ! Capital business maxim that, Mr. Mallory ! And as for our friend Mr. Mat being either shot, or t'other thing, you know, I think I could suggest another line of defence ; I *think* I could, with all deference to an authority doubtless more conversant with that department of business than our house can pretend to be," said Mr. Slowcome, with a most courteous bow to Mr. Mallory.

" Indeed, Mr. Slowcome ! And what may that be ? I should be curious to hear it, I confess ! "

" Well ! it is true I am but an ignoramus as to the practice of the criminal side of the court, Mr. Mallory ; but my humble notion is, that if I were in Mr. Mat's place, and

either you or your respected father were to say anything to me of so unpleasant a nature as felony, Mr. Mallory, I,—speaking in the character of our excellent friend Mr. Mat, you understand,—I should reply to either you or your respected father, *Forgery !* Mr. Mal-lo-ry, FORGERY ! For-ge-ry ! ! " cried Mr. Slowcome, speaking with his accustomed slowness, but with an energy that caused his chin and his pigtail and his watch-chain all to oscillate in unison.

" I do not know what you mean, Mr. Slowcome ! " cried Mallory, turning very pale ; " but I would advise you to be very careful of actionable words, Mr. Slowcome,— spoken before witnesses, Mr. Slowcome ! "

" Dear me ! dear me ! dear me ! To think of its being actionable to talk of forgery in the most abstract, and I may say hypothetical, sort of way ! See now ! I told you that I knew nothing about these matters ! But it's as well to be hung for a sheep as a lamb, now isn't it, Mr. Mallory ? So we will come to the concrete. I say the document you submitted to me, purporting to be an extract from this register, has been fraudulently altered, Mr. Mallory ! The *date* has been tampered with, Mr. Mallory ! The marriage between the late Julian Lindisfarn and your good sister, Mr. Mallory, was celebrated, as duly shown by this register, not before, but after the birth of the child now wrongfully called Julian Lindisfarn ; and that child is *nullius filius*, which means, strange as it may seem, Mr. Mat, the son of nobody at all, and therefore *à fortiori*, as I may perhaps be allowed to say, nobody's grandson, and in no wise heir to an acre of the Lindisfarn estates ! *Nullius filius,* Mr. Mallory ; and the rights of the Misses Katharine and Margaret Lindisfarn are in-dis-puta-ble, Mr. Mallory. That is all ! And a very good day's work you have done this morning, Mr. Mat ! I congratulate you with all my heart ; and between ourselves I don't think that Mr. Mallory will, under the circumstances, be hard upon us about the felony —under the circumstances, eh, Mr. Mallory ? "

" Can't say indeed, Mr. Slowcome ! We shall see, we shall see, sir ! " said Mr. Mallory, sticking his hat on over his ear, and taking a stride toward the door ; " you shall hear from me shortly, sir ! "

" I think not! I think not! " said Mr. Slowcome, shaking his head, as Mr. Sligo closed the door behind the discomfited foe.

" We shall here no more of them, sir! " he continued, turning to Mr. Mat; " Ha, ha, ha! Tantivy, tantivy! very remarkable chance. Tantivy, tantivy! " repeated the old gentleman, slowly as he rubbed his hands over each other softly,—" tantivy, tantivy! very good, very good indeed! "

Mr. Mat hardly waited to hear the end of old Slow's felicitations, before, rushing out of the office as precipitately as he had entered it, he sprung into the saddle, and astonished Miss Lucy by the unwonted style in which she was required to get over the ground between Silverton and the Chase.

" Forgery! Forgery! Forgery! " he shouted in view-holloa tones as he rushed into the drawing-room, where the ladies of the family, including Lady Farnleigh, were sitting.

Of course the news of the finding of the register, and of old Slow's decision respecting the facts resulting from its contents were soon made known to every member of the family, and were welcomed by them with rejoicing, slightly diversified in the manifestation of it in accordance with the characteristics of the various individuals. The only one of the party whose peace of mind was in any degree permanently injured by the events which had taken place, and the erroneous impressions arising from them, was Miss Immy; for the upsetting of the foundations of her mind by the statement, which had with difficulty been made credible to her, that the Lindisfarn girls were not the heiresses to the Lindisfarn property, was so complete and irremediable that it was found impracticable to convince her that the decision now once again arrived at that they *were* heiresses, was not liable to be again reversed to-morrow. It is a dangerous thing to disturb the ideas of those who have never accustomed their minds to the possibility that their *certainties* may turn out to be not certain.

Kate nestled up to her godmother's side, and whispered, " I do so hope that nobody will have told *him* of it, before he comes here."

" Oh! you would like to have the telling of your ' him '—as if there were but one of the sex in the world—yourself; would you? " said Lady Farnleigh, in the same whispered

tones. " Well, as he is at this moment probably in the *Petrel* off the coast of Moulsea Haven, and as the instant he can get away he will come here as fast as a horse's legs can carry him, I think you have a fair chance of being the first teller of your good news."

" If I can only make him understand how wholly my great joy at this change is for his sake," said Kate, drooping her face over her godmother's shoulder, and, putting her lips very close to her ear.

" I am inclined to think, my dear, that you will not find him obtuse on that subject," replied Lady Farnleigh.

Miss Margaret, after having partaken with the rest of the family of the general burst of mutual congratulations with which Mr. Mat's news had been received, quietly stole away to her own room and locked herself in. There throwing herself into a large chair, she remained for many minutes plunged in reflections which, it would have been very evident to any eye that could have watched her, were not of an altogether pleasurable kind. There were certain expressions flitting changefully across those lovely features, like thunder-clouds across a summer sky, and certain clinchings from time to time of the slender, rosy-tipped fingers of those long, beautifully-formed hands which denoted that other feelings than those of unmixed satisfaction and rejoicing were present and busy within that snowy bosom. We know that Miss Margaret had been shamefully and cruelly treated. She certainly had cause to feel anger and bitter resentment against a certain person,—and Miss Margaret was apt to feel resentment keenly. How far it would be justifiable to conclude that Madame de Renneville's lovely pupil was engaged, during those long minutes of self-absorbed reflection, in debating within herself what course would secure the best and sweetest vengeance and the severest retribution on the individual who had incurred her displeasure, must be left to the consideration of the candid reader. Supposing it should seem probable that such was in fact the case, we can only discover the decision on this point arrived at in her secret meditations, by observing and carefully piecing together her actions immediately reverie gave place to action, and those particulars of her subsequent conduct which yet remain to be recorded in these pages.

Now what Miss Margaret *did* immediately

on rousing herself from her meditations and her easy-chair, was to change the somewhat neglected attire which she had adopted, during the sackcloth and ashes days of disappointment and misery through which she had just been passing, for a very carefully arranged and tasteful *toilette de matin*. Miss Margaret's practice in the matter was quite oriental and biblical, it may be observed. The fact is, that sorrow manifests its evil influence very differently in different natures. In Miss Margaret it produced a singular tendency to slovenliness. She was like the cats when they are ill, and when under a cloud took, as the phraseology of the servants' hall has it, "no pride in herself."

She was curiously prompt in making this change, certainly. Nevertheless, perhaps this promptitude may be seen to have been inspired by that judicious and keen appreciation of men and things by which Margaret Lindisfarn was so remarkably distinguished.

CHAPTER L.

ARCADES AMBO!—CONCLUSION.

Just as Mr. Mat was hurriedly mounting Miss Lucy at Messrs. Slowcome and Sligo's door, the carriage of Mr. Falconer drove up the High Street of Silverton, on its return from Chewton. As soon as possible after that triumphant flight of Mr. Mat with his prize in his hand from the village in the moor, the worthy banker had taken his leave of Mr. Mallory, and had entered his comfortable carriage, charging his coachman, as he did so, to make all possible speed in returning to Silverton. But not only were the banker's handsome pair of carriage horses no match for Miss Lucy, but the road they had to traverse was some two miles longer. And it resulted thence that Mr. Falconer arrived in the High Street, as has been said, only just as Mr. Mat, after his important interview with the lawyers, was leaving it. The banker caught sight of Mr. Mat, as he rode away from the lawyer's door, and putting his head out of the carriage window, called to the coachman to stop at Messrs. Slowcome and Sligo's office.

"I saw Mr. Matthew Lindisfarn leave your door a minute ago, Slowcome," said he, making his way into the lawyer's presence in a much more hurried manner than comported with Mr. Bob Scott's ideas of the dignity of his principal. "Of course you have heard all about the strange adventure at Chewton. You have seen the book, I suppose, that he carried off in such a—I must say—in a somewhat unjustifiable manner. Is it a register? Is it *the* register? Does it prove anything?"

"I never am able to hear more than one question at a time, Mr. Falconer," said Slowcome, looking up very deliberately from a letter he was writing, "even when I am not interrupted in another occupation. Yes! I have seen the book Mr. Mat brought from Chewton. What came next?"

"Why, was it the register? Do tell me all about it, Slowcome, come, as an old friend; interested, too, you know, in the matter."

"Ay, ay, indeed. Still interested in the matter? Dear me! But to tell you all about it would really occupy a larger amount of time than I am able, with due regard to other pressing avocations, to devote to that purpose at present,—just at present, you see, Mr. Falconer."

"Only just one word, Slowcome," said the banker, absolutely writhing with impatience, under the severe discipline with which old Slow was wont to chastise that failing: "Did the book Mr. Mat found prove anything?"

"Oh, dear me, yes! It proves all the marriages and deaths in Chewton parish for a very considerable number of years, Mr. Falconer."

"It was the register, then? Come, Slowcome, do 'let the cat out of the bag' with one word. Come, there is a good fellow. You know that I have good reasons for wishing to know the truth. What does the register prove in the matter of the Lindisfarn succession?"

"Well, I have no objection to state it as my opinion—with all due reservations, you will understand, Mr. Falconer—with all due re—ser—va—ti—ons, of course—that the register now fortunately discovered and brought forward in evidence, does very satisfactorily and indisputably," and old Slow, who had risen from his chair, and was standing with his back to his office fire, with his hands under the tails of his coat, made at each disjointedly uttered syllable of those polysyllabic adverbs a sort of little bow, which caused his coat-tails and his watch-chain and his pigtail to move in unison, like the different parts of some well-regulated machine,—"very sa-tis-fac-to-ri-ly and in-dis-pu-ta-bly, Mr. Falconer, establish the clear, and, considering the age of the other parties named in the entail and other circumstances, I think I am justified in saying, in-de-fen-si-ble right of the young ladies at the Chase to their father's estates."

"You don't say so! By George, Slowcome, could you not have said so in half a word?" cried the banker, as he hurried to the door of the room.

"No, I think not, Mr. Falconer. I never make use of half-words considering entire ones to be more sa-tis-fac-to-ry."

But Mr. Falconer was half-way to the halldoor by the time old Slow had got through this last adverb, and was hurrying home up the High Street, before the earthquake that began to heave Mr. Slowcome's white waistcoat, giving evidence of the existence of hidden laughter far down below the surface of the man, had subsided.

"Fred, come here," said Mr. Falconer, as he passed hurriedly through the outer office of the bank into his private room behind it; "I want to speak to you."

Mr. Frederick, who had of late been far more regular in his attendance at the bank than had been the case for some time past, rose somewhat listlessly from his seat, and followed his father into his sanctum.

"Shut the door, Fred," cried the senior, hastily; "here's all the fat in the fire again, and we shall burn our fingers at last, if we don't mind what we are about. They have found a parish-register which proves that the girls up at the Chase are the rightful heirs after all. No mistake. Old Slowcome has just told me; took me half an hour to get it out of him."

"By Jove! If you had not sent that old fool Gregory to spoil all, I should have been all right by this time," said the unreasonable young gentleman.

"Yes, and if it had turned up t'other way? A pretty job. But it's not too late. If you are half a fellow, you will be able to put it right again. But sharp's the word. No time to be lost."

Freddy shook his ambrosial curls with a very decided expression of doubt. "I am afraid it wont do," said he, "I am afraid *that* game is up. Nothing, you know, sir, has passed since my letter to the squire withdrawing from the engagement."

"Dictated by me, of course," rejoined his father, "you make it right with the girl, and I will undertake the squire."

"I am almost afraid it wont do," replied his son; "it is worth trying though, anyway. I'll try it."

"Not an hour to lose, my boy; and, Fred," he added, as his son was leaving the room, already meditating his high emprise, "lay the blame on me, as thick as you like, you know. That will be your plan."

Fred nodded, and hastened to his own room to prepare for marching on this forlorn hope, having asked one of the juniors in the bank, as he passed, to have the kindness to order his horse to be saddled for him without delay.

In a few minutes he came down dressed altogether in black, with his face looking a good deal paler than it had been half an hour before, and with his left arm in a sling.

Thus got up for the occasion, he mounted his horse as gracefully as could be done by a man who had the use of only one arm, and made the best of his way to the Chase, arriving there about an hour and a half after Mr. Mat, and as near as might be about the time when Margaret had shown her admirable tact and knowledge of mankind by making the improvement which has been mentioned in her toilet. She was, in fact, in the act of descending the staircase which opened on the front hall at the Chase when our friend Fred entered the house. No more inevitable meeting could have been arranged for them. The groom, who had taken Frederick's horse from him, had opened the door for him, and had then gone away to the stables, leaving him, as a well-known and familiar guest, to find his own way into the drawing-room, after the unceremonious fashion of the house. And thus it happened that there was no servant present to mar the privacy of their interview.

Fred did it very well, certainly. Hurriedly advancing two or three rapid strides toward the foot of the stair, where Margaret stood, magnificent in the accusing majesty of her haughty attitude, he stopped suddenly; and made a partially abortive effort to clasp his hands before him, which, painfully impeded, as it evidently was, by the maimed condition of the arm supported by its black silk sling, was—or at all events ought to have been—exceedingly touching.

"Margaret," he said, in tones rendered low and husky (so much so indeed as to be inaudible in the neighboring drawing-room) by his evident emotion,—"my own, my adored Margaret, oh, tell me that I have still the right to call you so! Oh, Margaret, if you could only know what I have suffered during these dreadful, dreadful days! Again and again I have thought that my reason must have sunk under the horrible mental torment I have suffered. It would, I feel sure, have done so, had I not at length forced my way to you despite the orders and efforts of nurses and all of them. Thank God, I can at least see and speak to you once again!"

"I see that you have hurt your arm, sir," said Margaret, coldly and haughtily; "did it ever occur to you that there might be worse torture than that of an injured limb? You tell me of your sufferings. Did you ever give a thought to mine?"

"Oh, Margaret, is it necessary to tell you, does not your own heart tell you, that what has been driving me mad has been the thought that you were suffering"—

"Oh, indeed, Mr. Falconer? Your trouble on that score might have long since ceased; you made me pass a very, very miserable hour; but the agony was soon over; you do not suppose that I could feel aught but contempt for a man who could treat a girl as you treated me, or consider it anything but a matter for self-gratulation that I had escaped all ties with one who could be capable of such conduct?"

"You are unjust to me, Margaret. Your displeasure is natural; but it renders you unjust to me. Can you suppose that anything save physical impossibility,"—and here he glanced piteously at his maimed arm,—"could have prevented me from keeping the appointment it had been such rapture to me to make?"

"The post-chaise, then, was not, as I had heard, countermanded by your father's clerk?" sneered Margaret.

"Assuredly it was," replied he, "in consequence of the unfortunate accident which happened to me as I was on the point of hastening to the *rendezvous*. It was necessary to provide against your being compromised by leaving the chaise standing all night at the garden-door. That was the only idea that remained firm in my mind when the

agony of the dislocation took from me all power of thinking. Can you harbor resentment, Margaret, against the victim of so cruel a misfortune?"

"Cruel as the misfortune was, it must be admitted that it was opportune, Mr. Falconer, —almost as strikingly so as the first moment at which you are able to get out to bring me the assurance of your unbroken affection."

"Opportune, Miss Lindisfarn? What do you mean?" said Frederick, with a well-feigned air of utter perplexity.

"Simply this, Mr. Falconer," replied Margaret, with an expression of withering scorn,— "simply this: that the abandonment of your proposed elopement coincided with very curious accuracy with the moment when the information in all probability reached you that I was not entitled to any portion of my father's estates; and that your reappearance here follows instantly upon the discovery that that information was quite erroneous. That is all."

"Now, Margaret!" said Freddy Falconer, in a tone of friendly remonstrance, and not appearing at all overwhelmed by the accusations of his beloved,—"now, Margaret," he said, stretching out both hands toward her, the injured one, too, curiously enough, "is it not unworthy of both of us to suppose that either you or I could be influenced in our conduct by such considerations? Blakistry, I hear, declares that he has the certainty that both you and your sister were aware of the facts that were supposed to oust you from the inheritance of the Lindisfarn property at the time when you first made me happy by accepting the offer of my hand." And Frederick looked at his beloved with a very peculiar expression as he spoke these words. "Now the low-minded Sillsbire gossips might make a very disagreeable story out of that. But we know each other better. We know that you in first accepting my offer and then in consenting to an elopement before the secret of your Cousin Julian's being alive had become known, as well as I in apparently suspending my hope of calling you mine for a short interval,—we know, I say, that neither one nor the other of us was influenced for a moment by any unworthy considerations? We know, each that the other is incapable of any such baseness. The world, my Margaret, the vulgar outside world, may talk of these things; but we know each other. I might have told you that I have induced my father to give Slowcome directions to make very exceptionally liberal arrangements in respect to pin-money. But it never occurred to me to mention it, knowing how little space any such matters would occupy in your thoughts."

"Little, indeed, Frederick," said Margaret, whose dark liquid eyes had begun, during the course of her Frederick's last speech, to turn on a service of glances of a very different quality from those with which she was regarding him at the commencement,—"little, indeed, would any such matters occupy my mind, except as affording a proof of your thoughtful love. Ah, Frederick, you know not, may you never know, what I have had to suffer since I doubted it!"

"But you doubt it no more, my Margaret?" he cried, advancing one stride toward her.

"To think of your having been so watchful over my future comfort, as to have persuaded your father to have the papers made differently. I must make that odious old Slowcome explain it all to me, that I may be able to say in days to come, Frederick, 'This I owe to the loving thought that remained true to me during the dark days.' May I ask old Slowcome to explain it to me?"

"He shall, my own Margaret. May I not once more call you so? It shall be explained to you, my Margaret," answered Frederick, who perceived that he was pardoned and restored to his former position, but that the little peace-offering he had mentioned must be really and absolutely paid, and not used only as dust to be thrown in the magnificent eyes of his Margaret.

"Ah, Frederick," she rejoined, allowing him to take her hand between both his, which he did with no impediment, apparently, from the maimed condition of one of his arms,—"ah, Frederick, these have been very painful days, a dark and miserable time! And we may be very sure that unkind and envious eyes have been watching us, and will not be slow to draw their own malicious conclusions, and make their own odious insinuations."

"But what need we care, dearest, for all the malicious tongues in the world, when we are mutually conscious of each other's truth and affection? Are we not all the world to each other, Margaret?"

"And that must be our strong and sufficient defence against all calumny; for you may depend on it we shall have to endure it. People are so envious, dear," she said, looking up at his handsome face and figure with all the pride of proprietorship.

"And well may all Sillshire be envious of me, my Margaret," murmured the gentleman, duly following lead.

So Margaret and Frederick understood one another very satisfactorily and completely, and, bold in their mutual support, advanced toward the drawing-room door.

"Take that handkerchief off your arm, Frederick; I am sure you can do without it," whispered Margaret, as they were on the point of entering; and Frederick did as he was bid.

I do not know that there is much more to be added to this chronicle of Lindisfarn. The most remarkable fact to be told in addition to what has been written, is that all four of the principal actors on the scene are yet alive, though it is forty years—ay, more than forty-one years by the time the lines will meet the reader's eye—since what has been related took place.

Admiral Ellingham, K. C. B., full admiral of the red, is a year or two on the wrong side of seventy; but he can still walk up through his own woods to the Lindisfarn Stone; and is altogether a younger man than Frederick' Falconer, Esq., who, though a year or two on the right side of seventy, begins to find his daily drive from Belgravia into the city rather too much for him, though made in the most luxurious of broughams. His regularity in making this journey is not attributable, however, at all events, to any unsatisfactory state of things at home, due to the presence or conduct in his home of Mrs. Frederick Falconer; for she is not resident there. One child, a daughter, was born to them after a year of marriage. She is still single and is the natural heir to the great wealth of her father. Kate is the happy mother of a much larger family, and when all of them, with their respective wives and husbands and children, are collected at Lindisfarn, as is sometimes the case at Christmas, it would be difficult to find in all merry England, a finer, happier, merrier, or handsomer family party.

The loss of the *Saucy Sally* was eventually the making of Hiram Pendleton, and consequently of his brave and faithful wife, instead of being their ruin. A good deal of admiration had been excited in the neighborhood by the gallant manner in which he had rescued his two passengers, Barbara Mallory and her child, from a watery grave, at the imminent risk of his own life ; and partly by the assistance of others, but mainly by the exertions and influence of Captain Ellingham, he was put into possession of the neatest fishing-smack on all the Sillshire coast, on the condition—most loyally observed—that she was to be used for fishing in the most literal sense of the term.

Julian Mallory was also indebted to Captain Ellingham for his first start and subsequent protection in a career which has given him his epaulets in the coast-guard service, and enabled him to offer a home to his mother during her declining years ; old Mallory died very shortly after the events above related ; and Barbara lived for some years, the first of them with her boy, and the latter of them all alone, in the large stone house at Chewton, which her father left to her, to the exclusion of her brother Jared, and to the breach of all communication between the brother and sister.

I do not know whether it may occur to any readers of the above history that any case has been made out for an exemplary distribution of poetical justice. If so, I am afraid 'that I shall not be able to satisfy them within the limits of the few words which I have yet space to write.

Poetical justice often requires at least a volume or two for the due setting forth of it.

And perhaps if I had an opportunity of relating even compendiously some of the life experiences of the four principal personages of our story, it would be found that all the antecedents which have been either related or indicated in the foregoing pages bore fruit very accurately after their own, and not after any other, kind. Stones thrown into the air *always* fall down again according to the laws of gravity, and not sometimes only.

As for any more immediate and dramatic action of Nemesis, I am afraid there is little to be said. Each lady of our principal *dramatis personæ* married the man whom she wished to marry, and each gentleman had the lady of his choice. Assuredly no one of the four would have changed lots with the other. It is true the squire marked his sense of the difference of the way in which his two daughters had conducted themselves in the very peculiar and difficult circumstances in which they had been placed, by so arranging matters that the old house and the old acres fell wholly and absolutely to the share of Kate, a charge on them, equal to half their money value, being secured to Margaret. But although the old banker had originally dreamed other dreams, it was not long before Frederick and his wife had both learned to think that the arrangement made was such as they would have chosen. So there was no Nemesis in *that*.

But then does she not—that sly and subtle Nemesis—habitually find the tools for her work rather in our choices gratified than in our choices frustrated?

HARPER'S

LIBRARY OF SELECT NOVELS.

☞ *Mailing Notice.*—HARPER & BROTHERS *will send their Books by Mail, postage free, to any part of the United States, on receipt of the Price.*

☞ *HARPER'S CATALOGUE and new TRADE-LIST may be obtained gratuitously, on application to the Publishers personally, or by letter, inclosing Five Cents.*